"Robbie looked at that hand and thought: It is the hand of the murderess. This was not the one which had struck Angus to his death, made of Laurie a hard and dominant and remorseless trollop, driven Bertie into his negation of life and perhaps into his grave. It is the hand of the murderess . . ."

In all her life there was only one person whom Janie Cauder truly loved. The others she savaged with her imperious will—this one she would have spared. But it was too late. Even Janie's love destroyed . . .

Novels by Taylor Caldwell in Pyramid edition

TAYLOR
CALDWELL

The
WIDE
HOUSE

"It is better to dwell in a corner of
the house top, than with a brawling
woman in a wide house."
—Proverbs 21-9

 PYRAMID BOOKS · NEW YORK

THE WIDE HOUSE

A PYRAMID BOOK ·

Published by arrangement with Charles Scribner's Sons

Copyright © 1945 by Janet M. Reback

Charles Scribner's Sons edition published April 1945
Pyramid edition published September 1963
Fourteenth printing, March 1977

Printed in the United States of America

Pyramid Books are published by Pyramid Publications (Harcourt Brace Jovanovich, Inc.). Its trademarks, consisting of the word "Pyramid" and the portrayal of a pyramid, are registered In the United States Patent Office.

PYRAMID PUBLICATIONS
(Harcourt Brace Jovanovich, Inc.)
757 Third Avenue, New York, N.Y. 10017

To

BELLA & ROCKY

with love

Contents

As she spoke, her cousin had a sudden and aching vision of the clear dim twilight of England in the Spring. As vividly

BOOK ONE

"THE GETTING OF TREASURES"

"The getting of treasures by a lying tongue is a vanity tossed to and fro of them that seek death."—Proverbs 21:6

CHAPTER 1

JANIE DRISCOLL CAUDER, in the later years of her life, would often say, with that simper and arching of her head that her daughter, Laurie, could not endure without pressing her nails into the palms of her hands: "I landed here, a young widow, with twenty trunks and bags, three lads and a little lass, with none to care and only the help of God to sustain me. Ah, if it hadn't been for the good Lord, what would have become of me, a young widow, landing alone in a strange country, with nae hoose nor kinfolk to comfort me?"

Janie, of course, confronted by an admiring and servile audience, would fail to mention that in addition to the "twenty trunks and bags, three lads and a little lass," she was also in possession of some fifteen thousand pounds sterling, given to her by her infatuated Irish mother. Had she mentioned the fifteen thousand pounds, it would have considerably dimmed the picture of the pathetic young widow thrusting out her tiny foot so gallantly, and so bravely, upon the unfeeling shore of a "strange country," surrounded by her children and her enormous luggage. Janie always pictured the circumstances about her as large and overwhelming, so that the audience could see her in contrast, so little, so slender, so childlike, and so undaunted, against the grim gray backdrop of New York in March, 1850, a fluttering small creature with chin held high above the ribbons of her bonnet, her gay eyes bright with a quicksilver humor.

New York had had a snowstorm the day previous, and snow lay in sodden soot-streaked heaps on the wooden pier. Against a sky the color of wrinkled lead the masts of the great ship were tangled with rope, and between them squatted the broad chimneys that had smoked so sturdily, but so intermittently, across the boiling Atlantic. Hundreds of immigrants, surrounded by squalling children who whimpered and tried to warm their red hands under pinafores and meager shawls, surged over the pier, dragging bundles of bedding rescued from the dank holds of the ship, frayed carpet bags and various knobby bundles. In contrast to these frightened wretches, Janie, in her sable cape and her trim gray woolen frock, her tiny bonnet covered with velvet violets, was a pleasant sight. She had come first class, of course, and had acquired, as usual, a flock of admiring and loving friends, who assisted her with the luggage, and snatched some of the smaller bags from the hands of stewards. The friends were all gentlemen, because ladies were not apt to be overly cordial with Janie after a day or two of acquaintance. So Janie's handsome little French bonnet was all bobbing animation among tall stovepipe hats and broad, fur-collared shoulders, and her laugh, arrestingly loud and hoarse and jovial, boomed out rollickingly. Sometimes she would withdraw a little mittened hand from the warm confines of her great sable muff, and she would then strike some urgent gentleman soundly on the chest or arm, as if to reprove him, and sometimes she would coquettishly twitch a thick Scotch shawl from the shoulders of another gentleman.

Her children stood a little apart from her, well-dressed and comely, and silent. The eldest boy, Angus Driscoll Cauder, held his little sister's hand in a firm if chilly grip. He was the least well-favored of Janie's lads, unusually tall, dark and dour-faced, and thirteen years old. His expression was reserved, cold and lightless. His complexion was sallow, his features were meager and small, his nose short and sharp, his nostrils compressed and narrow, his mouth thin and drawn. He had a good chin, however, firm and dimpled, and if one cared to look closer after a first careless glance, he would see Angus' eyes, a clear and very shy gray, the color of smoke.

His little sister, clasped so firmly to him, was a beautiful child of about six. Under her beaver bonnet with its wide brown ribbons, flowed a cascade of hair so flaxen yet so radiant, that it was like a cape of pale gold over the fur-bordered capes of her bulging coat. Her big and smiling eyes were a translucent blue, shadowed by golden lashes, and she had a sweet round little face the color of milk and tea-roses, and a large pink smile that trembled easily into a myriad of dimples. The fact that the bitter wind sweeping in from the sea had turned her tilted nose quite red, and made her sniffle, did not detract from her touching loveliness, and her air of shy but eager gaiety.

Though the four children stood together in a circle, a quick eye would have discerned that in reality they formed two distinct groups—one, Angus with his sister, and Bertram (Bertie) Coleman Cauder and Rob Roy (Robbie) Duncan Cauder, the other. Strangers were apt to be much taken by Bertie, his mother's darling, for the eleven-year-old lad was almost as tall as Angus, but better formed, exceedingly solid, and extremely handsome. He had a large round face, all life and ruddiness and laughter, with big white teeth that flashed with constant and innocently malicious smiles, and bright blue eyes, a trifle small. His head was large and round and strong, covered by auburn curls that glinted with gold, and all his ways were quick and vital and restless.

Robbie was the "black one," as Janie would say, with candid disfavor. He was little; he had inherited Janie's smallness and wiriness of body. He looked hardly older than Laurie, his sister. Nevertheless, there was nothing childlike or pathetic about his compact lean little body; in truth, there were times when he resembled a sinewy gnome.

As Janie continued to dally with her admirers, and her voice, so hoarse and rollicking and coarse and hearty, continued to boom out over the bedlam of other voices, even Bertie, the effervescent, became miserably quiet. The wind grew in intensity; the sky became more lowering. It was nearly five in the afternoon, and darkness was running in long waves from the sea and over the huddled city beyond the pier. A dull roaring came from the ocean; wind whistled through the masts of the ship, and the crew scuttled along the decks. The crowd was beginning to disperse, slowly. From the low broken banks of New York, yellow lights began to twinkle. The wooden pier bent and echoed with hurrying feet.

A tall, slender young man, his long fawn coat caped in sable, his tall hat set at a fashionable angle on his high small head, sauntered through the crowds. His saunter was graceful; he was all fashion and favor. His tight fawn pantaloons were fastened by straps under his thin, polished black boots. He carried a gold-headed ebony cane, very slender, with which he lightly moved aside urchins and shivering women and even men. His coat was open, and swinging, revealing a flowered silk vest, and crisp white ruffles. He had a dark full face, bright and keen, with a subtle smiling mouth, and black eyes, very large and piercing. His black hair, sleekly brushed back, curled at the ends in a most engaging manner. His air was careless, composed and arrogant, and between the fingers of one gloved hand he carried a long cigar. He was a great gentleman, doubtless, thought many a woman as she cringed from his path.

He stopped, not far from the four children of Janie Driscoll Cauder, and studied them. He put his cigar to his lips, and smoked idly. Then he said: "Good God!" He began to walk again, more quickly this time. He came back to the children, and smiled at them, his very white teeth glistening between his lips. "Are you Janie's brats?" he asked, genially, his restless eye searching each face.

They stared at him, sunken in their chill wretchedness. Only Robbie spoke, and he came forward courteously and composedly, removing his hat. "Would you be our cousin Stuart?" he asked, in his light voice, without inflection.

"I would, indeed," the man said, lightly, with a deep amused bow. "Or rather, your mama's cousin, Stuart Coleman."

Little Laurie bobbed automatically in a curtsey, and the other children bowed stiffly. Bertie had recovered his ruddy gaiety. He approached Stuart and tucked his hand in his arm. "We're damn cold," he said, frankly. "Will you get Mama away from those gentlemen?"

The smile left Stuart's face. He looked down at Bertie thoughtfully. He patted the small firm hand on his arm. "I will that," he said, with much kindness. He turned his attention to Laurie, who was staring at him with her great blue eyes, so wondering and so calm. "Hello, pet," said Stuart, softly. He reached out and gently pinched her cold round cheek. She smiled at him radiantly, blushed, and buried her head against Angus' arm.

"Tell me your names; which is which?" said Stuart. Robbie, as usual, took command. He indicated his elder brother, and in a quiet competent voice, said: "This is Angus." He indicated Bertie, clinging so affectionately to Stuart: "That's Bertie, Bertram. I'm Rob Roy, Robbie. This is Laurie, our sister," and he waved indifferently at the little girl.

"Four of you, eh?" said Stuart, meditatively. "I didn't quite know there were four." He smiled a little. "Janie was careless. I thought she might bring two, at the most. She only mentioned Bertie and Laurie."

Robbie shrugged indifferently, and Stuart eyed him with shrewd quickness. He turned and surveyed Janie, still laughing hoarsely, she and her gentlemen now quite isolated on the wooden pier. "Janie as usual," commented the young man. He gave the children a reassuring nod and smile, and left them, sauntering, amused, towards his cousin and her covey of admirers. He stood on the animated outskirts, swung his cane, and smoked. Then, quite suddenly and alarmingly, he shouted: "Janie! For God's sake!"

The gentlemen jumped like startled fawns, and parted instinctively to reveal the little vivacious woman in their midst. She stared at Stuart, then rushed in tiny lively steps towards her cousin, shrieking, holding out one mittened hand, the other clutching the huge sable muff. Her sable cape streamed after her, her little French sandals twinkled under her gray skirt, her purple veil blew back from the velvet violets of her bonnet. She flung herself into the laughing Stuart's arms, the while the uneasy gentlemen huddled together and scowled. She was all extravagant kisses, little hoarse cries, and perfumed embraces. "Ah, Stuart, my darling!" she exclaimed, her face running with her easy tears. "And where have you been this long time?"

He held her gently from him. "Let's look at you," he said, fondly. "Yes, it's the same old Janie, though I haven't seen you since the day you were married."

Stuart Coleman was now twenty-eight, and he had been only fourteen years old when he had last seen his cousin. But he remembered very clearly the small triangular face with its somewhat sallow complexion, and the thick array of brown freckles over a nose frankly large and Roman. He remembered the wide mobile mouth with its crafty grin, audacious and merry, and the little square white teeth, glistening and perfect. He remembered the long glinting green eyes, merciless, sly and always twinkling with incipient laughter under their streaks of tilted auburn brows, and the sharp specks of amber in them, which gave them a feline and untamable quality. And he had never forgotten her bright red hair, naturally straight and always tortuously curled into smooth gleaming sausages about her animated face, and just touching her shoulders. Janie had not changed much. She was now thirty-two, and did not possess the slightest beauty, for all her neat trim little figure and high taste in somewhat flamboyant fashion, and candid use of rouge and powder.

Stuart Coleman, who was astute, knew all about Janie. But he was amused by her, charmed by her. He kissed her heartily, as she clung to him, knowing the hypocrisy of her tears of joy. A false baggage, he observed to himself. But a merry soul, he added. He knew at once why she really had come to America. She intended to marry him. He laughed, inwardly.

"Come, I've got a carriage waiting, and I'll take you all to your hotel, my darling," he said, chucking her under the chin. "Is all this your damned luggage? All of it? My God!" He indicated the trunks and bags with his cane. He glanced carelessly at the discomfited and deprived gentlemen, who began to slink away into the gathering darkness like beaten hounds.

Janie clung helplessly to his arm, and adored him with her green dancing eyes. She became suddenly limp and very female. She sighed, and touched her dry eyes with her kerchief. "My love, what should I have done without you?" she whimpered.

Stuart smiled broadly. "I really don't know, my pet. But we must hurry. The carriage is waiting. Gather up your pretty brood, and we'll be on our way."

CHAPTER 2

WHEN Janie wished to make an impression, as she did now upon her cousin, Stuart Coleman, she suffered a few apprehensions. Her mother had been cousin to Stuart's dead father, and Gordon Coleman had been no admirer of Janie. What, then, she asked herself, watching Stuart warily, had the young man heard of her?

Stuart had heard a great deal, but being a wise gentleman he allowed Janie to "stew in her own juice," as he inelegantly put it to himself. He knew all about Janie. He would continue to stare through the spattered windows of the huge stage-coach which was bearing them all to his home in Grandeville, N.Y., and he would affect to be engrossed in the dun flat country that fled beneath the groaning wheels.

His father had been a loquacious and petulant talker. He had been much attached to his cousin, Bridget Murphy, Janie's mother, and had been infuriated at her marriage to that "damned Scotsman, Duncan Driscoll." Gordon Coleman was a "wild Irishman," in the family's opinion, and would come to no good end. He had married Stuart's mother, now dead, and had gone with her to America to make his fortune, when Stuart had been fourteen years old. The family, in relief, had contributed generously towards the fund which made his exile possible, and though they had loved the young Stuart, they had been glad to be rid of relatives that had been a constant drain on reluctant purses. When they heard of Gordon's amazing success, they did not change their personal opinion of him, but said, enviously, that apparently it was possible for the most foolish lout to make money in America. It was by reason of Gordon Coleman's pettish diatribes that Stuart had learned so much about Janie and her family.

Janie's father, Duncan Driscoll, "a lowlander" from Barhead, Scotland, had, with the aid of a considerable inheritance from a dead uncle, purchased an unusually large farm just across the English border. That was reprehensible enough, that he had bought land in England, but that he, a seaman, should make a resounding success of it was enough to make any self-respecting Scot indignant. What did he know of cattle and sheep and other "beasties"? Duncan apparently knew much, and as he was a man of resolution and intelligence he throve from the start. But, when he married the buxom Irish Bridget Murphy, his own family abandoned him with thoroughness and dispatch.

Duncan, with the rocky serenity of a Scot who is prosperous, betrayed no worry over this situation. He was amiable to everyone, though not particularly fond of anyone, and was agreeable and friendly to his wife's people. He even allowed her cousin, Gordon Coleman, and the latter's wife and son, to occupy a small cottage on his land. Gordon was lodge-keeper, and exerted his Irish love for overseership on the other farm-laborers, but he had none of the Irishman's geniality and friendliness and good-fellowship. In consequence he was hated by his underlings.

Duncan's wife presented him with seventeen children, of whom Janie was the youngest. While Gordon Coleman (who hated Duncan more wildly than he hated anyone else, doubtless due to the fact that he had received endless benefits from the Scotsman) disliked Bridget's children with a dull and heavy aversion, he particularly detested Janie. His own son, Stuart, born some five years after Janie, soon revealed a disgusting fondness for the girl, and she for him. She would run down from the great gray house on its knoll, and invade the little gray cottage at the gates, her carrotty hair fluttering, her green eyes dancing, her mouth one broad grin.

Janie became an obsession to this gloomy and frustrated man. As hatred has a memory as boundless as love, he compiled quite a dossier about the young lady. It was this dossier, which even in America many years later, he laid before his son. He forgot nothing. Much of what Stuart had not learned by actual contact with Janie, he learned from his father.

Janie had been coddled by her father and her elder brothers and sisters, though they had understood all about her from her first lisp. Her mother, however, worshipped this child of her old age, and nothing was too expensive, too inappropriate, for the wily little creature. Bridget, fat, aging, illiterate and adoring, found nothing more fascinating than this last child of her womb, and nothing that Janie could do was reprehensible in her fatuous eyes. Janie had a tiny sable cape, stole, bonnet and muff when she was barely five years old. Janie had her own Shetland ponies, her own garden, her own maid, her own gold watch, her own little jewelry case filled with rich rings and bangles and chains. Her velvets and silks were imported from France, as were the delicate laces on her cambric underwear. Her boots came from London. She was early taught the use of lotions for her complexion, which, despite the most anxious efforts of maids, remained distinctly yellowish in cast. Though no sun was allowed to touch her bare skin, her large and predatory nose gathered to itself a crop of thick brown freckles every spring, bathe them as she would with buttermilk.

The servants hated and feared little Janie, from the lowliest scullery maid to the special Oxford tutor engaged to teach her. For she was full of cruel pranks, which she vehemently denied when her tearful mother gently reproached her. Janie had the ability to look her accuser directly and straight in the eye, without flinching, and declare that she had done no such thing. Once, after a particularly outrageous trick upon a stableman, by which he was almost gored to death by a bull which Janie had slyly let out of its compound, Duncan thoroughly thrashed his little daughter. In consequence, Bridget did not speak to him for a month, and was not appeased until the harassed man presented Janie with three new lengths of velvet and an ermine cloak.

Yet her ways were so winning when she desired, so meek and sweet, her expression so innocent, that she could "come over" anyone whom she wished to placate. She had coaxing little manners, also, and she could even, upon occasion, subdue the loud and raucous hoarseness of her voice so that it was almost soft. She might pull fat Bridget's mobcap strings from under her chin, and tie them in hopeless knots as the good-natured woman slept in her chair before the fire, she might put pins into her mother's favorite red velvet cushion so that Bridget would arise with an anguished cry, clutching her great buttocks, she might do any number of such knaveries, yet she was always forgiven when she could induce a large tear to fall over her cheek and make her thin wide mouth tremble.

She was hardly ten years old when her doting mother began to search anxiously among the neighboring "gentlemen farmers" for a proper husband for her child. Her sisters had all been married before they were seventeen to comfortable and sturdy young men of the neighborhood, and well-settled on excellent farms. To Bridget's increasing distress, Janie took no apparent interest, during her adolescence, in eligible youths of the countryside. It was not until she was nineteen that her avaricious eye fell on young Robin Cauder and her desire fastened on him.

As Janie was so abysmally greedy, her lust for Robin Cauder was inexplicable. For Robin had only the garments on his back, and a thin collection of shillings and pence in his tight, frayed pantaloons. He had been born in the dark and violent highlands of Scotland, one of numerous sons of a starveling shepherd. Robin, at a very early age, was set to work as a shepherd also, and in the deep snows of the black mornings he would take the flock out to forage for the meager moss under the snow. Then it was that he sang to the lonely star of the morning, and in such a voice, so golden, so strong and sure, that it seemed the gnarled rocks listened, and the twisted trees. Even the sheep lifted their heads, as if enchanted. He sang the Highland lays, full of wild melancholy, full of death and lovesick girls and fated young men, full of war and glory and hatred for England. He would wrap his shawls about him, oblivious of the terrible winds that swirled his kilts about his reddened young legs, and he would lift his face to the paling morning sky, and sing like a veritable angel.

He also had an angelic beauty. Tall, sturdy, full of grace, he had a dark clear skin, fine black eyes, the Hebraic nose of the true highlander, and a mop of curling black hair. The girls soon loved him. But Robin loved nothing but his savage mountains and the sound of his own singing. He was only sixteen when he left the highlands and made his way, a minstrel, through the towns and hamlets of Scotland. His voice, though untutored, charmed and intoxicated his poor listeners to such an extent that they would produce numerous pennies, and even shillings, for him. They loved to hear his laughter, rich and rollicking, full of joy in life.

He wandered through Scotland, this singing young vagabond, for a whole year, living gaily with strangers who would
give him shelter, even though it were only the hearth before
the meager pit fires or in a barn with the cattle. He was seventeen when he reached Barhead, Scotland, and cast his eye
curiously across the English border. Englishmen, he knew,
were more lavish with shillings and pence, than his own cautious countrymen. He wandered across and sang in English
taverns until even the prosaic English tenant farmers would
raise their heads from their warm beer and listen, open-
mouthed. It was in one of these taverns that the reckless son
of the local minister heard him sing, and induced him to visit
his father. The minister, overcome by such a glorious voice,
persuaded Robin to learn the dull hymns of respectability,
and to sing in his chapel. Robin found it all very boring, for
he had a restless and wandering foot. He decided to stay until he had collected ten pounds. In the meantime, he slept in
the garret of the minister's house, where the blankets were
clean and adequate.

Janie heard him sing in the chapel. She watched him from
the family pew. From the first day she desired him, with vo-
racity. She would marry this seventeen-year-old youth, and
no other, she vowed. She broke this appalling news calmly
to her parents, who were thrown into desperate perplexity.
Duncan stormed and raged; Bridget exuded buckets of tears,
the brothers and sisters sat about in their woolen breeches
and frocks, and lifted their hands in wailing horror. Janie was
firm. She would remain a spinster, reviled by the neighbors,
unless she had her Robin.

Robin, in the meantime, remained happily ignorant of the
fury that engulfed Stronghold, the Driscoll farmlands. He
had noticed Janie in her pew, her slight little body arrayed
in velvets, furs and silks, bejewelled like a Jezebel, and with
a suspicious coloring on her sallow cheeks, and though he
was aware that she looked at him steadily with her long green
eyes, and smirked at him coyly as he sang, he was not taken
by her. He had never loved money. He desired only to sing
his way through life, careless, restless, and full of merriment.
Janie's position did not impress him in the least.

It was not until she contrived to waylay him on the road
home to the minister's house, that he began to look at her
with interest. He was not a lad to forego any promised pleasure. But Janie was astute. It was marriage or nothing. She
dressed herself in her best, and was so gay, so amusing, so
full of hoarse laughter herself, that the lad found himself

waiting for her on the winding road. Janie soon saw that sables and silks and the best beaver bonnets had no power over him, and subtle as always, she found the way to his quicksilver heart. She would sigh and murmur that she was but a little fluttering bird in a golden nest, that she desired nothing but to see the world, that her spirit was smothering to death at Stronghold. When Robin spoke of far places, of his own highlands, Janie would cleverly contrive to make her eyes sparkle with green light, or tears, and she would vow that she must see those highlands.

Still, it might have come to nothing had not Duncan, with fury, visited the awed and trembling minister's house, shouting that he would see that jackanapes immediately, or, with his own hands, he would tear the very beams from the ceilings. Robin, hearing the uproar, came negligently and gracefully from his garret. He was not intimidated by Duncan. When he finally, through the imprecations and threats, caught the gist of the old man's words, the lad threw back his head and laughed with huge enjoyment.

Nevertheless he was also angered, for he was both stubborn and proud. So, he was not good enough for Janie, was he? He must leave at once, must he, with a pocket lined with pounds? Robin only laughed. When next he met Janie on the road, he asked her to wed him.

They did not marry for two months, and Janie was imprisoned in her home, Duncan finally overcoming the tears and pleas of Bridget. Janie went into a "decline." She would neither eat nor sleep, she wept, until she had her Robin. Her mother's tearful pleading had no effect. Janie locked herself in her room. Outside, the brown autumn winds tossed drying leaves against the closed shutters. She would sob loudly, and then listen. If, after some time, she did not hear the distressed shuffling of her mother's feet outside the door, or her deep sighing, Janie would go off into a tantrum, screaming and shrieking like a banshee, hurling herself violently upon the floor, kicking and drumming against the polished boards.

Duncan, who was of a considerable toughness, finally surrendered.

"Hae y'braw vagabond, then, and be damned to y'both!" he roared one morning, outside Janie's door. And then he thumped off crashingly out of the house, mounted his horse, and rode to the nearest tavern. When he returned, in a golden numb daze, Janie was seated before the fire sipping hot milk and brandy, while Bridget bumbled and flurried about her reconciled child.

Robin was waited on, a few days later, by two of Janie's elder brothers. They, they announced irately, had come to give their father's consent to Robin's marriage to Janie.

Now Robin had not seen Janie for nearly two weeks, and, in truth, he had almost forgotten her. He stared in amazement at her brothers, and then his clear dark skin flushed scarlet. Inwardly, he cursed the wild and stubborn folly that had brought him to this impasse. He said nothing to the young farmers, but when they had gone, he decided on flight. Wed a lass and be tied to the earth? Not Robin!

He tried to flee the next morning. But on the road back to Scotland he encountered the eldest and strongest of Janie's brothers, on horseback. Robin stared up at that large brown face with the relentless eyes, and burst out laughing. He shifted his knapsack, turned about, and went back to the minister's house, whistling.

He was wedded to Janie six weeks later. Gordon Coleman did not come. But his wife and Stuart were there. Stuart had followed the course of Janie's wooing with a schoolboy's great curiosity, mingled with amused affection for his older cousin. In truth, he was delighted at her artful success, and her cunning, and thought her a bold and venturesome baggage whose life would be interesting to observe and follow. No more would he and Janie scamper through the woods, searching for butterflies, and feeling the soft moss under their feet as the slanting red light of the dying sun fell through the columns of the trees. No more would he watch with Janie the dim white light of spring in the evening sky, nor would they run down to the river again and skate upon the black ice glittering in the noonday winter sun. He remembered Janie scrambling up the tilted trunk of some old tree, then, reaching a low branch, grasping it and swinging herself out into space, hanging by her hands. How her petticoats would flutter in the cool forest wind, and how thin and active her legs looked, in their long frilled pantaloons! For indeed, Janie was as lively as an insect, and as noisy as a cricket, and as daring as a squirrel. No one could be dull in her presence, slyly malign though it was. Then too, for Stuart, at least, she had a boisterous affection, for all her tormenting ways, her cruel little teasings and malice.

Remembering how she had endlessly entertained him, how she had violently clouted him one moment then fawned on him the next, remembering the coarse and rollicking laughter, obscene in its tones, echoing in the dark woods, remembering her avarice and her impulsive generosities of the instant, he felt his sadness growing.

It was a raw brown autumn day when Robin and Janie were wedded, and the narrow-paned windows gushed with leaden water. The big gray house, gloomy as always with the exception of the kitchen and its copper pots glowing in the fire, had a dank chill smell. There was a wide window-seat beneath the back windows, and Stuart sat there, yawning and waiting with the others, for Janie and her groom to appear. These windows overlooked the kitchen and the herb gardens, bounded by a gray stone wall. In the center of these lush and untidy gardens grew a tree, sinewy and twisted. Pools stood about in the midst of tangled and drooping vegetation, trembling in the cold wind, rippling and wrinkling like miniature lakes whipped by a storm. Dirty brownish clouds scudded across the darkening sky. For a little while the rain had stopped. Drenched doves had ventured forth from the dove-cote, and now sat in a row on the low gray wall, their feathers ruffling miserably. They had a woebegone look, and made mourning sounds, infinitely melancholy. A dog was barking wretchedly. From some distance came the somber lowing of cattle making their way back to the barnyard. And now, as Stuart watched, a dim skirling mist began to rise from the black and ruined garden, twisting its way through dead stalks and grass, then lifting a little like an upflung drifting scarf, or in puffs like mushrooms.

It was not a day of good omen. Fires had been built in the parlor, which was seldom used except on grand occasions such as Christmas (though Duncan, the Scot, was against any "Papish" observance of the holiday), or a wedding or a funeral. In consequence, the very panelled walls had a damp patina over them, and in places farthest from the fire this dampness gathered in dots of water on the polished wood. The mahogany furniture, slippery with horsehair or hard tapestry or velvet, glimmered blackly in the firelight, and the wide Turkey carpeting stretched drearily from wall to wall. The many guests felt this despondent atmosphere, and huddled about the immense black-marble fireplace, their whiskey-glasses in their hands. The males had fortified themselves prodigiously, and their hoarse country voices were becoming exceedingly loud. The ladies, in their large velvet skirts and pelisses and fur-trimmed mantles, had withdrawn primly from their menfolk, and were chattering in the subdued voices appropriate to weddings or funerals. The lamps, thriftily not yet lighted, waited for the touch of a taper. Gloom thickened in every corner.

Near the north wall sat the minister's eldest daughter, a thin consumptive young female, dressed in dull brown, her bonnet hiding her lean pale face. Near at her hand stood a small organ, and by that organ miserably lounged the minister's only son, a very fat little boy about ten years old, who had been delegated to supply the air for the instrument which was to resound forth the wedding march. No one noticed these poor abandoned young creatures, though the boy had an attack of loud sniffles, and kept wiping his nose surreptitiously on his sleeve, and his sister made dismal clucking noises in reproach, tendering her handkerchief.

One of the brothers, annoyed at the thickening dimness, dared to light one lamp in a far corner, but this wan illumination only intensified the dusk. The fire could not warm the room. When the sad old minister entered, his caped coat damp and stained, his hat in his hand, all in the room glowered at him as if he was not the victim of their own cupidity but a venal serf rightly stricken by heaven with the direst poverty.

No one had as yet seen the bridegroom, that wild black lad of seventeen, and as time passed, and there were preliminary sounds upstairs, the company became restive, and some of the gentlemen went to the windows to stare out into the darkening evening. "Making a run for it, eh?" said one of the younger men out of the corner of his mouth to a companion. "Don't know if I blame him." The minister, venturing a word in a stammering tone, announced that Robin had arrived with him and would be in immediately.

At that moment Robin entered, attired in a fine pearl gray coat and lighter gray pantaloons, finery at which the company stared with frank amazement. On his arm he carried a tall gray beaver hat, and about his strong young throat the white ruffles were stiff and glistening. He brought with him such splendor, such freshness and high youth, that he appeared to light the room. Among those country horse-breeders and farmers, he moved with lightness and vivid grace, and though his face was soberer than usual, and very thoughtful, nothing could repress his natural air of brilliant vitality. The ladies turned stiffly on their chairs, and the dourest face of the most malign old woman softened at the sight of him. The men glowered, muttered greetings, and stared. But the minister stood by the youth he had come to love and smiled at him gently.

Everyone started when the minister's daughter heavily attacked the organ. And now there were footsteps on the polished wooden stairs. All rose, the ladies rustling, their bonnet strings falling on their firm bosoms. Now Duncan entered with his daughter on his arm, his expression ponderous and gloomy, and in their wake came fat Bridget, weeping copiously, and attended by her daughters.

Nothing could make Janie pretty, though she had rubbed her cheeks fiercely with a piece of dampened red flannel until they glowed suspiciously, and though she had rubbed her wide lips with the same material until they were sore. She appeared unusually childlike on her huge father's arm, drooping meekly and modestly as if she found the weight of the assembled regard overpowering. As Janie's toilettes were always awaited avidly, every female eye fixed itself upon her, and mouths became enviously and meanly round. For Janie's wedding gown, hastily rushed from London on the last stage-coach, was a French importation. Janie had always had *chic*, and an air of fashion. Her little but shapely body did justice to the creation, which was all white satin and point lace. From her tiny waist, the skirt was an enormous sloping bell, flowing about her feet, drifting with lace on which tiny pearls had been sewn. The basque, gleaming like moonlight seen through faint and delicate clouds, was fastened tightly with crystal buttons. The raw red curls were almost completely hidden in a mist of the finest point lace, crowned with artificial orange blossoms, and upon her little arms the white kid gloves wrinkled freshly.

And then, suddenly, all this glory was ruined. Duncan stopped so suddenly, and with violence, almost on the threshold of the parlor, that Janie stumbled and fell against him. He glared about the room, his face suffused with crimson.

"Where hae the damned lights, then?" he shouted. And he stamped his foot furiously, several times.

A confused murmur passed through the guests and the relatives. Bridget stopped her weeping; her daughters blushed furiously. Then into the room charged a housemaid in mob-cap and apron, carrying a taper, her petticoats billowing. She rushed at the fire, a path being suddenly made for her, lighted the taper and darted from table to table. Everyone watched her. The minister's daughter was so unnerved by Duncan's oath and the confusion that she burst into tears, and the little boy forgot to pump, let the organ music die on one last caterwaul, and gave a loud squall of terror.

Then all at once the oddest sound broke through the funereal and startled silence. It was Robin's laughter, a little wild, but loud and merry. He was leaning against a table, and was so shaken with his mirth that he had to cling to it, his head thrown back, his mouth open so wide that all his white and glistening teeth were visible. Now the attention of the stupefied company turned, astounded, upon the lad, and the lamplight showed distended and shining eyeballs. Stuart, near his mother, began to grin.

And then, as suddenly as Robin had laughed, he was abruptly still, and very pale. He stood up straight, and stared emptily at nothing. One of Janie's sisters had pinched the weeping minister's daughter, and she struck the organ keys with feverish energy. The little boy pumped. Everything was as it had been, but Janie was trembling with rage, and Duncan had the fixed dull look of a man who had been savagely kicked.

After that everything was anti-climax. Stuart guessed that Janie would never forgive her husband for that outburst of rude but uncontrollable mirth. The marriage, performed respectably enough, the repast afterwards, consisting of mighty hams and cold beef and ale and whiskey (all of which was hugely enjoyed by the gentlemen), would never eradicate from her mind the rough humiliation she had suffered. She smirked and simpered, accepted kisses and handshakes, her green eyes sparkling, but when she glanced at Robin, very white and apart now, her glance was virulent.

She made him pay. For two months, during which he first began to hate her, she balked him of the one lone joy of his marriage.

CHAPTER 3

SHORTLY after Janie's marriage to her "braw Robin," Stuart was taken to America by his parents. Thereafter, all his tales came to him from his father. Gordon, infatuated by hatred, corresponded with his cousin Bridget, mother of Janie, and it was from that barely literate poor woman that the spate of stories crossed the long green ocean, to lodge forever in Gordon's inflamed brain.

Duncan Driscoll, it appeared, had some gloomy sympathy for the young lad precipitated so unwillingly into the bosom of his family. At any rate he did not press Robin for a time to take his "proper place" in the household, and learn the art of gentleman-farming. Robin wandered restlessly in and out of the great stone house, spending his time in the taverns, or sometimes, with strange obedience, following his father-in-law about the land and listening abstractedly to his rich, though brief, comments on farming in general. Duncan did not yet insist; Robin came and went, often returning slightly the worse from the inns, and, from the very beginning, becoming daily less given to conversation. But not until the end of the first year of his marriage was it noticed that Robin rarely sang now, and when he did sing, it was in a low and melancholy tone.

Then he began to develop another trait which had lain deeply beneath his careless youth. By the time he and Janie had been married two years, he was given to somber fits of violent depression during which he raved and screamed wildly. And afterwards became abruptly and blackly silent for many days. His young face grew heavier, yet paler; the flash of his dark eye was no longer gay fire, but passionate and malefic rage. It was not all Janie's fault. She had caught this savage young hawk in her rapacious hands, and though she held him, bewildered and resentful at his struggles, trying to pet and coax him, she deserved some pity for the wounds he inflicted on her with his lacerating beak, so sharpened with despair. It was not she alone that he hated. He hated this warm, smug farmland, this quiet country, this land of close green meadows and sun, and the hopelessness of its peace. It had captured and imprisoned him. He hated it and its jailer. In the beginning, he had tried to be patient, even docile, with shrugging Scot resignation. But it was too much for him; he was too young.

"He'll be off one of these fine days, my lass, mark my words," said Duncan to his wife, and there was hope in his pitying voice.

But Robin stayed, though neither his irritable brothers-in-law, who despised him for his wild ways and his scorn of money, nor poor, fat and loving Bridget, nor Janie, knew why. Only Duncan understood. No matter if Robin left now, he would never be free again. The memory of the prison would forever remain with him. His wings were broken. The wild things, Duncan understood, must never know a prison. Their memory is too long. Scotsmen never forget grief nor hardship nor pain nor injustice nor despair, no matter how far it lies behind them in the past.

The first child appeared thirteen months after the marriage: dark, feeble little Angus with the long legs. Robin looked at him sluggishly, then turned away. But later, touched in his own youth by this little snuffling creature, he began to play with it, for he was so young and so desolate. By the time Angus was two Robin was devoted to him, and would carry him in his arms far from the house into the nearby forest, and would not return for hours. It was whispered in the village that Robin was heard to sing in the forest, and that sometimes he would climb a distant hill, his child in his arms, and fill the clear and empty air with his wild songs. Janie did not care. She had never been fond of little Angus, and hating Robin by now, she affected to believe the baby resembled him. Too, she had another baby in her arms, her darling, her Benjamin, ruddy Bertie with the laughing blue eyes.

Two years, and Robin still was doing nothing whatsoever to assist Duncan. Nor was he asked. It was enough for him to take the "bairn" to the forest and the hills. He never lost his dark melancholy, but something like peace had come to him in these days. When Rob Roy was born Robin did not appear aware of the fact. Later, when he did become aware that he had a third child, he appeared dazed, and was very silent. He was barely twenty-three and the life had left his face forever. He had that pathetic and confused gentleness of wild things that have been broken but not tamed. Rare, now, were his furious quarrels with Janie. He seldom spoke to her, even in bed. Days would go by without a word passing from him to his wife's kin. By this time the family had given him up as "a bad job," and left him alone and forgot him.

Duncan was very old by the time Laurie was born, and he found the chatter and crying of children too much for him. Janie had become a shrew, and quarrelled viciously with her father. Bridget, as always, was adoring, and one or another of the babies was always in her arms.

For the second time, when Laurie arrived, Robin was interested. This beautiful little girl-child with the golden hair and eyes like Northern winter skies fascinated him, caught and fixed his attention. Angus, now nearly eight, was his young father's constant and silent companion, and he walked beside him through the meadows while Robin carried Laurie, singing to her softly.

No one but Angus and Laurie knew what he sang to them, or how joyously he played with them, when he was alone with his children. Sometimes a far glimpse of them was seen,

Robin running, the children stumbling and racing behind him, frantic with shrill laughter and joy, Laurie's long golden curls streaming in the bright wind, Angus' thin gaunt legs flashing, Robin's black locks dishevelled.

For some reason, Robin never sang his Scottish ballads to the children. He sang other songs, lovely, terrible, rich and majestic, and it was not until she was a woman that Laurie knew that these songs had come from Robin's heart, and not from any folklore or the pen of any composer. Each of the children had a favorite song. Angus' was "O Morning Star!" And Laurie's was: "O Love Greater than Life!"

Laurie was four years old when Robin died. He had taken a touch of "rheumy cold" and was dead in two days. His illness had not been severe; it amazed and confounded his physicians when he suddenly spoke no more, and they found he had left his prison forever. Not even his two beloved children could keep him. Just before he died he had sent for little Angus, who had waited for hours outside his father's door in the tragic and tearless silence of mortal grief. And Robin said only, holding his son's small thin hand: "Ye'll not forget our songs, then, ma little lad, and ye'll help your wee sister to remember?"

Angus, speechless, had nodded, and had bent to kiss Robin, who was smiling. When Angus lifted his head and tried to speak, Robin was still smiling and gazing at him. But Robin was dead. Only Duncan knew why he had died. Only Duncan, looking at the young and vivid face, strangely wild and free and happy now, was glad. Only Duncan wept, though Janie had used an onion copiously to induce tears.

For Janie was not displeased at the death of this hating lad she had married. He had been a burden and a shame and a soreness to her for years. She was free of him. With characteristic vigor, she began to plot her new life.

She lived with her aged parents for two more years, but her acquisitive and avid mind was never still. She was a born adventuress. Her restlessness and ill temper grew as her vigor mounted. Nothing satisfied her. Duncan broadly hinted that there was a fortune in it for any man courageous enough to marry his youngest daughter. Many presented themselves. But Janie had had enough of the quiet life.

Letters still arrived from America from Stuart. His parents had died. He said little about his mode of living, and only once or twice mentioned a "shop," which, he declared, was doing well in the struggling but vital city of Grandeville, N.Y., on some outlandish body of water he called "the Great

Lakes." A shop? queried his kinsmen, discontentedly. Who ever heard of a man making much of a living in a shop? But when Stuart carelessly mentioned having made over ten thousand dollars the last year (ten thousand dollars hastily calculated was apparently two thousand pounds!) his kinsmen were dumfounded. Janie was very proud of the letters. She carried them in her reticule for days. She remembered Stuart with fondness. When, one Christmas, he sent her a miniature of himself, she was entranced by his handsomeness, by the deviltry in his black Irish eyes.

It was on a blustery January morning that Janie announced that she would take her children and be off to America.

Bridget was prostrated with grief. But Duncan listened with sour interest and dawning hope. Janie had made a hell of his house these past years with her quarrelling, her screams, her bad temper, her tricks, and her greed. She had filled the old man's house with children who were always crying or demanding or sulking. Duncan prayed to his gods that Janie was serious about this, and for the first time in many years he was tender with his daughter, and began to discuss with her large and elaborate plans.

Janie hid her fury and disappointment. She had, in the beginning, decided to leave all her children save her darling Bertie with her parents. Four children to America! She had fully expected that her mother, at least, would demur, would demand that the children be left behind to comfort her old age. But Bridget had been quite savagely warned by Duncan that he would not put up with it, and that Janie would go with her children, all of them, or remain at home with all of them. He gave way to senile but violent rage when alone with Bridget. "She'll nae leave her whelps in ma hoose!" he cried, "to free herself, the besom! from her responsibilities! Ah've had frae enough of her antics, ma lass, and Ah'll die in peace in ma ain bed with nae sight of her face!"

Janie, confronted by her father's ultimatum, almost gave up her gay plans. She had written to Stuart, however, some time ago, and now a letter arrived from him, full of laughter, full of urgings that she come. So Janie announced that nothing could separate her from her bairns, and she would be off, a lone widow with no home of her own.

Bridget gave her all of the fifteen thousand pounds left to her by her own father. And Janie went to America, with the heartfelt blessings of her parents.

CHAPTER 4

JANIE, during the first few hours in the stage-coach had filled her cousin's ears with horrid stories of the hardships she had endured during her crossing. How ill she had been! How she had lain in her hard bed, tossed to and fro through black and stormy nights! How hideous had been the slops fed to her, and how the stewards had neglected her, leaving her all desolate and at death's door for hours together! She painted a most lurid picture for Stuart, all dark and shifting shadows of suffering, in which she, a most brave and valiant little woman, had endured unmentionable things without complaint and only with gentle patience. She had been robbed of a precious ring by a steward, who had fawned upon her and gained her confidence. Her children had run about the ship untended, while their poor little mother had moaned and sobbed in her bed, all bewildered at the treatment accorded her, remembering the hardheartedness of her parents, and enduring her homesickness and desertion with meek resignation.

Stuart assumed a most sympathetic expression and pressed Janie's hand. He hid as best he could the black sparkle of his eyes. Janie was very diverting. But her children were even more diverting. For, as Janie sobbed out her story, touching very dry eyes pathetically with her perfumed handkerchief, Stuart watched the faces of Angus, Bertie, Robbie and little Laurie. Angus had aroused himself from his peculiar dim lethargy, and was gazing at his mother, his thin black brows knotted together in stern perplexity, his small white teeth worrying his lip, his hands twining nervously in his shawl. Bertie was grinning. Robbie, however, regarded his mother with indifferent contempt, and shrugged. When he met Stuart's eye, he smiled faintly, with amused disdain, turning away immediately afterwards to stare through the dusty and rattling windows. Little Laurie only stared at Janie, blinking rapidly, her blue eyes shining with worry and bafflement, young as she was.

When Janie paused for breath, quite overcome by the pathos of her recital, Angus stammered weakly: "But, Ma, you weren't very ill. Only the first night. Then you danced. Don't you remember, Ma? All the gentlemen coming to the

29

door of our room, and quarrelling about who was to dance
with you first? And Ma," he added, shrinking as her baleful
and murderous eye fell fully upon him, "you had such fine
gowns and rings and bangles and chains, and you wouldn't
come back until it was almost morning. I remember," he
added with hysterical loudness and haste, as Janie's infuriated
look increased in hating virulence upon him, "that it was
morning, often. And you would be singing, and the lady next
to us would knock on the wall, and you would shout back at
her and laugh, and the gentleman at the door would laugh,
too. And the ring wasn't stolen. You found it this morning."

"Oh, shut up," said Robbie, disgustedly, without turning
from his contemplation of the wet and wintry landscape outside. Bertie chuckled, kicked his elder brother vigorously in
the shins, and winked at him with good-natured warning.

But poor Angus, apparently firmly under the belief that
Janie had innocently forgotten, and was only making mistakes which she would be grateful to him for correcting,
went on with even wilder haste and loudness, looking at his
mother earnestly:

"Don't you remember, Ma? And the stewards were very
good to us, bringing us our breakfasts in the morning when
you forgot to take us to the dining-room, and were sleeping
so soundly. And you tipped them, and they cried the last
day, and you kissed them all around, and thanked them. And
everyone said you were the Belle of the Ball, and the captain sent you a basket of fruit with his compliments?"

There, thought Stuart, suppressing his laughter, is an innocent who will never learn, never in his life. He looked compassionately at the young lad's eager intense face, at his
urgent gray eyes and trembling mouth. He saw how white his
knuckles had become, and how his fingers were entwined in
the shawl, and how he was quivering. His earnestness was
astounding.

But Janie looked at him with rage, her tight and sallow
face suffused. She was beyond speech, except for a hoarse
and animal-like grating deep in her throat, like a growl.
Then, without warning, she darted, crouching, from her seat
beside Stuart, and clouted poor Angus violently over the
head with her clenched fist. He tried to evade her blows,
crying out, sheltering his head with his thin arms, but she
found openings in his guards, and punched and thrust cleverly. Her eyes were all glittering green madness under her
red curls and the bobbing purple violets of her bonnet, and
she had caught her lip between her teeth and was uttering

ugly panting sounds in her furious exertions. Her skirts fluttered and swayed; she kept her footing miraculously in the lurching coach, which, fortunately, had no other passengers but the Cauders and Stuart. Her agility was remarkable; she pounced, feinted, struck, recoiled, slashed and beat, with such speed, such dexterity, such telling and energetic blows, that one could hardly follow her movements and could only see the fluttering and swaying of her petticoats, the frenetic bobbing of her bonnet and the dancing of her little feet.

During all this, the two other boys, with great deftness, had lifted their feet from the gritty floor of the coach, and had huddled their knees under their chins. Little Laurie, sitting beside her assaulted brother, had not moved. She sat very still, stark and white, and looked at her prancing and feinting mother. And there was horror on her little face, the frozen and appalled horror which is without fear, and is akin to loathing. As for Angus, he uttered no cry, nor did he gather himself into a hard tight ball, like a bug, seeking to expose little vulnerable surface to his mother's blows. He only feebly kept his arms above his head, shrinking only a trifle, and his attitude, tragic, humble, despairing and resigned, made Stuart's careless heart beat with a voluptuous rage against Janie. Still, he might have done nothing, shrugging fatalistically, had it not been for a sharp glimpse of little Laurie's face, with its remembrance of many such scenes.

Then it was that he reached out, caught a large thick wad of Janie's petticoats in his hand, and wrenched her violently back upon her seat. Just at that precise moment, the wheels of the stage encountered a particularly obdurate rock, and the occupants of the vehicle were thrown about like dolls in a box. In consequence, Janie was hurled about somewhat roughly, and as her rage was not spent in the least, and she apparently felt that Stuart had contrived the rolling of the stage, she turned on him with blind and insensate fury, striking him a sharp and vicious blow on the cheek. Stinging from that assault, Stuart acted with instinctive anger, lifted his hand and vigorously boxed his cousin's ears, and then thrust her from him with an exclamation of disgust. Her bonnet fell over her brow, so that only her gibbering mouth was visible, and apparently it firmly wedged itself there. She had fallen into a corner of the stage seat on which she was sitting, and there she sprawled, frantically clutching at the bonnet whose stubborn brim had flattened her nose. She accompanied her struggles with stiff and spasmodic jerks of her outflung legs, and much raucous puffing. Her skirts had rolled back above her knees, displaying small but pretty legs tastefully enclosed in white silk stockings, and Stuart, recovered from his anger, regarded them briefly with automatic admiration. Then the sight of the struggling and maddened woman, battling with her stubborn bonnet, struck him as singularly funny, and he burst into a shout of laughter. He reached for Janie's skirts, pulled them down decorously, gave her bonnet a yank, and revealed her distorted face, which was all blotches and malignance and glittering green eyes.

"You're a big lass now, Janie," he said, with high good humor. "Keep your skirts down, in public at least. And be thankful for that big nose of yours; it kept you from smothering to death." He touched his cheek, and clucked. "You're a damn little bitch, Janie, and need a thrashing."

Panting, Janie lay back in her corner, glaring at her cousin with the maddest hatred. He smiled back at her easily, and shook his head, clucking again. "Truly, you must do something for that complexion, my girl. Yellowish-green doesn't go well with hair the color of young carrots."

Janie opened her twisted mouth and emitted an oath, an ugly and obscene series of words. Stuart, in spite of himself and his amusement, was shocked. He put his hand over her mouth. She promptly bit it. He withdrew his hand with a howl, lifted it instinctively to strike her, and then, in the very downward swoop of that hand, he caught it back. He muttered something which only she heard. Then, suddenly black of face and narrowed of eye, he drew himself away from her, as far as possible, and stared before him.

Janie burst into tears, loud and heart-breaking. Tussles were no new thing with her. She had often fought with her brothers and sisters, those who were nearest to her own age. She had invariably triumphed over them, frightened them, or reduced them to abject appeasement. She had never before encountered anyone who withdrew himself from her with such contempt as Stuart's, and who heard her cries and sobs with such disgusted indifference. She cried louder. Stuart did not even shrug. He looked at Angus and Laurie.

Bertie and Robbie, who had regarded the swift assaults that had taken place between their mother and their cousin with deep and absorbed interest, were not at all disturbed. They had often seen their mother strike their uncles and aunts with violence, whenever they disagreed with her, or tried to advise her.

It was not at Bertie and Robbie that Stuart gazed, then. It was at Angus and Laurie. Angus had dwindled, so that his long lean length appeared much smaller than before. He had fallen back against the dusty leather seat of the coach, in an attitude of tragic collapse. His small dark face was ghastly, with a bone-like luminosity in the spectral dusky light that came through the windows. His gray eyes were half-closed. He seemed hardly to breathe. His hands lay beside him, palms upturned, and flaccid. He appeared barely conscious. From his nose twisted a thin rivulet of blood, of which he seemed completely unaware. Janie must have scratched him savagely upon his right check, for this was oozing slow red drops, and there was an ugly darkening spot on his right temple. Stuart, with strange and unfamiliar pity, guessed that it was Janie's display of murderous hatred and madness which had caused this collapse of the poor lad, rather than her physical assaults upon him.

Little Laurie, trembling, her lower lip caught sternly between her small white teeth, was kneeling beside her brother and attempting to stay the flow of blood from his nose with her tiny kerchief. Her beaver bonnet had fallen on her childish shoulders, and the setting sun, striking through a thick layer of gray clouds, lay like a coppery nimbus on her long golden hair. She was very quiet, and all her movements were old and tender and gentle. She wiped away Angus' blood, pressed the stained kerchief firmly across the bridge of his nose, and held it there. Stuart was amazed, and achingly touched. When Angus sluggishly opened his eyes and looked dazedly at his little sister, she smiled at him eloquently and with courage, and bent and gently kissed his cheek. But not for a moment did she stop the strong pressing on the bridge of his nose. Angus sighed. He rolled a little towards the child, and closed his eyes again. Laurie murmured softly, over and over.

My God, thought Stuart, with pity. The little darling, then, the little darling!

He became aware that Janie's sobs and groans were mounting in ferocity, that she had begun to writhe on the seat, that she was doing all she could to attract his bemused attention. He turned to her with a violent and threatening gesture. "Be still, you besom!" he shouted.

Janie was so shocked at this very queer reaction to her rages and hysterics that she immediately and abruptly became silent. This, then, said her cunning mind, was no way to win Stuart. She sat up, meekly. She allowed real tears to drip pathetically over her cheeks, one of which was jerking spasmodically. She looked at Stuart, with imploring humility.

She made her mouth shake. Her head drooped. She cried quietly. Stuart, in his turn, regarded her intently, his black eyes kindling and flashing, his mouth harsh and thin.

She sobbed gently: "Stuart, my love, you don't know what I've had to put up with, with that sneaking, snivelling hypocrite and liar! No one but God knows! What have I done that heaven should have punished me like this? It's no wonder, God knows! that I forget myself. I've had thirteen years of him, turning his poor dead papa against me, sneaking behind my back to my own papa and mama with his lies, distressing me and humiliating me."

Her hoarse voice was very plaintive and beguiling. She reached out timidly and laid her hand on his arm. It stiffened under her touch. But he did not shrug her off.

She clasped her hands together, and implored the wooden roof of the coach, the whites of her eyes shining malignantly in the dusk. A subdued but patient frenzy had her.

"Such a liar, Stuart! You can't imagine. It's beyond you. A pious liar, always slipping off to his kirk with his prayer-books under his arm of a Sunday! Always praying and snivelling, and slipping about with his sly eyes, turning my nearest and dearest away from me with his false meeknesses and his whines." She turned to her pet, Bertie.

"My darling lad, tell your cousin this is true, that—that serpent of a brother of yours has made my life wretched, and a burden, with his tales and his lies and his impudence! Tell your dear cousin, Bertie!"

Bertie had been grinning widely as he listened to his mother. "He does contradict," he admitted, with a broader grin.

"Contradict!" cried Janie, in simulated and frenzied grief. She put her hand to her heart and panted. "It is more than female sensibility can endure! Before Heaven, I swear it! I, who have been the best of mothers to my orphaned bairns, who have prayed all alone for them, with my heart breaking in my breast, humbly seeking out how best I might protect them from a cruel and unfeeling world, and then only to discover that I have nourished a viper in my bosom!"

Her hoarse and croaking voice thickened with the rough accent of her forebears, and hearing that accent, which unwillingly brought the young Janie to his memory, and the dusky hills of home, Stuart felt his disgust and anger abating. He was annoyed at this. He wanted to hate Janie, but when he heard her speaking he smelled again the smoking peat fires of his youth, saw the darkening evening sky with its single white jewel of a star, the long lonely stretches of moor, silent under glimmering purple shadows, and heard the sound of cow-bells, melancholy in the twilight, and the laughter of those homeward bound from the fields. It was nostalgia that softened him towards Janie, and he sighed a little.

Janie heard that sigh, and her shrivelled heart leapt. She glanced at him cunningly from beneath her sparse and yellowish lashes.

"Still," said Stuart, trying to speak roughly, "you were too hard on the lad, even if what you say is truth."

Janie wept. "You may be sure it is true, Stuart. I forgot myself. I always had a high spirit, God forgive me, and I can't control myself when I hear lies. 'Speak the truth and shame the devil,' my dear papa used to say. I hate a liar, Stuart. I love truth. It is a weakness in me, I admit. I go quite frantic in the presence of a liar. 'Janie will speak truth, always, no matter the consequence,' my dearest mama always said. 'Even if you kill the lass, she will stand before you and look you boldly in the eye. She'll have no lies about her.' O Mama, Mama!" sobbed Janie, uncontrollably, clasping her hands to her breast in a most touching gesture, and rolling her eyes upwards again. "To think your child has come to this, in a strange land, among strangers, practically orphaned, driven from her home to seek a new home for her helpless little ones, unbefriended and neglected, widowed and helpless!"

"Well, well, then," said Stuart, patting Janie's hand. "It's a hard way you've travelled, it seems. There, now, cease your blubbering, my pet, and here is my handkerchief for your tears. You've quite ruined your own."

His one desire, now, was to soften or prevent any private punishment which might be inflicted upon those two poor children. If he were to remain obdurate and contemptuous and cold, Janie would visit her hatred and frustration upon Angus and Laurie. Of this, Stuart had no doubt.

"You've practically murdered the lad, Janie," he said, moving closer to his cousin, and, with false tenderness, wiping away her tears. "It's hard lines for you, I know, coming like this. But you've got to promise to be easier on the little wretch. Come on now, promise. If I hear of any more of your tantrums, I'll turn you out in the snow, so help me God." He added, rallyingly: "Look at the lad: he's bloodied like a fox after the hounds have been at him. They hang women for that in this country, Janie."

The crafty Janie, still weeping, then displayed her admirable talent for acting. She used no finesse. Dazedly, she allowed her eyes to widen in complete amazement as she turned them upon the suffering Angus and Laurie. She stared violently. She put her hand again to her breast, and said, in a suffocating murmur: "No! No! I cannot believe it! Oh, dear Heaven, it was not I who did that! Tell me I did not!" and she grasped Stuart feverishly by the arm and sank against him, all tears and anguish, and implored him with her green eyes, which were now glaring in cleverly simulated horror and anguish. "Oh, how can I be forgiven? Stuart, my love, help me, help me!" She burst into loud and broken sobs quite piteous to hear, and so moved was she by her acting that she actually turned quite white under her sallowness, and her face quivered and jerked. "My temper, my odious temper! To think that I have so vilely attacked my puir bairn, by puir wee wean!" She put her hands over her eyes and groaned hoarsely. "Oh, tell me I did not do this!"

Much as Stuart enjoyed this little scene, and silently congratulated Janie on an excellent performance, he was embarrassed before the dancing eyes of Bertie and the cool, watchful distaste of Robbie. He wanted to say to her: "Come now, enough of that, my lass. You are making a fool of yourself." But he dared not. He said, therefore, very gravely: "You did, indeed, my girl. And it's ashamed of you I am. There, now, save your tears for your children, and comfort them."

Though he knew the speed with which Janie usually acted, he was yet startled when she flung herself bodily from the seat and fell before her abused children on her knees, taking care, meanwhile, that her frock and cape had time to drape gracefully about her, and that her tight red curls should fall back upon her small sloping shoulders in a beguiling fashion. (Very touching, observed Stuart to himself.) She flung wide her arms to Angus and Laurie. She sobbed loudly. Then she seized Angus in her grasp and dragged him forcefully to her breast. She clutched him frantically, pressing his bruised and bleeding head to her shoulders, patting him, kissing him wildly, murmuring, groaning, sobbing with utmost despair and contrition, flinging back her curls, imploring Heaven for forgiveness with streaming eyes, crying out incoherently.

Again Stuart glanced at Robbie and Bertie. Bertie was giggling silently. Robbie raised his thin black slashes of brows, and shrugged. But little Laurie had shrunk as far as possible from her distraught mother, had curled herself into a small ball in the corner of the seat. There she crouched, visibly trembling, her tiny face white as linen, her blue eyes shining deeply in the dusk. She appeared quite ill, her golden hair disordered over her shoulders and neck.

Ah, my little darling, darling, thought Stuart again, with deep compassion.

He turned his attention again to Janie and Angus. The boy lay supine in his mother's frenzied arms. He allowed her to minister to him in her rough and febrile way. He endured her kisses.

Then, to Stuart's supreme astonishment, the boy broke out into the wildest sobs and cries, and began to return his mother's embraces with despairing abandon.

"Oh, Mama, Mama!" he cried. "Oh, Mama!"

CHAPTER 5

Though Janie had known that America was a "braw land," and considerably larger than England and Scotland combined, she was dismayed at its apparently endless reaches as day after day passed in various coaches, and amid varying discomforts. The insular mind could not grasp far horizons, eternally changing, and boundless.

By the fifth day of miserable travelling, she had begun to despise all Americans, who were, most certainly, not gentlemen. As for their ladies, they were dun and dull, prim of mouth and thinly raucous of voice, bearing all discomforts with pious resignation. They would sit with their mitted hands in their laps, their black or brown bonnets stiffly upright on their heads, their pale tight faces very set and grim, while their husbands, obviously finding the company of their consorts suffocating, resorted steadily to the bottle in every tavern and hotel at which the stages passed. Eventually, however, coming with delighted surprise upon the colorful and lusty Janie, with her false meekness and her sparkling long green eyes, they drank less and peeped at her, fascinated. They made timid and awkward overtures to her, in spite of the presence of the four children and the amused Stuart.

She was all tenderness and softness and solicitude with her children now, understanding that Stuart was pleased by this. When Angus timidly "contradicted" her (and he could never seem to refrain), she would say, sweetly and archly, lifting a gloved finger at him: "Now, my lovey, perhaps

Mama is mistaken, but it is very naughty of her little lad to say so." When she would find Laurie staring at her fixedly, in her strange unchildish way, she would not shout at her, as usual: "Ye wee toad, I'll clout ye for your impudence!" She would merely smile at Laurie tenderly, and ask her if her head ached.

Her lusty delight in life survived steadily through all the punishing days, and as she was possessed by a deep curiosity about all things, she was rarely afflicted with ennui. Nor did the journey exhaust her, for despite her tininess and thinness of body she had been blessed by the finest of constitutions. Even her attacks of "bile" seemed to testify to a hardy endowment, and though her complexion suffered and became extremely yellowish, and her suppressed temper rose to heights of gall, her endurance was remarkable. While other ladies became faint and exhausted, and had to discontinue the journey temporarily, or became quite green when the gentlemen resorted to cheroots and pipes and whiskey, Janie thrived on it all. Stuart's admiration grew.

In the meanwhile, the landscape which had begun by being dreary, dull and dead, running with brown March mud and streaked by oily leaden water, became increasingly desolate beyond the windows of the coaches. Now the flat land was black and stricken, as they travelled north, smoking with gusts of dry and whirling snow. The foothills, too, were black as coal, low and empty, with here and there a dusky pine struggling to live and stand upright against gray and gaseous skies. The farmhouses huddled near the highway as if for protection, their wooden walls seeming to tremble in the harsh and howling winds. Their smoke lay flat and long along their eaves, boiling mournfully from the chimneys. The coaches passed frozen pools and little lakes, the black water just beginning to seep through the gray ice. Woods, twisted and sinewy, bare of every leaf, sluggishly rolled behind them. Also, the air was becoming steadily colder, so that the occupants of the coaches shivered, and the ladies clamored for hot bricks at the hotels, with which to alleviate their suffering. The roads were rougher now, full of frozen ruts or thick oozing mud, and the children, who had crossed the Atlantic without sickness, now retched miserably in their corners. The vehicles tossed and heaved, accompanied by the shoutings and curses of the drivers, and sometimes not more than ten miles would be covered in a day. Bad as the days were, the nights were worse, moonless and starless, filled with a leaden and crepuscular shadow, and often the travellers lost all track of time and came to believe that they had been tossing like this for ever in deep gloom and chill and misery.

The country became wilder as it touched the borders of Pennsylvania. Now, in the dun and dreary light of day, the travellers could see the distant striding of black, snow-veined mountains, over which boiled purplish or ashen clouds. The road rose higher, so that some of the travellers were terrified at the glimpses below of far narrow valleys twisting between the mountains, of spectral icy lakes glimmering in the quick-silver and fugitive light of the infrequent sun. Sometimes, at sunset, a mauve and misty shadow fell over the gigantic and desolate landscape, giving it an eery and terrible air of doom and solitary immensity, while the dull crimson western skies outlined the mountains like an awful fire. Now there were no signs of any habitations at all, only this stark and terrible grandeur of frozen white earth and tremendous black mountains and gray dead rivers, and, at sunset, this frightful cosmic conflagration which reduced the world to pale, purplish fog and formless chaos.

Janie, who was rarely aware of anything beyond the warm and cosy and immediate moment, now fell silent, staring out at the landscape with a look of fear on her pinched and shrewish face. The insular soul of the lowlander was filled with horror, nameless and shivering. Remembering the low soft hills of home, she was terrified at this gigantic grandeur. Her voice was very muffled when she said to Stuart, beside her:

"It fair takes my breath."

Stuart glanced through the window, and said with the patronage of the seasoned traveller: "Oh, this is nothing at all. Mere foothills. I've seen the Rockies, when I went to California a year ago. I've done a bit of pioneering, myself."

"So big, so braw," said Janie, unconsciously using the idioms of her Scottish father. "My God," she added, "is there no end to this land?"

"My darling, you've seen only the fringe," said Stuart, indulgently. "The damn country's as wide as the Atlantic. You've no idea."

He thought to inspire Janie's amazement and interest, but she only shivered, huddling in her sables. She sighed, and moved as if her breath had been taken from her. The bloody light of the sunset outlined her narrow profile, with its large, predatory nose and wide thin mouth with its expression of cruelty. She murmured: "At home, the fields are white with daisies, and the lambs are on the hills."

As she spoke, her cousin had a sudden and aching vision of the clear dim twilight of England in the Spring. As vividly as though he gazed at it with his physical eye, he saw the soft green hills against the dreaming silence of the heliotrope sky. He saw the low and peaceful valley with its low white farmhouses. He smelled hawthorn and the fresh scent of the fields and heard the distant tinkling of gentle cow-bells. He heard the faint calling of lambs and the melancholy answering of the ewes, echoing in the tender stillness. Ah, England, England! thought this young Irishman, who had never seen the land of his forebears.

Did these children remember, with pain? Laurie was sleeping on Angus' shoulder, and the boy was staring mournfully through the window of the coach. Stuart was suddenly startled. There was the most remote and absorbed expression on the lad's small and quiet face, as if he saw nothing of the wild and desolate scene outside. His face was the face of a dreamer, unchildlike, still, and heavy with sorrow.

Bertie was dozing, with an amiable smile curving his lips. Stuart smiled a little, involuntarily. He was already fond of Bertie, who laughed so much and never complained, no matter how weary he was. The lad found everything humorous; his good temper never failed. His ruddy hair lay dishevelled over his handsome head. There were several deep dimples trembling near his lips, though he was dozing comfortably and unconsciously.

When Stuart glanced at Robbie, his smile grew broader. For Robbie was trying to read by the failing light. Stuart observed to himself that the lad was always reading. Robbie read coolly and methodically, withdrawn in himself. Yet he did not give the impression of being a scholar. There was a purposefulness in his reading, an unpleasant concentration. Stuart tried to crane his neck far enough to catch a glimpse of the title of the book. Then he was astonished, and highly diverted. The title was: "Famous Cases at Law at the Assizes at Old Bailey."

Law! Stuart began to chuckle to himself, but he eyed Robbie with more interest, and a curious and wary dislike. A sprig of a lad like this! His dislike grew.

CHAPTER 6

ON THE morning of the next to the last day the hills had become lower, like walls in the distance, but the cold was more intense. Now all about them lay flat land, stark and black and motionless as death. Settlements were thicker, however, and little towns and villages. Janie, assured that the long journey was almost done, became very interested. She had not heretofore questioned Stuart much about his home or his affairs. She had been too intent on ingratiating herself with him, of amusing, diverting and fascinating him. Now she began to eye him with furtive speculation, though, when he turned to her suddenly, she smiled charmingly.

She must know all about him. Grandeville—what manner of city was this? Stuart explained. A raw and overgrown village, rather than a city. But boisterous and vital, expanding rapidly, situated on the bleak and brawling waters of Lake Erie. Here it was that the famous Wells-Fargo Express had originated. (Eighteen of Janie's trunks had already gone ahead to Grandeville on that express, much to Janie's bewildered admiration.) A bustling town, this Grandeville, the point of exchange between the unfathomable West and the East. Traders were here, and shippers came and went constantly, arranging passage for themselves and their goods on the Great Lakes. Yes, said Stuart, to one of Janie's inquiries, one could see Indians there, coming and going silently, and across the narrow channel of some outlandish river one could catch glimpses of Canada. Canada! Janie felt comfort. An outpost of England still flying the old Union Jack! Ah, it was guid, it was guid, she said, again with the accent of her fathers, which always returned to her in rage, under stress, and at the height of emotion. Stuart promised to hire a boat and take her to Canada at the first opportunity.

He warned her, however, that she would not find that finished and urbane quality of English towns in Grandeville. It was a raw and uncouth hamlet, though bustling and riotous and full of the air of commerce, and the sound of wild growing. The streets were not yet cobbled; they were filled with mud, and the walks were of splintered and tilting wood. Most of the houses were of wood, also, and ugly as hell, he

41

told her frankly. Only a few of the houses were of brick, or stone, and, he added complacently, his own house was one of them. "With a fine view of the river, too," he said.

But Janie, her heart beating faster at his depiction of Grandeville, of savage men fighting for new gold in this new land, of "saloons" and raucous women and raw drink, of struggle and vehemence and strangeness, was not at all depressed at the picture Stuart drew for her. She was a natural adventuress, without delicacy and shrinking. She felt her blood stir. She listened with delight to the tales Stuart told her of his house. It was filled with mahogany, he bragged, gently, and fine rugs from the Orient, and she would be "at home" there. "We aren't entirely uncivilized," he boasted, "and we aren't exactly a frontier settlement. Why, Grandeville is old, for America! The British burnt it in 1812, and it was old, then." When he spoke of the wild and untamed West, it was with patronage. Grandeville was very cosmopolitan. Janie would find Germans there, as well as Indians, and a Jew or two, and peculiar folk from Eastern Europe, peddlers and shopkeepers, tailors and artisans, all enthusiastically working to transform Grandeville into a roaring city of commerce.

He told her of two of his friends, a Catholic priest called Father "Grundy" Houlihan, and Sam Berkowitz, a German Jew, and a rival shopkeeper. Janie raised her sandy eyebrows, and shrugged, regarding her cousin with a superior wondering smile. "A Papist!" she exclaimed. "And a Jew! O my God, my darling Stuart!"

Stuart was annoyed. "Damn it, you're half Irish yourself, my elegant little besom!" she said. "Your mama was a Papist, remember, and so was my papa." As for Sam Berkowitz, by God! he was a man of genius, and a devil at poker, and could beat Father Houlihan eight times out of ten. The three of them spent almost all of their evenings together, and damn pleasant evenings they were! They, his friends, were men of sense and shrewdness. He, Stuart, would be desolate without them, with not a damned soul of any intelligence to console his leisure hours.

Yes, he acknowledged, angrily, there were "gentlefolk" in Grandeville, also, but as dull and dead as a cold herring. There was, for instance, Joshua Allstairs, a grasping old swine who had mortgages on almost all the property in Grandeville. An Englishman! Who could expect anything better of Englishmen? Stuart's face was deeply flushed when he mentioned Mr. Allstairs, to whom he owed ten thousand dollars.

"And no ladies of elegance and fashion?" asked Janie, slyly, watching her cousin with acuteness.

Stuart was silent. The flush did not recede from his face. And then his eyes began to twinkle. He winked at Janie. "Ah, there are, indeed!" he murmured. "A fine house of them, and the ladies very gay and handsome." He coughed, significantly. Janie squealed coyly, and lifted a mittened hand to her face, and over her fingers she peeped at him with ribald modesty. Then she gave him a sharp and painful jab, and croaked: "You dog!"

She asked him if they ever gave any "balls" in Grandeville, and with defiance Stuart assured her that many "soirées" were held, that the music was excellent, and the toilettes of the ladies truly remarkable. "We have quite an aristocracy. The ladies import their gowns from Paris, itself, by God!"

He also told her that Grandeville was a city of the "Underground," to which escaping slaves of Southern planters fled on their way to Canada. "A thriving business," he added, with some regret. In order to impress Janie he told her of the Virginia cavaliers, of the fine gentlemen and stately gracious homes of the South. "We'll go there, some day, on a visit," he said, and continued mysteriously: "I have plans. It was only a month ago that Sam suggested something— Of course, it is not thought out, yet, but the idea is very exciting. Sam is full of ideas."

Then he became curiously silent, and watched Janie with tentative thoughtfulness. Sometimes he smiled, and his black eyes would sparkle with something like malice. In some way, he communicated his thought to Janie, for she became very careless as she said:

"And, my love, you've found no lady of your own, yet?"

Stuart coughed. He pretended to shyness. He looked away from his cousin.

"No," he murmured, thoughtfully, "though Miss Marvina Allstairs, the only daughter and darling of old Joshua, appears much smitten with me. And she is a young lady of fortune."

At this, Janie was sick with consternation. She regarded Stuart searchingly. But the rascal only hummed pleasantly to himself.

As he had much regard for Janie, after all, he was suddenly depressed. He had anticipated this moment with malicious pleasure. He looked forward to watching Janie's face when he told her of Miss Allstairs. It would be very amusing, he thought. But now it no longer appeared amusing. Janie had come a long distance to him; she had brought these miserable young puppies with her across the endless miles of ocean. Then he was angered against her, in his self-protectiveness. Surely to God she had not seriously believed that a man seven or eight years her junior could become her suitor, for all their earlier years together! Surely she had not thought that childhood associations and a present considerable fortune could make him overlook her age, her children and her unvirginal state! It was damned impudent of Janie, and shameless! And very insensible, too, and brazen! Janie was a fool.

But Janie, herself, was speaking, her hoarse voice sly and soft:

"Is Miss Marvina a great beauty, then?"

Stuart made his face serious and meditative; he made his mouth curve gently. He did not look at Janie when he said: "Indeed, that she is! A rare beauty. A young lady of consequence, and very accomplished."

Stuart thought of the loathsome Joshua Allstairs, who had not looked very kindly on his suit. Joshua was an Englishman, who hated all foreigners, and particularly hated Irishmen, whom he contemptuously considered slightly lower than "niggers" and Indians. He had permitted Stuart in his house only because the young man was aggressive and had the gift of making money, and despite his race was no Papist. Moreover, old Joshua loved to play whist, and Stuart was an accomplished player, and also knew good whiskey from bad, and was no mean opponent at chess. Stuart, seeking to ingratiate himself, had invented all manner of Irish and Scottish illustrious forebears, and even a "County seat." Mr. Allstairs, who had no forebears except shopkeepers and small artisans in London, had been unwillingly impressed, especially by the "County seat." "My father was a North Irishman," Stuart had grandly lied, "and an indirect descendent of Lord MacIlleney. My cousin, the present young Lord, frequently visited my parents in England. He is married to the Hon. Amelia Courtney, whose father, Lord Devonshire, is very potent in the House of Lords." He had added, believing in the principle of being hung for a sheep: "Dickie—that's my cousin, Lord MacIlleney, has vowed to visit me in America, and you will find him very gracious and condescending."

Still, old Joshua, who jealously guarded his lovely Marvina, was dour on the subject of Stuart's suit. One could not get

away from the damning fact that Stuart was Irish, and it
was well-known that the Irish were an inferior race, and
schemers, and liars, and cutthroats and thieves and vaga-
bonds. Worse, they were still under the influence of their
abominable and bloody Church, and worshippers of "graven
images." (Joshua was a very devout Presbyterian.) Despite
all Stuart's advantages as a suitor, his skill at whist and chess,
his expanding fortune and his elegance and gracious manners
and wit, Joshua gloweringly hesitated. He had made a huge
fortune in this hated America, by reason of the fact that he
was, himself, a thief, a charlatan, an exploiter and a ruthless
scoundrel. He had intended to return to England with his
only child, his darling, and marry her off to some nobleman,
or at least to gentry.

Stuart thought of all these things, and his gay and lively
face darkened somberly. Janie saw this. Her sinking heart
rose. Her queasy stomach relaxed. She wet her lips, and
studied her cousin craftily. Then all was not sunshine and
roses. Her courage and will, always stupendous, rallied to her
assistance. While there is life there is hope, she thought,
smiling inwardly. Stuart had said little of Joshua Allstairs,
but the subtle and crafty Janie had learned enough from his
expression to guess that the suit was not regarded by the old
man with overmuch favor. Janie's mind continued its spider-
like spinning, and now a dreamy smile touched her lips.

She changed the subject, amiably. She was all affable and
naughty jokes again, bestowing vigorous slaps and arch
glances upon Stuart, until she had him laughing once more,
and delighting in her.

Later that night, through the thin rough wooden walls of
the hotel, Stuart heard the sound of Janie's shrieking and
blasphemous voice, the crash of blows upon some silent
victim, and then Laurie's high and terrified cry: "O Mama,
Mama, you've hurt him! Don't hit him, Mama!"

Stuart understood. Boiling with impotent rage, he could
only despise himself for the suffering inflicted upon the helpless little Angus and his sister for his, Stuart's, fault. A dozen
times he could hardly restrain himself from bursting into
Janie's rooms and striking her violently, and rescuing the
children. Then he shrugged, despairingly. There was no use
at all. He could do nothing.

But he muttered over and over, through his clenched teeth:
"Oh, the trollop! Oh, the bitch!"

All his pity for Janie was gone. He hated her virulently
now.

CHAPTER 7

LONG before dawn, on the last day, Stuart uneasily awakened from his dozing and moved himself with considerable painfulness on the leather seat of the couch. Anxious to return to his home, he had, after consultation with Janie, decided not to stop off at any hostelry for the last night, but to continue the journey in order to arrive at Grandeville before sunset.

The close and dusty air in the coach was bitterly cold and penetrating. Despite rugs heaped over his legs, Stuart was chilled and miserable. There was a faint moon in the black sky, a recumbent crescent of a moon, and brilliant stars. By their light he saw the humped and huddled forms of Robbie, Angus and Laurie lying under their own rugs on the opposite seat. The children slept in attitudes of complete abandonment and exhaustion. Stuart could not see their shadowed faces, but a long strand of Laurie's golden hair glimmered in the wan light. Beside Stuart slept Janie, leaning against him, and beside her, her darling, Bertie.

There was no sound but the rumbling of the coach on the rough road. Even the coachmen drowsed on their boxes, lulled to sleep by the darkness and the wooden wheels and the soft thud of the horses' hoofs. Once in a while the harness jingled dimly. The coach rolled like a boat; the windows rattled a little in their frames; the doors squealed gently.

Stuart was suddenly and horribly depressed. His volatile nature was either high and jubilant, or sunken into black depths. Accustomed though he was to these curves of exhilaration and despondency, he thought each a permanent state whenever he was engrossed by it. Now he was certain that this heavy melancholy was to be his for all eternity. He moved heavily and tried to peer through the mud-stained window. He saw nothing but the dark and shining heavens, the formless flat darkness of the earth. He sighed, pulled himself cautiously away from Janie, who grumbled in her sleep, and leaned against the side of the coach.

The sick and nameless despair of the Celt fell on him like a crushing weight. He had long learned that it was useless to search for a cause, or at least a significant cause. The smallest things were often enough to plunge him into profound dejection. Large and formidable events often exalted him, for they were matters which he could grapple with and overcome. They never depressed him. It was the gnat in the ear, the slight prick of the flesh, the way the wind blew, or the look of the sky, or a word, or a glance, or, sometimes, even the movement of a woman's skirt, that had the power to overwhelm him with that mysterious horror of complete depression, which was wordless and reasonless. Sometimes he thought he was going mad.

Not being reticent, he had complained volubly of these states of mind to his friends, Father "Grundy" Houlihan, and Sam Berkowitz.

"Weltschmerz," said Sam, sighing. He had explained the word to the impatient Stuart, who had laughed contemptuously and noisily. "World-sickness!" It was laughable. What had Stuart Coleman to do with "world-sickness?" He loved the world very much, and found it full of enjoyment.

Father Houlihan had said, soberly: "It's the soul in ye, Stuart." Stuart had laughed hardly less contemptuously than he had laughed at Sam. His soul! By God, he had nothing but his strong young body and his appetites, and if he had a soul it was hidden in him like a sleeping seed, or a small stone, and as far as he cared it could remain that way. "I do nothing I later regret, for I do nothing I could regret," he said, feeling quite clever, and winking at the priest.

He now thought his two friends very dull, and very old, though Father Houlihan was less than ten years his senior, and Sam only seven. Stuart was already patronizingly referring to others as "foreigners." "Foreigners" in his opinion were those who were less concerned with making money than they were with their own minds and their memories.

Hideously wide-awake now, he went over the events of the recent days. He saw little Laurie's bright hair, the boys' faces. Then he clenched his fists. It all came back to Janie.

I never think, he said to himself, with rage. I get myself into the damndest scrapes, and then wonder afterwards how they occurred. I'm a fool, by God! What am I to do with her? I've run from responsibility to others all my life; I've cavilled at marrying. I've gracefully skirted the slightest threat of involving myself with others and their problems. Yet, here I am, with this strange woman, and her children. What am I to do? I never thought she'd take me seriously.

It bewildered and infuriated him to remember that he had been pleased when Janie had written him that she was coming to America. As if coming to America were a day's journey by chaise, and after a pleasant meal or two the visitors would return whence they had come! He had not looked ahead beyond the mere fact of Janie's arrival. Further, he had not given the children a thought.

Wait, said his mind, suddenly coming to a halt in its rushings-about. Janie had money. Fifteen thousand pounds of money, sterling. He had not thought of that, and for an instant he felt some justified self-complacency. Then his lips pursed in a soundless whistle. Roughly, Janie's fortune amounted to more than seventy-five thousand dollars! He would have little trouble in borrowing ten thousand from her, and paying off that blood-sucker of a Joshua Allstairs. Once paid off, in a round sum, Joshua would have considerably more respect for the suitor of his daughter.

Stuart became excited. His cold flesh warmed. He suddenly saw all the possibilities of seventy-five thousand dollars.

In his jubilation and excitement, Stuart brushed aside the warning thought that perhaps Janie might not be willing to lend him the money, if it led eventually to his marriage to the beautiful Marvina. He could manage Janie. He would have her fortune secure before he became formally betrothed to Marvina Allstairs. All he had to do now was to win the green-eyed bitch, cajole and flatter her, and lead her to believe God knows what. He thought of Janie callously. Had she not come to trick him into marriage with her? He owed her nothing. If he tricked her in return, then the better man had won. Besides, she would find her fortune more than doubled, and that was much too good for the besom.

Stuart was exhilarated. His depression had fled. He was thrilling, warm, vital, strong again. He looked through the window impatiently, could not wait for it to be done.

To the east, now, the sky was changing. It had become the purest, softest dim blue, changing to indigo overhead. Along the line of the dark earth ran a line of bright clear fire, motionless but faintly quickening moment by moment. In the very middle of the pellucid blue hung a huge and brilliant spark of light, the lucid star of the morning, restlessly radiant and burning whitely. And above that star lay the crescent moon, palely silver and vivid, its horns upturned, its luster dimmed by the glowing star. How still was the sleeping earth, how black and chaotic in its formlessness, and how very silent! It was as if it still had borne no life, and knew no quickening as yet. The silence had a quality deeper than the stillness of night or sleep. There was a prescience in it, an imponderable waiting, no longer insensate, but prepared for living, for the word which would give it form, and being.

The wordless majesty of the sky caught Stuart's careless attention, and the soul of the Celt was strangely moved and awed. It was humbled, made immeasurably sad. All at once it seemed to Stuart that nothing was of significance, and especially not himself. He had not prayed since he was a child; now, there was a fumbling in him, as if heavy coarse hands trembled to lift in prayer. Faint words from his childhood came to him: "When I consider Thy heavens, the work of Thy fingers, the moon and the stars, which Thou hast ordained, what is man——?"

Stuart's sadness rose to the acute arc of sorrow, and then his healthy resistance came to his aid, and he shrugged a little. He heard a stirring sound. Angus and Laurie had awakened, and the two children were staring with rapt pale faces at the eastern sky. Stuart looked at them uneasily, and furtively. He saw Laurie's pure little profile, the mouth open, the blue eyes distended, in the wan light of the brightening morning. He saw Angus' stained and sorrowful face, so young, yet so timidly tragic. The two children held each other's hands tightly. Over Laurie's shoulders streamed her golden hair, dishevelled and tumbled. She was only a child, but she had the look of a woman.

Janie was yawning and muttering, as she began to awaken. Bertie was already awake, rubbing his eyes vigorously. But Angus and Laurie were aware of nothing but the morning, leaning towards the window with the sad eagerness of exiles who see the shadowy outline of the shores of home.

Then Stuart started involuntarily. For Laurie had begun to sing, so very softly, but with pure clarity. She had the sweetest and most innocent of voices, but oddly strong and true for so young a child. She sang as if to herself, a strange song in Gaelic, as if repeating to her inner spirit the words some other had taught her. Stuart had forgotten almost all the Gaelic he had ever known, but he caught a few words. It was a hymn to the morning star.

The sweet and beautiful young voice filled the coach like a gentle harp. Even Janie, surly from sleep, listened, but with suppressed impatience. Stuart was not aware of her. He saw only the singing child, who sang as if alone, and meditating. Angus was listening, his eyes fixed on the star, and the fading moon.

Angus was seeing a strange sight with his inner eye. He

saw black and chaotic hills, broken in the first light of the morning. He saw those lonely and desolate hills smoking with white veils and clouds of snow. He saw that sky, and the star, and the moon, above them, silent and awesome. And he saw the singer, not Laurie, but a strong and slender lad, singing to the morning star, his face uplifted, his black eyes wild and ecstatic, filled with the humility and rapture of boundless adoration. Suddenly Angus began to weep silently, his tears running over his cheeks. He felt no rapture; he felt only bereaved and exiled, and full of pain. He was only a child, and he had no words for his suffering. He only knew that his heart swelled with agony.

Now Laurie had reached the end of her song, and was very still, leaning against Angus' shoulder. Janie yawned prodigiously, and said, with ill-temper: "Stop your yowling, so early in the morning, lassie. You fair wake the dead."

Stuart leaned towards Laurie. He had the strongest urge to touch the child. But somthing held him back. He said, very gently: "What is that pretty song, my darling?"

Laurie turned her head slowly to him. The brighter light of the rising day fell across her lovely little face. Her blue eyes were bemused, as if seeing something beyond her mother's cousin, and though she smiled vaguely, Stuart knew that she did not truly see him.

"It was a song Dada taught us," she said. "It was Dada's song. He made it for Angus. He made a song for me, too."

"Yes?" said Stuart, even more gently. "What was the song he made for you?"

Laurie hesitated. The lightest of blushes touched her cheeks. She dropped her eyes. "It was called 'Love that is Greater than Life.' "

Stuart raised his eyebrows. He felt a return of his old wry humor. "That's a strange song for a little girl," he said, with gentle raillery. "You don't know what it means, do you?"

But it was Janie's strident voice that answered him: "Robin fair coddled the brats! Such nonsense. He was no father to his family, that I can tell you. And now, Laurie, you'll comb your hair and sit up like a lady, and Angus, you'll stop mooning through the window and weeping like a baby. Where is your hanky?"

Stuart had noticed Robbie little during the journey from New York, but now his eyes involuntarily met the young boy's. Robbie was smiling his dark and twisted smile, sardonic and faintly ribald. It was a gnome's face that stared at Stuart, old and satirically amused, and impersonally cruel, as if he found Stuart very interesting and very naive, and just a trifle stupid.

Bertie was yawning widely, his ruddy curls tangled, his handsome and pleasant face smiling as always. He looked at his brothers and his sister, and for one intangible instant there was a quick and facile darkening of his expression, as if with compassion. It was incredible. Stuart could hardly believe it. He felt disoriented, as if he had wandered into a strange country peopled with the strangest creatures.

The day wore on, and the exhaustion of the travellers increased as they approached Grandeville. The sky to the northeast was steadily darkening. The travellers became more silent as the hours passed, as if they were beyond speech. Even the voluble and vivacious Janie had sunken into heavy speechlessness.

Stuart lurked in his corner of the coach, scowling and thinking. He was not given to long meditations. But now his mind was curiously engrossed with the effort to disentangle himself from the wavering disorientation of his impressions. And, peculiarly, he was not thinking so much of the lovely little Laurie, or of Janie, or of Angus and Bertie, but of Robbie. He could not forget the singular expression of the lad when he had looked at him that morning, nor the humiliating sensations in himself.

Angrily engrossed with his compulsion to think about Robbie, he recalled that he had spoken very seldom to the lad during the journey. Robbie was so silent, so well-satisfied with himself, so thoughtful and withdrawn, that one was apt to overlook him. His small and meager stature, his colorlessness and reserve, contributed to that overlooking. He never asserted himself. He sat in the coach for long days, and never appeared to be one with the other travellers. Never had he complained or acted in a childlike manner, cajoling for sweets or favors like Bertie, or sunken desolately in himself like Angus, or moving in timid bewilderment, like Laurie.

Rapidly losing his equilibrium and common-sense, Stuart could not look away from that slight and quiet figure in its corner of the coach. Stuart recalled Janie's remark that Robbie was "the black one." Yes, thought Stuart, a black one indeed. Everything about him was black, from his smooth sleek skull to his tilted black eyes with their startling expression of cold and impersonal ferocity, from his pale dark skin to his pale fixed mouth, which was hard and quiet and strongly delicate. He had delicate small hands, pale and firm, also. He did not look like a child. He was too compact and aware, and too still. Stuart looked at his hands again. They held the thick book without awkwardness. "The black one." He doubtless possessed a black heart, also, thought Stuart, vengefully.

What did the little wretch see in that absurd book? It was all pretense of course. He wished to impress others with his taste for great learning.

It was only at sunset that Stuart could finally bring himself to speak to the object of his compulsion and detestation.

"Come, now," he said with a smile, and in a rallying tone, "what is so interesting in that big book? Too big for so little a lad."

Robbie lifted his black eyes slowly, and fixed them disinterestedly upon Stuart. He did not speak for a moment or two, in which Stuart felt his gorge rising and his cheek coloring. Then Robbie said, in his firm quiet voice: "It's very interesting, Cousin Stuart. I think I told you once. It's about the murder trials at Old Bailey."

"Murder trials!" repeated Stuart, raising his eyebrows in an attempt at amused and indulgent archness. "And how would they be interesting a lad like you, hardly out of his napkins?"

He thought to embarrass Robbie, to reduce him to helpless childhood. But Robbie only regarded him with that inscrutable thoughtfulness so infuriating to the young man. The slightest of smiles touched his fixed lips. He shrugged almost imperceptibly, as if he found Stuart tedious and childish.

"They do interest me," he replied, with quiet reserve. "I'm going to be a barrister, some day. I like to read about murder trials. The judges and the barristers are so stupid. They never see anything." The dimmest of warmths now pervaded him, and the cold fierceness of his black eyes kindled. "Why, anyone could see that Jervis murdered his wife!" He tapped the book with a little hard finger. "Yet they acquitted him for 'lack of evidence'! Even a fool could see how Jervis diddled the jury!"

Stuart was dumb. He leaned back in his corner, his mouth opening slackly. Robbie calmly returned to his book. Janie was chuckling hoarsely, and with pride at the precosity of her abominable offspring. She did not like Robbie in the least, but she had a rough admiration for him and his efficient ways which relieved her of many responsibilities.

"A sharp one, that!" she said.

But Stuart was again confused with his disorientation and

sudden wild hatred for Robbie. He brooded over it for half an hour longer.

Bertie, the good-natured and sweet-tempered, was becoming bored. He teased his mother for a moment, but when she gave him a sharp slap, and shouted an oath at him, he desisted, and yawned. Then his bright blue eye lighted on Robbie like a gay and winging fly. He reached out and snatched the ridiculous tome from his brother's lap and threw it on the dusty floor of the coach. Robbie started up with a muted but enraged cry, and fell upon his brother. Janie shouted, and struck at them indiscriminately as they rolled against protesting feet, and raised a cloud of dust, and punched each other furiously. Stuart helped Janie to disentangle the welter of young arms and legs and wrinkled jackets. "Now then, now then!" he cried, dragging Robbie from Bertie, who had begun to get the worst of it. He flung Robbie violently back upon his seat, while Janie, conservatively belaboring Bertie, pushed him back beside her, and smacked his clothing free of soil.

Robbie sat on his seat, and panted, straightening his clothes with silent fury. He glared at his brother with inhuman rage. He passed his hands over his shining black hair, smoothing it back into place. He was trembling.

Bertie, properly subdued by Janie, but still laughing uncontrollably, glanced at Robbie. They stared at each other for a moment or two. Then, to Stuart's amazement, Robbie began to smile. He brushed off the last chaff from his trousers, fastidiously. His smile widened. His cold black eyes were actually dancing. "I'll give you something to remember, one of these days," he said, and his voice was the voice of a child.

But he did not resume reading. He and Bertie began to chaff and threaten each other in the meaningless and ferocious accents of childhood.

CHAPTER 8

JANIE was no complainer, no matter what her thoughts. Now that she had something to gain she was all affability and good nature. She minimized discomforts, joked about them raucously, and accepted everything.

From the first she hated America, not passionately or

vengefully, but in a matter-of-fact fashion, and without personal bias. Nevertheless, she soon accustomed herself to the country, and looked about for advantages for herself.

She had been agreeably surprised at Stuart's house, where she was now lodged with her children. "It ought to be something," Stuart said grudgingly, in answer to her admiring ejaculations. "I borrowed ten thousand dollars from old Allstairs to build it." Janie, who felt surprised contempt that anyone would borrow money to build a house, made no comment on this. She could very well understand borrowing money to buy land, or to create a business, but the borrowing of money to buy "gee-gaws" was practically blasphemous. There was something feckless in a man who loved beautiful things, and would put himself in jeopardy to purchase them. Because of her secret contempt for Stuart, she felt herself gaining mastery over him, and confidence in herself. She had had many bad hours on that journey from New York. Now her apprehension was almost gone. She was again Stuart's gay senior, indulging him, laughing at him affectionately, and exchanging ribald stories with him.

It was indeed a strangely lovely house, built of clear white stone, and facing the river. It was also extremely large, which amazed Janie, and of beautiful proportions, possessing sixteen rooms, each one more alluring and restful than the one before. There were three lofty stories; the windows were all high and narrow, with grilled work protecting them. It had the look of a Grecian temple, for eight white pillars soared upwards the entire height of the house, supporting a graceful balcony at the top. The stone had been brought to Grandeville on a barge, by way of the canal, and Stuart never tired of telling the story of its arduous journey. So exquisitely were the blocks fitted that it took a close glance to see the lines of their joining, and so gleaming and bright was their texture that they appeared to be formed of the purest white marble. One entered the central hall and saw the floating and curving grace of a winding staircase, which reached the third gallery. From the ceiling hung a huge chandelier, crystal and gilt, and glowing with lustre. At night it blazed with candles, whether or not guests were expected. Janie found this extravagant, but Stuart said, irately: "I built this house for my own enjoyment, and not to flabbergast strangers."

The floor of the huge hall was amazing, being constructed of an apparently seamless piece of brilliantly polished black granite, which, like the exterior of the house, had the look of marble. Many of Stuart's acquaintances were appalled at the startling effect of this house, which was deliberately black and white, and were revolted at so strange an idea. It was fantastic. No one but an Irishman, they said, would conceive of anything so odd. The woodwork was pure and gleaming white, the fireplaces polished black stone, immense yet curiously delicate in their structure and carving. The lofty ceilings were of white molded plaster, dimly touched with pale gilt. The great parlor, cold yet exquisite, had a parquetry floor, partially covered by an Aubusson rug of the most soft and faded tints of blue and rose and faint crimson. The furniture, exquisite also, was of austerely perfect lines, the graceful sofas and chairs being covered with silken damask and dimmed tapestries and velvets in shades to match the rug. On every carved table stood crystal lamps and strange brilliant boxes, and on the white walls were excellent paintings of flowers and country scenes. "No portraits of illustrious ancestors," said Stuart, grinning, "though it's thinking I am of buying some in London to impress the local gentry."

The great dining hall was panelled in pale wood, and was all crimson and subdued blue in its furnishings. The furniture, in the best Chippendale tradition, was flawless. There was a library too, the walls lined with impressive books, which Stuart candidly confessed were quite beyond him, as he was "no scholar." Their quiet backs, crimson and blue, also, repeated the colors of the rug and the velvet draperies. Here, too, was a fireplace, always burning, even in summer. "Damned cold climate," said Stuart, "and miserably damp."

There were eight huge bedrooms, most of them facing the river, four, with their dressing rooms, on the second floor, and the last four on the third. Two of the larger rooms possessed small sitting-rooms, also. All were fitted with fireplaces, but because of the short summers and the long inclement winters of this northern land, Franklin stoves stood on the hearths. Here, too, the furniture was in perfect taste, with huge canopied beds, soft rugs, and the best of wood and hangings, all brought, with the other furnishings, from England and the Continent.

Unfortunately, Stuart's ambitious plans for his house had not been able to extend to large grounds; his money had disappeared in the most disconcerting way. He had been able to purchase only two acres from Joshua Allstairs, after the cost of the house and its furnishings had been estimated. Nevertheless, on this small plot Stuart had demonstrated amazing and unexpected taste. He allowed no trees or high shrubbery to hide the vista of the river, which flowed below the strong slope from the house. From the doorway extended a gently winding path of flagged white stones, so that the river seemed part of the house and its grounds, and a delicate extension of them. But on each side of the house, and behind it, grew high and noble elms and chestnuts, established trees which gave the house a look of agelessness and security. Stuart had made most of the land behind his home, and so artfully were the gardens and the paths and the grottoes arranged that they appeared much larger and more extensive than they were. Then, as the house was in an isolated plot, quite a distance from the center of the town, the outlying land was still unsettled and wild. Stuart never informed new acquaintances that these woods and these stretches of tangled brush were not his. He enjoyed them serenely, and indeed, he had plans for extending his property from time to time. He hunted in them with a good conscience, despite the fact that Joshua had grimly posted them, and conducted his guests through the glades and the thick forest of virgin timber.

He had even gone to the extent of situating his stables on the very borderline of his property, and even slightly beyond it. Fond of horses, he had eight of them, of good blood and breeding. He also had four carriages, of the best workmanship. Near the stables stood a small building where he housed his servants, all five of them.

Stuart cared little for the opinion of those who could neither help nor harm him, and would naively quote the cost of his house and its furnishings to anyone who had the impudence to ask. Therefore, when Janie craftily suggested that all this splendor must have cost more than two thousand pounds, he readily agreed. "I had ten thousand dollars of my own," he said, "and I borrowed ten thousand more from that old bastard Joshua. First mortgage on the bloody shop," he added, ruefully. Janie was tactful enough not to express her opinion. However, she remembered what her father had once said, in speaking of an extravagant new neighbor of no discernible antecedents and family: "A beggar always builds a palace when he can borrow a few pounds."

It was a constant joy, and justification, to Stuart to know that he possessed the finest and most spectacular house in the country. When, on a Sunday, gracious carriages drove nonchalantly along the path near the river, the passengers elaborately unaware of the lovely mansion on the high slope beyond, he exulted and chuckled. "Ah, it's not looking they are, the fools, but it fills their eye!" he would exclaim. When ill-natured comments were repeated to him, that he was a fool and would go bankrupt and eventually become a beggar, he was not infuriated. He was only delighted. Only when it was reported to him that old Joshua had sourly remarked that he did not like the black granite entrance hall, and would change it at once when he came into possession of the house, did Stuart privately grind his teeth. So passionately did he love the house he had built that he secretly vowed that he would burn it to the ground before it should pass into the hands of Joshua Allstairs. "It will break the heart in me," he would whisper to the darkness, as he lay in bed, "but that I shall do."

But in his heart he did not truly believe that his beloved house would pass from him. He would fight to the death for it. It was his treasure, his heart's treasure. It comforted him like a woman; it filled his life like a dozen children. It was the reason for his living and his work. It was the expression of his soul. He never tired of wandering through each room, and rejoicing in it, rubbing the wood with his hands, and exulting over its furnishings. In a way, it was his religion, the consoler of his weariness, the satisfier of his deepest instincts. Also, in an odd way, it had so completed him that he felt no need for any woman to share it with him. Sometimes, for long minutes, he would stand before the great gilt pier mirrors, and smile at himself with tears in his eyes.

Janie, suspecting much, was highly and cruelly amused at this folly, this devotion of a man to a house, and finally admitted to herself that there must be more behind this splendor and beauty than a mere revolt against a deprived childhood. In a sense, the house was Stuart's soul, part of the fantasy that lived in it, part of its mystical and dreamlike quality. Stuart might be hard and grasping, even greedy, in his desire for money. But this hardness and grasping greed were dedicated to a living beauty.

Stuart had inherited his father's store. Casual and light-hearted by nature, he would have been contented to make a small and easy profit, and to have gambled it away among happy companions, or to have roamed the country at intervals, or to have spent it on women. By temperament he was no clever business man, no bargainer. The house changed his nature, gave him restless and unsleeping and ruthless ambition. It was no longer his. He belonged to it.

The best rooms had been given to Janie and her children. Their presence hideously depressed and revolted Stuart. He shuddered inwardly when one of the boys scuffed a floor, or

ran across a polished expanse. He was in misery when the
children invaded the parlor or the study. He sweated inwardly when they sat on his furniture. He knew, then, that
he must rid himself of them, when, of course, he had acquired Janie's money on loan. In the meantime he kept his
grinding thoughts to himself.

Grandeville was an ugly city of some twenty-five thousand
souls. It consisted of a long middle street, called Main Street,
with smaller thoroughfares branching desultorily from it on
each side. The "old" section of the city was grouped along
the river also, but at least three miles from Stuart's house,
and here lived the "old" families, who were rapidly becoming rich from the tanneries, slaughter-houses, horse-trading
stables and shops of the community. Some, too, like old
Joshua, made great fortunes in mysterious ways. Others were
traders, and owned barges and lake vessels that brought and
carried away commodities from and to other Lake cities. The
"old" families were no longer adventurers. They were the fat
bourgeoisie, smug and content, but rapacious, greedy and
opportunistic into the bargain.

They lived in the ugliest of tall, narrow, red-brick houses,
all with cupolas and turret-work and wide dark verandahs,
with stables and gardens behind and grim iron-fenced lawns
before. Here, in their section, they had their hideous churches,
gray-stone or brick or wood, filling the Sabbath air with a
strident iron clangor. Along their cobbled streets moved their
stately and gleaming carriages, filled with their haughty and
uneasy women. The walks were either stone or planks, and
were kept in a reasonably clean condition. The only aspect of
beauty was the enormous old elms and chestnuts which
bordered the streets, and filled the northern summer with
sonorous murmurs. However, they darkened a scene already
dark and gloomy, and gave to this section a somber and
desolate air, unfriendly and repellent.

The houses themselves were furnished in execrable taste,
to match the exteriors. The choice of the householders ran to
black walnut and heavy mahogany furniture, to horsehair
and crimson plush, to hideous ornamentation and Brussels
carpets, to curtains of stiff Nottingham lace and balled velvet.
"They'll be Manchester English if they suffocate for it," Stuart
had once said, laughing contemptuously at the stained-glass
doors and windows, so narrow and slit-like, whose draperies
rejected the last wan gleam of sunlight which penetrated
through the dark trees. He shuddered at the memory of oak-
panelled dining-rooms, of tall, vault-like rooms, narrow and

dim, of square oaken stair-cases and spectral narrow corridors. He remembered shivering in many of these houses on gaunt winter nights, curving his body towards meager fires lurking far back in marble fireplaces. Even the gardens were dank, on the warmest of summer days, smelling of mold and sour earth, and immense respectability.

The largest and ugliest red-brick house of all on the best street (which was called River Road) was the mansion of Joshua Allstairs, and all the hideousness of his neighbors' houses could be found here on a grand scale. Stuart swore to his cronies that when he left that house he would immediately fly to his own, there to change his clothing which had become green with mold and damp in Joshua's parlor. "It's plucking the worms I'd be, out of my hair, for an hour after," he would say.

Far from this stately quarter, on the other side of Main Street, was the "new" city, composed of little red-brick houses, or, in the majority of cases, of clapboarded shacks and cottages. Here lived the newcomers, the detested Germans, the boisterous and drinking Irish, and the other nameless and despised races. Here were strange names, alien and revolting to the fastidious descendants of English and Scottish adventurers who had settled here more than sixty years earlier. Here were the humble workers who toiled in the vile tanneries and slaughter-houses and the two little iron foundries and the shops, who kept the stables and cleaned the streets and the sewers, who labored on the docks during the open summer months, who furnished the female servants for the denizens of the great houses, and who were employed in many other capacities. As they were still fresh from Europe, they maintained towards their haughty employers that nice combination of servility and devotion so proper to their class, and when these were combined with a large dash of fear and the threat of imminent starvation upon the whim of their masters, they could be depended upon to remain docile. Here, too, in this section, were the thriving taverns (owned by the great) where a man, and sometimes a woman, could drink that draft of anesthesia which made life bearable. Joshua owned many of these taverns.

The one beauty in this depressed section was the tiny little Church of Our Lady of Hope. Stuart, though no Catholic, had, with one of his supremely reckless and generous gestures, supplied the frightened little Catholic community with the same white stone of which his own house was built, for their church. One reason for this gesture was his new friendship for Father Houlihan, but the strongest reason of all was that he loathed the inhabitants of the "old" city and hated their oppression of the weak and silent populace of the "new" city, for which, however, he had the same contempt. Flushed with the intoxication of his own amazing magnanimity, he spent his money heedlessly for the building of the church, furnishing half the cost. Father Houlihan, too dumfounded, too moved and full of emotion, could do little more than feebly protest at the young man's wild extravagance. Mosaics were brought from Italy, fine laces for the altar cloths, and a beautiful little organ was shipped to Grandeville all the way from New Orleans. It was only when Stuart enthusiastically suggested that Carrara marble be brought for the floor that Father Houlihan awoke from his daze, and roundly refused, though with tears in his eyes. Stuart it was who tried to buy the land on which the church stood from Joshua Allstairs, and was promptly refused. Nevertheless, Allstairs finally agreed to lease the land on the payment of a certain sum, which Stuart guaranteed.

Later, Joshua sourly asked the young man, with a sidelong glance from his wicked gray eyes: "Why are you so tender with these heathen Papists?"

Stuart had shrugged carelessly, but he could not prevent his cheeks from flushing with a kind of sheepish embarrassment. "Ah, how can I know?" he replied. " 'Grundy' is a friend, and a good one, and the poor devil has no decent place of his own."

He could not confess that he was already cursing himself for his foolhardy generosity, and as usual he sat down in bewilderment to scrutinize the impulsive blindness of it. He had more than a faint suspicion that his motive was an impudent and contemptuous defiance of the people of the "old" city, who had hardly accepted him, and still fastidiously despised him. When the priest suggested that the real reason for any action, good or bad, lay too deep in the soul for any analysis, Stuart scoffed, though secretly he was a little startled and pleased. He hoped, rather than believed, that the true impulse which had sent him furiously spending money in behalf of the "heathen Papists" was a reputable one, out of the deeps of some unsuspected stature of soul. He lost this one small hope when he glanced at his bank balance, and cursed himself. He simply did not know why he did certain things.

Nevertheless, there was hardly a Sunday when he did not drive his carriage slowly past the church during high Mass, and did not bring his horses to a halt not far from the door.

He would sit there, a strange smile on his lips, listening to the fresh voices of the choir, and the noble grandeur of the music which came from his organ. He would watch the sunlight glittering on the golden Cross, and turning the small stained windows to colored fire. But, though Father Houlihan had informed him that there was a tablet on one of the walls with his name upon it as donor, nothing could induce him to enter the church. Why this was, he again did not know. He only knew that the gemlike beauty of the little church inspired in him the same passionate affection—to a lesser degree —as did his beautiful house. It was his creation, his monument.

Stuart's repentances did not last long. When he was again solvent he paid for the Italian statues of the Virgin and St. Joseph. It was enough for him that the church was lovely, that it was like a white jewel shining in the mud.

Nor was he insensible of the fact that his generosity had resulted in his shop's prosperity. The people he had befriended patronized his establishment exclusively. But, to do him credit, he had not thought of that in the beginning, though he accepted, with a surprised smile of mock modesty, the compliments on his sagacity paid to him by many of his peers, and even by the redoubtable Joshua himself. Ah, they thought him a knowing fellow, did they?

The lower reaches of Main Street consisted of many shops and taverns. There were harness shops and clothing emporiums, feed stores and tool shops, boot shops and food markets and butcher shops. But they were like pigmies compared with Stuart's store, which was managed by Sam Berkowitz.

It was called "The Grandeville Supreme Emporium."

CHAPTER 9

In the beginning it had not been the "Grandeville Supreme Emporium." It had been, simply, "Sam's Shop," or, without prejudice, "the Jew's Shop." Fifteen years before, Sam Berkowitz had arrived in Grandeville with his old mother, and a peddler's pack on his shoulders. Grandeville had had an air of bustle and vitality even then, and here Sam, exhausted, had decided to stay. He had rented a small dusty harness shop, and had laid out his meager wares. He had not exactly prospered, for though he was full of brilliant theories which Stuart was later to exploit, Sam was no business man. It was not that he had no knack for trade. It was just that business, in its more sordid aspect of buying at as low a price as possible, and of selling at a price consistent with the incomes of customers, did not interest him. Moreover he was too old, spiritually, to care much for profits. A roof over his head, peace, bread and a little meat, was enough for him. His chronic exhaustion was more of his soul than of his body. And his old mother could no longer help him.

The Coleman family had arrived in Grandeville for no discernible reason. There were greater and more flourishing cities than this. But here they were: Gordon, with less than two hundred dollars, a young son, and a wife. Gordon might never have met Sam Berkowitz had it not been for the fact that, on a certain hot summer's day, he had wandered disconsolately down to the canal docks to watch the unloading of a big barge from down-state. Finally he became aware of some argument near him. He saw a tall thin man with reddish hair protesting to a sharp little dealer who stood near a pile of unloaded wares. Gordon scowled. The lean and red-haired man, so shabby, was speaking in foreign and uncertain accents. He had the gaunt and prominent features of a Jew. He was no match for the dapper little dealer, who blew clouds of smoke from his cheroot into the Jew's face, and shrugged his shoulders airily. "Price's gone up," he said, with high indifference. "Pay, or don't pay. Don't matter to me, bo."

Sam lifted his hands and shoulders in an attitude of resigned despair. He looked down at the pile of goods, and shook his head. "I can't pay," he said.

The little dealer grinned, shifted his tall hat to a jaunty angle, and looked very knowing. "Come off, come off!" he exclaimed. "You Jews've got all the shekels in the world! Don't I know!"

Sam said nothing. He lifted his despondent head, passed his hand over his face, and began to turn away. There was a look of suffering and hopelessness in his hooded brown eyes, and of ancient resignation.

Gordon Coleman was a taciturn and unfriendly man, full of gloom and suspicion. Had the dealer been less sharp and jocular, had he had less of an English accent, had he been possessed of a less self-satisfied and cunning air, Gordon would have turned away indifferently. But, being what he was, Gordon hated him instantly. All his life he had hated the keen and the self-possessed, the hard and the prosperous. It was this hatred which made him growl diffidently: "What's all this, eh?"

Sam, who had been about to pass him, stopped and glanced at him shyly. He touched the cloth cap on his head, and said with gentle courtesy: "My goods. Promised for fifty dollars. Now, the price—seventy-five dollars." He shook his head. "I haf only fifty dollars."

There was something about Sam Berkowitz, gentle, sad and simple, which made Gordon unwillingly sympathetic. He was not an impulsive man, but he hated the little dealer, who was watching them with a wide and glittering grin.

He said: "What goods? What are they?"

It was only angry curiosity which made him speak, and he flashed the dealer a dour and sullen look.

Sam lifted his hands eloquently, and let them drop. "I haf a little store. Goods for the vomen's kitchens. Pots. Pans. Thread. Calico. Such things. Now, I haf no goods. Tomorrow, I haf no store."

Gordon was somberly silent. He had less than two hundred dollars. He had no prospects. His interest was awakened. If he should lend Sam Berkowitz twenty-five dollars, there might be a profit in it for him. He hesitated. Then, he thrust his hand in his pocket and withdrew some money. He laboriously and deliberately counted this abominable American exchange. Sam, amazed, watched him. The little dealer drew near, like a small, compact and well-groomed rat, all alertness and interest.

"That's the ticket! That's the ticket!" he exclaimed. "Allus help a fellowman and make a profit! Thank ye, sir, thank ye! And, Mr. Berkowitz, what is your next order, sir?"

Gordon suppressed a desire to boot the dealer vigorously. There was a hot crawling in the roots of his hair, and all over his flesh.

In the beginning he intended only to remain in Grandeville until Sam had returned his money, with appropriate interest. He visited the store often, for he was very lonely and filled with nostalgia. Sam was his only friend. He would sit near the splintered counter in the miserable little shop, so filled with dust and hopelessness, and watch the wrangling transactions of the housewives, with their bonnets and baskets. As Gordon hated practically everyone, he hated these pinched-faced women with their mean eyes. He came to enjoy his hatred. But he did not hate Sam Berkowitz.

And that was a strange thing. Perhaps it was because the

gentle and courteous Sam was no match for the women with the tight and meager faces. Perhaps it was his own memory of being exploited by those who despised him. At any rate, he began to take an interest in the store. It was soothing to talk to Sam, who had boundless gratitude for him, and who thought him a very superior gentleman. He argued with Sam, pointed out to him that he was often cheated and had to sell his goods under cost. His egotism, so long bruised, swelled and flourished. And then one day he pushed Sam to the rear of the store, and confronted the next women himself when they entered. They were accustomed to Sam's shy deprecation and shrinking from them. Now they were faced by a truculent Irishman with a hard flushed face and a belligerent glare in his eyes. At the end of the day Gordon's exultation was unrestrained. He was drunken with his success. He had confronted the world, had struggled with it, and had conquered. Moreover, he had gotten almost twice as much for the goods as Sam might have got.

He became Sam's partner. Sam was only too happy. Now that he was released from the actual hideous necessity of dealing with the public, he was full of the most magnificent ideas. They were endless. After shop hours he and Gordon would sit in the tiny living-room behind the rear door and argue. Old Mrs. Berkowitz would stir a fragrant iron pot on the iron stove, and regard them lovingly.

Within a few months Gordon had moved his family from the dirty hostelry in which they had been wretchedly sojourning, and had transported them to a neat cottage not far from the shop. The young Stuart was pressed into service behind the counter, and for deliveries of the larger goods. Now every shelf was filled, the quality and the variety of the merchandise expanded. Stuart and his father sold the wares; Sam purchased them, poring over catalogs and bills sent him by dealers and manufacturers in other cities.

At the end of a year young Stuart was forced to attend a "gentleman's school" in Grandeville, where he first encountered the fat youthful progeny of the "old" city. It was there, too, that he first encountered the class distinction and racial hatred for which America was to be known in the future. He was a "dirty Irishman." He was a "filthy Papist." He was a "slum rat." Even when he had convinced his tormenters that he was no "Papist," he could not deny his Irish blood. However, when by his fists and his superior curses, he had made them take cognizance of the fact that he had been born in Scotland, of a Scottish mother, his life was more tolerable.

But he knew, and his enemies knew, that his father paid twice the tuition that the more elegant young gentlemen's parents paid for their education.

No retiring blossom by nature, he became a swaggerer out of sheer defensiveness. He was bigger and heavier than his contemporaries. He had made them respect his fists and his oaths. It was no desire of his that he associate with these young noblemen of families who drew their wealth from tanneries and abattoirs and venality. But Gordon, obsessed with the idea that his son must be a gentleman, forced him to attend. Stuart would much have preferred the shop, and the company of Sam, and the strange delicacies which Mrs. Berkowitz produced from her stove.

By the time Stuart was eighteen, and happily released from his school (where he had not in the least distinguished himself in Latin or literature or the arts), the shop had become the Grandeville Supreme Emporium. Moreover, it had absorbed two nearby shops, and was prospering. It even had a second floor, an astounding innovation. Sam was a shrewd and inspired buyer. Gordon was a hard but just retailer. It had been Sam's idea that perhaps the ladies of Grandeville might be interested in purchasing more handsome articles for their homes than had hitherto been available in the city. Why should the ladies import such things from Chicago, New York and Philadelphia, when they might be persuaded to purchase them, at a lower price, right at home in Grandeville? Besides, many of the ladies bought sight unseen from the distant shops. Here, they could examine and haggle and consider.

As a result, some fine lace curtains appeared in the shop. Only a few. These were gone in two days. Later, the daring Sam produced some excellent little Oriental rugs, a few sets of imported French china. The ladies were enthusiastic. They filled the shop to bursting. Moreover, there was a handsome young man behind the counter, as well as the hard and sullen Gordon who had never learned beguilement. Now carriages filled the street before the shop, and the ladies said some very pointed things to each other, when they jostled to buy. One day the Mayor's lady, herself, came in state, and swept away triumphantly with a set of Limoges china and a silver toasting fork, much to the awed rage of the other defeated ladies.

Stuart, it was, who suggested that the shop might be totally irresistible if it lost its dusty and unattractive air. He was a young man of much imagination and dash and color. (And, as the ladies had approvingly observed, he possessed excellent legs and the most enchanting manners.) So it was, over the angry protests of his father, that he actually laid a Brussels rug on the ground floor of the shop, and placed a few comfortable chairs about for the comfort of the lady customers. He, himself, kept the small windows sparkling. Once, in his enthusiasm, he had even suggested that tea might be served the ladies at certain hours, but here he was completely outshouted by his father, and deserted even by his warmest friend, Sam Berkowitz. He had to let the matter drop, but it by no means died in his mind.

By the time Stuart was twenty-two the shop was enormous, "almost as large as a Philadelphia shop, my dear, of the best clientèle," the Mayor's wife had graciously informed her friends. It filled three floors. It had been widened and expanded. Carriage blocks were placed strategically at the curb for the convenience of customers, and a small immaculate boy (not in the uniform the inspired Stuart had deliriously suggested, however) was always poised to race out to assist.

Stuart was not completely mad. He knew that the solid life-blood of a trade was the custom of the farmers and the lesser townsfolk. So, adjoining the more resplendent and elegant shop was a large, neat but simple store where bright calicos and humbler household wares could be purchased at a most reasonable price. Here the farmers' wives in their sunbonnets and their shawls, and the poorer women of the town, could shop without being awed and thrust aside by the more delicate ladies.

Stuart was no cynic. He had at first been a little fearful about his own idea of making class distinctions between one stratum of his customers, and another. Would not the farmers' wives and the poor townswomen be angered at the implicit suggestion that they were not fit for the elegant emporium, that their presence was more welcome elsewhere? But to his amazement, and cynical disillusionment, he saw that the poorer shop was greeted with pleasure and gratitude by its customers. He saw that it was appreciated, and considered most proper, by those who had by no means been subtly insulted. It was the oppressed then, that created the oppressors, who accepted oppression with a sense of appropriateness. It was the oppressed who perpetrated the class distinctions, and laid themselves humbly down before their "superiors" for the latter's boots, and who preferred to be treated as lesser beings.

Out of pity and contempt, Stuart, in dull hours in the elegant shop, would himself wait on the customers in the poorer shop. Here he was all graciousness and courtesy, with a slight touch of genteel patronage. He saw to it, however, that the cheaper wares displayed were of the best quality obtainable of their kind, and that the prices were reasonable.

By the time that Stuart's father died, when the young man was twenty-five, the Grandeville Supreme Emporium was absorbing almost the complete trade of the whole country-side. There were "departments" here, in adjoining subsidiary shops, where the farmers could purchase harness and tools, denim and boots, feed and tobacco. The Emporium had de-voured the little individually-owned stores in its path, and digested them. The first department store had made its appearance, though it did not as yet bear that name. "Every-thing for the Mansion and the Cottage," had become its slogan, sprung from the glowing brain of Stuart Coleman, ably assisted and abetted by Sam Berkowitz, who was buyer and treasurer.

Relieved of the inhibiting presence of Gordon, who always prophesied the direst results from expansion and innovations, Sam really displayed his mettle. Now there was an adjoin-ing shop where stoves were sold exclusively, and fireplace equipment. Sam and Stuart went on to dizzier heights. In one tiny shop, branching out from the mother shops, were sold goods exclusively for babies and young children, from the finest nainsook to yards of material to be cut into squares and prepared for the regrettable habits of children who were as yet unable to comprehend more sanitary arrangements. There were little fur bonnets and mittens, made of the softest white fur, and carriage blankets of appropriate sizes, and bassinets of the most cunning white wicker, and even wooden toys, and the most delicate French laces.

By this time the Grandeville Supreme Emporium had ab-sorbed one complete block of stores and shops, and stood grandly facing the sunsets, unchallenged and magnificent. Years later, other great shops were to declare that they were the innovators of the department store, but in fact the Grandeville Supreme Emporium was the first of its kind, and its fame had extended even as far as New York itself.

All this was not accomplished without gigantic stress and strain and consuming anxiety and debt. Because Stuart and Sam poured back their profits into expansion and more daring innovations, they were compelled to borrow money. As Joshua Allstairs controlled the First National Bank, and emphatically disapproved of the Grandeville Supreme Emporium for no clear reasons except that it was "high-falutin" and ridiculous,

Stuart was compelled to pay enormous interest. But the fantastic success of the Emporium, by reason of its novelty and its variety and its amazing innovations, always relieved Stuart of any doubts. When he was twenty-six, a year after the death of his father, he built his astounding house and borrowed ten thousand dollars for its erection. Then it was that he indeed had a reason for expanding success. He drew ideas from Sam's inexhaustible brain as magicians draw rabbits from hats. He often drew out rabbits from his own hat, also. He and Sam rarely disagreed.

Though Stuart was still "that Irishman," and was not fully accepted in the most elegant society of Grandeville, he was handsome enough and rich enough to be considered a great catch by the dainty young ladies of the best families. But Stuart had his house. It was enough for him. His more robust desires were ably satisfied in a certain discreet little house near the outskirts of the town, where he often met the sober husbands and fathers of the best society. Here, too, he could drink and gamble in elegant surroundings. Joshua Allstairs, as was understandable, drew a profit from this establishment also.

Two years before the coming of Janie to Grandeville, with her brats, Stuart had been allowed to make the acquaintance of Miss Marvina Allstairs. She had just returned from a young ladies' finishing school near Philadelphia, and was possessed of the most magnificent wardrobe and jewels. She was her father's Benjamin, the apple of his eye, the treasure of his heart, and, in a way, she represented to old Joshua what Stuart's house represented to him. She was the reason for his rapacity and greed, his mercilessness and evil, his ownership of brothels and banks, his steamships and his trade, his investments and his rascality.

Joshua guarded her jealously. He scrutinized every invitation that came to her, and accompanied her to every house. He was old and wicked, and almost infirm, yet he drove his vitality constantly so that she should go nowhere without him. There were few homes, however, to which he permitted her to go, and at every turn he directed her thoughts away from Grandeville to New York, Boston and Philadelphia, and beyond them, to England, where her destiny lay. She sojourned temporarily in Grandeville, but did not live in the little city.

Stuart might never have met this golden pearl of a woman had he not called unexpectedly one evening to visit old Joshua privately on the subject of a loan for his house.

Miss Marvina was sitting with her father in the enormous and somber parlor of the hideous great house when Stuart arrived. She was introduced to him.

It was Miss Marvina, rather than Stuart, who decided that she would remain in Grandeville, and that she would marry him.

CHAPTER 10

STUART had been conducted ceremoniously to the parlor where old Joshua lurked like a thin gray spider with his bright fly of a daughter. Nothing was on Stuart's ebullient and darkly fiery mind but his plans for his house. Like many of his violent and vehement temper, he could think of but one thing at a time, and that thing at this moment was the beautiful mansion he was planning near the river. In fact, as he saw, in the dim lamplight, the rising form of a female person, his first sensation was of irritable annoyance and frustration. This, then, was Joshua's daughter, and her presence would inhibit him from the persistent and dogged arguments he had already formulated.

A servant discreetly lit another lamp or two, and the long dark shadows retreated before their sudden beams, so that the full repulsiveness of the dark crimson and mahogany room was revealed in its utter dankness and coldness, its sweeps of somber velvet and Brussels rug, its oak-panelled walls and snarling scarlet fire under the shelter of the black marble mantelpiece. Stuart drew a deep breath. This room, so crowded with the ugliest and most immense pieces of mahogany furniture, so littered with small round tables covered with velvet cloths bordered with golden embroidery and balls, and holding upon them bronze and china lamps and a profusion of knickknacks and *objets d'art*, always suffocated him and threw him into the deepest despondency. As no air was ever admitted into this house, it smelled of mold and beeswax and dampness. There was an inimical and repellent atmosphere here, enhanced by the dark portraits scattered here and there on the walls. Here, one knew instinctively, were only suspicion and hatred of all others beyond this house, and detestation and sinister malice and unfriendliness. It was a hateful place, no less hateful than its master, and he who infrequently entered here was conscious of malevolence and rapacity and sly evil. Even the servants demonstrated the truism of the saying: "Like master, like man," and their faces, lip-licking, furtive, silent, their sidelong looks, gave the more impressionable visitors the feeling that they had inadvertently wandered into a dark ominous chamber of hell whose demon-master was served by lesser demons.

Stuart, remembering the quality and atmosphere of this terrible house, had fortified himself with whiskey before entering. Nevertheless, he could not restrain a shiver or two. He felt his warm blood congeal. He would not have been surprised had his breath left his lips in a cloud of vapor.

Old Joshua did not stir from his huge winged chair near the fire. He only tightened his gnarled hands on the ball of his cane and squinted at Stuart sourly. But his daughter, startled at an unexpected visitor, rose on a wave of dainty confusion and uncertainty. She knew that her father never wished her to extend any friendliness to the inhabitants of Grandeville, and her first thought was flight. And then she saw Stuart standing there, near the far doorway, and she drew a little quick breath.

For Stuart, in his best fawn pantaloons (so cunningly fitted to his long fine legs that they seemed another skin), so polished of narrow boot, so excellently garbed in a long brown coat and flowered waistcoat and ruffles and perfectly folded stock, with glittering rings on his fingers and the glitter of a heavy golden chain across his middle, was the handsomest sight she had ever encountered in the shape of young male flesh. He was so tall, his shoulders so broad, his hips so narrow, and his face, dark and youthful and glowing, was so compelling, that the girl stood, fascinated, her lips falling open, breathlessly.

As Joshua had always referred to Stuart, when infrequently mentioning him with contempt to his daughter, as "that beefy Irish animal," Miss Marvina could not believe for a moment or two that this was young Mr. Coleman. And so it was that Miss Marvina could only stand on the hearth like a beautiful and timid bird poised for flight, and stare at Stuart, with utter stupefaction.

Obsessed with his grim idea of persuading old Joshua to lend him ten thousand dollars, and marshalling all his arguments, and trying to breathe in this dank and smothering atmosphere, Stuart did not, for a moment or two, focus his attention on Miss Marvina. It was not until old Joshua grunted: "Good evening," and waved his wasted hand at the girl with a muttered word of angry introduction, that Stuart became aware of her in her entirety. He bowed to her indifferently, and then as he straightened up, he saw her distinctly, and was completely startled and amazed.

Never had he seen such perfect loveliness, such tall slenderness and perfection of figure, such grace and lightness. Miss Marvina was only sixteen, but her height and carriage made her appear several years older. She wore a gown of gray satin, tight to and revealing her tiny waist, from which it swelled out like an enormous shimmering bell to the floor, and it was draped and caught cunningly in a hundred ripples of silvery light. Her ivory shoulders were quite bare; they gleamed softly in the lamplight as if polished and carved and rubbed by a master artist, with the most loving attention. Her arms, too, were bare, and possessed of the luminous quality of ivory, and of the most perfect shape and delicacy, and Stuart could catch glimpses of her young breast, soft and gently pulsating in its ivory sweetness. About her throat was clasped a string of exquisite pearls, and as she breathed they glimmered with a lustrous life of their own against flesh no less perfect.

If her body was beautiful, her face was no less so, and Stuart stared at it, completely dumfounded. It was oval and sculptured, with fragile planes of extreme delicacy and flawlessness, and quite pale. But her mouth, full, yet not wide, was like a dark sweet plum, and her large brilliant eyes were of an astonishing golden shade, vivid and radiant, darkening and welling in the midst of thick black lashes, like golden fire. Her nose was short and almost translucent, with nostrils delectably flaring. Her hair, thick, black, shining and without the slightest curl, was drawn back from her low broad forehead and pearl-studded ears into a thick chignon at the base of her white neck.

So blinding was her beauty that it hid, like a dazzling light, any hint as to her character. It was impossible to tell what kind of spirit lived behind all this loveliness and perfection. She was static. Even the golden fire of her eyes did not betray a single clue. It was like the pulsing of stars, which did not reveal any quality at all. So it was that for almost everyone, even her father, she possessed a quality of mysteriousness and remoteness.

Old Joshua saw the stupefaction of Stuart. He was not displeased. He grinned wryly under his long vulture's beak of a nose. His egotism and his passion for his daughter were invariably exalted when he saw the effect she had upon others, as though she were a cherished *objet d'art* of his which he had brought from far places and set up to display. When

the servants looked at her with awed admiration, he was not
affronted. From the lowest and the highest he expected, almost demanded, astonishing worship.

So it was that he sat there in his chair, bent and withered,
almost palsied, like an emaciated gray spider, his knotted
hands folded on his cane, his evil gray eyes narrowed and
glinting as he gloatingly enjoyed to the full all Stuart's manifestations of frozen incredulity. He was a little man, almost a
head shorter than his daughter, and so afflicted with rheumatism, so twisted by the wrackings of his shrunken flesh and
bone, that he could not walk without his cane, and then in
only a creeping and sliding manner, bent and huddled. He
made a slipping, slithering sound when he walked, and that
sound, approaching down the corridors of banks or in the
houses he infrequently entered in the company of his daughter, struck a strange and shivering terror to the hearts of
those who heard. He had a narrow face, like a "gray flounder," to quote Stuart, but it was topped off by an amazing
round dome of a skull, large and full, and like polished gray
stone. His expression, wry, sardonic, wicked, sometimes
quickened to a frightful alacrity whenever he was enraged
or wickedly amused, or plotting newer profits or rascality, or
when he contemplated the helpless struggles of his victims,
who were many.

Joshua Allstairs had been married when he was over fifty,
to a frightened little girl of much beauty from Philadelphia,
whose father was hopelessly in Joshua's debt. The child had
lived only a month after the birth of her little daughter, and
had expired on one last relieved gasp of joyous escape. Now
Joshua was in his seventies. But age had only increased the
evil in his soul, and his sinister machinations.

He dressed in gray, with touches of silver, which accentuated his spider-like attributes of mind and body. His horrible house was like a motionless and stony great shell with
him living at its heart like a vigilant bright pulse of malignance, sleeplessly watching and menacing and without mercy.

This then, was the power of Grandeville. Even the cities
of New York, Boston, Philadelphia and Chicago knew of
him, and hated him, and feared him.

"Sit down, sit down, Mr. Coleman," he said, testily, after
he had glutted himself on Stuart's dumb amazement. He regarded his daughter, hesitated, then looked again at Stuart.
His glance was like a glittering thrown knife. It was always
his custom to dismiss Marvina whenever strangers arrived.
But he was in a mood, tonight, for amusement. It would be

diverting to watch the complete enslavement of Stuart. So he touched his daughter gently but firmly with his withered hand, and she sank speechlessly again into her chair. Stuart, moving as if he were numbed, lowered himself also into the chair Joshua indicated. The two young people continued to stare at each other in a kind of bewitchment.

Joshua lifted his shoulders so high that they almost reached his ears. He pressed his chin on the hands folded on his cane. He regarded Stuart almost with cunning affection.

"Well, now, and how is our wonderful shop, eh?" His voice, thin but malign, was filled with cackling indulgence.

"Splendid. Splendid," murmured Stuart, hoarsely, not looking away from Miss Marvina. What beauty! What devastating beauty! His heart was not touched. He was only blinded. Nor were his passions and desires aroused by the girl, no more than if she had been a painted portrait of incredible loveliness.

His thoughts were confused. He suddenly saw, with his inner eye, a floating white staircase, curling upwards like a light and marble ribbon, and down this staircase drifted Miss Marvina in a silver gown like moonlight, every motion and gesture bright and fluid as flowing silver. The picture was so exquisite that he felt a pang. Now his heart was beating with great rapidity. Such a picture was foreordained to come to pass, he believed in his confusion. Nothing could interfere with it. It was appropriate; it was finished. Now his pulses were suffocating in their speed and pounding. But still his heart was not touched, nor his desire, except for a wild determination that he must have his house and that staircase, and Miss Marvina drifting down it to complete it.

Joshua's eyes narowed glintingly. So, this beefy and bold young man had been jarred, had he? This impious and profane devil with his colorful wardrobes and his debts and his gambling and his trollops? Joshua furtively licked his lips, hunched his bony shoulders higher in his gray coat. Let him look at Marvina. It was as far as he would get.

"You'll have some tea, or some fresh cider?" he asked. "As you know, my dear Stuart, we serve no spirits in this house, and no wine."

Stuart turned to him, dazedly. He stared at Joshua a long time. "No, thank you," he said, somewhat hoarsely. His struggles with himself were evident. He drew himself up rigidly in his chair, pressed his lips together tight. They had become somewhat pale. Now they were grim, and there was a look in his eye of vivid hardness and determination. He said: "Thank you, sir."

Joshua glanced at his daughter. And then he scowled, shifted his body uneasily. What had come over the girl? She was regarding Stuart steadfastly, her lips parted, her eyes full of dreaming tawny light. What the devil!

Ah, no wonder she looked like this. She had never seen so much flamboyance and vigor before in her life. Stupid child. She must be shown, without delay, that under all this vitality and zest and coarse life was the most infantile mind possible, and the most reckless and imbecile. She must be shown what a fool was this, a fantastic and heedless fool. Later, she would laugh deliciously with her father.

Stuart was determined not to look at Marvina again till he had accomplished his purpose. He dared not look at her. He lifted his black head challengingly and fixed his eyes upon Joshua.

Joshua turned smilingly to his dreaming daughter. "My dear," he said, fondly, "you must visit Mr. Coleman's remarkable shop, or, I should say, Mr. Coleman's shops. Most remarkable! We are quite proud of the Grandeville Supreme Emporium, and endlessly astounded at it."

The girl turned her head slowly to her father. She appeared asleep, though her eyes were wide. "Yes," she murmured, and the white hands clasped in her lap tightened together.

"You will remember, my dear, that we passed these—shops, on our way home from church yesterday. You were quite diverted by them, you will recall."

The girl was silent. She looked only at Stuart, and Stuart looked only at Joshua. The grimness had increased on his face, and the darkness. Now his forehead glistened faintly, though the chill of the room had not lessened.

"Astounding, astounding," murmured Joshua, and he chuckled deeply in his corded throat. Then he raised a knotted finger and shook it archly at Stuart, and grinned. "But there is a limit to astonishment, eh? There is a time to conserve?"

His bushy gray eyebrows, so startling in contrast with the polished gray expanse that loomed above them, tilted diabolically over his malevolent eyes. Stuart, gazing at him, felt his pulses slow to a sick pounding. He never looked at this man without loathing, without senseless fear, and involuntary hatred. Yet his muscles tightened with increased obstinacy.

"I presume, sir, that you are referring to the mortgage you

hold on the last three shops? You have been receiving your interest promptly, I believe?"

Joshua shrugged, lifted one of his folded hands a little from his cane, dropped it. "Ah, yes, most certainly. I have had no complaints from the bank. I have nothing to reproach you with, my dear Stuart." He coughed gently. "You will forgive me for my paternal interest, will you not? I have always been deeply interested in your bold enterprises, and have admired them. Nevertheless, there have been some moments of uneasiness. 'Is this young man expanding beyond his ability to absorb the investment?' I have asked myself. So far, so good. I am proud of you, my boy. You will forgive an old man's concern, will you not?"

Stuart was silent for a few moments. But he regarded Joshua with that dangerous but helpless loathing. Now his face became darker than ever. He said, without expression: "Thank you, Mr. Allstairs."

Joshua inclined his head humbly. "I may be wrong, and sometimes too officious, but the welfare of my young friends is always close to my heart."

"Also, your money, sir," said Stuart, unable to control the blunt and insolent words.

Joshua was delighted. He looked sidelong at his daughter. The pale ivory of her cheek had colored a little. Ah, then, she had felt a stir of indignation, had she?

"Money," sighed the old man, tilting his head sideways. "The root of all evil, as the Good Book says. But I have a duty to my depositors."

You damned, psalm-singing old swine, thought Stuart, passionately. But this time he held his tongue. He was conscious of Miss Marvina's regard, like electric fire, though he did not turn to her.

"I have discovered the hardest thing in this melancholy life of ours," said Mr. Allstairs, in a sad and meditative tone. "It is the reconciling of the demands of the world with one's conscience. One must compromise, one must always compromise. One must render unto Caesar the things which are Caesar's, and unto God the things which are God's."

Such as your profits from a brothel, thought Stuart. He compressed his mouth even tighter. But in spite of his silence, there was a dark and violent tension about him, and Joshua, who was very subtle, felt it, and understood it. He was more and more delighted. So, the fool would not be goaded into some devastating remark, would he?

"Nevertheless, it is hard," mused Joshua, sadly, and he

dropped his head with a pathetic gesture. "Sometimes, one must be firm, in the face of the most urgent implorings. Such as for extension of credit from farmers and tradesmen. One is faced, on the one hand, with the touching prayers of those who cannot meet their notes, and on the other hand, with the trust of one's depositors. How to compromise? What to do?"

"I trust," said Stuart, with vicious irony, "that I shall never force such an afflicting need for decision upon you, sir."

"I hope not, I hope not," sighed Joshua, almost in a tender whisper. "I should not know what to do. I should be forced to take my decision to the knees of God, and humbly pray for a solution."

Stuart's gorge rose so that he almost choked with rage and disgust. His strong brown hands clenched. Momentarily, he forgot Miss Marvina in his desire to smash this evil pious thing.

Joshua regarded him tenderly. "You comprehend me fully, do you not, Stuart? Only a faithful man could do what you are hoping to do: build a church for our esteemed—er—Papist, Mr. Houlihan."

Stuart said, in a pent tone: " 'Father Houlihan,' I believe it is, sir."

Joshua carefully laced his fingers together, and balanced the neat tent on the head of his cane. "My dear boy, will you forgive me if I again urge you to visit my church, and partake of the comfort of the service, and the consolation of the Gospel?"

Stuart drew a deep breath. His black eyes were glowing. "Mr. Allstairs, I will go anywhere with you, even down into hell, if you will listen consentingly to what I have to propose to you."

At these astonishing and heedless words, Joshua turned to his daughter. He looked at her closely, as he said to Stuart in a voice of rebuke and sorrow: "I must remind you, sir, that there is a young female present, and I do not care for your oaths in her presence."

Marvina had turned very white. She had dropped her head, and her father could not see her face. But he could see that she was trembling. It was enough for him.

Stuart stood up. In agitation and fury, he exclaimed: "Sir! I present my apologies to your daughter. If she desires, I will conduct her from the room. But I have no more time to waste."

Joshua lifted his hand. "I am certain that Miss Marvina has

forgiven you, my boy. Let us not speak of it again. I am also certain that Miss Marvina understands. She has already forgiven you your Irish blood, and your associations with a heathen Papist. Is that not so, my dear?"

There came the faintest sound from Marvina. Then she lifted her head, turned it away from the two men, and stared fixedly at the fire.

"I judge no man," said Joshua, in a soft but awful voice, "for that is not within my province. I leave that to God."

"And very good of you, sir," replied Stuart bitterly, completely disorganized now. "The Almighty must be grateful for such condescension."

He was a shrewd man, and now he cursed himself, as usual. He saw very clearly that he had played into this fiend's hands completely. But just at this moment he could not care. He cried: "Will you, or will you not, sir, allow me to present an urgent matter to you?"

Joshua was silent. He regarded Stuart with a sweet fond smile. "My dear boy, do sit down. You quite disturb me standing so, with your hand clutching the back of your chair. But, you see, I am lonely. It is very rarely that I have an opportunity to discuss matters close to my heart with a friend."

Stuart, almost blinded with disgust and rage, sat down again, stiffly, and panted a little. His strongest impulse was to roar a few choice curses at Joshua, but expediency, coming to his belated rescue, quelled him. Nevertheless, waves of heat and violence flowed from him. He said: "Shall I get to the point, sir, and cease wasting your time?"

Though he was now extremely doubtful that his request would be granted, his determination that it should was all the stronger.

"Do proceed, dear Stuart," said Joshua, with a royal wave of his hand.

"I want a loan. Of ten thousand dollars," said Stuart, getting out the words with great abruptness, and savagery.

CHAPTER 11

IT WAS one thing to bait Stuart so that his hot and foolhardy Irish temper might display itself to his humiliation and disaster, and it was quite another to discuss business matters with him when Joshua might have to display his own cupidity and ruthlessness, to his daughter's bewilderment, and perhaps distress.

Joshua had never spoken to his daughter of any of his affairs. She was never to know that the money which purchased her the finest pearls and satins and furs and carriages and jewels and finishing schools came from brothels, usury, foreclosed farms, ruined little shops and businesses, and the slums of the growing city. He took advantage, therefore, of the old convention that females had no capacity to understand the intricacies of finance, that they were overpowered by them, and had no interests beyond their toilettes and their homes and their families.

Accordingly, he smiled with the utmost paternal sweetness at Stuart, and said, softly: "Ten thousand dollars, eh? A most precipitous young man! Ah, my dear boy. Well, we must discuss this, must we not?"

He turned to Miss Marvina, and said gently: "My dear, may I ask you to retire so that Mr. Coleman and I might talk very tedious business?"

Stuart understood, and did not repress his dark wide smile. He got up promptly, however, and bowed to the uncertain young lady. She rose, as gracefully as a dove rises into the air, and a deep blush ran over her cheeks and neck. She glanced silently at her father, who was painfully rising to his feet. She was evidently much confused. She bent and kissed Joshua's cheek, and her beautiful hands fluttered a little. He returned her kiss, and patted her cheek. "Good night, my love," he said, and for a moment there was a strange bright flash upon his gray face and in his evil eyes.

She turned toward the door. Stuart quickly went to her side and conducted her to the threshold of the hall. There he bowed to her again. She was very tall. Her eyes were only a little below his, as she lifted them slowly in a sweep of black lashes. He was very close to her now, and could see the living translucence of her pearly flesh, and the very red pulsing of her lips. And now for the first time he desired her. The golden light of her eyes dazzled him. He felt heat sweep over his senses, and heard a drumming in his ears. He looked deeply into that wide golden fire between the lashes, and then at the faint division of her breasts which showed above the line of her low bodice. He thought it was innocence that gazed out at him in such shining confusion and silence. He did not yet know it was only emptiness.

She colored again, so that even her ears glowed scarlet, and then she bowed her head and turned away. He watched her go. He saw her mount like a bird, flowing and sinuous, up the enormous oak and marble staircase, her hand on the banister, her silvery gray skirts floating behind her. She passed a lamp, and it glimmered brilliantly on the smooth blackness of her coiled hair. She did not look back, but she moved very slowly, with infinite and indescribable grace, knowing he watched her. It was only when the last flutter of her train had passed from his sight that he could turn away.

He came slowly back into the room. The chill dankness had gone from him. His whole big body was hot and vibrating. It suddenly occurred to him that he had not heard her voice, except for that faint murmur when her father had addressed her. It did not matter. He longed for this lovely thing with enormous passion.

"A pretty chit, eh?" said Joshua, with deprecation, staring at Stuart cunningly.

Stuart said nothing. He looked at the fire, whose heat now felt insufferable to him. He pushed back his chair, and breathed heavily. Joshua, who a moment ago had decided to inform Stuart, very casually, that his daughter was destined for a life far from Grandeville, now decided to hold his tongue. Let the beefy sweating fool entangle himself in dreams and lustings. His later humiliations and sufferings and ruin would then be the more intense.

"Ten thousand dollars?" said Joshua, shaking his head with loving rebuke. "A lot of money, Stuart. Remember, you still owe me twelve thousand dollars." He rubbed his dry palms together with a sound like the slithering of a snake through dry leaves. He chuckled benignly.

Stuart came to himself with difficulty. Then, remembering the house he wished to build, which would be so appropriate a setting for that divine creature now bedazzling his senses and enchanting his mind, his determination and ardor came back in a wild rush. He cried, rather than said: "You have no complaint, sir! You are receiving the interest and principal regularly!"

"Quite true, quite true," agreed Joshua, in the richest of voices, and nodding his head benevolently. "I do not regret lending you the money, Stuart. Money, like tools, rusts if it is not used. You have the highest credit with me. But you will forgive me if I satisfy myself, for the sake of our depositors—a sacred trust, Stuart—if I make some inquiries?"

"Make them!" exclaimed Stuart, intoxicated.

"May I ask what sort of new plan this is that will require ten thousand dollars, proposed so recklessly?"

Stuart leaned towards him. Regardless of the fire, he pulled his chair forward, his face and eyes aglow and blazing. "I want a house. A good house. A house such as doesn't exist in Grandeville at the present time. Something unusual. Not a house to live in temporarily, but always. I have the plans, mostly in my own head. I want only the best. The ten thousand dollars," he added, incautiously, and in his enthusiasm, "will be only a beginning."

"Ah," murmured Joshua, narrowing his eyes and regarding the other intently.

"I have eight thousand dollars, cash, to begin with. I wish it were more. But Sam and I put everything back into the shops. We have an order coming for which we have paid fourteen thousand dollars. But the eight thousand dollars will do for a start. I have already purchased the stone, for which I shall pay nearly five thousand dollars—out of my eight thousand. But all that is only the beginning. That is why I need the ten thousand."

Joshua's face revealed nothing. He said, thoughtfully: "Where do you intend to build?"

Stuart hesitated, then plunged in boldly. "I want to buy some land from you, sir. You have a large tract near the river. I thought about eight acres, perhaps more."

"Eight acres!" Joshua cleared his throat slyly. "Well, Stuart, I must explain. I had almost intended to build there, myself. Besides, I have some other plans. Docks, perhaps, when the city grows. Perhaps the railroad, which we expect to be laid through to Grandeville, might desire that tract of land, at a good price." He shook his head. "Buy another place. I should have to ask you too much for it. That would hurt me."

"How much?" asked Stuart, bluntly, hating him.

"That land," said Joshua, "lies at the narrowest part of the river. I've heard rumors that a better ferry service to Canada will soon be planned. Docks will be necessary."

"How much?" repeated Stuart, with a dark tight face.

Joshua tented his fingers, and regarded Stuart affectionately. "Four hundred dollars an acre," he said.

"Four hun—," began Stuart, and then was silent. His face became violent in its speechlessness. His fists clenched. Then, in a stifled voice, he said: "Why, you damned old—! You bought that land for one thousand dollars, all two hundred acres of it! And that, less than five years ago! Five dollars an acre! And now you have the audacity to ask four hundred dollars an acre for it!"

Joshua was not affronted. He grinned. "That was five years

ago, my boy. Grandeville has grown considerably since then. It is expanding down the river. In ten years, it will be worth twice what I ask. Why, only a week ago a grain man offered me five hundred an acre. He wanted to buy five. When I name only four hundred, it is as a concession to you."

"There isn't a piece of property anywhere in this country worth four hundred dollars an acre, and you are well aware of that, you, you—!" cried Stuart.

Joshua shrugged with Christian patience. "All right, Stuart. Suppose we don't argue about it? Four hundred is my price. I don't really want to sell. Why not build elsewhere?" he added, reasonably. "I have fine parcels of land at less than twenty dollars an acre which might suit you."

"And where would that be?" asked Stuart, grimly.

Joshua screwed up his eyes meditatively, and studied the vaulted ceiling which floated in melancholy shadow.

"Let me see," he muttered, thoughtfully. "Ah, yes! Certainly. A really lovely parcel of land, Stuart," he added, with delightful enthusiasm. "Not an eighth of a mile from the home of your friend, Mr. Houlihan—I beg your pardon: 'Father' Houlihan. The south section of the city. I admit that section is not excessively desirable, in some parts. But just beyond its immediate borders is a nice piece of property. Ten acres. I can let you have it for twenty-five dollars an acre."

"You mean, near the quarries, and the brickyards?" said Stuart, very quietly.

"Yes, yes, of course! You know the section, I see. How convenient, when you wish to visit your friend! Just a few minutes from his residence. And, as you are such close friends, the presence of his parishioners near by should give you considerable pleasure."

Stuart stared at him with darkly sparkling eyes. "My house! You think I would build my house near German swine and Irish dockhands and street-cleaners?" The ancient hatred of the Celt for the Teuton filled his face with dark blood. He seemed to be choking. He lifted his hands in a violent gesture.

"My dear boy, my dear boy!" exclaimed Joshua, lifting his hands in amazed horror. "I am surprised at you! Are not these men our brothers in the sight of God? Is this not a Republic where all men are equal? Besides, you are Irish, also, you must remember."

Unable to control himself, Stuart sprang to his feet. He looked down at Joshua with such rage that the old man involuntarily extended his hand towards the bell-rope that hung near his side. But he could not reach it. Stuart's look paralysed him, and he could only gaze at him with unblinking eyes in which fear had risen starkly.

"Near your brothels? Near your taverns? Near your dirty brickyards and tanneries and slaughter-houses?" said Stuart, hoarsely, clenching and unclenching his fists, and trembling with his savage fury. "Where I could watch your whores parading past my house at night, and the drunkards screaming as your hirelings threw them into the gutter? My God, I ought to kill you!"

"Softly, softly," muttered Joshua, casting a glance of sincere alarm and uneasiness towards the doorway. "My dear Stuart," he continued, trying to mask his fear, "do sit down, I pray you. Stop looking at me like a wild bull. If I have offended you by suggesting that you are no better than the men who live in that section, I apologize. But, you see, by your association with that debased Papist, Houlihan, and with the Jew, Berkowitz, you have almost forfeited the regard of society. Gentlemen with any pretense of genteel habits do not associate with such creatures. 'By their fellows shall ye know them,' to paraphrase the words of Our Lord, Jesus Christ."

"You dare mention Father Houlihan in the same breath as yourself?" ejaculated Stuart, almost beside himself. "You dare believe that you are the equal of Sam Berkowitz? You, who have never had an honorable thought in your wizened life, or a gentle charity, and who have never done one act to endear yourself?"

Joshua sat back in his chair, though his lean and shrivelled body was rigid with alarm. He assumed the air of forgiving majesty. He eyed Stuart with a look of profound agitated sorrow.

"My dear, dear boy," he said, "I am amazed, wounded, at your extraordinary passion. I never bear malice. I never nurse in my bosom any unworthy feelings of indignation or vengefulness. Did I ask you to come here tonight and request a loan of ten thousand dollars? Did I say to you: 'Mr. Coleman, sir, I beg of you to enter my house and there negotiate a transfer of ten thousand dollars from my pocket to yours?' Is it by my will that you came, and by my will that you have affronted me?"

Stuart was silent. All at once he was terribly sick. He cursed his tongue, which had led him into this trap, his ferocious tongue which was like an unbroken stallion, full of fire and danger. Now his house was gone. Miss Marvina was gone. Forever. Worse than all else, he felt himself a fool.

Joshua craftily studied him. He saw Stuart turn pale. He felt no pity for this impetuous, warm-blooded young man whom he had so humiliated. He was feckless. He was contemptible. He was less than dirt, less than a dog, to Joshua Allstairs. The foul Irish rascal!

Nevertheless, none of these malevolent thoughts showed on the old man's face. Instead, in a voice of grave long-suffering and kindness, he said: "Do sit down, Stuart. I am sorry we cannot come to terms. But I will tell you what I will do: I will sell you two acres of that land for seven hundred dollars. That is three hundred fifty dollars an acre, one hundred fifty less than what the grain feller offered. Come now, what more can I do?"

He spread out his hands in a timid and defenseless gesture. Stuart was not deceived. But a frightful wave of relief flowed over him, so intense that he felt weak. The house, and Miss Marvina, were not irretrievably lost, then! He did not see how completely he had played into Joshua's hands. He was to see that only later. He only felt a stiff and shaking gratitude that he was not to be thrown out before his mission was accomplished.

Again, Stuart sat down. Joshua beamed on him with sacred fondness. "There now, there now," he purred. "That's better. Much better. We'll do more by kind words and reason than by name-calling and anger. We are reasonable men, are we not, Stuart?"

"How do you want the seven hundred dollars?" asked Stuart, stifled with his warring emotions.

"Cash, Stuart, my boy. Cash. A small transaction. Too small for a loan."

"You shall have it. And—the ten thousand dollars?"

"That is another matter," said Joshua, with hesitating regret. "Now, let me think a moment."

He bowed his head over the hands folded on the cane, and seemed to pray. Nothing could have been more pathetic than his attitude, which seemed to suggest that he was wrestling with the more venal promptings of his mind, while his soul and heart pleaded for his young friend. And Stuart watched him with a profound and riotous loathing which he could not conceal. The fire crackled somberly. The long shadows seemed to creep back again around the borders of the lamps.

Finally, Joshua lifted his head, his gray and wizened face radiant. He slapped his knee, and chuckled.

"I have it, my boy! When you have laid the foundation of the house, and have started to build with your own eight thousand dollars, then I shall lend you ten thousand dollars! I will send you an agreement to that effect tomorrow. There now, isn't that capital? Isn't that excellent?"

Stuart regarded him somberly. "And?" he said, with grimness.

"Ah, yes, I presume you mean the interest." Joshua leaned back in his chair, and became thoughtful again. "You see, Stuart, I am in a delicate situation. You already owe me a vast sum of money. You can't give me another mortgage on your shops. I owe it to my depositors. One must protect and tenderly guard the trust of those depending upon one. One must cherish it. That is the Christian attitude. My only recourse, then, is to take a first mortgage on your house."

Stuart breathed unevenly. "Yes, I can see that. I am willing, though I thought you might increase the loan on my property. What interest?"

"Let me see," said Joshua. "A house such as you intend is a risky investment. Who would, in Grandeville, purchase a house which cost at least twenty thousand dollars to build? Where is the man who has the money, or the recklessness, or the extravagance? It would be a white elephant. Therefore, should you—er—default, through no fault of your own, of course, I would have on my hands a house without much probability of a buyer. I should face the loss of my ten thousand dollars. Or rather, my depositors would face that loss. That is too much to ask of these struggling farmers, my boy, these little tradesmen. Think of the dollars, too, deposited in my bank by the toiling workman, each coin stained with honest labor. I must protect them," he added, with holy and kindling ardor. "None of these shall ever say that Joshua Allstairs wasted their substance, or jeopardized the earnings of their sweat!"

"What interest?" repeated Stuart, in a low pent voice.

Joshua gazed at him tenderly. "In justice to those who trust me, I should ask twelve percent. However, because of my paternal regard for you, I shall ask only ten."

"Ten percent!" cried Stuart, half rising from his chair, and then sinking back into it. "That is criminal!" All his initial hatred and rage came surging back into him like a dammed river. "It is also illegal!"

"Illegal?" repeated Joshua, in a pained voice. "Illegal, considering the risk I shall be taking? Why, my dear feller, I ought to ask fifteen percent. However," and he struck the arm of his chair, "you are under no obligation to accept. If you wish, the subject shall be considered closed."

Stuart stood up. He was shaking all over. He felt very cold. Reckless though he was, the enormity of the proposal sobered him. Caution told him to leave at once, before he put himself into shackles forever to this devil.

And then he saw his dream of a house again, and Miss Marvina rising like a white plumed bird up its circular staircase, and he was completely undone.

He clenched his hands on the back of his chair. He looked at Joshua with strange glittering eyes. "Done," he said.

Joshua looked at him with loving fondness. "Done," he repeated, gently. "And much pleasure in your house, Stuart." He coughed archly. "Are you thinking of the sacred bonds of matrimony, my boy? Is that why you wish a house?"

But Stuart did not reply. Those strange eyes continued to fix themselves upon Joshua, and Joshua, frozen by their glitter, could only stare back, in a profound silence.

CHAPTER 12

JOSHUA ALLSTAIRS rarely entertained more than three or four guests at a time, and then only very infrequently. He had as his valid excuse his infirmity and age, and his lack of a hostess. It was true that he now had his daughter, but she was young and inexperienced, and it was not proper that she should as yet take her place as the gracious lady of the house. Moreover, he had no older female relatives in Grandeville.

However, his cronies and fellow-plotters often came to dinner, as did those who owed him money. As for the latter's visits, they came almost on command in order that Joshua might satisfy himself in subtle ways that his money was not in jeopardy. Stuart was one of these.

Stuart, though not given to delving into the motives of others, was yet sufficiently astute, and intuitive as only a Celt can be, and early suspected Joshua's invitations. It had been his malicious delight to refuse them, except when they became too peremptory or he had been unable to meet a note immediately. But when he felt secure and lordly and arrogant, and matters were proceeding well, he would decline ceremoniously, not even bothering to invent an excuse.

But now he came, upon every invitation, ostensibly to confide to his dear old friend the progress of work on his mansion. He had two motives, the first and temporarily the more important, the opportunity to ingratiate himself with Miss Marvina and to court her surreptitiously, and the second, to talk of his dear house and the wonders he had ordered for it. In the latter motive there was much of the braggart, much of the preening of the intoxicated cock, and also the desire to impress the girl and make her wish to be mistress of all this coming splendor. So it was that at least twice a week he dined with Joshua and his daughter in the horrible and lofty grave-vault of a dining-room where soggy potatoes and cold fish and pale eggs were served in a mysterious sauce on the most ugly and elaborate silver. It was an unending marvel to Stuart where Joshua had secured his plate and china. In a way they were unique, for no one in Grandeville had ever before seen such hideousness, even in distant shops. It was Stuart's opinion that they were made to order, and were the excrescences of Joshua's deformed soul, designed by him.

Usually, before going to Joshua's house, he would fortify himself magnificently with whiskey and dine on rich beef and pudding in his own neat brick cottage. Then, pleasantly in a glow, and feeling himself at least eight feet tall and prodigiously handsome and dashing, he would clatter over the cobbled streets in his most impressive carriage with its two black horses, and alight in the grandest and most swash-buckling of manners. Only by such preliminaries could he endure dining with Joshua, and avoid being attacked by nausea at the sight of his obnoxious viands. Fortified, fed and exuberant, he could decline the dishes and endure the dank closed chill of the dining-room and face the implacable old man with assurance and poise.

At these frequent dinners, he and Joshua would converse on many things. Joshua, who was learned and scholarly and deeply interested in politics and history, would propose many subjects. Sober, Stuart would laughingly have declared himself grandly ignorant on all these topics, but delightfully intoxicated both by whiskey and by Miss Marvina's golden eyes, there was no subject on which he did not profess at least a talking knowledge. As he was instinctively quick and imaginative and natively shrewd, he often baffled Joshua with his observations, which, though couched in simple language and without affectation, were sometimes possessed of that ancient subtlety of a man whose mind is uncluttered. When Joshua once declared that geography and history were one, Stuart's mind at once encompassed the idea, and he volubly argued the matter, much to Joshua's somber anger. Later, Stuart would not remember the discussion, except that he had been almost brilliant, and he would feel some smugness. But his mind remained beautifully innocent of what in more delirious moments had been keen observations.

He surpassed himself in Miss Marvina's presence, and though sometimes his remarks were naive, they were uttered with such savoir-faire, such an implication of deeper meanings, that they probably stunned the young lady, who had little mind of her own.

After four months, Stuart had no more knowledge of the spirit of Miss Marvina than he had had on the very first night, except that she had a voice like rich slow honey, a voice which she rarely exercised. It was enough for him, however, that she smiled like an angel, that she blushed when he gazed at her boldly, and that she was apparently docile and well-bred and not at all clever. She was also an accomplished harpist, and after dinner she would sing sweet innocuous songs for him, totally without expression, creating such a marvelous picture of loveliness as her white hands stroked the strings and her bosom was lifted, that the infatuated young man was completely dazzled. He would gaze at her with the proud and delighted air of a proprietor.

He knew, however, that Miss Marvina was not insensible to him. He knew that he could catch her eye and hold it, and he felt himself very much the muscular snake bewitching the helpless and fluttering bird. He would pity her for her entrancement—the beautiful and innocent creature! He would feel tender compassion for her because she could not resist him, as, indeed, what female could? He did not know that Joshua watched all this with sly enjoyment, and that he would rub his dry hands in gleeful anticipation.

For Joshua, like Stuart, and practically everyone who came into contact with the entrancing Marvina, knew nothing at all about his daughter. From childhood she had been silent, though not secretive. She had always been docile and pliable, smiling when spoken to, moving with exquisite obedience, and never venturing any opinion of her own. As with all others, it had been enough for Joshua that she was incredibly lovely. The truth of the matter was that Marvina, though she could write a perfect hand, and could read aloud with expression, and knew her sums and her geography enough to pass the simplest tests, and could embroider with exactness if without inspiration, and could play the pianoforte and the harp and dance like a fairy and discuss topics proper to a young lady of elegance and gentility, was almost illiterate. Her soul was faceless, her heart perpetually untouched, and there had been practically no occasions when deep thought had ever darkened the placid shallow lake of her mind.

Miss Marvina, then, was a primitive, and what she desired she obtained. She desired few things ardently. One of them was Stuart.

Later, in fear, Father Houlihan was to say that he would never have believed that a human creature could be born and live without a soul had he not met Miss Marvina. For that man, she became beautiful smiling horror, and out of the depths of his Celtic superstition he recalled stories of creatures who moved and smiled and talked and had their being like other human creatures, but who in reality did not exist at all, and who, when they passed from the perception of others into the illusion of death, were gone forever like a puff of mist, leaving no trace behind them, not even any memory of them. As they had no souls, no verity, even God was unaware of them, that they had lived, for never had they possessed the means of communicating with Him. Even Hell, itself, had known nothing of their existence; hence, they were incapable of evil.

To say that Stuart loved her would have been a gross extravagance. It was his blithe belief that no man could love a woman, with all that loving implied: friendship, communion, companionship, perceptive tenderness and profound devotion. A woman was a female with whom to sleep, and upon whom to beget, and, in daylight hours, a hostess and a housewife and a mother.

He brought her flowers and books. She would receive them with evident pleasure, holding the flowers in her lovely arms, or clasping the books in her white fingers. But the flowers made no impression upon her. The books were clasped in marble. Her eye was as blind as her mind. She moved and smiled instinctively, as others unconsciously agreed.

So besotted did Stuart become that he actually accompanied Miss Marvina and her ominous father to church every Sunday. He dissipated the tedium of the sterile Protestant service by staring at the girl, and imagining all sorts of delights. She would sit very primly, with her brown bonnets and cloaks and frocks and gloved hands, regarding the dull minister dutifully, her profile perfect in the gloomy dusk, gleaming like carved ivory. She never seemed aware of Stuart during her devotions. She filled that barren air in the church with a glow and a glory that was positively indecent, in the opinion of the more muddy ladies.

If Stuart drank more heavily Sunday afternoons and nights than was usual with him, he did not know the reason. He told Father Houlihan, wryly, that he had to get the dust of a Protestant Sunday out of his throat. But it was the dust of emptiness, of associating with emptiness, that made him so distraught and sent him to his whiskey.

A Protestant Sunday in Grandeville was a dreary and horrific affair. "They hide under the beds," said Stuart, "and pull the chambers over their heads." But it was true that Grandeville became a ghost town for twenty-four hours, echoing and gray, only the tolling of the church-bells resounding over dead roofs and empty streets. Occasionally, a discreet carriage rumbled, muted, over the cobbled streets, during the hours when no services were being conducted, and inside some of the houses the inhabitants, stuffed with heavy dinners, slept the somber and oppressive hours away. Only rarely did one see an urchin, sluggishly expiring of ennui, walking languidly over the boardwalks, or a family group out on foot for an airing. In the main, Grandeville huddled under its trees in heavy silence, and the sparkling river turned gold in the sunset with only a few eyes to observe it.

It had always been Stuart's custom to flee the confines of Grandeville Protestantism on Sunday and betake himself to that benighted section of the city called "Pope Town" by its haters. There, a subdued liveliness could be found. In the grimy streets youths would play ball, or lounge on corners to look over the sprightly girls who passed with their mamas or their brothers. Here one could see alien faces, still lively with the memory of European Sundays, which had been all bright gaiety and lightheartedness. Children would race over the broken wooden walks, shouting, and their mothers would stand in their shawls in doorways, exchanging gossip. Father Houlihan would visit his parishioners, children following him in an affectionate train. He always had a pocket of nuts, apples or sweetmeats for them. He was much loved. To this disreputable section, therefore, where life and simple happiness and released joy could be found, Stuart often made his way. Sometimes he would engage in pitching horseshoes with other benighted souls, or in arguing ferociously, and ignorantly, about politics with large red-faced young Irishmen. He would always end up with a cold glass of beer in Father

Houlihan's extremely modest residence, and accompany it with cold slices of good beef and hearty bread. There he would be joined by Sam Berkowitz, and the evening would pass happily in a game of cards, or in loud argument, and much laughter.

"The Sabbath," said Father Houlihan, "was made for man, and not man for the Sabbath. What joy have these poor people in their lives, for six days of a week? Nothing but work and toil and sweat and hardship, and uneasy exhausted sleep. The Good Lord made the Sabbath, I'll be thinking, that His children might be happy and gay for a little, and forgetting how hard are their lives and their masters."

His views were not shared by Protestant Grandeville, where Sunday was gray and arid and cold and bitter and completely dead. In fact, they had long tried to have certain laws passed by which it would be a misdemeanor to play games on the streets, or gossip loudly, or laugh in public places, or indulge in cards and other innocent pleasures on a Sunday. "It's cruel, and wrong, to make the Sabbath a wretched thing," said Father Houlihan, with a sad shake of his head, "and if they pass these laws, it's myself that'll be the first to be hauled to the jails. They have made the Sabbath a day of penal servitude and sorrow."

The laws were not passed. Grandeville relied on cold disapproval, ostracism and example to quell the happiness of the inhabitants of the pagan "Pope Town." They did not succeed overwell, though policemen passed through the dingy and forlorn streets and made arguing and laughing groups of young men move on to another spot of vantage, and warned the children to cease their noise. But they said nothing to Father Houlihan who watched them with a sorrowful and meditative face.

He had a small and poverty-stricken little church before Stuart built the white jewel of a chapel for him. It was nothing for gross hoodlums from other sections of the city to invade that quarter and break the windows regularly, and deface the statues and befoul the interior. When Stuart built the chapel, he hired a bodyguard for it for many years, armed with clubs and guns. Father Houlihan protested, but the guard remained. "God will guard us," said the priest. "It's assisting Him they are," said Stuart, grimly. "We have the law," said the priest. "Law," remarked Stuart, "lives in the pocket of the politician, and the politician lives in the pockets of the rich."

In the meantime, Stuart's house was rising near the river. More and more people walked casually along the tow-path to watch the process. Even the mule-drivers paused to stare, and the barges they convoyed slowed down almost to motionlessness in the turgid waters of the canal, and the chimney pipes of the boat-dwellers would send up their smoke in an undisturbed column.

Stuart often brought Miss Marvina and Joshua to see the house. The girl would pick her delicate and graceful way through heaps of white stones, assisted by the devoted Stuart, who would then turn to assist her father. The winter days became spring; the river turned bright blue under blazing blue skies. The summer came, all gold and soft cool breeze. Then it was winter again, with white snow and a strong blue light upon it, and the river was choked and gray with ice, and the Canadian shore was a black blur against fiery sunsets.

And now Stuart conceived his passion for his house, and dedicated himself to it. It was a living thing for him, a beautiful and perfect thing, an extension of his dreams. When it was finally finished, in the second February, he moved in and gave himself up to dark ecstasy.

Then, one Sunday, after Miss Marvina had retired, he asked her father for her hand.

CHAPTER 13

THIS momentous occasion occurred about four months before the coming of Janie. Stuart had been writing his cousin his usual highhearted and careless letters, and she had expressed her determination to "take up life anew" in America. Stuart, to tell the truth, hardly believed it. He had more important things on his mind at this time, and England was far away, and the creatures in that country scarcely existed in his consciousness.

On that Sunday when, with rolling heart and pounding pulses and with an exterior as debonair and flashing as always, he approached Joshua Allstairs on the subject of his daughter Stuart was not thinking of Janie in the least.

The dinner, as usual, was execrable. Stuart was even more heavily fortified than was customary by his frequent libations that morning. His repressed excitement, and the alcohol, got him through church services with magnificent oblivion. All through the dreary and protracted prayers and hymns and sermon he saw only Miss Marvina, lovely in brown velvet and brown fur, her face framed in the depths of a beaver bonnet lined with silken lace. Apparently she felt his excitement, for she kept glancing at him with her tawny eyes, in which a deep light was reflected. He did not know that it was indeed only a reflection of his own tumult.

He had only occasionally hinted to Sam Berkowitz about his plans for Marvina. Sam had only looked at him steadily with his inscrutable sad brown eyes, and had said nothing. Nevertheless, something made Stuart cry irritably: "Think what we can do with one hundred thousand dollars or so, Sam!"

Then Sam had said, quietly: "You think her papa agree, yes?"

"Certainly!" Stuart had exclaimed, quite irately. "Why not? Is there anyone more eligible than I? Why not, for God's sake?"

"I think," said Sam, "her papa say no. No."

As Stuart had some secret qualms himself, Sam's remark only angered him.

"I think her papa say yes. Yes," he said with some cruelty, mimicking Sam's accent and manner. Then when Sam was silent, Stuart shouted: "Why not? Because I owe him a few thousand dollars? The dirty rascal will get it back, and he knows it. Why shouldn't he agree?"

Sam gazed at him with compassionate despondency. "Mr. Allstairs is a wicked man, Stuart. A bad man."

"What has that got to do with it?"

But Sam said nothing. He only returned to the shops and walked through them slowly, like an uneasy ghost. The shops had not been doing so well, recently, perhaps because Stuart was so often absent these days, putting the final touches on his beloved house, and gloating over it. Sam had had to put quite a sum of money from his own private funds into meeting the last note on the house. Stuart had practically no reserve funds of his own. He had, with inner shame, and much outer irritability, offered to pay Sam an exorbitant interest, in fact insisted upon it. But Sam had only regarded him with eloquent affection and pain, and the matter had been dropped. "You'll take a mortgage on it, then, for a thousand dollars?" Stuart suggested. Sam wanted to laugh a little, but had refrained. He put his hand on Stuart's shoulder, and pressed it. "What is mine, my friend, is yours," he said. "Besides, haf you not said there is a corner in that house for me? I pay for that corner, yes? It is only right."

"There was that altar in Grundy's church, too," said Stuart, gloomily, after putting his fingers for a moment over Sam's hand. "It cost two hundred more than I expected. But the other was too cheap for the church. Why do churches cost so much, anyway?"

Sam studied him with profound love. What a child this was! Warmhearted and reckless, heedless and rapacious, wild and melting and fierce, all in one. This child should not be contaminated by the flesh of the Allstairs. It was evil and revolting. That maiden, with her empty eyes and her soulless body! He, Sam, could not endure the thought. But there was no arguing with this blind young man, who never suspected that evil was about to embrace him. The gates of hell are guarded by creatures who have no souls, and who contemplate with the eyes of dead statues those who descend.

And then Sam murmured aloud, in Hebrew, in slow sonorous phrases: "Rescue my soul from their destructions, my darling from the lions."

"What?" said Stuart, frowning. But Sam only turned away.

"You and your Talmud!" said Stuart, staring after him.

The whiskey, then, the intoxication of Miss Marvina, his determination that he should have her and her fortune, and the dark uneasy turbulence in himself, which was voiceless though ever-present, brought Stuart to Joshua Allstairs that Sunday afternoon four months before the arrival of Janie.

For some reason, Joshua was unusually affable and slyly humorous that afternoon. Stuart was quite exhilarated. He did not know that Joshua was well aware of what the young man wished to say, and that he was gloating over him in advance.

When Stuart with shaking hands put a cheroot into his mouth, Joshua did not rebuke him by reminding him that this was the Sabbath, and that tobacco was not permitted in "this house." He only regarded Stuart benignly from the depths of his chair, where he lurked in malignant grayness.

It took Stuart several moments to light the cheroot, during which he cursed under his breath. His forehead was damp. His face was crimson. Then, having succeeded in drawing a cloud of smoke from the tobacco, he turned to Joshua abruptly.

"Sir," he said without preamble, thoroughly forgetting the fine and elegant speech he had prepared, and which he was to deliver with a wonderful mixture of dignity and respect,

"I wish your permission to sue for the hand of Miss Marvina."

He paused abruptly. He did not know that he was panting quite audibly. His black eyes fixed themselves upon Joshua with a mingling of challenge, pleading and arrogance. His muscles tightened, as a preliminary to battle.

But Joshua continued to regard him with shining benevolence. He even chuckled a little, fondly, rubbing the palms of his hands against the polished head of his cane. Nothing could have been more indulgent and more affectionate than his expression.

"Ah," he murmured. "I suspected this. You love my daughter, eh?"

"I adore her!" exclaimed Stuart. He swallowed, and added: "I hope then, sir, that you do not disapprove of my suit."

"The chit," said Joshua, softly, "is hardly eighteen."

Stuart, suddenly quite delirious because of Joshua's mild manner and gentle attentiveness, cried: "But most girls are wives and mothers at that age, sir!"

"She has given you encouragement, Stuart?"

Stuart frowned. He cleared his throat. "Young ladies of breeding do not give encouragement, as you call it, Mr. Allstairs. But I have reason to believe that Miss Marvina is not insensible to me."

Now Joshua had already perfected his plans to take Miss Marvina to England before the end of the year, and he could afford to enjoy himself at Stuart's expense at this time. He prepared himself for complete gratification of his wickedness and hatred.

"Now Stuart," he said, archly shaking a finger at him, "let us be sensible. What have you to offer my daughter, who has been brought up under the most genteel and luxurious circumstances? Your shops? I grant you they are marvelous, marvelous! I have no doubt that you will be a very rich and enterprising man, one of these days. But just at this time, eh? What have you to offer? You are in debt. I fear, at times, that you are expanding beyond your reserves. In the last analysis, my dear boy, you are only a shopkeeper. I had hoped for more for Marvina."

Stuart colored violently. He compressed his lips.

"You are also Irish," said Joshua, his voice dropping almost to a whisper. "Now, I pride myself on no prejudice, please understand. This is America, where the strangest creatures become quite powerful. You must forgive an old man, Stuart, who has only one treasure. But I find your Irish blood repugnant——"

"My mother was a Scotswoman," said Stuart, grimly, hating himself.

Joshua shook his head in sad and gentle rebuke. "Well, we shall overlook your—antecedents, Stuart, for a moment. You see, I am quite tolerant? Who are you, Stuart? You have told me of exalted relatives in Scotland and England and Ireland, but I have seen none of them. Sometimes I have fancied that you were—er—elaborating. Forgive me if I wrong you unwittingly. I should, however, like some definite proof of these personages."

"You shall have them, sir!" said Stuart, rashly. He suddenly thought of Janie. "Why, sir, I had almost forgotten! My second cousin, Mrs. Cauder, is about to visit me in America. A lady of fortune and breeding."

"Indeed." Joshua was unpleasantly surprised. "May I ask who Mrs. Cauder is?"

"My second cousin. Her father is a gentleman of—large holdings, sir. Janie has a large fortune in her own right." Now Stuart's imagination came into play. "Her second cousin on her father's side is Sir Angus Fraser. You must have heard of him, sir. His paintings hang in the Royal Academy."

He cursed himself that he could not remember the other illustrious forebears and relatives that he had so blithely mentioned to Joshua in the past, and which he had invented on the spur of the moment to impress the formidable old devil. But his volatile spirits only lingered momentarily on this débâcle. He earnestly hoped that Joshua had also forgotten the august names he had picked out of the clean air. Janie, however, was tangible. She existed. She indeed had a fortune. Devoutly, Stuart hoped that she would fall in with his inventions, and admire them, for his sake. His confidence returned.

Joshua was eyeing him keenly. This, then, was an unexpected and disagreeable event, if true.

"You recall Sir Angus Fraser, sir?" urged Stuart, with rising intoxication. "His painting of her Grace, the Duchess of York, is considered one of the masterpieces in the Academy."

Joshua was perturbed. He coughed lightly. "Sir Angus Fraser? But, of course. I remember the painting—" He paused, frowning: "And Mrs. Cauder: she has children, I presume, who are travelling with her?"

"Yes, indeed," said Stuart, with enthusiasm, though he had not given Janie's children a moment's thought in the past. "I believe the eldest son, Angus, will inherit the title, as Sir Angus has no male issue." He was somewhat confused about the British laws of inheritance, but he shrewdly suspected that Joshua knew as little.

"There is no possibility, I opine, that you might inherit the title?" suggested Joshua, thereby confirming Stuart's suspicion.

Stuart paused. Now, there was a wondrous matter. But even his recklessness was not equal to this enormous invention. He shook his head sadly. "I am afraid not, sir. Direct lineal descendants, I believe."

Joshua aroused himself with sudden interest. "This son of Mrs. Cauder: what is his age?"

"Oh, a mere lad, sir. Possibly in his early teens."

Joshua was profoundly disappointed. Then he brightened. After all, a few years' difference did not matter. Marvina could wait. But, good Heavens! This was all a different matter, then. He struggled to regain his former detachment. He frowned.

"Well, then, it seems you do have exalted connections, Stuart. Let us proceed to another matter, then. You are deeply in debt, Stuart, not only to me, but to others, for certain large shipments of goods."

Stuart glared. His debts were a delicate subject. He said proudly: "I have never defaulted on payments of principal or interest. I am doing amazingly well. I hope to be completely out of debt within a year, your debt, also, Mr. Allstairs. I only owe you six thousand dollars on the original loan, and ten thousand on the house. The ten thousand I regard as a private matter, not connected with the shops, of course."

Joshua meditated. The fool Stuart had signed an agreement that a single default on the ten thousand dollars would make Joshua the owner of his house. He eyed Stuart absently. "Of course, of course," he murmured.

Now, if this Mrs. Cauder should make Stuart free and clear of this ten thousand dollars, it would be very disagreeable indeed, and very unfortunate. Nevertheless, there was no doubt that she could do this. Joshua's face became a mask of frustrated evil, webbed and cracked and grimacing.

However, a relative who had for a cousin the illustrious Sir Angus Fraser, portrait-painter to the kings of England and other noble personages, was not to be ignored, particularly if she had a son a year or two younger than Miss Marvina.

"Wait a moment, wait a moment," said Joshua, frowning. He sucked in his lips, and fixed his ophidian eyes intently upon Stuart. It would not do to antagonize this lofty Mrs. Cauder. One must wait and see, however.

Joshua tapped his lips thoughtfully with the head of his cane. He had had to revise many things in his mind. His eyes narrowed and glinted with a vicious light. Then he said: "Stuart, my boy, I cannot give you an answer about my daughter at this time. She is still very young, in experience, if not in years. Shall I merely say this: That I do not frown upon your suit?"

Stuart's exultation was hardly to be contained. His sanguine mind bounded over any disquietude. He would manage everything!

He sprang to his feet, his face glowing. "I have your permission to speak to Miss Marvina, then?"

"Not so fast, not so fast," rebuked Joshua, shaking his head, but smiling. (He must have hours alone, to think.) "I did not say that. I merely said I do not, as of this instant, frown on your suit. But there are many things to consider."

"I built my house for her!" lied Stuart, with magnificent dash and fire.

Joshua grinned. But he made no comment on this.

"I have said there are many things to consider. You must allow an old man time to make up his mind to relinquish his darling."

When Stuart departed, in a blaze of rapture and intoxication, Joshua sat alone for a long time, until his meager fire died down. Then he rose, groaning, and went up to his daughter's apartments.

CHAPTER 14

MARVINA was sitting before her own fire in her own small sitting room. She was attired in a loose robe of crimson velvet, bordered with fur. Her black hair lay on her shoulders. When her father entered she was looking at the fire, as motionless as a painted statue. She turned to him with a lovely smile, and lifted her face for his kiss. Her manner was tranquil, serene and without interest.

Joshua sat near her, and regarded her with passionate intensity. The firelight flicked over her perfect features, which were entirely without any expression at all.

"Thinking, my darling?" he asked, gently.

"Yes, Papa," she replied, obediently, in her rich slow voice.
"Pleasant thoughts, I hope?"

"Yes, Papa."

"You are quite contented, my love?"

"Yes, Papa."

"I did not disturb you?"

"No, Papa."

Joshua was silent. The words had come from his daughter with docility and calm, like unhurried echoes. For the first time since she had been born, Joshua felt a vague chill. The eyes, gazing at him almost unblinkingly, were completely empty, if radiant. He thought for the very first time: What is there behind that face? She was like a large and beautiful doll, mindlessly waiting to be taken and manipulated.

Almost with irritation, he said abruptly: "What were you thinking of, my love?"

She stared at him without expression, but there was not the slightest surprise in her regard. "Thinking, Papa? Of many things. How pleasant it is that spring is coming. Of my new sable pelisse which you bought me a week ago. Of the party next week. Are these thoughts wrong on Sunday, Papa?"

She said this, placidly, and turned back to the fire.

"Frivolous thoughts, I believe, my love," said Joshua, with stern fondness. But Marvina did not reply. She looked at the fire, and smiled emptily, with infinite sweetness. He had the sudden unpleasant thought that she had forgotten he was there. When he cleared his throat, however, she turned her eyes obediently to him again.

"Mr. Coleman has just left, my love. He sends you his regards."

"Yes, Papa." Was there a quickening of that exquisite face, a brighter tint on the lips? But the girl's manner was undisturbed.

"A fascinating young man, eh?"

"I believe that is the general opinion, Papa."

"But what do you think?" he demanded, abruptly.

"Mr. Coleman is very genteel, Papa. Quite a gentleman. His conversation is very clever."

"Umph," muttered Joshua. His eye-sockets stretched with the intensity of his study of his daughter.

"You do not find him repellent, then?"

"No, Papa." She was looking at him with her golden eyes quite wide, and waiting.

"You like him?"

"Yes, Papa."

"You find his conversation agreeable, Marvina?" His voice was strangely hoarse.

Her head was still bowed. A coil of her hair hid her profile.

"He is very civil, Papa," she whispered.

Ah, it was only a reticent young girl, then! Joshua sighed again, as if released from an unbearable pressure.

"Marvina, my love, he asked for my permission to press his suit with you."

He saw that she was trembling. Her head bowed lower. "Yes, Papa?" she said, almost inaudibly.

"You would not refuse him, then, I presume?" His voice was loud and harsh.

She lifted her head. Her eyes were actually filled with tears.

"Not if it was agreeable to you, Papa."

Joshua was silent, filled with black chaos. Only a few hours ago he had intended to dismiss Stuart with harsh laughter and mockery, and then to come to his daughter to renew his laughter with her at the presumption of that contemptible and nameless Irishman. He had even heard her sweet laughter in advance.

But now he could only crouch there, in silence. Many things had changed. A few moments ago he had felt the horrible presence of an incubus. He had been released from the ghastly visitation by the sight of Marvina's blushes and tears and agitation. He simply did not know where he was!

Certainly, he had not even dreamed of Stuart as a husband for Marvina. Yet here he was, now, almost urging him upon his daughter. He felt suddenly ill and devastated, and very old.

He stood up, and began to tap his way to the door. On the threshold he paused, and looked back. His daughter was regarding him with quiet breathlessness.

He cried out, in the strangest of voices: "We shall see! We shall see! But, in the meantime, Marvina, you are not to give him the slightest encouragement!"

He waited. If she had said: "No, Papa," he might have broken out into incoherent exclamations, and left her abruptly. But, to his most appalling relief, she only smiled, and the firelight showed her blushing face.

CHAPTER 15

Now JANIE had come, Janie with her many trunks, her fortune, and her brats.

During the journey to Grandeville, Stuart had thought more strongly and consistently than he had ever done in his life. It had become more and more obvious that Janie was hardly the "grand" relative expected by Joshua Allstairs and the others to whom Stuart had ebulliently announced her coming. She was raucous and coarse; she was boisterous and ribald. She was noisy. She had a hoarse voice, which she used roundly, with no regard for the decencies. Moreover, she was flamboyant. But—she had a fortune. She had the most astounding wardrobe, far surpassing, in quality and variety, even the exquisite wardrobe of Miss Marvina.

Nevertheless, Stuart had the gravest doubts that the prim and rigid ladies of Grandeville would approve of Janie Cauder. Janie, who hated the strait-laced and the pious and the affected, could be relied upon to shock and horrify them, to give them the "vapors." She swore like an artilleryman, and her opinions of the sacred things would have turned even a tolerant gentleman like Father Houlihan gray with terror. Let them once know that Janie was no stranger to whiskey, but would pull up her skirts before a fire to warm her legs and drink her grog, straight, and Stuart would be completely ruined.

Yet, he remembered, brightening, his father had told him tales of the British aristocracy. Duchesses who swore, who rode like men, who loved their beer and their whiskey and their dogs, were quite common. Perhaps he could pass Janie off as one of these. Who the hell were these American "aristocrats," anyway? he thought.

The picture, in his mind, became more subdued of tint, fading from the frightful scarlets of its original tone. He could hear himself saying, with high and amused indulgence, to certain ladies: "You must meet my dear cousin, Mrs. Cauder. Quite a character. A true type of the British aristocracy. They have no need to fear that someone might look askance at their family, or their titles, or their positions, so they can be entirely natural, you know. No affectations or simperings. Haven't you, my dear Mrs. So-and-so, observed that when a lady or gentleman is of the most elegant and irreproachable family, she or he need pretend to nothing, and does not fear the opinion of the more vulgar classes? Or even of their own?"

He rehearsed this, sweating. However, his apprehensions did not decrease. Janie had been with him a week. He could no longer keep her immured. One of these days, the ladies, in a body, would call upon her. She would be his dreadful secret no longer.

Nature came to his rescue, or, rather, bronchitis and rheumy colds.

On the seventh day, Janie obligingly had a "chill," and Robbie and Bertie followed suit. On the eighth day they were confined to their beds. The doctor expressed his anxiety. Stuart breathed easier. A reprieve had been granted him. Now his spirits soared again, and as he was safe for at least two weeks more, he thought nothing of the time beyond them.

He could even visit his shops and chat gaily with the customers without watching closely to see if one of them had heard some ghastly tale of Janie, through the medium of servants. He could even visit Joshua and Marvina with a free mind, shaking his head dolorously over Janie's sufferings, and expressing his regret that the party he had been arranging for her must be postponed. He could even be kind to Janie's other children, Angus and Laurie.

These two, he observed, were having a hard time of it. The servants resented them. Janie loathed them. They would drift about the grounds of the house, and through its forbidden rooms, like miserable little ghosts. Even Stuart, the careless, was not insensible of their wretchedness.

It was early April, now. The river was choked with drifting cakes of ice, which had made their way from the Lakes. The floes crashed and crunched against their shores, sparkling in the new sunlight. Between them the water was blue-black and foaming. From them came a wall of cold bright air, penetrating even the warm garments proof against winter blizzards. Endlessly, the floes extended back-and-forwards, hoary and broken, moving like an avalanche to the Falls. But the trees were showing the first swelling buds, and when the wind was still the air had a softness and freshness that lifted the heart. The sky, a clear and brilliant blue, stood over the earth like a pure arch of light. The ground was still barren and brown, oozing with moisture, but there was an odor to it at once strong and fecund. The first Canal barges and the first Lake steamers had not yet been able to penetrate the ice-floes, but rumors of them were rife. The first Canal barge had been sighted at Utica, a traveller announced. Within two or three weeks, it ought to arrive in Grandeville. Throughout the North country there was a murmur of high activity and hope, and one forgot the ice-floes thundering on their way to Niagara, and the wall of icy air that flowed almost constantly from them.

Now the sunsets were rarely cold scarlet. Instead, purest lakes of pale green stood in the west at twilight, and the last sunlight that fell on the black waters and cakes of ice was warm and crimson, though lonely still, and enormously silent. Some children had found crocuses in the woods, and the robins had returned, filling the quiet evening air with notes of melancholy silver which dropped as from a far height like rounded drops of pure water. It is true that the edges of ponds and puddles were rimmed with ice at night, and that sometimes flurries of snow whirled across the brown landscape and over the ice-floes. But noonday was almost gentle and festive, and the dull fire had gone from the sunset. At night, the stars were less sharp and blazing, and the moon had a soft look.

One evening, sweeter and balmier than the last evenings, Stuart returned from his shops, dutifully inquired, not too hopefully, about Janie's miserable state, and discovered Angus and Laurie standing in the brown wet garden listening to the robins. Stuart sauntered up to them, and when they turned their faces to him, and he saw their timid shrinking from his, his heart smote him.

"Well, well," he said, with uneasy heartiness. "Aren't you afraid of the night air, you two?"

Angus muttered something, Laurie curtseyed. Stuart looked with unwilling intentness at the little girl. All her bright color was gone. It was a small pale face there, framed in her golden locks and her big bonnet. She was shivering visibly in her small brown coat with its fur collar. Ah, the poor little love! She had heard nothing from Stuart since her arrival but reproaches when she ran through his precious house, or left her fingermarks on his balustrades. No wonder her eyes were so big, and so deeply sunken in mauve shadows. He recalled his first touching encounters with her in the coach. He had loved the poor wee creature then. He could not endure her expression: timid, sorrowful and afraid, nor the way she moved closer to the pale Angus and clutched his hand. They knew themselves unwanted and disliked and resented, these two poor children, and they could only look out upon the world in sad bewilderment.

"What are you doing here?" he asked, huskily, moving closer to them and trying to smile heartily.

"We are listening to the thrushes," said Angus, almost in a whisper. He pointed to the big robins hopping over the grass, and flying in the trees.

Stuart smiled more naturally. "Oh, we don't call them thrushes, in America. Of course, they aren't real robins: they are really thrushes, as you say, my dear Angus. But the first English settlers were reminded, by them, of the real English robin, which is much smaller and has a redder breast. So they called them robins, too."

The children smiled with painful politeness, and were silent. They regarded Stuart with big and uncertain eyes. His throat began to feel dry and tight. He looked up at the sky with affected ease. "A nice evening," he approved. He paused. "Would you like to walk down to the river with me?"

Laurie glanced up timidly at her brother, who pressed her hand tighter. The boy said, courteously: "Yes, that would be nice, Cousin Stuart."

He tried to walk beside them, but they drew behind, still uncertain and afraid. So he walked ahead of them, swaggering a little in his pity and uneasiness. They looked at the back of his tall figure with its fawn fur-collared coat and high gleaming hat, and cane, and gaiters and light pantaloons. They thought him magnificent.

In the summer, this long slope was covered by a layer of fine new grass, green and fresh. But the grass was still brown, and little trickles of black water writhed their way through it. Stuart's polished boots, he observed ruefully, were not exactly benefited by the mud. He paused. The children splashed hopefully behind him, so he went on. Automatically he cursed the impulse which had led him through this slime and oily brownness down to the river, from whose somber gray floes a bitter wind was rising. Well, these poor little devils were used to English mud. American mud was a poor thing in comparison. He turned up his fur collar and buried his chin deeply in it.

"Here we are," he said, cheerfully, as he paused some fifteen feet from the bank of the rushing and grinding Niagara. The black-blue water boiled through the cakes of ice, which tumbled headlong towards the Falls, but here and there, as the floes parted momentarily, one could see that the water was the color of a gleaming turquoise. Beyond this restless but implacable heaving lay the purple smudge of the Canadian shore, and above this smudge was a band of brilliant dark fire, almost too bright for the eye. And above this band lay a lake of the purest cold green, cloudless and motionless. One could almost imagine sails gliding over this lake, so perfect was the illusion. Far above this band the sky was darkening to a dim mauve, and in its depths sparkled and burned the evening star, silent and unstill.

High above the slope stood Stuart's white house, and in the pure clarified air of the spring evening it gleamed like a marble temple, seeming to rise airily from its base against the sky. On either side of where Stuart and the children stood, the shore broke away in stone and mud and gravel. The land about the house was smooth and cultivated, but on either side of it the woods loomed, the upper branches of the bare trees filled with brown light.

It was very silent here, and the savage river, the green lake in the west, the cold wind rising steadily from the floes, the distant smudge of the Canadian shore, the brightening sparkle of the star, all gave the scene a certain solemn desolation and wildness. Even the muted thunder of the rushing ice intensified the silence. Stuart, forgetting the children, looked at the river and the sky, and his warm soul became motionless and chill, filled with melancholy and unease. He began to shiver.

Then he heard Angus' quiet and timid voice: "It is very strange and beautiful, isn't it, Cousin Stuart?"

The young man smiled down at the lad; his face was stiff and numb with cold. "A damned unpleasant place, at this time of the year, my dear Angus. Wait till you see it in the summer."

Angus smiled politely. Little Laurie stared out at the river, and looked at the sky. Some faint beams from the fallen sun shone on her small face. The wind had whipped some color into her baby cheeks, and her blue eyes were radiant. The wind lifted locks of her golden hair and blew them over her shoulders, like strands of living brightness. Stuart could not look away from her. Her beauty pierced his heart with a kind of indescribable and aching sweetness. Almost timidly, he touched her cheek with his gloved hand, and then his fingers caressed her chin. She turned her face up to him slowly, and smiled. It was the loveliest smile he had ever seen, shy and innocent, confident and understanding.

Without knowing what he did, he bent and kissed her cheek, with great tenderness, and a kind of obscure sadness and love. She did not shrink, nor seem frightened. But very shyly, and with touching faith, she put her other hand in his hand, and she stood there, between her brother and Stuart, warm and trustful.

Poor thin Angus, with his haunted gray eyes and pinched pale face, saw this, and he blinked away sudden tears as he stared determinedly at the river. He was shivering quite violently in his thin black coat, and the wind whipped his pantaloons about his legs, which, as they were so thin and long and lanky, resembled the legs of a scarecrow. He wore a tall beaver hat, which he clutched to his head with his free hand. His profile, haggard and too mature for so young a lad, was rigid with his attempt to retain his composure. His poor desolate heart was shaking in him. He suddenly loved Stuart with an awful intensity.

His emotion, though repressed, impinged itself on Stuart, and the young man looked at him with furtive compassion. Good God! How could he have been so cruel and neglectful of these poor children, who, though unwelcome guests in his house, were there by no fault of their own! He felt a surge of angry and pitying heat in his chest. With his usual impetuousness, he vowed that he would do something to make them happy.

In a voice of muted kindness, he said: "How do you like America, Angus?"

The boy stared fixedly at the river, trying to control himself. He said: "I haven't seen much of it, Cousin Stuart. But what little I've seen is very beautiful—like this." He looked at Stuart timidly with his dimmed eyes. "Your house is beautiful, too. Much nicer than Grand-da's."

"Do you miss your grand-da?" asked Stuart, absently. "And England?"

Angus hesitated. He was afraid of offending Stuart, who was so kind to them all. Then he said, in a low voice: "Well, this is strange, here. We knew every lamb and every calf and horse, and all the people. We knew the kirk and the minister and the manse, and the meadows and the hills. We knew the—sound of people's voices."

"Yes. I understand." The ache in Stuart's heart was increasing intensely. "I was homesick, for a long time. You know the house where I was born, and lived?"

Angus brightened. "Yes. Mr. Kirkland lived there. He was Grand-da's manager. Grand-da is getting old. Mr. Kirkland had three little girls, and an older lad. We played with them." He added, politely: "It is a very pretty house."

"Would you like to go home?"

Angus hesitated again. Then he said simply: "We'll never go home, Cousin Stuart."

"Oh, now, I don't know about that! Your mama doesn't like America, I am afraid. She has been ill ever since she came here, and from the reports I receive from the servants, she'll be off with you all again."

At the mention of his mother, Angus' face changed subtly, and he sighed. He repeated, after a moment: "We'll never go home again."

Stuart was silent. He chewed his lip. Then, with false heartiness, he said: "Well, then, we must make the best of it. You'll go to school, the school I attended. You'll make friends. You can go to church again, soon. America isn't a bad place."

"I'd like to go to church," murmured Angus.

Stuart frowned a little. "Pious, psalm-singing little liar!" That is what Janie had called her eldest son. Stuart wondered if it were true. He had no high regard for truth, himself, considering it very tiresome at times, and to be used only sparingly, as one used pungent spices. People who professed a violent love for truth, he had observed, were singularly unpleasant people, and were rightfully avoided by the more civilized. Nevertheless, he thought dimly, truth-telling should be planted in the hearts of the young, whether their elders approved of it or not.

"Why should you like to go to church, eh?" he asked. "Tedious damn place, I'll be thinking."

Angus was silent. Then, in the strangest loud voice, he said: "It's peaceful in church, and God's there, and is so kind."

Stuart studied him in uneasy speechlessness. He rubbed his numb cheek with his knuckles. It seemed a terrible thing to him that a child should know the want of kindness, and could find nothing of it in the world of men but must go to a church for it.

He said, awkwardly: "Then, you must meet my dear friend, Father Houlihan. He is a good and gentle man, Angus, and loves young people, and all young creatures." Some iron sadness in him relaxed. That was it! Grundy must know these pathetic and desolate children. He had the holy gift of kindness.

But Angus was regarding him with round and solemn eyes. "He is a Papist, Cousin Stuart. Papists worship strange gods and idols. Grand-da said they were pagans and heathens. I don't know as I would like—Father Houlihan."

Stuart was suddenly furious. He shouted: "What damned nonsense! Your Grand-da's a fool, you poor little idiot! Grun—Father Houlihan is one of God's good men, with a heart of gold! Be thankful that ye'll know him, if ye ever will!"

Angus shrank back a little. "I'm sorry, Cousin Stuart. I didn't mean to offend you. I never knew any Papists. Perhaps Grand-da was wrong."

Stuart was immediately remorseful. He grinned, though his ruddy color was still high. "There, now, don't mind me. But it fair enrages me to listen to the prejudices of stupid people." He paused, then lifted his hand and pointed far over the floes of ice. "Look there, to my right, down the river. What do you see?"

Angus strained his eyes in the gathering dusk. Far down the river some two miles, hardly discernible in the twilight, was a vague dark bulk, right in the middle of the churning floes. "It looks like an island, Cousin Stuart."

"It is. It is called River Island. Quite a fair piece of land, full of woods and meadows and flat rich earth. Only a few people live there, a farmer or two, and some squatters. It is entirely undeveloped."

He paused. "You have heard me speak, no doubt, of my friend and business manager and partner, Mr. Sam Berkowitz?"

Angus murmured something politely.

Stuart pondered in his mind, briefly. "Well, let me tell you something about this world, Angus, especially what we call the Old World. It seems that in some countries, a man is hated if he has a nose of a different shape from that of the other men about him, or if his hair is a different color, or his ways are strange, or if he worships in a different way."

Angus interrupted eagerly, wishing to please Stuart with his own fund of knowledge. "I know! Grand-da told me how the Papists used to burn the Protestants at the stake, and about the Crusades, how the Crusaders used to kill and hang the Saracens."

Stuart frowned a little. "Well, yes, that's what I mean. In a way. It's all stupidity. It's beyond human comprehension, I'm afraid. We all kill what we are afraid of, and we are always afraid of a man who is slightly different from us. Why, I don't know. It's Original Sin, I suppose.

"Well, then, Mr. Berkowitz came from a country where he and his people were hated because they worshipped God in an old and ancient way. It was a country where the rich and powerful men oppressed the people, and wanted to keep them oppressed, for their own gain and profit, and to keep their rich fine houses and their silver. They were afraid of the people; they were afraid that some day the people might think, and they might ask themselves: "Why shouldn't we, too, have roofs that do not leak, and tables that are filled with good bread and wine and meat? Don't we work hard enough for it? Aren't they our hands that till these fields, and our labor which builds these rich houses, and our sweat that waters the grain?'"

As Stuart said these things, in a loud and ringing voice, he saw the face of Father Houlihan, and his lips moving in these very words.

Angus was watching him with eager closeness. Even little Laurie lifted her face in the gathering darkness, and listened, her mouth dropping open.

"Well," continued Stuart, with gathering ardor, "this was the way it was in Mr. Berkowitz' country. The people began to think, and to get restless, and to look about them, muttering in their throats. Their hearts were hot with a knowledge of injustice and cruelty and hopelessness. And so their voices became louder and more threatening, and the rich and powerful men were afraid.

"So they looked about them for some way to satisfy the people, who were so wretched and hungry and oppressed. They were too greedy and cruel to give the people bread and freedom and hope. That would have been money out of their pockets. And then their eyes lighted on Sam's people, who were poorer and more oppressed than the others. Sam's people weren't liked in his country, because they didn't believe in the prevailing faith, and because stupid people had attached all kinds of cruel and lying legends to them.

"So the rich men had a very clever idea. Why not tell their people that their suffering and coldness and hunger was the fault of Sam's poor people?"

"But the people wouldn't believe anything so silly!" cried Angus, surging closer to Stuart with a sort of eager impetuousness. "They couldn't diddle the people like that!"

Stuart nodded his head slowly. "But they did," he said, grimly. "You see, my dear Angus, the people believe anything, if they are in pain. They are blind and stupid, too, and in the mass they are crueller and more ferocious than any animals. They believed. Perhaps they wanted to believe. It gave them an excuse to murder and plunder Sam's helpless people. Besides, it was safer to do this than to revolt against the real cause of their suffering: their masters. None of their own blood would be shed, as it would be shed if they turned their hatred against those who oppressed them. In truth, they had the approval of their masters."

He could hardly see Angus' face in the dusk, but he felt the young boy's wild and horrified emotions, his incredulity and terror, his unreasoning fright in the face of his first knowledge of the enormity of the world of men. Something in him was profoundly shaken and broken.

He said, aloud: "The world's not what you believe, Angus. It's an evil place, filled with evil men. It's each man's duty to help in the fight against that evil." His heart soared with the strangest exhilaration at his own words. "We blunder, we go astray, but if we have faith that evil can be destroyed, we shall win. Perhaps not now, not in five hundred years. But sometime. Please God."

Angus was quieter. Stuart resumed. "But let me get on with my story. It is almost night now, and this damned wind is getting stronger. Pull up your collar, Angus.

"So the people in Sam's country turned against his people, in their pain and hunger and blindness, and the rich men sat back, smiling, smug and safe in their warm houses and before their fires, and eating from their silver dishes. The wrath of the people had been turned away from the real murderers and thieves. So—Sam left his country, and came here, penniless, with only his hands and his faith——"

"In God!" cried Angus.

Stuart said testily: "Well, then, in God, if you must. I really meant: his faith that somewhere in the world there was safety for the oppressed. He thought he had found it in America, where we believe, or profess to believe, that all men are equal. Except the Negroes, of course. And Sam came to Grandeville.

"One day, he looked out at River Island, down there, and had a wonderful idea. It was quite mad, of course, but it was beautiful. Why couldn't that big and unsettled island be made into a colony for others of his people who must leave their own countries to get away from the suffering mobs and the cruel masters? For, Angus, you must know that what happened in Sam's country has happened before in many other countries, and is happening now, and will happen again.

"Sam was quite taken with his idea. It became a dream to him, a wonderful dream. He talked to me and to Father Houlihan, and Father Houlihan thought it wonderful, too. He and Sam went to the Mayor, and talked about it to him. You see, that island is American land, and is owned by a handful of people who would be only too willing to sell it at a reasonable price. Sam and Father Houlihan went to these people, after talking to the Mayor, and they have named a price. And so Sam is working very hard to get this money. And one of these days, he hopes, he can give it to his people for their home."

It was so dark now that he could see the children's faces only as dim blurs in the heavy purple dusk. But he felt Angus' trembling intensity and eagerness.

"Mr. Berkowitz is a Jew, isn't he, Cousin Stuart?"

"Yes."

Angus was silent, but his emotions appeared to grow, and vibrate. Then he heaved a deep sigh, and said the strangest thing, in a shaking voice: "Thank you, Cousin Stuart."

Stuart was unbearably touched, but he did not quite know why. He pressed his hand on Angus' shoulder. The boy strained his eyes in the darkness towards the river.

He said: "But why does Mr. Berkowitz want that island, Cousin Stuart? America is free for all men, isn't it? He is safe here, he and his people?"

Stuart said with loud irony: "Oh, yes, indeed. Land of the free and home of the brave. We don't hate anyone here, except the Catholics and the Jews and the poor slaving blackamoors. America is free for all men, provided they are exactly the kind that is already here. Father Houlihan could tell you a pretty story."

He was sorry that he had had to shatter the last hope of this poor boy. But truth was necessary. Oh, damn truth! exclaimed Stuart, inwardly.

He said: "Let's go back to the house." He felt enormously tired and heavy and depressed. He wanted nothing but his solitary supper in his lovely dining-room, then an evening by the fire, drowsing and planning. He hesitated. Then he said: "Won't you and little Laurie have supper with me, Angus?"

CHAPTER 16

IT WAS a very cosy supper, and Stuart, after his first fears that Laurie might spill her milk on the Aubusson rug or stain the fine damask, felt quite happy in the presence of these children. Something childlike, vehement and simple in himself was satisfied, and warmed.

Laurie ate like a perfect little lady, minding her manners, and sitting straight and quiet and dimpling and smiling in her chair, her golden hair framing her exquisite little face. When Stuart spoke, or her adored brother, she would turn the sparkling blue of her eyes upon him, and listen intently, whether she understood or not. As for poor Angus, his gray pinched expression was gone, and even his thin cheeks seemed rounder, and there was an eager light on his face. His eyes were quite wide and luminous, and he laughed occasionally at some droll quip or other of Stuart's.

A queer lad, thought Stuart, of Angus, with pity and wonder. He had half believed Janie's stories, in spite of himself, that Angus was dull and stupid, crafty and sly, whining and psalm-singing, and an incorrigible liar. He had not taken the trouble to investigate her tales, for he had not been interested in Angus, or the other children, except to speed their going from his precious house. Now he began to doubt, and to hate Janie with fresh ardor.

And then, to his horror and indignation, he began to learn that Angus was blindly, frightfully and incredibly devoted to Janie.

At first, Stuart could not believe this revolting fact. Surely, a lad of Angus' wit and penetration must know what Janie was! He had his own experience of her, of her malevolence and slyness and cruelty, and lies.

Yet, Angus spoke of her simply and fondly, with the most touching shadow on his face. He loved his mother. That was enough for him. But why did he love her? Throughout the supper Stuart tried to fathom this puzzle. Then, slowly, he gathered that the boy was blind in many ways. He remembered only Janie's rare kindnesses, her laughter, her wit and gaiety. He remembered her frivolity, which must have appeared to him a dear thing. Her sins he did not see. When she was cruel to him and his sister, he believed that it was in some way his own fault, his own sin, or that she did not understand. What she said was infallible, all her opinions and prejudices.

Stuart was more and more revolted, as he listened to Angus, and more and more saddened. He saw, with a flash of intuition, that some day Janie would inevitably corrupt this simple boy, with his integrity and innocence, and that the corruption would be a most terrible thing. Yet what could he, Stuart, do? He perceived that should he begin to enlighten Angus he would only inspire distrust in him, or break his heart. Angus was the sort who must believe, and love, and who when his belief and love were betrayed would be forever shattered, and perhaps made evil, also.

Besides, Janie was all he had. Stuart had no illusions that Angus must inevitably impress his mother with his nobility and high integrity of spirit. Rather, she would pollute and ruin him, as she must, because of her greater and harder strength and her knowledge of wickedness.

Angus did not know that his mother hated him. He would know some day, but not yet.

As he talked to Stuart, quite volubly, in his new trust and confidence, he expressed his interest in the shops. Nothing was more agreeable to Stuart than to talk of his darling enterprises. He elaborated at great length, while Angus listened, fascinated.

Finally the lad remarked, wistfully: "You must be a very rich man, Cousin Stuart."

Stuart paused. For some reason, he frowned. He did not like Angus' wistful references to money. It was surely not in his character.

"What does that matter?" he asked, carelessly. "Do you like money, Angus?"

Angus hesitated. He looked down at his blanc mange, which a servant had placed before him. "I don't know," he murmured, distressfully. "I never had much of it, or needed it. But mama said when someone says that money is nothing it is either because he has never felt the need of it, or never hopes to have it."

Stuart frowned again. "Your mama has a very high regard for money, hasn't she?"

Angus looked up and smiled radiantly. "Yes. Mama says you might as well be dead and buried if you haven't it. And that you must work very hard to see that you have it, lots of it. Or other people will hate you, and not let you in their houses, and that even God despises a man who hasn't the gumption to work and get money."

"Why should God despise such a man?"

But Angus was quite illuminated. "There is the story of the talents, you remember, Cousin Stuart. One man had four talents, and buried them, another had two or three, and returned them without increase to his master, and another had only one, and made it produce more. God loved that man, and threw the others into the outer darkness, because they hadn't made them increase."

Stuart was highly irritated. "I don't think those 'talents'

meant money at all!" he exclaimed, irately. "I don't recall that God was ever in the banking business."

Angus shook his head, humbly. "Yes, they were, Cousin Stuart. They were a Hebrew coin."

Stuart had an inspiration. Suddenly it seemed very necessary to him to set this boy right, to keep him from the path of destruction. He said: "Well, then, it was used as a parable, that story of the talents. To make it clear to the people. I think it meant gifts of God, such as ability and goodness and faith and charity."

But Angus was very literal in interpreting the Bible. "Talents were Hebrew coins, Cousin Stuart."

Stuart was baffled. He was also very confused. He had the highest regard for money, himself, and thought it Heaven's supreme blessing and benediction on men. He had long ago determined that nothing should prevent him from getting it, in any way possible, and he had adhered to that determination. Nevertheless, there was something in him which was revolted and enraged at the spectacle of this boy's incipient corruption.

He said, darkly, feeling himself very puerile: "Money is an explosive, Angus. It can do the most awful things. It can devastate and destroy."

Angus smiled at him, and Stuart was confirmed in his own suspicion that he was puerile. For that smile was singularly adult and indulgent. Stuart was angered, and got up abruptly from the table, quite disliking Angus.

The children followed him docilely into the drawing-room. He had not bargained for this. He felt very tired. But he could not rudely dismiss them. They hungered after him as those who are chilled hunger for a fire. Laurie, in fact, came beside him, and took his hand trustingly.

He sighed. He sat down in his chair. Then, after a look into the little girl's lovely and shining face, he impulsively took her on his knee and began to twine her golden curls over his fingers. He kissed her. "You will be a heartbreaker one of these days, darling," he said.

Angus sat near him on the hearth, on a footstool. The warm and ruddy firelight fell on them comfortably. Fingers of red light danced and glided over the edges of exquisite sofas and chairs, and formed deep shining pools on the polished tables. The draperies had been drawn over the windows, and their folds glistened. The wind of the early evening had risen to a deep and minatory roar, shouting of strange places and strange lands.

Stuart listened to the wind. His Celtish soul was made restless and vaguely enormous. He saw the wind sweeping over the sea, roaring westwards, and his ancient blood was stirred.

It was this that made him say to Laurie, with great tenderness, looking into her eyes: "Would you like me to tell you a story, my love?"

"Oh, yes, yes!" she whispered, with shy eagerness, adoring him.

Stuart, coming to consciousness, was annoyed. The wind, for an instant, became only a disturbance at the windows and among the bare trees. Then its voice penetrated, again, every tumultuous cell of his body.

Stuart pondered. What was that strange story his grandmother had once told him, when he was scarcely older than Laurie? It was only the ghost, the mood of a tale, but he had not completely forgotten it, and it had strange meanings hidden in it somewhere. Stuart did not rightly know the meanings, but he had felt them. Angus, deeply interested and ardent, looked at him, waiting.

Stuart, with sudden inner clarity, saw his grandmother in her warm chimney corner, her shawl over her shoulders, her smoking pipe in her sunken mouth. He saw the dark and glimmering firelight on the red tile floors, the stained darkness of wooden walls, the gleam of polished brass andirons. He saw how the tiny diamond-panes of the high sunken windows trembled in the wind outside, and how, at times, the candlelight flickered as it was disturbed on each pane, so that it momentarily shone like a small dark mirror. It was a wild night outside, that old dead night, and there was a turbulent wailing in the trees so that they groaned mysteriously.

To Stuart's memory, that room with its ancient woman by the fire had taken on an occult agelessness, so that it all seemed more of a fairy tale than any real remembrance. So it was that as he told Laurie the tale, his eye was wide and dim, seeing his grandmother and the fire, and hearing the wind.

The story was really nothing, after all, but moods and dreams.

There was a small girl, homeless and wandering, who after many footsore days of travel, and much hunger and loneliness and sadness, came to the high wall of a strange garden. Over the top of that wall she could see the branches of the oddest trees, each leaf shining and polished like metal, and bearing among them round and golden fruit of the most uncommon kind. Birds sat among the leaves, motionless and dreaming, plumaged in yellow and red and blue and purple. The little girl longed for the fruit, and looked about her for a gate. She found it, sunken in the stones, and with fear, pushed it open. It made no sound. She entered the garden. There was no sound in it at all, and here the sunlight had a faint and gauzy light, as in a dream. Not a leaf fluttered. There was no breeze. The birds sat in the trees and slept. There were many flowers here, drooping in the dim but mysteriously clear radiance, which was like that hour just before dusk. The little girl saw roses, and pansies, and great lilies with open striped yellow throats, and hanging leaves. Paths wound among the flowers, paths of scattered stones, between which the thick green moss was growing.

The air, drowsy and dreaming, was filled with the most entrancing odors of flowers and shrubs, so heavy that the little girl could hardly breathe. There was the old and be-witched perfume of elderberry blossoms too, sweeter and more swooning than all the others. The little girl wandered down the paths, and looked at the sundials, and was vaguely surprised that, though the light was both soft and transparent, the sundials did not show the time. There was no shadow on them. Indeed, there were no shadows at all in this garden. Everything stood, soundless and breathless, in this garden without time. Everything slept. There was no wind, but the elderberry scent came and went in long sweet puffs as if disturbed. Not a bird uttered a cry, or broke the silence with the rustle of a wing.

The little girl came to a pond, sunken in the thick green moss. It was like a round shield of glimmering pewter, and nothing disturbed it, not a ripple or the shadow of a fish or the flight of an insect. Two swans, white and still, slept on its surface, which reflected the pale blue sky. Beyond the pond, the trees were thick and dark and ancient, bending their heads and showing their golden fruit, which shone like little yellow suns in the half-light.

And then the little girl was very frightened. She knew that she must leave this spellbound garden at once, and find her way back to the sunken gate and the highway. Perhaps her guardian angel had whispered to her urgently. And then she cried out that she was very tired and thirsty and hungry, and must eat of that golden fruit and rest a little. After that, she would resume her journey, and look for a home.

She climbed the branches of the nearest tree and plucked the fruit, and sank her little white teeth into it. She sat there in the branches, while the strange and beautifully-hued birds slept motionless near her, like fruit, themselves. The fruit was very sweet and juicy and delicious. It tasted like honey and wine, and its flesh was as satisfying as bread. And below the little girl lay the wide garden of flowers and pond and swans and trees, drifting in a faint and luminous mist like pearl and last sunlight, with the odor of elderberry sweet and swooning on the warm air.

The little girl, satisfied and rested, climbed down the tree and stood beneath it. "I must go," she said aloud. She hardly heard her voice, which seemed to drown on the air. And then she became very sleepy, as if overpowered. She sank down on the warm thick moss and slept.

She must not have slept long, or another day had come, for when she awoke, the garden was just the same as she remembered. She arose. She looked about her, dreamily. But she had forgotten who she was, and from whence she had come, and where she was going. She remembered nothing but the garden, enchanted and timeless, full of sleep.

Laurie and Angus had listened to this tale breathlessly. Laurie's blue eyes were like still fire in the soft dusk of the room.

"Didn't the little girl ever leave the garden?" asked Laurie, and now there were tears of pity for the child who remembered nothing but enchantment and dreams.

Stuart hesitated. "Well, yes, she did."

The little girl lived in the garden for a long time, but she never remembered the days, and there were no nights, except for the pearly mist which drifted through the trees. She was very happy, this child in a dream. She ate of the fruit, and slept, and talked to the flowers and the silent swans, and smelled the elderberry. She looked down the tawny throats of the lilies, and stroked the roses, which had no thorns and never faded. She walked over the winding paths, and gazed up at the birds.

And then one day, she found the old sunken gate again. She was very surprised to see it. She did not remember it. She pushed on it and it opened soundlessly. She stepped out onto the rutted road. She looked behind her. The garden was hardly to be seen, now. The pearly mist had fallen over it like a translucent cloud. And from somewhere the little girl heard the wind of Heaven, for the first time in endless ages. It was a loud and thundering sound, and it frightened her. She wanted to run back into the warm and silent garden, but the gate gently pulled itself from her hand and closed. She put her hands on it and tore frantically at it, but it would not open. She tried to climb it, but it seemed to grow higher and higher, and to be filled with wounding sharp edges. Finally, she fell down upon the ground, tired out, and memory came back to her, and she wept long and deeply, until she was exhausted.

And then she discovered that she was no longer a child, but a woman, full-grown. She got to her feet, and walked away down the highway. And it was winter now, cold and raw, with snow flying and the trees blasted and black, and not a bird to be seen.

"Did she find a home, and someone to love her?" cried little Laurie, quite pale, and very eager.

Stuart hesitated again. It was the strangest tale, he remembered, and it was not clear to him. He wondered, with mysterious intuition, whether he should tell the children the rest.

"No," he said, gently, looking into Laurie's wet eyes, "she never did find a home. She never did find anyone who really loved her. Not as she wanted to be loved, I am afraid. Worst of all, after the garden the world seemed very ugly and noisy and cruel and fierce to the girl. She could never get used to it. And one day she tried to find her way back to the garden and the elderberry scent and the golden fruit of dreams.

"She never did. And so she died of a broken heart, in the snow."

Again, he looked into Laurie's eyes. And then he had the strangest thought. He saw the garden reflected in her eyes.

Angus was silent. He had made no comment on the story. Stuart felt suddenly very tired and stupid. He gently set Laurie back on her feet.

"Bed time, my love," he said, and kissed her cheek.

CHAPTER 17

JANIE recovered from her influenza far sooner than did her sons, Bertie and Robbie. While the two boys still lay in bed, coughing miserably, and threatened with lung fever, Janie had risen gaily, and was sitting by her window, where she could look out over the greening slope and the river with its churning cakes of ice. She thought the sight forbidding, but her naturally vivacious spirits did not permit of any sense of desolation.

Dressed in a rich black velvet peignoir, bordered with white fur, her little feet on a white hassock, she looked with sparkling green eyes upon the water, her busy mind engaged with plots and counterplots. Again, her reddish hair had been tortured into ringlets, and she had applied rouge and powder to her sallow, freckled face. Despite her thinness, the result of her influenza, she appeared quite avid and animated. The April sun came through the bright windows and lay on her shoulders comfortingly. She could hear the strong, almost arctic wind, of this Northern spring, but it was safely shut out from her. She looked out, her wide thin mouth, painted and mobile, smiling faintly.

For Stuart had requested a few minutes with her. She lifted her mirror and studied her face. Not handsome, she reflected, but spirited and lively, as her dear mama had often said. And full of sprightliness and interest. Ah, if it were not for those freckles, and the big Roman nose with the predatory nostrils! She arranged her head in the proper attitude to minimize the nose. She had drenched herself with musk, and the deep dusky odor permeated the large and perfectly appointed room with its white walls, iron candlesticks, white doors and fireplace, delicate mahogany chests and wardrobe, round soft rug, white canopied bed and little pale blue-and-rose damask chairs. Her sense of luxury, very well developed, was complacently satisfied with what she saw.

Yes, Stuart had done himself well. She glowed at the thought of him, and smiled slyly. A braw laddie, and one of her own kidney. They would do well together. Her wizened heart stirred with something quite like warm affection and pleasure.

Suddenly, she thought of poor wild Robin with his strange and moving voice, his lighted face and quick wild gestures. Her mouth curled with cruel contempt, her eyes narrowed, and glinted. The feckless fool! The damned, ridiculous lark! She laughed shortly, and it was an ugly sound. She had gotten nothing from Robin but four inconvenient and unwanted children. In her youth, she reflected, a girl visualized a man in her bed. When she was older, she visualized money in the bank. But that was when she had acquired wisdom.

The door of the wardrobe was half open. Janie contemplated the endless neat rows of her frocks, her gleaming velvets, her purple pelisses, her sable and ermine capes, her silken cloaks. On the shelf above were the boxes that contained her wondrous bonnets, each more ravishing than the last, and her muffs. Why, in this raw frontier town, she would soon be the full gay leader. She would teach these boors and barbarians the amenities of polite and elegant society, the civil niceties of good breeding. She saw herself languishing on Stuart's arm, as they entered a shadowy drawing-room, all the drab ladies envying her magnificent toilette, all the gentlemen bewitched.

So absorbed was she in deciding the gown she must wear upon her first appearance in Grandeville society, that she did not hear Stuart's knock. It was not until she heard his hearty voice in greeting that she looked up, with a start.

Stuart stood in the doorway, a wide grin on his face. He was very uneasy, and covered it with affected gaiety. He came to her across the sunlit floor, and bent and kissed her cheek, affectionately. "Well, well! How pleasant to see you up, and hearty again, my love!" he exclaimed.

He glanced about the shining room complacently, his gaze sharpening to discover if anything had been marred during Janie's illness, and if the maids had left a speck of dust on any darkly gleaming surface. Ah, was that the mark of a glass on the bedside cabinet? He went over to it, bent and scrutinized the mark, put his head first this way then that, frowned, rubbed the mark tentatively with his finger. His brow cleared. It was only the grain of the wood. Relieved, he straightened up, smiled at the little rosy fire, and returned to Janie with more sincere heartiness than before.

She had watched him with her slanted eyes, a nasty little smile on her mouth. Nevertheless, she melted when she saw his beaming ruddiness and handsomeness. He put his hand on the back of her chair, and his grin became somewhat absent and thoughtful.

He had something on his mind. He must use a measure of duplicity. Sometimes he thought himself a very clever fellow indeed, shrewd and knowing, and he anxiously wished everyone to believe that of him. However, deep in his heart he loathed knowing and clever people, and was afraid of them. But he envied their serenity and peace of mind. Peace of mind, he had decided ruefully, was given only to idiots and the wicked, those too benighted to have a conscience, and those who had been conveniently born without one.

Janie's gaze was very sharp, and he felt uncomfortable under its tentative reflection. He patted her cheek, sat near her. He took her thin freckled hand. "You are feeling quite well now, eh, my pet?"

"Perfectly," she replied, in her loud hoarse voice. She coquetted at him. "How good and thoughtful you've been to me, darling Stuart. I'm fair humbled."

"Well, now," he said, expansively, leaning back in his chair and crossing his long fine legs, "it was nothing at all. I wanted you to be comfortable, in your illness. The children have been well cared for. I've seen to that. And so we can think of other things now, can't we?"

And then he was silent, studying her closely. Could he pass her off as an exalted relative? Certainly, her toilettes and her jewels and her scents, (and her money) were impressive enough. If he could just persuade her to watch her blasphemous tongue, and not to laugh so loud and so coarsely! He cleared his throat, and smiled uncomfortably.

"The Mayor's wife, Mrs. Cummings, sends you her deepest regards, Janie. She wishes to know when you will be well enough to attend a party given in your honor. Cummings and I are good friends, you know."

Janie, pleased, bridled. She was agreeably surprised, also. "The Mayor, Stuart? How very gratifying! Please inform his lady that I shall be well enough to accept her gracious invitation next week, at any time." She paused. "Is she a very handsome lady, Stuart? And young? And elegant?"

Stuart thought of Alicia Cummings, short, stout, gray, with round pink cheeks, twinkling blue eyes, the sweetest smile, and no style at all. "She is a lady," he said, emphatically, and with warmth, as if defending her from the Janies. "Everyone loves her. No, she is not young. But she is very good. Charitable works, without tiresome piety. It is a pleasure to be in her company, for she is always civil and kind, and genuinely concerned. And very witty and learned."

"No doubt it is easy to be kind to personable young men, and very concerned," suggested Janie, slyly, licking her lips. All at once, she made Mrs. Cummings appear to be a lascivious old beldame, full of obscene and crafty desires for young men, and possessed of all foulness. Stuart felt suddenly sick and enraged. He turned his inner eye away from Mrs. Cummings, as though she had been offended by his very look.

But he controlled himself. He only turned a little livid about his full and irritable mouth. He said, in a voice somewhat muffled: "Mrs. Cummings is very kind to everyone. She is the confidante of every young girl in her circle, and the friend of anyone who needs friendship in affliction. I have heard no word against her."

He wanted to get up and leave the room. He could not

endure Janie's silently laughing face, the flash of her sharp predatory teeth between her painted lips. All at once she appeared hideous and hateful to him, and loathsome.

She said, in a horribly soft tone: "I am sure that Mrs. Cummings is a delightful lady, and I shall be overwhelmed to accept her invitation. Please extend my regards to her, and thank her for her kindness."

"I shall, ma'am," said Stuart, in an unnatural voice.

"How would you like to drive with me to the shops, my love?" he asked. "It is a fine day, and the air will do you good. Wear furs, though. We have very cold weather here until well into May. The warm sun is deceptive."

"I should like a drive, indeed," assented Janie, with genuine pleasure. "How thoughtful of you, dear Stuart."

He rose, coloring uneasily. He said: "I've been in to see Bertie and Robbie. Bertie is very restless, but Robbie still reads his damned book of murders. The rascal is actually making notes! He draws diagrams. A changeling, that's what he is."

"A shrewd lad," commented Janie. "We'll make a braw lawyer out of that one."

Stuart hesitated. He looked at her with simple earnestness. "I've been talking to Angus, too. Nearly fourteen, he says. A big lad. Do you know what he told me the other night? He said that his Grand-da had promised to let him be a doctor. He was to have gone to Edinburgh, to study with Dr. Mac-Intosh, the surgeon. I've almost promised to see to it that he shall study with a fine doctor in America."

Janie's face narrowed with dark evil. "A doctor?" she said.

"He has it in him, Janie. He's the heart of a doctor. Self-sacrificing and devoted. I know it. I always recognize true goodness. There's some'at of the martyr about him."

"Pious!" exclaimed Janie, as if that were the most degraded epithet in her vocabulary, and the most shameful. "It's to the kirk he'll be going every day, if you don't watch him, and not minding his lessons."

"He could do worse!" cried Stuart, forgetting his purpose in coming to this room. "I'll be taking him to Father Houlihan for consolation and advice!"

Janie sat bolt upright in her chair, and her eyes were malignant in their green flashings. "You'll not make a snivel-ling damn Papist of my son!" she exclaimed. "You'll not have him worshipping idols and bowing to Holy Marys like a heathen, and go about burning people!"

"Oh, God damn it!" shouted Stuart, quite crimson. "You

talk like a fool! Grundy wouldn't harm the lad! He'll not be converting him! Grundy's got wit and intelligence, you besom! Have you no kind thought or word for anyone?"

Janie was not shaken. She was always invigorated and exhilarated in the presence of screaming voices, oaths and violence.

"You'll not take him to a priest!" she shrieked. "I shall give him my express command!"

Stuart's clenched fist opened and itched. He wanted to slap her viciously in the face. He ached to do it. Involuntarily, the muscles of his arm contracted, and the limb lifted.

Janie had another idea. She saw Stuart's involuntary gesture, and she was as excited by it as any wild tigress. "Consolation!" she screamed. "What consolation, you fool? Why does my son need consolation?" She could not resist goading him into a physical outbreak against her.

"Because he's got a hellion for a mother!" shouted Stuart, even louder than before. "Because you've made his life a curse, harrying him and cuffing him, and frightening the life out of him with your bad nature!"

Then, all at once, they were both grimly silent. They panted audibly in the quiet sunlit air of the warm room. They stared at each other unblinkingly. Janie was thinking that she had been a fool, that she had antagonized Stuart, when it had been her express determination to "soften all over him," and predispose him to marriage. And Stuart was thinking that he had quite kicked over his private applecart, and that nothing could now placate Janie. They both hated themselves, and cursed themselves inwardly.

Stuart was the first to recover. He made himself smile. His face was still crimson, and it was damp. He felt the moisture pricking all along the forehead line of his thick black hair.

He said, lamely, his voice somewhat hoarse: "There, now, we are fighting and yammering as we did when we were children together, aren't we, Janie? It makes me homesick for the old days."

Janie, enormously relieved, laughed raucously. " 'The old days!' " she repeated. "Ah, it fair makes me want to cry, Stuart." And because she was so excited, so stimulated, she burst into genuine tears.

Stuart, though he hated her, was not insensible to the tears of a woman. There was a core of weak softness in him. Besides, his own relief was so profound that he trembled. He went to her at once, and put his arm about her shoulders, and kissed her red curls. "Ah, come, come, my darling! You are breaking my heart. Won't you forgive me, Janie? I shall be inconsolable if you don't."

Janie could almost always detect duplicity. She saw that Stuart was sincere, and her spirits rose. She cried and clung to him, and protested that she was a bad thing and merited no kindness from him, and that he had been so thoughtful of her, and so kind, and that he must straightway put her out of his house and send her home.

"No, no," said Stuart, pitying her, and seeing her as she desired him to see her: a homeless widow with four helpless children, thrown upon a heartless world. "It was I who was wrong. This is my house, and you are my darling guest, and my dear love of a Janie. Forgive me, my pet."

They wallowed in their emotionalism. Stuart's, at least, was sincere. Janie grinned craftily to herself, her face buried against his shoulder.

Later, they sat close together, their hands entwined. Janie was all ardor and stimulation. Stuart felt vaguely sick and weak. But he was very kind to his cousin. He could now approach her on the subject of her exalted background. He was tactful, in his new duplicity.

"This is a vulgar new society, my love," he began. "The people here know nothing of elegant manners, or true aristocracy. You will laugh at their pretensions, as I do. They are raw and ignorant. Also, they have the most extraordinary ideas as to what constitutes a lady of the aristocracy. So, they are excessively genteel. They believe that a true lady or gentleman is very mincing and delicate in speech, and full of sublime hauteur and daintiness, and would swoon at the slightest hearty word. Never having observed at close range any real gentlefolk, they have been compelled to use their imagination. As they are low-bred, they imagine, with malice, how they would treat their inferiors should they have been born to nobility. Some of them are even thinking of pink coats and hounds, but there is an uneasy prejudice in America against British customs, even though the people are of British stock almost entirely. They think longingly, however, of the British ways of life, and envy them and ape them furtively, in their way."

"How excessively diverting!" exclaimed Janie, genuinely interested, and full of scornful laughter for these plebeians.

"It is pathetic, somewhat," remonstrated Stuart. "These low-born, ill-bred poor creatures have nothing but their affectations and their hidden desires to console them for the barrenness of their money-grubbing lives. To each man his peculiar consolation. We must not forget, too, that these pretenders are powerful in America. They are so powerful all over that they can retain slavery in the Southern States, and gouge the workers in their industrial factories, in the North. They browbeat, quell and oppress, in the true way of all low-bred men. It is very sad, though. Someone ought to teach them true gentleness of manners, and the simple kindness of those who are authentically well-born. Someone ought to convince them that gentlefolk are not concerned with money or money-getting. It would be a revelation to Americans."

Janie smiled irresistibly. What a darling simpleton was this Stuart, with his serious face and sad words! But she fell in with his mood.

"I see," she said, gravely, her quick mind already ahead of his.

He sighed with relief. "Well, then, should you, Janie, upon presentation to them, be your simple, natural, well-born self, without affectations and graces, they would immediately condemn you as being no aristocrat. They would look askance at you. Should you speak in your usual robust way, they would be horrified. Should you pretend to no exalted antecedents, and refrain from bragging and exaggerating, they would consider you inferior. You are a lady. But you must fill the frame of their imagination to convince them that you are. You must fall in with their idea of gentlefolk."

Janie, the natural actress, was delighted. "I shall simper, blush and cut attitudes, in the most amazing way!" she exclaimed. "I shall be so delicate that I shall swoon at a light word, and have the vapors if a man blows his nose in my presence! I shall invent the most illustrious ancestors, with portraits and ghost-haunted castles, and moats and drawbridges. Let me see: Lady Constance Vere de Vere was my maternal great-grandmother! She was so dainty that she fainted at a loud voice!"

"Splendid," said Stuart, though with inner doubt. He gnawed his lip. He had not admitted to any Lady Vere de Vere. He must tell Janie about Sir Angus Fraser. Smiling in a somewhat sickly fashion, he confessed to Janie his previous inventions.

She laughed uproariously, and slapped his knee so vigorously that he winced. He was ashamed, both of himself and of her. But he was relieved that Janie had understood him so completely, and that she was entering into the play.

"I only want them to appreciate you, and not misjudge or

deprecate you, my dear," he said, very lamely. "I want them to do you justice."

Janie winked. "Have no doubts, darling Stuart. They shall adore me."

"No naughty jokes, no tapping gentlemen on the arm with your fan, no tripping and showing your ankles, no swearing, no robust remarks," pleaded Stuart.

"None!" cried Janie, throwing herself back in her chair in the most elegant of postures, and half closing her eyes, and fanning herself with her kerchief. "I shall be the delicate genteel widow, of the purest blue blood, with a voice like an angel, and with fluttering lashes. You shall see! You shall be proud of me!"

Stuart had his serious doubts. But he sighed with relief, and got to his feet. Janie looked at him, then had another thought.

"This Mr. Allstairs you mentioned, lovey. Is he one of the local aristocrats, also? And his amazing daughter, Marvina?"

Stuart, calling on his easy duplicity again, made himself look her boldly in the eye, and smiled broadly. "Yes, my love. He is the richest man in Grandeville, one of the rich men of the State. A dreadful creature. You will meet him. Miss Marvina? Well, I confess I was at one time attracted by her pretty face. But, heavens! she is dull, dull! Like a varnished wax doll. Do be kind to her, dear Janie. The poor girl hasn't the wit of a newborn calf. Do not make fun of her."

"You haven't made any commitments with regard to the treasure, Miss Marvina, Stuart? Commitments that might be misconstrued by the ogre of a father?"

"None at all! None at all! As I said, I was attracted, as were a dozen other men in Grandeville. But life with an empty doll, I decided, would be a horrible affair."

His spirits soared again. He had come off very well! Janie was practically convinced. Her sharp green eyes were almost soft.

"But you did say, my pet, that you intended to ask for her hand," she pointed out to him, doubtfully.

He laughed. He colored. He patted her shoulder. "Shall we say I've changed my mind?" he asked, with false archness.

Janie was intoxicated. She had always believed that Stuart was a simple soul, without successful dissimulation, and that he could certainly never deceive anyone as clever as Janie Cauder. Why, he was a child, a lovable simpleton, a zany.

She looked at him coyly, and waited. He knew what she wanted. His body grew tight with repulsion.

But he made himself bend deliberately and kiss her on the lips with ardor.

He had accomplished his first step. The other would come later in the day. It was worth it. But when he left the room, he could not believe it, in his sickened heart.

When she was alone, Janie hied herself to the chest of drawers, unlocked the lower drawer, and, from under billows of lace and fine linen underwear, produced a bottle of whiskey, half emptied. She held it high in her hand, so that the golden sunlight glinted through its mellow contents. "Ah, ah!" she said, richly, smacking her lips, and chuckling with pleasure. She tilted the bottle to her lips and drank deep and long. "Ah," she said again, on a prolonged respiration of satisfaction. She replaced the cork, hid the bottle again, with slow and loving movements. "A wee drap is guid for the soul o' a mon," her father had often remarked, relating how his father would drink a full glass of whiskey three times a day with his porridge or haggis or bailed mutton. The old man had lived to the fine age of one hundred and ten, and never a morning passed but that, in shawl and kilts, he had climbed the snowy hills to look at his sheep, and to stamp about, vigorous and ruddy, in all the glory of his six feet three inches of magnificent health.

Janie, apparently, agreed with her grandfather that a "wee drap" was the elixir of life. It had that effect upon her, after she tenderly locked the drawer again and put the key in her bosom. She began to hum hoarsely under her breath, then to caper about the room like a female goat, exulting and laughing aloud, as if nothing could restrain her, her skirts flying about her thin little legs, her red curls bouncing, her face a bright mask of merry evil.

CHAPTER 18

STUART brought his finest equipage, drawn by two gleaming black horses, to the gravel side-drive of the house. Harness and wheels glittered in the spring sunshine. The coachman secured the reins, then jumped out. Stuart intended to drive. He stood by the vehicle, tenderly rubbing his hand over the black varnished sides, blowing on the silver lamps, and polishing them lovingly with his kerchief. The horses looked at him sideways, showing the whites of their eyes. He patted their watered-silk black rumps, and pretended to examine the silver harness. Then, satisfied and smug, he breathed deeply of the strong fresh air, glittering with sunlight, and awaited Janie.

She came out the side entrance, and Stuart anxiously scrutinized her, worrying about her maiden appearance in Grandeville public places. Then he relaxed. Janie, as if she had known what carriage awaited her, was all black velvet and purple. Her frock, elegantly draped and restrained, fitted her perfectly. A number of silver chains hung about her neck. She wore a marvelous sable cloak over this elegance and picture of fashion, and black kid gloves. Her huge, black-velvet bonnet had purple violets cunningly peeping out from under its brim, accentuating her bright red hair. She minced down the white stairs from the doorway, and pleased, Stuart gallantly extended his hand to her. She was the picture of a delicate and wistful little widow, all fragility and modesty. She had even used restraint in the matter of rouge, and under the very slightest coating of powder her freckles were evident, and a little touching in their simplicity. It was only when she grinned wickedly at Stuart, showing her sharp and predatory white teeth, that the picture became distorted.

She allowed him to assist her into the vehicle, where she sat with eyes demurely downcast, her gloved hands in her sable muff. Then he sprang up beside her. He began to laugh. "Don't put on so much," he warned, with a wide smile. "Just be a little natural."

She looked up at him, her long green eyes sparkling naughtily, and thrust out her tongue at him for an instant. He quite liked her now. This was the old gay Janie whom he had loved, whose wickedness had been so fascinating. "No swearing, remember, and keep your voice low and sweet," he said, but with fondness.

Stuart, himself, was very handsome and dashing in his many-caped brown great-coat, and his tall beaver hat, and his ruffles and gloves. He guided the spirited horses up the grade to the muddy roadway that led into town. He felt very carefree, for some reason. Beside him, Janie was quiet and graceful, but he could feel her repressed vitality and excitement, which was like an electric wave. Now, he thought, if she will just behave herself, all will be well.

Purposely avoiding the meaner streets, he drove, jingling,

through quiet sections under trees still bare and brown, and by hedges still black and twisted. Water ran between the rough cobbles of the road. The plank walks were still sodden. The houses had an ugly and barren look, their red brick or wooden façades grimy from winter rains and chimney soot. But the wind that came from the Lake and the river was strong and fresh, and had an exhilarating smell, and the sun was bright and clear, and the pale blue sky pellucid. Stuart had warned Janie that this would be a long ride. But she was not bored. She peeped about her with patronizing interest. She thought the town very ugly and muddy, with a raw lack of symmetry and beauty. The tall narrow houses, gloomy on their muddy lawns, were indeed excessively hideous, with cupolas and wooden fretwork and deep dark verandahs. Here and there a drab lady, in huge bonnet and blowing dun-colored cloak, minced along the walks, or children played spasmodically, enjoying the release from winter. Carriages passed, the occupants craning out to stare at Stuart's handsome equipage, to exchange greetings with him (as he touched the whip gallantly to his hat) and to scrutinize the demure little lady beside him, so preciously immured in her sables and carriage robes.

This, Stuart informed her, was Niagara Street, so called because it ran beside the river for some distance. It was a street of middle-class people, of the professions and the shops. He sat very straight on his seat, controlling his horses, chatting lightly with Janie, explaining landmarks to her, and pointing to them with his whip. Without stopping his exposition, he bowed repeatedly to the passing carriages, and smiled, his strong teeth flashing in the cool sunlight. Finally, he turned up another street to lower Main, and pointed down it. "My shops," he said.

Janie leaned forward to peer with unfeigned interest at the source of Stuart's income, about which she had spent many long days of absorbed guessing. And then she was quite impressed. The shops filled one longish block, and though uneven, and apparently built at different times by different owners, they had a grand and compact air, the windows polished and glittering, and carriages drawn up outside. Here all was busyness and comings-and-goings, with house-boys following well-dressed ladies to the carriages, their arms filled with boxes and bundles. As they slowly passed the first shops, Janie was impressed by the crowded interiors, the activities of clerks; and the milling bonnets and the constant opening and shutting of doors. She looked at the long gilt sign:

"Grandeville Supreme Emporium," and the red-and-white stripes and the snowy stars of the flag that flew from the flag-pole near the main shop.

Stuart was quite flushed with pride and swelling embarrassment. The ladies on the walks stopped to stare at the elegant equipage. They collected in groups. They watched Stuart grandly offering his hand to the strange little lady who alighted, modestly pointing her black slippers straight ahead, and bending her bonnet so that her face was hidden. They whispered together, furtively. This must be Mr. Coleman's elegant female relative from England. What sables, what velvets, what fashion and gentility! They craned their necks to study her wardrobe, and envied her. They tried to see her face, but could catch glimpses only of a red curl or two. The redness pleased them, for red hair was considered the supreme ugliness.

Stuart affected to be totally oblivious of the watchers. He seemed tenderly concerned with the little elegant creature, who put her hand timidly on his proffered arm and minced beside him into the rich shop, her velvet skirts flowing about her gracefully, the muff held close to her face as if to protect its delicate texture from the cold wind. They entered the main shop with a stately air, measured and majestic, as if about to go into the measures of a minuet. One of the street urchins, who had been watching, absorbed, broke into ironic applause as Stuart and Janie disappeared within the shop. The ladies, with whom it was a principle never to acknowledge the existence of the lower classes, nevertheless bestowed upon the perspicacious urchin the gracious acknowledgement of his demonstration, and were highly pleased with him. They lingered on the walks, discussing the newcomer, and speaking in unconsciously affected voices, as if practicing their grammar and correctness of speech in anticipation.

Janie was astounded, in spite of her planned supercilious smiles, at the really elegant and luxurious interior of the main shop, its Turkey-red carpets, its small, carved, comfortable chairs with red plush seats, the polished mahogany counters, the wide neat shelves with their burdens of a really amazing assortment of fine silks and linens and damasks and velvets, the tables of excellent Limoges and Haviland china, the silver, the assorted Dresden and marble ornaments, the laces and ribbons and scents, and all the other countless objects calculated to seduce the feminine heart.

She was pleased by the air of great prosperity in the large shop. There were three active gentlemen clerks all in black broadcloth and white ruffled linen and pointed polished boots waiting on the crowd of eager and examining ladies. Lengths of gleaming velvet, of shining silk, of glistening linen, lay over the counters, and there was a great and active sound of snipping. Ladies' hooped skirts billowed incessantly, and with much rustling, from counter to counter. Bonnets were bent together for consultation, muffs lifted to hide whispers and evaluations. Young boys went in and out to the carriages, with boxes and bundles. The bell sounded constantly in the bustle. The china being examined tinkled, and once or twice a lady disputed a price with a bowing clerk. The spring sunshine poured like a cataract through the shining windows, which were framed in dark blue velvet. There was a warm smell here of discreet sachet and rose-water, and the rich scent of luxurious fabrics. Over some of the chairs the ladies had thrown their tippets and furred cloaks, and the silk linings added splashes of purple and red and blue to the lively scene.

Janie had expected to make a grand and overpowering entrance, utterly cowing these barbarians, but for some time she and Stuart went unnoticed amid the activity. Stuart swelled with importance and complacency. He pressed the little gloved hand on his arm in eloquent and delighted communication.

A stout, middle-aged lady in black silk and black fur and a big black bonnet, turned, summoned her waiting boy, and ordered him to pick up some newly wrapped packages for her. She had a sturdy but exceedingly intelligent face with bright pink cheeks, twinkling blue eyes, and a humorous fine mouth with one corner chronically turned upwards in a gently satirical fashion, and a dark eyebrow that followed suit. Her smooth thick hair was quite gray, which gave her face a youthful freshness in comparison. She was all competence and precision of movement, and the ladies smiled at her respectfully as she prepared to take her departure.

Stuart caught her eye, and bowed deeply. Gently, he led Janie forward. The lady waited, eyebrow and mouth quirking upwards more distinctly as she studied Janie with candor and politeness. "My dear, dear Mrs. Cummings!" exclaimed Stuart, softly, "and how are you today? May I present my dear cousin, Mrs. Cauder? It is a great honor! Janie, my love, this is Mrs. Howard Cummings, the Mayor's lady."

The ladies curtseyed briefly. Then Mrs. Cummings extended her mitted hand to Janie, who took it in her narrow little fingers. She instantly hated Mrs. Cummings, whose hand was full and warm and strong. She hated the shrewd kind eyes that estimated her, and the eyebrow and the quirking sardonic mouth. As for Mrs. Cummings, her honest face took on a subtly bland expression, and there was a quick narrowing of one eyelid.

"How very nice!" murmured Mrs. Cummings. "My dear, I hope you will like our Grandeville. You have received my messages during your illness? And Stuart has conveyed to you my invitation to dinner?"

Janie's naturally hoarse and booming voice lowered itself to a discreet murmur. "Indeed! I am delighted to meet you, Mrs. Cummings. Stuart has spoken so extravagantly of his dear friends. It was kind of you to remember me, a stranger in a strange land, so far away from my dear mama and papa, and my brothers and sisters." She paused a moment, to let her eyes fall and a look of sorrow to come over her face. She was all meekness and defenselessness. Then she lifted her eyes again to look bravely at Mrs. Cummings, and to allow a brave smile to touch her mouth. "But I am not going to be unhappy! That would be impossible, in the presence of so much kindness and civility from dear Stuart's friends! I trust I shall not be ungrateful."

Mrs. Cummings smiled, but was silent. Her gaze was fastened thoughtfully on Janie, though it was not unkind. Then she said: "I understand that you have four children, Mrs. Cauder. How very comforting for you!"

Janie simpered, sighed, touched her lips with her kerchief. "Ah, dear Mrs. Cummings, you cannot imagine the comfort! I could not endure living without my darlings."

"You are to be envied," said Mrs. Cummings, and now she sighed a little, and smiled again. "I have only one child, my little Alice, who is ten years old, and very frail, I am afraid. It will be pleasant for her to know your children, Mrs. Cauder."

All at once the good woman appeared uneasy, and a little breathless, which was very startling as she was famous for her poise and composure. She said, hurriedly: "I must truly go. You will remember my dinner, Mrs. Cauder? And you, Stuart?" She turned to Stuart as she mentioned his name, and looked at him strangely, and the eyebrow and the mouth were not quirking now. Her fresh color had inexplicably faded.

Stuart bowed, expressing his deep gratitude. As he spoke, Mrs. Cummings' strange look deepened, and she touched his arm swiftly with her fingers, then turned away. Stuart gallantly opened the door for her. She smiled at him for an instant, a breathless and disturbed smile, and went down the steps followed by her boy, loaded with parcels. Stuart, after a moment's hesitation, and completely forgetting Janie, hurriedly followed in Mrs. Cummings' wake, brushed aside her coachman, and assisted her into the carriage. She made a big pretense of being engaged in adjusting her cloak, skirts and bonnet, while the boy loaded the carriage. Stuart's Celtish intuition murmured dimly. Frowning thoughtfully, he returned slowly to the shop. What had disturbed Mrs. Cummings? In justice, he could blame nothing on Janie, who had been all civility and discretion. Mrs. Cummings, perhaps, had had a twinge, a sudden headache. Ah, that must explain it! His volatile spirits rose again, and with a dashing swagger he closed the door behind him and stood again at Janie's side.

She gave his arm a secret but vicious pinch. He winced, uttered an exclamation. But she was looking up at him archly. "So, that is our old dear friend, Mrs. Cummings!" she muttered. "How fond she appeared of you, darling Stuart!"

"She is one of my best customers!" said the young man. He said heatedly, as if defending Mrs. Cummings: "Her patronage is very valuable, I assure you, Janie! I would rather any other lady in the city were offended but Mrs. Cummings!"

Janie interrupted sweetly: "I did not offend her, my love. Was I not all primness and respectability?" Stuart was at a confused loss.

Another lady, having concluded her purchases, turned. She was a huge fat woman, dressed in crimson velvet, her cloak bordered with black seal, her muff enormous, her crimson bonnet quite the largest in the shop. She was monumental; she was shapeless; she was completely overpowering because of sheer bulk. The bonnet framed a pink and white face of distinctly porcine cast, and her tiny black eyes had a piggish and repellent expression. Her mouth was thick and pursed in a chronically arrogant and belligerent look, and her short thick nose was like a snout. She jingled with chains and bangles; her cheeks and forehead were moist. She exuded a smothering scent of musk. Her hair was thick and yellowish and coarse. She was about thirty-eight years old, and she gave one an impression of complete insensibility, suspicion, coarseness and brutality.

Stuart bowed to her deeply, and beamed, though he hated her for her arrogance and insensate peasantness, her domineering ways and her pretense at gentility.

"My dear, dear Mrs. Schnitzel!" he exclaimed, warmly. "I have not seen you lately. I trust you have not been ill?"

Mrs. Schnitzel stared at him with porcine hauteur, as if suspecting his civil words of some ulterior design. She appeared to swell and bristle. Then she deigned a smile of supreme condescension. "I have been in New York, Mr. Coleman," she said, in a deep rumbling voice with a distinctly Teutonic accent. She lifted her big head impressively, then turned to stare unblinkingly at Janie, whom she immediately despised because of her small and graceful figure and style. Dislike glittered in the tiny black eyes.

"Ah, yes," said Stuart, flushing. "Mrs. Schnitzel, this is my cousin, Mrs. Cauder, just from England. Janie, my dear, this is Mrs. Otto Schnitzel, the lady of the owner of our largest slaughter-house."

The lady bowed with majesty, like an empress acknowledging the impudent presence of an inferior. Janie looked up at that vast swinish face. "Mrs. Schnitzel!" she began, in a whispering scream of incredulity and mirth, then caught herself quickly. She curtseyed. Mrs. Schnitzel did not curtsey. She swelled even more with her importance and condescension. She moved away like a ship in full sail, her crimson velvet skirts sweeping behind her, her cloak swaying. Stuart opened the door for her, bowed, and then watched the stately and shaking descent of the Teutonic dame. He returned to Janie, whose little face was convulsed.

"My darling Stuart!" she whispered, trembling with merriment, her eyes sparkling irrepressibly. "What an odious female! Schnitzell And what, in the name of God, is that name? Schnitzell"

Stuart could not restrain a grin. His Celtish soul hated the Teuton deeply for repression. "A German sow," he whispered, in return. "Grandeville has many of them—these Germans. A horrible people. Brutish. Slaughter-houses and tanneries and sausage factories. Appropriate to their natures. None of them are accepted in genteel society except a few like the Schnitzels, who are very rich and very pretentious."

"Schnitzel!" exclaimed Janie. "My dear God! What an appalling name! Do they all have such names?"

"Some are worse, like our Schnickelburgers, for instance," said Stuart. "Hush! We are talking too loud. Would you like to see the other shops now?"

Janie shook her head, still giggling. "Why does America allow them here, my love? Such names! Such faces! Such——"

"Such swine," added Stuart. His face darkened. He remembered, with anger, that it was Otto Schnitzel who had threateningly advised the Mayor to prohibit the building of any more Catholic churches in Grandeville, and to prevent the coming of nuns into the city. It was Emil Schnickelburger, too, who had insulted poor old Grundy publicly, on the main street of Grandeville, and had splashed him with mud from his carriage wheels. It was Gustav Zimmermann who had ordered Sam Berkowitz to move off the walk into the mud when the swelling German was passing. Sam had not so moved, and the German had refused to pass by him, turning away with an obscene Teutonic oath, and a lifted cane.

Stuart was now so disturbed that he decided not to introduce Janie to the other engrossed ladies, though they were eying them both furtively. He conducted Janie from the shop, with an air and much dash. He took her to the other shops.

As they went from one to the other, Janie was genuinely impressed. Her eyes blinked thoughtfully. Her manner towards Stuart became more intimate and fond and delighted. Her fifteen thousand pounds were safe, then, from any cousinly fortune-hunter. This vast and prosperous establishment was obviously not only on a paying basis, but the source of much revenue. Stuart, in spite of her previous opinion, was apparently possessed of an extraordinary amount of buiness acumen and enterprise. She saw that he had many employees. She saw the streaming carriages. She saw the activity. She heard the jingle of money. It was like a bee-hive about the shops, and Stuart assured her that on Saturday the streets about the shops were impassable. Every barge that came up the Canal was loaded with his goods. Twice a year he went to New York, where he negotiated for the import of the finest European merchandise from England and France, and even from Italy and the Orient. There was no limit to what he could do, he assured her. He had the most wonderful plans, he hinted, but that must wait a little. He had not finished expanding.

She saw that not all of this was bombast, but based on shrewd business intuition. It was a land for dreamers, for bold entrepreneurs, for imaginative adventurers who gambled largely and won magnificently. Her insular soul was shaken.

"You must save a lot of money, my love," she said, tentatively, moistening her lips avidly.

Stuart hesitated. He smiled down at her patronizingly. "That is not the way to make a fortune in America, my pet," he assured her. "This is not England, where you laboriously add penny to penny. 'Many a mickle makes a muckle,' to quote your esteemed father. No, that is not our way in America. In England, one puts pence in the bank and watches them grow to painful pounds. In America, we put our pounds back into our enterprises, and watch them make golden fortunes. This is a land of tremendous distances, not a narrow little island. One cannot estimate things here. One must venture, if one is to gain, and not venture with pennies, but with fortunes."

Janie was shrewd and intuitive, also. She was shaken to her foundations. She saw all the possibilities. Suddenly her fifteen thousand pounds were a meager thing, a miserable drop of water in a golden well that was bottomless. She had thought of herself as an heiress. She was apparently only a poor widow with a mite. Her heart burned with greed. She would be conferring nothing on Stuart with her wretched pounds, he who had hundreds of thousands of pounds in mind.

She leaned against him, clinging to him, as they went from shop to shop. Stuart had intended her to be impressed. He had exaggerated. He had hoped, at best, to put her into a state of mind in which she would be amenable to a loan of ten thousand dollars to him. He felt her to be impressed. Had he known to what extent, he would have been delirious with pleasure.

She met Sam Berkowitz in one of the shops, and she stared at him forbiddingly. Not knowing the full extent of his share in this dazzling prosperity, she thought of him as a hanger-on, kept here by the noble generosity of the gilded Stuart. She was very prim and reticent towards him, as befitted a Christian, while he looked at her silently with his hooded and lighted brown eyes, and bowed to her courteously. She did not know that he followed her with his long sad gaze as she swept from the shops, and that he shook his head a little.

CHAPTER 19

JANIE ate alone with Stuart that evening for the first time since her illness. The beautiful dining-room was golden with candlelight. Stuart had ordered an especially fine dinner. He plied Janie with excellent wines. Gradually her coldness of flesh warmed. The golden light swam all about her. She laughed louder and louder, sitting there in her best blue velvet and pearls, her curls red and shining on her thin shoulders. Her rowdy voice was rich with ribald jokes. Her glass was never empty. Never had she felt so deliciously free, so fascinating, so full of worldliness and poise, so clever and sparkling. She was in her proper place at last. Her old home was entirely forgotten. Her onerous children did not exist. She had no parents, no memories. She was an elegant lady of gracious salons and waltzes and music and fine toilettes, fascinating a handsome and beloved companion whom she was about to marry. Because of her exhilaration, she appeared quite intriguing, even to Stuart. How had he forgotten what a gay companion Janie was? How had he forgotten that one was never bored in her company, and that her effervescent and cruel little malices were so witty?

On a wave of huge and boisterous laughter, they went together into the lovely drawing-room, where a great fire burned and fresh liqueurs were set out. They drank each other's health again and again. The most tender affection and excitement pervaded them. Janie's croaking mirth could be heard in distant rooms. Suddenly she rose, pulled up her flowing and swelling skirts and waltzed about the room, showing her silken knees, and even her thighs, most licentiously. Stuart applauded noisily. Janie cavorted and swayed, kicked and pranced quite gracefully, while Stuart bellowed: "Bravo! Bravo!" The children, far up in their beds, listened, and Bertie, in his nightshirt, stole to the head of the stairs, grinning and snapping his fingers. "Mama's at it again," he whispered to Robbie, who was indifferent. Angus sighed in his bed, arose and shut the door of the bedroom of his frightened little sister, after kissing her and getting her assurance that she had said her prayers. The servants peeped in at the revellers and went away, snickering.

Janie at last collapsed, weak with laughter and exercise, and sprawled on a damask sofa. She allowed Stuart to take her hand and pull her upright. He bent and kissed her, out of sheer exuberance. She clung to him like a tigress, and so great was her ardor that he was suddenly warned. Gently, he disengaged himself and sat near her while she, laughing, smoothed her curls and pulled down her gown.

"Never have I enjoyed myself so!" she shouted, flinging out her arms. "Ah, it's a rare devil you are, Stuart!"

He sat, not far from her, his hands on his knees, laughing uncontrollably. His black eyes dwelt on her cunningly. It was really a pretty little piece, this Janie. His neck felt thick and pulsing; the veins started in his forehead. What the devil! She was no child, but a woman older than he, and ready. It was a lewd baggage, knowing and lusty. A night might be pleasantly spent with her, and no one the wiser.

She saw his eyes, and a long hot thrill came over her body. Ah, there was more than one way to skin a cat! There was no doubt that Stuart found her desirable. She knew a great deal about men. Once involved with her, he could not retreat. Besides, he had the kindest heart.

She lifted her arms with deliberate languor and rearranged her hair. Her waist was tiny and neat, in its stays. She regretted that she had not more bosom. Her green eyes narrowed seductively. Stuart moved on his chair.

But there was one thing that Janie did not know about Stuart. He was tenacious. He was crafty. He put first things first, most of the time. Later, he would consider other things. He had no scruples.

He went to the sofa and sat down beside her, taking her hand. He kissed it gallantly. Then, though the fumes of the wine were still boiling in him, his mind became clear. Janie looked at him ardently. She was very silent now. He allowed his face to become thoughtful, even grave.

"Janie, my love," he began, in a serious and considering voice, "you told me that you had fifteen thousand pounds. That is roughly seventy-five thousand dollars." He shook his head. "That is very little for America. I've been worrying very much about you." He cleared his throat, and appeared embarrassed. "Even should you remarry, that money is little enough. I should like to see you possessed of much more. It is the least I can do for you."

Janie sat up alertly, her eyes gleaming in the firelight. She wet her lips in the familiar covetous manner. Her hand tightened in his. "Yes," she said, softly.

"It's the least I can do," he repeated, in a firmer voice, as though challenging an unseen listener, who might be very admonishing. "Yes, the very least. So I've thought of a way. Mind you, I'll encounter much difficulty. But I'm prepared for argument and disagreement, and protests. We are a closed partnership. We've never considered such a thing—" He paused. He sighed and frowned, and averted his head.

Janie was tense. "Go on, Stuart," she commanded. "After all, we are cousins, are we not?"

He sighed, without answering for a time. Then, in a lower and reluctant voice, he continued: "Janie, even though your money was safe in the banks, consider the interest. Very small. Should you decide not to remarry, you could not live on that interest, in the pleasant manner to which you are accustomed. Not in America, at least, and not with four children. Money doesn't grow by itself. You would be compelled to live on the principal. Your fortune would soon go. Who, then, would marry an impecunious widow, with four children?"

Janie regarded him with gray fear. Her eyes blinked. She bit her lip.

Stuart was much disturbed. "Do not think it is easy for me to speak to you like this, Janie. I wish I could do something for you. I—I have spoken of it, to someone else, but he protests——"

"The Jew!" cried Janie, enraged, and beating the sofa with her clenched fist.

Stuart winced. He cleared his throat. "Janie, don't say that. It isn't quite true. But a man has to protect his interests, you understand. However," and he sat up, quite exultant, "I have thought of a way!"

"Yes!" exclaimed Janie, her face lighting up with eagerness. "Yes, Stuart!"

He turned to her, and gripped her shoulders excitedly. His hands were strong. His face was alight. He was an excellent actor. He cried: "Janie, would you be willing to invest twenty thousand dollars in my shops?"

A sudden cold wave swept over Janie, an old Scottish caution and suspicion. She leaned away from Stuart, but he still gripped her. She studied his face, and now she was sober. But she could find nothing there but excitement and generous affection.

"Go on," she whispered, thickly.

He could not contain his enthusiasm now. He started to his feet. He paced the room. He struck one clenched fist in the palm of the other. His acting was so convincing that all her suspicions were gone. Her excitement rose again. She sat on the edge of the sofa and watched him.

"Janie!" he cried, suddenly stopping and wheeling towards her. "I will tell you something that no one knows except, of course, the banks! Sam and I have an income of over fifty thousand dollars a year from the shops! It is a secret, and I am telling you this in confidence. If you invest twenty thousand dollars in the shops, you will have a handsome income of about five thousand dollars a year, as your share! If you invest more, the income will be in proportion. And all without touching the balance of your principal. You will be a partner in the Grandeville Supreme Emporium, whose possibilities are limitless! Later on, there is no telling what your income will be! I've told you how we intend to expand! You have seen for yourself!"

He watched her, his eyes kindling, his face dark with congested blood.

"Janie! Do you understand? Do you see what I am offering you, who must be protected?"

Janie twined a red curl about one trembling finger. She was very white. He plunged down beside her again, laughing silently, and with evident joy.

"I think I can persuade Sam, Janie! I think he will understand how I can do no less, you being my cousin. I will have the papers drawn up tomorrow, my darling! And then you will have no worries, and need only sit back, you darling little creature, and watch your income grow, and anticipate larger and larger profits as we expand!"

Janie spoke hoarsely: "But Stuart, you did say that you were compelled to borrow ten thousand dollars from Mr. Allstairs, for your house. Why did you not withdraw the money from your business?"

At this shrewd query, Stuart was taken aback. His brow wrinkled. He cursed himself for his loose tongue. I never think! he thought, hating himself. He forced himself to laugh boyishly, to look sheepish. He rubbed his cheek with the knuckles of his right hand.

He chuckled, as if embarrassed. "My pet, I spoke too loosely. You mustn't breathe that to a soul. You see, most of my money is in the business. Sam and I put back our profits into it. I suppose it is a little complicated to a female mind, but I will try to explain. If I had withdrawn that ten thousand dollars from my business, I should have cut into the profits. I don't want that. I don't want anything to interfere with that." He put on a knowing air, and winked at her in an engaging fashion. "I don't want anything to interfere with the expansion. It was a private loan from Allstairs. It has nothing to do with the shops at all."

He spoke his lies with so artless a manner, with such a boyish air of simple confession, that Janie, the astute, was completely deceived. In a way, also, she was seduced by her opinion of her own acumen. Stuart could never "come over" so shrewd a baggage as Janie Cauder!

"I see," she murmured, with a clever aid. She shook her red curls at him chidingly. "My love, you are very bad. Well, no matter." She drew a deep breath. Her eyes gleamed again. "You will draw the papers tomorrow, Stuart?"

He was almost beside himself with his triumph. Tomor-

row, then, old Allstairs would have his ten thousand dollars
thrown into his devilish face. Then a quick marriage to Marvina and her fortune. His mind whirled. It would have to be
an elopement, in a way. Before Janie was undeceived, and
without the knowledge of Allstairs. Marvina was of age. She
was her father's darling. He would rage awhile, and threaten.
But there was nothing he could do. Later he would be reconciled. The mighty fortune, in due course, would then fall into
Stuart's hands. He could hardly contain himself in his exultation and delirium. He had not dreamt it would be so easy.
His opinion of himself rose to rapturous heights. What a dev-
ilishly clever dog he was! What a brilliant blackguard! He
saw visions that made his senses swim.

He caught Janie in his arms and kissed her with violence.
She clung to him. Her mouth was hungry and tumultuous.
He was not thinking of her. He caressed her lavishly, but
mechanically. His heart was pounding and thick.

And then, slowly at first, but soon quickening, he became
aware of the hot and wild passion in his arms. His senses
gave a strenuous lurch. He drew back a little. Her arms tightened about him, sinewy. She pulled down his head and fastened her mouth on his, her fingers twined in his black hair.
The blood rushed to his neck and face and head, with a long
singing.

Later, in her dark room, as Stuart waited, she was glad
she had not lighted the candles. She did not wish Stuart to
see how meager was her body, despite the lewd flame which
burned in it like a conflagration.

CHAPTER 20

STUART COLEMAN did not have the opportunity,
the next day, of "throwing the ten thousand dollars into old
Allstairs' face," for the reason that both Joshua and his adored
Marvina had been taken ill a day or two before with the sea-
sonal influenza. Stuart's buoyant mood awakened him the
next morning. He suffered no regrets, no squeamish embarrassment. He was too healthy to harbor them, too realistic.
He hoped, in his generosity, that the "amiable indiscretion"
had been enjoyed by Janie as much as it had been enjoyed by
him. Janie was no defenseless young girl, a fragile guest in his

house, whose virtue he must respect. She had no respect for her own virtue, and was hearty and healthy enough to know that she possessed none. If any seduction had taken place, he said to himself, with a laugh, he, not Janie, had been seduced.

He ate alone at breakfast, and set out, very early, to confront and wheedle and browbeat Sam Berkowitz. His mood sustained him. Sam was apt to be difficult at times, and obstinate. The news that he and Stuart had a new partner was bound to be startling to him, to say the least. Stuart went over opening phrases in his mind as he swung through the silent sun-touched streets, tossing his cane up in the air and catching it, and whistling exuberantly. He bought a newspaper, glanced at the headlines, and went his way. A very happy and peaceable life was this! Certainly there were nasty rumbles from the South, and hot-headed and unconcealed threats against a North that did not understand the slavery problem. But this was nothing. Let the hot-heads call each other names, and peace would prevail. At least Stuart hoped so. As for Europe, he had done with it long ago.

It was not until he reached Sam's neat little gray house in a very unfashionable section that the first qualms came to him. He frowned in annoyance. He could not, would not, retreat. Sam must be made to see that at once. Doubtless there would be some unpleasantness. That was all that irritated Stuart.

He was admitted to the little quiet parlor by a sleepy maid-servant. Old Mrs. Berkowitz, confined now to her bed with rheumatism, no longer came downstairs in the mornings. But Sam was called, and he entered the parlor in his shirt-sleeves, tall and bowed and lean, with rough hair prematurely gray, his eyes alert and inquiring. But, as always, he was serene and still, his subtle dark face gentle and friendly.

"Ach, Stuart, this is early for you, no?" His voice, heavily accented and grave, nevertheless sounded pleased. If he felt some warning, he did not betray it. "You will haf coffee, yes? I am about to eat my breakfast."

"I've eaten, thank you, Sam." Beaming ostentatiously, Stuart lifted his coat-tails and seated himself in a velvet chair, leaning his cane against his knees. "It was a little matter of business, which I thought I ought to discuss with you before the banks opened."

Sam was instantly anxious. He sat down, slowly, and peered at Stuart with his short-sighted eyes. "Money?" he said, slowly, and with regret. "It is money again, Stuart? You need money?"

"Damn it!" exclaimed Stuart, irately, moving in his chair. "Do I always need money?"

"Nearly always," said Sam, with a smile.

"Am I a pauper? You are implying I am a pauper, Berkowitz?"

But Sam was undisturbed. "I am but implying, my dear Stuart, that you usually need money."

Stuart scowled. Then he could not help smiling. "Who doesn't?" he asked, frankly. "Besides, a business needs only one solvent partner. Yes, it is money. But not my need for it. Money that is about to fall into my hands."

Now Sam was truly alarmed. He knew Stuart very well. When he had this carefree attitude, this insouciance, matters were precarious. Then a greater alarm seized Sam. Was Stuart about to announce his betrothal to Miss Marvina?

"Don't look so haggard, Sam," said Stuart, laughing. His color was excellent. He was in high good spirits. "I mean it when I say I can get my hands immediately on twenty thousand dollars."

Sam pursed his lips, and his expression deepened into real concern. "When a man says he can get twenty thousand dollars, like a whistle, Stuart, it is time to call the police. Forgive me. I haf not interrupted. You shall tell me."

"I am trying to, God forgive me!" said Stuart, with irritation. "Twenty thousand dollars, at once. And no police, damn you. I'm not a bank-robber yet, though I confess it has its points. No, it is my cousin, Mrs. Cauder. She has consented to lend me twenty thousand dollars. Immediately."

Sam stared, in silence. Certainly, it was plain to see. Stuart was handsome and magnetic, and very ingratiating. It would be a little matter for such a one to persuade a susceptible woman to part with so large a sum of money. Sam was both relieved and regretful, and very sorry. He had not believed it of Stuart.

"That is very kind of the lady, Stuart," he said slowly. "And, as she is your cousin, she does not demand security?"

Stuart coughed. He had come to the difficult point. He studied the gilded head of his cane with great concentration. Then he put it aside and said blandly: "She does not demand it, no. But I offered it."

Sam could not help saying, with some somber mischief: "Your house, Stuart, which is so heavily mortgaged to Mr. Allstairs?"

"I resent that tone, Sam, and your sarcasm! It is uncalled for, and ungenerous. Am I a rascal, Sam, to deceive a poor widow, lone and forlorn, which she, herself, says she is? Do I rob orphans of their bread, and kick them in the backside to boot? Damn it, you have a high opinion of me!"

"There, now," said Sam, soothingly, but with a brighter smile, "I haf nothing but the best opinion of my friends. Do not be so angered, my dear Stuart. I haf said nothing at all. I haf been impertinent, yes, in inquiring about the security?"

"Well, no," replied Stuart, mollified, but still uneasy. "That is why I have come. To talk about the security. You see, I offered Janie a sort of partnership in the shops."

Sam was shocked. He got slowly to his feet. He looked incredulously at Stuart. He could not speak.

"Don't look so much like a hanged corpse, Sam," said Stuart, with an attempt at a laugh. "I will explain it to you, briefly.

"I have intimated to her—and it is no lie—that an investment of twenty thousand dollars in the shops will bring her at least five thousand a year, more or less. She was very avid about it, I assure you. Her lips dripped greedily. It was very edifying, this female cupidity. You and I draw hardly twice that much apiece, just at this time, from the business, and we have considerably more invested, as you know very well. Another partner, a silent and female one, who has placed twenty thousand dollars at our disposal, is to be welcomed with glad cries. You agree with me?" He paused. "I see you don't agree. Well, no matter. Hear me out.

"Think what we can do with twenty thousand dollars, Sam. You remember that bankrupt stock in New York, which we can get for a song? I am going to order it immediately. You remember how regretfully we discussed it the other day, and wished we might be able to negotiate a loan to buy it. Now, we can. I am still waiting for the glad cries."

Sam sat down, slowly. Now his brown eyes were no longer gentle, but penetrating and very somber. Stuart waited for his comment. But he only said, very quietly: "You haf not told me everything, Stuart."

"Well, no, I haven't. Not quite." Stuart hesitated. He chewed his lips. He did not look Sam directly in the eye. "I need ten thousand dollars, Sam. I need it very bad. I need it to pay off that old bastard, Allstairs. At once. I intend to do it.

"I will put the whole twenty thousand dollars into the business, and borrow ten thousand of it back, repaying it in a stated sum each month out of my own pocket. Once rid of the ruinous interest which I pay to that usurer, I can manage the payments easily. Janie will receive a sum at stated intervals, herself, as her income from the investment. I am to draw up the proper papers, today."

Sam looked at him steadfastly. "I shall offend you, Stuart, but I must. It is necessary. You repay Mr. Allstairs regularly because you fear to lose your house. Because you fear for your prestige with him. But relieved of that, you will not pay back regularly into the business. And the business will pay Mrs. Cauder regularly, in spite of the prosperity or the decline of the shops. You and I, Stuart, we can wait. We can be calm and patient. We can tighten what you call our belts. But she cannot tighten her belt. She is a woman, with children."

"Curse you, you are calling me an irresponsible thief!" shouted Stuart, crimson, covering his confusion with bluster. "You are actually saying that I shall default on my payments back into the shops! You are implying I intend to rob you of your damned profits!"

Sam lifted his hand. He said in a clear, firm tone: "I haf told you often, my dear Stuart, that what I haf is yours, when you need it. I do not resent the tone; I am not angered. I am only afraid. For you.

"You will listen to me, please. You and I—we can wait. Mrs. Cauder cannot. It is to protect her that I speak, and this you know, in your heart. You are in debt, Stuart. You haf debts everywhere. Last month, it was nearly one thousand dollars, in gambling and women. You haf told me yourself. There was that necklace for the handsome lady in Saratoga last year. Haf you paid that yet, Stuart? I think it is two thousand dollars more. And the horse-racing, Stuart. You cannot resist the horses. I know all this. You are angered with me. But you know it is the truth."

"I will sign notes!" shouted Stuart, furiously. "I will give you all the cursed notes you want! Turn them over to your usurers! Sell me out, damn you!"

But Sam only smiled sadly. He shook his head, over and over. "You know you talk wildly, Stuart. You know that if you go bankrupt, I go with you, gladly. What need haf I for money, except what I had planned for my people? What I haf is yours. But I cannot see you ruined. I cannot stand by while you ruin yourself."

Stuart got up, with a violent gesture. He said, vehemently: "I swear to God, Sam, that you misjudge me. I will pay everything back, promptly. I give you my word of honor. I've been strapped before. I don't mind being strapped again. No more debts, personal debts, until the money is repaid."

He smiled grimly. "There is something else, which will assure the payments. I intend to marry Miss Marvina Allstairs. Very, very soon. With or without her father's consent."

If Sam had been disturbed before, he was distraught now. But it was a dumb distraction. He wrung his hands together. He looked at Stuart with a kind of despair.

Stuart was recovering his good spirits. He did not notice the sunken expression in Sam's eyes, the wringing of his hands. He said, jubilantly: "Even if the old swine holds out, there will be other ways. Miss Marvina inherits quite a fortune in her own name when she is twenty-one, from her late deceased grandfather, her mother's father, from Pittsburgh. I believe it is nearly one hundred thousand dollars. You and I, Sam, could manage very well for three more years, even if things went badly with us, which they won't. The shops are growing more prosperous every day. You told me that, yourself."

But Sam said, in a low and shaking voice, his eyes fixed on the floor: "You will marry this lady, Stuart, because you love her, and not because of the shops?"

"Certainly." Stuart stared. "I am much attached to the young lady. I would not go so far as to say that I would marry her without a penny, for I would not. But I should prefer her with a small fortune to a lady with a larger one. Unless," he added, grinning, "the second lady had too attractive a fortune."

He sat down again, full of eager vitality. "The old bastard won't hold out for long, Sam. He loves that girl too much. I shall make a model husband. He will soon soften. I know it!"

Sam's despair increased. That strange, dead young woman! That Golem with the beautiful face! She would freeze Stuart's hot and vigorous heart; she would destroy his soul! It was not to be endured. Yet there was nothing to be done. When men were bent on destruction, the cries of friends were smothered in the winds of passion.

Stuart put his hand on his friend's numb knee, and shook it affectionately. "Why do you look at me like that, Sam? Don't you understand? Everything is going splendidly. I am sorry I insulted you. But you understand me, Sam, don't you? I wouldn't hurt you for the world. It is all my damned hasty tongue. I know what you are, in my heart. Sam, damn it, I love you."

Sam put his cold knotted fingers over Stuart's warm hand. He said nothing.

"Sam, you forgive me, don't you?"

Sam rose. He put his hand over his face for a moment. "There is nothing to forgive, Stuart." He dropped his hand. His haggard face was ravaged. "You will wait for me? And then, we shall go to the banks, and our lawyer."

But again, after all negotiations, the exuberant Stuart was frustrated, at least for the time being, in his plan to march boldly to Joshua and deliver him the cheque for ten thousand dollars.

For Joshua and Miss Marvina had been quite ill of their influenza, and immediately upon making recovery, went for three weeks to a mountain inn to recuperate in airs higher and sweeter than those that blew with hard cold strength in Grandeville.

While in the mountains, Joshua perfected his plans to take his daughter to England that summer and leave her there, a suitable chaperone and sponsor having been obtained.

Stuart was glad of the reprieve, though momentarily disappointed. He, too, laid his plans, and they were bold ones indeed.

Janie Cauder was now a silent partner in the Grandeville Supreme Emporium, and considered herself fortunate. She no longer had doubts that Stuart would marry her. He was all gallantry and affection. He was kind to her children, who apparently were very fond of him, except Robbie, who privately considered Stuart a simpleton. When Stuart suggested that the three boys attend the "gentleman's school" which he himself had attended, Janie was pleased. It was so kind and civil of dear Stuart to be interested in her children's welfare!

Little Laurie appeared to be his favorite. He walked with her in the late afternoons along the river, and from her windows Janie could see the pair of them, the tall and dashing Stuart in his tall hat and furred collar, and the child, in her cape and bonnet, walking hand in hand along the banks of the turbulent water.

CHAPTER 21

ANGUS looked about Father Houlihan's house with shy curiosity and uncertain wariness. It was not at all the "den of iniquity" he had been led to believe all priests' homes were, according to his grandfather, who had had a dour hatred of "Popery." It was, rather, a mild little white cottage with a picket fence about it, which enclosed a small lawn, turning steadily green now in the brisk May weather. Close to the house were flourishing rose bushes, already in full leaf. The small windows were brightly polished, and the draperies framing them were of some heavy cheap cloth the color of oatmeal. The white door boasted a brilliantly polished brass knocker in the shape of a ferocious bear's head. The cottage was next door to the beautiful little white church, and seemed to bask gently in its protection.

The inside was as simple, bright and unpretentious as its exterior. A Turkey-red rug stretched over polished broad boards, and the furniture was all of solid oak and leather, with here and there a small good holy picture on the oaken walls. There was even a small organ, and some oaken tables, and a bright little fire on a blue-tiled hearth. (Stuart had presented practically all the furniture in the house.) On some of the tables were blue bowls of narcissi and tulips, the pride of Father Houlihan's garden, which he cultivated himself, muddying his cassock and getting quite apoplectic in the process.

Over the mantel was a large crucifix (also a present from Stuart) all of ebony and ivory, and beautifully carved. Angus glanced at the crucifix, startled, then, to Stuart's irritation, averted his eyes as from something indecent. But the boy was very polite, and when Stuart indicated a chair, he sat down on the edge of it, his hat on his knees.

Stuart regarded Angus with an attempt at sternness. But in truth he was really worrying how he was to impress the lad with the necessity of keeping this visit a secret from Janie. This was Sunday evening, and Stuart was to meet his friend Sam Berkowitz here, for the usual card game after Vespers. There would be beer waiting, and some of Mrs. O'Keefe's good baked ham, and crusty bread. Now that he had brought Angus here Stuart, as usual, cursed himself for

147

his impulsiveness. That afternoon he had seen Angus languishing wistfully, and with a tragic face, near the river, and had impetuously asked him if he would like to go visiting a friend that evening with his cousin. The boy had eagerly and gratefully accepted. Stuart had not revealed the identity of the friend until almost at the door of the cottage. Now he almost forgot what impulse had moved him to bring Angus here, except that some faint instinct, born of pity, had suggested it. That instinct had recognized that Angus needed a friend, someone compassionate and simple and good, and as usual, when thinking of these virtues, Stuart thought of the priest.

He smiled irrepressibly. Perhaps, some day, he would tell Angus how he had come to know Father Houlihan. But that must be years from now.

The meeting had occurred under disgraceful circumstances. It seemed that two of Father Houlihan's flock were fairly wealthy men, a surprising circumstance. These two families had each a favorite and only son, handsome lads in their late teens, coddled and pampered by their parents and given entirely too much ready cash. As a result the lads were headstrong and wilful, and very extravagant. They had found their way, one Saturday evening, to the house of the town's most expensive and luxurious brothel (owned, of course, by Joshua Allstairs). Stuart had met them there. The ladies were very sparsely clad, and very young and gay, and the lads had begun to enjoy themselves immensely in the elegant parlor, each with a lady on his knee and a glass of whiskey in his hand. Stuart was in a similar position.

Someone must have informed the fathers of the lads of this nocturnal excursion into the realms of illegal Venus. As, apparently, the fathers themselves were too well known in this house, they had appealed to the priest, obviously unwilling to go to the police for assistance. Father Houlihan, that doughty soul, had invaded the brothel armed with nothing more than his indignation and regret. He had had no intention of upbraiding either the madam or her girls, but only of rescuing the misguided boys. Had he thought for a moment or two, Stuart reflected later, he might have acted less impulsively, and with a regard for his cloth. But Celt as he was, he acted first and regretted later. How he was able to force his way past the gargoyle that guarded the brothel, no one ever rightly knew, least of all the inflamed Father Houlihan.

At any rate, he had exploded vehemently into the parlor,

shouting, very red and swollen in the face from embarrassment and anger. The lads had turned white and dumb, had let the coquettish ladies slip from their laps, and had dropped the glasses with a crash to the floor. Father Houlihan, more and more embarrassed, and very enraged now, had struck each lad violently on the cheek, had stamped and shouted some more, and ordered them out of the house, uttering imprecations in a thick brogue.

During the ensuing confusion, one of the young ladies had shrieked: "Who is that, in the name of God?"

Stuart, laughing uncontrollably, had glanced at the long black cassock that swirled energetically about Father Houlihan's legs, and shouted: "Why, damn it, it's Mrs. Grundy!"

As Father Houlihan, overcome by his embarrassment and his anger, was exhibiting symptoms of even more complete mayhem on the lads who had caused him to come here, Stuart rushed to the rescue, almost beside himself with mirth. Father Houlihan's lusty vocabulary had aroused Stuart's intense admiration, and the priest's vigor, his shame, his utter blustering confusion, inspired Stuart with affectionate compassion. He had finally and dexterously pushed the boys from the house, and had returned to the priest who was panting hoarsely, and wiping his face with a huge white kerchief. Stuart took his arm. The priest resisted, and in a quite unclerical flow of language, had consigned him to hell. The two left the house together.

Once on the sidewalk, the priest had turned to him fiercely. "It's ashamed you should be before your God, leadin' young spalpeens like that to their doom and damnation!" he had exclaimed.

"I didn't lead them there." Stuart, still laughing, explained what had actually led the miscreants' steps to that house. The priest had stared, horrified, and then had begun to laugh helplessly, despite himself. Besides, Stuart pointed out to him, it was very unseemly for a priest to go roaring into a brothel, even for the rescue of misguided youth.

"I never think," confessed Father Houlihan, ruefully. He stared at Stuart, aghast. "D'ye think I was seen, eh?"

"No doubt," Stuart comforted him. He loved Father Houlihan immediately. "I never think" had a familiar sound. Stuart walked to the priest's cottage with his new friend. It was not white then, but a miserable bleak little shack with broken clapboarded walls. During that walk Father Houlihan bewailed his temper, and declared that he would have much to confess because of it. His manner was so earnest, so robust, and so childlike, that Stuart was more and more delighted.

As they stood before the sad little cottage, Father Houlihan looked up at Stuart, and sighed. "A fine young feller like you! And why should ye be going into a pit of hell like that? With a wife and all, eh?"

"I have no wife, and no 'all,' " Stuart assured him. Father Houlihan was slightly relieved, but he shook his head, sighing again. "A fine upstanding man!"

That had been the beginning of a friendship which was to last all their lives, a lovely friendship with frequent riotous quarrels and rages only enhancing it. At least once a month Stuart left the priest's house in a rage, advising him to go to the nether regions, and accompanied to the door by Father Houlihan's lusty voice using many sacred words but in a distinctly unsacred way. Then they would write each other a series of notes, abjectly apologizing, and meet the next Sunday.

Stuart was still trying to find words with which to warn Angus, when Father Houlihan entered, beaming, filling the warm little room with vitality, health and enthusiasm. He was always enthusiastic, and was rarely dampened in his simple buoyancy, for he devoutly believed in the innate goodness of mankind despite all his knowledge to the contrary. "Well, well, well!" he exclaimed, in a rich deep voice, and looked at Angus with friendly sympathy and curiosity. Stuart had already told him of this young lad, and he was prepared, as was always his way, to love the young and unprotected.

Angus rose diffidently, clutching the brim of his hat. His pale thin face flushed. He could not look directly at the priest, and his heart was beating hard. He had expected some dark, lean and subtle Jesuit with an evil glinting face, with whom he must be on rigorous guard. But this very short, very fat, immensely broad and completely bald man of forty years resembled Friar Tuck far more than he did any Latin dialectician of subtle machinations. He hardly came to Stuart's shoulder, and his cassock gleamed over his large belly and massive shoulders, so tight was it stretched. He had short fat hands, excessively white and well-kept—his one vanity—and very expressive. Everything about him was expressive and volatile, and full of zest. He exuded joy in living, and ardent affection for everything, even when he was sad, which was very often.

He had a great round head, the scalp polished, damp and

shining, and very pink. Only above his ears, and at the nape of his bulging neck, were there a few golden hairs, the last of a once very handsome gilded mane. He had immense rosy ears, which stood out from his head in an attitude of pleased surprise, alert and listening. His face was very round and broad, pink and clean, with a series of chins. His corpulence was a source of great despair, and the object of much sorrowful meditation, but he could not resist good food and beer, in spite of all his prayers for assistance and mortification of the flesh.

He had thick golden eyebrows over strenuous blue eyes, which shone restlessly and with huge humor. He also had a large bulbous nose. But he had the sweetest mouth, full and pink, with touching dimples always flashing, and a smile always trembling at the corners.

He was a simple soul. But he was also extremely intellectual, a fact which did not becloud his simple faith. Once he had told Stuart that he did not believe in much knowledge. He had said that too much knowledge stupefies and blinds the soul, and silences the heart's intuition. Nevertheless, his own wisdom had not stupefied nor blinded him, and his heart's intuition was as pristine in its clarity and prescience and loving kindness as though he had been newly born. He distrusted all subtle men, all dialecticians, all realists, all sophists, whether of his cloth or of the world, and this, in part, probably accounted for the fact that he was no favorite of his bishop's, and remained a lowly priest all his life. Perhaps he was too honest, too forthright, too vigorous and single-hearted, too pragmatic, ever to rise to high ecclesiastical heights. He was beyond hypocrisy. He spoke of that vice often, but could never really understand it, and was always appalled and dumfounded when he encountered it in others. He was also a bad businessman, and vague about his accounts, another thing which damned him in the eyes of his bishop. And he never set out to proselytize, for which he had been frequently reprimanded. He only knew, in his earnest bewilderment, that he loved God, and that other men doubtless also loved God, in their own peculiar ways. But he never got anywhere in his arguments with his severe bishop, and though he remained humble in the presence of that august man, he would leave the bishopric more confused than ever, his mouth moving dumbly with new arguments, his head shaking helplessly. Sometimes he would remain on the walk outside the noble house, staring at it vehemently for a long time, and then would leave in a very abased and confused state of mind, resolving to do better, though what the better was he had not the slightest idea.

His love for his God gave him a great and beautiful dignity, which his corpulence could not diminish, nor his lustiness and enjoyment in living. His faith was like a light on his huge pink face and in his lively blue eyes. He also had a wild and uproarious bad temper when aroused, and an unbridled and lusty tongue, and a violent way with him when convinced of some rascality or cruelty.

Because he was so unaffected and sincere, the priest always looked steadfastly and directly at everyone, but with such kindness that he rarely offended. He looked now at young Angus, very earnestly, but the boy, blushing and ill-at-ease, only peeped at him shyly, and kept dropping his eyes. There was a little silence in the room. Stuart stood apart, and watched, smiling a little. Father Houlihan continued to study Angus with his simple and open directness, and, then, very slowly but clearly, a shadow of sadness and affection came over the priest's face, and a dim sorrow clouded his violent blue eyes for a moment or two. Because there was no beam in his spiritual vision, he saw without distortion.

"Well, well, well," he said again, but in a gentle murmur this time. He was suddenly abstracted. The warm May twilight was darkening. Father Houlihan took a wax taper from the mantelpiece, applied it to the fire, then went softly about the room lighting the lamps, turning them up carefully so that their mellow bloom soon flooded every corner.

Stuart was annoyed at Angus. The boy had murmured an inarticulate greeting, and then had remained standing like this, frightened and stiff and uneasy, with God only knew what thoughts in his mind. Stuart had warned him he must address the priest as "Father," and he well understood how the word must stick in that young Presbyterian throat. Was it a mistake to have brought the young jackanapes here, to embarrass Grundy?

Angus furtively watched the priest moving lightly about the room, ambling comfortably from one lamp to the other. He seemed confused, himself. His picture was all awry. Father Houlihan, approaching the last lamp, complained that his sister had neglected to fill it. He bent over it, frowning and pursing his lips. He lit it. "And how would ye be today, Stuart?" he asked. He smiled. There was still enough oil. He beamed at it.

"As usual, well," said Stuart. "And you?"

"Oh, wonderful, wonderful! I am always wonderful!"

He stood up, the taper in his hand, and the clear golden light fell on his face as he turned to Angus. It was a beautiful face, for all its pinkness and big fat features and its peasant heartiness. He smiled at Angus; it was the loveliest smile of kindness and gentleness and warmth.

He blew out the taper, and waved it gently back and forth in his hand.

"So this is our Angus, eh? This is the lad who would be a fine doctor?"

Angus colored deeply. But he managed an uncertain smile, and shifted on the balls of his feet.

Father Houlihan neatly replaced the taper, pinched its blackened tip. He returned to Angus, and sighed enviously. "It was a doctor I dreamed of being, myself, in the old country." He shook his head. He moved towards Angus very slowly and looked at him. As Angus was a tall lad, and Father Houlihan was so short, their eyes were almost on a level. The priest looked into those young blinking eyes, so fearful, yet so hungry, and he saw their apprehension and distrust of him.

"It's eyes like gray Scotch mist he has," said the priest gently. "I spent many years in Scotland, near Inverness, where I had a cousin. He had sheep. I well remember it. And the Scotch mornings, just before dawn, and the morning star over the hills." His strong rich voice was very tender.

Angus lifted his head suddenly, and gazed at the priest without fear, and with excitement.

"My dada sang a song about the morning star!" he exclaimed, then colored again, more deeply than ever. His eyes filled with tears, and he jerked aside his head. The priest was silent. He looked at the lad, and his face was very sorrowful.

"Perhaps," he said softly, "he is singing that song to the angels now."

Angus was silent. His throat worked. Father Houlihan put his arm about the lad's shoulders, not quickly, so as to alarm him, but very slowly and comfortingly. "I shall say a prayer for your dada, tomorrow," he promised.

Angus moved restlessly, then, at the warmth of the loving arm about him, which he could not resist in his heart's hunger, he was still. But he looked at Father Houlihan with uncertain sternness. "We can't pray for the dead—sir," he said, with piping resolution. "They are in God's hands. They have no further care for our prayers, which cannot help or hinder them." The tears were bright in his eyes.

Father Houlihan was quiet a moment, then he patted Angus' shoulder. "I should like to know that my friends remember me, and send their greetings to me in the form of prayers, and that God listens to them in my behalf," he said. "And I cannot but believe that they know, and that God lends us His ear when we pray in love and sorrow."

"But we can't change their fate, which was fixed when they were born," whispered Angus, obstinately. "And even before they were born. Predestination."

Father Houlihan was not one to argue dogma with anyone, and especially not a hurt and suffering child. But he said, his voice ringing warmly and tenderly: "Ah, that would be cruel of God, I would be thinking, to condemn a man from his mother's womb. I cannot believe that God is less merciful than men. Ah, well," he added, his tone dropping, and sighing, "it is not for us to know yet, for sure. But we can trust in His eternal kindness and love. That is all we can know."

He pressed Angus' shoulder again, then removed his hand. He smiled brightly. "So, it is a doctor ye'd be, is it? And a fine one, no doubt. Good doctors are born, as priests are born, with their vocation in their souls."

Angus was still obstinate, but his resolution was fading. He regarded Father Houlihan with less sternness now, and less shyness. Something warm and sweet was pervading him, something like consolation. Then he remembered that his grandfather had often told him that the servants of Rome were like serpents, insinuating and soft of movement, seeking whom they might devour with seductive words and tender gestures.

"Thank you, Mr.—" he began, stiffly, then caught Stuart's hard look upon him. "Reverend," he amended, through dry lips. The poor lad hoped this would satisfy his mother's cousin. Priests were reverends, too, weren't they?

Father Houlihan beamed at him. "And how would you be liking our America, Angus?"

"Very well, thank you," replied Angus, politely. His fingers ached from their tight clutch on his hat. As if he knew, Father Houlihan removed it from the lad's clutch, and laid it beside Stuart's on a table. Angus stared at his hat, vaguely affrighted and uncertain, but there was nothing he could do.

The priest turned to Stuart. "Sam is already here, in the back room, with the shades drawn. You'll be liking a game, as usual?"

"What the hell do you think I came for, Grundy?" said

Stuart, boisterously. He could feel Angus' shocked and frightened eyes on him, and he had a momentary impulse to smack the lad heartily and put some sense into him. But he avoided looking at him.

Father Houlihan hesitated. He glanced at Angus. "And what will the boy be doing while we play?" he murmured.

Angus tugged at his pocket with trembling fingers. "I always carry my Testament with me on Sunday," he said, almost incoherently. He produced a small, black-bound book and held it in his small shaking hand, the fingers clutching it as if to protect it.

"Good, good!" exclaimed Father Houlihan. He hesitated again. Stuart wore an expression of violent patience, and nodded at the priest emphatically. Father Houlihan shrugged. He left the room, Stuart following him, and Angus bringing up the rear with the fearful step of one entering catacombs where all kinds of blasphemous horrors could be found. Father Houlihan fell back a moment. He touched Stuart's arm. "Ah, the poor, poor child!" he whispered, and there was a plea in his voice.

They walked down a dark little passage to a door that opened on a very comfortable little sitting-room, crowded, warm and lit with fire. Two dogs rose inquiringly on their entrance, and began to bark a welcome. They were curly black spaniels with impudent faces, and they rushed at the priest and pretended to devour him with love. They then turned their ministrations upon Stuart, who scratched the backs of their necks. Next, they turned, laughing, their tongues lolling, upon Angus, whose pale face had brightened shyly. Recognizing a friend, the dogs fell upon him with squeals of delight. He picked one up in his arms, and began to laugh. That laugh was reluctant and feeble, as if seldom used, but very childish. The dog kissed him heartily, while his mate tried to climb Angus' leg in an excess of jealousy. Angus struggled with the dog he held, trying to escape the kisses, and trying to retain hold upon the fat and ecstatic little body. He laughed again, eagerly. He looked over the dog's lively head at Father Houlihan, who was watching with compassionate and smiling intentness. "I'd love a dog!" said Angus, with unaffected longing. "But mama will not have it."

There was no strain in his voice now, no wariness.

He put the dog down, and it joined its mate in attempting to scale Angus' long thin legs. He looked down at them, loving their liquid and lively eyes. And then he saw that there

was someone else in the room now, someone who was rising slowly from behind a small green-baize table near the
fire, on which were two decks of cards and a wooden box.

Angus was startled, and immediately shy and reserved
again. This, then, must be Mr. Sam Berkowitz, of whom Stuart had told him. Angus was full of distrust and reticence
once more. He had never seen a Jew in his life, and from the
stories he had heard of the Hebraic race, he was prepared
to see someone closely resembling Fagin, from Mr. Dickens'
famous story.

But this was no Fagin, the boy observed confusedly. This
was a tall, very thin stooped man, with thick and premature
white hair and a long gentle face full of wisdom. The eyes
looked at Angus with his own shyness and reserve, and
faintly smiling. Apparently Mr. Berkowitz had no fashion, for
his long dun-colored coat sagged from his thin shoulders, and
his pantaloons were wrinkled. He held a pack of cards in his
hand, which he absently shuffled.

"My young cousin, Angus," said Stuart, carelessly, going to
the fire and rubbing his hands. "Angus, this is Mr. Berkowitz."

Sam bowed his shoulders slightly, and smiled at the boy.
"Good efening," he said, courteously, in his accented deep
voice. He gazed at Angus thoughtfully.

"Good evening," muttered Angus. He was again ill at ease,
and frightened. But Father Houlihan was bustling at the fire,
and had drawn up a chair near the friendly warmth. Angus
sat down with a murmured thanks. The dogs fell on him
again, and both attempted to jump into his lap. He forgot
his fear, and assisted them. They stood on his knees on their
hind legs, and kissed him with enthusiasm. He began to
smile, hugging them pathetically to him. Father Houlihan
went to the table, where Stuart had already seated himself,
and took his place. He winked at Stuart. His broad black
back shone in the firelight.

"Well!" he exclaimed, "and who will be winning tonight,
do you think?"

"We, as usual, as we always do on Sundays, you blackguard," said Stuart, darkly. "There's a law against card
cheats, you know. I could shoot you and be exonerated." He
tapped the wooden box, which had a wide slit in its locked
cover. On the side were printed the words: "Poor Box." "I'd
like to know how much you filch from it after Sam and I are
gone."

Father Houlihan laughed with a rollicking sound. "Now,
then, that's very bad of you, Stuart. I only open it once a

month, for the poor. There were one hundred ninety dollars in it last time," he hinted, wistfully.

It was the custom for the friends to come here on Wednesday and Sunday evenings to play cards. But the winner was obliged to put all his winnings into the poor box on Sundays.

"It's a funny thing," observed Stuart, still darkly, as he dexterously shuffled the cards, and began to deal them, "but you have a strange way of winning on Wednesdays, while Sam and I almost invariably win on Sundays. That would be due to your prayers, no doubt?"

"God always rewards those who help the poor," said Father Houlihan, with a chuckle. He picked up the five cards that Stuart had dealt him, and sighed. "Now, then, you will accuse me of cheating again, but these cards are remarkably bad."

"Oh, of course," said Stuart, with vicious emphasis. "Not even a little pair, I presume?"

"Not openers, at any rate," admitted the priest, laying the cards face down on the table. He looked at Stuart and Sam expectantly.

"I vill open," said Sam, tossing two blue chips on the table.

"Damn it. I will raise you two," growled Stuart, after Father Houlihan had shaken his head sadly and had thrown aside his cards with an expressive gesture of his hands.

"It's up to us two, as usual," said Stuart. "Grundy's out of it—as usual."

Father Houlihan leaned his black fat arms on the table and watched the betting with sparkling interest. In a moment there were five dollars in chips between the two men. "Three kings," said Stuart, fatally. Sam raised his eloquent eyebrows, smiled, shrugged, and shook his head. "You haf me beat, Stuart," he admitted.

In the meantime Angus had become aware of what sinfulness was transpiring near him, in the ruddy warmth of the firelight. His face became white and rigid with shock. His eyes were distended. The caresses of the dogs went unheeded. He had been right, then. This was a den of iniquity, in which his godless relative, Stuart, violated the Holy Sabbath with a black and evil priest and a Jew who had, from birth, been cast into the outer darkness. He felt appalled pity and terror for Stuart, Stuart who was too innocent and too kind to realize the fiendish nature of those who were seducing him into damnation. He wanted to cry out, to implore Stuart to flee from this fiendish place before it was too late. His agitation was so extreme that his mouth shook and tears of complete terror flooded his eyes.

The sensitive dogs, feeling his emotion, crouched on his knees and gazed at him with their liquid eyes. They whimpered a little. Automatically, his trembling cold hand soothed them. They cowered under it, bewildered.

"Grand-da was right," said Angus to himself, his heart quivering with fear. He looked at the gleaming black back of the priest, at the back of the huge rosy skull, which glinted in the firelight, at Sam's mysterious quiet face and gentle smile. They would devour poor Stuart, these two, and drag him into the pit with them. Angus clutched his Bible as though it were a talisman against the witchery of demons. His legs felt cold and paralysed. His throat and mouth were as dry as cloth.

Stuart had forgotten him. He was absorbed in his game, his handsome and mercurial face frowning and intent. He swore softly and obscenely under his breath.

"God damn it! You've never seen such cards!" he cried. He suddenly picked up Father Houlihan's discarded cards, and glared at them suspiciously, after exclaiming: "I'll bet you've got better, you scoundrel!" He added, with grudging surprise: "No, by God, you haven't! The devil's in it!"

"You *will* think I cheat, won't you?" remarked the priest, complacently.

"I don't understand it! If you aren't lying in your teeth, the only time you get decent cards is on Wednesday. The devil's in it!"

The priest was smug. He said, piously: "God protects the poor."

Stuart savagely drew one card, then screamed. Sam laid down his cards. "A royal flush!" wept Stuart. "The first time in my life, and probably the last! And it has to happen on a Sunday!"

The others burst out laughing. Father Houlihan leaned forward to gaze at the miracle, with reverence. He then looked at the pot. "Twenty dollars!"

But Stuart was beside himself, now that he realized the full extent of the calamity. He pounded on the table with his fists. "A royal flush! A royal flush! The first time in a thousand years! What I could have done with that at Mrs. Sheldon's! I'd have made a fortune! And it has to happen in this den of vice on a Sunday, for the poor box!" The chips and cards danced.

Sam and the priest rocked with mirth at this wild-eyed

grief. They clutched each other, as they were in danger of falling from their chairs. Tears spurted from the priest's eyes. He wiped them away, and went off into fresh paroxysms. Even the silent Jew was overcome. He laid his head on the table and sobbed weakly.

Stuart continued to keen over his ghastly luck, and with his fresh lamentations the agonies of laughter of the others increased. The dogs began to bark. They jumped from Angus' lap and began to cavort around, in the wildest excitement.

It was some time before the game could continue.

CHAPTER 22

COMPARATIVE quietness prevailed after a while, though Stuart wailed at intervals, and cursed. They had all forgotten, in the excitement, the silent white-faced boy staring at them with his distended eyes from the corner of the fireplace.

A soft spring rain had begun to fall. It whispered against the windows. The fire sung to itself on the hearth, and the light winked off the andirons. The little dogs slept on the hearthrug, and whimpered in their dreams. The lamplight burned with a merry glow. The comfortable little sitting-room was cloudy with smoke which poured from Stuart's and the priest's cheroots and from Sam's pipe. Across one wall were several shelves of books, whose crimson and blue backs bulged from much handling. It was pleasant and full of friendliness and comfort for all in the room except Angus.

A long time had passed, filled with the sound of spring rain, fire, the little whimperings of the dogs, and the slap of cards and clink of chips, and Stuart's colorful curses and the laughter of the others. Angus had sat for nearly an hour in a tense and rigid state, as if in a catalepsy, his fingers like iron about his Testament. He never looked away from the players. His eyelids stung and turned red with smoke and strain. At intervals, long cold rigors ran over his emaciated young body.

Then, at last, nature came to his rescue with a loud protest at the constriction of his muscles, and he was forced to relax. Sharp and aching pains invaded his legs and arms. His back felt broken. Against his will, he leaned against the back of his comfortable wing chair. For the first time, he was conscious of the warmth of the fire. But his heart was trembling, and there was a pounding in his head. His vision dimmed, and he closed his eyes. Long slow tears ran under his shut eyelids. He was hardly more than a flat shadow in the chair, one hand hanging vulnerably over the arm, and its whiteness was like the whiteness of death.

He was no longer frightened. He could not have told what his emotions were. He only knew that he felt lost and most frightfully lonely, even more lonely than usual. And agonizingly weary. The Testament lay shut on his knee. Another hour ticked away.

There was a brisk bustle at the door, and Angus, half asleep in his exhaustion, started up. The nicest little short fat woman was entering, with silvery hair and cheeks like pomegranates and a white apron over her black bombazine. She shouted: "Are you sinners ready for your supper, then?"

"One moment, O'Keefe," said Stuart, scowling at his cards. Sam half rose and bowed to the woman courteously. Father Houlihan was engrossed in his hand. "One moment, Sarah. Ah, no, Stuart, it's all yours, I am afraid."

"It's hotter than the bad place itself, in here," said Mrs. O'Keefe, removing her glasses and polishing them. "And no air, by all the Saints! You'll be smothering, that you will." She went purposefully towards the window, and, as she passed Angus, she started and stared at him. "Well, well. What have we here?"

Angus rose, though all his limbs creaked and ached. He peeped at her, prepared to be frightened again, but this little hearty woman with the wide smile and little twinkling blue eyes was no alarming spectacle. He returned her smile, and gave her his short stiff bow.

Stuart glanced over his shoulder, and stared at Angus as if he were an apparition. He had completely forgotten about him. He said: "Oh, yes, O'Keefe, that is my cousin's boy, Angus. Angus Cauder. This is Mrs. O'Keefe, Angus, Father Houlihan's sister."

His voice was apologetic and somewhat sheepish. He rose, pushing back a lock of black hair from his damp forehead. "Whew!" he exclaimed. "I'm running with sweat. Angus, I'm sorry I neglected you so long."

But Angus and Mrs. O'Keefe were regarding each other in silence. The poor lamb, thought the woman, it's feeding he needs, and a lot of it. She put her hand on the thin arm and patted it. She cocked her head and mumbled reprovingly between her lips, then said: "Well, now, it's ashamed they should be for leaving you like this, and me dying for a bit of company upstairs alone. They should have brought you up to me."

Angus tried to remind himself coldly that here was another Papist, and one inevitably doomed to hideous eternal torments. But he could not retain his stiffness in the face of such warm kindness and affectionate affability. "Thank you, ma'am," he murmured. "I—it didn't matter, truly. I—I was just resting."

Mrs. O'Keefe studied him shrewdly. "It's not resting you should be at your age, Angus, but laughing and playing."

Father Houlihan, feeling much distressed that he had been so remiss towards his young guest, wondered what to say. He was much afraid of his sister, and respected her tongue. He began to clear his throat. But Mrs. O'Keefe firmly ignored him, and said to Angus: "And would you like to stretch your legs a bit and help me bring in the supper for the sinners?"

Angus, in an agony of renewed shyness, wandered behind Mrs. O'Keefe into the brightest warmest kitchen he had ever seen, all red-tile and copper, and broad window-seats full of plants, and a black range fuming against the wall. There were platters of cold baked ham, spiced apples, cold beef, preserves, crusty white bread, and cold beer waiting.

"There, now, the platter, my lovey, first, and yes! the cloth for the table, and the silver, and those big napkins, the one in the ring for the Father, the one folded across for Mr. Coleman, and the square one for Mr. Berkowitz. They'd be liking clean napkins every time, but that's an extravagance. Here, lovey, another plate for you. To think they never told me, the wretches! You like ham?"

"Very much, thank you," said Angus, weakly. He sighed. The warmth and brightness invaded his cold limbs. He looked at the back of Mrs. O'Keefe's broad and active body, and for some reason the way the white apron was tied, in a huge starched bow, made him want to cry again. He winked back the tears. He swallowed. He almost whimpered: "Do they play cards—every Sunday, Mrs. O'Keefe?"

"That they do, the abandoned wretches!" she exclaimed, fondly. Then something in the boy's voice caught her belated attention. She turned about, quickly, and again her shrewd little blue eyes dwelt on him. "Why, lovey?"

Angus turned crimson. The plates almost fell from his hands. "Nothing. Only, in Scotland we don't do those things. The Sabbath is a day of rest——"

"That it is, Angus! This is their rest, the poor darlings."

She still watched him, with growing sympathy. "You don't like it, eh?"

"It—it's just that it's strange to me," he faltered.

Mrs. O'Keefe observed him with kind silence. Then, in a very gentle and maternal voice, she said: "My lovey, there is something everyone should learn, very early. It is only what a man has in his heart that's either good or bad. And if it's bad, and wicked, and malicious, and cruel and selfish, then all the church-going in the world, and all the praying, and the observing of the holidays is nothing. Nothing. And that's the God's solemn truth, child."

Her tone took on strength and quietness, and her blue eyes were piercing. Angus gazed at her, blinking his eyelids, trying to reconcile what he had heard with what he had been taught.

He stammered: "You mean that they—they are good men, and God will forgive them for desecrating the Sabbath?"

"Desecrating the Sabbath!" repeated Mrs. O'Keefe, roundly. "By all the Saints! They're doing nothing to the Sabbath except be a little happy! And that's what God wanted us to be on the Sabbath, and every other day, my poor lamb!" She added: "Did you think God wanted us to be miserable?"

Angus stared at her. Then a curious flash passed over his face, and he said, almost incoherently: "Yes. Yes, that is what I thought! I didn't know it before, but that is what I thought!"

Mrs. O'Keefe, an impulsive woman, came to him then and kissed him soundly, and hugged him in her short fat arms, which were so comforting and safe. He submitted, holding the plates out of her way, and enduring the most curious sensation of sweetness and consolation. He was blinded by his pathetic emotion; he felt his Grandmother Driscoll's arms about him, and smelled the same nostalgic odor of clean and gentle warm flesh, motherly and substantial, a help in trouble, a tenderness in pain. There was in him such a passionate hunger for love that he could hardly endure this great pang and swelling in his chest.

He carried in the plates, then returned to the kitchen quickly. He watched Mrs. O'Keefe cutting seed-cake. He said, stammeringly: "Mrs. O'Keefe, do Catholics hate Protestants?"

She looked at him quickly, and smiled. "I have no doubts that many of them do!" she said, vigorously. "And Protestants hate Catholics. That's the way with silly people. We all have to hate something, it seems, don't it? Why, I don't know. It's original sin, I'll be thinking. It's one of those things that one's got to accept, like sickness and worry and accidents and death."

Angus' mind was all chaotic. He moved closer to Mrs. O'Keefe, and alertly understanding his terrible need, she paused in her work and regarded him with compassionate gentleness. She knew the tumult in that unlearned young heart, and felt humble that it was given her to alleviate it in a measure.

"You see," he said timidly, his pale thin face quite scarlet and desperately earnest, "I've heard so many things. It—it all seemed simple to me. Good on one side, bad on the other——"

"And the good side, of course," said Mrs. O'Keefe, with gentle satire, "was the side of your papa and mama, and granddaddy, and England, too? And your church?"

"Well, yes, in a way," he said slowly, fumbling with his words as though they were unfamiliar objects, and very strange. "And it never seemed necessary to me to ask questions about it. It's very hard, asking questions, and very sad, too, seeing that perhaps your side wasn't right at all, and there was something to be said for the other. It—it makes things not so simple. I—I like it to be simple, you see."

He gazed at her with a desperate intensity. "Mrs. O'Keefe, I've read the books, too, how the Catholics burned and hanged the Protestants, and the Massacre of St. Bartholomew, and the persecutions of the Huguenots, in France. How does —Reverend Houlihan explain that? They aren't lies, you know. And what Philip of Spain did to the Dutch, with the priests behind him."

Mrs. O'Keefe laid down her knife, and slowly took Angus' cold thin hand. Her kind face was very grave. She said, slowly: "It's true, perhaps, what you say, poor lad. But the Protestants did that to the Catholics, too, you see. They did it to each other, in their hateful ignorance and folly. What does the Father say? He knows all these things, what the Church has done, and its cruel old priests. But the priests were human. They aren't above other men, in spite of their frocks and collars." She drew a deep, sorrowful breath; her bright blue eyes were stern and quiet. "The Father knows it all. But he has his faith, not only in God, but in all mankind, that someday it will be kind and gentle and full of love and pity. It was only last week that he said to dear Stuart: 'I've been asked why I am a priest in a Church that has so bad a history for blood and persecution and intolerance. And now I ask you why you belong to the Republican Party, and are now a citizen of the United States. Is the Republican Party without fault? Are the hands of America clean of all aggression and conquest and war, and other ugliness? If a man will not join a Party, or a Church, or a country unless it be without fault and without stain, then that man will join none of them, and he will stand alone in the world! No, we cannot be such fools. We cannot doubt the good in a Church, a Party or a nation because it has had its dark histories, and its wickedness. We can only try to help it develop its good, and overcome its evil. By our faith, and our daily acts, we can make a sweeter history, and a force that will help in the liberation of mankind through the long ages to come.'"

Angus was silent. He looked into the good woman's tender eyes. His hand slowly warmed in hers. They stood like this for several moments, smiling faintly at each other.

Then Angus said, softly: "Father—Houlihan—he is a very good man. I'm glad Stuart brought me tonight, Mrs. O'Keefe. I'm glad I know you, too."

An expression of light and peace came into the poor boy's face. He smiled again, and sighed. He carried more food into the other room, moving as if in a dream. Mrs. O'Keefe watched him go, with tears in her eyes.

Stuart was ruefully putting his winnings into the poor box, and making loud and bitter protests. But among them he dropped several gold pieces, surreptitiously. He said, darkly: 'Grundy, I'm going to watch what you do with all this money, some day. I believe you put it in your skirts, and smack your chops over it."

"Never mind," said the priest, soothingly. "Perhaps your inordinate luck will be excellent next Wednesday, my Stuart. Perhaps another miracle, eh?"

They all sat down to eat in the firelight. The fire sparkled on the silver and fresh whiteness of the cloth. Sam Berkowitz helped himself to the cold beef. Father Houlihan winked at Stuart, then said to Sam: "Now, then, why be intolerant, my dear Sam? Why do you not taste of this delicious ham, which Sarah has so kindly baked for us?"

Sam smiled slowly. A look of dark humor came over his features. "I shall no longer be intolerant, Father. Next Friday evening I shall join you over a plate of ham, and we shall eat it together."

Father Houlihan laughed uproariously, beating his fork handle on the table. "You have me there, Sam, you devil, you! It is worth a special dispensation, by all the Saints!"

The chatter became loud, sometimes acrimonious, sometimes violent, sometimes punctuated with bursts of laughter, sometimes turning serious and somber. Angus listened in a daze. He had entered a strange, warm Never-Never Land, which was bewildering but oddly comforting. He watched the three men, and Mrs. O'Keefe, drinking their beer on this Sabbath evening, and it no longer seemed sinful to him, but kind and harmless. He listened to political arguments, and when slavery was discussed he stopped his eating, and was all painful attention.

Father Houlihan pointed his knife at Stuart, who had just vociferously disagreed with him. "I tell you, Stuart, we shall have a frightful war over this question. I know it, like a seer. Nothing can avert it. The tempers of men are too high and too violent. There are large interests in the North which cannot compete in the labor markets against the South, with its slave labor. The cause of abolition is holy. Then, though the war will be fought, not as a holy crusade (though the people will believe that), but actually in the cause of economics, slavery will be abolished. Out of the greed of men a great wrong is often righted. I must disagree with Holy Writ in this one thing: a thistle can sometimes bear good fruit. Stones can become bread."

"I still don't think we shall fight for the sake of benighted blackamoors," said Stuart, thinking again, with regret, that he might have made a fortune in the Underground. "I, for one, shall not fight to free niggers. I shall mind my own business."

Father Houlihan shook his head, smiling. "I doubt that you could resist a fight, my boy."

A peculiar expression came over Stuart's face. He glanced furtively at Sam. There had been something bothering him lately. He cleared his throat, and said brightly: "Oh, by the way, Sam, I forgot to tell you something. It will interest you."

Sam looked at him with doubtful distrust. When Stuart assumed this air of boyish pleasure, this air of openness, skulduggery was well under way. "What is it this time, Stuart?" he asked, uneasily.

Stuart frowned at him. "You are a suspicious dog, Sam."

"I," said Father Houlihan blandly, "am also suspicious. You see, dear boy, you don't deceive your old friends."

Stuart flung himself back in his chair with an air of angry exasperation. He looked about the table with ire. "I've never known friends to have so little faith in a man! I'd best keep this to myself, it seems."

But Sam was disturbed. He said, quietly: "Tell me, Stuart."

"It's nothing at all, I tell you! Only a chance for an excellent profit." He leaned towards them, angrily. "You know, Sam, how I had the idea of advertising all over the damn country for large job lots of goods that were refused by retailers for one reason or another, including bankruptcy. It was a blasted good idea, you admitted yourself. That is how we got that consignment of china which was refused in Utica. We made a tidy profit. We paid cash for consignments, and bought them for a song. The news must have got around, and there is a lot of envy among retailers that they hadn't thought of it, themselves. They're rectifying their mistakes now, of course, after we showed the way."

Sam nodded. "Yes, this I know. Go on, Stuart." Father Houlihan was listening with shrewd interest.

Stuart was speaking quickly now, with irritation. "Well, then, though we are having more imitators all the time, we are still ahead of all the others. We offer reasonably fair prices. Our advertisements are better written, and draw more offers of refused consignments, or overstock. People have faith in us.

"Well, three days ago I had a visitor, at home. Two weeks before that I had received a letter from a certain growing arms and powder concern in Pennsylvania, a place called Windsor. I was requested to grant an interview to a certain member of the firm, a Raoul Bouchard, on a matter of confidential importance. 'Now what,' I said to myself, 'have I to do with this firm, called Barbour & Bouchard?' It is true we sell powder and firearms and rifles, when we can buy them in large lots, and make a tidy profit, but why should this concern, who manufacture these things themselves, wish to discuss a very confidential matter with me—us? I know that they use an excellent brand of steel, called Sessions. Remember, Sam? We bought a consignment of their firearms for cash, which was shipped to Syracuse, the retailer having just gone into bankruptcy? They were fine articles, you remember. We made a pretty penny on them. So, I said to myself, why does Mr. Bouchard crave this interview with me, in secrecy?"

Sam was silent. His long hands closed tightly over the edge of the table. His brown eyes were narrowed and fearful. Stuart avoided looking at him, directly. He waved his hand with a careless air.

"Mr. Bouchard came to my home three days ago. A damned grinning Frenchman, with curly black hair and eyes like a happy devil's. He brought with him a letter from the president of his firm, an Ernest Barbour. He made me promise that the matter would not be discussed outside of our own concern. Naturally, I gave him that promise, and I'm keeping it."

Father Houlihan smiled irrepressibly. But he said nothing. His expression became grave and thoughtful once more.

Stuart was more and more careless. His voice became enthusiastic and bold. "Mr. Bouchard made me a very interesting, and overwhelming proposition. I am to advertise, discreetly, for large lots of rifles, any kind, and obtain them. Ten thousand rifles."

"Ten thousand rifles!" cried Sam involuntarily. "But why does this gentleman need ten thousand rifles! And why do they not manufacture them, themselves, with their excellent steel of which you had told us?"

Stuart was embarrassed. He reddened. Then he blustered: "How the hell should I know? Perhaps they want a lot of cheap rifles, immediately, to sell cheaply, and as they have a certain prestige they don't want these rifles to bear their trade-mark. Nor, for the sake of their prestige, perhaps, do they wish to advertise themselves. It is apparent they do not wish their name connected with this transaction. No one must know," added Stuart, unguardedly, "that Barbour & Bouchard are involved in this."

Sam and the priest exchanged a long disturbed look. Then said Sam: "Mr. Bouchard, perhaps, told you all these things, very openly, of course?"

"Yes, he did! What does it matter? They want these rifles, bought discreetly. They want me to consign them, after purchase, to a certain border city, in Kentucky, not in one large lot, but in a number of small consignments. They have given me a certain name. Wherever I buy these rifles, I am to send directions for the consignment to that city, and pay cash. I will never see the rifles, of course; they will never be sent to Grandeville. My part is the advertising, the buying, the consignment. That is all."

He patted a pocket. "I have the name of the man, and the station, to whom the rifles are to be consigned. I have never heard of him. It is all very confidential. And—" he paused, impressively, "I am to receive exactly twice the cost of the rifles as my profit."

But Sam was looking with dark and heavy alarm at Father

Houlihan. "Ten thousand rifles, consigned to an obscure man in an obscure Southern city. Why? That is what I must know."

"Good God!" shouted Stuart, banging the table with his fist, "don't you suppose the Southerners wish rifles for hunting, too, and other things?"

But Sam was not intimidated. He looked at Stuart directly. "Why, then, cannot Barbour & Bouchard make these rifles, themselves, which they can do so much more cheaply, and keep the profits for themselves? I haf heard of them. They manufacture much. Unless," he added, gravely, "these are needed quickly—at once."

"That's it, of course." Stuart was relieved, though he was still flushed.

"But why all this secrecy, this confidence, this swearing to silence?"

"I don't know, I tell you! What does that matter to me? I am interested only in the profits!"

Sam looked at the priest. "Secrecy—arms—obscure consignments. I do not like this. I do not like this Barbour & Bouchard. They are evil men. Their odor reaches the nostrils of men everywhere. Ten thousand rifles, shipped in the deepest secrecy. It has a bad sound. And I think I know why all this is."

Stuart cursed himself, as usual, for his loose tongue. He said: "Ours not to question, but to advertise, to buy, to reconsign."

But Sam ignored him. He said to the priest: "It was only three weeks ago that I read in the papers that this firm has received an order from the Federal Government for twenty-five thousand new rifles, to be manufactured immediately. Yet it is apparent they do not wish these ten thousand rifles for the United States Government. They wish all secrecy. The rifles are to be consigned to a Southern city. What, my dear friend, is your conjecture on this?"

"The obvious one, my dear Sam, the obvious one," replied the priest, in great distress. He looked at Stuart, steadfastly. "You see, do you not, my son?"

"No!" shouted Stuart, violently. "I do not! I don't use my imagination! I take men's words for things! I don't pry and question into something which is none of my business!"

But Sam looked at him directly. "Do you not see, my Stuart? These men cannot involve themselves in this. They would disclaim any connection, in the event of a Governmental investigation. Yours will be the danger, as well as the profits.

Should you, in your danger, declare that they were the in- stigators, that you had this visitor and the proposition, they would explain that they had merely approached you, as a retailer, in order to sell you their rifles. Yours would be the name of the consigner, the instigator. They have power and prestige. They will be believed."

Stuart was momentarily nonplussed. Then he said, vio- lently thrusting back his chair: "I need that money. I need the profits. I intend to do it."

"I am your partner," said Sam, in a strong voice. "I can- not permit it."

"Then I shall use my own money! I shall borrow it! I know I can borrow it, with ease!"

His face was congested. He glared about him, his eyes glittering.

"You lend yourself to murder, to war between brethren?" asked the priest, sternly.

Stuart smiled at him darkly. He was breathless. "Did you not say that the cause of Abolition is a holy one? I'm willing to help in such a holy cause!"

The priest was silent. His pink face was now very pale. His eyes were earnest. Then he said: "The arming of the South is no holy cause."

Sam had no "loose" tongue. He rarely discussed the affairs of the shops with others than Stuart. But he was too dis- tracted now for reticence. He said, and in a voice that Stu- art had never heard before: "You speak of your need for money, Stuart. I know you need it—always do you need it. You will not live modestly, until you acquire a fortune. You live recklessly—for the day. When men are reckless, they need large sums, and they will haf them, no matter who suf- fers. It is no greed in you that desires this; it is necessity. I haf urged you to save, to guard, until it is safe to spend so, in your way. But you will not. Men like you are driven to evil things because of their need, because of their extravagance."

"Stuart, you are determined on this thing?" asked Father Houlihan, with great anxiety. "I could not endure it, Stuart, if I thought that what you have done for me has so indebted you to others that you must needs engage in a nefarious traffic to recover your losses."

Stuart, the mercurial, was touched by this simple distress. He pressed the priest's hand. He said airily, ignoring Sam and his unpleasant remarks: "Don't worry, Grundy. What I did for you cost me very little. No, I need a lot of money.

I always need it, damn it! And I'm not going to wait until I am shrivelled and crippled like that old fiend, Allstairs, before I can buy what I wish. I'm afraid I wouldn't want it, then. Frankly, I'm in difficulties. I see a way to turn a pretty penny. I'd be a fool to refuse it. I don't know what the rifles are needed for; I do not care. If I refuse the offer, others will accept. I shall have nothing but a moral conscience if I refuse, and moral consciences never paid off mortgages nor bought a man a woman, nor feathered a nest, nor, at the last, even bought bread."

Sam said nothing. He shook his head over and over, in the most somber dread and grief. Stuart, recovering his spirits, laughed at him. "You'll pay my bail, eh, Sam, if I am hauled in? You'll visit the poor prisoner with a basket, and, perhaps, a saw and a rope?"

His full handsome face was flushed heavily. They had all forgotten Angus, who had been listening in bewilderment and fear. Mrs. O'Keefe, unconcerned with the arguments of men, had been filling beer glasses, and had brought Stuart his extra glass of whiskey, which he always demanded.

Sam and the priest regarded him in silence. They loved him deeply. They saw him as a foolhardy child, not as a malefactor. If he had been naturally evil and rapacious he would not have been their friend; they would not have loved him. To them he was the perpetual boy, heedless and violent, who must be protected from his own unthinking predicaments.

"I shall pray that you will not do this thing," said Father Houlihan at last, in a weary voice. "For the sake of your soul."

Stuart laughed boisterously. "My soul, by God! I have no soul! But thank you kindly just the same, Grundy. If I feel any stirrings in my breast I'll run to you at once, shouting 'Eureka!' "

He became ostentatiously aware of Angus, who was staring at him with anguish. He put his hand on the lad's shoulder. "Almost done, Angus? We'll soon be off, then. It is getting late, and your dear mama will be worrying about you."

"We will talk about all this, tomorrow," said Sam, heavily.

Stuart waved his hand airily, but did not look at the other man. "No use, Sam. I've already accepted, and spent, an advance. I have agreed to the contract." He pushed back his chair.

With an effort, and a sad face which tried to smile, Father Houlihan looked gently at the pale Angus. He said: "So it is a doctor you'd be, my child. And why?"

Angus looked at him eagerly. "I've always felt so—Father Houlihan! It is so terrible to see people suffer. I don't want to make money sir, believe me. I only want to help people, to find out cures for their disease, to ease their pain."

Stuart laughed coarsely. "Aren't you the little feller who tried to persuade me recently that money was everything?" he asked, in a rallying voice.

Angus turned to him in confusion. "If I cannot be a doctor, then I shall want a lot of money," he said, with simplicity. "But if I am a doctor, then I shall not want it."

Stuart laughed loudly. But the priest was gazing at the boy with grave intensity. "I see," he said softly, "I see. If one cannot have his soul, he must have money." And in the depths of his heart, he murmured a prayer.

"What a damned sophistry!" cried Stuart, gaily. "I confess I don't follow the brat's reasoning."

But the priest put his hand firmly on Angus' shoulder. He turned his grave look upon Stuart. "Much will be forgiven you, my son, if you guard this boy, and give him his opportunity to be a physician."

Stuart stared, uncomfortably. "That's his mama's business, Grundy. I have an idea that she won't allow me to interfere. Besides, why a doctor? There's no money in it. And from what he told me, himself, he wants money, the damned greedy little Scot!"

But the priest said: "You will help him, Stuart? I charge you with it."

Stuart, annoyed, said: "Don't charge me with anything! I've got enough to do with myself, God knows." He added, more calmly: "I'll do what I can. But it's a lot of nonsense."

He pointed a derisive finger at Sam, with whom he was much enraged. "Look at Sam, here. Saves every penny. For what?"

Sam lifted his bowed head, and looked at him, directly. "You know I wish to buy River Island for my people, Stuart." His brown eyes were suddenly full of a mystic and vehement light, though his voice did not rise when he said: "I haf always believed that America is the Promised Land which Moses saw from the Mountain, for all suffering and persecuted and oppressed men, I think he saw it, across the oceans, and across time. I haf that dream in my heart, Stuart. I must help make that dream true."

Stuart laughed, much too loudly. "Look at the three of us! You, Sam, are dedicated to a dream, Grundy to his God, and I to my house! At the last, it comes to the same thing."

Sam said softly: "God has blessed this land. It will be great, greater than any land before, if it has its dream. Nothing can destroy a man, or a nation, if there is a dream."

Stuart smiled grimly, and rubbed his fingers on his glass. Father Houlihan smiled with passionate tenderness. And Angus listened, his heart beating in the strangest way.

CHAPTER 23

STUART stared blackly at Joshua Allstairs. His heart was fulminating, full of sick rage.

"What more do you want?" he asked, in a stifled voice. "I have repaid your ten thousand dollars. I have just made a contract which will bring me at least thirty thousand dollars; I already have a large advance.

"My shops are prospering. I have plans for expansion, which will be under way this summer. I shall soon control all the main retail business in Grandeville. There will be a branch of the railroad extended to this city within a few months. I can buy much more quickly, extend the field of my merchandising, when that happens. There is nothing to stop me. I have the finest house in Grandeville, of which Miss Marvina would be proud to be mistress. I shall be worth an amazing fortune in the shortest possible time."

Joshua leered. He was enjoying this immensely. He tented his fleshless fingers and regarded Stuart with evil benignity.

"My antecedents," continued Stuart, more strongly now, "are at least as exalted as yours. You have met my cousin, Mrs. Cauder, a lady of fortune. You have heard her story of our relatives, Lady Vere de Vere, and Sir Angus Fraser. Who have you like these in your family tree? Again, what more do you want?"

Joshua sighed, but continued to grin under his vulture's nose. "Stuart," he said with fond mildness, "if you were related to the Royal House of England, if you were a millionaire, I should still refuse to allow my daughter to marry a blackguard Irishman.

"And you are a blackguard, you know, my dear Stuart. You are faithless, churchless. You are impious, and blasphemous. God is an unknown word to you. You are also a drunkard, a consorter with lewd women. Your familiars are a Jew and a black priest. You are not accepted in the best of society, for these and a number of other reasons. You are not even honest. I am well aware of many of your dealings. You lack scruples——"

Stuart forgot that he was a suppliant, that he must placate this foul fiend. He sprang to his feet and shouted: "And you are a tavern-keeper, a brothel-keeper, a usurer, a gouger, and a thief! You draw your profits from these and from breweries, which you profess to abhor! You rob miserable black slaves on their way to Canada! You have financed the most nefarious things! I have done some dirty work, myself, but by God! I've never drawn my gold from a woman's body and bed, nor from a slave's starving hands, nor from the misery of bankrupt farmers!" His face was distorted with his fury.

"You swine!" he exclaimed, as Joshua cowered in his chair. "You dirty, misbegotten, filthy swine! You brothel-keeper and tapster! And you have the audacity to whine at me piously, as though your hands were clean and your crippled body as pure as snow!"

"You contemptible Irishman," whispered Joshua, his hand on the bell-rope. His face was a death's-head. "You come into my house and assault and insult me, because I refuse you my daughter. Go. Go, before I send for the police."

But Stuart was too insanely excited and enraged to hear this. He stood over Joshua with knotted fists, and his eyes leapt in their sockets. "There is no one who knows you that does not curse you! You are an abomination! You call me a blasphemer. Every breath that you draw is a blasphemy, you foul bastard!

"Look you, were I less of a man than I am, and more of your kidney, it's seducing your daughter I'd be doing, instead of coming to you like a gentleman, and praying for her hand. And, by God! I may do it yet, as a lesson to ye, ye scum and filth!" He paused, his voice breaking with his fury, then continued, shouting wildly: "D'ye thing it is a comfort to me to think that my sons might be like ye, with your blood in their veins? Or my daughter a trollop, with your soul?" The brogue, so carefully long absent from his speech, came back thickly, and it was a savage Irishman, indeed, who looked down on the bent and emaciated Joshua.

Joshua tugged the bell-rope with so much terror that it was torn down in his hand. But the butler, a tall gaunt man with a sly and lip-licking face appeared, smirking. Joshua saw him with mighty relief; he was trembling visibly. He pointed to Stuart. "Show this fop, this blackguard, this popinjay, to the door!" he squeaked, struggling for breath. "And never let him enter again."

Stuart flung back his head and laughed raucously and furiously. "Enter again, this den of thieves? This ante-room to a brothel? This usurer's pit of serpents?" He paused abruptly, and now his dark and swollen face gleamed. He bent over Joshua and thrust his fist under the shrinking old man's nose. Fascinated with terror, Joshua stared at him. "But you've not seen the last of me, I swear! You and I have a reckoning to make."

Fortified by the presence of his butler, and his hatred, Joshua squealed: "I'll have you in Court, I'll have you in bankruptcy, you puppy!"

Suddenly Stuart relaxed. His rage was gone, leaving only his laughter and contempt. "That is easier said than done, thief though you are. There is still law in America. The tale isn't finished yet. There is another chapter."

He looked down at Joshua as though he were an unspeakable obscenity, then swung away, arrogant and confident in his contemptuous strength and wholeness of body and handsomeness. He was exhilarated by his fury, as with whiskey. Never had he felt so buoyant and invulnerable. The butler, still smirking, accompanied him to the great and spectral hall, where the most pallid of light drifted. The man gave Stuart his hat and cane and gloves, peeping at him from under granulated lids, and bowing stiffly.

There was something in his manner which made Stuart pause and scrutinize him narrowly. Now he was more sober, though his emotions were still elated. He remembered that "Like master, like man," and recalled that thieves are always supremely devoted to their masters, with a devotion far beyond that given by a decent man to an honorable master. This butler, doubtless, continued the old tradition. Nevertheless, Stuart decided that he, himself, had nothing to lose, and decided to chance a broaching of the man's defenses.

Stuart glanced swiftly at the door beyond which Joshua crouched. Then he returned to the butler, who was watching him with his covert grin. Meeting Stuart's look, the man expressed silent tentativeness and watchful interest. Stuart, loathing him, bent towards him and whispered: "I am at home every evening at ten the balance of this week."

The man said nothing. He only bowed again, and smirked, and opened the door. Stuart stepped out into the cold brisk May air, and looked back. The door closed promptly behind him.

Now his assurance suddenly faded. He walked away, with his usual swagger. But he had sobered. The fumes of rage and triumph began to leave him. For years, he had ached to strike at Joshua Allstairs; his loathing had been like a festering poison in him. It had been a release. But now that it was over he was enormously depressed and sunken.

However, he reflected, had he continued to be all respect and deference to Joshua, it would have brought him nothing but continued oily and benign insults. The old man would not countenance him for his daughter. Stuart's respectful importunities, his controlled pleadings, would only have increased Joshua's malevolence, and he would have enjoyed himself. Stuart, then, had lost nothing at all, and had delivered himself of an unbearable load of venom.

His depression was very dark. But his natural ebullience of spirits would not let him fall too low this time. He proceeded to the shops, and by the time he had arrived there he was smiling again, and greeting the ladies with the utmost deference and affability. They adored him, condescended to him pleasantly, and the older ladies looked at his broad shoulders and narrow waist with wistful affection.

But Sam Berkowitz, subtle and sensitive always, soon discerned that there was something disorderly and pent about Stuart today, despite all his amiable chatter and eagerness with the customers. Stuart had once complained that one could have no ' secrets from his old friend, that he was a "witch," and knew all things by "divination." At any rate, Sam studied Stuart with careful earnestness, and after a little he was less disturbed. It was not money, this time, apparently. Stuart, when pressed for money, or in financial difficulties after some hideous extravagance, wore a certain sultry and preoccupied expression, was hasty and short of manner, and confused. He was none of these, today. To be sure, he seemed to be thinking deeply, was restless, and had a way of pursing his lips. He was scheming, doubtless, meditated Sam, with relief. It was not money, then. What was it?

Sam speculated. It was a woman. Only money and women could so turn Stuart's attention away from his beloved shops. Then Sam knew. Stuart had apparently spoken for Miss Marvina, and had been refused. Sam's relief increased tremendously. Some chronic tightness in him relaxed. It was a good thing! A very good thing, thank God.

At five o'clock that evening, Janie appeared, luxuriously arrayed, and in Stuart's most formal carriage. She minced into the main shop, her downcast lashes brushing her cheeks, and gowned in rich purple velvet and ermine. At the sight of her, Stuart colored, but he came forward gallantly and seated his cousin in an empty chair. The few ladies now in the shop bowed to that pathetic little widow, and smiled at her amiably. So far, Janie had been a great social success, and she had managed to ingratiate herself even with those with whom Stuart was no social favorite, and who had only grudgingly accepted him. Her meekness, her amiability, her professed gratitude for the kindness of new friends in this "strange land," her admiration for everything, her fascinating conversation and careful diction, had impressed all very favorably. Moreover, it was evident that she was a lady of fortune, and had the most remarkable jewels, and the most elegant of Continental airs.

Sam had retired to the office behind the shop, and had begun to look over the day's accounts. He was surprised when Stuart suddenly entered, shutting the door abruptly behind him. "Look here," whispered the young man urgently, "come out into the shop and tell me in front of Janie that I must not forget our dinner together tonight."

"But we haf no dinner," said Sam, in surprise.

"Oh, damn you! Who said we have?" Stuart glared at him with ire. "But I'm not in the mood to dine tête-à-tête with the strumpet tonight. If I do, there'll be fireworks, I vow. I can't afford that, just yet. I'm in a bad state. Besides, your mama can give me a bite or two, if I appear. If you think not, I'll go to the tavern."

"I see," said Sam, thoughtfully. It was very sad, this good Stuart constantly involving himself with women. Sam remembered how one distraught and hysterical married lady had haunted the shop every day for several months, merely to see Stuart, and how there had been many distressing scenes in this very office, behind closed doors.

Stuart left the office, and returned to his dwindling customers, for it was approaching the dinner hour. Janie decorously awaited him, all modesty and tremblings. He ignored her, putting all his charm into his ministering to the belated ladies. Janie smiled under her long nose, and bit her lips vigorously to increase their color. Sam's door remained obdurately shut, though Stuart kept glancing at it with fury. The last customer was now preparing to leave. Stuart coughed loudly. The male clerks, folding up the silks and velvets, and murmuring among themselves, were relaxing at the end of a long hard day.

Stuart conducted the last lady to her carriage, and lingered on the walk with her. His anger increased. Damn Sam, anyway! Finally, there was nothing to do but to re-enter the shops, and to say to Janie: "Well, my love, shall we leave now?"

Janie rose, simpering coyly. Just at that exasperating moment, Sam's door opened, and he entered the shop. Stuart glared at him, with relief. Sam was apparently surprised to see Janie there. He bowed to her. "Good efening, Mrs. Cauder," he murmured.

Janie regarded him with haughty but pleasant condescension. "Good evening, Mr. Berkowitz," she said. She laid her mittened hand on Stuart's arm. "It is late, my dear. Shall we go now?"

Sam cleared his throat diffidently. He pretended to regard Stuart with confusion. His unhappiness, however, was sincere. He said, in a low and hesitating voice: "But, my Stuart, haf we not a dinner together, tonight, to discuss some financial matters in quietness?"

Stuart, happy, affected to start. He frowned. "Damn it, yes! But Sam, can't it wait until tomorrow night? Janie's come for me, and I had something in mind for the evening."

Sam, unused to duplicity, stared unaffectedly at him, wondering. But Stuart winked impatiently. Sam cleared his throat again. He shook his head, sadly. "The banks—they haf the auditors tomorrow, and will consider those matters, Stuart. It cannot be delayed."

"O hell, then," said Stuart, pettishly. "If I must, I must." He turned to his cousin, and took her hand. "My love, you can see how it is. Business affairs. Always business affairs. Sam is very obdurate. But he is right, of course."

Janie turned her green eyes upon Sam with hatred. He was more and more confused. He murmured something very feebly, and made an expressive motion with his hands. He was afraid of Janie, as he was afraid of all heartless and cruel people.

Janie spoke with hoarse loudness: "There is nothing to be done, it seems. But I do deplore that you are at the beck and call of the most unfeeling—persons, my darling Stuart."

Stuart flushed. He regarded Sam sheepishly. But Sam betrayed no reaction. "Ma'am," said Stuart, with formality, "there are matters which are beyond female comprehension. Shall I conduct you to your carriage now?"

He led Janie with ceremony to the street. The May evening sky was pure mauve, shining with the last sunlight. The cold North air rushed through the streets, like a wall of fresh water. Stuart assisted Janie into the carriage. She was enraged and disappointed. But she managed a seductive smile, as she looked down at Stuart. "Early?" she whispered, languishing at him.

He smiled at her gallantly. "If possible," he whispered in return. He watched the carriage as it rolled down the cobbled street. She waved her kerchief coquettishly to him. He waved back. He felt sick and hot when he returned to the shops. He was already tired of Janie, and her knowledgeable ways, and some fundamental decency in him was revolted. He slammed the door angrily behind him. The clerks had slipped away. Sam was waiting in the warm dusk, and Stuart could see the clear brown shining of his eyes. They were like a dumb but wise reproach.

"I thought I'd never rid myself of her," Stuart fumed, setting a chair into place. "Damn it, how do I get into such abominable scrapes? What do I do? Nothing! Nothing, I swear to you! But the women hang about like damned fainting sheep, smothering a man until he can't breathe for the likes of 'em."

Sam smiled faintly. Stuart did not look at him. Then Sam said, gently: "You are to marry Mrs. Cauder?"

At this revolting suggestion Stuart forgot his embarrassment, and swung on his friend. He burst into violent laughter. "Marry her? For Christs' sake, Sam! Am I an idiot? Do I impress you as an idiot, an imbecile?"

"Yes," said Sam, firmly.

Stuart stared at him, astounded.

Sam continued, with more gentleness: "In your affairs with women, my Stuart, you exhibit no intelligence at all. You do not learn. Every man may haf one bad time, but more than one bad time a wise man does not. This lady, Mrs. Cauder: was it necessary to haf a bad time with her, in your house?"

Stuart's face was crimson. He laughed abruptly. He glanced at his watch. "It wasn't such a bad time. On the contrary. But enough is enough. That is the hell with women: they never have enough. They gather the rosebuds where they may, but insist on embalming the damned dried leaves forever, and push them into a man's face on all occasions. I'm finished with them."

Sam sighed. He said, tentatively: "You haf promised Father Houlihan to look favorably upon his niece, whom he loves so much. Marriage might be excellent for you, my friend."

Stuart still scrutinized his watch. "I think you are right,

Sam." He turned to Sam, and his mercurial face now expressed nothing but blandness and innocence. "Shall we go? Thanks for extricating me."

"Tonight, there was the extrication. But am I to invite you to supper every night, without end?"

Stuart had recovered his good temper. "Who knows?" he said, affectionately. "Sam, what would I do without you?" He took his friend's arm. But Sam resisted. His face was now grave.

"You haf not forgotten that Mrs. Cauder is now our partner? Embarrassment will not cease."

"O hell, let the future take care of itself. In the meantime, I have things to do. Shall we go?"

He whistled gaily as they left the shops, and locked the doors behind them. All at once Sam was ill with uneasiness.

CHAPTER 24

AT HALF past nine that evening Stuart let himself softly and furtively into his house. It was most horrible, he fumed, that he must creep into his own darling house as though he had no right to be there, and all because of a strumpet with lascivious green eyes. He tiptoed up the stairs, and peered down the hallway. Janie's door was open a mere crack, but a light shone out into the darkness. He cursed her silently, retreated, and rang for a servant.

"I may have a visitor tonight," he said curtly. "I wish you to stand by the door, and watch, until half past ten at least. I do not wish a bell to ring. It—it is a matter of importance and privacy."

The servant immediately suspected the coming of a woman, which was not unusual. He nodded silently, and withdrew, grinning to himself in the hall.

Now Stuart cursed himself for his indiscretion. He ought not to have suggested that Allstairs' butler come to the house. Janie would eavesdrop, if she heard voices. I never think! thought Stuart, fuming at himself. He went into the great white hallway, where the servant had taken up his vigil. Stuart glanced up the stairs, then whispered, frowning haughtily: "It is a gentleman I expect. You will conduct him quietly to the sun-room, where I will await him."

He marched away, and then cursed himself again. The

servants of the city doubtless knew each other very well. The
rumor would get about that Mr. Allstairs' man had visited
Mr. Coleman that evening, on a secret matter. There was
nothing to do now but work fast.

The sun-room was cold and brilliantly empty. Stuart sat
down and glared at his watch. Fifteen minutes to ten. He
folded his arms across his chest, and frowned. All at once he
felt certain that Allstairs' man would not come tonight. Or
on any other night. He had been a fool to think so. His gorge
rose. He crossed his knees and swung a long leg. Its suave
outlines, under the strained fawn broadcloth, pleased him
with their symmetry. He cocked his head, the better to observe the silken flow of strong muscles shimmering under the
crystal chandelier.

Then he was despondent again. There were other ways, of
course, through which to approach Marvina. But in a week
or less she would be gone from Grandeville. His volatile despair rose to a high pitch. Was he to be balked? Never! He
had never been balked in his life. He would not be so now.
 — He heard whispering footsteps on the rich rugs outside
the room. His heart began to beat. His servant entered with
Joshua's man, lank and gaunt in black broadcloth, his hat
clutched in his two hands against his lean breast, his bald
head gleaming in the candlelight. He was smirking respectfully. He bowed to Stuart. Stuart, sweating with relief, dismissed his servant. He sat down again, with languid grace,
and surveyed the butler with a haughty smile.

What a vulture it was, fit servant for fit master! The cadaverous face was long and sunken and livid, the nose a
curving thin hook, the eyes the eyes of a weasel, without
conscience or faith, and lit only with the avid light of greed.

"What is your name, my man?" Stuart asked, condescendingly.

He very well knew what it was, but when the man murmured: "Grimshaw, if it please you, sir," Stuart inclined
his head regally.

"Excellent, excellent," he said. He hesitated, then with
a royal gesture indicated a chair. "You may sit down,
Grimshaw."

Grimshaw was only amused by this elegant show of im-
perialism. He sat down on the edge of a rose-damask little
chair, holding his hat on his bony knees. His attitude was
all humility.

There was a little silence. Stuart began to feel uncomfortable. The man was not looking at him, but Stuart was un-

easily aware that all his affectations had not in the least impressed the slinking cur. Stuart stared at the floor. The black-and-white stone was exquisitely polished, so that all objects were reflected in it. The dim rose of the draperies stirred at the windows as the night wind rose strongly.

"You are probably conjecturing why I suggested you come to me tonight?" said Stuart.

The man coughed deprecatingly. "I considered perhaps, sir, you wished to make a change?"

Stuart scowled. "Well, no, I am well satisfied with my own man, Grimshaw. It was not that. It was something more important. Something that would benefit you in the extreme, beyond mere wages."

"Indeed, sir? How kind of you, sir." The man's face expressed nothing but respectful bewilderment. But he sucked in his lips with an ugly sound, and his tiny brown eyes gleamed.

Damn you, thought Stuart, you know very well why you came! But he smiled condescendingly, and continued: "How would a thousand dollars suit you, Grimshaw?"

The man was shaken. But he recovered himself. "A thousand dollars, sir?" He shook his head, gently. "That is not enough, sir."

Stuart stared at him, paling furiously. Then he said, in a low voice: "Then you do know why I sent for you?"

The man smirked, and dipped his head. "In a way, sir. But it is worth more than a thousand dollars. It places me in jeopardy. I shall never have another position in Grandeville, if the matter is ever revealed. A man must guard his livelihood."

Stuart's heart swelled in his chest with loathing and fury. But he said, with hoarse wildness: "I assure you that I shall protect your interests. Nothing shall be learned from me. No one shall ever know."

The man sighed. "But Mr. Allstairs, sir, is a very astute gentleman. Nothing escapes him. He will put two and two together. He is a dangerous gentleman, begging your pardon, sir. I should leave Grandeville immediately, for fear of his wrath. Therefore, sir, you will understand one thousand dollars is not near enough. I have thought of setting up a small shop, myself, sir, in a distant city."

The man grinned at him slyly. Suddenly Stuart's rage got almost, but not quite, beyond control. The filthy dog, with his insinuation about a shop! It was that, more than anything else, which made Stuart's gorge rise and his fists clench.

But there was too much at stake now for an outbreak, and he swallowed the thick salty bulk which had risen in his throat.

He said, and his voice had dwindled, though his eyes were on fire: "I offer you one thousand two hundred dollars."

The man sighed again, sorrowfully, and moved on his chair as if to rise.

"What then, damn you?" cried Stuart, turning scarlet.

"Three thousand dollars, sir."

Stuart started to his feet, maddened. "Three thousand dollars! Why, you unspeakable cur! You reprobate! You stinking dog!"

The man rose slowly, in one swift movement, and retreated a step. His face was ghastly with fear. He looked at the infuriated Stuart, and licked his lips. He backed away, still farther.

"May I leave, sir?" he whispered.

"Leave?" shouted Stuart. "Get out of my house before I kick you all the way back to the house of that fiend!" He advanced on the man with doubled fists.

The man backed away still another step or two. But he was shrewd. He reached the shelter of the doorway, and paused. "Miss Marvina is well guarded, sir," he suggested, in a piping tone. "You will never see her again, sir. She will be extraordinarily well guarded, hereafter."

Stuart, in the very midst of rushing upon him, halted. Everything was lost now.

He began to pant. His rage made everything dim before him. And in that dimness, Grimshaw was a floating black shadow, hovering in the doorway.

Stuart groped for a chair. He fell into it. He looked at Grimshaw with malignancy. "Sit down," he said, stifled.

The man, not looking away from him, fumbled for another chair, and again lowered himself on the edge.

In the midst of the noise of his pounding pulses, Stuart's mind began to function. Where would he lay his hands on three thousand dollars now? He had less than three thousand in his private account. He would have to borrow from Sam, to make the payments on the ten thousand he had borrowed back from the shops. But he thought of this only briefly. With a shaking hand he withdrew a sheaf of banknotes from an inner pocket. His damp fingers trembled as he counted out five hundred dollars. He flung the bills at Grimshaw, who avidly bent and picked them up. The man counted them, making sucking sounds with his lips. Then he folded them and put them inside his coat.

"Five hundred dollars, sir," he murmured, reproachfully.

"You will receive one hundred dollars more each time you bring me a note from Miss Marvina, written in her own writing, with which I am well acquainted," said Stuart. "And on the day that Miss Marvina leaves with me to marry me, you will receive the rest."

The man was silent. Then he sighed and smiled. "You will give me notes, and an agreement to that effect, sir? Tomorrow?"

Stuart suddenly felt quite ill. The man rubbed his chin thoughtfully.

"If I may be allowed to say so, sir, the young lady weeps in her room each night. I have it on the authority of her maid, sir. She pines for you, sir."

Stuart did not speak. His face blackened. But he listened.

"I would suggest nothing of this, sir, no hope, if I did not know that the young lady would be amenable. She vows, in tears, that she will marry no other but you. She has said this to her respected father, in my own hearing. You cannot fail, with my help, sir."

Still Stuart did not speak. The man murmured deprecatingly: "I know of a small minister, sir, in La Grange, who will marry you at the drop of a hat, sir."

Stuart found his voice, but it was strained and dull. "You will accompany us as a witness?"

The man appeared simply surprised. "But certainly, sir. I shall leave Mr. Allstairs on that day."

"When you appear with Miss Marvina, I shall give you the rest. An agreement will be delivered to you tomorrow, to that effect."

He could no longer sit in his chair. He looked down at Grimshaw with murderous eyes. "Do not think to diddle me, you dog. If you fail me, or betray me, you shall not escape me. I swear to that. Do you understand?"

Later, he crept up to his room, his boots in his hand. The light still shone from under Janie's door. He heard the rustling of the pages of a book. When he finally closed his door silently after him, and locked it, he was trembling.

CHAPTER 25

THE HARD and nimble air of the Northern early night blew strongly through the streets of Grandeville, gushing in from the Lake and the river. Yellow lights glowed from the massed houses. Street lamps burned vividly. As there was still a hint of frost in the evenings, though it was May, the stars glittered like white fire, and the slow white crescent of a burning moon rose with majesty. The streets were quiet and full of peace.

And now carriage wheels echoed in the evening hush, the horses' hoofs striking sparks from the cobbles. The carriage made its way down the hard mud slope towards the river, and approached Stuart's house. It stopped at the front door. Stuart leapt out, and extended his hand to a lady within the carriage. She took his hand and alighted. She was tall and slender, heavily cloaked, and wore a bonnet with a thick veil. Still holding her hand, Stuart led her to the door, and pulled the bell. The carriage rolled back to the stables.

The day had been febrile and exciting. Stuart was exhausted and very nervous. He was not one to brood on the future, however immediate. He left that evil moment to its own time. He had that evil moment now. In a few seconds, he would be inside his house, and confronting Janie with his new wife.

The girl beside him was very calm and docile. Since the marriage this afternoon she had said little, only smiling sweetly and placidly, her hand in Stuart's. He was profoundly grateful for this. In his infatuation he believed her serenity was strength and wisdom, and he wished to live up to her opinion of him, which was doubtless excellent. He did not as yet know that she never possessed any opinions at all.

The thing to do, he meditated, waiting for the door to open, was to consummate the marriage without delay. A daughter who was no longer a maid was not worth rescuing. Only if that daughter could be rescued from her marriage bed with her virginity intact was the expedition sensible. Stuart resolved to obviate that possibility at the first feasible moment. The thought exhilarated him. He turned to the girl with a smile, and his black eyes glowed in the darkness. She returned his look with serene fondness.

The door opened, and his man stood there. When he saw the young lady his mouth gaped, for he had often seen Miss Marvina on the streets. The man stepped back and Stuart and Miss Marvina entered, she moving like a dream of beauty, full of floating grace, her tawny eyes shining. She waited like an exquisite statue for the next command of her master, her Pygmalion, her gloved hands clasped before her. Stuart gallantly removed her cloak. She gave him her bonnet. Then he took her hand again and led her into the magnificent drawing-room, and called his man, who had been following them, bemused.

"Briggs," said Stuart, in a tone of authority, "this is your new mistress, Mrs. Coleman."

In a louder and more genial voice, he said: "Is Mrs. Cauder at home? Please convey my regards to her, and ask her if she will grant me a moment in the drawing-room. And Briggs: don't mention this surprise to her."

Before the man could recover, Stuart turned to Marvina. "My love, will you be seated near the fire? It is chilly tonight."

"Yes—Stuart," she murmured, seating herself with a rustle of rich brown silk. Her black hair shone in the firelight. Her ivory face and golden eyes were expressionless. Even when she smiled, the smile was empty. She obeyed. Had he told her to stand up and dance, she would have done it without surprise, and with calm. Her mouth, so like a dark gleaming plum, released its smile automatically.

It was lovely to have a quiet wife, reflected Stuart, abstractedly. Not one of these horrible chatterers. But he was not really thinking of this actively. He was listening for Janie's step on the stairs. And now his heart began to beat most unpleasantly. What would Janie say? He had some slight idea, and this was the cause of the disagreeable prickling at the roots of his hair, and the sudden dampness along his spine. He prayed to his profane gods that she would at least retain some rags of civilized behavior. He did not want this innocent child to be terrified, this girl of eighteen who, though of a mature woman's age, had been so immured. He did not want her maiden ears to be assaulted by blasphemies shrieked by the rowdy and vulgar Janie, who was the foulest thing when aroused.

He heard the opening of Janie's door, and her light swift tread upstairs. He rose and stood beside his wife, his hand on her shoulder. "My love," he said hurriedly, meeting the golden beam of her obedient eyes, "my cousin, as I have told you, is a little strange sometimes, and not quite herself. You will not be alarmed, ma'am?"

"Oh, no," she said softly. And now, odd to say, her eyes were filled with a brilliance which he had never seen before. "I have met Mrs. Cauder, you know, Stuart, and I thought her very civil."

Most damnable phrase! thought Stuart. "Very civil," the chit had said. So she disposed of hurricanes and tempests and ravening beasts. All at once he wanted to laugh, quite insanely.

But Janie was entering, in white foulard scattered with vivid pansies, her shoulders bare, her red curls painfully and carefully disposed on her little bony shoulders over which she had thrown a white lace shawl. She bounced into the room, all vitality and gaiety, shrieking: "Stuart, you dog! Where have you been! And dinner cooling the while!"

And then she stopped short, frozen, and stared at Marvina. Her small and narrow face turned quite pale, and the freckles on her big bony nose sprang out.

Marvina, all brown silk and demure white lace collar and smooth black chignon, rose with a stately movement, smiled, and waited. Nothing could have been more composed. The bad moment had arrived. Stuart was definitely sweating, though he grinned.

He advanced a step or two, involuntarily putting himself between his wife and his cousin. He tried to speak, but his thickened throat would not permit a sound. As for Janie, she stood there, petrified, and now her face had become as ugly as sin, and as vicious, and as malevolent. She must have had some prescience. Her shoulders bent a little, her back curved, as if she were about to spring. When Stuart, in anguish, cleared his throat, she turned upon him swiftly, arching more than ever, and her eyes were savage.

"Well?" she said, her voice cracking, "well? What is *she* doing here?"

With a tremendous struggle, Stuart found his speech, and tried to bluster: "How dare you speak to me in such a peremptory tone, ma'am, as if this were not my house?"

"Curse you, Stuart!" she cried, with furious scorn, "stop this nonsense, and tell me why this strumpet is in this house, this house which you have as much as promised me will always be my own?"

She stamped her foot. Her cry had risen to a shriek. She knew, now. A girl like Miss Marvina would never have come to this house, unchaperoned, unless the incredible, the impossible, the frightful, had happened. She screamed: "Why do you bring your women to this house, Stuart Coleman, this house which I have presumed to be respectable and sacred, the roof under which my helpless children live?"

One part of Stuart's mind was thankful for this appalling outbreak. It gave him an opportunity to return in kind, and with similar ferocity. He had, that afternoon, had a disagreeable vision of Janie swooning, of Janie in agony, of Janie in tears, weeping out her reproaches, of Janie broken. He could not have coped successfully with such a Janie. The whole thing would have degenerated into a wallowing mess. But a Janie enraged and shrieking and brawling was easier to contend with, and need be spared no pity, no embarrassment, and no remorse.

So now he shouted, lifting his fists: "Mind your tongue, ma'am, or I shall mind it for you! This is my wife, ma'am, the mistress of my house, and I demand that you treat her with the respect and civility and courtesy due her!"

Janie's pale face immediately became livid. She looked at Stuart, and despite his fury, despite his shame, he quailed before that look, so insane was it, so malignant.

"Your wife?" she repeated, and now her voice had fallen, but was all the more terrible for its quieter tone. "This—this creature is your wife?"

"Yes, ma'am, my wife. We were married this afternoon, in La Grange, a small village some ten miles from here. It may be a surprise to you, but we had planned it for some time."

Afraid to look at his wife, he nevertheless turned to her. He was amazed. She was not in the least disturbed. Her fixed smile had not passed. She might have been alone, so aloof, so detached, was she. She regarded Janie with the wide and empty gaze of a smug child, who has not yet learned to feel much emotion. It was apparent that she was not horrified or frightened.

In the sudden hiatus which followed Stuart's words, Marvina's honey-rich voice entered with tranquillity: "Good evening, ma'am." And she curtseyed gracefully.

Stuart and Janie stared at her, their faces becoming idiotically bland, incredulously robbed of all expression. "Good evening, ma'am," in the face of chaos and excitement and shrieks and threats!

All at once Stuart began to laugh. He could not control himself. He bent double, almost collapsing in his mirth. He laughed until he wept, until tears rolled down his cheeks.

He slapped his knees; he choked; he whimpered; he struggled for breath. And each time that he glanced at the serene Marvina, regarding him without puzzlement or wonder, and at Janie's blank staring face, he went off into fresh paroxysms. Finally he staggered weakly backwards near the wall, and fell against it, speechless with agonies of laughter. He could not endure to look at the women; he swung himself face to the wall, and gave himself up to convulsions.

"My God!" he groaned between times, when he could catch his breath. "My dear, dear God!"

Janie recovered herself. But she was silent. She was clever enough to know that any word she could say just now would only throw Stuart into new hysterics of hilarity, which would render her more and more ridiculous. She turned, instead, to Marvina, who looked at her with courteous and faintly smiling attention, as if all this were nothing at all, but happened in the normal course of events.

"So," she said, in a vitriolic voice, "you've married my cousin, eh? You strumpet!"

If she thought to goad Marvina, to break that smiling and impassive calm, she was mistaken. Marvina smiled at her radiantly, though again that odd brilliance shone in her eyes. "Indeed, yes," she said, mildly. "This afternoon. So precipitous of dear Stuart, was it not? We ought to have invited you, and so I mentioned to Stuart, but he declined, as you had been indisposed." She smiled even wider. "The minister was so kind, though I should have preferred Mr. Hawkins, of our own dear little church."

Janie stared at her, her face becoming rigid and completely evil with hatred and malignancy.

"Were you aware, ma'am," asked Janie, "that my cousin promised me marriage, after taking advantage of my helpless state and giving me vows of his intention?"

For the first time, a puzzled gleam touched Marvina's eyes. She glanced at Stuart, then returned with equanimity to Janie. "I do not know of this," she confessed, without distress. "I only know that Stuart spoke of you most kindly. Are you certain you were not mistaken, ma'am?"

"Mistaken?" screamed Janie, beside herself again. "You fool, do you not know what I mean when I say that he took advantage of my helpless state? Do you understand, you zany, that he slept with me, after his promises?"

She caught her breath on a deep gasp of rage, then waited for the girl to cry out in horror, to hide her face with her hands, to retreat. But Marvina merely gazed at her tranquilly, and said: "How very reprehensible."

There was not even revulsion of the slightest kind in her voice, or disbelief. Having said her say, she waited most politely for Janie to speak again.

But Janie, confounded, was beyond speech. She looked at Marvina with distended eyes, disbelieving what she saw, as if she faced a nightmare. She looked at that beautiful face, the passive deep mouth, the golden eyes, which surveyed her with the utmost detached friendliness. She could not believe it!

And then all her frustrated hatred, her wrath, her disappointment, her lust, her wild and real anguish, were too much to be borne. She sprang upon Marvina, her fingers dangerously flexed, like talons, her teeth bare and glistening, her eyes mad. She uttered horrible sounds. Her movements were swift, but Marvina instinctively recoiled before this fury, and flung up her arm to protect her face at which Janie's ferocious attack was directed. The claws fell impotently on the thick brown silk of the rounded arm, and though the fabric was torn, the skin was not even scratched. Nevertheless, the girl staggered backwards under the assault, and cried out, feebly, like a kitten.

Stuart, drawing deep gulping breaths, heard that cry, and turned about. He saw Janie preparing to attack again. He saw Marvina's torn sleeve, and her bewilderment. In an instant he had seized Janie by the arm and had wrenched her about. He lifted his hand and struck her savagely on the cheek, first one side and then the other, with the back of his hand. And she turned upon him, fiercely, like an untamable cat from the jungles, trying to tear at his eyes, his cheeks. Once her nails actually reached his cheek, and a long bleeding gash appeared.

She was tiny and he was big, but she had the strength of a dozen devils. She slipped out of his grasp again and again, twisting sinuously, trying to dodge about him to get at Marvina, who was now really pale and frightened, and who was actually whimpering. The girl's chignon had become loosened; her long black hair began to uncoil on her shoulders. "Stuart! Stuart!" she cried faintly.

But Stuart, cursing between his teeth, was too busy to heed her just yet. He tried to grasp Janie's arms, to pin them to her sides. He shook her violently when he could, until her teeth chattered. But she was almost too much for him. A kind of horror overwhelmed him; her face floated beneath his own, the face of a demon, flashing white and wild, and full of insensate madness. Never had he seen or confronted a thing like this in all his life. It was as if he had become entangled with an obscene loathesomeness, which threw his senses into appalled abhorrence. He could not endure it that she touched him. His cheek smarted as though venom had been poured into it. His very soul sickened, and became frenzied. He retched, through his curses, through his panting cries: "Now then, you she-devil, now then!"

He hated her, abominated her. Finally he was able to catch both of her flaying arms and pin them together before him. Even then she wrenched and tore, turned one hand inwards and raked his wrist. He could not bear to look at her face, so distorted was it.

"Oh, you bitch!" he grunted. "You bitch!"

He was driven almost to insanity by his horror of her. He wanted to kill her. He twisted her arms until she screeched, and the servants crowded at the doorway, trembling. She flung back her head and screamed like a demon out of hell. Her children, who ate their dinners in the servants' dining-room, heard, and huddled together on the stairs. Even the composed Robbie was weeping. Angus held his little sister in his arms, and tried to cover her ears with his hands.

Then Stuart, his horror mounting, his eyes dazed with faintness, clapped his hand on Janie's mouth. She gurgled and choked under it; she tried to bite it. But he was inexorable. He wanted only to still that ghastly noise of hers. It made him frantic. Shuddering though he was, he dragged her tightly against him, and increased the pressure on her mouth with his other hand. Only her legs were free now; with one sharp toe she kicked his shins over and over. He did not feel it. He closed his eyes; only the blubbering sound she made against his smothering hand filled the room.

It was on this pleasant scene that Joshua entered, accompanied by the Sheriff.

He saw the servants, who had not heard his furious ringing, who had not opened the door. He saw the huddled children on the stairs. He saw Stuart struggling with the maddened woman; he saw his daughter standing at a distance from them, her eyes wide in her white confused face, her hair on her shoulders, her gown torn.

He looked at them all, incredulously. He stood there, leaning on his cane. Only the Sheriff moved. Stuart was an old friend of his, and the tall stout man was greatly embarrassed. But he knew what to do in the face of violence.

He put his hand strongly on Stuart's arm, and caught at Janie with the other. He wrenched them apart. Janie, free, gulping, saw only another antagonist, and turned upon him. He struck her smartly in the face, and dexterously sent her whirling in a billowing of petticoats. She fell into a chair.

"Now, then, what's all this, eh?" he growled. "What is the meaning of it? Come now, man, speak up."

But Stuart could not speak. He pulled his kerchief from his pocket. He dabbed at his bleeding cheek. Janie, in her chair, sensing what had happened now, was weeping noisily.

She pointed a shaking finger at her cousin. "He tried to kill me! He tried to strangle me to death!"

White and mute as a ghost, Stuart continued to wipe his cheek. The Sheriff, understanding not a little, looked at him compassionately. Then he turned to the servants. "Bring some whiskey, you fools," he ordered, in a tone of authority. He turned back to Stuart. "Come, man, sit down. Take hold of yourself. That's right. Here's a chair."

Stuart sat down. He appeared deathly ill. He bent his head on his hand, his arm supported by his knee. The Sheriff sighed.

"I've got a warrant for you, Stuart, for kidnapping. Have you anything to say?"

Stuart found his voice. "Tell that woman to cease her screeching," he implored, dully.

Janie's wails were increasing in strength. The Sheriff turned on her abruptly. "Stop that!" he bellowed. "What's going on here, anyway?" The servant returned with a glass of whiskey. The Sheriff pressed it upon Stuart. "Drink this," he ordered. "You need it."

In the meantime Joshua had edged and crept towards his daughter. He looked at her expressionlessly. "Come home at once, my dear," he said. "This is no place for you. Where is your cloak and bonnet? Come, my dear, Papa will take you home."

But Marvina did not appear even to be aware of him. She looked only at Stuart, who was drinking the whiskey. Mechanically, she put up her hands and rewound her hair neatly.

"You don't want him arrested, do you, my love?" Joshua said softly. "He will spend the night in jail if you don't come home at once." He chortled evilly. He pointed to Stuart, and the sobbing dishevelled Janie. "Do you want to live here, with them, with these dreadful creatures? Come at once, lovey, and Papa shall not mention this again. Papa and his little girl shall go away, far away, and forget all this."

He, too, understood what had happened. He squinted at Janie, and chortled again. Lady Vere de Vere and Sir Angus Fraser, indeed! He was voluptuously delighted. Nothing could have gone better for him.

"That is his fancy woman there, my little love. That is what innocence has led my darling child into, this abominable house. This is the scoundrel who persuaded you to leave your papa for him, this den of iniquity. But Papa has rescued you. We shall forget all this. It never happened. In the meantime, he will get his deserts."

Stuart handed the glass back to the Sheriff, who still regarded him with compassionate regret. "Thanks, Bob." He breathed deeply, over and over. "I wasn't about to kill her, Bob, though I wanted to. She attacked my wife."

The Sheriff moved a little. "You married Miss Marvina, Stuart?"

"Yes, this afternoon." Stuart became aware of his wife now. He stood up, weakly. He turned to the girl and held out his hand. His stiff face broke into a feeble smile. She left her father immediately, and came to him without hesitation. Her serenity had returned. She put her hand in his, trustfully, and smiled up at him.

The Sheriff stared at them both. Then he scowled. He looked at Joshua. "You said that he had kidnapped her, and was forcing her into marriage, Mr. Allstairs."

Joshua grimaced at him, malevolently. "The girl is under age!" he exclaimed. "I don't believe he married her! He only wanted to bring her to this house!"

"You can prove this, Stuart?" asked the Sheriff, sternly.

"Certainly. I have my marriage lines here." Stuart fumbled at his pocket. "We were married today by a Methodist minister in La Grange. Here are the names of the witnesses. The girl is not under age. She is nearly nineteen. She is a woman, not a child."

The Sheriff examined the paper closely. His embarrassment grew. He looked at Stuart, standing there with his young wife. There was a quiet dignity about him, despite his disordered array and bleeding cheek, a kind of splendor which was one of his strongest physical characteristics, and very magnetic. There was a sudden silence in the room, broken only by Janie's dull sobbing and her hysterical appeals to the Almighty for justice.

"This seems correct, Mr. Allstairs," said the Sheriff. He

was an honest man, and he hated Joshua. His voice took on roughness. "Your daughter is past eighteen. She is of age; the law permits her to marry. She was not kidnapped, but came with Stuart of her own free will. You could not have restrained her. She has married Stuart, and I am afraid there is nothing we can do."

Joshua hobbled up to the Sheriff and Stuart, shaking as if with a palsy. He looked slowly from his daughter to Stuart, and then at the Sheriff. Then he cried: "Is there no justice for this seduction of my daughter, who has been guarded in her innocence and protected from such scoundrels? Is there no redress for a man entering another's house and stealing his treasure? Had the girl not been so guarded, so innocent, this would never have happened. She may be of age, so far as years are concerned, but her mind is still the mind of a child! I demand justice!"

The Sheriff made a wry face. "Mr. Allstairs, the law does not consider it kidnapping when a young female is of age, physically, and consents to marry her suitor, and is not concerned with what her male parent considers her correct mental age. You are not inferring that your daughter is an imbecile, and incompetent under the law?"

Joshua ground his teeth. His daughter gazed at him with that pleasantly smiling emptiness with which she surveyed all things. "Dear Papa," she murmured fondly, as though everything were natural, and her father had just delivered himself of commonplace remarks.

Joshua lifted his cane, swayed, shook his cane in the air, and cried out furiously: "I demand justice! There is a moral law as well as that written on the books! This man is a thief and a scoundrel, a lecherous roué whose name is a byword in detestable places, a mendacious and larcenous black-guard! He married my daughter for her fortune. He is in dire financial straits, and has used this innocent child to obtain money from me! That was his sole purpose in seducing and carrying her away!"

"Careful, careful", said the Sheriff sternly. "It will be Stuart who may have redress under the law for these remarks, and I give him this information freely."

But Joshua was beside himself with frustration and hatred and grief. "He suborned my employee! He induced, with his wiles, this man to deliver my daughter into his hands, my daughter who knows nothing of men! He bribed this man! This I learned only two hours ago, from a maid in the confidence of the wretch. Is there no justice for a robbed father, for a violated house, for a ruined child?"

He thumped his cane on the floor with uncontrollable rage. Tears ran over his withered cheeks. He lifted his cane and pointed to the sobbing Janie.

"Look at that woman, the woman he alleges is his cousin! He has attacked her feloniously, with homicidal intent! This took place when he brought by daughter to this iniquitous house. Ask her why this attack upon her person, a defenseless female, a widow with helpless children?"

The Sheriff automatically turned to Janie at Joshua's command. He muttered: "This does not change the matter." In a louder tone, he said: "Mrs. Cauder! A charge has been made. Will you kindly cease your weeping for a moment, and reply to a question or two?"

Janie had been well aware of what had been taking place, though she had continued to wail and beseech Heaven. Now she went off into fresh paroxysms of anguish, flinging herself back into her chair, covering her face with her hands, and praying in long thin screams. The Sheriff, very harassed, scowled at a staring maid and demanded that she bring smelling salts, and while efforts were made to calm Janie, the poor man turned to Stuart and shook his head with somber reproof. "How you do get into scrapes, Stuart," he said in a low, regretful voice.

Stuart grinned. But he was uneasy, and extremely embarrassed. He put his arm about his wife. He said: "Though it may appear ungallant, truth compels me to say that my cousin, Mrs. Cauder, is not always truthful in her allegations. I ask you, Bob, to bear this in mind when she recovers her delicate breath and can curse and lie with her usual dexterity."

Janie, having decided that she had displayed enough agony, flung back her tangled curls, wiped her cheeks, bowed her head, and was suddenly the silent picture of shame and distraught sorrow, all bereft and defenseless. The Sheriff took a step or two towards her.

"Mrs. Cauder, I beg of you to maintain your composure and answer a question or two. You have declared that Mr. Coleman made an attempt upon your life. Why was this?"

Janie's head bowed lower. Her breast heaved. "O dear God," she whimpered, "that I have had to come to a strange land, without a natural protector, for this! I am only a poor widow with four helpless children, and I listened, with all faith, to my cousin's importunities that I join him in America."

The Sheriff interrupted. "He promised you marriage, Mrs. Cauder?" he asked, incredulously.

Janie lifted her head. She was an excellent actress. She revealed a brave white face, quivering, pure, wet with tears. She looked at the Sheriff, humbly. She made her eyelids tremble, her lips shake. Very quietly she said: "Yes, he did that. He has promised me marriage several times, and as I am alone and defenseless and unaccustomed to the ways of the world, having always been protected by my dear papa and mama, I believed him."

She allowed fresh tears to run down her cheeks. "I believed him, sir! I believed him to such an extent that I gave him twenty thousand dollars of my small fortune, the fortune my dear mama gave me when I left England!"

"Oh, the rascal, the unprincipled creature, the monster!" groaned Joshua. "The thief and murderer! This robber of helpless widows and children, this seducer of pure young females!"

"Twenty thousand dollars!" exclaimed the Sheriff, in distress. He looked at Stuart, who had flushed heavily.

"Let me explain, Bob. She did not 'give' me the money. She knew that her fortune of approximately seventy-five thousand dollars would not last long in America, with four children to sustain. I offered her a share in my shops, though my partner was very reluctant. I was moved by only the highest motives, as she is my cousin, and I am her only male relative in America. An agreement was drawn up in proper terms, of which she is possessed. A copy is in our bank, where it may be examined at any time."

He continued, with rising anger and excitement: "As for my promises of marriage, that is a lie, and she knows it is! I made no promises to her!" He paused. A cunning look narrowed his eyes. "Ask her under what stress she claims I gave her these promises! Was it under seduction? Is she ready to confess that she cohabited with me in this house? Is she so ready to foreswear her good name—for a lie? For an advantage, is she prepared to make her name a byword in this city, her position untenable?"

Janie opened her mouth to scream, and then suddenly met Stuart's narrowed and gleaming eye, his nasty smile. His words rang in her ears.

The unpleasant expression increased on Stuart's face. He chuckled. "You can see, Bob, that my cousin is a virtuous woman, and though somewhat disturbed that her secret plans have gone awry, she cannot, for her own sake, falsely declare that she has been seduced by me in my own house, which she, a mature woman, entered of her own free will and desire. However excited she may be at this time, and disappointed, you will readily discern that she is all virtue and modesty, and that she spoke only under the stress of a vehement and hysterical emotion."

The Sheriff regarded Stuart suspiciously. He understood. He frowned. He shook his head, saying under his breath: "You should be more careful! Someday there will be a reckoning."

Triumphant now, filled with the toxins of excitement, Stuart turned to Joshua, who stood, blinking his eyes, confounded:

"As for you, you old dog, only the fact that you are now my father-in-law restrains me from decisive action against you. Thank your God for that. You have called me a thief. I can bring you to account for that, and sue you for a pretty sum. You have made false accusations against me, for which I could shoot you with impunity." He made a grandiose gesture, and smiled disagreeably. "But I am filled with Christian charity tonight. Out of the kindness of my nature, I shall refrain from prosecuting you, and giving you your deserts."

Janie was so filled with hatred, with insensate madness and frustration, that she could only cower in her chair and look at Stuart with an expression that resembled lightning in its menace and balefulness. It was a look that might have killed.

Stuart was rising very rapidly to the occasion. He continued, to Joshua: "I owe you very little, now. Within four weeks I shall receive a large sum resulting from a certain business transaction. I shall repay you all my just debts. You declared that I married your daughter for her fortune. Why, you gray old dog, I shall soon be able to sell you half a dozen times over!"

"Oh, the odious wretch! Oh, the liar and the rascal!" moaned Janie, wringing her hands.

But Joshua looked in silence at Stuart. He began to speak, almost whisperingly: "You have won just now. But this is not the end. There will come a day when there shall be a reckoning, and with God's help, I shall speed that day."

He turned to his daughter, and his voice was sincerely broken. "My love, you have seen what has taken place in this house. I am an old man, and you are my treasure, that

I have loved and guarded. You have deserted me, not of your own will, but because of your innocence. I ask you, for the last time, to leave this villain, who will destroy and ruin you, and return with me to your own dear home, where you will be protected against him." In strangled tones, he continued: "Come home with your papa, my darling!"

Stuart tightened his arm about Marvina. She leaned against him. She smiled fondly at her father. "Dear Papa," she said, in her honeyed voice. "Good night, dear Papa."

Joshua gazed at that empty face for a long and piercing moment, his heart in his wicked eyes. Then he bowed his head and turned away.

Stuart, glowing like the sun at midday, saluted the Sheriff. "Now, Bob, will you be kind enough to clear this house for me? I am weary, and I must put some medicine upon this hell-cat's scratches, or I shall surely die of the hydrophobia." He paused. "As for this woman, my cousin, and her children, they may stay in this house for twenty-four hours longer. Then they must leave. That is my order, which I can enforce."

He took Marvina's hand and led her from the room, past the servants and the Sheriff, and Joshua and Janie. They watched him lead her, watched the silken grace of her flowing garments, her dazzling smile, her look of adoration for her husband. She did not glance backwards, not even at her father, who groaned as if death had suddenly seized him.

The children were still on the stairway. They moved aside in dumb and stricken silence, as Stuart and Marvina ascended slowly. They looked at Stuart with pale young faces and wide eyes. He smiled at them benignly, and with indifference. He reached the stair where Angus and Laurie were standing, their arms about each other. The little girl's face was streaming with tears. But her blue eyes regarded Stuart steadfastly, shining in the warm dusk.

He never knew what made him pause there, beside the child. He only knew that something held him, made him stand there looking down at her, with the most curious plunging of his careless heart. And then he bent gently, and kissed her white cheek.

"Good night, my love," he said, softly, touching her golden hair.

As for Marvina, she stood looking at the children with her amiable and meaningless smile, nodded to them agreeably, and went on, Stuart following her.

They reached the door of Stuart's apartment. Stuart, his

pulses throbbing, stopped there on the threshold, and again took his wife's hand. He looked at her with intense significance and passion. She smiled at him, placidly.

"What nice little children, Stuart. I am sure I shall love them," she said.

Stuart could not speak. For the first time it dawned on him, faintly and disagreeably, that his wife was stupid. Abysmally stupid.

BOOK TWO

THE CHILDREN IN THE GATE

"His children are far from safety, and they are crushed in the gate, neither is there any to deliver them."—Job 5, Verse 4.

CHAPTER 26

ANGUS CAUDER picked up his medical books from under the counter and laid them on top of it. He passed his thin hands over his face, and sighed. All the juice and life were squeezed out of him, so that he felt dry and brittle and flaxlike. Even his mind was dry and dusty, laid over with the grime of old despair and hopelessness and acquiescence. He moved his tongue in his mouth, to alleviate the parched sensation which came from his soul.

The last customer had gone. Even the clerks had long ago closed the door behind them. Angus ran his finger over the top of his books, and sighed again. Then, with a tragic gesture, he pushed the books aside, and went into the back room which served as the offices of the shops. He walked with a slight stoop, for he was not strong, and he was too tall and thin. Nor were his movements full of the vitality and sprightliness of youth. He walked like an old man, heavy with years and stiff with ancient dejection.

Stuart, frowning over the ledgers, looked up and saw the youth. He smiled slightly, leaning back in his chair. He, too, was very tired. He smoothed his hair with both hands; there were a few wiry streaks of gray in its heavy long blackness with the curling ends.

"Finished, Angus? But, of course, it's nearly seven. What are you doing here so late?"

"There were some bolts to rewind, Stuart, of the new foulard."

The lamp on the desk threw its pallid light over the ledgers, and over the new panelled walls, for even here Stuart must have his elegance, his reassurance of luxury. In that wan circle of illumination, Angus stood in silence, his gray

199

eyes hidden, his pale and suffering face, lined even now though he was still so young, full of chronic reticence and pride. His mouth, always reserved and thin, was now a wide tight line with rigid corners, as if it was an iron gate forever barred against the spirit within and the joy without. His fine brown hair, sleek and longish, lay flaccidly on his narrow skull, and two or three strands streaked across his forehead with its noble contours and strong protuberances.

Stuart peered at him with furtive uneasiness. He lit a cheroot, and frowned at the panelled ceiling.

"You've been here six months now, Angus. How d'you like it, eh? The shops and all?"

"Very well, Stuart. It—it's very interesting. Isn't it?"

"Is it? You find it interesting, Angus?"

Angus hesitated. He moved on his long thin feet. He wore the black broadcloth and white linen of the other clerks, and they gave his emaciated body a funereal look. Against that blackness his hands, so slender and tapered, appeared waxen and lifeless.

He spoke formally: "People are always interesting, Stuart."

"Are they?" replied Stuart, wryly. He examined the end of his cheroot. "I think they're a damned nuisance, most of them. However, I'm glad you aren't dissatisfied.

He knew that the young man had come to him for a specific purpose, and he wondered what it was. Angus never volunteered any communication between them; his attitude was entirely withdrawn and negative, as a rule, in his dealings with Stuart.

When Angus remained silent, Stuart looked at him directly. "You are satisfied, aren't you, Angus?"

Angus dropped his head. "Please forgive me, Stuart, but I'm not. You see, Mama thinks I should have a little increase."

"Ah. She does, eh? And what does Mama suggest?"

At the note of irony in Stuart's voice, Angus flushed. He lifted his head and looked at Stuart arrogantly, though there was a faint quivering over his thin features. He said, and his voice trembled defensively, and with a pale affrighted anger: "Mama says that as she is a partner in the shops, and that as I work here, I ought to receive more than the other clerks." He hesitated. "She thinks I should receive at least three dollars more a week."

Stuart studied him curiously. "And what do *you* think, Angus?"

The youth was resolute, however. His gray eyes suddenly gleamed in the lamplight. "I think it should be five more, Stuart."

Stuart suddenly turned his attention again to his cheroot. He scowled, and cursed inaudibly. "The tobacco we get these days! Look at the damn thing!" He removed the chimney of the lamp and applied the tip of the cheroot to the flame, which wavered and darkened. "You have to have a conflagration to light cheroots now." He replaced the chimney, and puffed vigorously for a few moments. Angus watched him. A slight grim smile deepened, rather than alleviated, the hard straight corners of his young mouth. All at once he was complete steely hardness, and it was Stuart now who was on the defensive.

Stuart smiled on his young relative brilliantly. "Very well, then, I think I prefer your opinion—to your mama's. We shall make it five, beginning Saturday. How is that?"

"Thank you, Stuart," said Angus, coldly. He moved, preparing to leave. But Stuart turned to him fully, in his chair. As always, his movements were impetuous. Yet as he met Angus' hard gray eyes he was suddenly silent. He frowned, and it was not with annoyance. He coughed, with embarrassment.

"Angus, will you sit down a moment? I want to talk to you."

But Angus stiffened. "I am late now, Stuart. We dine at half past seven, you know. Mama will be annoyed if I delay her."

"Oh, we mustn't annoy Mama, of course! But I am expecting my carriage, and I'll drive you home. In about five minutes. You couldn't walk it so fast. I won't keep you long."

Angus did not speak for a moment, and then into his voice, neutral and indifferent, there crept a proud note. "Very well." He sat down stiffly on the edge of a chair near by, and waited, looking at Stuart with a dimly inimical expression. Stuart saw it. His embarrassment increased. But also his pity.

"You'll think it none of my business, certainly, Angus. But you and I were friends, once, a long time ago. I was always very fond of you. You know that, don't you?"

Angus was silent. But the harsh corners of his mouth moved in a repudiating smile, cynical and cold.

Stuart colored. He struck his palm on the desk. "You've

listened to false tales, Angus! That is evident. You must believe me that I've always been fond of you."

The lad moved, as if affronted, and appeared to be about to rise. But he said nothing. His eyes were like pale and polished stone as he regarded Stuart, and waited.

Stuart was becoming excited. That was bad for his liver, he recalled angrily. Well, to hell with his liver just now! He would make one try only, to rescue this young fool, to break down his ridiculous defenses.

"When you were fourteen, Angus, you confided in me that you wished to be a physician. A—friend, urged me to look after you; he charged me with encouraging and helping you. I resented the charge. Nevertheless, for his sake I remembered it—and for yours. Last June you were graduated from your school. I was surprised when your mama requested that you be admitted to the shops."

He paused. His low forehead wrinkled uneasily. Angus had listened, in wary silence, and while Stuart had been speaking, his young face hardened, become like shining steel. He still waited, his eyes fixed on Stuart.

"You've done good work in the shops, Angus. You have a keen mind and an understanding one. You've helped me with the books, and I look forward to turning more and more of them over to you. I find them onerous. Sam usually attends to them, but as you know, he hasn't been well since his lung fever last March. It will be some time before he can do a full day's work on the ledgers.

"Yes, you are doing well. You will eventually do excellently. But that isn't what I had hoped for, for you. You've left school now, and I fully expected that you would go to study with some good doctor. Like Dr. Dexter. I spoke to him last Spring, and he agreed to take you. You know that. What changed your mind? Aren't you interested in medicine any longer?"

Angus was still. But Stuart saw with what a convulsion his hands suddenly clasped themselves together in a movement as if he were wringing them. And then his hands were still, also, though still rigidly clasped together.

He said, in a voice without intonation: "It doesn't matter whether I am interested or not, or what I had wanted, or planned, Stuart. Mama can't afford to keep me in idleness any longer, and it is my duty to assist her."

"Damned nonsense!" cried Stuart, with his quick rage. "Your mama is receiving nearly six thousand dollars a year from her investment! Why, last year, if I remember correctly, it was over that. She hasn't touched her principal at all. Then, two years ago, when her father died, she received ten thousand dollars as her legacy. She has tucked that away, too, in her damned strong boxes. She can very well afford to let you do what you had always dreamt of doing."

Angus had straightened in his chair. His eyes sparkled with bitter affront. "Stuart, you don't know all my mother's affairs, and I—I consider it presumptuous of you to criticize her. You have forgotten there are three other children. She can't afford to pamper me. Bertie is only seventeen, Robbie is not yet sixteen, and there is Laurie, who is only eleven. The boys aren't finished with their school. Mama is sometimes very pressed. I must help her. It is my duty. To complain would be immoral. We must each put aside our hopes when they conflict with duty. We cannot ask others to suffer for us, and to deny themselves. Such selfishness is sinful and cruel."

Stuart's full face was dark with congested blood. "You mean you consider it sinful and cruel to oppose the unfeeling and insensible demands of a rapacious woman? Just because she is your mother?"

Angus rose. He had begun to breathe in short breaths. "Good night, Cousin Stuart."

But Stuart rose also, and stood before the door. "Angus, by God! This is the last time I shall appeal to you, and try to make you see what your mother is doing to you. I will have my say, and then you can go, and be damned to you!

"Your mother has always disliked you. You've never admitted it, in your fatuous devotion to her. She intends to ruin your life. She has already made you a dirty little money-grubber. Look at you! You're sick to death, to the very depths of you, you puppy! I've watched you in the shops, from this door. I've probed to your heart; I've seen your misery. Angus, you are dying on your feet. It wouldn't matter so much if it were only your damned miserable flesh. But you're dying inside, Angus. And you're letting a woman who hates you, who enjoys thwarting and murdering you, do this thing to you. To the idiot thing you call your soul. She is using your best instincts, your devotion and honesty and sense of duty, to destroy you."

He stopped, running out of breath. His treacherous heart was pounding in his chest, with great pain. Now, curse it, he would have to forego his whiskey tonight. He put his hand to his chest, and pushed it there, with instinctive pressure.

Angus had retreated from him, to the other side of the desk, and now only the lower part of his body was in the light. His face was in shadow. But out of that shadow the gray steel of his eyes flashed with scorn and cold outrage.

Stuart was trembling with violence. He drew a deep breath, tried for his own sake to control the vehemence of his voice, and said:

"You speak of duty. Damn it, you would agree with me that a man has only one soul. He must guard and protect it, lest he die. You will agree with me, there? And to guard and protect it, he must yield to its instincts. He must never step aside. You have always wanted to be a physician. You have the emotions of a devoted man, self-sacrificing and dedicated. That is the temper of your soul.

"Yet you are allowing this woman to destroy your soul, to make a grasping and greedy animal of you, an avaricious miser. I've seen you fondle the gold pieces that passed over the counter to you! I've seen you jingle them in your hands, and smile. You've put them away, lovingly. I've watched you. But they didn't put any light in your miserable face. They put ugliness there. The ugliness of a dying soul, Angus."

He had to stop. His breath failed him again. But his black and restless eyes, usually so careless and selfish, were bright with earnestness now, and impatient anger, and pleading.

Angus looked at him in silence. Stuart could hardly see his face. But he felt the boy's implacability and contempt.

Then he heard Angus' voice, thin but firm, and harsh. "Cousin Stuart, you speak to me of 'souls.' But you don't believe in souls, or in God. You are a bad man, and you know that in your heart, Cousin Stuart. I can't listen to you. Your words mean nothing to me."

He paused, while Stuart stared at him with incredulous hopelessness and fury.

"I've done my duty here, Cousin Stuart. I'll continue to do it, if you allow me to stay after this. You can always trust me. I want to learn the business, as my mother is one of your partners. I intend to make the shops my lifework. I want it that way. That is all I want. And I can't listen to anyone, least of all you, who would lead me astray, away from God and what I know is my duty. Holy exhortations never came from a faithless instrument. I can't believe that from you would ever come any sound advice or righteous guidance. What your motive is I do not rightly know, but I do sense that you are advising me to repudiate and defy my poor mother, who has devoted her life to her orphaned children. You are advising me to turn aside from my duty, and selfishly to pursue my own frivolous and unsanctified desires."

At this imbecility, Stuart was not freshly angered, but only sick with despair. He lifted his hand, as if to brush aside a swarm of gnats that meaninglessly buzzed and stung. He said, with passionate quietness:

"Angus, if your mother should refuse to allow you to study medicine, and you are afraid you will be left penniless, and thrown out of her house, you can come to me, with pleasure. I will help you. You can live in my house, and study with Dr. Dexter.

"I am your friend. I have never urged good deeds on anyone else but you. It is distasteful to me. A man should choose his own life. But you are so badgered, so confused, so fatuous, that you need help. I am offering you this help, from my heart."

But Angus cried, in a thin and shaking voice: "You have no heart, Stuart! You are a bad and faithless man! It is a sin to listen to you!"

He caught up his hat, and plunged towards Stuart, who instinctively moved aside, aghast. The boy seized the door handle, wrenched open the door, and fled. Stuart, standing there in the office, heard his wild and retreating footsteps running through the empty shops. He heard one last cry, as the outer door opened and shut.

He moved slowly towards his desk. He fell into his chair. His face was damp. He wiped it. Then he began to curse aloud, viciously, to curse himself and his folly. He felt weak and sick, after this encounter with this blinded young man, whom he had tried to help.

He opened a drawer in his desk, and recklessly produced a bottle of whiskey. He drank long and copiously. He needed it. He put the bottle away, and cursed aloud again, with richness and despair and rage. Oh, the damned young idiot, the cursed imbecile! Damn him to hell, and his mother with him! He deserved nothing better.

He locked up the desk. It infuriated him that his hand was shaking.

CHAPTER 27

STUART went out into the dead and ashen quiet of the November evening. A faint fog had drifted in from the Lakes, and every street-lamp floated in a rainbowed aura. The board walks were slippery and dark with moisture; the cobbled streets gleamed with a wet black luster. Every house showed rectangles of orange light. From a distance, carriages and wagons rumbled faintly, and with dim echoes. Not a soul could be seen.

Stuart, locking up the doors, glared at his full block of shops with that swelling rich satisfaction which never failed him. During the past five years or so, he had torn down the uneven line of chaotic little shops and rebuilt them on an even height of three stories, so that they appeared one long shining establishment. Indeed, he had cut doors in the walls so that one could travel from the main shop to the last on the street, without stepping outside. One could pass from the ladies' luxurious establishment into the boot shop, where ladies, choosing their own fine leathers, could be fitted for excellent boots by expert shoemakers and where their husbands and children could also be fitted; and from the boot shop to a fine millinery shop, a wonderful innovation for Grandeville ladies, who were accustomed to patronizing a pet dressmaker, who usually starved between hats. Stuart had employed these impecunious females, and had paid them miraculous wages, to their eternal devotion and gratitude. Now marvelous bonnets stood on stands in the windows, surrounded by lengths of gleaming velvets and heaps of artificial flowers and ribbons and feathers. Beyond these effete shops were hardware establishments, harness makers, furniture emporiums, feed shops, pantry staples, and even a meat shop. One of the larger shops was in the nature of a "general store," where the farmer could find almost everything, and could order anything from careful catalogs compiled by Stuart and Sam Berkowitz. In short, a family could enter the first shop and come out of the last, completely surfeited and supplied, and laden with bundles.

In a conspicuous spot, framed in a thick golden frame, were excerpts from large newspapers sent Stuart from several distant metropolitan centers, all praising him for his innovations and merchandising genius. These hung on the brocaded walls of the Ladies' Shop.

Stuart now employed twenty clerks, female as well as male, an innovation that had made Grandeville gasp. All were well-trained and elegant, and aware of their responsibilities as employees of America's strangest and most wonderful shop. They conducted themselves with the hauteur of nobility. To work for Stuart was not only to receive wages beyond the dreams of avarice, but to have a certain exclusive social patina bestowed upon them. They were not "degraded" by their employment. Nor was their love for Stuart the result only of his wages. They found him kind and understanding, tolerant and sympathetic. When he passed through the shops, he was followed by their adoring glances. He knew them all, and their families. He was never too busy to inquire about a sick member of these families, to send regards, to listen with concerned interest.

It was natural, therefore, that Stuart should be hated, justifiably, by other employers of labor. He was a "revolutionary, a Whig," a traitor to his class. He gave the working people, born only by the grace of a wise God to serve their masters, a false idea of their importance in the social scheme. Some ministers declared that it was sacrilegious to pay a clerk fifteen dollars a week, an incredible sum, when the usual just wage was about six or seven. He was making his employees stiff-necked, giving them strange ideas, and implanting in them sentiments unbefitting their station.

But despite these condemnations, and threatened boycotts, Stuart prospered. He had introduced another strange idea into merchandising: the Customer is Always Right. Heretofore, in Grandeville, among other merchants, and among merchants everywhere, the prevailing religion was *caveat emptor*—let the customer beware. But Stuart had another idea entirely. He sold sound merchandise at a sound price, and received a sound if modest profit. Should the merchandise prove faulty he exchanged it cheerfully, and with apologies, or refunded the money. The people of Grandeville, stupefied at first, came to trust him implicitly.

But Stuart was also very shrewd. He sold for cash only. No matter how high-born and wealthy the lady, she paid on the counter as did the small laborer or farmer. No credit was extended. The farmers, accustomed to running bills, might have complained ferociously had they not known that the lady in ermine, bowling along in her carriage, was compelled to open her reticule and disgorge as quickly as themselves.

"No bills, no arguments, no lost customers," said Stuart. "Besides, as they know, a man who sells for cash can sell cheaper, taking a smaller profit, and giving better goods."

At Sam's suggestion he started another innovation. A farmer, after harvesting, could deposit with Stuart a certain sum which he believed would cover his purchases for the year. (This cash-account was also extended to other urban customers.) At the end of the year the accounts were settled, and any surplus moved over to the next year, or refunded.

The great expansion of the Grandeville Supreme Emporium had, in the main, come from the one hundred thousand dollars which Mrs. Coleman had inherited on her twenty-first birthday.

Stuart was now a rich man. And, in proportion to his income, his expenses increased inordinately. As a result, he very seldom had a large sum of ready cash. The profits went back into the shops, and a considerable proportion was spent in his own peculiar fashion.

The railroad had been built to Grandeville, and Stuart used it at least twice a year to visit New York, there to arrange for shipments of new goods, to tour the shops for new ideas, and to amuse himself. The latter activity often cost him a small fortune. He was much esteemed by the lighter and more luxurious ladies of New York. Chicago, that great fulminating city on the Lakes, also knew him, as did Saratoga and the horses, of which he was very fond. New Orleans had seen him, too, and other Southern cities. One summer, not accompanied by Mrs. Coleman, he had gone to Paris.

He lived lavishly, with his wife and his one child, little Mary Rose, almost five years old now, whom he adored. He spared himself nothing. Therefore at thirty-four his girth had considerably thickened, his full ruddy face had become florid, his liver had shown angry indications of its outraged existence, and he had had one or two bouts of gout. Always a "fine figure of a man," he was now very imposing in his new weight and extremely flamboyant wardrobe, and the splendor of manner and appearance which had always distinguished him had now become lavish and overemphasized, much to the amusement of his enemies, of whom he had very many. Also, his generosity, his magnanimity, his reckless extravagance, did nothing to endear him to the conservative and the pious.

Stuart had built the compact and comfortable little convent behind the church of Our Lady of Hope, and had established a parochial school adjoining the convent. Here the children of the poor could be adequately educated, taught trades and needle-work, other revolutionary ideas which shocked the community for a long time. Stuart had offered to build a similar school for the Protestant poor children, and it was only after three long angry years that his offer was accepted, and then only after exhausting pleas on the part of Mayor Cummings. "He'll be opening schools for niggers, next," said many of the people, bitterly.

He had ideas for a public hospital, but this innovation had aroused so much opposition and horror that he had temporarily refrained. However, he discussed it often with Father Houlihan, who was enthusiastic. The nuns would nurse in the hospital, the priest had promised him, and Stuart had doubtfully considered the idea. Nevertheless, he studied plans for the hospital, and his determination grew.

No one but Father Houlihan and Sam Berkowitz understood this wild and contradictory man, this man of large and colorful inconsistencies and rages and blasphemies, of mercies and kindnesses and furies, of selfishnesses and obtusenesses and brutalities. They knew that his huge faults came from the excess of his virtues, that he could not endure to see suffering, so that for his own peace of mind he must alleviate it.

With it all, he was an eternal child. It was this childlikeness that made him stand, as he did now, this November evening, and stare smugly and joyously at his shops, never tiring in his admiration for his own accomplishments.

He had momentarily forgotten Angus. But when he saw his carriage waiting, he swore under his breath, and moved towards it, viciously striking the walk with his gold-headed cane. His temper was not soothed by the fact that he was having difficulty in fastening the middle button of his many-caped coat. Damn it, he had refrained from much drinking, and too much food, lately, yet his girth was not decreasing. He felt, with apprehension, the heat under his stock, and the wave of heat that ran down his back. It was that copious whiskey he had just taken, of course, and it was all that cursed young puppy's fault. His face, as he passed under a street-lamp, was very florid and sullen. In the folds of his cheeks the crimson was almost purple, as was the thickened roll of flesh under his chin. It was an over-full and dissipated face, reckless and violent. Fast living and indulgence made it a little difficult for him to spring with the old lightness into his carriage, and his anger against himself and Angus increased.

There had been an ominous throbbing in his right, and gouty, foot. Now it was subsiding. As the carriage rolled through the empty streets he became conscious of a healthy hunger. He must really begin to walk a few miles every night, as his doctor had ordered. He would begin tomorrow. He would drink nothing more tonight. He would have but one helping of good roast beef at dinner. He felt very virtuous, all at once. It was a villainous way for a full-blooded man to live, he meditated gloomily, especially that prohibition against too much dallying with the ladies. However, after leading the life of a monk for about six months, his doctor had assured him, he might resume a more normal way of living.

He had a visit to make before going home. The carriage turned down one modest street after another, in the south side of the city. After about half an hour, it reached the pretty white cottage of Father Houlihan.

The priest had been ill recently of an intestinal complaint, which had much exhausted him. There had been considerable typhoid fever in the city that summer. The priest was convalescent now, but his duties for some time had been taken over by his young assistant, one Father Billingsley, who also lived in the cottage. Stuart did not like Father Billingsley, who was young, intolerant, bigoted, overly zealous in making converts, and very severe and pious. In his turn, Father Billingsley did not like Stuart, though he was overawed by him, and afraid of him.

"A damned budding Jesuit if there ever was one!" Stuart had called him, and in his presence. He rarely addressed the young priest directly, but always referred to him in the third person and with rudeness and brutality. Father Billingsley was tall and emaciated in his black robes, with a long thin white face burning with religious ardor, and too-brilliant black eyes as fiery and restless as Stuart's own.

When Stuart entered the cottage tonight, not at all in a happy frame of mind, he took no pains to hide his black scowl of annoyance at seeing Father Billingsley beside Father Houlihan, before the parlor fire. The older priest, in dressing gown, shawl and slippers, was still very pale and flabby, and revealed, in his tired but still strenuous blue eyes, the effects of his recent illness. He was apparently weary. He greeted Stuart with simple pleasure, holding out both his hands. Father Billingsley, with a censorious expression on his white young face, silently testified that he had been "annoying" his senior, to use Stuart's expression. Stuart never understood the nature of the "annoying." He only knew that when he came Father Houlihan would sometimes appear weary and exhausted, but patient and sweet as always. Now Stuart scowled at the younger priest, ignored his formal greeting, and angrily demanded why his friend should resemble a damned skinned turnip again.

"My dear Stuart," said the older priest, fondly, pressing his friend's hand in both of his own hot palms. "I am really doing excellently. I gain strength every day. Perhaps I did too much reading this afternoon," and he rubbed his eyes apologetically.

"You look," said the rude Stuart, with a darkling glance at Father Billingsley, "like the underside of a flounder dead for a week. Hasn't Dr. Malone been in to see you again, as I ordered? He promised to be here every day, the cut-belly!"

"Now, Stuart, you know that's no name to call Dr. Malone, just because he insists that surgery can be extended to the abdomen, in defiance of medical opinion," said the priest, with an irrepressible smile. "Cut-belly, indeed! And it's you that was the lad that suggested that Dr. Malone shall head your hospital."

"He'll head nothing but the workhouse if he doesn't take better care of you!" exclaimed Stuart. "I'll be damned if I'm going to let anyone neglect you, or annoy you, or harass you in any way, whoever he is!" And again, his ireful eye glittered on Father Billingsley, who, frightened, drew himself up to his tall thin height and looked dignified and severe.

In gentle pity, Father Houlihan touched his junior's hand, and smiled at him. "No one can annoy me, as you say, Stuart, or neglect me, with this lad about."

Stuart, shrugging rudely, glared at the fire. The whole attitude of his big body suggested that he would prefer Father Billingsley's absence just now. But the younger priest, who for his conscience's sake could never forego an opportunity to sway Stuart's soul, would not leave, despite his own passionate desire to do so. He seated himself slowly, and his youth was suddenly revealed in his look of uncertain distress and melancholy. But his pale mouth set severely, and with dedication.

In an effort to restore the precarious peace, Father Houlihan said: "Dr. Malone has agreed to allow me to use your carriage, beginning tomorrow, if it is no imposition, Stuart."

"It shall be here promptly at two," Stuart replied, pleased

at the verdict. He sat down, and suddenly beamed on his friend. "God bless you, you old pirate! It'll be good to see you about again. And the Sunday and Wednesday games, too."

As Father Billingsley most decidedly did not approve of the Sunday card games, and had been horrified at them, Father Houlihan peeped at him apologetically.

"The poor box could be filled again," he suggested, "and with benefit."

There are men who can insult delicately. Stuart was not of this exalted class. His way of insulting Father Billingsley was to ignore him entirely, to speak over and about and around him. He did so now. He glared again at the fire.

"Well, it might soothe you to know you've given me the gout again, and set my blasted liver to doing capers, Grundy."

"I?" Father Houlihan was deeply concerned. He sat up in his chair, dislodging his shawl, which Father Billingsley, who really deeply loved him, adjusted with a sigh. "What have I done, my dear Stuart?"

"Oh, don't look like a startled corpse," said Stuart, with a short laugh. He reached over, took Father Houlihan's knee in his hand, and shook it gently. "I shouldn't have said that, you innocent. I only mean that I took your advice, and spoke to that puppy of an Angus."

"Yes?" said the priest eagerly, dropping the shawl again, and giving his junior another opportunity to readjust it. "And what did he say?"

Stuart began to laugh unpleasantly. "He practically consigned me to hell. Oh, I gave him all the arguments you had so carefully rehearsed to me. It did no good. I was a 'bad and godless' man. I had no 'faith.' I was leading the lamb astray, in suggesting he disobey his darling mama, God damn the bitch! He's as proud as Lucifer, the insolent popinjay, and as dull and dead as ditch-water. I tell you, he's done with all of us, and it's that strumpet's doing. She hates me like sin, though we've had an armed truce for the past few years, and everything is sweet and affable between us again. She had to do that, of course, or she'd never have had one invitation to dinner in the city again, or been accepted among my friends."

Father Houlihan lifted his hand with a pleading and painful gesture. Father Billingsley looked aghast at this coarseness and vulgarity and sinful talk.

"Stuart, please tell me all about Angus."

So Stuart told the whole disagreeable story, with gestures and profanity. Father Houlihan watched him. And then the priest knew that Stuart was deeply hurt, much more hurt than he would ever confess, even to himself.

"Curse it, I liked the lad! Grundy, you know I did. He and that poor darling little Laurie. I loved the little lass. I saw her with her mama in the shops, a week ago, a love of a child. Ah, what a beauty she will be, what a belle, what a heartbreaker! It's no use, Grundy. Janie's poisoned the children against me. I can't help them again."

"The children in the gate," murmured the priest, with deep sorrow. He wrung his hand in the shawl.

"Eh?"

"Never mind, my boy. It—it is very sad. You cannot keep after him, then?"

"No. I'm convinced that if I try it he will leave the shops, in spite of the increase in wages. He's that sort. Proud, stiff-necked, stupid and righteous. I'm afraid his soul's gone to damnation, Grundy." He grinned, wryly. "You should see him around the tills! With the devil's own look of gloating."

Father Billingsley cleared his throat timidly. "One mustn't desist in the saving of souls," he muttered, looking at Stuart.

But Stuart looked only at the older priest, and said with brutal sarcasm: "I think, Grundy, the saving of souls should be left to those competent to do it."

Father Billingsley flushed. He dropped his eyes; his mouth drooped. Father Houlihan said, pleadingly: "I wish you could do more for the lad, Stuart. I know I'm not competent enough to tell you how to do it. You know all the circumstances better than I. I can only pray. And some day, I feel, my prayer will be answered. In the meantime, do what you can, if it is only a little."

Stuart stood up. He said, with brutal insinuation: "I'm no busybody. Let a man save or lose his soul in his own good time, and by his own choice, and be damned to him. That's his own affair. Any man who tries to interfere is a —— in skirts. In skirts," he repeated, with heavy emphasis.

Father Houlihan saw, with compassion, that his junior's pale young lip was actually quivering, that he was trembling. He leaned back in his chair and closed his eyes. "Ah, well," he sighed. "We shall see what prayer can do. In spite of what you say, Stuart, I know you won't neglect the lad.

"And now, Stuart, that other matter. Have you found out anything about this organization which calls itself the 'Know-Nothings'?"

Stuart was aroused by the previous conversation to new heights of insult. "I've talked about it with other men, and done some questioning. All I know so far is that it is, as you have said, an anti-Catholic, an anti-foreign, organization. And a nasty, disgusting, brutal organization of cut-throats, liars, ignoramuses and dolts. Led, believe it or not, by our clergy. There have been some inflammatory sermons in the churches, even in Grandeville."

He continued: "I know nothing about it. I know only that when the country's seething, as this one is seething about the slavery question, lunatics try to divert the national temper by finding it an easy victim, one that can be murdered and hung and beaten without any bloodshed on the part of the attackers, and without danger of the law. The country's getting roiled up about slavery, and there'll be hell to pay very soon, I'm thinking. The powerful fellers know this; they don't want war, or any other trouble, with the South. So they've thought up the Catholics to divert the people, and give both North and South something on which they can vent their rising tempers with impunity. Intolerance, as you told me, is like a leech on a bad bruise; it sucks out the blood. The powerful fellers have thought up the Know-Nothings as a leech, to keep the people from war over the blackamoors."

"Yes, yes, of course," said the priest, in anguish. "It is an old device of the oppressors, this diverting of the people's righteous indignation into harmless if bloody paths, this finding of a victim whose sufferings will not matter. It is done in Russia." He smiled up sadly at his friend. He patted one of the hands on his shoulder. "Stuart, you are a good man. I know. God bless you. Do what you can."

When Stuart had gone, he turned to Father Billingsley, who was now at the exploding point, and he said sternly: "Our hands are not clean, Father. God knows, they are not clean. There was much in what Stuart said. Let us take it to our hearts. For the sake of our souls. For the sake, perhaps, of our very lives." He added, in a suddenly clear and passionate voice, ringing and strong: "There is room for all of us here, all men with good will in their hearts, all the oppressed and the suffering! Let us not hate each other, and incite one against the other, because we differ in our gods and our ways of life. Who is so presumptuous as to say who is right, and who is wrong? Let us beware of hatred, lest it turn and rend us who give it birth!"

CHAPTER 28

IT WAS not in Stuart's nature to be meddlesome. He detested those who were continually anxious about the welfare of others. To him, that was presumption. Further, he believed that those who cannot help themselves are in some way contemptible and weak. To aid them was to increase their irresponsibility.

But Father Houlihan's gentle, or angry and bellowing importunities (returned in furious kind by Stuart) finally reduced him to the point where he decided that he would call upon Janie to desist from her pressure upon her son. After he had made this decision, he was so enraged that he was unendurable. God knows he had troubles enough of his own, financial and private. Was he not married to humanity's worst example of congenital idiocy? Did he not have a darling child whose health did not improve despite the waters of Saratoga and long sojourns in the mountains? Were not women hell's own brew, exigent and bottomless and inexhaustibly rapacious? Had he not his own liver to contend with, and a damned partner who was always going over ledgers and meanly advising less borrowing and less extravagance? It was the devil's own life. His plans were all awry. Joshua Allstairs had not relented. Stuart seldom saw him, and then only at a great distance. He heard no ominous rumors of him, but Stuart could see him, like a gray spider, crouched in his horrible house, biding his time, plotting the hour of vengeance when he could hurl Stuart down forever. It was nerve-wracking to think of him in that house, silent, watching, waiting, and sometimes the suspenseful vision was intolerable so that Stuart had wild dreams of rushing to that house and crying out that he move now, speak now, do what he would, and God damn him, anyway!

"You haf only to be calm, to be careful, not to spend foolishly, conserve and watch," urged Sam. "Nothing can hurt you then, my Stuart."

It was useless to explain to anyone, and especially to Sam with his disciplined dream, that for one like Stuart to "conserve, to be careful," to be thrifty and provident, was worse than dying, that he would choke in the atmosphere of pennywatching, that he would stifle should he have to guard his

215

expenditures. When he merely considered that a diamond bracelet for a favorite lady might be an extravagance, or a lovely piece of French glass or an ancient rug might better not be purchased just at this time, he was thrown into a veritable frenzy of melancholy and despondency, so that he became frantic and life seemed one vast prisonhouse of crusts and water and drabness. He filled his house with gorgeous and beautiful things, feverishly piling them up as a hunted man piles furniture high against an oaken door, to prevent his pursuers from breaking in and seizing him. Only Father Houlihan and Sam knew that these were the frantic gestures of a man terribly afraid of poverty and of life, most terribly afraid of other men.

He was often completely and artlessly surprised to discover that there were other things to fear besides poverty and starvation. Incredulously, he almost believed it when it was explained to him that some men feared the loss of prestige, of love, of health, of family, of friends, of position and of power. Some men, he was hugely amused to learn, even feared the loss of the love of God!

He hated those who had no money, for they subtly threatened him, said to him silently: "So is it possible for you to be, without dignity, hope, pride or salvation, the prey of the foulest man with gold in his pockets." And out of this hatred was born his compassion, and not paradoxically.

The more money he obtained, the wider and wilder grew his extravagances, for he needed constant assurance of his invulnerability. With this drunkard's need upon him, and his mystic terror of Joshua, and the imbecility of his wife, and the frailty of his little daughter, and Sam's constant and anxious cautioning, Stuart could irately, and with truth, declare that he had "enough troubles of his own, curse it, without meddling with the lives of others."

Nevertheless, one pewter-bright December Sunday he went to Janie's house.

He had set out calmly enough, in his carriage, grumbling and cursing under his breath, gnawing his lip and glowering about him, but able, at moments, to bow to some passing acquaintance, and to wink at some properly chaperoned young girl bowling along in her own carriage with her oblivious mama. But the closer he came to Janie's house, the more ireful he became, the more embarrassed. Finally he passed a favorite saloon. It was closed on Sundays, of course. But for regular and favored patrons it preserved a discreet backdoor. It was early, hardly four o'clock, and Stuart had grimly followed his doctor's advice that there was to be no drinking until the evening dinner had been eaten. However, when he saw the saloon he recklessly decided that he needed a drink, several of them, before approaching Janie.

He left his carriage, went through the back alley to the rear door, knocked on it three times with his cane. It opened immediately, and he was admitted to the rear room. It was already filled with his particular cronies, who hailed him with delight.

Soothed, happy and flattered, as only a simple man can be soothed at the signs of favor of his contemporaries, Stuart seated himself at a large round table and lavishly ordered drinks for himself and the five other men about him. A violent political argument was in progress, and Stuart soon, and exuberantly, found himself participating.

He, himself, had been an ardent Whig, but had joined the new Republican Party after its formation in 1854. He had energetically campaigned for its first Republican candidate, who had been defeated a month ago by James Buchanan, Democrat, and fifteenth President of the United States. Stuart felt personally affronted and outraged by the elections, and now he darkly hinted that he was privy to some secret confidence about them. "Mind my words," he said, glowering about him, "there was dirty work there. I'm not at liberty to reveal what was told me by an exalted personage of high importance, but I was given to understand that the South had much to do, and not honestly, with the election of a Democrat. The pro-slavery clique. That isn't the worst of it, either. This personage, this close friend of mine, always in touch with Wall Street, earnestly assured me that next year we shall have a financial panic. We always have 'em when a Democrat is elected."

"You mean," said a friend cynically, "that the Democrats just come into a depression caused by your friends, the Whigs, and so get the blame for it."

The argument became hot. This Buchanan, with his love for the Southerners, would stimulate the already inflamed ill-feeling between the Southern States and the North. Hadn't pro-slavery men just sacked Lawrence, Kansas? Hadn't John Brown, that madman, recently massacred five pro-slavery men by Pottawatomie Creek? How much more of this could go on without the whole country bursting into flames? It was all the doing of the Democrats of course.

"It's your nigger-loving Republicans that're causing all the trouble," disagreed another man.

"I don't love niggers!" cried Stuart, after a fiery gulp of whiskey. "But I don't want any goddam war, and unless we keep our heads we shall have it!"

Another man nodded gloomily. "What about this here Dred Scott decision? Throw the whole damn country into turmoil. You'll all see."

"All I want is to make money, fairly, and in peace!" bellowed Stuart, banging on the table with his fist. "I don't want to get embroiled in any sanctimonious sentimentality about the Rights of Man, and slavery, and high principles! Damn it, there's trouble enough in the world without going out with swords and banner to find it, and all in the name of God and justice, too!"

But a young man, with a serious and lighted face cried: "That is the credo of all the bloated and selfish men in the world! 'Am I my brother's keeper?' they asked, elbow-deep in money. 'Go away; don't bother me. I have my business, my shop, my factory, my mill, to attend to, and my notes to meet. God? Justice? Mercy? Decency? What are they? Will they bring me money, increase my bank account, my property? No? Then I'll have none of them.'"

He looked at them all, somberly, at Stuart, who was grinning sardonically, and at the other three men. "And then," he added, "comes the chaos, the ruin and the death, the just punishment for such selfishness and greed. Do not think for a moment, my friends, that when the day of reckoning comes, as it will, you will escape."

The thought was so depressing that Stuart ordered another round of drinks. He reiterated: "I don't want war. Who does? Why can't fools shut their mouths? I'm not interested in slavery. I've never thought much about it, except as a bone of contention. I have an idea! Why don't the sanctimonious anti-slavery fools pay every planter for his slave, a decent price, and then free the blackamoors? After all, the planters have a huge investment in their slaves. It's wrong, and incredible, that anyone should suggest they free their slaves without just recompense. It—it's un-Constitutional, by God!"

"Listen to the foursquare American patriot!" jeered another man. "How long've you been in this country anyway, Coleman? What do you know about America? You, an Irishman!"

At this insinuation as to his Americanism, Stuart started from his chair with clenched fists, his face suffused. Two of his friends rose with him, and grasped his arms. Others in the room, delightedly smelling a violent fight, stared and turned their chairs about. That Coleman! That Irishman! He couldn't remain in a room five minutes without exploding. It was very diverting. One of the barkeeps hurried out of the room to call reinforcements.

Stuart, struggling with his captors, who exhorted him to calm himself, let his furious eyes dart about the room. And then, all at once, he was rigidly still.

At a far table, oblivious, sunken into a drunkard's stupor, sat a very young man, his head bowed, an empty bottle and glass before him. The glimmering lamplight shone on his head of thick, light auburn curls, and on his slack and ruddy young face and closed eyes. He was a big fellow, dressed in the height of fashion in fawn-colored pantaloons and darker coat and elaborate ruffles. He sat there, in his stupor, unaware of the riot which had suddenly started at Stuart's table. Beside the bottle lay his tall beaver hat, his cane and gloves. On his finger a rich jewel glittered.

Stuart stood and stared at him, paling, while his friends loosened their grasp on him, uneasily, and then followed his eyes. One of them began to laugh, uncomfortably.

"He's here all the time, soaking it up," he said. "A damn young drunkard. Spends a fortune; always alone, too. Haven't you seen him here before, Stuart?"

But Stuart flung off the arms of those who held him, and went over to the table of the young man. The others in the room, sensing his great consternation, and seeing his grim silence, watched with intense interest. Stuart was unaware of any of them. He stood by the table and looked down at Bertie Cauder, Janie's Benjamin, Janie's darling, sleeping the sodden and drivelling sleep of drunkenness.

Stuart pulled out a chair and sat down. He felt sick. He had very rarely noticed Bertie, but on his infrequent encounters with the youth he had liked his debonair air, his merriment, his constantly twinkling blue eyes, his attitude that life was an extremely good joke, and very enjoyable. Nothing ever seemed to disturb him; Stuart had never seen him without a wide smile, and a laugh. He was very popular in his school; he had many friends. His ways were winning and charming, and he softened everyone, even the most suspicious and dour. He laughed at his mother's rages; he laughed at Angus, with his solemnity, and bitter pride and silences. He laughed at his favorite brother, Robbie, and the "black one's ambitions." He laughed at everything. He was like a smooth silver mirror dancing in sunlight.

And now he was here, in his drunken sleep, and evidently not for the first time. It was not to be wondered at, thought Stuart, bitterly. He had no other occupation; he had no ambitions. He was a weakling, and a sot, like many charming, laughing people, whom everyone loved.

Nevertheless, Stuart's violent heart was stricken, for some nameless reason. He felt angered, and full of pity and disgust.

He picked up the empty bottle, and flung it from him, with a crash. He looked at the drooling, half-smiling mouth of Bertie Cauder, at the reddened and flabby cheeks. Yet all at once he was no longer angered. It was such a young face there, unconscious, fallen into a drunkard's dream, a vulnerable face, and tragic.

He laid his hand on Bertie's shoulder, and said in a low voice: "Come on, come on now, Bertie! Let me take you home."

But Bertie merely tilted gently on his seat and would have fallen to the dirty floor had not Stuart caught him in his arms. The lad's head rested against Stuart's ruffles, like the head of a sleeping child. Stuart looked down at the moist bright curls, and he cursed inwardly, almost with a sob.

He saw the shadow of someone else beside him, and he looked up, blinking the dimness from his eyes. Bertie's brother, "the black one," Robbie, stood there, composed and reticent, and with such damnable and indifferent assurance. Robbie was still undersized, though he was nearly seventeen, with a mature if small dark lean face and with wise and cynical black eyes which saw everything and were disturbed by nothing. Everything in that face was delicate and attenuated, full of a peculiar aristocracy, a carved refinement. His expression was reserved, but without Angus' harsh pride and melancholy, and his delicate mouth, mobile and thin, smiled slightly. He did not follow the prevailing mode of longish hair; his own black sleek head was cropped very short, and gleamed like a seal's. One saw every fine bone of the thin temples and the sharp small cheeks and chin. His nose was fragile, excellently cut. In his garb, also, there was reserve and aristocracy; his pantaloons and coat were all of the best black broadcloth, his linen severe and white, without ruffles, his folded black stock without a pin.

"So," he said, "he's at it again. I often come here for him. There is a room at the side, Stuart, where he—'rests'—until I can take him home. With your help I'll take him there, if you please."

A dark flush of hatred suffused Stuart's hot face. Robbie,

as always, made him feel clumsy, too large, stupid and heavy, and very, very gaudy and absurd.

"If this has been going on, why hasn't your blessed mama done something about it?" he shouted, oblivious of the interested audience. "And you, you popinjay! I thought he was your pet brother. Why haven't you done something?"

Robbie looked at him with indifferent gravity. "That is what I am trying to do, Stuart," he said quietly, with a note of reproof in his toneless voice. "If you please!"

He took one of Bertie's arms; Stuart seized the other roughly. They hauled the unconscious Bertie to his feet. Half dragging, half carrying him, they opened a door and entered a chill dark little room in which there were a number of chairs, a table, and a sagging sofa. Robbie was all calm. He craned after them as they entered the outer room. His manner consigned them to the limbo of creatures who do not matter, who have no existence unless it is granted to them by those who might acknowledge it. He closed the door quietly behind him. His gestures were all authority and composure.

They sat Bertie on the sofa, his sagging back against the wall. From him came gusts of sour whiskey. He dropped his head on his chest and sighed. His hands hung down limply beside him, large white hands, jewelled and well-kept, like a woman's.

Stuart stood helplessly beside the sofa, his disgust and rage rising. He was still burning from the hated small Robbie's manner. Quite viciously, then, he lifted his hand and struck Bertie smartly on first one cheek then the other. "You dirty sot!" he exclaimed. "You miserable, worthless young jackanapes! You puppy! Wake up, you young dog, and be ashamed of yourself!"

Robbie seated himself on a stiff chair near by and studied Stuart with a faint dark smile. One of his little hands played with the chain of his watch, which stretched across his waistcoat of flowered black silk.

"He wakes up quite soon, Stuart," he said composedly. "Don't agitate yourself, I beg of you. If you will sit down for a little while, unless, of course, you have other and more pressing engagements, you will have the pleasure of having him hear you."

Savagely, Stuart tore a chair away from the table, thumped it down at a considerable distance from Robbie, and stared at the youth with fury.

"Your pet brother! He is so much your pet that you cannot watch him!"

Robbie glanced at his brother quietly. For an instant, only, his keen black eyes softened, and his smile faded. Then he said, still looking at Bertie: "I am indeed very fond of him. He is happy. Who am I to interfere with his happiness?"

"You can say that?" said Stuart, aghast, fulminating. "You think a drunken stupor is happiness? You think if a man makes a spectacle of himself, and degenerates into such degradation, no one should try to prevent it?"

Slowly, calmly, Robbie looked at him. He studied him in silence. He appeared all meditation. Then he said: "It is apparent that you do not understand, Stuart. You think it can be prevented, that he can be aroused to shame, that exhortations can save him. I tell you, nothing can be done."

Again he studied Stuart, who stared at him stupidly. "For example, Stuart," he continued, his hand delicately playing with his chain. "you drink. But you are no drunkard, in spite of the undoubtedly large quantity of spirituous liquors you consume. You see, then, there is a difference between you and Bertie: you, who drink, and Bertie, who is a drunkard. Is the distinction too fine?"

"You talk like a conceited young ass," said Stuart rudely.

Robbie smiled, and shook his head in polite denial. "Perhaps I have not made myself clear, Cousin Stuart. I have made a study of such matters. I have talked long with our physician, Dr. Gibson. There is a literature of sorts on the subject, which I have closely inspected.

"For instance, as I have said—and with no offense meant —you are a drinker. But you always have a reason for drinking. You are angered: you drink a few glasses. You are depressed, and always for a good and sufficient reason: you drink a certain amount. Whiskey is an anodyne for you, numbing the too sharp sensations which afflict you. When they are numbed, you no longer drink. You drink with friends, for joviality and good-fellowship. In short, you drink, but always for some reason." He paused. "But Bertie needs no reason, no reason at all. That is why he is a drunkard."

Stuart continued to stare at Robbie intimidatingly, but also with confusion now. He felt his whole big body awkward and too cumbersome, in the presence of that small and precise elegance, which was too wise.

Robbie continued calmly: "There is another distinction between you and Bertie, not too subtle a one. You like the taste; you enjoy it, not only for the effect when you are disturbed or in good company. No drunkard enjoys liquors. He loathes them; they gag him. A man who enjoys his drinks is always in control of himself. But a man who drinks, and drinks alone, for no discernible reason, is a man who cannot stop."

This was all too much for the simple Stuart. His head whirled. He glowered at Robbie. "I suppose," he said with elaborate and futile sarcasm, "that none of you has ever exhorted this young fool to be a man?"

Robbie's smile was gently thoughtful. "There you have it, Stuart. Bertie does not want to be a man."

"Eh?"

"Exactly, Cousin Stuart. He does not want to be a man. At intervals, he feels the pressure upon him to be a man, the pressure within himself. He resists. His resistance is drink. When he drinks he becomes utterly irresponsible, incapable of being a man, freed from the necessity. He becomes a child again, one who must be cared for, guarded, loved and protected. No one expects him to 'stand on his own feet.' He becomes again the heedless child."

Now he folded his hands slowly on his lap and contemplated Stuart with detached reflection. "Who can make Bertie strong? He was born with that soft core of weakness in him. Nothing can strengthen him. Nothing can harden that cheesy core. We are impotent to help him. He alone can help himself. And I doubt even that. The inherently weak man has no will. He does not want a will. He does not want to face the hardships and adversities and duties and responsibilities of adulthood. Nothing can make him want to face them. It is useless. We can only keep him happy until he dies of his affliction."

"You are a cold-blooded young devil!" exclaimed Stuart.

Robbie shook his head in gentle denial. "I am a realist, Cousin Stuart. I am not insensible to the misery of our poor flawed Bertie. But there is nothing I can do. I can only stand by, and assist him when his childishness leads him into such predicaments."

Stuart stared at Robbie in silence, with something like humble fear, and with much helpless hatred.

Robbie looked at his brother with a cool anxiety. "He must have drunk a great deal, this time. He has been away from home since morning. This bout began four days ago. Usually four days are enough. Yet this is the fifth day, and he is still drinking. I suppose I shall simply have to wait until he is able to walk."

Stuart stood up. His depression was heavy upon him. "I have my carriage near by. I was going to call upon your mother, anyway. We can take Bertie."

"Why, thank you, Stuart," said Robbie, composedly. "That is a relief. Will you assist me? I think we can carry him out, between us."

He stood up, also. Stuart hesitated, scowling. "Your—mother. What does she think of all this, eh?"

Robbie shrugged, delicately. "Sometimes she thinks he is a 'braw laddie.' That is when she is in a good temper. She admires a man who drinks; it is manly, I believe is her opinion. Then when she is not in a good temper she berates him, even strikes him. I have seen her beat him with her slipper, and have heard her curse him. That is because she does not understand."

"She gives him too much money!"

Robbie smiled, as at some absurd remark from a child. "I assure you that if Bertie were not given money, he would sell anything, or rob anyone, for the money with which to drink. Mama has some regard for my opinion. I have persuaded her that withholding money will do no good, so, for the family name, and for Bertie himself, it would not be wise to limit his allowance, or completely deprive him of money. He will only bring disgrace upon himself, and upon us. No, it is better for him to be able to buy what whiskey he needs. And I assure you, Stuart, he desperately needs it. After such bouts, I always take home a bottle for him, or he would surely die, or go mad."

"Have you had your minister talk to him?" demanded Stuart, fuming, unwilling to accept the cold and terrible verdict which Robbie had pronounced on his brother.

Robbie compressed his lips, to keep from smiling again.

CHAPTER 29

It was Angus' custom to read to his mother every Sunday afternoon. He did not approve of her choice of literature, but he had the gift of resolutely closing his very consciousness to that which he did not desire or wish to acknowledge. He could read aloud for hours, in a grave, well-modulated and excellent voice, and not have a single conception or memory of the thing he had read. The voluptuous scenes narrated in the yellow-backed "French" novels passed over his awareness like unnoticed clouds. The amorous bedroom encounters did not make a solitary blush rise to his pale and virgin cheek. Sparkling and witty dialogue left him immune from humor. Janie would sometimes watch him with wry and amused interest as he read, and was always baffled at the lack of disconcerted embarrassment or discomfort. She would lie on her chaise-longue, her lacy scarf or shawl over her thin shoulders, and help herself to a plate of bon-bons, or sip tea, and listen attentively and with enjoyment.

She was nearly forty now, and needed spectacles to assist her lengthening sight, her inability to read small print. But her vanity, her hatred and fear of age, would not submit to this need.

So she would half-recline comfortably, and have Angus read to her. He did not find it onerous, though a few times he had gently suggested passages from the Bible and decorous books suitable to the Sabbath. Janie's prompt, and very rowdy and very blasphemous, rejection had made him wince, and he never mentioned the subject now. She would sometimes study him idly or with cynical conjecture as he read, sitting near her in a stiff armless chair, his hands holding the book high, his somber young face expressionless through all the tawdry or passionate text.

On this particular Sunday Janie was in quite good humor. Outside, the sky was like polished pewter, brilliant with diffused sunlight. The black and sinewy arms of trees formed an intricate pattern on the shining panes of window glass near which she lay on her chaise-longue. She could glance down at the Sabbath silence of the street below, and bemusedly watch the glittering carriages that occasionally rumbled over the cobbles. In the distance, the cross on the steeple of a church flashed in reflected light. Soft bells announced Vespers. A fire crackled on the marble hearth, and threw long rosy spears on the solid black furniture, which was all comfort and pleasant ugliness. Her canopied bed was white, covered with lace flounces and little pillows. The draperies at the windows were rose-strewn silk, and very rich and heavy, in accordance with Janie's taste. By her elbow stood a little table on which reposed a tea-tray and contents. (She had taught her cook the art of making scones.) There was marmalade there, a pitcher of thick cream, hot tea in a Limoges teapot, the scones, a plate of seed-cake, and a round silver bowl of sugar. The tea steamed; the fire chuckled; the pewter sky brightened; the bells filled the air with a sweet murmuring; the house was quiet. Only Angus' voice went on, fluid, eloquent, and very clear. It took only a little imagining to make her half-believe that she was home in England, and not in an alien land at all.

She had bought this tall narrow brick house shortly after leaving Stuart's fabulous mansion. In a spirit of contrition (for he was warmhearted), he had been able to purchase this house for her at a substantial saving over the original price. It was ugly, three stories in height, with narrow dark halls and unexpected thin staircases, and tall box-like rooms. But it was also very comfortable, warm in winter, cool in summer, and for Grandeville, amazingly dry. Gloomy, dull, blank-faced, with a wooden verandah, high slit-like windows, carved fretwork and little stone excrescences at those windows called balconies, it was properly respectable and stood on the second-best fashionable street, surrounded by almost identical neighbors. The lawn before it was narrow, enclosed in privet hedges (brown now, in December), and surrounded by huge dank trees. But there was considerable ground, and a garden in the rear, and a good stable and other buildings. The street was called Porter Avenue, and was quite near the river. It was also near The Front, where a garrison of soldiers was maintained, suspiciously aware of Canada, and Janie could hear the evening taps very clearly, and sometimes the morning reveille. This never failed to excite and interest her. Quite often the garrison would march through the river streets, very rigid and stern, with drums beating and fifes playing and flags fluttering, and the officers very handsome indeed on their black horses. There was one, especially, with great black mustaches and excellent shoulders, who always saluted her when he pranced by, as she leaned from her upper window to watch. It was very romantic.

She had only two servants, and did much work herself, polishing the many silver articles, mending, embroidering and doing considerable creation in needle-point with her skilled needle. She loved order and cleanliness, and was not in the least averse to assisting in obtaining this desirable state. Her natural vigor, which had not abated with the years, found a happy outlet in this work.

All in all, she was quite content. She had the happy faculty of adjusting herself to circumstance, and enjoying herself wherever she was. She was much admired in Grandeville, especially by the gentlemen, and as she was hospitable, amusing and gay, invitations to dine with her were eagerly accepted. For the first time in her life she had been careful to cultivate female friendship, and had many sincerely devoted friends, and practically no enemies. Janie was not one to kick against the pricks. Like wine, she filled the goblet of her environment, and sparkled invitingly in it.

At first she had thought she might marry. But none had pleased her among these beefy merchants, tanners, horse-traders, butchers, bankers and manipulators of land. Moreover, Grandcville air seemed conducive to longevity among Grandeville females, so there were few widowers.

She carried off her old humiliation very well. After a short interval she had invited Stuart and his new wife to dine, and gave a party for them. During that dinner she had been a most perfect and engaging hostess, showering beaming looks of affection on "dear Marvina," chiding Stuart affectionately for having neglected his "family" during the period of his ecstatic honeymoon, gently forgiving him with an arch look, imploring her guests to love and pardon him, with glances that were very touching. All in all, she carried it off excellently, and Stuart, red-faced and confused, was grateful to her.

She even deceived Stuart, so that he invited her alone, artlessly believing in her reformation. His first visits had been received with abuse, upbraidings and curses. He had vowed never to come again. But Janie, with a crafty narrowing of her evil green eyes, had burst into laughter, and had shouted: "You would not dare, you blackguard!" However, though he did visit her alone, for the sake of appearances his visits were few and far between. Later, a precarious peace prevailed between them, and then Janie began to enjoy his company. With him she could be natural. She knew he was afraid of her, that he hated her. But she also knew she could amuse him.

She visited him and Marvina, and was openly affectionate with the girl, so that Marvina quite adored her. And always she brought one of her children, sometimes more.

The prosperity of the shops assured her quite a respectable income, which she administered shrewdly, for she had a natural business acumen. The rest of her money reposed in one of Joshua's banks, and brought in a pleasant interest. She had even bought some land, on Stuart's advice, and had sold it at a profit.

There was much reason for her contentment, then. If her

mind continually schemed and plotted, the evidence was not yet. Her great health and vitality made her enjoy life, enjoy every day, as no "truly virtuous" woman would have enjoyed it.

She enjoyed these Sunday afternoons when Angus read to her for hours after an enormous, well-served, well-cooked dinner. Sometimes she drowsed; she would lean her red head back on the pillows, and smile softly in her half-dreams. She was mistress of every situation.

She did not drowse today. The novel was too exciting, and the incongruity of Angus reading the purple passages too amusing.

She watched him, grinning, as he read:

"And now, attired for the night in a loose white silken robe, which revealed all the pearly and innocent wantonness of her limbs, Lady Isobelle moved to her casement and looked down upon the moonlit gardens. Her black hair flowed over her marble shoulders in streams of ebony. She flung open the casement, and the moonlight streamed in silver fire over the gentle roundness of her half-concealed breasts. She raised her eyes to the stars, and implored aloud: 'Let him not come to me tonight, dear loved ones who guard my purity and my honor, for surely I cannot resist him further!'

"But, alas, there was a quick and furtive knock upon her chamber door, and instantly it was flung open, for this lovely and unsuspecting creature had neglected to lock the last barrier which protected her from the lustfulness of her suitor, who, despising her defenseless state, and knowing that no cry of hers would arouse her sleeping sister, and understanding that never, never, would she allow that sister to suspect that her adored husband was in licentious pursuit of the gentle and unprotected Lady Isobelle, had audaciously taken advantage of all these things. He saw her as she cowered in the draperies of the moonlit casement, palpitating like a fawn at bay, all her limbs shining through the diaphanous fabric of her single garment, her head thrown back, her lovely breast revealed, her face as white as snow. With a single savage moan, he was upon her, pressing his hot lips deeply into her lips, her throat, her bosom, while she lay in his arms, fainting and sobbing under her breath, unable to resist him. When he lifted her in one sweep, and moved towards the bed, she knew no more."

Angus paused, to turn a page. His movements were quiet and abstracted. He cleared his throat, automatically, for he had been reading for hours of the pursuit and seduction of the desperate and defenseless Lady Isobelle. His pale and austere countenance was like a statue's, changelessly reserved and dignified, his regard unhurried. His long thin figure, in its funeral black broadcloth, aroused Janie's risibilities. She began to chuckle.

He glanced at her with cool surprise. "That is the end of the chapter, Mama. Shall I begin another?"

But Janie was convulsed with mirth. She flung back her head and screamed. Angus watched her, bewildered. "Was it amusing, Mama?" he asked, with a slight ruffling of his thick dark brows. He glanced down at the book, uncertainly, and with disapproval. Janie's convulsions increased.

She looked almost young as she laughed without restraint. The years had sharpened her features, made them more lividly vicious in color and contour. But her eyes were still vivaciously green and restless and glittering, her hair still undimmed (though secretly assisted), her airs and graces still lively. She wore a dark green velvet peignoir, with a white lacy shawl over her shoulders, and her throat and hands sparkled with many jewels.

"Oh, go on with you, Angus, you stone of a man!" she cried at last, when she could get her breath. "My God, you are past nineteen, and you know no more than a chick in its shell! Good heavens, lad, give me my smelling salts. You've fair choked me!"

Angus, bewildered, brought her the jewelled vial of smelling salts from her dressing table. He removed the stopper, gravely, and courteously handed the bottle to his mother. She sniffed, strangled on the strong perfumed fumes, sniffed again, laughed, shook her head, and replaced the stopper. She sank back against her cushions, exhausted with her merriment, and stared at him with bright hard speculation.

She said, in a suddenly quiet and ominous voice: "Sit down, Angus."

He sat down obediently, for obedience was his cardinal sin.

He looked at his mother attentively. His inexplicable devotion and passion for her had increased rather than decreased, with the years. His stern and austere egotism made it still impossible for him to believe ill of those on whom he had cast his love like a glittering mantle.

He knew all about "sin," did this poor and wretched youth, but he knew nothing about the world of men, and their immortal wickedness. He was ripe to become a great Messiah, or a great villain. It was Janie's intention that he become this villain, in order that he might serve her. She was very clever. She knew his devotion to her, and though it amused her, filled her with loathing derision, she understood what a weapon it was to be used against Angus, against those she hated.

What a booby it was, to be sure! She smiled at him, and her pale and sallow cheeks wrinkled like canvas, in the afternoon sunlight.

"How are the shops, my love?" she purred, with a sudden change of tone.

He moved on his stiff chair, and answered her eagerly: "Splendid, Mama. We can hardly take care of the orders." And then his thin tongue licked his lips, furtively, and his gray eyes glimmered. Janie smiled to herself, satisfied.

"You were quite right to speak as you did to Stuart, my pet," she said, in a considering manner. She frowned thoughtfully. "I am proud of you. To think that he dared try to persuade you to disobey your poor mama, who has suffered so all these years! But let's not speak of that. I hold no grudge against him. My own papa always said that it was impossible for me to hold a grudge." She laughed a little. "It is so tedious, Angus. And one must have the most prodigious memory, you know!

"Let it be, then. You know my own secret little plans for you, that some day you shall be the owner of the shops. We must leave the way in God's hands. One of these days, I hope, I shall be able to buy a larger share in the shops, and the shares, of course, will belong to my children."

She sighed. Angus was rigid on his chair. He gazed at her with passionate intensity.

Janie was silent a moment. Then, in a firm and resolute tone, she said: "My love, I have always told you that money is everything in this wicked old world. You believe your mama, don't you, your mama who has lived so much longer than you, and who has had experience of life? Thank you, my love. I see that you understand.

"And that is why I must, even though perhaps accused of indelicacy, come to the subject of Miss Gretchen Schnitzel."

It was then that Angus turned quite white, and he looked aside, even his lips pale. He said, in a strained faint voice: "But Mama, Miss Schnitzel, though no doubt very exemplary and worthy, does not appeal to me."

Janie, shocked at this folly, lifted herself upright on her lounge and glared at him, the shawl slipping from her shoulders. She cried, with hoarse outrage: "' Does not appeal to you,' you puppy! How odious of you, how indelicate, how improper! What do you mean by it? Answer me at once, you fool!"

Angus cringed. He pressed his back against the chair. His long white hands trembled, those hands which bore the fingers of a surgeon. He moistened his parched lips, and whispered: "Please, Mama. Your heart, you must remember. Mama, I don't like Miss Gretchen. She—she is repulsive to me. She—she is fat and white, like lard, and short, like a keg. Her hair—it's like coarse flax, and her little hard blue eyes are like a pig's. She—she is a German, Mama. You never liked Germans, you know."

Janie, still glaring at him, slowly lowered herself again. A muscle twitched in her dry cheek. Her eyes were vicious.

But she said, quietly and brutally: "I like everyone who has money. Have you so easily forgotten my lessons? I've looked, with you, into the Bible, which assures us that God loves the man of wealth and property, and despises the poor. Did not that convince you? A dog, or a German, who has money, is respected both by God and the world. I shall not repeat all that to you. You know it, and you are a fool if you've forgotten it."

She laughed abruptly, and the sound was ugly. "Miss Gretchen is her father's heir, the heir to his tanneries, his bank accounts, and his property. She is the catch of Grandeville. God knows why she ever looked with favor at you, Angus! And God knows why her respected papa and mama have not turned you out of doors whenever you called upon the family! I am not one, however, to quarrel with the smiles of fortune. Miss Gretchen favors you; her papa and mama favor you. That is enough, it seems."

All at once she uttered a loud sob, and covered her face with her jewelled and corded hands. Angus started to his feet, and took a step towards her. She flung aside her hands. Her eyes were authentically wet. She clenched a fist and beat upon a cushion with it. She cried out, savagely:

"You would destroy all my hopes, you, my son! Is money to be plucked out of the air? Is the sustenance of a poor mother to be denied? Are your brothers, and your sister, to starve? Are we to be the butt of the laughter of idiots and scoundrels? How are we to rise above our enemies, without money?

"Don't you understand, you young blackguard, that if my ambitions for my children are to be accomplished we must have money, not a niggardly few pounds, but thousands of them? The shops! How are we to inherit them, to make them our own, unless we have money? And the money is there for you, in the person of Miss Gretchen Schnitzel, and you have the audacity to tell me that she does not 'appeal' to you!"

"Mama!" he cried.

But she regarded him with noble detestation, and elaborately shrank away from him. "Do not touch me, Angus! You, my undutiful son, whom I have brought up in tenderness and love, building all my hopes upon you, praying for the day when you will avenge the slights put upon us! Go away, Angus. Go from the sight of your afflicted mother; spurn her love and devotion. Laugh at her sorrows and her dreams. Turn your back on Miss Gretchen, and her money, which could save us!"

He gazed at her with the hopeless and awful despair which would have stricken a less resolute woman. But she, seeing it, looked at him only with righteous anger and inconsolable grief. She cowered on her lounge, as if very cold and completely abandoned. She shook her head, sighed, leaned back, and closed her eyes.

"Go, Angus, I implore you," she said, in a fainting voice. "Send Daisy to me. No, send Laurie, my daughter, my little daughter. There must be one in this house who is not insensible to my sufferings."

But Angus sat down on the edge of his chair. His hands were spread open on his knees. He shivered, quite violently. His head was bent. Suddenly he thought of Miss Gretchen Schnitzel, and a vast retching sickness filled him. But he subdued it with fanatical sternness. He swallowed the salt water that oozed into his mouth.

And then, all at once, for the strangest and most mysterious of reasons, he heard the far echo of a heroic song, and for one blinding instant he saw the wild white face and glowing black eyes of a young man he had been taught for many years to hate. It had been years since he had heard that song, had seen that face, and his heart suddenly rose and expanded in him involuntarily, like a bird rising from a dark pit into the light.

And then, so twisted had he become, so lost, so bedevilled and distorted, it seemed to him that that face and voice were evil, and the vision a warning to him. Ah, it must be so, he thought. There was no other explanation. The last time he had seen and heard them with his mystic inner eye and ear

was when, at the age of fourteen, he had made his final plea
to his mother to be allowed to study medicine. How loud
the voice had been then, how wicked and triumphant! He
had fled from his raging mother to his minister, who had
solemnly assured him that his first duty was obedience to
his poor mama, who was wiser than he, who had "sacrificed"
so much for him. It was God's command that parents were to
be honored, and obeyed. Whatsoever, or whosoever, seduced
a child into contrary behavior had been visited of the devil.

That old rising and expanding of his heart, then, had been
subdued and crushed by him, in righteous exaltation. It had
never come again, until this day.

He straightened himself in his chair. The face and the
voice faded, as on a last glimmer, a last faint echo, sinking
back into the abysses of despairing forgetfulness. He had
conquered his own inner sinful self again. He was whitely
exultant.

"Mama," he said, clearly, "please, please listen to me. You
are right. I was wrong. Forgive me."

But Janie did not stir. She lay, as if broken and lost. But,
slowly, her eyes opened. She looked at Angus. She saw his
strained and ghastly face, his feverishly burning gray eyes.
She saw his humility, his exaltation, his love for her, his
conquest of his deepest and most profound instincts, his
violation of himself. She saw his innocence, which—strangely
for Janie—now seemed to her a terrible and pathetic thing.

She had no conscience. But there was a sick and curious
churning in her, which for several moments she could not
control. She had never loved Angus. She had always despised
and derided him. Nevertheless, as she stared at him, unblinkingly, the churning invaded all her flesh, and there was
a choking in her throat. She had the most ridiculous impulse
to shout at him: "Oh, go away from me, you fool! Go away,
but never look at that fat white tub of lard again, and be
damned to you!"

But fortunately, as these incredible words trembled on her
shaking mouth, her reason and her commonsense returned.
She forced a tender and forgiving smile to her face. She held
out her languid hand to him.

"My darling lad," she murmured, feebly. "Do forgive your
mama if she was too stern, and too stricken by her emotions.
I should have known that my love would always see his
duty."

She was trembling, and for the first time this trembling
was not assumed for effect. It was genuine. How close she

had been to ruin, then! How grateful she was that she had been silenced before the foolish and dreadful words had left her lips! What had possessed her? What folly, what stupidity!

Angus rose swiftly, and took her hand. He looked down at her, smiling tremulously. "Oh, Mama. It is I who should ask forgiveness, not you." He drew a deep breath, and said, strongly: "Tomorrow I shall ask Mr.—Schnitzel—if I may press my suit with Miss Gretchen."

She smiled at him with that liveliness and animation of hers which was so fascinating, all her white teeth sparkling, her eyes dancing vivaciously. She patted his hand, and said with anticipatory joy: "We shall see! We shall make them bow down to us! They'll rue the day they made fools of us! We'll show them!"

She sprang quickly to her feet, moving like a young girl. She walked quickly up and down the room, chuckling glee-fully, throwing back her spirals of reddish hair. She was all vitality and life, her skirts swirling about the low heelless black sandals which covered her tiny feet, and sometimes, as they swirled and tilted, her little calves, in their white silk stockings, were fully revealed. She appeared quite pretty in her gay vehemence, and Angus watched her.

She had forgotten him. But when she finally did see him, she almost loved him for the triumph he was about to give her. She stopped before him, and patted the arm in the black broadcloth sleeve, and laughed aloud. If she was aware of the thinness of the arm in that sleeve, she did not show it.

"You are a good lad, my love," she said fondly, and sighed. "What should I do, a lone and abandoned widow, if I did not have such a man about the house?"

Then her face became pinched and uneasy. She glanced about, as if looking for something. "Where is Bertie? Where has he been these days? I never see him."

Angus hesitated; his expression darkened. He had become quite adept in protecting his mother from knowledge of his brother's drinking bouts, until the final day of extremity when he collapsed. So it was that Janie was still unaware that this collapse was the finale to the days of drinking. Incredible though it seems, she as yet believed that the day of collapse was the first day, and that Bertie, though a "toper," could not carry his liquor like a man.

When Angus still hesitated, picking his painful way be-tween truth and evasiveness, she glared at him. "Where is he?" she demanded, in a loud hectoring voice. "He isn't drink-ing again, is he?"

Angus said, weakly: "I believe he spoke of visiting Miss Alice Cummings this afternoon, Mama."

The glare faded from Janie's eyes. She smiled. "So that is it, eh? Well, then. But it is only a chit, still. How old is the lass, Angus?"

He turned away. He said faintly: "I believe she is fifteen, Mama."

"Yes, yes, so her mama told me. I had forgotten." Janie looked pleased. "Not a chit, after all. Bertie could go far and do worse, it is true. There is money there." She chuckled again. "Trust Bertie to use his head, the rascal!"

She mused on her Benjamin, and a look almost of sweetness softened her eyes. "He does well in his classes, too, I am told. And with ease, though the wretch never studies. Mr. Braithe assures me he has never had a cleverer lad."

"He does well," said Angus, mechanically.

"Next year," said Janie happily, "he will go into the shops, also. No nonsense about Bertie."

Angus glanced down at his hands. He said nothing. Janie stared at him impatiently. She made a dismissing gesture. "My head aches, Angus. Send Laurie to me to brush my hair. She never remembers, the little besom, until reminded. What it is to have a neglectful daughter!"

Silently, Angus turned and walked slowly to the door, erect, almost emaciated in his black broadcloth. "Like a damned undertaker," thought Janie, viciously, and with nasty amusement. Perhaps she should have apprenticed him to the grave-diggers, after all. Her Bertie, and even that disgusting "black one," Robbie, would have served her better in the shops. But no, she reflected, neither of her younger sons had that inherent rapacity and greed which stirred so strongly under Angus' pious and dutiful and gentle exterior. What was it that that damned Stuart had said to her about Angus, which had so surprised her with its unexpected subtlety? "He has substituted duty for the love of God and man." His Scots rigidity of character was still unshaken, though Stuart had called it "terribleness." Yes, the lad was dour, but he was weak. Janie, watching him leave the room with his noiseless and stiff tread, laughed in herself. Trust the virtuous and the stiff-necked to be the greatest scoundrels of them all!

She threw herself again on her couch, and gave herself up to pleasant meditations. The December afternoon was paling and darkening. The firelight was more vivid in the room. She could feel its warmth on her feet. She hummed a little, hoarsely, under her breath.

She had done well for herself. That she knew. She had come far, in a strange land, with no help from anybody. She was enjoying herself, and she had vivacious plans for the future. She felt in herself a sense of power and invincibility, very agreeable sensations.

CHAPTER 30

ANGUS made his way down the narrow slit-like corridor towards his sister's room. It was very dark and dank here, smelling of wax and chill airlessness. The servants were sleeping in their quarters on the third floor, after the arduous labors of the big Sunday dinner. In an hour they would arise and prepare the evening tea. But now the house was silent except when gloomy hollow echoes reverberated through it, like echoes coming down long and empty tunnels.

Angus could hear those disembodied echoes, that roamed through all the corridors and rooms seemingly without human origin. They boomed and dwindled, enhancing the dark, cold and crepuscular melancholy of the day and the house. Angus stopped suddenly, and his hand reached out and leaned against the wall. He felt the paper dampness of it, its chill. Its very texture impinged itself with a curious intensity on his palm, so that, as he stood there in the semi-dusk of the hall, he felt himself surrounded by living entities that gazed at him with immobility. It had always been this way with him: from his earliest childhood he had been suddenly seized, at intervals, by the strangest and most affrighting sense of awareness in the most ordinary objects about him, and his heart had risen on an arc of confused terror and dread. A slight shift of plane had come to him, and with it a sensation of disorientation, of nameless fear, of lostness, and he would look about him with the eyes of a frightened and bewildered alien. He never could understand the horrible despondency which would come to him then, the hopelessness, the iron weight which would replace the slow quiet beat of his heart.

Now he slowly rubbed his thin palm on the paper, and looked about him, too burdened even to sigh. He could not see the design of dull red roses on the wallpaper, or their coiling green leaves. He could see nothing but the dim shallow light that filtered through the small window at the end of the corridor, where it made a bend at right angles to the part in which he stood. He could hear nothing but those long running echoes that traversed the corridors of the house like drifting ghosts. He could feel nothing but the agony of his despondency and dread and unidentified anguish, and the texture of the wall under his chilled hand.

But all at once he wished for death with an overwhelming intensity. This desire, too, was a familiar one to him. It had in it a black urgency, a will to flight. It was an agony that cooled his lips and set his lungs to laboring. For, by then, terror would take him, though his despondency was none the less. A battle would rage in him, with hopelessness and despair and grief on one side, and fear and the will-to-live on the other.

During all this time, he stood as silent and motionless as a ghost himself, there in the dusky hall with the little window a rectangle of pale light in the gloom. He looked steadfastly at the window; its wan illumination lay on his features, which were rigid and white, and in his eyes, which were empty and distended. He could not move. His stiff arm, with the hand pressing against the wall, upheld him. He was petrified with his suffering.

Finally, as if breaking free of chains, he stirred, and said simply, and aloud: "Oh God." In the past this had been the word to free him from the horrible enchantment. It did not free him now. It was like a heavy stone hurled into black and bottomless depths, into which it sank without a trace, with not even an echo of its passage. He said it again, over and over, and again it was like falling stones, cold and shapeless and without meaning.

It seemed to him that an hour or more passed as he stood there, washed over by the darkest waves of anguish on which no star shed any light at all. But it could have been only a few moments. When he could resume his walk down the corridor, he felt as weak and broken as though he had just risen from a sick-bed, and the huge pain that pervaded him was a low fire all through his tired body. He ached as if stricken by an endless sorrow.

He reached the little window, and stopped involuntarily. He looked down at the blasted gardens two stories below. He saw the wet bricks of the winding walks, over which bent the cold and iron branches of empty trees. He saw the white walls beyond, the ruined flower-beds. He saw the paling pewter of the December sky, as silent as death itself. Not even a sparrow twittered over the brown grass, or swung on a limb. There was no wind at all, though this was a land of almost constant wind. Everything stood frigid and without movement and life.

He stood with his hands grasping the window-frames, and said aloud, and very simply again: "I cannot endure it." He said it over and over, with a dull and heavy vehemence which was yet without passion or meaning. He did not ask himself: What is it I cannot endure? Instinctively he knew that to know the answer would be too terrible, would make life impossible for him. He only listened to the sound of his voice, and its dogged rising and increasing swiftness, and the very sound of it, while expressing his enormous agony, also dulled it. It was an incantation. After a few moments of listening to his own words, his own cold and meaningless frenzy, he could straighten up and go on again, weaker than ever, but dizzy rather than frantic, as he had been before.

Nevertheless, his face was wizened, dried into the planes and wrinkles of voiceless torment. He tapped on Laurie's door, and at the sound of her clear young voice he opened the door, and peered within. He smiled. It was the smile of an old man.

Laurie sat crouched on the hearth, reading by its red and uncertain light. Her little room was in gathering shadow. The firelight was like a pool on the thick shagginess of the hearthrug. The andirons and the fender glittered with bright brazen reflections. Laurie wore a black woolen frock over which was tied her ruffled pinafore of white muslin. Her long golden hair, which reached far below her waist, was held back from her face by a band of crimson ribbon. She looked up at her brother, smiling faintly; her small face was serene and full of dignity. She stood up, tossing back the lengths of her hair, and her smile grew brighter. She was a tall girl, nearly twelve now; there was an air of calm and gentle authority about her, and a maturity greater than her years.

"Is it time for tea, Angus?" she asked.

But he stood on the threshold and only gazed at her with a poignant acuteness which was the aftermath of his enormous despondency. She was warm and young and alive. She was the denial of his melancholy and his despair. She was the normal voice calling over the blackness which had almost drowned him; she was the voice awakening him from nightmare. He could feel the nightmare retreat to a greater distance from him, held at bay by her very existence. He shivered.

He came into the room, feeling that he had just returned

from an age-long journey. He rubbed his hands together. "It is cold," he said. He stood on the hearth and bent to the fire eagerly, urgently. She watched him in silence, and now her face, daily growing more beautiful, more closed, more dignified and withdrawn, looked almost fluid in the firelight, and full of mature pain.

Angus lifted the coal scuttle and threw more coals upon the crimson embers. Now the fire leapt and spluttered, throwing off radiant sparks; it roared up the chimney. Angus stared at it, with his urgency hot upon him. It was like a fever in him, like the febrile fire that races after a deathlike chill. He turned to his sister, and smiled upon her.

"What were you reading, Laurie?" he asked, and his voice was tender and deep, as it always was when he spoke to her.

She did not move, but there was a curious restlessness about her, which showed itself in the sudden flicker of her golden lashes and the half movement of her red young mouth. She said, almost coldly: "I was reading *Bleak House*. By Mr. Dickens."

And now Angus' look matched her voice in coldness. "A novel, Laurie! On the Sabbath! Where are your Sunday-school books, and your Testaments?" But there was a lifelessness in his tone which he could not overcome.

Laurie shrugged slightly. "I have studied my lesson, Angus. I've read the texts."

"But you haven't meditated upon them," he said, and it seemed to him that his words were thick and heavy in his throat.

She shrugged again. "Enough. I can't 'meditate' on them all day."

"It's little enough to give—God—one day out of seven," he rebuked her.

But she was silent. Finally, he glanced about the room and looked at her bedside table. There lay the lessons and the Bible. He said in the dull and abstracted voice of complete listlessness: "Would you like me to hear your lesson, Laurie?"

"No, thank you." If there was irony in the quickness of her response, he felt rather than heard it. He regarded her with distressed dourness. She smoothed back her hair calmly with the palms of her lovely large hands, so white and perfect. But she continued to return his regard impassively.

"Where did you get that novel, Laurie?" he asked, not understanding the pain in his heart.

The faintest of smiles passed over her lips, a smile of cool irony and disinterest. "Cousin Stuart gave it to me for Christmas. It is one of four of Mr. Dickens' books which he gave me. They're very interesting. Angus. You should read them."

"I have no time for nonsense," he said, with proud severity. "Nor should you, Laurie. The world is a grave and serious place, and there is no room in it for frivolity."

The girl was about to reply tartly; the first forewarning of her words was already quick and unusually vivid in her large dark-blue eyes. But she held them back even when they had risen to her lips. Instead, a gentle look, tender, even maternal, replaced the first hard sparkle between her lashes. She came to her brother and took his dry cold hand. "Never mind, Angus. I promise you I've got my lessons. Is that enough?"

He made a movement as if to withdraw his hand; he tried to let her see his displeasure. But he could do neither, for her expression was so gentle and loving, and her young hand so warm. Against his will he smiled at her. With his free hand he stroked her smooth and shining hair. He said, irrelevantly: "It is so pretty, your hair, Laurie."

That reminded him. He added: "By the way, Mama wants you to go to her and brush her hair for her. Her head aches."

Instantly, and intangibly, her features hardened, became aloof and impregnable again. But she said indifferently: "I had forgotten. I'll go to her at once."

She smoothed down her pinafore, straightened the ruffles at her neck, and went out of the room quickly, walking with a steady effortless gliding motion which was one day to entrance thousands of people. Angus watched her go. When the door closed behind her it seemed to him that the room was suddenly invaded by a deathly coldness and emptiness, which not even the renewed fire could dissipate.

He looked about the little room, which quivered with silent crimson. The corners were lost in shadow. The dark ceiling moved in the firelight. The furniture was plain, but good and somber mahogany. The narrow little canopied bed was white and nebulous. The draperies at the tall thin windows stirred in a rising wind. All about were scattered Laurie's school-books, and other books. Angus frowned sadly. He looked down at the hearth where the maligned novel lay, open and face down. He picked it up, and distastefully, holding it as far from him as possible, he scanned a page or two.

He read: "She is like the morning. With that golden hair,

those blue eyes, and that fresh bloom on her cheeks, she is like the summer morning. The birds here will mistake her for it."

Angus lifted his gloomy gray eyes from the book and stared at the door through which his sister had gone. There was the strangest rising in his heart, like a voluptuous pain, almost a pain of joy and overwhelming tenderness. He forgot that this was the Sabbath, and this the reprehensible book of Mr. Dickens. "She is like the morning"! The lovely words were a dazzle of light before his dimmed eyes. Little golden Laurie, his darling. The book shook in his hands. Who cared for Laurie, but himself? Who loved her, but him? She was his treasure, his responsibility; she was all he had.

He sat down on the stool near the fire, feeling a weight behind his eyelids like tears. His sorrow was on him again, formless and huge. He knew Laurie loved him. But she was changing in these days. She had always been scant of words, but she had always smiled. Until lately, until hardly a few weeks ago. What had happened to his Laurie? There was a coldness and hardness about her now, hardly ever broken, a chill surface, impervious and silent. Her mother called her "a self-satisfied and selfish minx, with no heart in her." Angus recalled those words. "With no heart in her." But no, he almost cried aloud, there is a heart in Laurie, but it is dying, it is being killed!

What was killing the sweetness, and the heart, in Laurie? What was making her as smooth and featureless as a stone? Laurie's heart, that heart of a child! He could not endure it. He was wild with his pain.

She rarely sang now. The pianoforte down in the lofty parlor hardly ever filled the house with its sweet notes, accompanying Laurie as she sang. He could hear the echoes of her full and beautiful voice, that voice which was too strong, too clear, too majestic, to be the voice of a young girl. It had suffered some training at her young ladies' school, but the prim and hampering methods of her teachers had not changed its fullness and life and roundness. It had broken away from them like a full flood over a feeble barrier of little stones, a golden flood that could not be restrained. How it had filled the house when she sang; it was the voice of an angel, tranquil but triumphant, sounding effortlessly like a trumpet in all the rooms. She could sing the most inane ballad, and it was a celestial rhapsody. She could trill a few exercises, and they were the movement of a symphony. Every room would seem to listen, breathless, as the strong rapture invaded it. Even the servants would listen, halting in their work and freezing into statue-like attitudes.

How long had it been since Laurie had sung? Angus, in his desperate intentness, could not remember. But it had been a long time. With the freezing and dying of Laurie's heart, her voice was dying also. It had become silent, like bounding waters frozen by quick and gathering ice.

"Oh, Laurie, Laurie!" he cried, and Mr. Dickens' maligned book slipped from his knees with a crash.

He stood up, quite wildly. He looked about him. He walked up and down the narrow little room. What had happened to Laurie? Why had he been so blind and so deaf? How had he been insensible to her silence, to the freezing of her face, to her stillness? It had been a long time since he and she had walked together, of a Sunday afternoon. How had it happened? He could not remember. He could not tell. He only knew that in his own black blindness of voiceless despair he had wandered away from his sister, had forgotten her. Her voice had been powerless to follow him. Or perhaps she had just remained behind, of her own will.

And then he remembered that last Sunday when they had walked together near the river. The memory came back on a rush of light, poignant and clear. It had been a cold spring Sunday in the latter part of May. The day was very bright, polished and chill, typical of the northland, and though the wind was like a wall of invisible ice, strongly pressing against cheek and breast, the memory of the seven months of bitter winter, black and bound, made this day seem festive and brilliant and gay. It was a release from months of endless snow and blizzards, and gales that rushed through the dark air like thousands of cutting scimitars. The banks of the river were wet and brown, smiling with half-liquid mud; the trees were only half-leafed; the grass, while greening slowly, was still short and uncertain. But the sky was pure and immense, filled with radiant light, and the rushing river waters were almost indigo in their intensity of color. So clear and pellucid was this north air that one could see the farm-houses and the little white cottages on the Canadian shore, and the faint greenness of the trees. Here and there a rotting cake of ice drifted swiftly with the current, tilting, catching on its surface blinding reflections of the sun. There was a wideness and a promise in the air, a murmur of brief but fervent life, and though the wind turned Laurie's cheeks to crimson, and though she must clutch her big beaver bonnet with her gloved hand or hold down her whirling skirts, she laughed with pleasure that the winter had gone. She stood beside Angus, and though he was tall, and nearly eight years older than she, the top of her head reached to his eyes.

A cloud of white gulls circled against the sky, catching sunlight on their wings. Their melancholy calling echoed in the clear silence, mingling with the voice of the constant strong wind. They blew down on the water, a swirl of giant snowflakes, and then rose again with small fish in their beaks. Wide flat rocks, bleached by the winter, shone in the sunlight, their edges lapped by restless green waves. Angus and Laurie picked their way carefully over these stones, and stood near the water, their bright eyes looking at the Canadian shore, the gulls, the river. Behind them were thick woods, full of the cries of busy birds. They could hear the many churchbells of the late Sabbath morning. It was very peaceful, very brilliant, and very cold.

Angus had found some violets in the wet woods, where the spring light had been white and misty. These were now fastened to the collar of Laurie's billowing brown beaver cloak. The sweet color was hardly less vivid than her eyes; her mouth was warm and living scarlet.

And then she had begun to sing, very softly, meditatively, as if she were alone and singing only to herself. Her voice seemed part of this bright and rushing desolation of wind and river and stone and blazing cold sky. Angus had listened reverently. How her strong voice rose, bell-like, powerful, yet pure and leisurely as flowing gold, so that all the air seemed filled with it! It was their father's song, so long forgotten by him, "O Morning Star!" And Angus listened, his heart swelling enormously one moment, the next squeezed by a sudden and overwhelming anguish.

He wanted to cry out to her that she must not sing that song, which was an agony to him, an amorphous despair. It was the song of a man whose memory he was convinced was a power of evil for him, turning his thoughts to the most joyful and pagan of things, seducing him from what he knew was his duty. But he could not speak. He could only listen.

He did not know when she stopped her singing. Only slowly he became conscious that she was silent, that now the voices of the wind and the river and the gulls had returned with overpowering intensity, as if awakened by the rapture of that song. Angus was very cold; his whole body was petrified with chill. He shivered.

He looked at Laurie, his lips numb, his eyes smarting. And she was looking up at him, so gravely, so intently, that he was startled. Her blue eyes shone in the cataract of light that fell from the sky; her mouth was serious, even a little hard, and very sad.

"Dada's song," he stammered. He could not look away from her, from that strange watchfulness of her eyes, and the hard sadness of her young mouth. She seemed to accuse him, not with anger, or disdain, but with sorrow and sternness.

"Yes," she said softly. "Dada's song. You remember it, Angus?"

But he could not speak. He could only loosen his hand from hers, and half turn away. Now he saw nothing of the sunlight but its desolation, nothing of the river but its threat of bitter green death.

"Angus," said Laurie, "you never go to the kirk with me any more."

He looked at the icy waters almost at his feet. He saw their emerald reflections, their bubbling foam. And then he said quietly: "No."

"Why not?"

"I don't know," he said, in his lifeless and neutral voice. "There seems nothing for me there, any more. Besides, Mama needs me on Sunday."

Laurie said nothing. When he glanced at her furtively he saw that she was smiling with a new grimness, and that her eyes glinted through her lashes.

She said: "There never was anything there, for anybody, in the kirk. God can't be as bitter and as harsh as the minister says. When I am old enough, and my own mistress, I shall not go, either."

"Oh Laurie, that is a fair wicked thing to say!" he exclaimed, dully. "You are only a little girl, yet. You cannot judge."

She regarded him shrewdly. "You have judged, haven't you, Angus?"

But he did not answer that. He looked at the river.

"But you haven't forgotten your Presbyterianism, though, have you?" Her voice was soft, and a little derisive.

"Laurie! You mustn't talk like that! What can you know? You are so young. Why Laurie, you are only a child."

She shrugged, indifferently. "Grand-da's mama was only two years older than I when she was married," she remarked idly. "I am not so young."

She pulled her blowing cloak about her tightly, and stared grimly at the river. "Angus, when I was little you talked to me about being a doctor. I haven't heard you mention it lately. Why not?"

He became rigid in an iron silence, then he said, very coldly: "That was all nonsense, Laurie. I am in the shops now. Mama convinced me it was ridiculous, and that she needed me there, to protect her investment."

He was startled when he heard her laugh. It was a soft laugh, yet it was derisive, and not pleasant to hear. "Everything is ridiculous when Mama doesn't want it," she said. "She doesn't want Robbie to be a lawyer. But Robbie *will* be a lawyer. She wants Bertie to go into the shops, with you. But Bertie will not have the shops. You wanted to be a doctor. But you have gone into the shops."

"Laurie!" he said, and his voice was full of pain and anger.

But she shook her head at him, scornfully. "She wants nothing of me but to be a fine young lady and make a good marriage. I am not a fine young lady, and I shall not make a 'good marriage.' I shall do what I wish. Only you are a bowl of porridge, Angus."

She had turned away from him abruptly, and had begun to pick her way over the stones, holding her skirts high, before he followed her. Now his face was dark and tight, his gray eyes flashing. He reached her. He took her elbow. "Laurie, you are cruel. You don't know what you say."

She pulled her arm away from him, and looked at him with glittering disdain. But she only said: "I can make my way alone, Angus."

And now, as he stood there before the fire he remembered that Sunday, and Laurie's words. They seemed enormously significant to him. He said aloud: "But I do not understand." Yet, when he tried to understand, he was filled with fear and complete desolation. He turned away from the memory, sick and trembling.

Laurie had not sung again, he remembered. Nor had she walked with him, or even talked with him for long. The cold hard imperviousness had slipped over her. Had she been avoiding him? He believed it now.

But he was not concerned with himself now, nor with the pain he was suffering at the memory of Laurie's words. He was thinking only of Laurie, Laurie who had been his darling, his little sister. All at once, he was terribly afraid. He was filled with a nameless conviction of guilt. "I can make my way alone," she had said. The phrase was full of grim significance, of sorrow, of repudiation.

He listened to the echoing gloomy silence of the day. It was evening now. The wind had risen strongly. It muttered restlessly at the windows. He lit a candle and put it on the mantelpiece. He looked about the room. It was strange and empty and alien to him, and unfamiliar.

He walked about the room, looking at Laurie's few possessions. But it was the room of a stranger, which disliked him, which willed him to leave. One of her ribbons lay on the bed. He picked it up, absently. It slithered softly through his fingers, as if to escape him. But he wound it through his fingers, feeling its silken texture, its warmth, as if it remembered what long lengths of gold it had tied. Without knowing why he did it, he put the ribbon in his pocket, thrusting it in with fingers that seemed too aware, every nerve exposed.

Then, as if in great haste, he left the room, half-running back to his mother's apartments.

CHAPTER 31

"BE CAREFUL!" said Janie, vindictively, pulling her head away from the brush which Laurie wielded. "You are an uncommonly awkward besom, Laurie. And careless as the devil. Haven't you remembered yet that you must take a strand smoothly from my head and brush it gently? Go away with you! Give me that brush."

Laurie surrendered the brush calmly. And, calmly, she lit the lamps about the room, going from table to fireplace with unmoved serenity and dignity. Then she pinched the tip of the wax taper, and replaced it in the vase with the others on the mantelpiece. She yawned, brushed her pinafore free of her mother's loose red hairs. Janie watched her.

"You are completely worthless, Laurie," she said, with viciousness. "You aren't even clever at your school. God knows why I pay one hundred pounds a year for you there! You aren't worth it. A great awkward girl like you! They tell me you will never be graceful in the dance, if you practise for a thousand years. You have no deportment. You resist all the efforts of your teachers. Your French is abominable. I had hopes for you at the pianoforte, but Miss

Humphreys tells me now that you show no more interest, and are very dull. Nor is your singing improving. They tell me your voice is rusty for lack of conscientious training. As for your needlework, it is the work of an infant. You are disinterested in charades. Your exercises with the backboard do nothing to improve your carriage, for you are a great stupid girl, like an ox. Wherever did you get that gigantic height? The women of my family were all petite and full of grace. You are as graceful as a cow, Laurie, and I am ashamed of you.

"I realize," continued Janie, with gathering excitement, "that you are not to blame for your deficiencies of appearance, and your big feet and hands, and your overgrown size. You will never be attractive to gentlemen, for gentlemen do not admire young ladies who top them by a head, and must wear enormous boots, like a stableman. But you could at least make some small effort to be proficient at your studies. I understand that you are not to leave your form this year, but must remain with the little girls several years younger than yourself. I cannot believe that a child of mine is by nature stupid! If you would but make an effort you could be as proficient as any other girl of your age with the globes, and in languages and music, and could at least learn to walk like a lady."

Unmoved, her face as expressionless as tinted wax, Laurie stood on the hearthrug and stared at her mother. Her feet were apart in a somewhat ungraceful position, her hands clasped behind her back. Janie could see the girl's strong and study ankles, her Scots virility and health, and impassiveness.

Janie's rowdy voice was loud and hoarse, when she cried: "There you stand, like an ox, utterly without grace or ladylikeness! A great stupid girl! Your only occupation is novel-reading and day-dreaming. You walk about this house with your heavy and lumbering tread, and do not even deign to keep your room in order. Are you popular with the other girls of the proper society, miss? No, they are too milk-and-watery for you, you have said! Do you invite them to tea, as I have urged upon you? No, indeed, they are too dull and 'young' for my grand and elderly minx! You prefer the horses in the stable, and the stable boys, and your novels, and your long rambling walks along the river, stumbling and climbing over the stones like a lad too big for his britches. Do you take an interest in your wardrobe? No, my lovely daughter must chaff and stamp and fume before the dressmakers and cause them to give up in despair. You would prefer linsey-woolsey, I presume, made in the fashion of a sack, so long as it covered your nakedness.

"My God!" resumed Janie, flinging the brush from her into a corner where it crashed loudly. "To have a daughter like this, utterly without style, with enormous feet and big clacking boots and a dull and lightless face! Whatever is to become of you? Who will want you? The only proper ambition of a girl is to make a good marriage, to repay her parents by doing them proud. By setting up her own establishment and taking her place in the world of fashion and style and accomplishment. But it seems that I must be saddled for life with your ugliness and obstinacy and lumbering feet and uselessness."

Then Laurie spoke, calmly, without perturbation: "You are right, Mama. I shall never make a good marriage. I know that. The lads do not admire me. It is annoying, but it is a fact. I do not know yet what I shall do, but I shall choose my own way."

Janie glared at her, enraged. "'Choose your own way,' did you say, miss? What way? What is there for you to do?"

Laurie smiled. "I suppose there could be less pleasant ways than managing a household for one's mother."

At this absurdity, Janie burst into raucous laughter. She flung herself back on her couch. Her mirth was ugly, full of hate.

She shouted: "You'll manage no household for me, you daft fool! You are incapable of it, if nothing else. Do you visit the kitchen to inspect the cooking pots? Do you show any interest in the marketing? Do you call the attention of the housemaid to dust under the beds? Do you count the linen and the silver? God knows you are old enough for all this, but you do not do it, skulking in your dirty room with a novel on your big bony knees. You do not even watch over your own cambrics and laces and ribbons and frocks. And this is the one, by God! who would manage a household for me!"

"It seems that I am entirely useless," agreed Laurie.

But this only further infuriated Janie, who jerked upright on the couch as if to rise and smack her daughter soundly. Laurie regarded her serenely. There was a wicked glint in her blue eyes.

"Of course I can always be a governess, or a schoolma'am, Mama."

Outrage stupefied Janie. Laurie remained tranquil and

apparently unaware. She mused. "But, no, as you said, Mama, I am no scholar, and can be neither a governess nor a schoolma'am. I am afraid that I can see no hope for me."

Janie let out her pent breath on a gust of rage. "Well, let me tell you now, miss, you shall not live the rest of your life on my bounty! I do not intend to keep a buxom young female in idleness the rest of her life! You can well look about you in a year or two, to see what inferior man might be willing to have you, though not as an ornament, God help you! Gentlemen of fashion and position demand females of fortune or comeliness to grace their homes, and not louts and japes and numskulls."

Laurie was silent, and undisturbed. Her impassivity was one of the most hateful things about her, to her mother. She looked indifferently across the room, and regarded her reflection in the opposite mirror with unconcern. She saw her strong and beautiful face, with its brilliant and intelligent eyes and stoical bright mouth. She saw the breadth of her young shoulders, which were square, and not sloping in the admired fashion, and the Grecian column of her throat with its creamy skin. Idly she admitted that everything about her was on too majestic a scale, too large, but she was not regretful. Once, in a moment of rare affection, Janie had called her a "braw lassie." She was indeed very "braw," she acknowledged. Health was too ruddy in her lips and cheeks, vitality too passionate in the glance of her blue eyes; even her nose, well-formed and straight and white, was too big, for all its classical outlines. She was one for heath and hill, for mountains and crags, for the roaring seas. She would never learn the gentle art of swooning, of the frail fainting voice, of graceful vapors. She thought of all this with her usual cold nonchalance.

She lifted her child's arms, and felt the smooth flowing of good muscles. Her flesh tingled with strength. She dropped her arms, and again clasped her hands behind her back. She spread her feet a little farther apart.

Angus opened the door. He was breathless and flushed. Laurie glanced at him; there was an imperceptible tightening of her features, and she turned away her head. Angus looked at his mother, her face dark with malevolent rage. In his usual abrupt fashion, which knew no tact, he said to Janie:

"Mama, it has just occurred to me that Laurie doesn't sing anymore."

Janie gaped at him. Was he daft, this ninny? She uttered

a rough oath, and threw herself with fury back against the cushions of her lounge. As for Laurie, she turned her head very slowly and gazed at her brother with icy inattention.

But Angus, excited, still under the spell of his misery and pain, approached Janie, and said with stammering eagerness: "All her teachers have said they never heard such a voice, Mama. There—there is a fortune in it." God knew what subtlety lay behind his trembling words, and his manner, but he was successful in causing Janie to cease her profanity and to stare at him, licking her lips.

He stood at the foot of her lounge, and spread out his hands helplessly. "It is true, Mama. Laurie can be a great singer. She can go everywhere. There is a fortune in it. It is wicked of her to neglect such a talent."

"What is all this?" asked Janie roughly, covering her feet with her shawl.

"Mama, you must have heard of the great female singers, who are famous in New York, in Paris and London." He paused. "Mama, you've told me how you heard Jenny Lind in London, in 1847, and how prodigious was the applause. You remember, you said she was Alice in Meyerbeer's *Robert le Diable,* and that later she appeared in operas in Manchester and Liverpool. Then she was in Berlin, and Paris, and all over Europe, and everywhere she travelled and sang she was greeted with adulation by all the crowned heads. Didn't I also hear that she sang in America, too, superbly? She made a fortune, Mama, you remember, and lives most luxuriously."

But Janie burst into a great shaking roar of laughter, ribald and hating. She pointed a finger at the immobile Laurie, standing there on the hearthrug, with a peculiar gleam upon her face.

"Are you trying to tell me, you ninny, that that great hulking lump of a young female is another Jenny Lind?" cried Janie, when she could get her breath. "Look at her!" Like a cow in a pasture! You are out of your wits, lad!"

But Angus was stubborn, afire with cold flame. He looked at his mother steadfastly. "Mama, you know I am right. You've heard her teachers. You've heard her sing. I've watched you. You—you were entranced. We all were. Mama," and he clenched his damp hands tightly together in his terrible earnestness. "I beg of you to listen to me. Take her to a clever teacher. Take her to New York. Let others be the judge."

Janie laughed uproariously again. And then she stopped,

abruptly. Her eyes slid about to fix themselves on her daughter. She was silent. Again she licked her lips. "What do your teachers at that damn school say about your voice these days, you obstinate wench?" she demanded, in a threatening tone. "Tell us. Tell your daft brother." Derision was crude and violent in her tone.

But Laurie did not speak. She was still looking at Angus, and the look was hard and watchful.

"I can tell you what they said!" Janie continued, with harsh excitement. "They said she never sings, that when she is finally forced to do so she makes havoc of the sweet ballads, that her voice is like a roaring calf's under the moon. That is what they said, you zany."

Angus turned and regarded his sister somberly. He said, almost reflectively: "What can they know, those female chirpers, who have never heard a real voice? They think a girl's voice should be sweet and inane, like little bells. How can they judge a voice like Laurie's, so pure and strong and rich? Have they ever heard an opera? Have they ever heard Jenny Lind, as you have done, Mama? What do they know of volume and greatness and presence? Laurie's voice has the volume, the greatness, the purity. She has the presence for the boards——"

"Are you suggesting I make my daughter an actress? An *actress?*" exclaimed Janie, grinning with her contempt. But her eyes were cunningly thoughtful.

"I am suggesting that you allow some competent authority to hear Laurie, and that if they agree that she has a great voice that you will send her to the best music schools in New York——"

"And with what, my fine planner and spinner of dreams?" screamed Janie, infuriated as always whenever it was suggested that she spend money.

Angus slowly fixed his eyes upon her. He said, with dignity: "Then I would be willing to pay for it, Mama."

Again, Janie shrieked with laughter. She rolled her head on her cushions, with her lewd mirth. Angus, very white, waited, until the noisy laughter abated a little. Then he said very quietly:

"I have enough to take her to a real teacher. After that, ma'am, it is in your hands. Later, perhaps, I can help. But it might be too late."

It was then that Laurie stirred. Her voice, slow, quiet, rich and full of resonance, filled the room. She said: "Mama is right, Angus. It is very foolish of you. I have no voice at all, though I thank you for the compliment." She paused. Her tone became louder, firmer, but more hurried: "I tell you, I never sing now. I shall never sing again!"

"The besom has more sense than you, Angus," said Janie, sourly. But her eyes were still narrowed, still thoughtful, and she still licked the corners of her lips. Her imagination was powerful enough to allow her to hear again Jenny Lind's magnificent voice, echoing through His Majesty's Theatre, in London. And now her heart, her wizened nugget of a heart, began to beat heavily.

But Laurie had come to life, on her hearthrug where she had been so obstinately rooted. She took a step or two towards Angus. Her young face was fluid again, beautifully violent and moved. Her blue eyes flashed like flame. She said: "I'll thank you to mind your own business, sir, and keep your silly opinions to yourself."

For a moment he was petrified by her look, by her manner, by her vehemence. He felt a sick pounding in himself. Never had he seen Laurie like this, his gentle silent sister whom he loved so deeply. It was a stranger, an inimical stranger, who repudiated him now, looked at him with bitter scorn and detestation, with accusation and contempt.

"Laurie," he began, holding out his hands, in fear.

But she turned away from him with a loathing gesture. She had just reached the hearthrug when they all heard the confused mutter of men below, the opening and shutting of doors, the sound of dragging footsteps, a fall, and Robbie's cool light laughter.

"What—" began Janie. She swung her little feet to the floor. She caught up her shawl. She ran to the door and flung it open. She called down angrily: "What is this? What is the matter?"

And now Stuart's voice, sullen but loud, came up the well of the dark stairway: "We've brought home your son, ma'am. Your drunken son. And will you come down and give him a look?"

CHAPTER 32

JANIE flew down the stairs, her skirts sailing behind her. She clutched the bosom of her peignoir. Stuart watched her come. On the lower steps Bertie lay sprawled, with a foolish sleepy grin on his suffused face, his ruddy hair damp and disordered. Robbie stood over him, with a detached expression. A servant had lighted the lamp on the newel post, and its bronze light hovered over the tableau on the stairs.

But Janie saw no one but her Benjamin. She rushed to him, then stopped just above him, and stared down in silence. Angry and furious words began to move Stuart's tongue, and then he could not speak. For never had he seen such a look on Janie's face, wizened, still, and full of stark tragedy. She stood there, in her disarray, her slippered feet on the same step that held the lolling head of the grinning Bertie, and was as motionless as a carved figure. Her lips worked; her thin and freckled throat pulsed; the hands that held her velvet garments trembled. Now she was an old woman, with red hair that flaunted itself over her stricken eyes.

Stuart's warm heart, so treacherously always at the edge of melting, now betrayed his anger into pity. He mumbled: "We've brought him home, Janie. Don't mind, ma'am. He's only a lad. Lads do foolish things."

He turned to Robbie, and said irritably: "Stop staring like a dolt. Give me a hand with the lad. Under his arm, there. Careful now. Come on, Bertie, you've got legs, not gristle; you can stand. Put your arm around my shoulder." He saw Angus at the top of the stairs, and shouted furiously at him: "Come down here, you! Give us a hand with your brother. Get him to his room."

Angus came slowly down the stairs, proud and silent. He looked at his brother, dangling between Stuart and Robbie. He saw the lolling head, the drooling grimacing lips, the half-closed eyes of drunkenness. He shuddered. Then he turned to his mother, and his face changed. He put his arm about her stiff and trembling shoulders. "Mama," he said, "please go upstairs, to Laurie. She mustn't see him like this. Mama, it doesn't matter. You know what you've always said: it is just his high spirits."

But Janie, apparently, did not hear him. However, she pushed his arm from her with rigid violence. She shrank against the balustrade. Then she put her hands silently over her face.

Stuart, with irate eyes sparkling, looked at her, then at Angus. He exclaimed: "Come on, you! Take his legs. He can't stand up, and I'm damned if I'm going to sprain my back hauling him up these stairs! Take his legs; that's it. Slowly, now. Up we go."

Struggling, sweating, bumping, staggering, they got Bertie upstairs. Halfway up he began to sing, incoherently and with stammerings. It was a gay and ribald song. Once or twice he became aware of his carriers, and he kissed Stuart, and then Robbie, with grateful enthusiasm. "Stout feller," he would mutter, approvingly. "Bit of trouble with the legs, you see. Not responsible." And then he would burst into loud and rollicking song again, throwing back his head and bawling lustily. He was heavy, well-fed, and seemed all flesh, boneless. His legs, in Angus' arms, were leaden, his polished boots glimmering gaily in the lamplight. Just before they reached the top he appeared to recognize Angus, and he burst into huge laughter, which exercise almost unbalanced Stuart and Robbie who, for a moment, hung precariously, and with teeterings, over the long flight behind them. Bertie's laughter increased in volume as he continued to stare at Angus' white strained face and averted eyes.

Janie stood below, crouched against the balustrade, her hands still over her face.

They carried Bertie into his room, and flung him roughly across his bed. It was the handsomest room in the house, with many windows, the softest rug of all, the most pleasant pictures framed on the white walls, and a pleasant fire already burning warmly on the black marble hearth. Robbie lit a lamp.

Stuart mopped his steaming face with a dazzling-white kerchief. He took off his tall hat and flung it on a table. He ran a finger around his choking stock. He exclaimed: "If I don't have a heart attack after this, or break a blood vessel somewhere, it'll be a marvel! Damned young scamp! He needs a kick in his backside, and a clout in the jaw."

But his rough words, as always, concealed distress. He could not forget Janie, there on the stairs. He fumed. He glared at Bertie, kicked aside one dangling plump leg. He grimaced as he saw the stained striped silk of his own waistcoat. "Dirty puppy," he muttered, rubbing at Bertie's droolings with his kerchief. His mouth twitched disgustedly. He stood at the foot of the bed, and cursed Bertie with vigor. But all this was to forget Janie's face on the stairs.

Robbie listened to him with cool amusement. Angus stood near the bed and regarded his drunken brother with bitter moroseness. Stuart glanced at the two young men, then compressed his mouth. He disliked both of them immensely.

They were both very thin, and dressed in their funereal black broadcloth. But Robbie was all exquisite aristocracy; the somberness of his cloth increased his look of elegance and gentlemanly assurance. Angus, on the other hand, looked like a "damned gravedigger," as Stuart thought, with considerable vindictiveness.

"What do you do with the dog, now?" he asked sullenly, of Robbie.

"We undress him, naturally." Robbie's voice was all quiet competence. He hesitated, smiled faintly at his brother Angus. "I've never asked you before, Angus, but I think I'd like a little help."

"Not me, this time," said Stuart. "I've enough vomit on me now, I'm thinking. Careful with him. If I'm not mistaken, he's about to puke."

Calmly, Robbie bent and produced the chamber from under the bed and set it on the floor close to Bertie's lolling head. He and Angus then dragged and pulled at Bertie's pantaloons, throwing the soiled and fashionable garments onto a chair. These Robbie soon folded neatly in a small bundle and put away in the wardrobe. He was all serenity. He directed Angus, who obeyed in that grim silence of his. All his actions were remote. He sternly repressed his shrinkings. He was very white.

They put Bertie between his cool sheets, after dressing him in his ruffled linen night shirt. There he lay, his handsome hair red and thick on the smooth embroidered pillows, the grin still fixed on his face. But now his eyes were wide open, and their bright blueness was fixed on the lamp. "Ho, it's night!" he said with pleased surprise. He rolled his eyes and looked at Robbie. "Good ole Robbie. Nice boy. Stout feller. Where's the day gone, Robbie?"

"In your cups," said his imperturbable brother. Robbie came close to him and smiled his chill smile. "How do you feel? Head ache?"

"Damnably," said Bertie, after a moment's serious consideration. "Stomach like a ship at sea. All hands on deck," he added, with a broad and happy smile. "Pipe all hands. Southeaster comin' up. See her pitch, lads." His face changed, became absorbed and serious. Robbie promptly lifted the china chamber, graced as it was with a wreath of pink roses, and held it near his brother's mouth. He was none too soon. Stuart retreated to a window and opened it, letting in the cold December air. He closed his nostrils in nauseated disgust. He put his head outside the window, the better not to hear the ugly retching in the room. He looked down at the dark street, saw the flickering lamps glimmering across the cobbled pavements. The stark trees outside were silvered with the moon. But still Stuart could not shut out the memory of Janie's face.

He returned to the room. Robbie had left with the chamber. Angus was standing as Stuart had left him, near the bed. He was gazing down at his brother with his pale closed look which told nothing at all. As for Bertie, he lay on his pillows, and panted, white and drained, with leaden lips and sunken eyes. The room reeked of sour and vomited whiskey.

"Don't look so damned censorious!" said Stuart, impatiently. "It's not a matter of life and death, Angus. The lad's got a good heart. We must make allowances for high spirits. He's young, y'know, and thinks it prodigiously manly of him——"

But Angus only regarded his brother with bitter steadfastness, and said quietly: "He's profligate and wicked. He's a waster and a drunkard. He brings shame to this house, and heartbreak to his mother, and disgrace to his sister. There is evil in him, and godlessness and faithlessness and impiety."

Stuart stared at him with repugnance and anger. "Don't talk like a fool," he said roughly. "Or a bloody parson. Damn you all, anyway! My father used to say that every Scotsman was either a lawyer, a drunkard or a deacon, and I'm blasted if he wasn't right! Who are you to judge this lad, you white-lipped 'wee minister'? How do you know what drives a man to drink?"

Angus raised his gray rigorous eyes and regarded Stuart with someberness. And those eyes shone in the lamplight like granite. "Why should Bertie drink?" he asked, sternly. "What drives him? He is our mother's darling. He has unlimited pocket-money. He is given everything he wants. Nothing is denied him."

Bertie, during all this, had been panting noisily on his pillows. Now at Angus' words he smiled brilliantly, and with childish affability. He nodded his head slowly, and pursed up his lips. "Right, right," he agreed, in the soft and slurring voice of agreeable drunkenness. "Quite right. 'Everything he wants. Nothing denied.' Quite, quite right. Everybody loves Bertie. Bertie has heart of gold. Bertie wants nothing." Suddenly he laughed and laughed, wallowing on the bed, and his rollicking mirth was a loud and bacchanalian riot in the room.

Robbie, in the meantime, had returned to the room, and had replaced the chamber in a handy spot. He wiped his hands fastidiously on his kerchief and glanced at Bertie with impersonal fondness. "Better now?" he asked, when Bertie paused for breath in his peals of joy.

Bertie immediately became serious again. His eyes were gentle as they fixed themselves on Robbie. Then, all at once, they filled with easy tears. He lifted his hand and Robbie took it, chafing it in his small dry palms. "Robbie," blubbered Bertie, "you're ma ain brother, are ye not?" Now his accents roughened, and the old forgotten dialect came to his swollen lips.

"I am that," said Robbie, soothingly. "Now, be a good lad and try to sleep."

But Bertie was suddenly excited. "Ye'll not turn from me, Robbie? With the drink and all? It's the divil in me, Robbie, and there's no guid reason for't. Ye understand, Robbie?"

"Of course, of course. Now, rest ye, Bertie. It'll do you good."

But Bertie could not be restrained. He began to sob, clutching Robbie's hand with a wet despair. He raved. He accused himself. He wept. His excitement rose, while Stuart watched him in alarm, and saw how damp that pale and swollen face was, and what an ominous color was spreading through his large full lips.

Just then Janie entered, creeping in, huddling in her shawl as if most awfully cold. But her livid face was both tight and drawn, and filled with virulence. Her green eyes darted viciously and warily at Stuart and then at Angus, and lastly at Robbie. She came to the bed, and sat down abruptly at Bertie's left. She caught his hand from Robbie. She clasped it to her breast, and glared at them all like a sharp and deadly weasel at bay, protecting her young.

"Be off with you,—all," she cried. "Leave me to my lad. You're none of you doing him good, with your japes and your taunts. The poor lad! He wants to be alone with his mother!"

Stuart's first reaction was anger, and then he saw her despair, her hopeless defensiveness, her shame and her fear. "Calm yourself, Janie. We've done what we could for him." He hesitated. He was full of pity for her, for this new Janie, so cold, so wretched, so broken-hearted. For he knew with the strong intuition of his primitive nature that Janie had at last realized what her son had become, and that she could no longer hide the hideous knowledge from herself.

He said, impulsively: "I'll help you, Janie. I'll do what I can——"

But she screamed at him, her face malignant with remembered hatred and frustration: "We'll have no help from you, Stuart Coleman! You who left a poor widow and her bairns to face the world alone!"

"Now, Mother," said Robbie. His voice was quiet, but it had authority. "You should be grateful to Stuart, who found Bertie and brought him home."

But Janie's shame was made only more violent at this. She waved one arm stiffly but menacingly at her cousin. "Be off with you!" she shrilled.

Disgusted indignation and compassion warred in Stuart. He picked up his hat. Robbie shook his head at him slightly, and with amused apology. Angus seemed fallen into some dull despondency and unawareness of his own. He was like some dark ghost unseen by the others, and unseeing.

Then indignation got the better of Stuart. He pointed at the recumbent Bertie, and his eyes sparkled with excited temper upon Janie.

"Look at your son, ma'am, and blame no other but yourself for his disgraceful condition! It's pampered him, you have, and coddled him, until there's no manhood in him, no proper restraint or self-control! The blame's on you, my good woman, and none else, no matter where you'd like to put it, in your damnable evil humor."

He paused. His voice had thickened with his rage. "I brought your blasted son home in my own carriage, hauling him from his den like a sack of flour. I've been puked upon by your son, and strained all my organs. I'd thought to come to this house today to plead with you to release your blessed son, Angus, from your commands, and allow him to pursue his natural bent for medicine. I'd planned to plead with you to allow me to assist him, to give him help offered by certain personages who can aid him profitably. And yet, for this, I receive nothing but insults!"

Angus had stirred suddenly at Stuart's words. He lifted his heavy gray eyes and stared at him strangely. In the wavering lamplight, his face appeared to dwindle and shrink.

Janie stared at Stuart, and nothing could have been more evil and watchful than her glinting eyes. She cowered beside Bertie, his hand still clenched to her breast.

Bertie had been muttering in his drunken delirium, then

in the silence which followed Stuart's words, he spoke out, loudly and clearly, with bubblings of mirth. "I'm a wise fellow!" he cried. "The wisest in the world! You all want something. Everlastingly you want something. But not Bertie Cauder. He is the wise fellow. He wants nothing at all, never anything at all, the darling!"

They were suddenly silent, looking at him. He had fallen abruptly into a deep sleep. His breathing was harsh. But he was smiling.

All at once, Stuart's anger was gone. He felt tired and heavy. He looked at them each, slowly, with frustrated weariness, and irascibility. He saw the chill Robbie, who looked at him with the faintest of smiles. He saw the gloomy withdrawn Angus. He saw Janie, hating him in the most violent silence. He saw the sleeping Bertie. He felt something inimical in the whole atmosphere, something which rejected him with contempt.

Then, in quite a shaken tone, he said: "You are a cold, grim and secretive people, you Scots." He pointed first at Angus: "It's always stiffening your moral backbones you are, with your frightful religion, or plotting and brooding in your cold rooms against better men." He turned to Janie and Robbie again. "There's something terrible about you, too much for the likes of me."

He went from the room. He walked down the corridor. A door was open, and on the threshold stood the young Laurie with her golden smooth hair and her still blue eyes. Stuart hesitated. They looked at each other in the dimly lit silence. Stuart wanted to speak to the girl, but he could not. He went down the stairway. He had almost reached the bottom step when he felt a touch on his arm. He was so certain he would see Laurie that he was quite startled when he saw it was only Robbie.

"Don't mind," said the young man quietly. "Mama's upset. Oh, damn it, I'm not apologizing for her impoliteness. You know Mama, Stuart. As for Angus—" and he shrugged. Now he smiled bitterly.

"You find it all amusing, I presume?" said Stuart bitterly. "You, with your smiles, and your confounded coolness. There's no heart in you."

Robbie shrugged again. He said: "I don't find it particularly amusing. I very seldom laugh at anything." He smiled again. "I'm like the Ephesian philosopher, Stuart, who laughed only when he saw asses eating thistles, in the midst of grass."

Stuart stared at him. His thick black brows drew together. He went away without speaking again.

CHAPTER 33

Angus was now one of the eight bookkeepers and office workers employed by the Grandeville Supreme Emporium, having served his apprenticeship in the shops. The original office behind the main luxurious shop had been enlarged to house several high desks and tables, where, under flickering oil lamps suspended from the ceiling, the clerks labored at the ledgers and wrote letters. Angus was not yet in charge, though Stuart was preparing him for that position. He worked doggedly, in remote and courteous silence, and was much feared, disliked and respected by his less august associates. It was nothing for him to work to nine and even ten o'clock at night, all alone, his small brown head bent over the ledgers, his neat pen adding or subtracting rapidly, the white pages turning methodically. If his stern and austere face took on a drained and exhausted look, it also increased in quiet harshness. Sam Berkowitz, whose own office led from the main office, would often pass the young clerk and stand near him, unseen, and watch him with sad eyes and furrowed face.

Christmas came and went. This was one of the periods when Stuart and Janie were "not speaking." Like all the other periods, it would continue until some chance encounter in the home of a mutual friend, or a meeting on the street, or in the shops, brought them face to face and forced them to speak politely to each other. They would greet each other quite imperturbably, and with genuine smiles of pleasure, and an affable conversation which ignored past unpleasantness would ensue. Then Stuart would call casually upon his cousin, or she would call upon him and his wife, and all would be forgiven and forgotten, until the next time.

Stuart had ostentatiously refused to allow his wife to include his name on her gifts to Janie at Christmas, though he permitted her and his little daughter to call upon the Cauder family at New Year's, the traditional celebration of the Scots. When Marvina returned, all golden smiles and placid simpers, Stuart questioned her closely about the behavior of his cousin. (He was always forgetting that his wife was a fool, who never found anything unusual or disturbing.) But Marvina would only gaze at him amiably and remark that Janie was very civil and kind. Stuart fumed.

Stuart did not carry his rages at Janie to her children. If he met Robbie accidentally, or Angus in the shops or the offices, he might be somewhat stiff and stately. But he would not mention their mother to them, nor show them his displeasure.

However, he had been deeply wounded this time, and so it was that for several weeks he did not speak to Angus, and elaborately ignored his existence. The "row" on this occasion had not been confined to Janie and himself. Her children had shared in it, which was unique. They had heard him ordered from her house like a whining beggar, had heard their mutual vows never to be aware of each other's presence in the world again. For dignity's sake, if nothing else, it was necessary for Stuart to be lofty and cold towards Angus, whom he genuinely disliked now, anyway.

The frightful North winter was upon Grandeville again, to last well into April and possibly into May. Walls of snow, sometimes seven feet high, bordered every shovelled walk. A layer of mingled ice and snow, well-packed and beaten, covered the cobbled streets for at least twelve inches. Every roof was weighted and thatched with blazing white, over which flowed the blue smoke from the embedded chimneys. An iron cold, an almost constant and violent wind, engulfed the city. Every few days a blizzard would blow up, swirling, blinding, the air chokingly filled with particles of snow like white sand, which cut and flayed the flesh of those unfortunate enough to be abroad. Huge dunes, also sand-like, would pile up against fences and houses and in open places, carved and rippled by the winds. Then would come an interval of fiery blue cold, utterly calm and silent, with skies incredibly still, and the snow so dazzling that the eye could not look upon it without tears. Every house would lie immured and petrified in banks of whiteness, the windows blind with white frost, and only the purplish plumes of smoke drifting along the frozen roofs testified that in these warrens there moved any life at all. But, during the bright and bitter days, sleighs would appear, gliding along the rutted streets with gay jinglings, the occupants covered to the noses with fur robes. The city stirred under its tomb of ice and snow, and emerged, shivering, and went about its business. To newcomers, these winters were unbearable. They lived as far from the gray and ossified river as possible, for from those desolate and bleak surfaces came winds like knives and scimitars, flaying unwary skin.

It was incredible to almost everyone that summer had ever smiled upon this country, and when the first days of spring appeared with warming sunshine and streets gushing with melted snow, a kind of hysteria seized upon all the inhabitants. For nearly seven months they had endured agonies of cold, of unremitting gales, of blizzards and black cracking nights, of constant struggles to keep warm in their houses. Then, in late April, perhaps, if fate was kind, the frost would leave the stark windows, mud would appear between heaps of dirty snow, and, if one had acute eyesight, one could discern that buds were actually swelling on the rigid trees. The sight of a robin was good for two columns in the local newspapers. The skies would soften, grow misty and even faintly tender, and though snowstorms would blow up under swiftly darkening clouds, and the windows would again show a layer of frost, one could confidently declare that winter was about over. In May the snow would be entirely gone, except for plaques of blackish ice against the houses which faced north. By the first of June one could rest assured that there would be no more snow until October, and the citizens would leave their houses and plan feverishly for the summer.

The winters, however, were so melancholy, so blackly depressing and full of iron hopelessness, that any quarrels, misunderstandings or enmities begun in the seven desolate months would inevitably have to wait for the thaws, to be forgotten. So it was that not until late February, during the occasion of the first treacherous thaw, did Stuart become aware of Angus Cauder. Even then, he would not have become aware if Angus had not actually entered his office.

Stuart was in an ill-temper. He had just recently returned from New York, where he had examined a new shipment of laces and velvets and feathers and bric-a-brac from France. The shipment had been in order, and the freight charges had not been too outrageous. But shortly before leaving for New York, Stuart had sworn to himself, and to Sam, that his expenses should be as economical as possible, that he would attend only to his business, and return promptly. No ladies, no dances, no festivities, no jewelry, no extravagance. Sam had gravely approved, though with not much hope. His pessimism was justified, though Stuart had not yet brought him the bad news. But Stuart's dignity, his refusal to discuss the journey, his stately manners and his conduct in shutting himself up in his office for hours at a time, justified Sam in his foreboding. Also, Stuart's face was more florid than usual, and bore the marks of strong dissipation in the dark circles about his eyes and in the furrows about his mouth. Moreover he limped a little, and could be heard swearing painfully behind his door. There was a suffused and gritty look about him, a swollen look, also. His disposition matched. Angus could not have chosen a more inauspicious time to invade Stuart's office.

But he saw that it was indeed a bad time, for Stuart, flushed, heavy of eye, looked at him with impersonal rage. His right foot, unbooted, was extended upon a chair. The ruffles at his neck were open, as if he had been stifling. His flowered waistcoat was unbuttoned. There was an atmosphere of pain, heat and disorder all about him. Angus, who knew nothing about Stuart's escapades in New York, believed, with the egotism and conceit of the narrow and self-absorbed man, that the black sparkle of distaste and annoyance in Stuart's eyes, his expression, so dark and kindling and bellicose, was a personal violence caused only by the sight of himself.

"Well?" exclaimed Stuart. His face wrinkled spasmodically at he felt a sharp pain in his hot and throbbing foot. Angus was taken aback. That wrinkling of countenance, he was certain, was caused by his advent, and he was alarmed.

But he said with proud formality: "I'd like to speak to you for a moment, Cousin Stuart."

"Ah! You would, eh?" said Stuart, with loud irascibility. "Well, speak up, then."

But Angus discovered that his throat was suddenly dry and tight. It was always hard for him to speak to almost anyone. Stuart, staring at him irately, decided that he liked Angus less than ever. "Pity him," eh? What damned nonsense on the part of old Grundy!

"Well, speak up. I'm a busy man," said Stuart. He added, with heavy sarcasm: "Would it be more money you'd be wanting? If it is, I can save your breath. You won't get it. And that's final."

Angus said nothing. But an expression almost of torment passed over his face. Stuart regarded him, fulminating. But his subtle instinct was aroused. What was wrong with the fool? Why did he stand there, as if condemned to the gibbet? Stuart scowled. "Well! Well!" he cried. "Say your say and be off with you. I've work to do even if you haven't."

Angus put his hand on the high back of Stuart's desk. For

some reason Stuart's wandering and glittering eye was caught by that gesture. He saw how the knuckles rose whitely in that spare lean hand so heavily veined. Everything about the taut fingers suggested misery and silent repression and pain.

Now Stuart heard his voice, faint but firm, not pleading, but full of quiet hauteur: "Cousin Stuart, I believe I owe you an apology. I misunderstood you before. It was very wrong of me, and insensitive."

Stuart raised irritable eyebrows satirically. "An apology, eh? Well, that's very nice, very nice indeed. And very civil of you, I'm sure. But what the hell do you want to apologize for?" he added, on a rising tone of impatience. "Are you referring to my suggestion that you study with Dr. Dexter, and your impertinent refusal, and your insults? If so, I have forgotten it all. Is that enough for you?"

The gouty foot was giving him hell now. His features screwed up with sharp pain. His glance at Angus was fuming. "You haven't reconsidered? If so, I wish to inform you that I am no longer interested. Go to your precious mama."

Angus flushed. He flung back his head with embittered pride. "No, Cousin Stuart, it is not for myself that I have come here, to hear your ungenerous remarks." He hesitated. "Forgive me. That was uncivil. I—I know you to be the most generous of gentlemen. The most kind. You—you believe that I have forgotten your past kindness to me. And to my sister. I have not. There have been misunderstandings. But it is not even of that that I wish to speak."

Stuart saw, with acuteness, what agonies this little speech had caused this rigorous young man, for he knew that to such a temperament apology, admission of wrong, was pure torture. For always Angus lived and thought and said only that which he considered righteous and justified.

But Stuart was softened in spite of his physical pain and his dislike for Angus. "Well, that's all very nice," he grumbled. "I accept your apology, then. Is that all you wish?"

Angus hesitated. He was nerving himself supremely to speak again. He looked at Stuart fixedly. "No, not all, Cousin Stuart. I wanted to talk to you about my sister. Laurie."

"Laurie! What's wrong with the little lass, then?" Stuart's attention was distracted from his pulsing foot. He stared at Angus with interest.

Angus hesitated again. The hand on the desk clenched

as he forced himself to speak. "There is nothing wrong, sir."
Always inarticulate, he desperately searched among betraying and unfamiliar words for the proper expressions. Stuart
had a mind's eye view of Angus picking up word after word,
discarding it with despair, sorting among baskets of others as
a color-blind man might sort among colored pebbles whose
sharp edges cut his fumbling fingers. The older man discerned that it must be he who must suggest, if he were to
know what Angus wanted.

He said with some shrewdness: "Well, if Laurie is not ill,
and there is nothing wrong, you need have no worry. Unless
you think all is not well with the girl?"

Angus looked at him with flashing but reserved eagerness. "Yes, that is it, sir. All is not well with her."

"She is unhappy, then?" Stuart frowned thoughtfully.

"Yes," almost whispered Angus, "she is unhappy."

"But why? She looks like a healthy little baggage. Too tall
for her age, perhaps. But a lovely face." Stuart paused, and
then he added softly: "But a lovely face."

He wondered why he felt such a sad pang at the thought
of Laurie, and such a tenderness. With more gentleness than
he had used before he said: "What troubles you about
Laurie, Angus? You were always so fond of each other. She
trusted you."

Angus could not answer. His head dropped; Stuart could
not see his face. But he sighed.

Stuart leaned back in his chair, and even more gently
than before he asked: "She does not trust you now? That
is it?"

"Yes," said Angus, in a low tone.

"You know why she does not trust you?"

Angus looked up. His face was full of anguish, but he
said quite firmly: "I have some idea. I believe she thinks I
should have gone into medicine, instead of into the shops.
When I was young I used to speak to her about it, and
make my plans. Laurie does not know that sometimes—
circumstances—prevent one from continuing with his dreams
and hopes." And now he looked at Stuart with desperate
and wretched defiance.

Stuart shook his head. "I am not going to urge you again,
Angus. I shall not argue with you about it. You know what
you wish to do, better than I."

"Thank you," whispered Angus. He was silent a little.
Then he said, dully: "But Laurie is still very young. She
does not understand. And I—I have no words with which to

tell her. I never have any words. Laurie—is a little hard. She would not understand even if I could explain. Laurie, I am afraid, is sometimes selfish. She loves me, I know. It is her love that makes her selfish—for me."

"I see," said Stuart thoughtfully. "An intolerant little piece, eh?"

He gazed at Angus with compassionate curiosity. "So, because Laurie believes you have—violated—yourself, she does not trust you. She is vexed with you. I always suspected that Laurie was unbending. There is something of you in her, Angus. You Scots are always like iron. Never mind. To surrender to the inflexible is to add rigor to their tyranny. You must do what you wish, Angus."

He was more curious than ever. He waited for Angus to speak. But Angus only looked at him with sad somberness.

Stuart, his intuition putting words into his mouth, went on: "So Laurie does not trust you because she feels you have betrayed yourself. She does not confide in you any longer. Worse, her character is changing under her distrust, and her withdrawal from you. Is that it?"

"Yes. Oh yes!" Now Angus' coldness dissolved. He was all pathetic eagerness and dim fire. "You have expressed it, Cousin Stuart."

Stuart was quite excited now. He even put the swollen foot down on the floor and was not conscious of any twinge. "And this does nothing good for Laurie. I can see that. But what good do you desire for Laurie, Angus, which she will not heed if it comes from you?"

Angus was trembling. He left the desk. Unbidden, he sat down on a stiff chair near Stuart. He was very close to the older man. He seemed to vibrate with his repressed and inarticulate passion. He leaned towards Stuart. His pale cold features were working strangely.

"Cousin Stuart, you have heard Laurie sing?"

Stuart frowned, considering. Then he brightened. "I have, that! A lovely, lovely voice! And so strong and pure, for so young a girl. But I understand she has teachers in her school who are developing her voice."

Angus leaned even closer to him. In his extremity he put his hand on Stuart's big knee. Now Stuart's compassion was very strong.

"But Laurie will not sing at her school. Her teachers have given her up. She will not sing at home. She never sings any more."

"She does not sing, eh? And she will not sing because she

is unhappy. There is a grimness in Laurie, Angus. I can see you know that. She is unhappy because of you. Because she is defiant and wretched. Am I right?"

"I believe so. I know it is so, Cousin Stuart!"

Stuart sighed. "But you cannot give in to Laurie's obstinacy and childish ignorance. That is understood. So what is it you wish me to do?"

Angus' head dropped again. He looked broken and sick. He began to speak in a mournful and very tired murmur: "There is no love for Laurie in our house, Cousin Stuart. No one loves her but me. And she will have none of me now. So she will become harder and harder, and more withdrawn, and more obstinate, Stuart. It—it will be a kind of death for Laurie, for by nature she is loving as well as strong."

He lifted his eyes and fixed them with desperate pleading upon Stuart. "It will be the death of Laurie's beautiful voice, Stuart. And it is a voice that should be given to the world. For Laurie's sake, as well as the world's. I—I cannot bear to see what is so wonderful in Laurie die.

"Stuart, you know that Laurie has always been very fond of you. She has never spoken much of you at home because of—Mama. But I know that she is fond of you, and admires you prodigiously. You could have influence with Laurie. She would listen to you. If—if you could urge her to take your help, and assure her that it would give you pleasure, she would do what you would ask."

Stuart studied him in silence. Then very softly he said: "What is it I would ask, Angus?"

Again eagerness flushed into Angus' eyes and cheeks.

"That—that she should sing for some great teacher you would procure for her, and that if that teacher's opinion was that Laurie had a wonderful voice, worth cultivating, that she should study with that teacher, or go to any school suggested."

Stuart was astounded. He leaned back in his chair. He frowned.

But Angus went on, the words now quite tumbling from his lips: "I do not mean that Laurie's voice should be cultivated just to give pleasure to her family and friends. I mean it should be cultivated for the world. Laurie could be another Jenny Lind. Perhaps greater than Jenny Lind!"

Stuart's head whirled. He put up his hand. "Wait a moment, Angus. You are suggesting that Laurie be an actress? On a stage? Behind footlights? I can't believe it of you, Angus! Where is your piety, your religion?" And he smiled

mockingly. He could not help that thrust, but he was immediately sorry when he saw Angus' sudden misey. He continued: "I am surprised, Angus. Do not heed me. But you
are suggesting that Laurie be an actress, and you know
what the world thinks of actresses. I have seen, and known,
many in New York." He smiled with happy reminiscence.

"No, Cousin Stuart," said Angus, with desperate quietness,
"I am not suggesting that Laurie be an 'actress.' Jenny Lind
is no actress. She sings in the wonderful operas. She is a
great artist. That is what I wish for Laurie."

Stuart was more confounded than ever. He tried to smile.
"You have no way to judge, Angus. You cannot know if
Laurie has a voice like Jenny Lind's."

But Angus said quickly: "But you know, Cousin Stuart!
You are a man of the world."

Stuart, in his simplicity, was flattered. He bridled a little.
"We won't discuss that, Angus," he said, almost with coy-
ness. "Let that be for a moment." He was silent, trying to
recall the full measure of Laurie's voice. It was ridiculous,
of course. Most young girls had sweet voices. He would not
confess it to Angus, but he had never heard Jenny Lind
sing, his own taste running rather to music halls and gay
soubrettes, whose voices were not usually the best. He was
forced to compare Laurie's strong pure voice with the rather
hoarse but merry croaking of actresses in provocative tights.
He did not know exactly what an opera was, either. Perhaps operas preferred voices like Laurie's, to their own loss.
Did opera singers wear tights? He frowned. If Laurie wore
tights, and thus attracted the attention of predatory gentlemen, then he, Stuart, must protect her. He would break the
head of any hopeful gentleman who found Laurie's legs
attractive.

He said somewhat angrily: "I can't understand you, Angus.
Would you enjoy seeing your sister in—in tights? Revealed to
the whole world?"

Angus was confused. He stammered: "Mama did not
mention tights when she spoke of Jenny Lind. She spoke
only of her voice, and Miss Lind's beauty, and the marvel of
her fascination."

Stuart saw that his reputation as a man of the world was
in serious jeopardy. He sat upright again, with a stately
expression.

"Oh, Jenny Lind," he said loftily. "I had forgotten Jenny
Lind. Certainly that lovely lady does not wear tights. It

would be beneath her. So it's another Jenny Lind you would have Laurie? Without tights?"

"I suppose so," admitted Angus, still confused.

Stuart remembered something. He said alertly: "Apparently you have discussed this with your mama. She was not revolted at the idea of Laurie in ti—, I mean behind footlights, as an opera singer?"

Angus faced him fully. In a hard and bitter voice, he said: "Mama understands that Miss Lind makes a fortune, Cousin Stuart. Miss Lind has sung for the crowned heads of Europe, for the President of the United States. She has an almost royal entourage. Mama listened to me very closely, and with consideration."

Stuart was all intent interest. He smiled. "Well then, you have no need to trouble yourself. Your mama will procure the proper teacher to pass judgement on Laurie's voice."

Angus twisted his hands together. Then, in low and halting words he told Stuart of the scene between his mother and sister, and himself. Stuart listened, acutely absorbed in the stumbling recital. When Angus had finished, overcome with misery, Stuart's thoughts whirled rapidly.

"This is a very ticklish thing, Angus," he said, after a long considering interval. "Laurie has asked you to mind your own business. Your mama has shown her interest. That is to be expected, when one remembers that she must recall the fortune Miss Lind is accumulating. And the fame and glory. However, your mama is not quite convinced. Her doubt is enhanced by Laurie's obstinacy, and her repudiation of you.

"If I should go to the enormous expense of bringing a teacher from New York here to listen to Laurie, there is always the probability that Laurie would refuse to sing, or refuse to accept any verdict that was favorable."

Angus held out his hands to Stuart, and the gesture was infinitely pathetic.

"She will not refuse, Cousin Stuart. Not if you ask it. She is fond of you. And—you must not mention my name in the matter. That would be fatal."

Stuart stared at Angus' moved and tremulous face. He bit his lip reflectively.

"You think I could have any influence on Laurie? Perhaps you are right." He paused. "But suppose the teacher's verdict is favorable, even enthusiastic. Laurie would need years of voice cultivation. Possibly in New York. Your mama, you think, would be willing to go to this expense?"

Angus was silent for a moment or two. His features became grim and more embittered. Then he said: "No. She would not be willing. I know that. Not even if she were convinced that Laurie would make a fortune with her voice. I—I almost believe that—that she would frustrate Laurie." Now he flushed crimson. He flung up his head. "Not that Mama would mean to be cruel! Please believe that. It—it is just that Mama is a female, and might not understand about the operas. She might believe that it would be—immoral—for Laurie."

"Oh, don't be a damned fool!" shouted Stuart, coloring with his fury. "You know bloody well that she would oppose Laurie because she hates the lass! You know she has always hated all of you, except her damnable drunken Bertie! You are a fool, man! And a liar to yourself." He continued, with increasing violence: "I thought you meant to talk to me, man to man. If you think you can come over me with your sickly pieties and your disgusting loyalties to your mother, then you can be off and never bother me again!"

Angus sprang from his chair. He retreated a pace or two from Stuart. He almost turned and ran from the room. But he stopped himself. His love was greater than his outrage. Stuart glared at him. He burst into nasty laughter.

"Your delicate mama might think it 'immoral,' eh?" he exclaimed. "Why, you young imbecile! What do you know about your mama? You have some maudlin painted-glass picture of her in your mind, or it pleases your confounded vanity to have such a portrait, and to believe it."

He got heavily to his feet, and winced at the agony in his foot. He looked at Angus with detestation and contemptuous outrage.

"Take your fairy stories away, and be damned to you! 'Immoral,' indeed! I won't have a man about me who lies to himself! Let us be honest, curse you. If you don't know what your mama is, I can forgive you. But you are no child. You know what she is, or you blind yourself to the knowledge. I can pity ignorance; I cannot forgive wilful blindness."

He fully expected Angus to leave him now. But Angus only stood there, shaking, looking at him with despair and agony, with overwhelming shame.

Stuart made a violent gesture with his whole right arm. "I am sorry for you, Angus, for what you are. You love your sister or you'd never have stood there like that, while I told you the truth about your mother. Yes, I am sorry for you."

He paused for breath. His treacherous heart was melting again, for all his rage. He could feel its softening, its pity, its weakening sadness. He tried to make his voice stern and harsh when he continued:

"You came to me to ask me to help Laurie. I have not said I would not. I have asked you if your mother would help your sister. You say she would not. Now then, suppose that I brought such a teacher to your sister, and the verdict was good. Suppose, then, I offered to send Laurie to a school of music and voice culture in New York, and your mother refused to allow her to go? What would you suggest then?"

Angus half turned from him. Stuart could see his bowed head, his thin and trembling shoulders. Then Angus said, in a faint and muffled voice:

"When Mama is convinced that Laurie will make a fortune with her voice, and the teacher has told her so, then Mama will not refuse. There would be too much money——"

"Ah," said Stuart, and then was silent. But he looked at Angus with pity.

"But Mama would not advance the money. She—she says she does not have it. But she would allow you to—to spend it, Stuart."

"Doubtless. Doubtless." Stuart's voice was hard and sardonic. He sat down again. He tapped on the desk with the fingers of one of his big strong hands. He regarded Angus' averted face and body with increasing compassion.

He said: "You have asked me for a great deal, Angus. Have you any idea what this would cost me?"

Angus turned fully to him. Now his face was white and proud again. His gray eyes shone like frozen stone.

"It would not be for long, Cousin Stuart. And I would repay you. You see, I am to marry Miss Gretchen Schnitzel when she is seventeen years old, which will be in about a year and a half. Her father has given his consent."

Incredulous, aghast, Stuart fell back into his chair. He turned quite pale with his disbelieving consternation. "The devil you say!" he exclaimed, thickly. "The devil you say!"

Angus was prouder than ever. He flung up his head, and replied steadily: "It is quite true, Cousin Stuart. Our betrothal will be announced in June, when Miss Gretchen is sixteen. We shall marry a year later. I can then repay you for any expenses you advance for Laurie."

But Stuart was furious again. "Do you actually mean to say that you will marry that repulsive, lardy, squat young female, you, Angus Cauder? That—that German creature, with the disgusting and odious parents? The tanners?"

Angus was silent. But his proud and haughty eyes did not leave Stuart's face.

"Where is your pride?" cried Stuart, still incredulous, still unwilling to believe, still enormously concerned. He could not endure the thought. "Where is your honor, your self-respect? What has this young female but money? There is no grace in her, no accomplishments, no charms. She is ugly, hideous. She is the proper daughter of her parents. And tanners! My God! If she had beauty of person, one might overlook her parents, and the tanneries. But she has nothing at all! My God, Angus!" He got to his feet again, and limped over to the petrified Angus. He put his hand on the young man's shoulder, and he shook him vigorously. "Angus. Look at me. Tell me it is a farce, a lie. Angus, I cannot bear it. After all, you are my kinsman."

But Angus quietly removed Stuart's hand, and faced the older man.

"It is not a lie, Cousin Stuart. And I must say I take offense at your remarks about Miss Gretchen."

Stuart stood there helplessly, his hands at his sides, his face wrinkling. He shook his head over and over, numbly. Then he said: "You love this—this Miss Gretchen, Angus?"

Angus compressed his pale lips. He answered, at last: "I intend to marry Miss Gretchen, Stuart."

Stuart became excited again. "But why, why? In God's name, why?"

Angus was silent. Then Stuart had a stunning thought. He caught Angus by the arms. His expression had become terrible.

"It's your mother, isn't it? Angus, it is your mother's doing?"

Angus tried to break free, but Stuart held him with painful strength.

"I resent your questions, Stuart. It is none of your affair." The young man's voice was faint but steady. "And, if you please, I should be glad if you would release me."

Again, Stuart's hands dropped. He was very grim.

Then he limped back to his chair and fell into it weakly. He put up his hand to cover his eyes.

He said: "I see it is all no use. Go away, Angus. And about Laurie: I will send for a teacher for her. We must wait for the decision."

He dropped his hand. Angus was still there, looking at

him. "Oh my God!" cried Stuart, overcome. "Oh, may God have mercy on you, you wretched young fool! Go away, for God's sake. It's sickening you are, to me!"

After Angus had gone, Stuart was left alone with his murderous and passionate thoughts. He whispered over and over to himself, beating on his desk with his clenched fists: "Oh, the besom! The black-hearted bitch! The horrible bitch!"

CHAPTER 34

OFTEN, on Friday night, Stuart would go to Sam Berkowitz' house. When he went to that house, it was usually because he was sick to death, bewildered, dimly frightened and lost. Or when he was fulminating with anger, and on the search for a sympathetic ear and kind concern. He did not find Father Houlihan's company, on these occasions, especially soothing, for the priest was so certain of God's eternal loving-kindness and eternal wisdom and mercy that he irritated, rather than soothed, Stuart, who saw too many instances to the contrary.

He preferred, then, when full of impotent rage, to go to Sam's house, where melancholy lived and patience was leavened with sadness and wit and brooding questions. Sam would listen to his raging and incoherent diatribes, sometimes faintly smiling, often sorrowful, and he would nod his head silently, smoking or gazing steadily at a little point just to the right of Stuart's head. Then, when Stuart was quiet for sheer lack of breath, Sam would open his Scriptures and read. Stuart did not always understand, but he felt soothed by the cries of the prophets, the laments of Job, the vehemences of Elijah, the sternness of Isaiah. Here was wisdom, pain, sorrow or rebellion from the hearts of the old prophets, and they were nearer the turbulent heart of the Celt than the sweet hopefulness of the New Testament saints.

Mrs. Berkowitz, old and afflicted with arthritis, would insist upon being carried or helped downstairs on Friday nights, where she could preside over her table and light the candles. Earlier, from her bedroom, she would relay the intricacies of Jewish cooking to the small German maid who bustled in the kitchen. Mrs. Berkowitz was especially insistent on the nights when Stuart came. He would watch her as she stood behind her candlesticks, tremulous with age and illness, so tiny, so gnarled and old. He would listen to her murmuring her prayers and her blessings behind the lighted candles, her wizened hands over her face, sometimes a tear or two dropping between her fingers. The candles would bloom in the darkness of the warm little room, and Mrs. Berkowitz' frail and trembling voice would rise in strange words of prayer over the yellow radiance. This ancient and mysterious ritual would kindle another light in the Irishman's uneasy and violent heart, and his old Celtic blood would be stirred unbearably, as if in nameless remembrance.

His strong Celtic imagination would see similar lights blooming in quiet or sorrowful or fearful homes all over the world, following the waning light of the sun, carrying the illumination into the darkness as the earth turned. The trail of the lighted candles was like a chain of awakening stars, full of message, of faith, of eternal hope. A thousand thousand dark nights might come, with oppression and fear and dread and madness, but the candles would stand there, frail but dauntless, like voices of comfort calling to brother and brother across the borders of every land, affirming their faith in God, their remembrance of His mercy and love, their belief in ultimate peace and brotherhood.

Though he had no faith at all, and really no hope or belief in anything, Stuart found a deep and mystical comfort in the lighting of the candles, which not only were an affirmation of God, but a light to the heart and the eyes of those who sat about the tables. There would be a stiff white cloth on the Berkowitz' table, and newly polished silver, and crystal glasses of wine. There would be strange rich dishes and new bread, warm and white in the light of the candles. The fire on the hearth, the candles, the seductive odors of boiled chicken and hot yellow soup and dark old wine would give Stuart a sense of timelessness and strength, and he would look about the closed room with the tired satisfaction of one who had found refuge.

Mrs. Berkowitz, with her kerchief over her head, and her tiny black eyes twinkling, and her worn face smiling eagerly, knew little English. But she would listen to the grave voice of her son and to Stuart's angry heated words with the greatest of wisdom.

Stuart knew that he must not speak, however disturbed he was, until dinner was done. By that time much of his anger and misery had abated, and he could discuss matters with Sam with more calm, and less incoherence. He would look at Sam's brown and furrowed face with the tight quiet lips, the gentle wise brown eyes, and his more infuriated exclamations would die away unspoken. Then it would seem to him that he had been very foolish, that he had given significance to things which did not matter.

He came, on this Friday evening, still sore and wretched and infuriated from his interview with Angus. Sam, after one look at his dark and twisted face, led him into the small dining-room without speaking. Then he went for his mother, carrying her downstairs in his arms, while her eyes eagerly searched for Stuart.

They talked of nothing but casual trivialities during the meal, while Mrs. Berkowitz anxiously filled Stuart's plate over and over with yellow noodles and chicken. She was firmly convinced that he had a poor appetite and needed nourishing. Only when he could eat no more would she subside, with a sly smile of satisfaction.

She was very tired tonight, so Sam carried her upstairs again while she feebly cried blessings upon the guest over her son's shoulder. The little maid departed with the dishes and brushed off the white cloth. A February storm was rising. Stuart could hear the hissing of the blizzard against the windows; the draperies stirred in the bitter gale, and from some crevice under a door came the sharp whisper of icy cold. He drew aside a curtain and peered out into the thick darkness. By the flickering light of a street lamp he saw the whirlpool of little white flakes rushing beyond the faint yellow circle which that lamp cast against the furious background. And then even that struggling circle was almost obliterated by the thickness of the snowflakes. It was a bad night. Within an hour or two the streets would be drifted with hard white dunes, and the air would cut into the flesh like knives. Not a soul was abroad. The street was all desolation.

Stuart returned to the fire, abstractedly cursing the Northern winter, and remembering the fur-lined warmth of his great-coat. He heard the distant wailing of a train as it shuddered its way through the choking darkness, and then that sound was abruptly shut off by the gale that swept over the frozen Lakes. It roared over the snug shingles of the roof; it battered the sturdy walls. It cried off into the night like a terrible voice rushing towards the sky. The fire leapt higher on the hearth.

Sam returned, to pour old brandy into little glasses. Stuart and he sat by the fire and sipped the liquor in companionable silence. But Sam watched Stuart with furtive acuteness. He felt the other man's dark unease of mind, his confusion.

"A bad night," suggested Sam, listening to the wind and the rattling of the window-panes.

"It's always a bad night, for eight months of the year, in this blasted country," said Stuart, with gloom. He pushed his hand through his thick black hair, and recalled that he had noticed a few more gray threads in it that morning. Now his face was both surly and uneasy, its florid color deeper than usual. Sam saw the discolored pouches under the black eyes, which had lost none of their irate sparkle with the passing of time, and he sighed to himself.

"It is always a bad night," repeated Stuart, and now he talked as if he were alone. "I'm sick of it."

Sam said nothing. Stuart rose and threw more coal upon the fire with a brisk rattling. He returned to his seat.

"I think," Sam said, in his slow accented voice, "that we are sick of the things in us, or of the things we think we see there. It is our belief in them that makes us sick. If we do not believe—" and he spread out his hands and lifted his shoulders in the old immemorial gesture of his race, which was a combination of humor and sorrow.

Stuart looked at him with temper. "God," he exclaimed, "you talk gibberish! I presume that if I do not believe in Janie, or the imbecility of her brats, they will not exist!"

"If you think that perhaps what you believe of that woman is not true, then it will not be true. For you, my friend," said Sam, thoughtfully. "For you. It will not be true, for you. If you think she is a good woman, and her children are good, also, then they will be good—to you."

"Oh, damn," said Stuart, turning from the other in disgust. "You still talk gibberish. It still remains that that trollop is a dirty animal, and that her children are idiots."

Sam leaned back in his chair and looked before him reflectively. "There was a man I knew once. He was a bad man. He was cruel and harsh, and a murderer in his heart. That is what others knew of him, or believed they knew. The evil he did was all about him. One saw it. But there were his wife and children—they thought him the kindest and most just of men. To them, he was all that. Who, then, was right?"

"You are getting as bad as old Grundy," said Stuart. "You are trying to come over me with all sorts of metaphysical nonsense."

But Sam was still reflective. "It is all a matter of where we stand, what view we see. The man on the mountain says:

'The valley is low.' The man in the valley says: 'The mountain is high.' The man at the foot of the mountain sees a height he cannot climb. But the man at a great distance sees only a low hill."

But Stuart was looking at him irascibly. "Oh, damn," he said again. "You are a wonderful help to me, Sam."

Sam smiled. When he smiled, the ancient furrows in his tired face disappeared, and his expression was all gay sweetness and amusement. Even his weary eyes danced. "Perhaps you are wiser," he said. "The more one thinks, the more one loses the outline of reality. You are like a child, Stuart. You see simply. That is why, perhaps, you are wiser."

But Stuart was still bewildered, and more and more impatient. "Let's get down to facts," he said, in an angry tone. "Haven't you noticed something, recently? Our sales are falling off. Fewer farmers are coming into town. The customers are more prudent, and they are buying cheaper articles, and fewer of them. What is the matter? Where has the money gone? There is no less money in the damned coun'ry. Where is it hiding? Where has it gone?"

Sam was serious again. "Let us ask, rather: 'Where has the confidence of the people gone?' Something has affected the confidence of the people. What is it? When you can answer that, during each falling off of confidence, then you can solve the riddle of panics. Sometimes it is but a rumor. Sometimes there is a whisper that crops have failed, or are smaller. Sometimes one suspects the political Party which is in power. But again: it is like the man who looks at a big distant mountain and finds it small, or the man who looks up at a small mountain and decides it is large. Money is very intangible. It is an imaginary thing. It is at hand if the confidence of the people remains, and it is lost if the confidence fails. I may be wrong, indeed. But I fear I am right."

Stuart stared at him irascibly. "You are still talking gibberish. I only know this: that our indebtedness is enormous, and our sales are falling off. That is the fact we must face. Damn you, sir, and your 'intangible' mountains! Philosophy never put decent amounts on the right side of the ledger, and never made red ink disappear on the wrong side. You can look at things calmly, and talk riddles. But I'm not calm, damned if I am! I see bankruptcy staring us in the face if things go on this way."

Sam was very grave. "You are right, Stuart. People are beginning, already, to talk of a 'panic.' Wall Street speaks of it as an inevitable thing. But I am no financier. I am no student of business history. I am only a shopkeeper. I know nothing."

He paused, then said, almost as if in apology: "Do you know what I think we should do? Retrench. Conserve. Economize. Sell what we haf, and buy replacements only with cash. And those replacements small. We should operate in a narrower, a more cautious, circle. In the meantime, we should hurry to pay off our indebtedness, as fast as we can. What do you call it? 'Pull in the belt.'" And he smiled at Stuart gently.

He knew, even before Stuart's face took on a frightened and enraged expression, that what he had said must raise furious resistance in the other man. He said hurriedly: "Please understand me. With no debts, we can afford to make smaller profits. Even in a panic, people must live. They buy smaller, cheaper. But they still buy. The shopkeeper who weathers the storm is a man who has no debts, sells what he can, and lives frugally on the small profits, until the storm passes. He is what you haf said: 'marking time.' That is the wise thing: 'marking time.' For, inevitably, financial storms pass. There are many wrecks left behind. But the man who has hurried to make himself solvent is not one of the wrecks."

Stuart looked at him, appalled and incensed, full of his old nameless fear. "You talk like a coward, Sam! It is people like you who make panics! You have no confidence!"

But Sam said, very gravely: "I haf confidence that the storm will pass, but unless I take care I haf no confidence that I shall not be wrecked. I wish to take precautions. I shut my doors and my windows, and bolt them, so that the storm will pass by with as little damage as possible. To leave open the doors and the windows is to invite destruction."

Stuart felt in himself the old sick sinking that always accompanied any suggestion of economy or caution. He exclaimed: "Oh, what a niggling soul you have, Sam! What an over-cautious, tiptoeing, miserable soul! You would count pennies. You would measure out each yard of calico before you buy it, and then buy half a yard. Is that the way great enterprises are continued, and expanded? By mean little souls who are afraid to buy two yards because they are not certain they will sell them immediately? By those who have no confidence that a customer has the cash with which to buy two yards?"

But now Sam's gravity had become stern. He said slowly: "You do not understand me. It is you, now, who are talking

what you call gibberish. If a customer does not haf the confidence that tomorrow he will haf two more dollars he will
not spend one dollar today. That is what is happening. The
customers of the country do not believe that tomorrow they
will haf two dollars, so today they spend one dollar, or
nothing. That is a fact which must be understood. Why they
fear they will not haf two dollars, I do not know. I haf said
I am no student of financial histories. I only know I am confronted with the frightened woman who is afraid that
tomorrow she will not haf the two dollars, so she will hoard
what she has to buy bread for her family when the next day
there are no dollars."

Stuart, in his ancient fear, got up, and began to stride
about the room, running his hands through his hair, rubbing
his hands together.

"You are afraid," said Sam, watching him grievously. "You
know, in your heart, that ladies in the shops spend fifty
cents, not two dollars, for already they fear that tomorrow
they will need the money for bread. Yet you will not listen.
You will not buy only one yard today because you will not
believe that tomorrow you cannot sell two yards. Yet you
may not sell half a yard. That is what I am telling you: buy
only one yard today, with cash, and pay, if you can, for the
many yards you bought yesterday. And quickly."

"Oh, the fools!" cried Stuart, swinging upon his friend.
"Don't they understand, using your damned idiotic metaphor,
that if they don't buy two yards today they won't be able
to buy half a yard tomorrow?"

Sam smiled sadly. "Perhaps the poor ladies do not understand economics," he said. "And, as we deal with the poor
ladies, we must cut our cloth to the measure of their fears."

Stuart stood before him, his face working furiously, his
color very bad. "All right, all right!" he cried, with elaborate
bitterness. "What is your solution, then?"

Stuart poked the fire again. Sam's face was wrinkling with
his grave thoughts. Stuart watched him, the fear thicker on
him than ever, his fists clenching. Then Sam sat back in his
chair and stared somberly at his friend.

"I haf been wondering, and hoping," he said. "I haf been
waiting for you to talk to me. I haf given you my advice. But
I shall not use the metaphors. I shall speak plainly. But first,
I must ask you a question: What is your cash, in the banks?"

Stuart flushed. He bit his lip. Then he said furiously: "I
can raise——"

But Sam lifted his hand, slowly. "I haf not asked what you can 'raise.' I haf asked what your cash is."

Stuart exploded. "In actual cash, damn you, about ten thousand dollars!"

Sam stared at him in grave silence. He shook his head a little. Then he said: "And your own indebtedness, my poor Stuart, is over one hundred thousand dollars."

He sighed. He put his little brandy glass to his lips, but took it away again, untasted.

"From the shops, from the last six months of custom, you shall haf but five thousand dollars," he continued. "That will be nothing to pay on your indebtedness. For, unfortunately, a man must live, also, as well as pay his debts."

Bitterly, Stuart exclaimed: "You are afraid that I will ruin you, as well as myself!"

Sam looked at him, and before that look Stuart colored. "Always, you accuse me of bad things," said the Jew sadly. "Yet, in your heart, you do not believe it."

Stuart made a disordered gesture. "I'm always apologizing to you, it seems. I won't, now. You know I have a rotten tongue."

He fell into his chair. He clenched his hands grimly on his knees. He glared at the fire, his face twisting. "Oh, damn, damn," he muttered. Then he turned his glare desperately upon his friend. "I can always borrow, again," he said. "My house is practically paid for. Besides, curse it, haven't we a huge amount of stock on hand, which ought to be worth something?"

Sam appeared a little more eager. "That is what I am saying! Sell what we haf. Pay off the indebtedness. Buy a little more, and that only for cash, when we can. That is the way of 'pulling in the belt' until the table is set again."

"But you've forgotten that we have a shipment coming in soon, amounting to at least twenty-five thousand dollars!"

Sam shook his head. "We cannot accept it. The shops in New York will buy it, perhaps, on the docks." He stood up. He said sternly: "I haf meant to tell you that. We cannot accept the shipment."

Stuart looked up at him. His face was dark. "Sam, you have money."

Sam was silent. Then he turned away. "Yes. I haf the money. For my people. I cannot spend that money, to buy goods which we shall not be able to sell, perhaps for a long time. I cannot take that money, which belongs to my people."

Stuart said, in an evil tone: "You will not—lend—that

money, to save me. And in the final event, to save yourself."

For the first time in many years, he saw anger in Sam's brown eyes, as the other faced him fully. "You speak of saving yourself, and me, Stuart! But there would need to be no talk of saving, if you had not been rash, and foolish, with your money! Always haf I warned you. But no, you would not listen. You must spend. It must be a house of useless treasures, or women, or jewels, or horses, or other lavishness. And now you speak to me of 'saving' you! You would eat the substance that does not belong to you, that was gathered slowly, and painfully, for the use of those who haf no hope, not even of life, if I do not use my money for them!"

Stuart, in his shame, was defensively enraged. He shouted: "If I go down, you go also, remember! Or perhaps you would buy me out, at your own price! You would throw me out!" He sprang to his feet. He stood there, violently trembling, before his friend.

But Sam only gazed at him with the quiet anger increasing in his eyes. For one moment Stuart saw contempt in them, and then great compassion mingled with the anger. Sam went to a table in a corner and brought out a single sheet of paper. He looked at it steadily, sat down by the fire. He said, not glancing at Stuart:

"Here are the figures, my Stuart. Simple figures. They can be understood. They will not take time to explain. Then, if you will, we can forget them.

"For the shops, we haf seventeen thousand dollars, in the banks. That is all. Our indebtedness: it is eighty-two thousand dollars. Our stock in the shops: we haf ninety thousand dollars invested. The stock, it is moving slowly. Slowly, slowly, like a river in the early winter, freezing, until it will not move at all, before the spring. The clerks, they must be paid. The indebtedness, it must be lifted, the payments on the debts made regularly. Next month, Stuart, you will draw as your share less than four hundred dollars. I, also. Yet you haf your personal debts to meet, to the banks. Your mortgages, your expenses. And always the clerks, who live on their wages, which we give them. It is the clerks, just now, of whom I am thinking."

Stuart looked down at him in silence, then he sank heavily back into his chair. Sam lifted his eyes and regarded him with the utmost gravity.

"You haf spoken of my private funds, in the banks, for my people. I haf told you before that if you needed my money, it is yours. I haf a fund—it is seven thousand dollars—above that which I haf saved for my people. It is yours, Stuart, if you will haf it. If you need it."

Stuart did not speak. He stared heavily before him at a point between his polished boots.

Sam sighed. Then he said in a more cheerful tone: "Your ten thousand dollars, Stuart, and my seven—it can help you. But only if we do not buy. If we economize. If we live frugally. If we sell what we haf, and buy no more. Until the river melts in the spring, and moves again."

Stuart glanced up at him with the upflinging of the head which told of desperation.

"All our profits, Stuart, they must go to pay off the indebtedness of the shops. We must take nothing. Your ten thousand dollars, my seven, this must serve us for our private expenses, until the river moves again."

"My God!" cried Stuart, "I spend nearly two thousand a month, myself! How long will the money last me?"

But Sam said with gentle inexorableness: "You must cut your expenses, my friend."

"But how?"

Sam sighed again. He hesitated. Then he looked sternly at his friend. "You haf showed me the diamond necklace and earrings which you haf bought for a certain lady in Chicago. They must be returned. There will be a little loss. They were twelve thousand dollars, Stuart? They must be returned. The jeweler—surely he will give you eleven thousand dollars for their return, if not the full price."

Stuart glowered. He looked away. "I paid only two thousand down on them, Sam."

Sam's head dropped wearily. "Return them. He will, perhaps, give you fifteen hundred dollars for their return. Then you will not be in debt."

Stuart pondered this gloomily. Then his fear, like a mad animal, leapt at his throat again, and in the extremity of his panic he jumped to his feet. "I can't, I tell you! I can't live like a niggardly beggar! I can't economize! It—it would kill me! What do you know? Nothing! How can you understand a man like me?"

But Sam only regarded him somberly, and compassion again changed his face. He said, looking up at his partner:

"Stuart, what is it you are afraid of? What is it that frightens you so?"

And Stuart said, his words leaping from the dark subconscious depths of him without volition: "I'm afraid of the world."

He sat down again, and looked at the fire. He said, almost inaudibly, as if he were speaking in a dream, "There is something you've forgotten, or haven't mentioned. I owe you fourteen thousand dollars, which you lent me. It was seventeen. I have paid you three. You didn't speak of it. You haven't forgotten it?"

Sam said softly: "Haf I asked you for it, Stuart?"

Stuart put his hands over his face. "No! No! You never would, Sam."

Then Sam said again, with deep compassion: "You are afraid of the world you say, Stuart. What is it that makes you afraid?"

Stuart dropped his hands. They fell between his big knees in a gesture of exhaustion. He stared again at the fire, and his handsome dissipated features were stricken and grim.

"I know what the world is, Sam."

"I know too, Stuart. But still I am not afraid of it. I know the worst it can do. But still I am not afraid. When one knows the ultimate, one knows that beyond it there is nothing worse, there is no more terrible thing to face."

Stuart did not seem to have heard him. The firelight filled the sockets of his staring eyes, and gave them a despairing appearance. He began to speak, and his voice was mechanical, as though those subconscious depths were speaking now through his mouth, without the knowledge of his alert mind:

"I was never a very bad lad. I—I was somewhat like a puppy. I was ready to be friendly with every man. If a man spoke kindly to me, I loved him. The world seemed a beautiful and exciting place to me, full of friendliness and adventure and goodness. That was when I was a young lad. Even when I saw evil things, and saw the twisted mouths about me, and the nasty eyes, I thought it only an accident. A rare thing. A troubling thing. But not universal. Never universal. I read the lies of the good men who had died long ago. The 'dignity of man,' the 'brotherhood of men,' the 'fatherhood of God.' They had been said so often that I believed that everyone knew them, and practiced them. They seemed lovely things to me, things universally accepted. Sometimes, perhaps, there were errors committed, but these were committed by only a few who had never heard of the things I believed were true, and understood. Those who were in error were criminals, just hated and rejected by the whole world. And I believed all this until I was nearly twenty years old!"

He laughed bitterly. Sam had listened to that grim and monotonous voice with deep and unmoving attention. He waited.

"I understood lies. I was an uncommon young liar myself," Stuart's voice went on, meditatively. He still looked only at the fire. "But they were harmless lies, never calculated to hurt a soul. Yes, I understood those lies. They were spice to life, or said in kindness, or in merriment, and no one was expected to believe them as truth. But lies said to injure, to maim, to cause suffering or destruction, or spoken out of viciousness or cruelty—these I never believed existed. I did not believe it until I was nearly twenty years old!"

Sam still waited. Again, Stuart passed his hands over his face with a tired and rubbing gesture. His skin, after their passage, was mottled and drawn.

"I understood the little malices, the annoyance of temper, the antagonism of one mind to another. I indulged in them myself. But I did not believe there were enormous malices without cause, which would set one man against another to the death. I did not believe there were cruelties which came only because one man was stronger than his neighbor, and he wished to destroy that weaker neighbor out of beastlike and reasonless malignance. I did not understand that cruelty and malignance were human attributes as much a part of the nature of men as the color of their eyes and the shape of their noses. I still believed, until I was nearly twenty years old, that there was goodwill in men, and a better part!"

Sam made a faint involuntary sound, but Stuart did not hear it. A sick excitement possessed him. He twisted his fingers strongly together, as if in great pain. He went on:

"But there was one thing I did not know at all, until I had grown to manhood. I did not know there was hatred. Oh, there were some lads of my age whom I disliked, whom I avoided, even in England, and when I came to America. I had my fights with these lads, when they called me 'dirty Irishman,' and other things. But still, I did not believe in hatred. But now I know that there is only hatred in the world, and cruelty, and murderous greed and enmity. I know that every man is set against his neighbor, like a mad wild animal, and that there is no decency or kindness anywhere."

Sam had the sensation that he was talking to a man in delirium, in terrible agony, who would not hear him. But he said: "My Stuart, have you forgotten Father Houlihan? Is he one like this?"

He was dimly surprised to learn that Stuart had actually heard him, for the younger man said: "Father Houlihan? I believe him a good man. But how can I know? He is 'good' to me. But what is he to others? You spoke to me about the mountain, which looks different to different men from different vantage points. I've thought you a good man, too, but how do I know? What do you appear to others? You and old Grundy are only two men, anyway, and I have met no other good men—if you *are* good."

Sam stared at him, and his own eyes were full of pain. He felt Stuart's simple suffering all through his own flesh. His heart was weighed down with suffering.

Stuart shrugged despairingly, still not looking at his friend. "And so, there it was. It was a bad time for me, when I understood. And then I was afraid. You can't understand how afraid I was. Then I began to see that a man had only one defense against other men: money. The more money he had, the higher the wall that guarded him against his fellows. That is why I knew I must have money. A very great deal of money. That is why I must have properties: to show other men that the wall is very high about me, and they can never scale it, to reach me and destroy me."

Now he turned to Sam and smiled. It was both a sad and an evil smile.

"I've told a little of this to Grundy, when he tried to come over me with his noble platitudes. He has talked to me of 'Christianity.' My God! As if there ever was any Christianity in the world! Somewhere I've read that there was only one Christian, and He was crucified. But I know there was only one Christian, and He was a Jew. And if the story is true, there was only one Christian, and He was God. He could never have been a man."

He lifted his hands for a moment, then dropped them. Again he smiled, and to Sam, it was a touching and very tired smile.

"No, He could never have been a man, not even in His flesh. If He ever lived at all, which I doubt. There are times when I know, in my heart, that He was only a beautiful myth. Someone invented Him, as they invented the older prophets. He came out of the mind of Jews; they are excellent inventors of excellence. I have seen that invention in you, also."

Then Sam said a strange thing, but in a clear voice of mysterious relief: "I haf always known, my poor Stuart, that you are a good man."

Stuart stared at him blankly. Then he shook his head numbly, as if he had heard words in a strange language, which had no significance for him.

Sam stood up. He went to his friend, and pressed his shoulder with his hand. He bent over him, and said quietly and strongly:

"Stuart, it must be that you must listen to me. I haf said you are a good man. To others you do not appear to be a good man, only to a few. You are only part of the flesh of other men; you do not stand apart. What is in your mind, and your heart, is in the minds and hearts of others, also. No one is created of a different—substance—than other men. So what is true of him, in greater or smaller measure is true of all.

"If there is good in your thoughts, and this I know, and good in your intention, and if there is kindness in you, and gentleness, and some justice, then these are in others too, greater or smaller. One stone in a field is no different from another; they came from the same earth, though some are of a larger size, and some of a different shape. So, you are no stranger in the world, looking at strange creatures who do not share your flesh."

Stuart looked up at him, and was silent. His forehead wrinkled, as he tried to understand. But he smiled darkly.

Sam went on: "There is not only blackness in the world, my poor friend. Let us look about us. We haf invented some measure of law and order. We haf justice. We haf some mercy. We haf some trust in others, and in their word. We haf hospitals and asylums, as well as jails and gallows. Great books are written, and men read them, and think. Even among ten thousand liars, there are a few honest men. There is hope in men for a better world, and even in the hearts of the murderers and the liars there is a hidden belief that the better world can come. All is imperfect, yet. All is still confusion and darkness. But if all men were evil, and there was only evil in the world, there would not be even the little law and order we haf, and life would be impossible."

He went on: "If all men were only evil, then the Scriptures would never haf survived to this day."

He took his hand from Stuart's shoulder, but still stood beside him. He lifted his whitened head and looked before him, and smiled.

"You haf spoken of your fear. But I do not fear. For I know that other men are like me, even if they are better, or worse. We are all the same. That is something we must learn.

When we haf learned it, then we shall haf understood that we haf nothing to fear from each other, that no one would do ill to another except in his fear. It is fear that is the darkness, and the cruelty, and the murder. When each man says to himself: 'Why should I fear my brother?' then the world we dream of shall be here."

Stuart did not speak. But he shook his head over and over.

Sam smiled, as if at someone invisible. "I believe, in America, that there will be the end of fear. And then there will be peace and goodness and the fatherhood of God. Yes, I believe that of America. The time will come. Perhaps not for many years. But it will come. That is my belief in America."

The candles which Mrs. Berkowitz had lighted had burned to their sockets. But all at once, in one last burst of light, they illuminated all the room. There was triumph in that last light.

But Stuart saw only the darkness that followed.

"I don't believe in America. I don't believe in anything. You talk like old Grundy, Sam. All I know is that I am afraid. We must come back to the shops."

Sam said, cheerfully: "Perhaps it will not be so bad as I think. But there is always a way. We shall find a way. No, it is never so bad as we think."

CHAPTER 35

JANIE sat in the warm ruddy kitchen, and carefully sorted out a heap of her worn but still luxurious gowns. Those that she discarded, after meticulous scrutiny, were destined for the daughter of her cook, Mrs. Gordon. Sometimes she hesitated, then with a quick gesture, she added a better frock of velvet or foulard to the heap. Now that heap, all crimson, purple, blue and violet, stood richly at her small feet.

There were few among her own class whom Janie ever trusted. But, with an odd democracy, she trusted her servants, who adored her, particularly Mrs. Gordon. For she was generous to them, and laughed sprightly with them, in her hoarse rowdy voice, and was always full of jest and gaiety except when she was abusive. Even then, they found her abuse fascinating, and greatly admired her profanity. It was nothing for her, when coming on a housemaid polishing the brass lifts on the stairs, to sit down a step or two above, and begin an interesting and amusing conversation with the girl. She would sit there, draped in one of her endless velvet peignoirs, her thin little arms folded on her knees, and exchange all manner of jokes and gossip with the maid. Both refreshed, then, they could continue with the day's work, parting with friendliness on one side, and deep appreciation on the other. The gardeners were always delighted to see her, as were the stableboys, for there was such an insouciant air about her, such zest, such ribald slyness, that they could count on at least half an hour of fun and laughter. She paid them well, and was generous with them in other ways, such as the granting of a holiday, and a deep interest in their personal affairs. Nevertheless, they took few liberties with her, for they had learned that a certain flash of her eye meant "wicked" temper and ruthlessness, which did not pass away too quickly.

She enjoyed their company, illiterate though it was. For they were almost always simple and earthy and honestly licentious, and their remarks were pungent, if lewd. In their presence, she never had to pretend to be a fine lady. She could be one of them, some fundamental roughness and robust crudity in her satisfied and stimulated. However, none of her children overheard any of her conversations with her menials, for these conversations were conspicuous for a lack of reticence and were often highly improper. But sometimes Laurie or Angus might hear the far rich booming of her naughty laughter, and the accompanying shrieks of Mrs. Gordon, in the kitchen, and then the door would be closed abruptly. The servants were great friends with other servants in the city, and after each night off they would return with spicy gossip to pour into their mistress' receptive and eagerly malicious ear. This backstairs scandal was the light and interest of Janie's life, and if an item was particularly exciting and scandalous the bearer was often rewarded with a velvet pelisse or a silver fifty-cent piece or an extra evening off. It was not truly bribery; it was just that Janie would be so delighted and pleased that she could not resist the reward, and gave it with grateful generosity.

The kitchen was her favorite spot in the house. It was a large wide room, one of the biggest under that roof, and the floor was of red tile, the walls of white plaster. It had a huge sunny window looking out on the back gardens, with a wide window seat full of plump linen cushions. Along the wall hung the many copper saucepans, all gleaming like gold in the brisk light, and against another wall was the huge iron and brick stove, fuming warmly, the kettles hissing, the lids lifting under the pressure to emit good rich odors. There were three comfortable rockers in the room, and one was Janie's favorite, for it was small and well padded, and her feet could touch the floor.

It was summer now, the brief fresh summer of the North, and the opened window admitted the sweetest bright wind and the chattering of birds. The trees sparkled in the sun; the grass was green and vivid. Roses climbed against the white wall of the garden, and yellow marigolds and purple lobelia and pansies and phlox were mingled in riotous color along the brick paths. A weeping willow tree was like a green and fragile fountain in the center of the garden, its strands floating gently in the moving and radiant air, and far to the right stood a noble elm, its branches gilded with gold. Pigeons fluttered over the gray slate of the roof and over the red shingles of the stables and outhouses, and flew up brightly against a turquoise sky full of wide summer light. All was very still and peaceful. The pans boiled briskly on the stove; the curtains at the window stirred. Mrs. Gordon moved about heavily, but quickly; she was a huge fat woman with a hairy mirthful face and little blue eyes shining with malice and wit and contentment. Her gray-black hair was bunched untidily over her head and about her full pink cheeks with their hirsute sproutings. She had a big and bellicose mouth, a nose like a snout, and a billowy breast, and enormous hips swelling under her full black skirts. A crisp white apron was tightly tied over her quivering belly. She looked competent and alert, with no nonsense about her, and was a prodigious talker, emphasizing her remarks with gestures of a polished ladle or fork. She was Janie's best friend, and had a rough and ribald tongue and a fund of shrewd tales that endlessly delighted her mistress. Her tales were never good-natured or kind, but full of lasciviousness and scandal. Mrs. Gordon thought the worst of everyone, and the worst was always biological.

Janie sat in her little rocker, and went over the gowns and frocks to be given Mrs. Gordon's daughter, who was married to a "poor stick of a creature." And, like all women married to such creatures, she had many children, of whom Mrs. Gordon was not in the least fond. They were "brats" and "bastards" to her, though the unfortunate mother was quite legally wed to her chronically ailing spouse. Laurie's outgrown frocks and underwear and pinafores went to clothe the older girls, and her brothers unconsciously contributed to the same family, their garments industriously cut down to fit the numerous male brood.

Mrs. Gordon always had a remark ready anent her son-in-law. She watched Janie's sorting with approval. She said: "You'd think, wouldn't you, that a feller that can't get out of bed except at the call of nature, and is always whinin' like a beat dog, wouldn't have the gumption! Yet there she is, gruntin' out a young un every ten months, regular as clockwork, while he lies there, bleatin'. And she gettin' out of bed in three days to take in washin' again! It's hell, I tell you, Miz Cauder, it's hell!"

"I always say that is the last part of a man to die, and even then you can't be sure," chuckled Janie. She laid a white batiste frock of Laurie's on the pile, and picked up her own last summer's foulard, a pretty blue.

She looked very neat and pretty this morning, her red curls piled high for coolness on her small head, her freckled cheeks flushed, her green eyes sparkling with humor. She wore a thin loose frock of dotted Swiss, and her arms were bare to the elbow, below a series of wide crisp ruffles. Below the flounces of the frock peeped her little feet in their heelless black sandals and white cotton stockings. She was good-tempered today. Mrs. Gordon had just finished regaling her with several juicy tales about her neighbors, and she chuckled in remembrance. When she laughed like this, showing her white even teeth, she looked young and gay, and one hardly noticed the web of fine wrinkles beginning to overlay her face and deepen about her malicious eyes.

She said: "That's a fine tale, about the Mayor! Four terms in office, and still pinching the girls behind the doors. Who'd think it of the decorous Mr. Cummings!"

"And he a churchman in the best standing," nodded Mrs. Gordon, with a grin. "And as fine a wife as a man could have, and a pretty girl for a daughter."

Janie frowned quickly. "One can't blame him, with a wife like Alicia, Gordon. A priggish creature, with high and mighty ways. I've never liked her. I'd thought of her Alice for Bertie, but the lad'll have none of her. And now it's Robbie, mooning about her, though mooning is hardly the word, he's so cold-blooded. And Alicia watching them like a hawk, and frowning to herself, as if my lads are not too good for her puling brat! I should be the one who should look askance, not Alicia, for who are the Cummings', anyway? His father was a tavern-keeper and horse-trader, and he's done some clever horse-breeding himself. We have different ideas in England, Gordon. Anyway, Bertie shows good taste. None of a horse-trader's for my aristocratic Bertie!" And she nodded in grim satisfaction.

Mrs. Gordon's mean little eyes narrowed shrewdly and knowingly on her mistress, and she smirked to herself. She said: "Well, Miss Alice is pretty, and her dad's got a fortune, and Mister Robbie could look farther and do worse. Though there's not much choice in Grandeville, and perhaps your boys would do better in a bigger town, Miz Cauder."

Janie nodded, and sighed. She pretended to be down-hearted, but Mrs. Gordon saw through her pretense. "And there's my Angus, marrying that tub of white lard in November, Gordon. Oh, that Gretchen Schnitzel! And her dada's tanneries that smell to high heaven! It's like marrying a stink, Gordon."

"But a rich stink," said Mrs. Gordon, wistfully.

Janie looked resigned, but also smug. "He'll go far, my Angus, with the money. No foolishness about the lad. He's been well trained. He's already got his plans. If he can only hold his nose."

"Maybe he'll go into the tanneries," suggested Mrs. Gordon.

"Oh, God, no! Schnitzel—(Heavens, what a name!) has two lads of his own, you know. And Angus has other ideas. And his mama, too," she added with a chuckle. She continued after a moment: "Angus *will* have the lass. Gordon, though I can't abide her. Did you ever see such a face? White and lardy, with little pig eyes, and hair the color of bleached straw. And a nasty nature, too. Dull as lard. She'll be as big as a keg in a few years."

"Maybe Mr. Angus'll help with the bigness," said Mrs. Gordon.

Janie giggled. "I have my doubts, Gordon, I have my doubts. I fear the lad lacks the parts. Besides, he'd perhaps think it sinful. Everything's sin, to Angus. Though he never goes to church any more. Like as not he thinks the only proper way to replenish the earth is through immaculate conception, or through the bees, like flowers."

She and Mrs. Gordon went off into a loud gale of laughter, with many supplementary remarks, all exceedingly improper. They rehearsed Angus' wedding night, with appropriate squeals on the part of Miss Gretchen, and sweatings and agonies on Angus', and much shame. They were quite breathless for several moments after this.

"Now my Robbie," said Janie, when she could get her breath, "would be very judicial with his Alice. It would all be logic, and serious discussion, prior to the event. Alice would be put through a severe catechism, sitting there in her nightgown, on the bed, while he walked up and down the bedroom with his hands behind his back, in the best Napoleonic manner. What did she think of the matter? he would ask her. Had she any reasonable opinions on the subject? Had she come to any sensible conclusion? That would be my Robbie!"

They shrieked again, Mrs. Gordon taking the time from her pots to sit on a chair, which represented the marriage bed, and to smirk in imitation of the bewildered Alice. She put a huge greasy finger coyly in the side of her mouth, and bridled, and pretended to blush. She threw her apron over her face. Janie was convulsed at this. "That would end the discussion!" she cried.

Mrs. Gordon returned to her pots. "When is Mr. Bertie expected back from his rest cure in Saratoga?" she asked, casually.

Janie glanced at her broad back sharply. But her face saddened. She bent over another frock, and her voice was gentle when she answered: "Next week, I believe. The poor lad! So big and hearty, who'd have suspected that he had a lung condition? And a bad stomach? But there it is." She sighed. "I never thought, all these years, that he was delicate. But one can't tell, even with a fine body like his. I'd have thought it likelier of that miserable Angus of mine, or even my little wizened Robbie. But never of Bertie, so big and handsome and merry and braw. He writes me, however, that he's quite recovered, and is just on edge with impatience to see us all again."

"What did Mr. Robbie say, after his visit to Mr. Bertie?"

"Oh, Robbie thinks Bertie is doing excellently. He was quite encouraged, he said." Janie sighed again. "Who'd ever have thought it, so gay and good-tempered, and never a care in the world—my darling Bertie."

Her rough voice was sweet with love and sadness, and very low. Her hands trembled above the lengths of the bright frocks on her knee. She blinked for a moment, and was quite blind with the dazzle in her eyes. Mrs. Gordon, who really loved her, glanced at her furtively with deep sympathy. That drunken good-for-nothing! To break his mother's heart like this! But then, he was such a love, he was, and like sunshine in the house. She echoed Janie's sigh.

There was a little heavy silence in the kitchen, and it seemed darker, though the sun still danced on the copper pans on the white wall, and the red tile was ruddier than ever. A fresh new breeze blew through the windows, sweet with summer scents and the odor of the damp grass. The blowing willow lifted its drooping fronds like a green wave, and then subsided. The pigeons cooed softly, spread their wings against the sky. The kitchen was full of the good odors of roasting beef and boiling broth. A length of taffeta hissed on Janie's knee as it slid towards the floor.

Then, in the distance, came the soft notes of a piano. These were followed by the sudden pure rising of a lovely voice, so beautiful, so rounded, so full and strong, that it seemed like the meditation of an angel. Mrs. Gordon, at the stove, paused in the very act of putting the ladle in a pot, and lifted her head. A look of tenderness stood on her coarse big face.

"Ah, Miss Laurie at her practicin'," she murmured.

Janie frowned. "Does she have to yowl so early in the morning?" she muttered. She threw down another frock with a vicious gesture.

But Mrs. Gordon heard nothing but that perfect and celestial voice, rising and falling on a simple practicing scale, and making of that scale a beautiful sound full of glory and sweetness and gravity. Tears rose to Mrs. Gordon's eyes. The breeze died. The pigeons were silent. It was as if the whole earth listened.

And now the voice became grave and slow, like meditative organ notes, murmuring of angelic prayer. Even Janie was compelled to listen. "The lass does have a good voice," she said, grudgingly. "But I doubt she'll have the ambition to make anything of it. She only took Stuart's teacher to please him. Not from any desire on her part. He's the only one who can do anything with the minx. Didn't I hear her, myself, tell him that she would take his teacher, and practice, only because she wanted her voice to be good enough for him! The nasty little wench! If she had been even two years older I'd have clapped her in a closet for that, and minded her like a hawk, and put good tight drawers on her! She sounded like a mewling lass, all lovesick and languishing."

She got up suddenly and shut the door with a loud and furious bang. The voice faded away behind that door to a deep murmuring. "Yowling, so early in the morning!" Janie repeated.

Mrs. Gordon was annoyed. She said: "Mark my words,

Miz Cauder, that girl'll do you proud one of these days! There's good money in that voice."

Janie, however, was not displeased. "I hope so," she said sourly. "With all that money spent on her. Though it's not my money. If that fool wants to waste two thousand dollars a year on a teacher for her, that's his affair. He always was wasteful and quixotic. I don't know why he does it." She chuckled evilly. "If he thought that he'd make a profit on my lass, later, he was damned mistaken. I took care of that, wisely. I made him sign a contract that he'd expect nothing at all from her later earnings, and he had to sign it before I'd let the minx breathe a note to his fine teacher from New York!"

There was nothing kind in Mrs. Gordon's hard eye as it dwelt briefly on Janie.

"And he boards and keeps Mr. Berry, too, besides the two thousand dollars," she said thoughtfully. "I wonder why he does all this, for your girl?"

Janie shrugged. "He's beyond me. But he was always picking up lame birds and putting them in trees. Wasn't he after me about Angus, until the lad curtly told him to mind his own business? Didn't he fume and fuss about Bertie, until I agreed to let my darling go to Saratoga? With him, Stuart, footing the bills?" She chuckled hoarsely. "If the damned ass wishes to waste his money on my children, who am I to stop him? Better my children have some of his reckless money than the trollops of the town. 'Why does he do all this?' I don't know. A busybody, a meddler, that's what he is."

"Perhaps he has a good heart," suggested Mrs. Gordon.

Janie snorted. "He's just a fool, I tell you, Gordon. A snivelling damn fool. Can't help doing for others. He'll end in the workhouse, and it's glad I'll be to see him there!" She flung a dress from her, and stamped on it, involuntarily. "That's where you'll find all the do-gooders, in the workhouse, and be damned to them for jackasses and dolts!"

She stood up, shaking out her Swiss flounces. "There you are, Gordon. Five of my frocks, and six of Laurie's, for your daughter." She paused. She put her hand in the pocket of her dress. She drew out a roll of bills, and selected one. "And you can give the lass this, from me. With that new baby, and all, she'll need it."

CHAPTER 36

BERTIE and Robbie Cauder strolled idly together, this Sunday morning, along the banks of the river, on the Canadian side. They had taken the ferry an hour ago, and were now on the way to Frenchman's Creek, where they contemplated hiring a small flat-bottomed boat for a few hours of rowing. It was a favorite sport for them; Bertie carried a knapsack with sliced bread, cold beef, and a bottle of wine.

It was a resplendent early autumn morning. The river, to their right, was a brilliant indigo under a sky hardly less colorful. Grassy banks sloped to the water, fretted with the shade of elms and maples. The latter trees were just turning into great fiery bushes, burning vividly against that indigo sky. There was a soft rustling in the still and shining air, the twittering of birds, the last busy humming of bees. Butterflies, yellow as butter, rose and fell gently on the softest and winiest of winds. The river murmured and whispered against its banks. The American shore beyond the waters was sharply etched in clear green, and in the distance the young men could see the squat little ferry steamer plowing determinedly, a toy boat, across the river, its lacy white wake spreading out in a fan across the heaving blue.

A high and musical bugle sounded through the silent and radiant air. A short way down the rutted and dusty country road was stationed the Canadian garrison. Against the strong indigo sky fluttered the Union Jack, all its colors blazing proudly. The young men could see the gray and ancient walls of the garrison, fretted with sunlight and treeshade. But they saw no one at all. As they approached the garrison, and Fort Erie, white farmhouses and little white cottages were clustered closer together, and the soft Sabbath was made even more silent by the occasional lowing of cattle, the bark of a distant dog, or the cackling of fowl. Now a few gardens faced the road, carefully enclosed in white picket fences. Beyond them burned last roses, zinnias and late summer poppies. Once they heard the creaking of a pump, or the squealing of a gate, or a faint far voice. But still, they saw no one.

They passed the garrison. In the yellow dust of the yard

three or four Canadian soldiers talked idly together, leaning on their muskets. Their young mustached faces turned with empty curiosity on the young men. Robbie and Bertie lifted their hats, smiled. The soldiers saluted, watched the walkers out of sight. Behind them the Union Jack streamed in the wind.

Now they had the rutted dusty road to themselves, with not even a cottage visible, only trees, grassy banks, and the river, and the wide and brilliant air. They had not talked for some time. Then Bertie cleared his throat, turned his sweet and charming smile on his much loved brother.

"Y'know, when I looked at that old damn flag there, the Union Jack, it fair touched me. A curious feeling. You'll thing me a fool, Robbie."

But Robbie said coolly: "Why should I? Patriotism, or chauvinism, is an old emotion. Primitive. Rooted in the race. Atavistic. A survival of the herd instinct. We'll not rid ourselves so easily of early instincts, Bertie. It'll take generations of reason and education. Not in our time, I am afraid."

Bertie, as always, was vaguely baffled and disheartened at Robbie's logical and quiet disposal of emotion. Robbie hid that emotion, when it was displayed to him, as one quickly hid offal or any other unpleasantness, for decency's sake. Bertie, in consequence, was a little depressed. He scuffed his polished boot in the yellow sifting dust. He said, somewhat petulantly: "Damned if I can ever make out what you mean, Rob. I only meant that when I saw the blessed old rag I realized I was far from home. A long way from home."

Robbie smiled with affectionate cynicism upon his brother. But he said, and there was a little sadness in his level voice: "You'll always be far from home, Bertie. Never mind me, though. We're out for a holiday, and that's all that matters."

He was sorry that he had depressed Bertie. But he simply could not help scotching silly emotionalism. Robbie firmly believed that the millennium would arrive when men acquired reason, and then only. All this balderdash, all these fetishes! No wonder man's mind still groped in the dark subterranean forests of primordial history, like a blind fish nosing amid sunken vegetation and dead roots! What did that mind discover in the watery and weedy desolation? Mermaids and seahorses, green monsters and flashes of phosphorescent decay. Sunken minds in shadowy forests!

The two young men were dressed in their Sabbath best, Bertie resplendent and handsome in light gray broadcloth pantaloons and darker gray skirted coat. There was something of Stuart Coleman's large splendor about him, though he was slightly thinner and shorter than his kinsman. His ruddy bright curls glimmered under his tall gray hat. In his gloved hand he carried a silver-headed cane. His ruffled linen was immaculate and crisp. He had apparently recovered his buoyant health, though there were still dark lines under his gay blue eyes, and a pallor about his mobile and almost constantly smiling mouth. Because he lacked Stuart's violence and fierceness, his glances were never quick or ireful, but always sparkling and amused or tender. His quick color had almost completely returned, except for that slight lividity about his red mouth, the underlip of which was so full and soft.

As for Robbie, he wore his uniform of black broadcloth with startling white linen, plain and glistening. He moved beside his brother, elegant and compact, the figure of aristocracy and judicious neatness. Even his gloves and his hat were black. He carried an ebony cane, with a gleaming gold head. He walked effortlessly; his movements were a little stiff and considered. Janie, angrily seeing them depart that morning, had said ill-temperedly: "There goes my darling with the black manikin! Whatever does my Bertie see in that undertaker?"

There were many others who wondered about that, for surely in the smiling and careless Bertie there could be nothing that would inform or stimulate the cold and precise intellectualism of Robbie's mind. Bertie's conversation was always gay, light and inconsequential, though never cruel or malicious. He could be amusing, almost always. Perhaps Robbie found this lightness and gaiety delightful, though one would never have suspected that.

They reached the mouth of Frenchman's Creek, where two ancient fishermen kept the little flat-bottom boats and fishing tackle for occasional customers. They were sleeping blissfully in their weatherbeaten shack when Robbie pounded on the rotting door, for Saturday night was a festive occasion for them, necessitating all of the Sabbath for recovery. One of them, in a dirty night-shirt, came grumbling to the door, and opened it with loud complaints. The door creaked loudly in the sunlit silence. Robbie smiled at the old man. "Hello, Bob. How about a boat for me and Mr. Bertie? And some fishing rods, and some worms?"

He and Bertie sat on the warm bench, their backs against the soft rotting wood of the shack, while old Bob pulled on a pair of trousers and swore lustily, within. Then the fisherman came out, stooping and haggard, his matted white hair streaming down to his shoulders. Cursing even more loudly, he carried a spade to a moist spot and began to dig for worms. His mangy old dog came out and sniffed at the two young men, who swung their neat legs idly in the autumn sunshine. Robbie leaned back, fastidiously, as far from the dog as possible. But the smiling Bertie scratched the old animal's neck with his white and jewelled fingers until, entranced, the beast put both forelegs on his knee and fawned on him with drooling adoration. His bleared eyes brightened lovingly; he rubbed his eldritch head on Bertie's immaculate knee, slobbering on it to Robbie's complete disgust.

"Ah, the puir auld lad," murmured Bertie, in his soft rich voice. "It's a puir auld creature, that it is. A fine auld man, in his last days."

The poor animal was beside himself. He wormed his skeleton muzzle under Bertie's flowered waistcoat, and tried to embrace the young man with his balding paws.

"You'll have fleas," Robbie pointed out. "And God knows what else. Look at your pantaloons now. Full of dirty gray hairs."

But Bertie put his arms about the dog and hugged him tightly, laughingly evading the kisses from the pale dry tongue.

Robbie said sharply, with an anger he could not define except that it was quite warm in his cold breast: "He may have a disease, Bert. You remember, he had some kind of scurf last summer. Do you want to be ill?"

Suddenly, and with a haste unusual for one who was so precise and considered, he seized the scruff of the lean and dirty neck and yanked the dog from his brother's embrace. Then, with a well-placed kick from his little pointed boot, he sent the animal howling and sliding from his brother, with such haste and force that its hindquarters and threshing legs stirred up a cloud of white dust. The dog came to a sprawling halt, then swung about for a new charge upon the adored Bertie, its face expressing only bewilderment and pain. Robbie raised his cane threateningly. The dog stopped in its tracks, panting, its eyes tortured. "Get away!" cried Robbie. "You filthy devil!"

The dog looked at him, and cowered. Then, dropping its withered head and almost hairless tail, it slunk behind the shack, whimpering.

Bertie turned to his brother, whose pale dark cheek was actually flushed. He shook his head gently. "You shouldn't

have done that, Robbie. No, you shouldn't have done that."
He still smiled. But his blue eyes were strangely bright and
fixed.

Robbie shrugged. He brushed off with a capable small
hand the gray hairs that clung to Bertie's knee. "You have
no intelligence, Bertie. If you don't have nasty sores soon,
or worse, I'll be surprised."

But Bertie, still smiling, only continued to shake his head.
He looked at the restless blue river and the distant American shore. Then again, he gently shook his head. His profile
expressed nothing.

Robbie was very irritated. Abruptly he rose, dusting himself off in annoyance, and went to see how the worm-digging
was progressing. He stood beside the old fisherman with the
fluttering white hair, and criticized the proceedings coolly.
"Less dirt, more worms," he advised, touching the battered
old pan with the tip of his cane. "We're not paying for mud,
Bob."

The fisherman cursed him without pausing in his work.
Bertie still sat smiling on the bench, looking out at the river.
All at once, there was an air of desolation about him, in the
sunlight.

But he was quite cheerfully voluble when he and Robbie
were once in the little boat, rowing up the creek. Sometimes he burst into a rollicking song, throwing back his
handsome head. He had carefully removed his coat. The
ruffled neck of his fine white shirt was open, and his full,
milk-white throat was exposed to the sun. The sunlight shattered on the diamonds on his fingers. He sang, and the water
echoed back his voice merrily.

Robbie, who would save his exertions for the return journey, down the creek, leaned back in the stern of the boat
and looked idly about him.

It was strange, the difference in the scene which the two
brothers saw. Robbie felt that the warmth of the autumn
sun was agreeable on his bared head and shoulders, and the
water calmly blue and the sky very clear. But that is all that
met his eye, all that impinged on his senses. He was occupied by his own abstract thoughts.

But Bertie saw something quite different. The boat glided
deeper and deeper into the creek waters, and, as the stream
left the turbulent river it became narrower and quieter.
Now the still grassy banks sloped steeply to the water, dark,
green and transparent and the long fronds of weeping willows swept the surface with frail fingers, their shadows a

lighter and more delicate green, airy and intangible. The bottlegreen of water-lily pads floated on the still surface, and their lovely flowers lay like stars among them, full of pure scent. Dragon-flies skimmed through the dim green air, jewelled and brilliant, and birds called from the dusk of the thickening trees. Now one could glimpse broken fragments of the burning blue sky through the willows. At one place the creek widened suddenly, to enclose a tiny island on which stood a motionless heron, streaked with rose in the sudden down-pouring of open sunlight, unnaturally vivid against the surrounding gloom. All about the boat sounded the vague ploppings of frogs as they dived from the water-lily leaves, and as the trees closed over the narrow creek again, and the watery green dimness engulfed the boat, one could hear the shrilling of tree-toads in the hidden damp fastnesses of the woods. Here and there a finger or a flash of light struck the water, hurtingly vivid. And over all was the clear and spectral silence.

Bertie was quiet now, though his lips were pursed as if about to whistle. He looked about him. His face was quite serious. It was like a beautiful marble face fallen into pure green water, in the shadow of the trees and in the reflection of the stream. He saw things Robbie did not see, or would not condescend to see. His blue eyes were opaque now, and moved more slowly.

They found their favorite spot. There was an opening in the trees, and the bank was less steep, and more gentle and thickly tufted with grass. They pulled up the boat, gathered up the knapsack, and climbed the bank. There, under a clump of trees some distance from the creek they sat down, leaning their backs against the brown trunks. They were enclosed in motionless, rustling peace, listening to the twitterings and the songs of birds in the thick branches above. They lit cheroots, spread their legs before them, and smiled at each other.

"Nice here," commented Robbie. He opened the knapsack, and withdrew two books from it. One was his "Discussions on Criminal Law," and the other, Bertie's Keats. He glanced at that thin volume, and tossed it indulgently to his brother. "Why you read poetic trash is beyond me," he commented, but with affection. He opened his book. He glanced at his watch. "We'll eat in an hour," he said. "Just time for a couple of chapters. Judge Taylor is to question me about them tomorrow."

Bertie took his book. He sighed and smiled. "I'll miss you, when you leave for Harvard, Robbie," he said.

Robbie shrugged indifferently. "That won't be until after Christmas," he answered. "I'll be home often. The winter will pass very soon."

Bertie's smile was more vivid. "Not for me," he commented. He opened his book. "Not for me," he said, in a lower tone.

Robbie said: "Yes, I know what the damned winters are here. There'll be snow in hardly another month. But you'll quite probably be very interested in your portrait work."

"Oh, of course," said Bertie, a shade too enthusiastically. Robbie frowned. He looked at the end of his cheroot. "You could go to New York to study," he remarked.

Bertie shook his head. His smile was very gay. "No, not for me," he said cheerfully. I've brushed an ash off his knee. "I'm not interested in New York."

Robbie regarded him with grave thoughtfulness. No, he thought with secret pain, you'll never be interested in New York. Or in anything. Never, never interested in yourself, or in living, or in anything in the world.

But Bertie seemed quite at peace, and happy, beginning to read his poetry. There was not a line in his body, in the bending of his head, which was not beautiful and perfect. Robbie could not understand the deepening of his pain. He began to read, but at first he could grasp nothing of the small text. Then, summoning his stern self-discipline he soon became absorbed in the intricacies of criminal law "as practiced in the sovereign State of New York."

Now there was nothing at all but the whispering woods and the echo of distant lapping water and the calls of the birds and the shrilling of late locusts. The light under the trees became softer and clearer, yet more spectral.

Robbie, to his irritation, began to discover that his book did not interest him very much. His thoughts ran away with him, a most unusual thing. He began to think about his brother, and finally he did not see the printed page before him.

He thought of Bertie with the sadness and heaviness with which one thinks of the dead or the inexorably dying. But his thoughts were without words. They were only a sad enduring, a faint sick restlessness like formless grief. There was nothing he could do for Bertie. There was nothing anyone could do for Bertie. For Bertie could do nothing for himself. Within that shining head there was no will, no desire.

He was like a bright leaf in the sun, which when that sun was gone was without a light of its own, nor cared for any light. It only waited.

He had known women, but he had known them as one knows food and then forgets it until the next exigent hunger. He could not love. Robbie even doubted that Bertie had for him more than a childlike affection and attachment, a little stronger than what he might feel for anyone or anything.

Then, quite suddenly and with hurting vividness, Robbie recalled that scene with the disgusting old dog. From the cool and colorless depths of his heart there rose a great silent cry, like a burst of anguish: Bertie! Bertie! There is something you have not told me! There is something you could tell me, and I would try to understand!

Bertie felt his intense look, and glanced up. He smiled broadly. "Look here now, Robbie, I know you hate poetry, but you've simply got to listen to this. Two excerpts. I've marked them. I'll read them to you, damn you, and you'll listen!"

He expected Robbie to protest abruptly, and wave him off. But to his mild surprise Robbie said with unusual gentleness: "Yes. Read them to me."

Bertie began to read in a voice Robbie had not heard before:

> "Darkling I listen; and for many a time
> · I have been half in love with easeful Death,
> Called him soft names in many a mused rhyme,
> To take into the air my quiet breath;
> Now more than ever seems it rich to die,
> To cease upon the midnight with no pain,——"

His rich voice stopped, and he looked at Robbie with his unchanging smile, and in silence.

Robbie did not speak. His black eyes did not leave his brother's face. But he felt a frozen stillness in him like death itself.

Bertie bent over his book again. "Here is another excerpt:

> "Heard melodies are sweet, but those unheard
> Are sweeter; therefore, ye soft pipes, play on;
> Not to the sensual ear, but, more endeared,
> Pipe to the spirit ditties of no tone:
> Fair youth, beneath the trees, thou canst not leave
> Thy song, nor ever can those trees be bare——"

Robbie did not hear when Bertie's voice stopped. He heard only:

> "Fair youth, beneath the trees, thou canst not leave
> Thy song, nor ever can those trees be bare———"

And then he knew that Bertie had a song, but it was not one he could ever sing to anyone, not anyone in all the world. He had no words for it; he had only pain, which he confronted with his brilliant smile and his gay eyes.

And Robbie also knew, with the mysterious prescience that came to him so rarely, that he would always see his brother, like the youth in the poem, singing his unearthly song under trees forever in full leaf, forever unchanging, himself forever dead.

He came to himself with a start. He had heard a curious sound.

Bertie had bowed his head on his knees and was weeping.

CHAPTER 37

IT WAS Angus' custom to accompany his sister, Laurie, to Stuart's house every Sunday afternoon in order that the girl might play for an hour or so for her benefactor.

But on this particular first Sunday in November he had taken ill with a feverish cold, and Junie commanded her youngest son, Robbie, to convey his sister to Stuart's home. Robbie, gloomy and exhausted, did not find this a pleasant prospect, but he was not one to argue vindictively, and was too adult to refuse a favor or even a peremptory request, if it did not inconvenience him too much. He saw no adequate reason, then, why he should not accompany his young sister through the streets of Sunday Grandeville.

Robbie did not particularly care for Laurie, though he had a casual affection for her because in some ways she resembled their brother, Bertie. She had Bertie's blue eyes, and her hair was only a few shades more golden, and she also possessed his fresh coloring and tall classic stature. But she and Robbie had had little conversation together, for he thought her rather a "dull piece" for all her beauty. Moreover, though she was but thirteen, she was almost as tall as he, and as he was irritably aware that his own stature was hardly impressive it annoyed him that so young a girl could almost meet him eye to eye.

However, he was prepared to be kind to her, uninteresting though her conversation would probably be, during the mile walk to the home of their kinsman. Also, he wished to speak to Stuart privately. In a paternal voice, therefore, he urged Laurie to dress warmly and to take her muff. For the streets were already filled with snow and ice, and a stiff gale, arctic and numbing, swept through the desolate streets under a low and angry gray sky.

The endless Northern winter had set in late in October. Until the middle of the following May the city would be gripped within the frozen hands of the Lakes and the bitter river. Robbie, whose blood was thin and cool, hated this northern clime, and contemplated the next seven months of rigorous winter with complete gloom and disgust.

So sentimental a term as "heaviness of heart" was not appropriate for Robbie, yet he was now suffering a very similar affliction. Too analytical and logical for a real surge of emotion, it annoyed him that he could experience such a dragging weight in his chest, such an aching stiffness in his limbs. Yet, discipline himself though he would, he could not rid himself of his weary malaise, his deep hopelessness. I have made my decision, he would say sternly to himself, and with self-disgust, and I shall think no more of it. But his denied and repressed emotions (though he would not acknowledge their existence) refused the decision made by his mind.

Reviewing all this, he walked with his sister through the deserted, windy streets. They had covered over half the distance before he became aware that he had exchanged no words at all with Laurie. He was too polite and civilized not to feel some discomfort over this. Therefore he glanced sideways at her, as he clung to his tall hat, and smiled frigidly, "Horrible weather, isn't it, Laurie?" he asked, courteously, and immediately felt complete ennui.

She turned her face to him, and returned his smile. It was a very lovely face, he noted absently. "Yes," she murmured. Her cheeks were flushed and cold.

"I'm afraid I'm not an interesting companion," he conceded. "Unfortunate that Angus has his chill. He would have much more to talk to you about."

Laurie turned her face away. She said, with cool tranquillity: "Angus and I never have anything to talk about, anymore."

Robbie was politely surprised. He bent his head in order

to get a glimpse of Laurie's face. It was quite rigid and tight under the beaver bonnet, he observed, and unpleasantly mature in its expression. Now he felt a stir of real interest.

"But you were always such friends, Laurie," he suggested.

She did not answer. She only walked a little quicker, with her long and smooth glide. For a moment or two Robbie was humiliatingly forced to trot to catch up with her. He was quite convinced, now, that tiny Alice Cummings was the young lady for him, and he immediately discarded his former admiration for statuesque females. Laurie would be quite a giant, he thought irritably.

"Angus was always your guardian," he remarked, further annoyed that his breath was a little hurried. "And you two were quite close."

But Laurie said clearly: "Angus has changed."

"Yes?" said Robbie, with increasing interest.

He was somewhat discomfited when his sister glanced at him with an odd smile, and a dimple appeared in her cheek as if she found him naive. "Angus has changed, that is all," she said.

"We all change," he commented coldly. "Did you expect him to remain a little lad?"

"No," she said, very quietly, "but I did not expect a man to become a little lad."

Robbie was amazed. He thought this a very peculiar and provocative remark to be made by a young lady not yet fourteen. Had he heard rightly? If he had, then his preconceived notions about Laurie were all wrong, and he would be forced to revise them. That would make for mental messiness, and take time. He preferred to analyse, index, and file all his conclusions permanently.

"I don't understand, child."

Laurie compressed her lips, and her young face appeared older and harder. She said with some coldness: "Why should you be interested, Robbie? You and Angus were never concerned with each other. Or are you just curious?"

"Curious!" exclaimed Robbie, annoyed. "I was only making conversation."

Laurie said: "I don't like making conversation. It is a waste of time."

Robbie, before he could discipline himself again, was conscious of a really hot dislike for his sister, and a renewed sense of humiliation. These were aggravated by her cold and unpleasantly amused smile as she stared steadily before her.

"It seems," he said severely, "that your polite education has been sadly neglected. Has no one told you that pleasant conversation is a necessity in civilized society?"

Laurie laughed suddenly. She touched her brother's arm lightly, and her eyes danced. "Then how your 'polite education' has been neglected, Robbie!"

His mind said to him: The minx is impossible. But some unsuspected spot of humor in him was tickled, and he laughed involuntarily. "Yes," he admitted, in an unusually warm tone, "I'm afraid it has, Laurie. I was only speaking as an elder brother to a young sister. Frankly, I think we Cauders aren't very civilized, are we? But what can you expect, with such a delightfully uncivilized mother?" he added, ironically.

Laurie had been smiling. But at his last words her eyes darkened, her lips became tight and hard. She shrugged. She walked a little faster.

All at once Robbie was conscious of the most infuriating pain in his chest, a sharpening of his sickness. For there was a look about Laurie, now, of Bertie. Her walk, the smoothness of her steps, the color of her hair, the lines of her profile, were all Bertie's. As one clings to a portrait of one who is dead or who is forever far away, so Robbie wished to cling to Laurie with a quite unreasoning passion.

He said, and was shocked at his own involuntary words: "Laurie, do you know that you look very much like Bertie?"

Her walk slowed. She turned her head to him. Now her young blue eyes were grave and gentle as they fixed themselves upon him. Stupefied, he saw compassion in them, and a new and thoughtful tenderness.

"Do you think so, Robbie dear?" she asked softly. She took his hand and held it, as they walked along more slowly.

He could not control himself. He said, with rare simplicity: "Yes, my dear. You do." He paused. "I—I am very fond of Bertie," he added, in a low voice.

"I know," she whispered. Then she said: "I am glad I look like Bertie."

He was silent. Their hands held together strongly. Robbie's mind said: This is ridiculous. But the sickness continued to lighten in his heart, and he felt the warmth of his sister's hand.

They did not speak again until they reached Stuart's house.

Here, by the river, the wintry air was heavy and sluggish, massive with cold. The river, gray and ruffled, reflected the somber light of the dark afternoon; the Canadian shore was lost in a gloomy mist. One could hear the rushing of the waters, the groaning of the wind in the bare trees. There was nothing but gray desolation and the monotonous flow of the river as far as eye could see, and heaven tumbling with dusky clouds. Occasionally a bronze or scarlet leaf, dry and crumpled, blew through the heavy and laboring air, or a gull rose, crying dolorously, a pale leaden light on its curving wings. All the grasses round about had turned a rusty brown, and bent in the wind with a crackling sound. Along the shore, waves hissed against the stones, left on those stones a skin of thin and breaking foam. Here and there were patches of snow, white as bone, and frozen.

Above them stood Stuart's house, the "Irishman's Folly," bleached and gleaming white against the rolling gray sky, a lonely temple of beauty incongruous in that wild setting. Laurie and Robbie climbed the flagged walks and opened the fretted iron gate. When they lifted the knocker clamoring echoes followed the sound, too loud in that immense and desolate silence.

But the shining black and white hall was warm, filled with a sweet and languorous scent, and lamps bloomed about, softly. A maid helped Laurie with her cloak and bonnet. While Robbie was similarly assisted, Laurie smoothed her ruffled golden hair with the palms of her hands, and glanced down at her crimson merino frock. Then she walked with Robbie into the great and lovely parlor, all her composure and serenity returned, her head high.

Stuart and his wife, Marvina, and his little girl, were waiting for them. With them was Mr. Richard Berry, the "fine teacher from New York," a very little dark man with a full black beard and a fiery black eye. He came forward, pointing his narrow polished boots like a dancer, and bowed deeply. Though he was pure New Englander, he affected a fierce and Continental manner, appropriate to a teacher of voice. He might even have kissed the young Laurie's hand had she given him the opportunity. He glanced restlessly at Robbie, and when Stuart came forward to introduce the two, he bowed again. He heartily disliked small men, and he did not like Robbie's cold and derisive eye.

Marvina, a radiant vision in blue velvet, came gracefully across the Aubusson carpets to greet Laurie and her brother. She kissed the girl on the cheek, and beamed emptily on Robbie. Wifehood and motherhood had done well by Marvina; she was quite plump now, and statuesque. But they had not put maturity into her beautiful vapid face with the wide golden eyes. It was the face of a child, forever.

"Oh, my pet, you are quite cold!" she said, in her rich voice, which had no expression in it at all. "And our dear Robbie is with you today, and not our Angus. Why is this?"

"Angus has a cold," said Robbie, politely, bored already. He did not like fools. But even a fool was better than this charming woman with the shining black hair who did not even possess folly. She made him uneasy. It was like addressing a statue, to speak to her. It gave him a sense of surprise when she answered a remark, for he was certain that anything said to her was unheard, and aroused no response in that perfect breast or behind that smooth white forehead.

He glanced curiously at Stuart, standing and smiling fixedly beside his wife, and he wondered idly, as he had wondered a dozen times before, how this violent and tempestuous man could endure the society of this empty woman who was nothing at all but a great doll echoing the thoughts and words of others. But, he thought, perhaps she was soothing.

Little Mary Rose came up now, shyly, smiling at Laurie, whom she deeply loved. The child took the older girl's hand confidently, and looked up at her. She was a very frail little creature, with a pointed and elfin face, white and thin. Her mouth was too wide, and too sensitive, and very tremulous at the corners, and a mass of lusterless dark hair tumbled over her fragile shoulders. Her straight little nose had quivering nostrils. But her eyes, enormous and black and full of sadness, were also radiant with sweetness, bright as dark stars, and trembling with light. Over her red wool frock was fastened a ruffled pinafore. She was so fairy-like, so frail and tender, that even Robbie could not look at her dispassionately, and he smiled at her frigidly and touched her cheek with his finger.

The great and exquisite parlor was warm and soft with lamplight. A fire crackled and roared on the marble hearth. On the pianoforte stood a crystal vase of hot-house roses. Roses were everywhere, from Stuart's precious conservatory. Robbie glanced about him approvingly. Everything was so tasteful. As always, when he entered this house, his respect for Stuart increased surprisingly.

Stuart insisted on being present at Laurie's lessons. He sat down and took his daughter on his knee. She nestled her head against his chest, and lay weakly in his arms. Sometimes she glanced up at him with shy and shining adoration. Marvina seated herself with the unconscious grace of an actress, her lustrous blue velvet draping itself perfectly along the lines of her thighs and legs, her white neck gleaming in the lamplight. Her usual lovely and empty smile was already graciously fixed on her face. Robbie sat neatly and stiffly in his chair of pale French satin, and prepared for an hour of complete boredom. He did not understand music. He did not care for it. But he turned his face politely and expectantly towards Laurie, who stood by the pianoforte while the vapid Mr. Berry played a few flowery chords. All about them bloomed the lamps, brightening the delicate colors of furniture, draperies and carpets, touching pale carved wood with fingers of soft light, mingling with the rosy lances of the fire.

Laurie had not yet begun to sing. Robbie glanced about him. Stuart's face was haggard and somber, and abstracted. He played slowly with a lock of his child's dark hair, and caressed her cheek with absent fingers. Her little legs were flaccid against the buff pantaloons that covered his fine good legs. His rings glimmered on the fingers of his big hands. It had been a hard year for him, reflected Robbie, with some involuntary sympathy. And the bad year was not yet up. He, Robbie, knew a great deal, from his mother's malignant remarks. The "panic" had done Stuart no good at all, and would do him still more mischief if he were not careful. Doubtless, he was thinking of it. There were deep and irascible clefts about his gloomy mouth. His eyes were sunken and heavy. He was a rash and foolish man, Robbie's reflections continued, and a turbulent one. But there was something about him——

Mr. Berry turned dramatically from the piano to the audience. "Schubert's *Who is Sylvia!*" he announced. "Miss Laurie has been practicing this for some time, and now she will give us an elegant rendering, for your pleasure!"

Robbie saw an irrepressible smile touch Laurie's lips. The minx stood beside her teacher, tall and composed and so damnably assured! Robbie was amused. There was an air of calm detachment about Laurie, too mature for her age.

Then her mouth opened, and from its rosy cavern came her voice, pure and effortless, full of sweet strength and melancholy. Now her detachment was gone. Her whole body became part of her voice, and it seemed to vibrate. Everything about her, now, was alive and rapturous, intense and vehement with ardor. She had forgotten those who listened.

She flung back her head; her face was lighted and ecstatic, strong with passion. Her hair fell down her back; her young breast arched. She lifted her hands, and they remained before her, lifted, palms upward, as if pleading. She was a woman, no longer a girl. Slowly her head turned, as if drawn by an irresistible wild attraction, and she looked at Stuart, her voice pouring from her like a golden stream.

And Stuart looked at her in return. His slowly moving hand faltered, then lay passively on his child's shoulder. Across the width of the lighted room his eyes met Laurie's. And now there was a tenseness about him, though he had not moved, and for all his quietness.

Robbie had heard Laurie sing at a distance in his own home, but he had not been interested, or even fully aware. His precise and orderly heart, so carefully free of emotion, had never been touched by music, for he lacked the organs to perceive so purely instinctual and emotionally noble an art. But now his cool senses were most enormously disturbed, and he felt the presence of an overwhelming passion and exaltation and terror in Laurie's overwhelming voice and her living young face.

He thought to himself: The money has not been wasted, then. She can really sing. But the thought was mechanical. There was something else in this room beyond a glorious voice, perfect and rounded and heroic though it was. There was something abandoned and more than a little terrible, something beyond reason, something which could overwhelm reason in one fiery flood, and demolish it, and set its little meaningless fragments to floating and rolling like jetsam on a roaring sea.

He looked at Laurie, as if the meaning of all this might be in her. He saw that her face was white and passionate, her blue eyes distended. He saw that she looked only at Stuart. Slowly, Robbie turned to his host. He saw the still hand on Mary Rose's dark hair. He could not see Stuart's profile, for it was turned away from him. But he sensed Stuart's passion which answered that in Laurie's face and in her voice.

Robbie frowned. Why, the minx was hardly fourteen! Fourteen in four weeks. He wondered, for an instant, why he remembered that. He had not even been aware of her age before. But this was not a child who stood there singing. It was a woman, unashamed, crying out, pleading, humbling herself, reaching out in an enormous hunger and rapture that would not be denied.

Robbie's contemplative frown deepened. He compressed his lips. It was all nonsense, of course. Would the damn song never end? He looked at Marvina, who was still smiling emptily, and nodding her head in pleased graciousness in time to Laurie's singing. She was fluttering a perfumed handkerchief before her lips. Her slipper tapped, under the flowing blue velvet of her gown.

When Robbie saw Marvina like this, he cursed himself for a fool, an idiot. And then Laurie was no longer singing. She was smiling down at Mr. Berry, who, with a judicious inclination of his head, was criticizing her effort. "A slight strain on the high notes—here," he said, striking a few loud notes. "A slight weakening at this passage, where it should be full." He commanded Laurie to repeat the criticized passages. She did so, out of context.

But now there was nothing wrong with the atmosphere of the room. It was all casual again, and ordinary. The repeated notes bored Robbie. He drew out his kerchief and wiped hands whose palms were ridiculously moist.

Stuart's hand had begun to play with little Mary Rose's locks again. He appeared suddenly exhausted. There was a weak and relaxed look about his long legs. He smiled down at his child; he was very pale. He murmured something to the little girl, and she nestled closer to him. Marvina yawned, caught herself, smiled about her vaguely and politely as if apologizing. Mr. Berry was pointing out a passage very irritably and severely to Laurie, and she was bending obediently over him. One heavy strand of her yellow hair fell across her attentive face. She warbled a few notes, nodding her head. It had become very dull and tiresome in the room. Robbie caught himself yawning.

Mr. Berry was giving Laurie instructions now, about her next practice. She nodded her head thoughtfully. Robbie glanced with boredom about the room again. He looked furtively at his watch. Through the half-drawn draperies he saw that it had begun to snow. Dark swirling flakes rushed against the polished windows. The fire crackled loudly, swept up the chimney touched with orange as it was caught by a heavy wind. Now, to Robbie, the room, the whole house, seemed empty for all its brightness and beauty, and a little cold. He wanted to go home.

And then he knew that he must talk to Stuart. He had contemplated this before, but had forgotten it in the ridiculous confusion of his thoughts. Stuart was talking quite loudly to Mary Rose, who was giggling. He hugged her to him, and the child shrieked, with delight. Marvina yawned again. Mr. Berry was closing the lid over the keys. He swung around to Stuart. "Did you enjoy the song, Mr. Coleman?" he asked smugly.

Stuart started. He looked over Mary Rose's head. "Eh? Oh, yes. Very much indeed. Laurie is coming along, eh?"

Mr. Berry paused portentously. He pursed up his lips. His black beard stuck out from his chin impressively. He contemplated the ceiling, screwing up his eyes. "She is improving, yes. She is growing, yes. But she will need much more before she can be accepted in our New York school. I suggest about a year more of close application. Yes, indeed. Very close application. No frivolity. No carelessness. A serious dedication, which is hard to find in the young. A religious dedication, Mr. Coleman. A thoughtfulness. A determination. But I think Miss Laurie has all these," he added hastily.

He then informed Laurie that he would have the pleasure of hearing her practice on Tuesday. (The practicing went on during the week. On Sundays Stuart and his family were regaled by the results.) A maid entered with a tea-tray, and the firelight glanced rosily on the silver. Marvina, all gracefulness and amiable twitters, seated herself before the tray and began to pour tea and dispense little slices of bread-and-butter and small cakes. All sat near her, about the fire. Stuart seemed to have forgotten everyone but his daughter. She perched on his knee. He would fold a slice of bread neatly and urge her to eat. At first she would refuse, gazing at her father pleadingly, but at his gentle insistence she would eat obediently, to please him. But her appetite was meager.

Mr. Berry had embarked enthusiastically upon the subject of operas he had heard in Berlin and Paris and London. As he talked, he waved the hand that held a little cake, and distributed crumbs copiously over the rug and himself. Stuart listened with real attention, now that the subject was a personal one with him. Marvina chattered amiably to Laurie, and the girl answered politely. Sometimes she would regard Marvina long and seriously, her fair brows knitted as if she had grave thoughts. She was young again, hardly more than a child, eating with pleasure, tossing back her streams of golden hair. Robbie drank tea, which he hated, and dispassionately disposed of cakes.

"Yes, it is definitely Wagnerian, that voice," Mr. Berry confided to Stuart. "Definitely Wagnerian. I can just hear Miss Laurie in *Lohengrin!* The lovely Elsa! She has a natural presence for the role. She will need no wig. The hair is perfect. She will have the stature, sir. Yes, very definitely, the stature! She will be a sensation, Mr. Coleman, a positive sensation! She will receive ovations in the capitals of the world! She will be received by crowned heads. As for America—" and he spread out his hands with somber significance —"who appreciates the arts in America? A barbarous country, sir, a barbarous country! There will never be anything here."

Stuart's face suddenly darkened with annoyance. He shifted his child on his knee, and she murmured. "What do you mean, sir?" he demanded irascibly. "What is wrong with America? It is a young country, yes. But you apparently forget that young countries are potentially capable of anything. When America has come of age, she will produce her own peculiar genius. What it will be I don't know. But produce it she will, I am certain of that. There is nothing impossible here."

Mr. Berry was taken aback. He said apologetically to his patron: "That may be quite true. But I have seen no signs of it, yet."

"It does not have to be the same kind of genius as that of Europe," continued Stuart, with rising irritation. "It may be something new. The signs are all about. America has a lustiness, sir. You may call it ugly. I call it strength. Have you forgotten your history? Rome was a barbarous young nation at one time. Greece laughed at her. But Rome had her splendor, later."

"A barbarous splendor, sir!" exclaimed Mr. Berry, proud to display his erudition. "You remember that, sir. It never even approached the 'glory' of Greece. Rome never produced the arts and the sciences of Athens, the philosophy, the— the—"

But Stuart interrupted rudely. "It was another kind of genius, I tell you. Why anyone has to think that only one type of genius is valuable, I don't know. It is as foolish as expecting every man to have blue eyes, just because blue eyes are admired. Have you no eye for variety, for change, for other colors? Does the whole landscape of the world have to be monotonous to be admired and enjoyed? Where is your appreciation of uniqueness, of difference, of individuality?"

Robbie was faintly surprised. It was a good argument, that of Stuart's, he commented to himself. But why the devil need he get so excited about it? His very excitement made his words seem puerile and ridiculous. When a man spoke heatedly, and stammered a little, and said his say in a loud and hurried voice, then men no longer listened to his words, however true and golden they were, and only smiled in superiority at his vehemence. It was very unfortunate, and people were asses.

A smug but furtive smile touched Mr. Berry's lips, and he inclined his head to hide it, discreetly. Robbie suddenly disliked him intensely. He entered the argument smoothly, his cool and neutral voice like a breath of damp air:

"I agree with you, Stuart. But men are unoriginal. What has pleased them once, and excited their admiration once, always seems to them to be the best. They disapprove in direct ratio to difference. A man with a new philosophy, a musician with a new idiom, a planner with a new idea, an architect with a new design, is always contemptible to the donkey world, which has its preconceived ideas, its devotion to the past. That comes from timidity, from a fear of change, inherent in human nature. To accept a new idea threatens its security, always precarious in a constantly changing universe."

Stuart listened, frowning. Then he said impatiently: "Yes, yes. That is what I meant. Thank you. That is why I say that American genius is different. It is just developing. It is in flux. We can't see the outlines yet. It is all so new."

He looked at his wife. All at once he seemed utterly exhausted and undone. He said, in a dull but gentle voice: "My dear, will you call the nurse? The child is asleep; she is very tired."

Marvina, smiling vacantly, reached for the bell-rope near her. Then, still smiling that vacant smile, she rested her tawny eyes on her daughter. The smile did not increase in mellowness or tenderness. It was only there, like the fixed smile of a painted portrait.

The nurse came in and carried off the sleeping child, whose mass of dark hair fell over her crisp white arm. Marvina watched her go. Robbie was reminded of a mindless kitten, involuntarily following with its shallow eyes any chance movement that attracted its attention. When the door closed after the nurse, Marvina graciously returned her countenance to those about the fire, and urged fresh tea upon them.

Robbie said to Laurie, who was now staring at the fire: "Shall we go, my dear? There is a blizzard out, and we have quite a walk."

Marvina said amiably: "Do let us send you home in the

carriage, my love." But there was no concern in her voice.

Mr. Berry bowed himself out of the room, after a last whispered instruction to Laurie. Laurie moved off into the hall, followed by the gracious Marvina, who belatedly congratulated her on her song. Stuart and Robbie were left alone. Stuart restlessly opened a silver box and brought out a cheroot. He lit it with a taper. He stood with his elbow on the mantelpiece and looked sideways at the fire. He appeared to have forgotten Robbie.

Robbie moved closer to him. He said, in a low tone: "Stuart, I want to talk to you."

Stuart lifted his head heavily, and stared in silence at his kinsman.

"I don't know whether anyone properly thanked you before for what you are doing for Laurie," said Robbie, with a tentative smile. "But I thank you now. It is excessively kind of you."

Stuart's brows drew together. Then he shrugged. He flicked ash into the fire. "Well, the girl has a voice. You admit that? And her mother said that she could not afford a teacher."

Robbie laughed, and the sound was unpleasant. "She was quite convinced that Laurie 'has a voice.' Had you only waited a little, discreetly, she would have coughed up the money for a teacher. But you did not wait. She waited. She is very clever."

Stuart scowled angrily. "I doubt it, that she would have 'coughed up,' as you say. She has no liking for the girl. Besides, I never wait." Now he smiled a little, quickly.

Robbie nodded. "My mother is ambitious. Once assured that Laurie could sing she would have spent any amount. I know that. It was unfortunate."

Stuart said nothing. He looked gloomily at the fire.

Robbie continued: "Another thing. I understand that you have suggested to my mother that you again send Bertie to Saratoga."

Stuart was silent.

Now Robbie approached him, and laid his hand with unusual urgency on Stuart's arm. "I must ask you not to do this, Stuart. Please."

Stuart regarded him with surprise. "Why not? Do you think your mother might 'cough up' for him, this time?" He smiled disagreeably.

"No," said Robbie quietly. "I do not. I know she will not. Because I have convinced her it is no use."

Stuart dropped his arm from the mantelpiece. He looked at Robbie curiously. The "damned little schoolmaster" looked gravely disturbed and grim.

"You convinced her? Why should you do that? Didn't the last treatment help the poor young fool? He was six months off the bottle after that. Has he gone back to it?"

Robbie looked away. But his voice was still level when he spoke: "Yes. He has. It's no use."

All at once he appeared very tired. "It's no use," he repeated. "Once, I had a different idea about Bertie. It is still partly right. But the reason was deeper than what I had supposed. I know now that if he has any desire for anything it is for death."

Stuart gaped at him. His features wrinkled with shock and repudiation. "Why do you say that? That's idiotic. You talk like a fool."

Robbie shook his head. But he did not look at Stuart. "I know I am right. And I know that nothing will give Bertie any desire to live. It is not because he is 'sick' of living. He just has no desire for life."

He turned to Stuart, slowly, and somberly. "Have you seen a mirror on the wall, Stuart? It hangs there forever. Sometimes the sun flashes on it. Or leaves it. Then it is in darkness. It only—reflects. It has no life of its own. It is perfectly static. Perhaps," he added, with a curious twisted smile, "if it could express its one opinion, it would ask to be taken down from the wall. It would perhaps say it is tired of hanging there, reflecting sunlight, or darkness."

Stuart glared at him. His intuition, which had no reason, understood. But his lusty mind violently rejected anything so horrible. "I don't know what you're talking about! It's all gibberish! Mirrors, by God! What has your blasted young bastard of a brother to do with mirrors, for God's sake? Look, you: I get fed up with living, and with problems, and wish myself dead, momentarily. But that passes. I never really want to die, though I get sick in the belly at times just because I am alive. But all that passes, like any other bellyache. One must go on living."

Robbie shook his head. He said quietly: "But Bertie doesn't want to go on living." He hesitated. Then he admitted a thing extraordinary for this young man of rationality: "There are some things which cannot be put into words. They must be felt. With the emotions, if you will." His mouth became wry at uttering the loathsome word. "I feel —things—about Bertie. I had a sort of talk with him, about two months ago. He didn't say much. It was more his—look. And then I knew it was no use. Nothing could ever make Bertie desire to live. It isn't emptiness, Stuart. It is more than that."

"But what does the young devil want?" cried Stuart, and his cry was a protest against the horror he felt in his warm and tempestuous heart.

"I have just told you, Stuart. He wants nothing. And he can't bear living, knowing he wants nothing. I—I can't explain it. I am telling you this very badly. I have no words for it. But I know it is there, like a nightmare, in his mind."

"But why should he feel like that?" demanded Stuart.

Robbie shrugged wearily. "I don't know," he almost whispered. "I don't know. Perhaps he was born that way. Bertie is pliant. He agrees with everything. He is charming and amiable. He is always pleasant and consenting. Why? Because, I think, he finds nothing important enough to oppose or to fight or to deny. I have listened to him agree to two entirely different opinions, nodding his head, as if his heart were in it. But—nothing was in it. He is not even *not* interested. It is something even more negative than that."

Stuart contemplated this ghastly idea for several moments. Then in a stifled voice he asked: "How is he now?"

"He has been drinking steadily for several weeks now. Ever since we had that talk. He is desperately ill. He hardly eats. He just lies in his bed, and drinks. My mother wanted, at last, to prevent him from getting his drink. I told her it was no use. He would find a way to get it, if he had to get out of his bed and steal it. Nothing would stop him. He would be like a drugged man, or a mesmerized one, searching for the one thing which keeps him alive. We can only let him drink, and die. That is what he wants. Who are we to say that it is better for him to live? Understanding what he is?"

"You would let him commit suicide?" asked Stuart, aghast.

Robbie shrugged again. "That is what he wants. Oh, I suppose we could get him over this, for a while. But he would return. It would just prolong his agony."

He sighed, and it was a strange sound from him. "So, there it is. I can't leave him, now. I was to go to Harvard, as you know, after Christmas. I have given up the idea, temporarily at least. I shall stay with Bertie."

Stuart was deeply concerned. "But why do that? You've planned on it, haven't you? You need to go?"

But Robbie was indifferent. "Yes, I suppose so. But it can wait. I can keep on with Judge Taylor. I really don't need to go, I suppose. It isn't absolutely necessary. There were some courses in philosophy in which I was interested, as well as on law. At any rate," he added, with a bleak smile, "I can be a lawyer without going to Harvard. In another two years, the Judge tells me, I can be admitted to the bar in Grandeville without all the other preliminaries."

Stuart stared at him with a new sharp interest. The lad was human after all. But he could not help saying sarcastically: "Now, isn't that against all 'reason'?"

Robbie smiled again, and there was something boyish in his smile. "There you have me. But sometimes, I am afraid, there are things stronger than reason."

All at once Stuart liked him, with quite a rush of warmth. He put his hand affectionately on the youth's shoulder. "How old are you, Robbie? Eighteen? Well, you still have plenty of time. Look here, if you ever need anything, will you tell me?"

Robbie regarded him steadily. "Stuart, why do you bother with us?"

Stuart pressed his hand strongly on the other's shoulder, then withdrew it.

"Damned if I know," he said frankly, and with a grin. "Just a cursed meddler, I suppose. I'm not really fond of any of you, damned if I am!"

Robbie laughed.

As he went towards the doorway, Stuart accompanied him. "Look here now, Robbie, you'd best stop your ideas about Bertie. They won't do you a bit of good, I'm thinking."

CHAPTER 38

Joshua Allstairs crouched over his cane and looked long and thoughtfully at his visitor.

The past seven years had not increased the old man's benevolence though it had had that salubrious effect on his piety. Time, too, had shrivelled his wizened frame even further, and he bore an even more startling resemblance to an ancient spider. His terrible musty house, so dark and haunted, loomed about him like a cavern in which he crouched malevolently. Everything about him was shadowy except for his bright and predatory eyes which fixed themselves immovably on Sam Berkowitz.

"Ah, yes," he murmured. He nodded his head and smiled benignly. "Yes, Mr. Berkowitz, you may smoke if you like. Though I do not indulge in the noxious weed, for moral and other reasons, I have no objection if others wish to jeopardize their immortal souls." He smirked slightly.

Sam lit his pipe slowly and gravely. He leaned back in his stiff chair. He regarded Mr. Allstairs with gentle reflectiveness. In his turn Joshua scrutinized the other. Why had this abominable creature visited him, written to him begging for a few moments of his time? Joshua licked his lips. He prepared in advance to enjoy himself.

Sam sighed a little. He made his face smooth and masklike, and then smiled at his host.

"It is a small matter of business," he said apologetically. He appeared embarrassed. "I shall not take up your time too long, Mr. Allstairs."

"I am not going to the banks today," said Joshua graciously.

"But I shall not take up your time too long," repeated Sam. He looked down at the toes of his boots. "Mr. Allstairs, this may seem strange to you. But I must ask you a question. I understand that you haf in your possession several notes given to the First National Bank, the Broadway Bank and the American Bank, in New York, by my partner, Mr. Coleman, in the amount of $21,000?"

He said this blandly, and his brown eyes now narrowed sharply upon Joshua.

Joshua was taken aback. His face wrinkled until it resembled the dried meat of a mummified nut. His eyes glittered at Sam inimically. Then he cleared his throat, and said pompously: "Mr. Berkowitz, sir, this is a most extraordinary question. Indeed, most extraordinary. And, you will agree, quite astonishing, also. I do not know where you have gotten your information." He paused, tentatively. But Sam's expression was still bland and unreadable.

Joshua was infuriated. "I can't understand this, sir! You will realize that I am astounded. Business transactions are not usually the common knowledge of—uninterested parties."

"I," said Sam seriously, "am an interested party."

Joshua stared at him. Then he grinned. "Yes, yes, of course. Please pardon my impetuous words, Mr. Berkowitz. I understand that what affects your partner inevitably affects you." He coughed gently. "But I am afraid you are under a misapprehension. Not about the notes, which I assume you believe I possess, but in your assumption that I would enlighten you about them."

Sam puffed slowly on his pipe, and was silent. He rocked one knee which was crossed over the other. He was not disturbed. Joshua regarded him with malefic emotions. His claws tightened on the head of his cane.

Then Sam spoke again, still very gently: "I haf reason to believe, Mr. Allstairs, that you possess these notes. You must not ask me who has informed me. I shall not tell you. But I know you possess them. The only one who does not know this is Stuart."

Joshua glared at him. He sucked in his lips. His head sank a little deeper into his bent shoulders. Now he was all evil.

Sam smiled kindly. "I also know that you purchased these notes, sir, at a discount, as the banks who held them were greatly embarrassed during the panic, and they must haf their money. You bought them, though they were not due."

"They are due in another two weeks!" cried Joshua, before he could prevent himself.

But Sam only nodded seriously. "Yes, I know this. And doubtless you will press for payment."

Joshua did not speak, but his whole withered face became alight with a wicked radiance. Sam nodded again.

"I am prepared to buy those notes from you, Mr. Allstairs, at a profit to yourself."

Joshua gaped at him. He threw back his head, so that his twisted neck was visible, like a bundle of ropes. He could not control himself. He cried hoarsely: "'Buy them' from me! No one shall buy them from me! I would not sell them for twice the money! Do you think, you crawling Jew, that I would give away my long-awaited chance to do vengeance on that godless blackguard? Do you think I have waited so long to be thwarted now?"

Neither his evil sparkling eyes, his color, his madness, nor his vicious words, had any disturbing effect on Sam's equanimity. Sam merely gazed at him quietly, as if he had made the most ordinary of remarks.

His quietness, his air of gentle waiting, had their effect on Joshua. He gasped a few more times, and then was suddenly still. He stared at Sam a long time.

"Why do you wish to buy these notes?" he asked.

Sam said, looking at him steadfastly: "That is my affair, sir. But I haf said: I am Stuart's partner. You haf not forgotten?"

Joshua worried his lips. He sucked them in and out. He bent over his cane. His ancient head trembled as though in

a palsy. Then, all at once, he began to smile, and that smile
was more malignant than ever.

"Ah," he said, very softly. "I see. You are not insinuating,
sir, that you are weary of Mr. Coleman's conduct? His debts,
his crimes, his putting your firm in constant jeopardy?"

Now Sam's eyes became hard and motionless, and unreadable. He said: "You may assume that, sir."

Joshua studied him. And then the vilest expression flashed
across his shrivelled features. He began to chuckle. The
chuckle rose to a virulent cawing. He rocked back and forth
in his chair. He looked at Sam cunningly.

"I thought so! I thought so! I warned him, years ago! I
warned him that a Jew was a dangerous partner! Not, Mr.
Berkowitz, that I am condemning you. Oh, dear no! I am
really admiring you. You, like myself, have been looking for
your opportunity. Is that not so?"

"You may assume that, sir," repeated Sam. He smiled.
His look became confidentially amiable. "But all this, Mr. Allstairs, is entirely between ourselves?"

Joshua nodded, delightedly. He leaned closer to Sam. "I
am aware of many things, Mr. Berkowitz, which would surprise you. I know all the affairs, and debts, of the Grandeville Supreme Emporium. I know that you have not yet
weathered the storm of the panic. I also know the exact
amount which is in your private name, in the banks. Mr.
Berkowitz, I admire you. You are a cautious and expedient
man, and a thrifty one. Doubtless Mr. Coleman's extravagance and criminal negligences have infuriated you."

"Doubtless," agreed Sam, with a sigh.

"And you wish to rid yourself of him?"

Sam inclined his head.

Joshua leaned closer to him. "You need a partner, Mr.
Berkowitz, a silent partner."

Sam reflected, briefly, that a silent partner would be very
good indeed.

"How much, Mr. Berkowitz, when Mr. Coleman is safely
out of the way?"

Sam did not speak. Again, his eyes narrowed shrewdly
upon the other.

Joshua nodded, with admiration. "Mr. Berkowitz, as your
banker, I have long admired your business acumen, your
genius. I know it is you who have made the Emporium
what it is, what it could be, if you were rid of Mr. Coleman.
I know how much more you can do. That is why I have
asked if you might consider a silent partner."

"I would consider such a partner," admitted Sam. His voice became earnest, even eager, but very cautious also.

Joshua nodded again. He rubbed his hand stogether. "It will be easy to do. I shall present my notes to our admirable and reckless friend, and will force him out of the Grandeville Supreme Emporium. Then I shall be your silent partner."

He looked at Sam with delighted and affectionate conspiracy. "I think, Mr. Berkowitz, that this solves our problem to our mutual satisfaction."

Sam was very quiet. He pulled placidly on his pipe. His eyes, now, were bits of shining brown stone.

Joshua became impatient. "It is all solved, Mr. Berkowitz." He grinned. "I realize, of course, that this causes you to pause, to think. You had intended, had you not, to present these notes to Mr. Coleman, and throw him out yourself, leaving a completely free field in which you would have no partner at all?"

Sam looked away. He appeared embarrassed.

Joshua shook an arch finger at him, and chuckled deep in his throat.

"What an expedient rascal you are, sir! But I admire you! On my word, I admire you. But I am afraid I cannot accede. I want a share in the Grandeville Supreme Emporium. If you are afraid that I shall interfere with the management, set your mind at rest. I have given the matter long thought, sir. When I purchased the notes it was with this idea: that I would be your partner. I trust your judgment, sir. I trust you implicitly."

He laughed with more richness. "He thought he could trust you, too. But he is no Joshua Allstairs, the unprincipled lecher!"

His face changed again, became vile and murderous. "He took my daughter, the only creature I had in all this world. Was he a good husband to her? Did he cherish her? No! He is breaking her heart. He exhibits his shamelessness to her boldly. His loathsome affairs are common knowledge. Think, sir, what this is doing to the heart of a gentle girl, who trusted him, and placed her life in his care!"

Sam sighed deeply. He looked at Joshua with intense sympathy. "This I know also, sir. I cannot express my regret."

Joshua became excited. He throttled his cane, as if it had been flesh. He was beside himself. He lifted the cane and shook it violently.

"I shall not rest until I have brought him low, until he

grovels at my feet in penitence for his outrages against God and man! I have sworn this. I have waited and planned for this. And nothing shall turn me aside!" He struggled for breath. "Only when he is a beggar in rags, imploring mercy, hungering for a crust, shall I be satisfied. When he is ruined, when my daughter is my own again, and her child sheltered in my arms, shall I know forgiveness."

Sam listened. His expression was sad and full of sympathy. He nodded repeatedly. "I understand," he murmured. "It is only to be expected.

Joshua, exhausted, fell back in his chair. He looked at Sam fixedly. He slowly fondled the head of his cane. He said: "You are a gentleman of heart and perspicacity. You understand me."

"Yes," said Sam, reflectively, "I understand. I sympathize. Nevertheless, you must sell me those notes."

Joshua aroused himself again. He was trembling. He cried: "I shall not sell you those notes! Haven't I made myself clear, yet, and what I want? Are you asking me to deliver my vengeance into *your* hands?"

"Yes," replied Sam, soberly.

"Then, sir, you are a complete fool, and I must revise my former opinion of you!"

Sam folded his arms on his chest. "Haf you forgotten, sir, that I may have a little vengeance of my own to satisfy?"

Joshua stared at him, moistening and sucking his lips.

"Stuart," continued Sam, "owes me over eighteen thousand dollars on personal notes. I shall never receive it back. There are other matters, too. That is why I must have his notes."

"But cannot you see, you obtuse creature, that we shall have a mutual revenge!" exclaimed Joshua. "Is that not enough for you?"

"No," said Sam thoughtfully. "It is not enough."

Joshua subsided. He rubbed his chin with his cane. He began to grin again. "It is true, then, that a Jew's vengefulness is bottomless, and without mercy."

Sam's eye began to sparkle strangely. But he said nothing.

"He has been your friend. He trusted you. He has been helpless in your hands," Joshua meditated, deliciously. "He trusted you above all others. He delivered himself to you, without reservation. Yet you would do this to him."

"Yes, I would buy his notes. At a profit to you," agreed Sam.

Joshua sighed. "Much as I admire you, sir, for your resolution, this cannot be. I am afraid that our revenge must be mutual. I assure you that it will not be the easier for him. I should like to see his face when he understands that his dear friend has betrayed him! Yes, I must see his face. I must be present. That is my one stipulation."

Sam stirred a little on his chair. It was the slightest movement, but it was eloquent.

"I shall pay you twenty-four thousand dollars for these notes. There is no interest due. Stuart has paid the interest promptly. You will haf a clear profit of three thousand dollars." He added: "No, more than that, sir. You bought these notes for seventeen thousand dollars. That is seven thousand dollars clear profit. It is not little, Mr. Allstairs."

Joshua forgot his pleasure in a surge of annoyance. He struck his cane up and down on the carpet. He shook his head angrily. "You are obstinate, sir. I shall not sell you those notes. Even though I lose three thousand dollars in immediate profits."

Sam stirred again. He looked down at his folded arms. "You must," he said, with the utmost gentleness. "I assure you, you must. For if you do not, I shall inform the proper authorities of your small traffic in the Underground. I shall inform the proper authorities that at the present moment there are twenty unfortunate negroes in a certain building known to you, owned by you, and that you haf exacted much money from these unfortunates for their passage to Canada, and that you haf made a fortune under similar conditions. Your confederates, sir, are known."

Had the house suddenly burst into flame about him then, had the walls and the ceilings collapsed with a thunderous sound, had Sam suddenly changed into a fiend before his eyes, Joshua could not have been more stupefied. Nor could his color have become more ghastly, nor his look more appalled. He fell back in his chair. He stared at Sam with a terrible look.

"Yes, I must haf those notes," said Sam, regretfully. "For if I leave this house without them, I shall go from here to the proper authorities. I had not thought I must say this to you. I thought it might all be done with kindness and understanding."

"You blackmailer!" whispered Joshua, and that whisper was as terrible as his look.

"I am much afraid, sir, that I am indeed a blackmailer," sighed Sam.

Joshua did not speak. The little fire snarled on the dark hearth. The gloomy walls drew closer. The early April wind whined at the windows. The old man might have expired in his chair, so motionless was he; even his fixed eyes had a look of death in them. He began to whisper again. It was like the rustling of leaves, that sound, like the scrabbling of a rat through straw. Sam heard it. But he could not hear the words for several moments.

"I have been betrayed. I have been delivered to my unbelieving enemies. I have been trapped by a godless Jew, a killer of the Christ. I, a Christian, have been delivered into the hands of the Saracen, of the abominable one, of the murderers of the beloved of the Lamb."

At these frightful and loathesome words, Sam was not disturbed at all, except that his eyes became brighter and clearer as he regarded Joshua steadily. His seamed face might have been a little paler, but that was all.

He said, with his usual gentleness: "I must haf those notes. Now."

Now Joshua became mad. He began to shriek. He struck at Sam with his cane. Sam merely pushed his chair out of range. Joshua gibbered. His face was horrible to see. It was distorted out of all resemblance to humanity. He writhed on his chair. His head rolled sideways on his shoulders.

He began to pant in his extremity. He screamed: "I shall have my own revenge for this! You shall not live in my country, for which my fathers died, and pollute this sacred earth any longer! I know what I know! You shall die like the Jewish dog you are!"

Sam said: "I shall haf those notes now. Now."

He stood up, calmly. He took out his watch, and glanced at it. "I haf taken up too much of your time. You shall give me those notes, now."

He took out his book of cheques. He glanced about him for a pen and ink. Then he pointed to the bell-rope beside Joshua's hand. There was a sudden terribleness about him, inexorable and merciless. "You will ring for ink. For a pen. I shall write you a cheque for twenty-four thousand dollars. Now."

CHAPTER 39

SAM OPENED the door of Stuart's office, silently, and stood on the threshold.

Stuart had not heard him enter. In fact, had Sam entered noisily he would not have known. For he was staring at the wall above his desk with the blind dry eyes of a man in extreme desperation. A smoldering cheroot was held flaccidly in his fingers.

Sam looked at him for a long time. He saw the haggard profile, frozen and motionless. He saw the ever increasing white threads in Stuart's hair.

He coughed gently. Stuart started. He turned his head slowly. Then a most painful smile touched his mouth but not his stricken eyes. "Come in, Sam," he said, and his voice was faint and hoarse. He nodded towards a chair. Sam sat down, and regarded his friend with deep sadness and understanding.

"You must know that this month you will not haf more than two hundred dollars from the shops?" he asked, in a low tone. "I haf just gone over the books."

Stuart did not speak. He had turned his head away again, and was again regarding the wall.

Sam lifted his hands and his shoulders, in his ancient gesture, then let them drop expressively.

"You haf not taken my advice," he said.

Stuart groaned. He put his hands to his face. There was silence in the office. Beyond the door there was that heavy and listless silence of shops which are empty. Sam could hear the murmur of frightened clerks and the shuffling of their feet as they dusted counters already dusted that day. He knew that they would wander to the windows and stare eagerly at any chance passerby, in the pitiful hope that she would enter.

Stuart said thickly: "There's no use. The people have no money, or no confidence. Our trade is steadily dropping."

"It is no worse than last month. And it is better than three months ago," Sam remarked, sighing. "We begin to see light."

Stuart turned to him with furious despair. " 'See light!'

But not soon enough to save me! No, not even if business recovered completely in six, five, four months!"

Sam said nothing. Stuart sprang to his feet, knocking over his chair. He began to walk up and down the office with distracted steps, pushing his hands repeatedly through his hair, and sometimes pulling it. He sighed. Sam watched him, not moving. Back and forth went the heavy and lumbering steps, quickening as his disordered thoughts quickened. Stuart stopped before his friend and cried out: "It is nothing to you, of course! Why should it be? But why must you sit there like a bloody image and watch me die? Are you gloating over me, by any chance?"

Sam said with extreme calm: "I haf said, Stuart, that we are recovering. Very slowly. Most slowly. But, we are recovering. We are paying off our debts. Each month sees us meet our debts completely, if painfully. We are acquiring no others. In two months, we shall be even. Does that not give you some joy?"

Stuart was silent. But as he stood there before Sam, he looked violent. He still ran his hands through his hair. Then, with slow blind movements, he felt for his chair and fell into it. But he did not glance away from Sam.

"Yes, what you say is true," he said in a muffled voice. "About the shops. But not about my private debts. I owe money. You must have guessed that."

Sam looked at the floor, and waited.

Stuart began to laugh, and it was not a pleasant sound. "Did you think I was living off the shops?" he asked wildly. "If you did, you were a fool! But you always were a fool, Sam."

Sam glanced up quickly. Now real anger flashed in his eyes, real disgust. He pushed back his chair as if he could not restrain a violence of his own. The gesture was instinctive. He said sternly: "I am tired of this, of being called a fool! I shall not haf it. It is finished. It is enough."

He stood up, also. He faced Stuart, who had begun to pale. Then Stuart turned from him. "Forgive me," he said, in that thick voice. His hand fell on his desk. "I don't know what I am saying. But you don't know——"

He fell again into his chair. He covered his eyes with his hands.

Sam stood behind him. He began to speak in a strangely quiet yet strangely passionate voice:

"Always, they say 'forgive me,' when they haf had their way with us, Always, when they haf taken our substance, and our blood, our labor, and even our lives. Always, when they haf defiled us, and degraded us, and used us, and inflicted suffering upon us, and driven us away into darkness and exile and pain. Always, when they haf struck us in the face, and trampled upon our children. Always, we must be subject to their madness and their hate, their superstition and their greed, their cruelty and their abominations! Always, when they haf glutted themselves upon us, and they haf become tired of the poor sport, and their own terribleness has frightened them they say 'forgive me.'"

Stuart dropped his hand. He turned in his chair and looked at Sam. He saw his friend's face as he had never seen it before, moved, stricken, but most enormously stern and unrelenting.

Sam raised his hand as if in invocation. He said: "'Forgive me!' And always, we answer: 'Father, forgive them, for they know not what they do.' But I say that you know what you do! You always know what you do! And because you know, you lift your hand again and again, and we die under it, world without end!

"But I say now that some day we shall cease to forgive. Some day, when the burden you haf put upon us is too heavy, we shall cry out to God, and there shall be only anger in our hearts, and not our long patience. And then, and then," he continued, his voice dropping into deep quietness, "God will answer us, and look upon our afflictions, and do His justice."

Stuart stared at him. And then a deep wash of color ran over his face, and his eyes fell. He said: "There is nothing that I can say. Except that I am ashamed. I shall not ask your pardon, Sam. That would be insulting you." Again, he covered his face with his hand, as if to hide himself.

After a long moment, Sam sat down near him. His tired face was very pale. Wearily, he brought out a few sheafs of paper and laid them near Stuart's elbow. "Are these the things which are worrying you?" he asked sternly.

With exhausted abstraction, Stuart dropped his hand and looked down at the notes beside him. Then suddenly he became rigid. He turned very white. He sat in stupefied silence, his eyes fixed. Then, still not looking away from the notes, he muttered: "Where did you get these?"

Sam said coldly: "From our friend, Mr. Joshua Allstairs."

Stuart came to life. He swung violently upon his friend. "From Allstairs! From Allstairs!"

"Yes," said Sam, undisturbed. "From Mr. Allstairs. I

bought them from him yesterday. For twenty-four thousand dollars. He had purchased them from the banks for much less."

Stuart put his hand to his forehead, and rubbed it savagely, as if to awaken himself from an impossible dream. He stared dazedly at Sam. And Sam returned his dilated regard impassively.

Slowly, then, Stuart began to realize. He whispered: "He bought them. He bought them to do me in. He intended to ruin me. That is what he was plotting."

"Doubtless," agreed Sam.

"And—he would have done it."

"Doubtless."

Stuart glanced down at the notes again, in stupefaction. He picked them up, examined them, as if incredulous. He dropped them on the desk. Very slowly he turned to Sam. He tried to speak.

Sam picked up the notes with measured movements, tore them neatly across, walked over to the fireplace, and dropped the fragments into the fire. He watched the flames devour the paper. In a moment there was not even an ash.

Stuart looked at Sam's back. He tried to walk. He put out his hand and caught the back of his chair. He was trembling uncontrollably.

"Sam," he whispered.

But Sam did not turn.

Stuart passed his shaking hands over his face. When he had withdrawn them his eyes were full of tears.

"It was the money for the Island," he said. "For your—people."

"Yes."

Stuart's throat and mouth were dry as death.

"You did that, for me," he said.

Sam turned from the fire. He was faintly smiling, though he appeared sad. "Yes, for you. You are a fool, Stuart."

They looked at each other. Sam's tired smile grew broader. He shook his head.

"Forgive me," he murmured.

Stuart sat down. He put his arms on the desk, and his head bowed on them. There was no sound from him.

Sam hesitated. He looked down at this broken man whom he had saved from complete ruin, at such a terrible and heart-breaking expense to himself. He tried to speak. But he could not.

Very quietly, then, he turned and left the room.

CHAPTER 40

RIVER ISLAND was afire with crimson, amber, scarlet, gold and bronze, under a sky of brilliant Chinese blue-green that appeared painted with an enormous flat brush against a high and arching dome. The few white clouds in it were white and carved and still, their edges outlined in sharp light. The river, a shining jade green, translucent and soft, lapped the grassy banks gently, on all sides. The Island, itself, was all flat wooded land, burning with color in this early November. Winter had been delayed. The land was basking in a golden Indian summer, and the mild air, soft and scented with woodsmoke, was filled with a dreamlike haze in which the far reaches of the river were lost and only its murmuring voice was heard. Dreamlike, too, was the enveloping peace. The autumn sun possessed a gentle warmth, though the light wind was cool and fresh. Sometimes the haze lifted a little, so that the streaked jade waters could be seen running swiftly towards the Falls. The American shore, on the left, the Canadian shore on the right, were only soft green-and-scarlet blurs beyond the waters that enveloped the Island.

The trees rustled faintly, with a dry sound, and now and then an amber or crimson leaf floated through the air. In the thick brush and thickets and woods, rabbits and squirrels scampered through the heaps of vivid leaves already fallen. Horse-chestnuts lay in the high and fading grass, moist and brightly brown in their open green shells. Red flowering vines climbed over stones, and little yellow wild-flowers grew in warm spots. The robins and other summer birds had incontinently flown, but gulls with glittering wings swept over the river and the banks, and uttered their melancholy cries, and sparrows were still brisk in the blazing trees. Sometimes, carried a long distance by the wind and water, one could hear the long whistle of the little ferry-boat, and hear its minute chugging.

Sam Berkowitz and Father Houlihan were walking on the Island this late Sabbath afternoon. They walked alone. The Island was quite large. Once or twice they saw the gray clapboards of a lonely farmhouse, heard a distant dog, or the rumbling of a wooden cart. But even these were lost as they plunged into the woods and came out on the north side of the Island where there was nothing to be seen or heard but the Canadian shore and the jade river. Here, on a small knoll, they sat down.

There was a deep understanding between these two friends that needed few words. Both might love Stuart with a paternal passion, and yearn to protect him. But for each other they cherished a long, compassionate and complete friendship, as equals, as men.

The priest removed his flat black hat and began to fan himself with it, for his girth had not decreased with the years. Also, his bunions hurt him. He rubbed them frankly, and frowned at his dusty boots. His great bald head glimmered in the reflected light under the trees. His big pink face was beaded with sweat. But there was a look of peace and meditation in his strenuous blue eyes.

Sam, in dusty brown, stretched out his long lean legs, and lay back on his propped elbows. His seamed gaunt face was tired and very quiet. His white hair lifted in the sweet breeze. A squirrel ran near their feet, carrying a bright chestnut in his mouth. He paused to look with wild and glancing eyes at the two men under the trees.

"It's four o'clock," said Father Houlihan, examining his huge silver watch. "How long will the boatman wait for us?"

"Until five, Father."

"Yes. Yes. Of course. In the meantime, we have nearly an hour." He sighed with peace. "It is very pleasant here."

And then he was sad. He glanced sideways, quickly, at Sam, who remained silent. Sam looked at the water. He sat up and plucked a few blades of grass, absently. He and Father Houlihan often walked here on the Island, full of plans for the things about which they would talk. But they never talked much, orally. However, their minds exchanged profound conversations, and they invariably left the Island refreshed and further confirmed in their affection and joy in each other.

But today Father Houlihan was very sad. He wanted to speak to Sam, and fumbled in his mind for words. But he had no words, and as he possessed great delicacy, he hesitated to speak of what was in his sore and simple heart.

So he looked out over the river, pursing his wide red lips, and praying a little. Sometimes he glanced furtively at his friend, on whose tired face there was a large resignation and despondency. Father Houlihan sighed, over and over, wrinkling his eyes, struggling in himself, praying to his favorite saint for the proper phrases in which to comfort the other man, who had not spoken, or told of the enormous trouble in himself.

Then the priest cleared his throat, and said casually: "Of the Old Testament, the Psalms are my favorite."

Sam looked at him courteously, but with abstraction. There was no interest in his eyes.

The priest clasped his hands on his knees and looked thoughtfully at the river that shone and sparkled with emerald lights. "There is one Psalm that always makes me think of you, Sam."

"Yes?"

The priest smiled, with a shy and childlike look, almost pleading. "Do you mind if I repeat it? Of course, it is very familiar to you.

" 'Lord, who shall abide in thy tabernacle? Who shall dwell in thy holy hill?

" 'He that walketh uprightly, and worketh righteousness, and speaketh the truth in his heart.

" 'He that backbiteth not with his tongue, nor doeth evil to his neighbor, nor taketh up a reproach against his neighbor.

" 'In whose eyes a vile person is contemned; but he honoreth them that fear the Lord. He that sweareth to his own hurt, and changeth not.

" 'He that putteth not out his money to usury, nor taketh reward against the innocent. He that doeth these things shall never be moved.' "

He repeated the majestic words slowly, with deep and subdued passion, and his voice was like a gentle prayer. At the end, his eyes were dazzled with moisture. He put out his warm hand and touched Sam on the shoulder.

Sam's face was unreadable. He did not look at the priest. He stared somberly at the river. Then, very wearily, he smiled. "That is so good of you, Father. But it is not true. There is no man like that, nowhere in the world. Except you."

Father Houlihan blushed brightly. He said eagerly: "Oh, no, no! You must not believe that of me! I am really a bad man, a sinful man. There is no controlling my heart, and my thoughts. Sometimes I even wish to kill! You do not believe that? Oh, there are times when I could do many a mischief,

I'm thinking, when I see how cruel man is to his brother, and how relentless, and how brutal, and how stupid. No, no, Sam, you must not believe good of me. I am weak and vulnerable, and I never think until after the event, and I have a tongue like a saw."

He shook his head vehemently. Sam's smile had become broader. He laughed a little. He regarded his friend with affectionate interest.

"I am so busy doing penances," said Father Houlihan ruefully, "that I really have no time to examine my soul, and understand God even in a small measure."

Again, there was silence between them, and Father Houlihan was helpless again. What had he done to comfort his friend? Nothing. His favorite saint must be busy on other affairs just now, and impatient of any interruption. Father Houlihan felt very humble and depressed.

Time passed.

Father Houlihan, in brushing off his black garments, felt the bulk of a small book in his pocket. He removed it. He smiled at it, pleasedly, looking at Sam. Perhaps a few excerpts from this book might redirect Sam's somber thoughts. He uttered a small and tentative sound.

"Have you read much of Thoreau, Sam? A very wonderful philosopher. One of my favorites, and so full of the life and vitality of America, and its underlying spirit. Would you mind if I read you a little?"

"Please," said Sam politely, and though his heart was too heavy for thought, he turned on his elbow to listen.

Father Houlihan had a good and flexible voice, sturdy and full of sincerity. He waved his small black book at the water and the trees. "Thoreau has words for this: 'When we walk, we naturally go to the fields and woods; what would become of us if we walked only in a garden or a mall? Even some sects of philosophers have felt the necessity of importing the woods to themselves, since they did not go to the woods.'"

He paused and contemplated the water again. "Sometimes," he said, meditatively, "I have thought that in a spiritual sense more deeply than in any other, that passage refers to America. This wonderful, wonderful America! This land of width and forest and air and water and glorious skies. See what Thoreau says: 'The heavens of America appear infinitely higher, the sky is bluer, the air is fresher, the cold is intenser, the moon looks larger, the stars are brighter, the thunder is louder, the lightning is vivider, the wind is stronger, the rain is heavier, the mountains are higher, the rivers longer, the forests bigger, the plains broader.'

"Yes," said the priest, his face kindling, "and the heart is greater, the soul is larger and stronger, the mind is freer, hope is without boundaries, and faith is nobler. There is no end to what is America. You, Sam, have called it the Promised Land, the Promised Land for all men."

"The Promised Land," repeated Sam slowly. He looked about him at the Island he had loved and coveted for the oppressed. His eyes closed on quick pain. The priest saw it, and his heart swelled with responsive suffering. He turned to his book, sighing.

"Thoreau speaks of America as the 'holy land.' Hear what he says: 'So we saunter toward the Holy Land, till one day the sun shall shine more brightly than ever he has done, shall perchance shine into our minds and hearts, and light up our whole lives with the great awakening light, as warm and serene and golden as on a bankside in autumn.'

"Yes," said the priest gently, "that is the future of America. She will go through much sorrow and agony, much darkness and distress and hopelessness, much error and pain and bewilderment and stupidity, but at the end, there will be the 'great awakening light.' Nowhere else in the world will that light be, for the darkness is too thick in the Old World."

Sam looked at him steadily. The weariness lifted from his eyes a little, and they had begun to brighten. "Yes. Yes. I haf always believed so."

"We are all Pilgrims, to America," said Father Houlihan. "We have come from wicked places and tired places. We have come here naked, with only our hope. With all the other races of men which form America, we will band together in brotherhood, and create a new destiny. In this land, all men will be brothers."

Sam sighed. "Yesterday I read in the paper that a man called Mr. Stephen A. Douglas has defeated Abraham Lincoln for the senatorship from Illinois. The papers make much of it. They foretell many gloomy things from it. I haf read much of this Abraham Lincoln. I believe he is what you say: 'an American.'"

Again they sat in silence. Sam had relapsed into his reflective despondency. Annoyed at his favorite saint, and abandoning tact and delicate approach, Father Houlihan burst out impulsively: "Sam, Stuart's told me what you did for him, and what it has meant for you!"

For a moment or two Sam's face expressed only annoyance and impatience. "He talks too much," he commented.

"You did not mind him telling me?" asked the priest, anxiously.

"No. No, certainly. But I thought——"

"That he might have more reticence?" suggested Father Houlihan, when Sam paused. He laughed a little. "Neither Stuart nor I belong to a reticent race. We speak from the heart, quickly, or from the devil in us, rashly. We bluster, roar, curse, weep, love or praise, at the top of our voices. Yes, we're a noisy people. But we never plot. For that, perhaps, God might forgive us our clamorous tongues."

When Sam only smiled faintly, the priest continued impulsively: "It was a kind thing. It was such a kind thing! And Stuart wasn't insensible to the cost to you, Sam."

Sam's thick white brows knitted quickly, as if with impatience. His hands touched the earth of the Island, and a flash of pain ran through his eyes. He could see, with his inner eye, this fine fair Island settled, the neat white cottages surrounded by gardens, by plowed fields, by thick orchards, by meadows filled with fat cattle. He could see the burnished roof of a synagogue here, off in that green mass of towering pines. He could see the brick wall of a school. He could hear the laughter of children, the happy voices of women, the deeper tones of freed men who lifted their eyes to a free and peaceful sky. Now the pain was deeper in his face, like an inner pang of agony.

He said, out of his pain: "Kind! Do not think it gives me pleasure to know that I haf paid for the diamond necklaces of Stuart's ladies, and their carriages, and their sable cloaks, for which he went so heavily into debt! Paid for them all with the lives of tortured men and the tears of little children!"

The priest regarded him with bitter sorrow and understanding. He put out his hand and pressed the hand of Sam, whose fingers were clenched in the soil and grass of the Island, which would never shelter the exiled and the wounded now.

"I have no words of comfort for you, Sam, nothing that could ease you. Anything I could say would be foolish. I can only say this, that I've never heard of a kinder or more selfless thing." He gathered courage and strength now. "God will not forget. God will understand. God, in some strange way, will, and must, help you."

But Sam only smiled dimly. The furrows beside his mouth deepened.

Father Houlihan said with passion: "You did it for Stuart, not for his ladies! You did it because you loved him. He was your friend. Do you think this is easy for him, Sam? Do you think he is completely insensible?"

Sam replied heavily: "If it would haf taught him a lesson, it would not be wasted. But I do not think it will teach him a lesson."

The priest shook his head sorrowfully. "Stuart is as he was made. With all his faults, he is the kindest man. Otherwise we would not love him so. He, too, has his burdens, and they are none the less heavy because he puts them on his own shoulders, himself. He is a child; he will never understand the cruelty and wickedness of others."

"No," said Sam, staring gravely before him, "he will never understand."

They stood up, now, and began to walk back to the little dock where their boat waited. The autumn day had turned bronze with the coming sunset. The haze was deeper, the river a brighter, slower green, and its voice was louder. The scent of woodsmoke came stronger towards them on the richer wind.

They paused for a moment on the dock, where their boatman sat and smoked lazily. They looked at the water, and then at the land behind them. Father Houlihan spoke, then, almost exultantly:

"We don't need islands and hidden places in which to hide the suffering and the oppressed! All of America is here for them, from one border to the other, from sea to sea! It is here, waiting, filled with the promise of God, with the hope of God, under the shadow of God's wing. It is the Promised Land."

At that very hour thousands of anxious men were reading Hinton Rowman Helper's *The Impending Crisis*, and listening, with strained ears, to the distant thunder of mighty steel wheels rolling from outer space upon a land soon to be torn in a bloody agony.

CHAPTER 41

JANIE sat beside Bertie's bed. The dark and spectral December day stood outside the house like death itself. Mounds and dunes of snow curved and sloped over the dead lawns to the streets, and the branches of the empty trees were weighted with heavy white. It had begun to snow again, slow whirling flakes rushing past the windows in a dusky silence. Janie, wrapped in her shawl, shivered, held out her feet to the low fire.

There had been two months of peace in that house on Porter Avenue, when Bertie had been gay again, and well, courteously refusing even a small glass of wine at dinner, and watching visiting friends and relatives drinking their brandy or whiskey with complete disinterest and indifference. But no one ever knew or heard the gatherings of the storm within him, the first lightnings, the first dim thunders, the first dark gales. One day he would be as usual. The next, he had rushed away from them into his own maelstrom of destruction, and they would not see the old Bertie again for a long time. When he would finally emerge, after days and even weeks of complete annihilation, it was as if a battered traveller had returned to them from far and terrible places, bearing in his eyes and in his manner the memory of most dreadful and nameless things.

Then would come the long nursing, the despair, the hopelessness, until the traveller could look about him again, smile, and begin once more the long upward journey to health and tranquillity.

On this day, Bertie was very ill. He had returned to his family only a week ago from his own secret and nightmare excursions. Each time that he returned, the painful climb to health and normality was longer, more tedious, more dangerous. The doctors could prescribe nothing for him but rest, quiet, casual treatment, and bromides. It was then that Janie nursed him, sleeplessly, cooked the little dishes he loved, coaxed him to eat, read to him, laughed with him, and brooded over him when he slept fitfully.

But she was too realistic, when off guard, to believe that anything now could be done for her darling.

A little lamp flickered in the corner of Bertie's handsome

room, throwing small wavering shadows on the white walls. By its light she could see Bertie's sleeping face. She could see the thinness of that face, its sunken eyes, the drawn mouth, the convex cheeks. It had a strange expression, remote rather than peaceful, stern and austere, an expression that it never wore in consciousness. She did not know this Bertie, Bertie who laughed, sang, whistled, made jokes and danced, who twitted and teased and filled the house with a kind of bright sunshine. The ruddy hair on the pillow was the only thing she recognized, and as she looked at the soft and glimmering curls in the lamplight, seeming so vulnerable, so beaten, a dry ache burned in her throat and her eyes were full of liquid fire. The room seemed full of bitter cold. She rose and poked at the red coals on the hearth, and stood there, looking down at them with anguish in her meager breast. The rising firelight quivered on her pale freckled face, and in her green eyes.

She went to the smooth white bed where Bertie lay as still as if he had died, only the faintest breath and the slightest quivering of his nostrils testifying that he still lived. She bent over him. Her hand touched his hair with the softest touch.

She sat down again, near him. She looked at his gaunt profile. She began to think.

Dear God, she said to herself, what is wrong, what has happened to my Bertie? What have I done? What has anyone done? Why does he do these things?

For now she knew that no mere zest, no mere buoyancy of spirit, no mere recklessness or heedlessness or folly lay behind the unconscious attemps at suicide which sent Bertie into his black country of lightnings and furies. Something drove Bertie to destruction. What was it?

As she sat there in the cold room, with the day outside slowly revolving into night, she searched her heart and memory with that dolorous and mournful honesty of a mother who sits beside the deathbed of her child. Where, she asked herself humbly, have I failed Bertie?

Her weary and tortured mind slowly crept, like a broken and weeping penitent, back through the echoing years of Bertie's life, pausing at each dim milestone, searching about it to discover whether, in the midst of the dead grass and landmarks of the vanished years, a clue lay there, waiting to be seen. Back, back to the day of Bertie's birth, where the baby, warm and pink and crowned with ruddy curls, lay in her arms.

Other milestones passed slowly in the dim procession of her mind. Bertie at three toddling after the dark and wizened Robbie he loved. Bertie in the garden, his small arms full of flowers. Bertie enraptured with his baby sister. Bertie laughing at the dour and timid Angus. Bertie, always laughing and playing, generous and affable. Bertie, whom everyone loved, and admired for his sweet nature and his pretty round face. Only his young wild father had not noticed or petted him. Robin, with his black eyes and distorted face and ringing voice: was there a clue there?

Janie huddled in her shawl, wet her dry lips, stared fixedly into the gloom of the shadows. She could see Robin again clearly, so young, so restless, throwing up his head like a savage colt terrified at the sight of strangers. She could see him standing vehemently before her, endlessly quarrelling, infuriated and broken-hearted. And the little four-year-old Bertie stood near his father, looking up at him with strange laughing blue eyes, but silent as he was never usually silent.

She could even hear Robin's voice, stilled these many years, but crying out now as fresh and clear as if he might be in that room where his son lay in his most awful unconsciousness: "Ye take the heart out o' a mon! The heart and the soul! Ye squeeze it dry, for ye will ha' your way!"

Robin had gone, gone back into his grave, and there was only silence in the room, and the dropping of coals.

No! she cried in her soul, I did not squeeze Bertie's soul dry! I gave him everything he wished! I denied him nothing! I would have sacrificed the lives of all of them, for him! He must have understood that nothing was valuable but my darling, that there was no value anywhere but him!

In the faded blowing grasses of the dead years lay a clue, faintly bright, faintly glimmering, near the milestone.

She plodded on. Another milestone. Bertie was only fourteen. He had come to her one evening, in his laughing, coaxing way, to kiss her goodnight. He stood beside her, outlined against the blue summer sky that shone against her window. There was a pale crescent moon in that sky, and one twinkling star, and the air was full of the warm scent of dew and grass, and the trees were shadowy green. He had kissed her. He had leaned against her chair. And then he had said, quite suddenly: "Mama, I'd like to go to sea."

How clear and vivid his eyes had been! She had never seen them quite like that. She had taken his strong young hand, and had patted it indulgently.

"To sea! Whatever for, you rascal?"

Had he trembled, or was she only imagining now that he had trembled? He had said, strongly, and with a kind of quiet desperation in his voice: "I want to go to sea! I've always loved the sea. You remember how I've always asked for books of sea stories, and how I love the water? Mama," he had said, after a still pause, "I'll find myself at sea."

She had looked at him, surprised at his vehemence, and she had laughed. Did she imagine that he had stared at her in the strangest way? And then he had cried out, pulling his hand from hers: "Don't tell me, Mama, as you always tell me, that there is no sense in it! Don't tell me that it is stupid and silly! Mama, I've got to believe that something is of value, somewhere!"

She had been very tender and gentle. She made fond fun of him. He, her darling Bertie, a smelly, ugly sailor! Who cared for sailors? What good was there in being a sailor? How ridiculous. She, his mama, could hardly keep from dying of laughter at the idea of her Bertie going to sea. And whatever did he mean that he had to believe "that something is of value, somewhere"?

He had not answered. He had kissed her gently, and had gone away. His head was bent; he walked as if dazed, and lost.

Janie shook her head, over and over, and shivered under her shawl. Was that a clue? Had the foolish darling boy really wanted to go to sea that much? Had his frustration turned him to drink? She shook her head again. It was not enough. If he had really wanted to go, he could have gone. Eventually she would have denied him nothing. But—he had not had the courage.

She made this admission to herself with a tremendous sinking pang of agony. Bertie had not had the courage. He had never really wanted anything very much. However, on that night he had wanted to go to sea. He had wanted it as he had never wanted anything before or since. He had wanted it because he had felt that at sea he might find himself, might discover "that something is of value." But later he had not wanted it.

Tortured by her thoughts she started to her feet and went to the bed. She bent over it. She stood there, bowed over the bed, in the most hideous grief she had ever known.

She knew now that she had determined, almost from Bertie's birth, that he must never leave her, never have another interest but her love for him. So it was that when he had advanced any desire which would remove him even a little from her influence, or any wish which would set him free in a world where men must make their own decisions and choices, and in which he would be an emancipated individual with a life of his own, she had opposed him, not in anger or obstinacy, but with loving laughter and jealousy. She had made him see the absurdity of his desires. She had stripped all value, purpose and dignity from any life or dream upon which his very young eyes had looked in yearning and wistfulness.

She had kept him, yes. He had not left her. But what remained with her now on that bed was a ruin, who believed nothing was of verity, nothing of importance or dignity or beauty, and who was dying of his knowledge.

Was it too late? she asked herself now, with bitter and rending anguish. Could anything convince Bertie that there was value in life, meaning, purpose, strength and truth? She did not believe these things, herself. She thought them absurd. But she was strong. She could live and enjoy life with zest and passion, because she found pleasure in every passing moment, and that pleasure was enough in itself, and a reason in itself. Bertie was "weak." He must believe that grandeur and validity and a hidden meaning lay in life. When he no longer believed, then there was nothing for him in living.

Had Bertie lost all capacity to believe in the lovely lies which weak men had invented to conceal the truth? She must discover whether there was any hope for him, whether it was possible to arouse in him the falsehood that life is of value, and God is in His heaven, earnestly interested in the affairs of mankind.

She wiped her eyes, sighing deeply. She turned, and saw Robbie standing near her, watching her intently. She had not heard him enter. She could hardly see him now, in the thick dusk of the room, for his neat slight figure blended with the darkness.

She looked at him for a long moment, and he returned her look quietly. How she had always hated this "black one," whom Bertie loved! How jealous she had been, out of her greediness! She did not like Robbie any better now, but in him she saw some hope for Bertie. She stretched out her hand, and clenched it strongly on his slight arm. "I want to talk to you, Robbie," she whispered.

She rustled out of the room, after one last look at Bertie, and Robbie followed. She went into her own apartments, and Robbie lit the lamps and stirred up the fire. Janie sat stiffly on a chair, wrapped in her shawl. She looked old and haggard and beaten. But her green eyes were glittering determinedly.

Robbie sat near her, and politely waited, one precise knee crossed over the other. She stared at him with intense thoughtfulness. Yes, she had always hated him. But she had always admired him, too. Of all her children, this was the only intelligent and reasonable one, the only one who was not befuddled by his emotions nor choked with his passions. He saw things clearly; he saw them whole. That is why he was never disturbed or agitated. He was the strong one.

She said abruptly: "Bertie is no better."

"He is sleeping all right?"

"Yes. But when he recovers, he will be off again, after a few weeks."

Robbie nodded reflectively, and with objective regret. "Yes. I know."

Janie said abruptly: "You've been close to him, Robbie. I've never asked you before. Is there anything we can do?"

Robbie was silent. He regarded his mother meditatively. She was a baggage, yes. But she was an honest woman, and demanded an honest answer.

He said: "No. I think not. Perhaps you won't understand this: but Bertie doesn't want anything. He drinks because he finds nothing of value, and nothing he desires."

To his great surprise his mother only dropped her head a little, and said, in a low tone: "Yes. I know. He is a weakling, Robbie."

His surprise was so great that he could say nothing for a moment, and could only look at Janie with new respect. He finally spoke: "Yes, you are right. He is a weakling. He never had the wit, or the courage, to disbelieve you, Mama. He never tried to find out for himself. He trusted you. He never knew that no one should trust anyone else, about himself. Perhaps he never wanted to distrust you. It was easier to believe you."

He expected her to look at him with outraged fury, to become abusive. But he was further surprised when her green eyes remained calmly desperate and honest.

"How right you are, Robbie. We have it now, that Bertie is a weakling, and wants nothing. It isn't necessary for me to explain things to you. You are the only one of my children who has sense. You understand what I mean?"

"Yes, Mama." He was suddenly very sorry for her, and felt very gentle towards her.

She spread out her hands in a gesture infinitely pathetic for the wiry Janie. "Robbie, what can we do?"

He got up then, and walked up and down the room, his head bent meditatively. His neat pale features were not loose and distorted as the features of men less strong and secure are apt to be under stress. Rather, they tightened, became smaller and clearer.

"I've given it a lot of thought, Mama," he said, pausing before her, and looking at her with the respect and consideration which one accords to a mental equal. "I've thought of it for years. Candidly, I don't think we can do anything. Even if you had given him his way about all his desires, I don't know whether it would have helped. Weak people, who are given all their way, almost invariably end up in confusion, running about like rabbits from one heap of fodder to another, unable to make up their minds which to eat. They wander all over, dissatisfied, hungry, idle, confused, a burden to themselves, an expense and anxiety to others."

She fixed her eyes on his, and a faint mournful smile settled on her thin and mobile lips. She shook her head a little. She sighed, smoothed out the fringe of her shawl. She said: "You persuaded me not to send him to Saratoga again. It would have helped him a little, prolonged his life and health. But you said I mustn't."

"No," he said quietly, "you mustn't. Why prolong his misery?"

She glanced up, very pale, very still. "That is a cruel thing to say, Robbie." Now frantic grief leapt to her eyes again, and she started from her chair.

"We can keep him comfortable, and protected, Mama. That is all."

He saw, suddenly and vividly, Bertie sitting under a tree with the green and watery light upon his face. That tree had lost its leaves twice now, but its dream-image remained, its leaves unshed, and Bertie under it, unchanged, "forever young."

Now all of Robbie's reason was swept away in an arching flood of pain. He cried: "Mama, let him alone! Let him go! I don't know what I mean; I can't make you understand because I don't understand, myself! But I know we must let him go. That is what he wants. That is the only thing he wants, and it will be the last."

312 | The Wide House,

him, and the child shrieked, with delight. Marvina yawned

CHAPTER 42

ANGUS CAUDER was married to Miss Gretchen Schnitzel five days before Christmas, in an atmosphere of great pomp and circumstance. The wedding took place in the Bethlehem Lutheran Church in the presence of such a huge Teutonic gathering that the Celtic Cauders and Colemans felt completely alien. The Schnitzels had many cousins, aunts, nieces and nephews, all huge, bellicose, pouting and brutish, all of a bleached sameness of countenance and suspiciousness of dull eye. Further, they were all employees of more or less rank in Otto Schnitzel's slaughter-house, and were very censorious with regard to Angus, darkly suspecting that he might be put in command over them. They were divided between an impulse to fawn upon him, as a future officer, or to condescend to him, as a junior in rank. Consequently they were assailed by that confusion which so often afflicts the Teuton: the equal impulses to oppress or to truckle.

Gretchen's three brothers, Heinrich, Hans and Adolph, were there, as white, thick and short as herself, all in a state of porcine resentment and sullenness. They had tried to prevent this marriage, but their fatuous father had given his consent. They sat with their fat wives and offspring in the pews reserved for the bridal family, and glowered.

Among the guests were the Schnickelburgers and the Zimmermanns, curiously resembling the Schnitzels. Janie, looking at them all, commented to herself that she was lost among a barnyard of huge, scrubbed pigs, and that it would not surprise her if they suddenly broke out into a chorus of grunts, and drowned out the organ, or suddenly rose at the call of a distant farmer and galloped out, revealing cloven hoofs under their pantaloons and their skirts. It was appropriate, she thought, that they were almost all engaged in the slaughter-house business, in tanneries, or in sausage-making. Gross beasts! she thought, and looked at them with sly contempt and disgust.

She was glad when the ceremony was over. It had, for Janie's taste, too much the look of an innocent being sacrificed to Moloch.

The young couple went to live at the Franklin Street residence of the bride's parents, a huge, turreted and completely hideous red-brick monstrosity, dank and narrow-halled and gloomy, with tall, box-like rooms and black-marble fireplaces. The third floor had been fitted for their apartments, and was choked with black-walnut and cumbersome mahogany furniture, all crimson plush and horsehair, and red velvet draperies. Angus vanished into that house as into a tomb, and was not seen for three weeks, during which time he was doubtless enjoying his honeymoon. During the nights of those weeks, Janie ruefully and naughtily amused herself with many improper conjectures. When next she saw her son, she searched his face closely to discover any change there of a catastrophic nature. But Angus appeared the same, quietly and timidly arrogant, silent, grim and reserved, full of austere pride and coldness. Janie did not know whether to be disappointed or relieved. Her deep curiosity went unsatisfied.

Stuart, as Angus' employer, was also invited, but had refused with great heartiness and precipitant enthusiasm. Not for him the smell of slaughter-houses, and the company of great beasts whom he both feared and detested. Father Houlihan thought it unkind of him. "Have you forgotten?" asked Stuart angrily. "Have you forgotten that Otto Schnitzel and his friends have introduced the Know-Nothings into Grandeville, and that it was their influence that caused those hoodlums to smash three of your best stained-glass windows four weeks ago, right in the middle of High Mass? They cost me five thousand dollars, those windows, and now you think I should have eaten at the table of those squealing hogs, and listened to their insulting remarks about you."

"It's just ignorance," pleaded the priest. "Ah, it was a bad thing, the breaking of those windows! The east one was my favorite. Such a pretty thing. But it's just ignorance, I'm thinking, Stuart, and it will soon pass."

"Grundy," said Stuart, with fond irascibility, "you're a darling fool."

Father Houlihan was annoyed at this, as he had his own suspicions of himself. "You're a damned insulting animal, Stuart!" he shouted. "Have ye no respect for my cloth? A fool, indeed!"

Stuart saw no change in Angus at the shops, except that the young man was stiffer than ever, and colder, and more silent. Stuart did not know whether or not he merely imagined it, but as the weeks went by it seemed to him that Angus was becoming thinner and paler, and more grim.

These Scots! thought Stuart. They can be drawn and

quartered or burned at the stake, and they will utter only texts or empty words. He was angered with himself that he could still foolishly worry about the young man, whom he heartily disliked.

Late in the summer of 1860, less than a year after Angus' marriage, Stuart received a rather incoherent note from Father Houlihan, asking him to call at the latter's home.

Father Houlihan was quite aglow, and excited, and very mysterious. He aggravated Stuart's impatience. He insisted that his sister serve the guest with seed-cake and tea, and proceeded to stuff his mouth with crumbly cake and twinkle at Stuart exultantly over his own tea-cup. Stuart resigned himself, and waited.

"Oh, come on, Grundy!" said Stuart, at last. "What the hell is it that you've got up your sleeve? Stop nodding your head like a confounded Punch and Judy, and tell me."

Father Houlihan, replete and happy, leaned back in his chair and clasped his hands across his round belly. He eyed Stuart with excited delight. "You'd never guess, Stuart. It's really incredible."

"Tell me. Let me be the judge."

Father Houlihan deftly scooped up a handful of rich crumbs from his plate, and popped them into his mouth. "No one can equal Sarah's cooking," he remarked exasperatingly. "You must let her give you some to take home."

Stuart regarded him darkly. "Come on, Grundy, what is it?"

But the priest would not be balked of his news by any haste in retailing it. He began a rambling talk about the new hospital, which Stuart had financed, the Hospital of the Sisters of Charity, close to the church of Our Lady of Hope. The fine new equipment which Stuart had bought had just arrived, and Dr. Malone, the chief of staff, was exceedingly proud of it, and very grateful to Stuart. Mother Mary Elizabeth wished Father Houlihan to express her gratitude, also, and her hope that Stuart might soon pay another visit to see the results of his generosity. "For a lady of her reticence she was very enthusiastic," said Father Houlihan. He enlarged on her expression and her manner as she spoke of Stuart.

"That's very kind of Mother Mary Elizabeth," said Stuart impatiently. He, too, was much awed by the fine face and grand cold manner of the Mother Superior. "But you didn't get me here to talk about her and old Malone?"

"In a way, yes," said the irritating priest, with a smirk.

Then he could not control himself. "Stuart, I think my prayers are about to be answered!"

"And what the hell," asked Stuart, with elaborate and sighing patience, "have you been praying for now?"

Father Houlihan was hurt. "It isn't a new prayer, Stuart. It's an old one. About young Angus Cauder."

Stuart stared at him wearily. "Again? What about Angus, the gray-faced Scots parson?"

Father Houlihan sat upright in his chair so swiftly that his big round face turned crimson. His bright-blue eyes sparkled elatedly. "You wouldn't believe it, Stuart! But Angus visited the hospital about a month ago, for the first time, and in his shy way asked Dr. Malone if he could watch a few operations, and look about him!"

"No!" exclaimed Stuart, suddenly interested.

The priest nodded delightedly, pleased at Stuart's interest. "Yes indeed. And since then he has dropped in at least three nights a week for an hour or so, and on Sunday, too. He borrows Dr. Malone's medical books. He has been present at several operations. He visits the sick. And here is the best! Dr. Malone says his knowledge of medicine is amazing! He could almost practice on his own. He has had several talks with the other doctors, and it took much to convince them that he was not a physician, himself! I am not exaggerating. Dr. Malone was so impressed that he suggested that Angus study with him, and that in no time at all he could receive his diploma!"

Stuart was excited, himself. "No! And what did Angus say to that?"

Father Houlihan was suddenly deflated. He looked down at his shining black belly. He coughed. "Well, then, this is not so good, Stuart. He must have been frightened, or something. Anyway, after that he did not return to the hospital for over a week. Dr. Malone is a very clever man. He did not make the suggestion again. However, he allows Angus to examine the sick and to offer his own timid advice. Dr. Malone says that he has a marvelous way with the suffering, and that his suggestions are very acute and show a profound knowledge. Angus, says Dr. Malone, is very tender and absorbed, especially when with hopeless and suffering cases, and his very presence seems to bring cheer and hope to them. It's almost a miracle, Dr. Malone says. The patients look for him. They call him 'doctor.' They say you wouldn't recognize Angus, in the hospital. It's a changed face he has, all aglow, and kind, and loving, and sure."

"I'll be damned!" cried Stuart. "Well, well! I have noticed that he does carry an armful of big books around with him, but we're not very friendly, and I've never questioned him. Well, so that is the story!"

He looked at the priest. "What do we do now?" he asked practically.

"Nothing, Stuart. Nothing at all. He must find his own way, with God's good help. Anything you might say to him would only frighten him, put him off, send him into a retreat which might be permanent. Let him find his own way. God will help him. Nothing is ever wasted, with God."

Stuart had his very serious doubts about that, but he kept silent. He began to think, to offer suggestions. What if he, Stuart, talked to Janie? No, that would do no good at all. It was impossible to talk to Angus. Robbie? He, Stuart, had acquired quite a respect for Robbie. No, it would be useless to talk to Robbie, who had a contempt for his elder brother, and hardly ever was found in his company.

"Let God do all this," repeated Father Houlihan, who had a most annoying faith in the Deity, and a quite impractical one.

Stuart, who was a man of action, found this exasperating. He began to walk up and down the room, while Father Houlihan watched him anxiously, and pleaded that Angus must find his own way, with the help of God. Any interference would only ruin matters. The secret must be closely kept. If the Schnitzels found out that their son-in-law had private and odious dreams, they might destroy all hope for Angus. No one must know. And Angus must not know that his friends knew of his derelictions.

"What a struggle he must be having in himself!" said Stuart, gloomily.

"Yes, he is suffering, too, Stuart. But what man can resist the call of God? When God wills, man obeys, consciously or unconsciously."

The next day Stuart encountered Angus in the shops, and studied him with guarded curiosity. How pale the sour devil was, and how gaunt! But nothing could have been stiffer or colder or prouder than that haggard face and those fixed gray eyes. Stuart frowned. He said: "Angus, have you heard from Laurie recently?"

"No, Stuart. I have not. Have you?"

"Yes, I received a letter only last Saturday. She says she is very happy in her school, with all the other young lady students. She is learning French and German and Italian at a great rate, and her voice is steadily improving. I have had a letter, too, from Professor Morelli, who says her progress is remarkable, and that she will be ready for Italy and Germany within a few months. A very good report for a girl so young, isn't it?"

"She will soon be sixteen," remarked Angus, absently. He looked down at the floor. His expression was very sad and very weary. He sighed, unconsciously. He added: "She never writes to me, only to Mama, and sometimes to Robbie, about Bertie."

"Well, now," said Stuart, feeling awkward, "that is too bad of the minx. After all, it is due to you that she has had this chance at all. Doesn't she know that?"

Angus looked up quickly, and his eyes were full of quick pain. "She is grateful only to you, Stuart. She does it—just for you, because you wish it. My own part in it she found impudent."

He added, unable to endure the look of sympathy in Stuart's warm eyes, and taking on himself his old pride and stiff arrogance: "Do not think I have forgotten how much you have done for Laurie, Stuart. Someday, I shall repay you. And that is another matter. I think I can make a payment next month. One hundred dollars. And thereafter I shall make regular payments. You must give me a complete bill."

"Go to the devil!" exclaimed Stuart, with his sudden rage. "Keep your damned money! Have you nothing to say to me but insults?"

He glared at Angus, who had flushed dimly. "Do you think she would take your money, you conceited popinjay? Let her once know you are paying for her studies, and she will abandon them at once."

"You wouldn't tell her, Stuart?" asked Angus, with proud anger.

"I would that! Immediately. Well, damn you, do as you wish. I can't stop you. But on your first payment to me I shall write to Laurie."

He swung away on his heel, leaving Angus to look after him in desperation and complete misery.

CHAPTER 43

BUT unfortunately for Father Houlihan's innocently benevolent hopes, Angus' surreptitious visits to the Hospital of the Sisters of Charity abruptly ceased, for no understandable reason. Dr. Malone reported this, regretfully.

Father Houlihan was of too impulsive and passionate a nature to sigh with resignation and turn away from a problem, leaving events in the hands of Heaven. Though he had so simple and profound a belief in God, he was of the conviction that it did no harm at all to assist the Deity by direct methods, a kind of pious nudging of the Divine Ribs. By works, by prayer, by concentration and humble insistence, he earnestly believed that God's attention could be secured, however irritable, and that often the Lord was induced to accomplish many a miracle by the sheer tenacity of His beseechers.

When he informed Stuart of his plot against the peace of the Almighty, Stuart laughed. "Grundy, you are a damned, long-nosed meddler. It wouldn't surprise me if your 'favorite saint' up and smote you properly for your impudence. Leave Angus alone. Let the devil stew in his own juice."

Father Houlihan was outraged. "You don't understand the efficacy of prayer, Stuart."

"Well, pray. As far as I am concerned, I've washed my hands of him. Greedy pig that he is. If you could see him fondle the cash, you'd stop tormenting your pet saint, and consign Angus to hell."

Father Houlihan often wandered disconsolately near the hospital, and within it, much to Mother Mary Elizabeth's gratification. She privately considered the priest a very careless man, and did not approve of his frequent, booming laughter. Now he engaged her in pious conversations, exceedingly serious ones, and was much awed and depressed by her intellect and stern faith. He persuaded her, also, to pray for Angus and having slyly enlisted her in the service of tormenting the Lord, he felt considerable satisfaction.

One Sunday afternoon, Father Houlihan visited the hospital and had one of his profoundly depressing discussions with Mother Mary Elizabeth. (Sometimes he felt this, also, was in the nature of a sacrifice and this was his only cheer.)

Mother Mary Elizabeth was the daughter of an old New England family, and a lady of great intellect and crushing erudition. She could read and write fluently in six languages, and as Father Houlihan could speak only one with any fluency at all, and was deplorably uncertain in Latin, except for the prayers and the celebration of Mass, he would always retire from her effulgent presence convinced that he was both simple-minded and stupid, and that her eye had dwelt on him with chilly scorn for his scholarly attainments. As he was enormously fat and short, and Mother Mary Elizabeth was aristocratically tall and slender, his feeling of inferiority could not be relieved except in privacy, when he gave vent to many eloquent and pointless oaths, for which he later did distressed penance.

His faith, he came to believe, was very primitive and un-complex, and disgustingly childlike. Mother Mary Elizabeth could converse easily and eloquently on many obscure sub-jects, and was very mystical into the bargain. Father Houli-han found himself floundering in discussions which had a precarious resemblance to the old problem of how many angels could dance upon the point of a needle. As this was a problem which was utterly beyond him, and completely out of the range of his comprehension ("damned silly idea, I'm thinking") he would retire from the lady's august presence feeling excessively puerile and worthless.

Father Houlihan remembered the simple and ignorant nuns of his childhood, with their loving faces and worn, calloused hands, and he thought Mother Mary Elizabeth a great mistake, and had many dark meditations on the educa-tion of females. He disliked the Mother very much, and al-ways went smarting and blushing from her presence.

Accordingly, on this particular Sunday, he was in a very despondent frame of mind. He had gone but a few yards from the hospital when he was almost run over by a somber black carriage with glittering silver harness. The black horses reared suddenly and stood up momentarily on their hind legs as the coachman wrenched on the reins. Father Houli-han retired hastily to the sidewalk and brushed off his hat, which had fallen into the dust upon his retreat. This was the last straw. He began to curse, with regrettable audibility, and to look at the occupants of the carriage with a blasting eye.

"Why don't ye watch where ye're going?" he shouted. "Running down the populace in your damned cart! D'ye think ye own the streets, perhaps?"

The carriage did not go on. There was a flustered air about it. The coachman grinned contemptuously. But the young man sitting with the young lady seemed disturbed and embarrassed, and slowly climbed down to the walk beside the priest. Father Houlihan, with a rush of crimson to his face, recognized Angus Cauder. He grinned foolishly.

"Well, now, it's Angus," he stammered. "I didn't know."

Angus hesitated, then removed his hat with stiff hauteur. "How do you do, Father Houlihan," he said, formally. "I'm sorry. But you did come off the curb very hastily, you know. I'm sorry."

"It's my carelessness," said the priest. But he looked at Angus earnestly.

He had not seen Angus since his marriage a year ago. How grim and pale the young man was, and how emaciated. It was pitiful to see. He looked up into those frozen gray eyes under the straight black brows, and at the rigid mouth. Angus' funereal black emphasized his pallor, his haggard features. But he was prouder than ever, and quietly arrogant. He regarded his old friend with distant politeness and cold if secret aversion.

"May we give you a lift—Father?" suggested Angus, gesturing towards the carriage with his gloved hand.

Now this, thought Father Houlihan, with a rise of his simple heart, may be an opportunity extended to me by St. Francis. He looked hopefully at the carriage, and then his spirits sank again.

The young lady returned Father Houlihan's regard with stolid contempt and repudiation. She sat there, in her sable cape and huge brown bonnet, like a lethargic lump of deplorably young obesity, her hands in her sable muff. Under the shadow of the bonnet, and above the brown satin ribbons, was a round, moonlike face, as white as lard, and as featureless. It was smooth and flaccid, that face, and its only expression was dull superciliousness and brutality. The little thick nose turned upwards, the nostrils static. The mouth pale, thick and protruding. The shallow blue eyes were very big and round, and completely torpid and fixed. Stiff lusterless curls of a coarse yellow clustered about her heavy neck. Yet, she had the coarse prettiness of a stupid peasant girl and that girl's suspiciousness, and evidently considered herself a grand lady. As Father Houlihan stared at her with open surprise and regret, she ostentatiously shrugged, lifted a hand from her muff to display her many jewels, and turned away. She stared stolidly at the back of the coachman, and thereafter ignored the priest.

So, thought Father Houlihan, this is the lad's wife. God help him.

He turned to Angus, and said with a painful smile: "Thank you, Angus, kindly. But I am visiting in the neighborhood." He hesitated. He looked up again at the tall young man, and stammered: "I've missed you, lad. Will you come to me, soon?"

As Angus had not visited the priest's house for many years, this was a surprising remark. One of Angus' level eyebrows lifted. But he said gravely: "Thank you."

He glanced at his wife. His mouth became thinner and narrower, if possible. It was evident that he wished to be off. It was also evident that he felt the pressure of decent courtesy, and was considering introducing Gretchen to his old friend. But the set of her massive shoulders under the cloak, the flabby obduracy of her porcine profile, dissuaded him.

Father Houlihan put his hand on the young man's arm. Angus drew back a little, then restrained himself. "Angus, you'll be coming to see me, soon? I'll be looking forward to it. It's been a long time."

Angus looked down at him. He said, with reluctant formality: "Yes, it has been a long time, hasn't it? How are you?"

"Well! Well! But after all, I am not young any longer." Father Houlihan had turned bright scarlet, and his humble smile was painful.

"It has been pleasant to see you, Father—Houlihan," said Angus. Now he smiled, himself. But the smile was only a contortion, a meaningless grimace, and his pale cheeks were rigid. He put his hand on the carriage. "Do give my regards to Mrs. O'Keefe, will you not?"

"Yes, yes," stammered the priest. But the carriage was already bowling off down the street, glittering in the pale December sunlight. He stood there a long time, watching it, until it turned the corner.

He went on his way. He was sick at heart. His step was slow and feeble. His lips moved in soundless prayer.

It was just before Vespers, and he crept humbly into his beautiful little church and knelt down like any other suppliant before one of the altars. A few of his parishioners were kneeling in their pews, and some were making the Stations of the Cross. He knelt in dim shadow, his hands clasped on his broad breast, his head bent.

The smooth and arching walls of the church were like snow, spectral in the dusk, and glimmering. The white floor was awash in a crepuscular light, and vaguely reflected the pews, and the slender, towering columns that rose like the white trunks of trees to the exquisitely groined roof. The lovely little altars were ashine with the flickering starlight candles, and the air was pervaded with incense and the scent of roses from Stuart's conservatories. Here was peace and twilight silence and sacred meditation, broken only by a subdued cough now and then, or the shuffle of pious feet.

Father Houlihan, whose mind was never profound or devious, and who had no high opinion of dialectic and obscurantism, believed as Emerson believed, that "the meal in the firkin; the milk in the pan; the ballad in the street; the news of the boat; the glance of the eye; the form and gait of the body; show me the ultimate reason of these matters— and the world lies no longer a dull miscellany and lumber-room, but has form and order; there is no trifle, there is no puzzle, but one design unites and animates the farthest pinnacle and the lowest trench." This was his belief. Let the philosophers argue their obscure and scholarly philosophies. Let the learned priests discuss their dialectical matters, until they lost themselves in a cloud of words and lifted their feet above the common earth. Let a million angels dance on needle-points in their unknowable essence. Let God be so discussed, so argued, so meditated upon, so dissected, that He become tenuous and dissipated and finally vanish and explode into a thousand intangible fragments and be no more. This was not for Father Houlihan, who could know only "the meal in the firkin and the milk in the pan" which explained everything.

But now, with chaotic suddenness, things were no longer so simple.

For the first time in his life Father Houlihan had a hideous and ominous prescience that the world was too much for men, and perhaps too much for God, also. His innocent mind was invaded by the most terrible thoughts, which affrighted him. He saw himself in a universe filled with strange beings, among whom he could not discover a single familiar face. Those few moments with Angus had been like a door in a comfortable room, filled with affection, and the furniture of friendliness. And that door had opened, without warning, showing him the boundless and dreadful country outside, which he had never suspected of existing. He stood on the threshold, dumb and trembling, feeling awful winds upon his frightened face, and even the stars were not the stars of his knowledge. He could not explain it to himself. He could only know fear, and wonder, and suffering.

He had thought the human soul as uncomplicated as his own, eager and hungry for light, willing to abandon its burden at the word of a waiting God, willing to discard its sins and errors if only the way were shown. But now he saw that human soul in its unfamiliar and frightful lineaments, and it was like the moon to him, showing only one face to the world, a face artificially lit by circumstance and exigency and convention, the dark side enormously suggested in its full dreadfulness and mystery, but never to be discerned.

"The meal in the firkin, the milk in the pan." No, there was no longer such a kind and artless explanation for the world of men and the Heaven of God. While he suffered, Father Houlihan felt a profound humiliation and contempt and desperation in himself that he had been so guileless. Perhaps God also had been scornful of his elemental philosophy.

He was filled with a prostrating grief and despair. He could not even pray. He clasped his hands humbly and besought the altar. Its eternal light flickered at him, remote as the farthest star. Then his vision was dazzled and splintered, and a moisture inundated the sockets of his dejected eyes.

For many years he had sought the explanation of wars, of cruelties, of madnesses, of insanities and treacheries and the insensibility of hearts. He had encountered all these things, and they had distressed him. But he had thought them errors, committed only by the blind and the foolish and the unenlightened, and he had displayed anger and indignation in their presence, and had been eager to teach and to guide. Now he said to himself, I know I have been a fool. There are terrible abysses and chasms and strange and awful countries in the human soul, and I have never known of them, or believed in them.

A great terror seized the priest. He looked about him. All was strange. He cried out, aloud: "O God! O God!"

His voice was like a screaming arch of agony, and the few worshipers in the church started, uttered little cries, and stared at him in the white dusk.

CHAPTER 44

UNAWARE of the bottomless suffering and despair
which he had inflicted on his innocent old friend, however
inadvertently, Angus continued the drive with his wife, the
former Gretchen Schnitzel. He sat beside her in his frozen
silence, as stiff and arrogant as an image, and stared fixedly
ahead of him. So well disciplined were his thoughts in these
latter years that almost never was he afflicted by his old
malaise of the spirit, his old despondency and terror. When
he felt the darkness moving towards him like an unseen and
fearful tide he would resolutely and sternly turn his face
from it, and his consciousness. He had a way, now, of
substituting clear and ordinary thoughts in his mind, as
householders light the little familiar lamps, while the earth
rolls inexorably into the unknowable and frightening night.
And, as those householders draw the heavy draperies across
the windows to keep out the cold and the sickening sunless
air, so he drew the curtains of discipline across the awareness of his subconscious soul.

He did not allow himself any reflections on his wife. She
was there; he had married her. She had brought him a po-
tential fortune. He resided with her in the house of her
parents on Franklin Street, and though the house was repellent, and very damp, it was at least fairly comfortable.
Mr. and Mrs. Schnitzel, though dull as to conversation and
boorish of manner, were worthy people, and he hoped that
he would steadily increase the regard they had for him.

He was now assistant manager in the shops, and was receiving fifty dollars a week, out of which he scrupulously
paid twenty-five dollars for his and Gretchen's "keep" in the
Schnitzel mansion. Mr. Schnitzel had grunted his refusal,
but when Angus had insisted, the slaughter-house owner had
eyed him with hoggish respect.

He never asked himself whether he liked or disliked his
wife. He gave her courtesy and respect. He never questioned
whether she was a lady, or intelligent, or if she had any
thoughts of her own, or what kind of a creature she was.
They were polite to each other, and apparently indifferent.

Janie might have been interested in their private life behind the dull door of their duller bedroom, huge and crimson

and completely hideous. As a connoisseur of life, and a lover of life, and full of zest as she was, Janie might have been appalled. For passion in its most joyous sense, its deepest completion, its love and ardor and tenderness, had no part in the conjugal atmosphere in that bedroom. It can only be said that Angus and Gretchen mated, with as little wildness and madness as can be imagined, and with only enough to make the act possible at all.

Stuart had disgustedly called him "a graven image."

Angus had only one passion now, and with the single-heartedness of the disciplined and sterile man he had directed what bleak desire he still possessed towards that one passion. And that passion was money. But he did not lust for it as Stuart lusted, for what it could bring in pleasure and security and peace of mind. He lusted for it as a thing in itself, a beginning and an end.

His mind was like a castle of airless and sunless towers, ordered and quiet and inhabited, with no echoes murmuring in the towering halls and no sighs heard in the corridors. Whatever remained of his youth lay entranced and chained in the black dungeons under the solid stone floors, and no voice came from the fastnesses.

But there was one room, which like Bluebeard's chamber was never opened, and in that room lived Laurie, his sister. He dared not put the key in the lock; he dared not swing wide the door. He dared not look at her face, and her body, dressed in the garments of his memory. He had, he reminded himself pompously, "done his duty" towards her, and assured her future. Then he closed the door upon her eyes and her voice.

With regard to others of his acquaintance and family, Angus was not even so positive in his attitude. He considered Stuart, contemptuously, as a wild and profligate fool, bereft of the well-bred moralities and the decencies, a man not to be considered seriously, and always to be suspected. (Nevertheless, he still feared Stuart, though he would have denied this.) He considered Sam with equal contempt, and suspected him even more than he did his kinsman, though he acknowledged Sam's capabilities and caution and thrift. Both of these, eventually, he would remove from the Grandeville Supreme Emporium, not in a spirit of vindictiveness, but with a quite impersonal detachment.

For Bertie, Angus had a cold and remote disgust. He was like something indescribably indecent and contemptible, of which no intelligent and civilized man could think. So far as

Angus was concerned, Bertie was dead, or dying, wallowing in his own corruption, and from the loathsome spectacle he resolutely turned his consciousness. He only prayed that Bertie would never impose his existence upon the awareness of his elder brother, and so long as this was granted Angus would do him the honor of forgetting him.

Robbie was somewhat different, and this obscurely infuriated Angus. However he might ignore his younger brother, however he might gaze at him with icy withdrawal and disinterest, Robbie's personality impinged itself uncomfortably upon him. He had always the unnerving suspicion that Robbie was amused by him, and disregarded him as one of no active importance. He felt Robbie analysing him with scientific detachment, curious about him academically. Robbie, felt Angus, saw him as a "specimen," an object, a casual phenomenon, without any personal entanglement whatsoever.

In short, Robbie was not impressed by Angus.

Angus felt no humiliation. He felt only scorn that his brother was so obtuse and unobservant. He saw that Robbie's coldness and precision came from no self-discipline, as did his own, but were natural manifestations of his character. He told himself that he despised Robbie, that Robbie was but an earthworm, tranquil and undisturbed in the midst of events. When Robbie once casually remarked that money was but a means to an end, and that if a man did not particularly desire any end money lost its value, Angus felt a kind of congealed joy and satisfaction, and was confirmed in his disdain for his brother. The fact that Robbie had now been admitted to the bar, and that old Judge Taylor had jubilantly announced that the young man would soon be a judge in his own right, impressed Angus only mildly. Some day, he thought to himself righteously, he might admit Robbie as a consultant in the legal affairs of the shops. This gave him a sense of virtue, and inclined him more magnanimously towards his brother.

It was, therefore, a frozen statue of a young man that rode beside Gretchen this blue October day, as upright as a steel rod, as uncompromising as a stone, and as lifeless. He had completely forgotten the existence of his wife. A faint frown marked the smooth harshness of his forehead. Now, under his quiet, his breathlessness, the entranced captives in the dungeons had begun faintly to stir, to breathe, to sigh. He quelled them. They subsided, but he felt the mournful regard of their imprisoned eyes. A dim light showed under the door behind which Laurie was hidden.

Then, suddenly, he was seized by a curious physical phenomenon. During the past year or so, when "aroused" like this, it sometimes happened that a quite hideous pain would flash through his skull, not once but many times, at intervals of about ten seconds. It would start at his right temple, rush across his forehead like a knife of lightning, and seem to emerge at his left temple. The first few pangs would be endurable. But the fifth and sixth, and those that followed, would be more than he could bear. He would clench his fists, close his eyes, grit his teeth, and endure in a breathless silence, uttering no exclamation even when alone. For the pain was too intense for a muffled cry, or indeed, for any motion at all. The final pain would seem to rend his brain apart into dazzling fragments, open like a crushed egg, and he would feel all through his flesh the quivering impulses of dissolution. Finally, he would open his eyes, to look out at a swimming world, unreal and tilted, and his whole face would be livid and moist, his heart roaring, his breath labored.

He had gone to a physician, who had prescribed spectacles "for close work," and sleep and rest, and attention to diet. None of these had helped.

During these seizures, he was removed from consciousness as though he had died. So it was that when he opened his eyes, and had seen the rocking backs of the horses and the fiery October sky, and had surreptitiously wiped his face with his kerchief, he became aware that Gretchen had been talking petulantly in her lowered and sullen voice. She was staring at him with her shallow pale eyes and scowling a little.

"Does your head hurt again, Angus?" she asked resentfully. "Dear me, it does seem that Dr. Schultz' pills ought to have done something!"

Angus swallowed stiffly, drew a deep breath, straightened himself. He glanced at his wife with haughty apology. "Nothing relieves it, my love," he replied, and his voice was faint but firm. "But Dr. Schultz assures me there is nothing really wrong. An affliction of my nervous temperament."

"Well, you don't appear nervous to me," said his loving wife, flatly, with a disagreeable shrug. She added, accusingly: "It's very odd, to me. You've had most of the attacks when we have been conversing together, like this, and nothing about to agitate you. Do you find me tiresome, Angus?"

"Nonsense, Gretchen," he replied with hauteur. There was a deep trembling all along his veins. But this, he knew, would subside shortly. "There is no reason, apparently, for these seizures. Doubtless, they will pass."

She looked without favor at his white repressed face and grim quiet eyes. Then she scowled again, as her thoughts veered. "That odious priest! How dared he speak to you, Angus! Like a beggar."

"Extremely impudent," agreed Angus. He drew out his gold watch, gift of his father-in-law, and murmured an exclamation. "It is almost five, Gretchen. We must return, I am afraid. Tea at six tonight, you know."

He gave an order to the coachman, who touched his hat with his whip, then turned the horses about.

Gretchen had begun to smile with sly satisfaction. "Papa tells me that at the last meeting of the Know-Nothings a resolution was passed to outlaw the Roman Church in America. How agreeable that will be, and how necessary it is! But Papa said you did not go to that meeting, Angus."

"If you will recall, my dear, I was engaged with the books at the shops," said Angus repressively.

"After all," continued Gretchen, "we must realize that this is really a German country."

Angus looked at her. His heart, which had begun to quiet down, beat fast again, and heat flushed to his face. He said coldly: "I am misinformed, then. I was under the impression that the founders of the American Republic were Englishmen, with a few Scotsmen, and Irish. Perhaps, Gretchen, you think it preposterous that we speak the English language in America, and that the laws of America are based on the British Common Law?"

Gretchen glared upon him with dislike. "Well, Englishmen are really Germans," she said, with the quick and sullen rage of the Teuton. "And I don't recall that there were many Scotchmen or Irishmen. Odious creatures!"

But Angus was suddenly exhausted. He sat back in the carriage and said nothing until they arrived at the ugly mansion on Franklin Street.

The Children in the Gate | 329

bought them from him yesterday. For twenty-four thousand

CHAPTER 45

THE HALL in the house of Otto Schnitzel was high, dark and cavernous, execrable with Turkey-red carpeting, gilt and plush chairs tortuously carved, and crimson draperies. It smelled heavily of beeswax and repellent chill, even on this blazing October evening. A sly-faced German maid took Angus' caped coat, hat and cane, and divested Gretchen of her cloak and bonnet. She announced that "Herr Schnitzel and Frau Schnitzel" were awaiting their daughter and her husband in the parlor, and that dinner would be served within an hour.

Angus thanked her gravely. He glanced at his wife, and saw the glimmer of her large white face in the dusk. The top of her rough flaxen head reached only to his chin. Her figure was thick and clumsy, and she had big pudgy hands heavily jewelled. Her brown velvet dress, with its enormous hoops, only accentuated her obesity and solid shapelessness. As her head was set so closely upon her massive shoulders, the neck was indicated solely by a small collar of lace fastened with a pearl-rimmed cameo brooch. Over this collar was more than a suggestion of a thickened double chin. Her bosom, like her shoulders, was massive and matronly, and sagged for sheer weight. Her upper arms almost burst the velvet of her sleeves. When she walked, the floor creaked, sturdy though it was.

She glanced at Angus with her customarily sullen and bellicose look, which was also sluggishly challenging. "Shall we join Mama and Papa, Angus?" she asked, and her tone was commanding. She moved towards the folding doors that shut off the parlor from the hall. Angus, walking slightly behind her, appeared cadaverous and unbending in his black, towering over her like a frozen tree, his step silent and slow.

The long narrow parlor stretched the length of the house and was pierced by windows eight-feet high and narrow as slits, shrouded in the ubiquitous crimson draperies. Dimly flowered Brussels carpet covered the floor. The gloomy black-walnut furniture was upholstered in horsehair and purplish or scarlet plush. Heavy and ponderous tables, covered with velvet cloths bordered with gilt fringe, held dimly lit crystal lamps whose bases were of intricately twisted brass or gold or silver. A fire smoldered on the black-marble hearth, and over the mantelpiece was a glimmering mirror in a thick gold frame, which reflected back the ugly and oppressive room.

Mr. Otto Schnitzel, slaughter-house owner and solid citizen and wealthy burgher, sat before the fire reading and rustling the local daily, *The Commercial*, and grunting out ill-tempered comments to his wife, in a rumbling and snarling voice. He was a short and enormously bloated man, with a huge bald skull and red, outstanding ears. In that great square head one might have expected a face to match, on a large scale. But, curiously, it was an exceptionally small and piggish face, the blunt little features suffused and highly colored, the lips pursed in a cruel and suspicious expression, the little pale blue eyes glittering meanly behind thick spectacles, which had a way of slipping incongruously down his low-bridged, pudgy and upturned nose.

Frau Schnitzel, near him, was a giantess in comparison. Time had not decreased the sulky swinishness of her vast countenance, nor softened her bristling manner, though it had laid harsh ribbons of gray through her dull light hair. She had a brutish and merciless look, arrogant and insensible.

As Angus and Gretchen entered, Mrs. Schnitzel regarded them with her usual domineering and suspicious look, and said ill-temperedly: "You are half an hour late. Where have you been?"

Mr. Schnitzel dropped his *Commercial*, and glowered at them. "Late," he commented.

Gretchen's stays creaked as she bent to kiss her mother. She giggled disagreeably, and said with ill-nature: "It wasn't my fault, dear Mama. But that horrible old priest, Mr. Houli-han, would stop Angus and converse with him at length. We almost ran him down. Perhaps it was unfortunate that we didn't." She giggled again.

Mr. Schnitzel and his affable wife stared at Angus, accusingly, and waited in bristling silence for his explanation and apology.

But Angus returned their regard with formal reticence and pride. "I am sorry if we are late," he said. "Father Houlihan was preoccupied and stepped into the path of our carriage. I was forced to apologize to him, though it was his fault. We had a short conversation, then drove on."

Mr. Schnitzel grunted, and planted his feet on the crack-ling newspaper. He pursed up his lips. Mrs. Schnitzel shrugged massively, and snorted. "Did he try to convert you again, Angus?" she asked maliciously.

Angus compressed his lips. He regarded his mother-in-law coldly, with a look that often quelled her. "Father Houlihan has never tried to convert me, Mother. He is a close friend of Stuart's, and was very kind to me when I was a boy."

Mrs. Schnitzel snorted again, and tossed her head. Mr. Schnitzel cleared his throat with a bestial sound. "Kind to you, was he? They're always looking for converts, those people! I'll have nothing like that in *my* family."

I must control myself, thought Angus. Father Houlihan is nothing to me. I do not even like him. But a thin and sickening pulse began to beat in his throat, and a thread of pain wriggled through his temple. He said haughtily: "I am not aware that I have ever shown any partiality to Catholicism, Father."

"He did ask you to call upon him, Angus," said Gretchen, moving closer to her mother. Her parents, at this, eyed Angus with surly accusation and wariness.

"So he did," agreed Angus. He sat down at a little distance from the others and looked straight before him.

"Do you intend to go?" demanded Mr. Schnitzel, in a bullying tone.

Angus slowly turned his eyes upon him, and appeared to meditate for a long time, during which Mr. Schnitzel became quite crimson with baffled rage. Then Angus said deliberately: "I do not think so. I may. But at present, I do not think so."

As always, the Teuton was intimidated by a cold and unmoved front. Mr. Schnitzel, after a wavering glare at his son-in-law, let his eyes drop. He muttered: "Well. Well, then. Don't think of it."

"Coffee, Angus?" asked the affable Mrs. Schnitzel, with bluster.

"Please," he returned, neutrally. Mrs. Schnitzel rattled the coffee cups, in a great temper, while Gretchen carefully inserted some loaf sugar into the brown fluid, and added some thick cream. Mr. Schnitzel shoved a plate of rich little cakes at his son-in-law. He respected Angus. He greatly admired his gentlemanly ways, and his integrity. He also feared his chilly gray eye and his lack of intimidation. He smirked at the young man, now.

"I see, by the *Commercial*, that the betrothal of your brother, Robbie, to Miss Alice Cummings, is to be celebrated by a dinner at the Mayor's home next month," he said in a heavily friendly tone. "He's doing well for himself. Money there. When's the wedding to be?"

"I'm not certain, Father. I think, in November. By the way, I understand that Robbie is to be appointed to the Bench as junior judge in January. So we have been informed by Judge Taylor. Then, next year when Judge Taylor retires, he will seek election."

"Good, good," grunted Mr. Schnitzel. But Mrs. Schnitzel was envious and annoyed. "He's too young," she said flatly. "Much too young. And not at all an amiable young man, but very presumptuous in spite of his quiet ways. I never liked him, I'm sorry to say, Angus. He has no social graces, and never tries to be overly civil. As for Alice Cummings, she is a very colorless young woman, very artificial in her manner, and entirely too sweet. I suspect such sweetness as hypocrisy."

Angus said quietly: "Miss Cummings is considered an excellent catch, and Robbie is fortunate."

"I never voted for Cummings," said Mr. Schnitzel, belligerently, glaring anew upon Angus. "He's too smooth for me. I've always thought him a liar. That library, now, what do you call it? The Grosvenor. Open to the damn public. Dirty smeary hands of day laborers handling books. What do they want books for, the pigs? Let 'em do their work well, and go back to their shacks, and never let us see 'em. That's what I say, and mean it, too. Books! Books for pigs and dogs! All a lot of nonsense. Cummings' doings, with his highfalutin' idea of public education. And your cousin, Stuart Coleman, giving two thousand dollars to it, and being made an officer, and he with all his scandalous debts!"

"Scandalous!" echoed Mrs. Schnitzel, nodding her head grimly.

"It's anarchistic!" shouted Mr. Schnitzel, with a violent surge forward in his chair.

"It's un-Christian," Gretchen chimed in.

Angus looked at them all, with a hard repressed look. His face was very white and still. I must control myself, he thought. He said in a low tone: "I'm not qualified to pass on the wisdom of the library."

Mr. Schnitzel was now almost beside himself, apoplectic of color. He wagged a fat finger at Angus, and shouted: "That Cummings! And your Stuart is no better! Accusing me of harborin' my laborers in pigpens! They're my shacks, aren't they? It's my land, near the slaughter-house, ain't it? Is this a free country or isn't it? Agitatin' scoundrels! Havin' me up in Court, and tryin' to force me to clean up my property, when the cattle's satisfied with the way things are, anyway!"

"It's always that way, when people associate with Jews," agreed Mrs. Schnitzel, somewhat obscurely.

"Are you going to clean up, Father?" asked Angus, unmoved. The thread of pain had become a wire in his brow, boring and burning.

Mr. Schnitzel was silent for some moments. He sat in his chair, a big lump of infuriated flesh. He looked at Angus with a minatory scowl.

"When they get an injunction," he said at last. "And not until."

"They will. Robbie's preparing it," Angus informed him, with a chill smile.

Mr. Schnitzel clenched his meaty fists and roared out an oath. Gretchen covered her ears with her hands, and giggled. Mrs. Schnitzel squealed.

"I'll fight it! I'll fight it, so help me God!" shouted Mr. Schnitzel, brandishing his fists and shaking them in the air. "We'll soon see who has the most influence, and the most money!"

Angus sipped his coffee. He remarked: "You are quite right. I shall help you fight it, if I can."

Mr. Schnitzel subsided, breathing noisily. But his scowl lightened. "Good. Good. You have sense, Angus. After all," he added, with a sly smirk, "you'll have an interest in that property, yourself, some day."

Angus nodded with dignity. Mrs. Schnitzel eyed him with approval. Gretchen regarded him almost fondly.

"I cannot see the sense in attempting to elevate the common people above their instincts and their natures," continued Angus, precisely. "It is very stupid."

Mr. Schnitzel had another thought. He glared down at the paper at his feet and stamped upon it as if it were alive. "And another thing: it looks like that back-country Abraham Lincoln will be the next President. I've got my uneasy thoughts about that. Common trash aspiring to the presidency! It's an outrage. Something that wouldn't be allowed at home. We have a decent regard, there, for family and breeding and ancient tradition. If he is elected, we'll have a war with the South on our hands. They're gentlemen, there. They won't allow it, I tell you."

Angus glanced up with slow alertness. "Perhaps he will be defeated. I cannot believe the American people so lacking in propriety and a sense of proportion as to elect a farmer and backwoods lawyer to the presidency."

Mr. Schnitzel was wrought-up. "Those niggers! I'm warnin' you, we'll have trouble about those niggers yet!"

"It's this awful country," offered Mrs. Schnitzel. "No appreciation of blood and breeding and education. A country of fools and boors."

Gretchen uttered her acid giggle and glanced at Angus maliciously. "Do you know what Angus said today, Papa? He said this is an English country."

"Nonsense!" roared Mr. Schnitzel, striking his fist on the arm of his chair and staring at Angus balefully. "We've got Germans here, many of 'em, too! More and more of us'll come, you'll see! We'll make something out of this country, a German country, and teach it proper manners and proper government! You'll see. It's destiny. You can't stop it. We'll put an end to this chaos, and put people in their proper places."

Angus put down his cup, and carefully wiped his fingers on his serviette.

"We'll have this damned country in the palms of our hands!" said Mr. Schnitzel, even more violently.

"Otto, your heart," reminded Mrs. Schnitzel, with a threatening glance at Angus.

Angus said calmly: "Your family, Father: did they belong to the military class in Germany? The Junkers, perhaps? Or, perhaps, to the old German nobility?"

Mr. Schnitzel, puffing and wheezing, opened his mouth, then closed it. His look at Angus was murderous.

Angus smiled his brief and chilly smile. He turned to Gretchen. "I believe it is time to change for dinner, my love."

"Another thing," said Mrs. Schnitzel, censoriously. "Is no one going to oppose the building of that Catholic college on Main Street? Canisius, I think they are going to call the dreadful place. Has no one regard enough for this country to prevent that?"

"Where did they get the money?" screamed Mr. Schnitzel, squirming in his chair. "Out of their starvin' people! Out of their criminal manipulations! And I understand your relative, the honorable Mr. Coleman, is giving five thousand dollars to it, too! And his Jew friend, that Berkowitz. And Cummings, if I'm not mistaken."

Angus rose. "Gretchen," he said with quiet command. He turned deliberately to Mr. Schnitzel. "I know nothing about the college. But they've bought the land, and the rest is no business of mine. If you think you can stop the building, you are at liberty to do it. But as you have remarked, Father, this is a free country."

Gretchen, unwillingly, followed him out of the room, with a last apologetic and sympathetic look at her parents.

Mrs. Schnitzel settled in her chair, ponderously. She said: "I often wonder what Angus' true sentiments are. He is very caustic, at times, and unimpressed with your sentiments, Otto."

But Mr. Schnitzel, who was really very fond and proud of Angus, glowered at her. "What do you women know?" he asked contemptuously. "I know Angus. No matter what he thinks, he'll never let it stand in his way."

CHAPTER 46

HAD ANYONE told the happily ignorant Stuart Coleman of the thoughts that were methodically forming in the mind of Angus Cauder, his relative and junior, he would have been astounded, and then would have burst out into incredulous and raucous laughter. It is true that he felt an angry uneasiness in the young man's presence, and betrayed this in a cavalier manner towards him, was careful to exaggerate a contempt he hardly felt at all, and to ignore him elaborately upon the proper occasions. "The puppy's lost every emotion but the lust for money," he would say to himself, with disgust. "A few years ago he was human. Now he's only a stone image of himself."

But that he, Stuart, and Sam Berkowitz, were already discarded in Angus' mind as inferiors whose day in the shops would soon be done, would have seemed to Stuart the dream and libel of a madman. He might have got the faintest hint had he seen the grimly faint smile of Angus as that young man inspected the books and saw the large sums drawn by Stuart against future earnings.

He might, too, have felt some disquiet if he had known that Joshua Allstairs and Angus had become discreet and distant friends, and that Joshua made it a point to have long and rambling conversations with his client upon matters that touched only slightly on the shops and its accounts and debts. If he had known, he would have cried: "Where is the young blackguard's loyalty and gratitude?" But Stuart could never have understood a man who felt no disloyalty or ingratitude in his plotting, but only righteousness. He could not have understood a man who believed that the man of virtue had been granted the power to destroy and discard those who were without "virtue," and so were beyond the pale of dignity as human beings, and the consideration and tolerance and justice of "better" men.

For Angus believed that the favorites of Heaven were ordained to order the affairs of those who did not bask in the approval of the Deity, and to dispose of them arbitrarily, without mercy or doubt or kindness. Wiser men could have told Stuart that a man might find some kindliness and generosity in men who were avowedly rascals and scoundrels, but that the same man would find nothing but mercilessness, cruelty and stoniness of heart in those who believed they had the approval of God, and right and justice, for their oppressions and their crimes against their fellows.

Unfortunately, the ingenuous Stuart knew only that his young assistant manager was very competent and intelligent. Stuart, who hated to give orders, delegated this unpleasant duty to Angus, who had inspired the clerks and other employees with hatred and profound respect for himself. A certain casual and enthusiastic air disappeared from the shops, a phenomenon that distressed the observant Sam Berkowitz, and was replaced by strict attention to business and automatic industry. Angus was feared, if abominated, and in consequence order prevailed, accounts were rigorously kept, and no one was trusted. As a result friendliness disappeared from among the employees, and every man watched his advantage to advance himself at the expense of those from whom he only lately entertained fellowship and sympathy. Angus had introduced the poison of suspicion and ambitious exigency into the shops, and while discipline and order prevailed, the light of devotion had left forever, and was replaced by greed. For Angus was lavish with rewards, and equally lavish with punishments. He also encouraged spying.

Sam saw all this. He was depressed and saddened. But he knew it was of no use to talk to Stuart, who would only have stared at him uncomprehendingly, and with indignation.

Angus now had his own small and clean and austere office, in the rear of the third shop. Most of the decisions regarding the personnel of the shops were made there, without consulting either Stuart or Sam Berkowitz.

"There's a certain falseness in the shops now, in spite of

the surface desire to please and to oblige," Mrs. Cummings remarked to her husband, the Mayor. "I just can't explain it. The clerks are always polite and deferential and alert and neat, eager to offer service and to perform it. No, I can't explain it, Frank, but I have seen the smiles suddenly disappear the minute one turns one's back, and the customer is no longer a friend, whom it is a delight to serve, but only a source of cash. And, somehow, I don't believe poor Stuart knows a thing about it."

"You've got to admit the slackness and easiness has gone," said her husband, frowning. "You've said that yourself, Alicia. Service is prompt and efficient."

"It is true, Frank. But something more valuable is missing. It used to be a pleasure to shop there. One met one's friends around the counters, and could sit and gossip for hours, and discuss the goods. Now you are served briskly, and if you pause to chatter the silks are swept away, and you are given the impression that if you have no serious business in the shops your absence would be welcomed, so as to make way for an open reticule."

"Well, it's all more businesslike," said Mr. Cummings, doubtfully.

"But a lot less agreeable, my dear. Nothing has changed in the shops but good will and friendliness, I admit. As for myself, I find them more delightful than fast and efficient service."

Stuart, friendly soul, saw only that his customers were uneasily anxious to be off when he encountered them, and that they eyed him guiltily and apologetically if they lingered. This made him apprehensive. But still he did not understand. He saw that the comfortable little chairs were rarely occupied now, and dimly feared that no one any longer cared to linger and chatter and diffuse perfume and laughter.

"Change! Change!" muttered Stuart angrily. "Why won't people remain as they are, instead of busying themselves with silly things?"

He was contemplating this restless thought one morning when Angus knocked upon his door, and entered his office. Stuart, who was expecting Sam, had looked up with a pleased smile. When he saw Angus the smile soured, and he grunted: "Oh, it's you. What is it now?"

Angus was not disconcerted at this uncompromising tone and glance. He sat down deliberately near his kinsman, and quietly crossed his knees in their black broadcloth. His icy

gray eyes contemplated Stuart dispassionately and with severity, though still with the respect a civilized man accords
his superior, however reprehensible. Grimly he observed Stuart's flushed and haggard face, the fold beneath his chin, the
sunken lines of dissipation around his black and irascible
eyes. He knew that Stuart was often compelled to walk with
a cane to ease his gouty foot, and it was with satisfaction
that he saw the widening patches of grayish-white at his
employer's temples. Yes, indeed, Stuart was aging, though he
was hardly past forty. He is almost done, Angus reflected to
himself.

Stuart, intuitive as always, saw that hidden scrutiny, and
he said quite suddenly: "Damn you, Angus, every time I see
you, you change some more. Once you were a fairly decent
lad. But now—" He gestured with angry restlessness.

"I trust," said Angus coldly, "that I have not changed for
the worse, and that you find nothing culpable or unsatisfac-
tory in my work?"

Stuart stared at him, blinking. Then he exclaimed: "Oh,
damn you! Never mind. What do you want?"

Angus did not look away when he said quietly and firmly:
"It is nothing about the shops, Cousin Stuart. It is, in a way,
more personal." He paused. Stuart glowered, his lips twitching. "Cousin Stuart," continued Angus formally, "it is in
connection with that petition, signed by you and others, presented to the Court with regard to a certain property held by
my father-in-law."

Stuart stared again, then began to smile unpleasantly.
"So?" he asked, in a treacherously soft voice. He began to
drum on his desk with his jewelled fingers.

Angus regarded him with impassive censoriousness. "I do
not think, Cousin Stuart, that you are completely in possession of the facts. If you were I am sure that you would order your name removed from that petition."

"And what," asked Stuart, still very softly, "are 'the
facts'?"

At this reasonableness, Angus proceeded, more confidently:
"The facts, Cousin Stuart, are that it is a very foolish idea,
revolutionary, and unjust to Mr. Schnitzel. The idea, I might
say, is even unconstitutional. It is an infringement on the
rights of property."

"Ah, so we've become enamored of the 'rights of prop-
erty,' have we?" asked the unimpressed and darkly amused
Stuart. "I thought you would get around to that, eventually.
But go on. You interest me."

The very faintest of flushes touched Angus' white cheek at this open ridicule. His lip rose slightly with contempt.

He began to talk, in slow and precise words, as if speaking and explaining to a dim-witted creature.

"Mr. Schnitzel bought that property about the site of his slaughter-house some thirty-five years ago. He built small—houses on that site, neat, clean and utilitarian. Three rooms to each house. They were somewhat close together, it is true, without room for a garden or a lawn, but they were clean. His workers were pleased with them——"

"As most of them had just come from the pest-holes of Europe," said Stuart, "even a three-room pigsty looked like Heaven."

Angus lifted his head haughtily, but otherwise ignored this interruption. "I am not saying, Cousin Stuart, that these houses are palaces. But in the beginning, I am informed, they were at least clean. Unfortunately, the kind of people who inhabit them are by nature filthy, inferior and base. If the—houses are now in a deplorable condition, it is not the fault of Mr. Schnitzel. The fault lies with the heedless and uncivilized persons who inhabit them. It is they who have created the dirt, rubbish, slackness and abandoned look of the premises."

"Have you been there, Angus?" asked Stuart.

The slightest expression of loathing involuntarily touched Angus' features. He said in a level voice: "I have. I admit they are foul. But that is the way these workers and their families desire their environment. They would be comfortable in no other."

"How do you know? Have you asked them?" demanded Stuart, with scorn.

Angus compressed his lips. "It is not in my province to question the employees of Mr. Schnitzel. But from what I have heard, the workers do not in the least object to the dirt and the odors."

"Which neatly relegates them to a status lower than that of hogs," commented Stuart.

"People of that class are indeed no better than animals," agreed Angus, unconscious of his kinsman's irony.

Stuart looked at him with exasperation. Insolent young jackanapes, humorless and stupid! He said: "Well, I have a fact or two for you, also, Angus. The people don't like their dirt and their odors. Some of them, in fact, have desperately attempted to clean up their horrible premises. But, very regularly, your lovely father-in-law has had heaps of entrails and other offal thrown into the very back yards of his shacks, and there they lie, stinking for weeks, until the people, themselves, are forced to cart them off, or bury them.

"As they are under a despicable labor contract with Herr Schnitzel, which binds them to live on those premises near the stinking slaughter-houses, they cannot leave without penalties, each very onerous. I believe there is some sort of intimidation going on there too, by agents of Schnitzel. Many of the people believe, perhaps it is the truth, that if they break the contract with Schnitzel, they may face fines, prison, or deportation back to the kennels from which they came. I haven't looked into the matter thoroughly, I admit. Perhaps the belief of the people is wrong. At any rate the agents, in their dealings with them, tell them it is quite true.

"The privies haven't been cleaned out in years. The shacks are never repaired, except when the people themselves can borrow, beg or steal a few feet of lumber, or a piece of glass. The roofs leak; the floors sag. Each heavy rainfall brings the water within the houses. Rubbish and dirt pile up relentlessly. The smell is horrible. The water supply is polluted. Flies and other vermin swarm there in all seasons. The whole district is a focus of disease. It is a disgrace to this city. It is a stench in the nostrils of the decent."

Angus regarded him with cold disdain and immovability. "I grant you many of your accusations, Cousin Stuart. But the fact remains that the people desire nothing better. Should the shacks be pulled down, the filth removed, and better habitations built, the aspect of the place would be exactly the same in less than two years' time."

Stuart leaned back in his chair. He looked at Angus long and thoughtfully, his eyes narrowed. His fingers drummed steadily on the desk.

"The people," continued Angus, his courage increased by Stuart's silence, "would be quite content there, in their humble abodes, were it not for agitators who tell them that they are abused, and that they deserve better from their employer."

Drum, drum, drum, went Stuart's fingers on the desk, and faster now. But Stuart smiled a little. "Angus, I will tell you something else. There have been no agitators, from outside. The people themselves, in their desperation, formed a committee which forced its way to the Mayor and demanded alleviation of their misery."

He stood up, towering over Angus, who looked at him with icy fortitude.

"Angus, I am speaking beforehand. But I tell you this: Go

to your amiable father-in-law with this message. Unless those shacks are cleaned up immediately, the worst pulled down, the offal removed and kept removed, the privies cleaned, the water supply purified, new roofs placed on the houses that need it, and everything else granted that has been demanded, —and all this within the next three months—the matter will go to Court in the care of the best lawyers in the country, and not only will Mr. Schnitzel be forced to do all this, but his contracts with his laborers will be abrogated. For at this very moment, these excellent lawyers of whom I have spoken are examining the whole matter in Washington. They are coming to the conclusion that Mr. Schnitzel and his ilk have been practicing serfdom in America, a virtual kind of white slavery, in violation of the laws of the United States."

He paused. He smiled down at Angus, and to Angus that smile was black and evil.

"You will tell Mr. Schnitzel, Angus, that he will clean up and repair at once. You will tell him to cancel his contracts. For if he does not, we shall ruin him, I am afraid. Yes, quite ruin him."

Angus got to his feet swiftly. He confronted Stuart, and his face was white and rigid. "You are a lawless man, Cousin Stuart," he said, in a hard still voice. "You have no respect for law and order, and the rights of citizens such as Mr. Schnitzel. You are a revolutionary, an agitator, a Nihilist. You are not a true American, Cousin Stuart. The rights of property mean nothing to you, the sacred rights of property guaranteed by the Constitution and upheld by Holy Writ. You profane these rights ordained by Almighty God, and would overturn the work of centuries. You are blasphemous, Cousin Stuart."

Stuart, incredulous, looked into the young man's eyes, and could not believe it. Was there craftiness in those eyes, hypocrisy, cynicism? No, there was not! Those eyes were burning with righteous indignation, with profound conviction. Stuart could not believe it. He was amazed.

"Why—why, you imbecile!" he stammered, quite struck. He stared at Angus, at the countenance whitely vehement like an affronted angel's. The lad believed what he had said! He believed, actually believed, that he had the sanction of God and the justice of men to uphold him. At this, Stuart was horrified. He began to shout, out of his confusion, his frenzy of disgust and dismay:

"Get out of here, before I boot you out, you fool! And tell your master what I've told you! Did I say three months?

It's two months now, and be damned to you, you idiot and pig!"

He seized Angus by the shoulder and literally dragged him to the door, then struck him in the face. He flung open the door and hurled the young man violently out into the shop itself. The distant clerks turned to stare, the customers to gape. Then, with one loud last clap, Stuart slammed the door and fell into his chair, gasping.

CHAPTER 47

STUART sat with Father Houlihan under the wide branches of the pear tree in the priest's old garden. The fruit hung in rosy-golden globules above their heads, smelling sweet and luscious in the warm autumn sun. The garden was long and narrow, with brick paths winding by rich and untidy beds of yellow and scarlet flowers, which grew with a kind of hearty exuberance found nowhere else. Between the sunken and uneven bricks grass and moss sprouted. Along a brick wall were matted the canes of thick climbing roses, and as these were a special kind unknown in that region except in this garden, they were blooming in heavy crimson clusters. Father Houlihan had a way with flowers. His rose-garden was ablaze with scarlet, white and gold and soft pink, and there were even a few bushes bearing upon them blooms so dark that they seemed purple, or almost black. Here and there, along the paths, stood crude small statues of white stone, Madonnas in pious attitudes surrounded by little low bright flower beds. A bird-bath in the center of the garden was riotous with birds, chattering of their autumnal migration. From the chicken-pens at the end of the garden came a loud clucking. Father Houlihan also possessed a dove-cote, and the white and purplish birds cooed mournfully to themselves, and lifted their wings to catch the clear and lucid light upon their feathers. It was amazing what that rather small garden could hold. Besides the pear tree, there were three apple trees, heavy with scarlet fruit, and a maple burning like a sacred bush. Formless, yet kind and lovely in its color and plenitude, that garden appeared the most peaceful and shining spot to Stuart, and as he sat under the pear tree with Father Houlihan he felt some of the black despondency in him lighten and become more bearable.

He and the priest were fondly observing little Mary Rose as she wandered among the rose-gardens, cutting blooms which she deposited in a small basket. The child, her little triangular face flushed with a rare color, would pause delightedly to exchange conversation with excitable squirrels in the trees, or to examine some extraordinarily beautiful rose. She was part of that garden, in her blowing white frock covered with a blue cloak, a blue bonnet over her dark thick hair, her little sandalled feet tripping lightly along the paths. She was nine years old, but because of her smallness and slenderness appeared much younger, as if she had been absorbed in timelessness when she had been six and had grown no older. She was preoccupied with her own shy and wondering thoughts, and had forgotten her father and her old friend. She removed her bonnet, and the fresh warm wind lifted her long hair and blew it about her face in heavy tangles. She laughed a little, a sweet and gentle sound, and put back her hair with tiny hands, looking about her.

"The child seems better," murmured Father Houlihan, beaming.

"Yes. And her cough is less. I'll have to send her away with her mother before the winter comes, however," replied Stuart, a worried frown appearing between his black brows. "The winter here is too much for her. No sun. The mountains will be better."

Mary Rose began to cough on a sudden spasm. She pressed her hands to her throat, and bent down in the paroxysm. Her face became contorted, scarlet. Stuart moved as to rise and go to her. Then the spasm was gone as suddenly as it had come. The child brought a kerchief out of her pocket and wiped her damp brow, shaking back her hair. She sighed. They could hear that sigh above the soft breeze. Her eyes were suffused. Then her attention was attracted by a particularly impudent squirrel, and she laughed weakly. She resumed her walk along the paths.

Father Houlihan's hand crept to Stuart's beside him on the white bench, and he pressed that hand with deep comfort and sympathy. He said brightly: "Yes, her cough is much better. Shorter, less hard. She will be quite well when she has reached her teens."

Above them, the sky was a brilliant dark blue, completely cloudless, filled with light. All at once everything was vivid with color, blazing in the last fire of the passing summer. But Stuart's despondency had suddenly increased.

He poked at the moss between the bricks, and said, dourly: "Grundy, you'll have me in jail one of these days."

Father Houlihan glanced at him, alarmed.

"What do you mean, Stuart?" asked the priest, with increasing dismay.

Stuart laughed abruptly. He poked at the moss with increased viciousness.

"Well, I threw that frozen stick of an Angus out of my office yesterday. I also clouted him—hard, not once, but several times, in the face. If I know him right, he'll not forget that. It's an excellent thing that he is my employee, and my kinsman; otherwise I'd be sued for assault and battery."

"But why, Stuart?" asked Father Houlihan anxiously. He passed an agitated hand over his great bald head on which the last splinters of golden hair near his neck and ears had turned white in the last few years.

Stuart told him the story, in harsh, amused words. But it was evident that his own violence had disturbed him. He added: "If it hadn't been for you, Grundy, yelping about Schnitzel's pig-pens, and insisting that I help you no matter what, and driving me mad with your naggings, I'd never have cared nor bothered. My God, why do you have to meddle? You've your own parish, Grundy. Isn't that enough?"

"But Stuart, some of my parishioners live in those stinking sties. I've seen them die, Stuart. I've seen their children cough and choke themselves to death, and vermin and other filth. They've begged me to help them." He paused. Stuart's smile was heavy and disagreeable. He continued to poke the moss more viciously. The priest put his hand urgently on his friend's arm. "Stuart, you know very well that you have been almost as concerned as myself. I told you the story, and you visited Schnitzel's property. Stuart, I'm sorry. If I had known—" he added, in a humble tone, and with a sigh.

Stuart could not let this pass. He laughed shortly. "Never mind, Grundy. You are right. Damn you, you are always right. But one of these days I'll have to pluck you out of a mob, or wipe the tar and feathers off you. You're making Hog Schnitzel very annoyed with you, and knowing humanity as I do, it wouldn't surprise me but what he'd induce the very people you are attempting to rescue to knock your brains out or burn down your house."

He expected Father Houlihan to deny this, vehemently, with his usual passionate belief in the inherent goodness of human nature. But instead, to his surprise, Father Houlihan seemed to dwindle, to shrink. His head sank between his broad fat shoulders. He sighed deeply, over and over.

"You haven't been receiving more threats?" demanded Stuart angrily.

The priest shook his head. He passed his hands over his face. He tried to smile. "Not more than usual, Stuart." All the brightness and comfort had gone from him. He looked blindly before him, his strenuous blue eyes, filmed now, automatically watching the fluttering of Mary Rose's white frock and blue cape. He seemed to sink into sad meditations.

He said, abstractedly: "They have done bad things to our Angus, I'm thinking. They are killing his soul."

"Damn his soul! He never had one, or it was a wizened little lump of clay if he did! Grundy, you are an ass, with your talk of souls. And your meddling with the 'welfare' of creatures who are quite contented as they are."

The priest said musingly: "Father Hauser of St. Louis' Church visited me yesterday. He is a very elegant man. He sat in my parlor like a gentlemanly wax dummy and informed me that I was 'embarrassing' my brother priests with my 'crusades' in behalf of the people. He inferred I was 'noisy.' At least that is the impression he gave me. He is much too polite to be openly insulting. He uses lavender on his kerchiefs, and looked about my parlor with a significant smile. He suggested that I was a poor man and that perhaps it was because I was 'incorrigible' and was not supported by my wealthier parishioners, who might be offended by my 'radical' ideas. In a way, he suggested with the utmost courtesy, I was injuring Mother Church in these delicate days, and inspiring distrust against her, and antagonism. He assured me that other priests were of his opinion. He hinted, therefore, that I confine myself solely to ministering to souls, and close my eyes to evils and injustices and exploitations and miseries which could be alleviated."

Stuart exclaimed, explosively: "What a damned fool he must be! Doesn't he understand that it is obligatory on every man, clergyman or layman, to fight for the welfare, health and peace of a community?"

Father Houlihan laughed softly. His blue eyes were gentle and shining. He put his hand on Stuart's shoulder and pressed it fondly. "You have answered yourself, my dear Stuart," he said, with love.

Stuart laughed, embarrassed. "Well, you have me now, Grundy, you confounded wretch. Go on, then. Do what you want. As things are moving now, we'll have Hog Schnitzel's pig-pens cleaned up shortly. What next," he added, with elaborate sarcasm, "do you desire to attack? And who? I'm your man. I'll sharpen up the battle-ax."

They laughed together, with affection. But Stuart shrewdly observed that the shadow did not entirely leave his friend's large tired face. There was a weariness about him, an abstraction, a pathos, which had never been there before. He sighed, even when he smiled.

The priest began to talk of the troubled times.

"There'll be no doubt that Abraham Lincoln will be elected," said he. "He is a good man, a noble man, from the reports, and most of the people in the North will support him. But what of the South? South Carolina has threatened to secede from the Union if he is elected. These are bad days, Stuart, bad days."

"Let them all secede if they want to," said Stuart, indifferently. He was anxiously watching his little daughter, who had suddenly ceased her play, and was lying under the maple with closed eyes.

Father Houlihan turned to him quickly. "But Stuart, you don't understand. Suppose that many of the Southern States secede and form their own union. Then we shall no longer have a strong and single nation, but two smaller nations, vulnerable to attack by their enemies. As in Europe. Only a single confederacy can retain freedom in America, defying a whole envious world to destroy it. I know my history in a measure, Stuart. A divided America will be a weakened America, prey to any adventurer nation which will covet it. Europe is hoping for division, and plotting future attack. I know."

"Well, we'll be infernal fools, North and South alike, if we permit such a division, and such a danger," said Stuart restlessly. Was the child asleep? Should he go to her? "Besides, why should we war with each other for the sake of blackamoors?"

"The negroes are men," replied the priest, with quiet urgency. "The enslavement of any man by another is a crome not only against the slave but against all men everywhere. Wherever a single man is oppressed, the world of men is oppressed in his oppression. Wherever a crime is committed, anywhere in the world, every man is guilty."

"I suppose you've told that to your parishioners," said Stuart, amusedly, still watching his daughter. "And that is why Schnitzel and his friends are calling you a troublemaker. Grundy, I can't be interested in the blackamoors.

I've seen only one or two, and that is perhaps the reason. More important than all is the unity of America. If the negro must be sacrificed at present to maintain that unity, then he must be sacrificed. Time will solve all things, believe me."

"The laissez-faire of the hard-hearted and cruel man!" cried the priest, indignantly. "You don't know what you are saying, Stuart. It isn't like you. You are merely repeating the sly insinuations of lesser and more venal men. The Southern people, in their hearts, know that slavery is hideous and unjust, a crime before the face of God."

"I understand that they're not as interested in that as they are at the threat of the usurpation of their sovereign rights. If they secede, Grundy, they will be acting in accordance with the provisions of the Constitution. It is their right."

"There are certain rights, Stuart, which must be abrogated in behalf of the safety and peace even of those who seek to abrogate them."

"Now you are becoming too subtle for me, Grundy." Stuart's voice was kind. But the signs of dissipated exhaustion was increasing in his expression and manner. He rubbed his eyes. "Damn it, there mustn't be war. What will happen to trade? And, Grundy, I can't afford another panic," he added simply. "I'm in debt, above my head. I've repaid Sam only three thousand dollars in the past four years. What'll we do if our European shipments are cut off, as they will be in the event of war? Grundy, I'll be ruined."

Father Houlihan, in his concern, forebore to point out to Stuart that his misfortunes were the result of his extravagances, which had not decreased. He only regarded Stuart with sympathy. He said, trying to comfort his friend: "Perhaps there'll be no war. Surely differences between kinsmen can be settled amicably, and in peace."

Stuart said, after a moment: "Did you know that Laurie is going to Europe next April? For two years' study, I believe." His black eyes smiled. "What a wench it is! I have such excellent reports of her. She will be home before she leaves, and I shall give her sundry warnings, as a man of the world."

Father Houlihan, watching his friend, was disquieted for some nameless reason. For at the mention of Laurie's name, Stuart's face had become secret and gentle, and abstracted. The priest said: "Laurie needs no warning. She is armored against the world. She is armored with bitterness and hardness and contempt."

"Nonsense. Why should a minx not yet seventeen be bitter or hard or contemptuous? She hasn't learned all that in New York, Grundy."

"No," said the priest sadly, "she learned that in her cradle, I am afraid. What a lovely face it is! Like an angel's. It is a face of golden metal. Only the finger of love, and God, could touch her heart, which is golden and cold and hard, also."

Stuart moved restlessly. His eyes were full of pain which he did not understand. He saw Laurie before him, and the strangest pang divided his heart. He took two cheroots out of his waistcoat pocket and gave one to his friend. He struck a lucifer, and lighted both cheroots. His big brown hand was trembling slightly. The blue smoke curled from their lips and floated in the warm air.

Then Stuart said suddenly: "There's something wrong with you, Grundy. I feel it. What is it?"

He expected his friend to deny this. But the priest's face changed, became old and flaccid. He said simply: "Stuart, I am afraid. I am full of fear."

"Fear?" Stuart stared. "Of what?"

But the priest did not answer. He was watching Mary Rose, who was rising feebly from the grass, and brushing off her cloak. The child lifted her basket of roses, and smiling, came towards her father and the priest. Father Houlihan's smile was like the sun, tender and warm and beaming. "Little love," he called, "are you tired?"

The child approached them, stood before them. The color had gone from her cheeks; her eyes were heavy. But she smiled at them shyly. She looked down at her flowers and said: "They are so pretty. Prettier than ours, Father Houlihan."

She picked one up in her frail fingers and held it to her little nose.

"Careful," warned the priest. "They have sharp thorns, my darling."

She still held the rose against her lips, and looked at him wonderingly. "But, Father Houlihan, I don't look at the thorns. I look only at the flowers."

Stuart laughed with fond indulgence. But the priest had forgotten him. A strange expression appeared on his large coarse features. He leaned towards the girl. He said softly, eagerly: "What do you mean, child?"

But she was not puzzled. She stood against his black plump knee and looked down at him artlessly. "I know the thorns are there, Father Houlihan. Under the leaves and along the stem. Sometimes there are worms in the roses, too. But I don't look at them. I see how pretty the buds are, and how fresh, and how sweet they smell. I think God's mind is so beautiful, in the roses. I don't think He wanted the worms and the thorns there, but only the scent and the petals, and so we musn't look at anything but the roses, and forget the others."

The priest murmured inaudibly: "The thorns and the worms are there, but the roses are there, too. If we look only at the thorns and the worms, we shall never see the roses, or know them." He blinked a dazzle from his eyes. He took the child's weak cool hand and held it passionately. "At the last, then, the world will be full of thorns and worms and darkness and decay and pain, for us." He put his arm about her and held her to him, burying his face for a moment in her cloud of dark hair. She relaxed against him, and shyly slipped her arm about his neck.

Stuart was perplexed. What was wrong with old Grundy? Why was his head bent like this, and why did his chest heave? The priest looked up at him, and he was pale, but his blue eyes were shining with peace and joy.

"Stuart," he said, "your child has saved my faith, and perhaps my reason. You see, Stuart, I had begun to see only the thorns and the worms."

"Damn," said Stuart, baffled.

But the priest said, with quickening ardor: "I had forgotten something I once heard, in my youth. There is a saying of Rupert, Abbot of Deutz, which touched my heart with the knowledge of its truth and eternal beauty. 'The heavens and earth and sea and all that is in them are the works of the Lord, but man is His work in a special sense, for to make him the Lord used His hands. For the other things it sufficed for the Lord to speak and they were made, but for man He took clay and fashioned it with His own hands.' Stuart, I had forgotten that. I had forgotten that the thing which the Lord had made with His own hands could not be entirely corrupt and evil and full of vileness."

Stuart stared at him blankly for a moment. Then his intuition, which was always greater than his reason, or his mind, understood. He laughed boisterously, but with affection. "So even you, Grundy, have your wrestlings! You'd begun to prick your fingers on the thorns and to smell the worms! I'd never have believed it of you!"

He stood up, still laughing. He put his hand on his daughter's head. "Kiss Father Houlihan now, Mary Rose. We must be going home."

Father Houlihan remained on his bench for a long time after his friend had gone. He sat very still, his clasped hands between his knees. But upon his tired and peasant face there stood for the first time in many weeks a look of shining peace.

CHAPTER 48

ROBBIE sat with his brother, Bertie, before the fire in the latter's bedroom. It was a gray and streaming November day, the wet air acrid and cold, the wind a stertorous bellow against the windows. The leaden rain stalked by those windows; mingled with it were flakes of heavy snow. The sky boiled with gray and rushing clouds. The fire spluttered on the hearth. Robbie had lit a lamp or two, but their light was feeble against the early darkness. He took the pipe he now affected out of his small and delicate mouth and remarked idly: "Winter again, curse it."

Bertie sat near him, in his favorite chair, his dressing gown wrapped about him, a shawl around his shoulders. He turned his head politely, and said: "Yes. Horrible. I hate winters. They never end, here."

He was very thin now, almost emaciated. His face was hollow and sunken. But his bright and ruddy curls were still thick and gay, and his blue eyes were shining. He coughed a little, weakly. After his last prolonged bout, in October, he had been taken ill with lung fever, and his life had been in jeopardy. He was now recovering. But his strength was slow in returning. He watched Robbie pour himself a glass of sherry, and his mouth, always ready with a smile, puckered with aversion. He turned away his head and looked at the fire. His profile, amiable, perpetually half smiling, was serene and still, with always that childlike expression of friendly interest and potentially eager waiting. His hands lay peacefully on the arms of the chair, beautiful hands, but hands without significance. They expressed nothing. They were dead hands, thought Robbie, but they were hands without peace, or even the lack of peace.

As if Robbie had spoken, Bertie turned his head politely. Robbie sipped his sherry. Bertie controlled an instinctive grimace, then hastily smoothed it from his features lest his brother be offended. On Robbie's lap lay the *Commercial*, and he glanced down at it. "Well, Lincoln's elected, and watch the fur fly now. There'll be war, as sure as hell. You'll see."

Bertie smiled again, courteously. He said: "Don't be so gloomy." But his voice was without interest. He spoke again. "In a week from now, Robbie, you'll be a married man. I'll miss you." Again he smiled, but it was without regret.

Robbie laid down his glass. He wiped his lips daintily. He refolded his napkin, and said quietly: "Miss me, hell. You won't miss me, Bertie. You'd never miss anyone."

Bertie regarded him with fond amusement. "Oh, I'll miss you, Robbie. I'll be visiting you, until you kick me out as a nuisance."

No, thought Robbie, you'll live in your vacuum of shining glass and smile out at me and at the world, and there'll never be anything within that glass but your own black and soundless storms. He said: "I hope you will be strong enough to be my best man, as you promised. But it would be just like you to decide that it would bore you." He laughed a little.

Bertie's words were concerned, but his still and smiling face did not change. "Nonsense. I am never bored."

You are never anything, thought Robbie.

"Judge Cauder," said Bertie, and he laughed slightly, as if genuinely amused. "Black little Robbie. Well, you are fitted for it. Did I ever tell you I am proud of you?"

Robbie looked at him with sudden gravity. "Are you, Bertie? Are you?"

"Of course." Bertie lifted one of his fine hands in a vague gesture. "I'm sorry I was too ill to be present at the ceremonies. But I was there, in spirit."

You have no spirit, thought Robbie, and the thought was a sick pain to him. You move and drink and sleep and smile, but there is nothing in you. If there ever was, it died long ago, and blew away like dust.

He wanted, as he had wanted so many thousands of times, to approach Bertie, to cry out to him, to seize him with his hands and force comprehension into those serene and untenanted eyes, to arouse recognition in them, and pain and life. If he would only die! he thought to himself, almost vehemently. There is no peace for me, until he dies. Until he returns to the void from which he came, and is nothingness. I shall never be able to feel anything, until he is dead.

I shall never be a human being, a full creature of vitality and eagerness, so long as he lives.

He loathed himself for this abysmal confession, for his helplessness, and suffering. He could not understand his incompleteness while Bertie lived. Little Alice awaited him. Doubtless he loved her. But he could feel nothing. He had nothing to give anyone, so long as Bertie was alive.

He said abruptly: "Bertie, do you remember Alice's cousin, Agnes Clayton? She was quite smitten with you, and I thought for a time that you liked her. At least, you paid her court. I remember that when she returned to Syracuse you used to correspond. What happened?"

Bertie laughed gently, and again he made that aimless gesture. "She was too good for me," he said amiably.

"But didn't you like her?"

"Of course I liked her. She is a very sweet girl. A charming female." But Bertie's voice, though musical as always, had no inflection in it of regret or sadness.

"Well, then," said Robbie, tentatively.

Bertie shrugged. "I'm quite contented with life as it is. Why should I complicate it? Besides, I said she was too good for me, didn't I? What have I to offer such a nice girl?"

"You could offer her something if you wished," said Robbie, abruptly. And then he knew it was no use. Bertie was smiling at him affectionately. "I don't want to offer anyone anything, Robbie," he said.

Robbie began to speak, annoyed, wanting to struggle against the impossible, and then he met Bertie's eyes. They were still shining. Robbie felt a curious lurching in himself, and he bent forward the better to see his brother's eyes in the lamplight. Was it only his imagination, or was there something strange and fixed in those blue depths, something warning and cold and sharp with pain?

If only there were! If only there were! But Bertie was smiling again, and there was nothing there now but bright emptiness.

Shaken by what he had seen, or imagined he had seen, Robbie continued with harsh earnestness:

"You talk like a confounded fool, Bertie. What do you mean, you don't want to offer anyone anything? You're an infernal egotist, Bertie. You don't want to dissolve the love affair you have with yourself."

Bertie flung back his head and laughed delightedly. "How clever you are, Robbie! It is nothing for you to turn out epigrams by the hour."

But Robbie was enormously shaken all through his cool reason and detachment. It was now or never, he thought. He must break that glassy and brilliant shell about his brother. He must plunge his arm through it, to seize on that strange and furtive something he had seen in its depths only for an instant.

He made his voice calm and neutral, but oddly penetrating: "Bertie, I've wanted to talk to you for a long time."

Bertie looked at him affably as he paused, and said; "Yes? What is it, Robbie?"

"I'm not going to ask you whether you have any affection for me, Bertie," Robbie went on. "You'll always tell me you have." Bertie nodded amiably. Robbie shook his head with the nearest approach to violence he ever manifested. "Try to think, Bertie. Try to understand. We've been very close. At least, I've tried to be close to you. We've been friends, Bertie. Oh hell, this means nothing at all to you, does it?"

Bertie said quickly: "Of course it does, Robbie. But what are you getting at?"

Robbie was silent. He chewed his pale underlip. He stared at his brother with something like desperation.

"Bertie," he said at last, "I'm going to be married. We'll be separated, you and I. We'll see each other often, but not so intimately as this. I'll have enlarging interests, in my work."

And then, helplessly, he knew it was no use at all. He could not smash that glass. There was nothing there, or if there was, it was forever removed from him. He stood up and poked the fire in the silence that followed his words. He shook coal upon it. He sat down again, and regarded the fire grimly. No use. No use at all. He could feel Bertie near him, tranquil, untouched, unapproachable.

And then he heard Bertie speak, very quietly, and it was not for some moments that he realized the significance of what he was hearing.

"Leave me alone, Robbie," said Bertie.

Robbie started. Slowly, cold as ice now, he turned his head. He looked full into Bertie's pellucid eyes. He saw the smile on Bertie's lips. But he saw, with a shock, the inexorable warning, the thing that was almost a stern threat. He held his breath. The two brothers regarded each other in a terrible silence.

"Leave me alone, Robbie," Bertie repeated, very softly. "Don't touch me, Robbie. Go away and forget me, Robbie."

And then, to Robbie's anguished amazement, he saw that

Bertie's hands were tightening on the arms of his chair, flexing, arching, the fingers lifting rigidly.

"O my God!" whispered Robbie.

Bertie inclined his head gravely. "Yes, 'O my God,'" he said.

Something was clenching, crushing, Robbie's heart. He dropped his head. Again he whispered: "I can't. I can't 'go away.'"

Bertie's voice was serene and low. "You must, Robbie. You really must. You must leave me alone. Perhaps it won't be long. But you must leave me alone."

The door handle rattled, and they heard Janie's hoarse, demanding voice. Robbie stood up. He felt very weak. He was trembling. He looked at his brother. Bertie's face was untenanted again, turned to the door, smiling a welcome.

CHAPTER 49

MAYOR and Mrs. Cummings lived in a classic white mansion on Delaware Avenue near North Street. It stood on the heights of a stately ascent of green land, embellished by numerous trees and carefully tended flower beds. All its rooms were high, broad and gracious, with lovely majestic staircases and immense fires. Mrs. Cummings (the former Alicia Clayton) had been the only daughter of an exceedingly wealthy freebooter, and as the majority of the gentry of Grandeville were composed of tanners, sausage-makers, slaughter-house owners, Lake traders, horse-breeders and "swappers," quarrymen and shopkeepers, grain merchants and canalmen, the defunct Mr. Clayton had acquired a kind of royalty by reason of being an adventurer. He had presented his daughter with this land and this perfect house upon the occasion of her marriage to one of his associates, who no longer bore the splendid aura of the freebooter. In fact, no one could have had a more respectable air than did this little, wise, rotund man with the serious brown eyes and the gentle tongue, and the passion for justice and decency. He had brown aquiline features, and was suspected, by the malicious, of possessing Indian blood.

He was serving his third term as mayor, and as he was generally loved by the less venal citizens, it was generally conceded that he would soon be elected to a fourth term.

Despite his lack of stature, he had a certain dignity and quietness that conferred a largeness upon him. It was to be expected that he was virulently hated by many, and respected by all.

His daughter, Miss Alice, resembled him in that she had inherited his brown eyes and a certain aristocratic cast of feature. But she also had shining brown hair the color of new chestnuts, and a fair complexion. Her figure was dainty and exquisite. She had a low light laugh, very musical and kind, and her father's quick and reserved intelligence. Her accomplishments were many, for her mother was a sensible wise woman, and Alice had been reared in a bookish but alert atmosphere which set her singularly apart from the apathetic young ladies of her acquaintance. She also had the warmest and most modest heart, a brilliant humor, clever perceptiveness and the quiet graciousness of a great lady. Her father's passion was law, and Miss Alice had become so proficient in that science that the Mayor sometimes regretted that she was a female. Between father and daughter was the deepest sympathy and tenderness, and he thought it the loveliest sight possible to see the swift bright changes of her animated mind reflected on her pretty oval face, as sunlit water throws its trembling shadow on quieter leaves. Mrs. Cummings would often wryly remark that she had given Alice birth but that the girl was really her father's daughter.

Cherished and adored as she was, her suitors were closely scrutinized by the Mayor, and it was not until Robbie appeared that the older man felt complete relief and satisfaction. Alice, he would think to himself, was the most sensible minx possible, and possessed of the most level head, but, even so, females were unpredictable when it came to the heart. The girl was now barely nineteen, and had betrayed no signs of any unthinking involvement with unsuitable gentlemen. Nevertheless, it was a great relief to the Mayor that she had finally chosen Robbie Cauder.

The marriage between the young people was celebrated the latter part of November. The Cummings' mansion, decorated with bowers of flowers and ferns and potted plants, was filled with life and festivity and that bubbling artlessness of youth so dear to the quiet Mayor. Alice's friends came from New York, and even from Boston, to be present at the ceremony. There were to be nearly two hundred guests, and as the *Commercial* editor lyrically observed, "this is the most important event of the social season of 1860."

However, even in that brightly lit and warm and happy

mansion, the shadow of the troubled year hung deeply. Gentlemen who ought to have applied themselves assiduously to the punch bowl, gathered in knots, and, with grave faces discussed "the situation." Where only laughter should have been heard, there were annoyed and disagreeing voices raised in argument. Mrs. Cummings, harassed and irritated, kept the Mayor in a ferment of busyness roving from group to group, urging them to "remember, gentlemen, this is a wedding, not a political caucus."

Fires roared in the chimneys. Great pier mirrors reflected the firelight and the many lamps and the laughing faces of the guests and the elaborate toilettes of the ladies. Stuart had been busy for three months importing laces and velvets and silks and feathers and perfumes for this event, and the dressmakers had been driven to distraction. The bride's gown, of white satin and faille, was a French importation, designed by Worth himself, and her veil was a cloud of French lace. About her small neck was a perfect string of pearls, her bridal gift from Robbie, and on her right wrist there sparkled her father's gift, a diamond and ruby bangle. Above the great bell of her gleaming bridal gown, her slender waist rose like the stem of a flower, and her pretty little bosom was smothered in pearl-strewn lace.

The bridegroom's mother, in crimson velvet bordered with ermine and draped with blue velvet roses, topped by a blue velvet bonnet, was resplendent and a wonderful figure of fashion. Janie's carroty curls were naturally threaded with gray, for she was now nearly forty-five. However, those betraying threads had been artfully dyed (by herself, in the privacy of her boudoir) and her complexion as artfully applied. She was the most vivacious lady present, and her hoarse and zestful laughter could be heard all over the mansion. She was excessively pleased by this marriage, and though she had had nothing whatsoever to do with it, she preened herself that she had been very clever in her guileful suggestions to Robbie ever since he had begun to grow a beard.

Stuart, who still retained a certain splendor in spite of his obvious dissipation, was present with his wife, the perfectly beautiful former Miss Allstairs. When that flawless beauty appeared, the most festive groups became silent in unwilling awe and admiration, though all felt that when Mrs. Stuart's tawny eye fell upon them with a gracious smile she really saw nothing at all.

Naturally the loathed Schnitzels were there, also, with

their German friends and associates, and Angus, as part of the clan, stayed near them. His tall thin figure, his shut pale face, his eyes which appeared closed even when wide open, set him apart from these stout and clumsy aliens, who muttered and grunted and smirked and snarled among themselves, with envy.

Laurie, Jane reported, though broken-hearted that she could not be present at her brother's wedding, sent her love and regards and regrets. Janie confided to Mrs. Cummings, with pride, that Laurie was deeply engaged in her musical studies, and must do an enormous quantity of work in order to be permitted to study in Europe the next summer.

No gentleman at that wedding was so handsome, so gay, so full of laughter and fascination as the best man, Bertie Cauder. The young ladies were devastated by him. Miss Agnes Clayton, niece of Mrs. Cummings, looked at him with swimming and swooning eyes, and was heard to sigh frequently. In black broadcloth, with exquisite ruffles and a flowered waistcoat, his tall and comely form set him apart as a resplendent figure, and his manners were so gallant, so courteous, so flattering and attentive and affectionate, that even the bellicose elder matrons succumbed to his charm. He was very affectionate with Robbie, and, after the ceremony, was seen to stay very close to him, his hand on his brother's shoulder.

It was a very happy wedding. At eight o'clock the bride and her groom departed for the station amid great confusion, congratulations, laughter and love. They were to pass their honeymoon in New York, and it was there that they would meet Laurie and spend some time with her.

No one was a spectator at the quiet leave-taking between Robbie and his brother. But Robbie had manipulated matters so that he had a few last words with Bertie in the warm dim hall near the staircase. Bertie had come willingly enough. The brothers stood near the newel-post lamp, and looked at each other, Robbie pale and grave, Bertie, as always, with his fixed and unreadable smile. The confused uproar of the revelry came to them from the distant parlors.

It was unlike Robbie to be so despairingly persistent. He faced his brother. A sudden silence fell between them.

Then Robbie, clearing his throat, said softly: "I'd like to know you'll be all right, Bertie. I'd like to know that, when I'm away."

"Oh, you mustn't worry! I shall do splendidly," said Bertie. He pressed his brother's shoulder affectionately. But Robbie's small and reticent face darkened. He shrugged a little. He was a fool. He ought to be convinced now that nothing was of any use at all. But still he persisted.

"Take care of yourself. We'll have some fine talks when I return."

"Of course!" said Bertie with enthusiasm. "We mustn't abandon our walks together, either."

"When it's spring, we'll walk again along the Canadian shore, and see your friend, Captain Willoughby."

"Good old Joe," assented Bertie, with affection.

"And Frenchman's Creek," suggested Robbie, with despair. Bertie nodded with bright gaiety. "We mustn't forget our fishing," he said.

Again there was silence between them. Bertie looked down at his brother, and his face changed a little. His hand dropped from Robbie's shoulder. A sudden strange expression glimmered in his eyes, compassionate but retreating.

"Be happy, Robbie," he said gently. Was there warning, pleading, in his warm voice? Robbie listened with painful and moved attention. "Be happy," Bertie repeated, and his tone was oddly urgent. "You have a new life. It is yours, all yours. You must think of nothing else. Promise me that."

"I can't cut off my old life, as if it had never existed," said Robbie, through a constricted throat. He touched his brother's sleeve. But Bertie, with an impulsive if gentle movement, stepped back a pace or two. Across that space he regarded Robbie as from an immense and impassable distance.

"You must, you must," he said. "There must be nothing else. Remember Lot's wife. She turned to salt when she looked back." He smiled; his handsome white teeth glistened in the dim lamplight. "Don't look back, Robbie. You must not."

He lifted his hand, touched his forehead with a gay salute, turned on his heel, and was gone.

Robbie stayed alone for several long moments after Bertie had returned to the festivities. All at once he felt a complete and overwhelming desolation and loneliness such as he had never experienced before in all his life. He could taste the dryness of his loneliness in his mouth, the sick dull ache of bereavement and melancholy in his heart. He was pervaded with despair. All about him was silent and empty wasteland, with not even a shadow to break its bleak and endless expanse. No voice could penetrate there, no movement.

He caught the newel post in a shaking hand. His grief

was more than he could bear, and his loneliness. Never had he felt so solitary, so abandoned, so set adrift in a universe without the smallest echo.

In those moments, he did not think of his bride.

CHAPTER 50

YOUNG Mrs. Robbie looked with absent approval into her mirror, and lifted her head to allow her thick weight of chestnut curls to drop in a shining mass on her shoulders. She scrutinized the flushed oval of her pretty face, and brought a smile to her mobile red lips so that dimples twinkled and sparkled about them. Her brown eyes, so lively and lustrous, gazed back at her solemnly, in spite of the smile. All at once she was amused at this dainty scrutiny, and she laughed to herself. She began to brush her hair.

Her pale-blue velvet dressing robe lay in folds over her slim thighs and knees, lay in a glimmering heap about her feet. It flowed and brightened with her movements. Reflected in the mirror she could see the gilt, plush, molded plaster, crystal, crimson and spacious walls of the bedroom of the bridal suite of the luxurious hotel. Sunlight lay on the wide but shallow windowsills, which looked out upon Fifth Avenue. The crimson velvet curtains, looped in blue cords and gold fringe, moved a little in the sharp wind which penetrated under the windows. A fire crackled in scarlet warmth on the black marble of the hearth. It was scented, quiet and peaceful in that room, the silence broken only by the soft swish of Mrs. Robbie's industrious brush, and the rustling of Robbie's newspaper.

Slowly the brush began to pause in its labors, and finally ceased. Now it gleamed in the motionless little white hand. Mrs. Robbie's smiling face became grave and still. She could see her husband in the mirror, as he sat near the window, his neat black knees crossed, his polished boots shining, his head almost obscured by the sheets of the *Journal*. He turned a page. His face had its usual reserved pallor. His small features were quiet and intent.

Mrs. Robbie thought: I love him. No one can tell how much I love him. I've always loved him. He is my heart, my soul. I've never told anyone. I can never tell him. He is shut away from me. Forever. Why? Oh, won't someone please tell me why?

Robbie turned another page, and soberly scanned it. A coal popped on the fire. Muted traffic sounds penetrated the quiet. The brush lay motionless in the girl's hand.

Alice spoke in her sweet low voice: "Robbie."

He glanced at her blue back, and smiled affectionately. "Yes, my love." He saw her young pretty face in the mirror, so serious now, so mature.

"Robbie," she said, and though her voice was still low, it was penetrating, "do you love me?"

He raised his tilted black brows as if with fond amusement. "Of course. Of course! What a silly, dear little question! Didn't I marry you?"

She lifted her hand and began to brush her hair again. Her hand was trembling. She did not speak for a moment or two, during which he watched her with that reserved amusement of his. Yet he felt some pricking of uneasiness. She put down her brush, and suddenly turned on the padded seat and faced him. The bright flush had gone from her smooth cheeks. Her brown eyes were somber, clear as brown water, but unsmiling. Robbie dropped his newspaper and looked at her in silence.

"Robbie," she said, "do you know you've never said to me: 'I love you'?"

He tried to smile lightly. "Was it necessary? Or am I a boor? I thought a young lady understood all that when a gentleman asked for her hand."

She did not speak. Her eyes never left his face. There were no dimples now about her mouth, which trembled at the corners.

She shook her head. "No, I did not 'understand.' I didn't think of it, I must confess. Until we were married. Until we came here."

"Then, why now? Have I been remiss?"

She shook her head again. He said: "You are a darling little child."

She lifted her hand listlessly. "Please, Robbie. There is something strange— It is true that I've never been married before. But something tells me there is a kind of strangeness, an incompleteness."

She waited impatiently for him to smile again. But he did not. He had dropped his head and was looking at his boots. Then he said softly: "My dear. My very dear. You mustn't be alarmed. It is just my temperament. I'm not very demonstrative, you know. You must take me as I am."

Once again her hand moved in a tired and listless gesture. "I know all that about you, Robbie. I've never expected, or even wanted, gallantry from you. You are so much like Papa. He isn't gallant, either. He and Mama are such happy friends, and love each other so, though I've never seen them exchange a kiss, or say a word of endearment in anyone's presence. It isn't that, Robbie, you see. Yet, I've always known how Mama and Papa love each other. There is something one can sense, something warm and close and dear." Her mouth quivered. But her eyes remained dry and steadfast, though in them there was a desperate pleading for reassurance.

Then Robbie said, so low that she could hardly hear: "You must give me time, my darling."

"Time?" she murmured. And then her heart began to beat with a loud sick fear, a terrible plunging. "Time?" she repeated. "Why, Robbie?"

He sighed. The papers slipped from his knees to the floor. He tried to smile, whimsically. He said: "I am a new husband, you know. We must grow together. Those things don't happen overnight. They take years of growth."

She caught the edge of the blue bench in clenched fingers. "Robbie," she said, "why did you marry me?"

She was very white, but her gaze did not falter or dim. Its pure brownness shone upon him from its strained sockets.

He stood up, and she had the dreadful sensation that he was about to leave her. Yet he did not move. He said, in slow and measured tones: "I married you because I wanted you, Alice. I love you as much as it is possible for me to love—anyone."

She shook her head, her eyes never leaving him. "No, Robbie," she said, gently, almost meditatively, "you don't love me. Not really. You try to. You try so hard. I can feel you trying. You want to love me. But something stops you. Something stops you from loving me as much as you wish. What is it, Robbie?"

He opened his mouth to speak. She saw the pale parting of his lips. But no sound came from them. He leaned his head against the glass of the window, his back to her now. He said quietly: "You are fanciful, Alice. Your female temperament demands too much, and is too imaginative."

She said: "You wanted me because you thought that

was an escape—from something. What is that 'something,' Robbie?"

When he did not answer, she was impelled to start to her feet, the long sick trembling running over her slight body. Her throat was dry; her eyes burned. She was full of terror.

"Robbie! I am only nineteen, but I understand so many things! I feel them in my heart, Robbie. That is why I must ask you: What is the 'something,' or the somebody, that keeps you from me?"

He turned to her slowly, against his will. She stood across the room from him, like a small and slender shaft of icy blue, her hair in disorder upon her shoulders, her eyes too bright, too desperate. He wanted to go to her. Something in him urged him to rush to her, to hold her in his arms, to hide those terrified young eyes against his mouth. But he could not. He felt as if a ton of stone had fallen upon him, had petrified him.

"Was there someone you loved before me, Robbie?" she asked, her voice clear and unshaking. "Someone you can't forget?"

He said, through parched lips: "My darling. I never loved any woman before. Believe me. You do believe me?"

She did not answer for several long moments. Her eyes burned into his. Then she turned her head aside. "Yes, Robbie. I do believe you. But are you telling me you can't love me with all your heart——?"

His voice came like a dry and painful rustle. "Perhaps it isn't in me to love anyone 'with all my heart.' I don't know. Perhaps I'm not made that way, Alice. You must take me as I am. I will do my best for you. You deserve that. You are the sweetest thing. There was never anyone like you."

He paused. From her hanging head the curls dropped and flowed, half concealing her face.

"You see," he said pleadingly, holding out his hands to her, "I've been so absorbed in many things. There was my study, my work. And my brother, Bertie. I've had to take care of him." And then as he spoke that name, he felt ill and hideously shaken. He leaned against the window.

Slowly, Alice raised her head. Her eyes were enormous, and very still.

Then, all through her swept the dreadful knowledge, flooding her sensitive perception without the aid of her shattered reason. Her eyes widened, looked beyond the room, beyond New York, back to Grandeville, through the years she had known and loved Robbie. Bertie. Bertie was beside him, always. Bertie, laughing, drinking, affectionate. Bertie, full of gaiety, never demanding, even a little affectionately bored by Robbie's absorption in him, even sometimes evading him. "The red and black of it," they had been called, by observant Grandeville citizens. Robbie rarely alone, except when he called at the Cummings' mansion, and often, not even then. Always, always Bertie. Why hadn't she known, before? She *had* known, in a way, and had been tenderly touched by this devotion in so cold and reserved a man. She had thought it admirable, a lovely thing.

Her lips felt like ice, and swollen. She moistened them. "Robbie, it's Bertie, isn't it?"

He still leaned against the window, but she felt his sudden rigidity. They looked across the room at each other again, intently. Then Robbie said: "Yes. I suppose so. We have been very close, Alice." He spoke simply, haltingly. "I don't believe I cared for anyone in the family, but Bertie. We were friends. I—I have had to take care of him, since we were children. He was, in a way, my charge. No one understood him but me, not even my mother, who adored him. And even I never understood. No one can understand him. I—I've had my glimpses, and they were quite terrible. He is like a child. Someone had to take care of him. Perhaps—Alice, perhaps I am as I am because I'm still not free from looking after Bertie."

He waited. She did not speak, but only looked at him desolately.

Then he cried out, the words torn from him forcibly: "I'll never be free until he dies!"

She stared at him for a long time.

And then there was a sudden huge breaking in her heart, a huge swelling and flooding, a great thunder. Her love rose up in her like a wave, crushing her, filling her, and it was mingled with an awful compassion, a passion to protect, to hide, to shelter and save him.

She flung out her arms and ran to him. She wound her arms about his neck, pressing her young body to his, drawing down his head to her breast. She held him as a mother holds a threatened child, crooning to him in wordless, sobbing murmurs. She kissed him, over and over.

He put his arms about her. He pressed his head to her breast, her warm young shoulder. She felt his tiredness, his loneliness, his despair.

But there was a triumphant, stubborn joy in her now.

She looked over his head at the sunlit window. She smiled.

I can wait, she thought. He needs me so terribly, my darling, my darling.

BOOK THREE

O MORNING STAR!

CHAPTER 51

ON DECEMBER 20TH, 1860, South Carolina seceded from the Union, and though the heaviest apprehension and gloom overspread many of the other States, the spontaneous celebration in South Carolina was an embarrassing demonstration that the secession was by popular will. Bedeviled, harassed and exhorted for years by the Northern States, the South looked defiantly towards Washington and muttered of other secessions. Temporarily, at least, the threat of bankruptcy which had hovered over the cotton planters with the heightening tempo of Abolitionism in the North, passed away, and a general air of optimistic vitality and quickening pervaded the South. Many believed there would be no war, but that the North would accede to the sovereign will of those States which decided to leave the Union, as guaranteed by the Constitution.

"Yes," remarked Father Houlihan, sadly, "the South has the 'right' to leave the Union, and its freedom to decide whether or not it owes allegiance to the central Government. But by the exercise of this 'right' the South has jeopardized the whole of America, perhaps forever."

To the consternation, dismay and despair of thinking men, not only in the North, but in the South, other States followed the example of South Carolina in a majestic and white-lipped parade. One by one the fair and flowery States rose and turned their faces from Washington, and in the White House Mr. Lincoln's kind and ugly face darkened with hopelessness even while his mouth set with passionate determination. Out of the House of America went the loveliest daughters, out into danger, out into threat and a terrible future, while Europe watched, smiling and malignant. The Constitu-

tion of the United States was the wide door through which
the daughters departed, and near that door stood Abraham
Lincoln, in prayer. He waited in silence; he said nothing as
yet. But he watched the emptying of his House. And he
looked at Europe.

"It was an evil day for the people when that man was
elected President," said Stuart, desperately concerned.

"It is an evil day for the people when God does not raise
up a leader in their desperate hour," replied Father Houlihan sternly.

The Southern senators left Washington. The Southern
States seized the property of the United States in their re-
spective States. Arsenals and forts were seized. Though war
was not yet threatened, a huge and mysterious supply of
arms appeared, and was distributed. Stuart, remembering
a certain dark-eyed and laughing man, Raoul Bouchard,
felt a burning in his cheeks and a sickness in his heart. Army
stores and other property were confiscated at San Antonio,
and the navy yards at Norfolk and Pensacola passed into
"Southern" hands.

In March, 1861, the seceded States formed their own
union—the Confederacy.

The South, intoxicated with its brilliant successes, with
its conviction that it had done only that which was permitted to it by the Constitution, with its aristocratic and contemptuous anger against the hard-fisted Yankees, who had
"brought this catastrophe upon America," with the gallantry
and simple dignity of its new President, retired into itself
amid a mass of flags and into a kind of happy delirium and
joyous resolution. No longer would it be the recipient of insults and threats from the Yankee industrialists, who saw
the inevitable exodus of industry into the Southern regions
of slave labor. No longer would the South be belabored by
accusations of "barbarism and heathenish practices." Only a
few Southern gentlemen heard the murmurs of a hungry and
rapacious Europe, and the stir in the capitals of the Continent
three thousand miles away.

"As the years pass," said a prominent Southern nobleman,
"the paths of the North and South must increasingly diverge.
The North, which will become ever more largely polyglot
and alien, will be to us a foreign nation, no longer one with
us in our Anglo-Saxon Protestant race, our aristocratic British traditions. It is for the sake of our race, our religion, our
traditions, that we must part company with the North."

The air of the whole country was electric with anger, dismay, fear, despair and treason. But no one yet believed that war would come.

Mr. Lincoln, himself, said there was no crisis but an artificial one, that nothing was really wrong, that nobody would be hurt. He pleaded with the people to "keep cool." And alone, in his great bedroom in the White House, he lay sleepless on his pillows and listened to the great rolling wheels churning down from the skies upon his country.

Grandeville received all the news with a certain dull apathy and indifference which was to mark all its history. A number of men were frightfully disturbed and afraid. But the mass of the people, and even the surrounding farmers, were inert. They did not believe in the possibilities of war. Or they did not care. The issues involved were nothing to the slum-dwellers and the laborers. They gaped at the newspapers, and forgot them. Even when it was rumored that Mr. Lincoln, in person, was to visit Grandeville during his tour of Albany, Poughkeepsie, Trenton, New York, Philadelphia and Harrisburg, few outside of "elegant society" were interested. They knew, vaguely, that someone, somewhere, was making "an awful fuss" about "niggers," but as they had rarely seen a negro, and knew nothing of slavery except their particular brand in Grandeville and their memories of another brand in Europe, the issue was to them as remote as the moon. Less than five hundred people in Grandeville had read *Uncle Tom's Cabin*. Less than five hundred talked in parlors and taverns of the coming terror. Less than eight thousand had even voted in the last elections. Less than one third of the people even knew the name of the President of the United States. Sunken in a kind of peasant lethargy, which knew nothing but heavy and unremitting toil and occasional mad drunkenness and constant breeding, they were as absorbed in their minute little affairs and lightless meager pleasures and crushing work as the very farm animals on the land beyond the city. Nor was this sunken attitude conspicuous among the "foreigners only." The Yankee farmers, laborers, dock workers and grain loaders showed little if any passionate concern with the state of the Nation. If a smarter neighbor spoke of it, his words were received with sluggish resentment on indifference.

The fact that if war came thousands of them would be compelled to engage in it personally had not yet penetrated their insular hearts, nor caused their slow pulses to beat faster.

Some few of these workers, however, did speak of it with concern and fear, and understanding. And these few were the Germans who had fled Germany in 1848, in loathing and disgust. Accustomed to alarms and calamities, to threat and insecurity, to despair and revolt, they smelled the first breath and heard the faint sounds of the coming frightfulness. It was ironical, then, that the children of these lovers of freedom were unconcerned with the approaching struggle, or, if they had opinions at all, these opinions were spiteful, sullen, resentful or traitorous. German fathers, remembering Bismarck, remembering a torn and gasping Germany, were helplessly appalled at the realization that their sons felt no passion for free America, though nurtured in America, and fed with the fruits of their parents' resolution and indomitable faith in the rights of man.

"Ah," said the priest, shaking his head sadly, "I am afraid that amongst us there will always be those who hate goodness and kindness and freedom, and yearn only for cruelty and madness and murder. What shall we do with them? There is something terrible for America in this thought, I'm thinking."

In the South was jubilation, resolution, courage, and fire, and a passionate patriotism. In many large cities of the North was only resentment, listlessness, stupid ignorance, unawareness and cold disinterest. The shopkeepers, however, the industrialists, the merchants, and others whose profits depended upon peace and commerce, were alarmed. They hated the threat of war; they feared it. They muttered angrily among themselves, and cursed Lincoln, cursed the abolitionists, cursed the mad disturbers of a peace that had steadily filled their purses. While patriotism ran like a bright flame through the cities of the South, the cities of the North sat in dark and lumpish surliness.

Mr. Lincoln knew of this. He saw the antagonistic faces that surrounded him during his tour of the Northern cities. He saw the thick, outthrust lips of resentment, the blank stare of bewilderment, the suspicion in empty or narrowed eyes. How was it possible for him to reach the hearts of this sullen people, to make them realize that the fate of America rested in them, and the hope of all the future? His heart sank deeply into despair. This people had no vision, no passion for justice, no patriotism, no pride, no courage, and no dream. It had only its rapacity. Rapacity, then, was the entrance to their stony souls. Let them once realize that if the South were victorious, their growing industrial empire might very well march South into cheap slave-regions, and their metallic fury might be aroused as it would never be aroused by the sight of a flag or the blare of a trumpet. A threat to a Yankee's purse would be heeded intently; inexorable economics spoke in a language he could understand.

It was not for some months that Lincoln realized that a strange and horrible phenomenon was beginning to take form in the North, and when he realized this he was aghast. Racial and religious hatreds had, so far, never stained the history of the Republic. Now, in the North, he saw the cobra heads of these hatreds lifting from the dank marshes of men's souls. At first he was incredulous. Who, among these many races, these diverse religions, had conjured up the cobras, had set their deadly heads to swaying? Who was the traitor? What was his design? Destruction threatened the Republic; she would need every hand, every firm heart, every stern voice, if she were to survive. And somewhere, in the black and steaming pits of men's spirits, a hideous tongue was whispering, a tongue that urged disunity, strife, hatred, violence and cruelty in the very face of the storm which was darkening over the nation. What was this traitor's design? What did he wish to accomplish? Did he not understand that such disunity would threaten the existence of America? Or was it possible that he knew only too well?

It came to Mr. Lincoln, slowly but implacably, that the traitor knew only too well. A nation in the throes of war could readily lose the war if diverted by regional hatreds and regional violences. That was the plan, then. Somewhere, in the Northern cities, there lived men who hated their country, who wished to see America die. And so it was that they plotted to disperse her strength, to confuse her, to weaken her with regional strifes, so that she would be destroyed. Destroyed by the South? No. For the South, inevitably, would suffer from this frightful disease, and go down to death with her Northern and alienated sister. It was against all America, then, that the plot was formed, against Southerner and Northerner alike.

Mr. Lincoln saw the shadow of the specter. He could smell its effluvia. But it vanished into shadows when he reached out his enraged and resolute hands to grasp it. Its lethal whisper was everywhere, but that whisper died into silence when a searcher approached. Its red eyes leered from every alley, from every street, from every corner, and even from the shade of elms on distant farmlands. But at the seeking stare of the angry hunter, the eyes closed and were gone, to reappear elsewhere.

Tolerance for the alien in race and creed was, Mr. Lincoln knew, most active in a homogeneous nation. From the homogeneous soil of England had sprung the Magna Charta, the Parliament, the belief in the rights of all men. It was the heterogeneous nation which was constantly in deadly danger, because of its inner and insulated groups who hated all other groups. The North was heterogeneous. It had long been the belief of romanticists that should diverse men live together, they would understand that all men are one, and differ radically in no way. This belief was shattered, in the Northern cities. The close association with strangers stimulated the natural hatred for their fellows which dwells eternally in all men. And some men, somewhere, were using this natural hatred of man for man to destroy America.

Some men, somewhere, with tongues in their cheeks and evil in their eyes and hatred for America in their hearts, had formed the organization known as the Know-Nothings, whose driving force was alleged hatred for the Roman Catholic Church. Finally, as its circle grew, it included in its hatred every man with a foreign name, a foreign birth, or a foreign religion.

While North and South looked at each other across the borders with fiery eyes of waiting suspicion and fear, the Northern cities knew anti-Catholic and anti-alien riots. The haters of America prepared for her death. They prepared for her death as they have prepared through all history for the death of all that is noble and lovely, grand and heroic, wise and tender and just.

To do this, then, they stimulated false and cruel hatreds, they invented perilous lies, they encouraged the North to remain confused and inert and resentful, they maligned Mr. Lincoln and hinted foul things about him. They used even the holy words of patriotism to accomplish their purpose. They talked of "saving America for Americans," of ousting the "alien in our midst." For the first time the phrase, "the alien element" was heard in the free and windy spaces of the Republic.

They, the real plotters against the Republic, used the very shibboleths of the patriots, the lovers of America. And the hatred increased like a pestilence.

The plotters crept Southward, death in their hearts. In the midst of the flags, the heroics, the trumpets, the mobilizations and the resolutions, the whisper circulated, and the

South, halting dazedly from time to time, heard the voice of destruction.

CHAPTER 52

IT IS a sobering reflection, thought Laurie, gazing steadily through the train windows, how nature repudiates the passions and the hatreds of men. All things live with nature, and are part of her, but man. He is the eternal pariah, the outlander, the alien, a stranger to this planet, surrounded by suspicious creatures hostile to him, fearful of him, hating him, fleeing from him at the very scent of his flesh or the sound of his step. They say it is the "herd instinct" which makes him band together with his fellows, even though he hates them. But it is something deeper than the herd instinct which compels him to build his terrible stony cities and crouch in them, like a besieged murderer, a hunted criminal, shut out from the deep and living heart of the earth. It is his knowledge that nature has rejected him, will not speak to him in the universal language of other beings, has denied that he is numbered among her children.

We are the evil, the dark and ugly thing. We were not created so. I know this. But, we have become so, with our wars, our horrors, our hatreds, our sleepless enmity for all things that live, our treacheries and our greeds, our monstrousness. We are the destroyers, the wicked and unspeakable enormity that the earth has cursed, and God forgotten. We are Cain, and have been expelled from the Garden.

Laurie shivered, and though the private coach was warm, she drew her sable cloak closer about her. The train was travelling with noisy swiftness through the still spring landscape. How beautiful it was! The brilliant greening earth flowered, undulating, to the distance, where amethystine hills, trembling with light, stood against a sky of the softest bluegray. Here and there, in pools of faint shadow, stood trees still empty, but brown, sinewy, bent, already flexible and blurred with the life that was beginning to pulse through their branches. A tawny light spread gently along their limbs. Among the green grasses of the quivering earth lay little blue pools of water, in which stood wild iris. Silent birds curved against the sky. If there were farmhouses about,

Laurie could not see them. An intense and moveless peace lay over the earth, undisturbed, forgetting.

When we are quiet, when we are not there, thought Laurie, the earth remembers peace, and forgets man lives. She stands in her beauty, dreaming and planning, with endless patience, creating and breathing, sighing with joy because she hears no man's voice.

Young Mrs. Rhinelander watched Laurie's still carved profile against the pure light that poured through the coach window. She thought how static and unchanging Laurie's face was, and had often wondered whether Laurie possessed any emotional warmth, any passion, any vehemence. She had known Laurie for four years, for Mrs. Rhinelander's deceased husband had, before his death, been New York's foremost patron of music. A strong friendship had grown up between the two young women, though Mrs. Rhinelander had never analysed why, or why she had been attracted to this cold, hard young girl who had made no overtures to her at all. Though Laurie could not be called secretive, she certainly never enlightened anyone about her thoughts, her desires, or her feelings. Even the ovation given her last week at the Astor Place Opera House, where she had made her American debut after her return from Europe, had not stirred or excited her. She had smiled, it is true, but it was a smile of remote ennui, and she had not bothered to thank the audience or to reply happily to the congratulations of her friends. When some enthusiastic young gentlemen had uproariously insisted upon unhitching the horses of her carriage, and had drawn that carriage themselves through the crowded streets, accompanied by other young gentlemen with torches, Laurie had sat back in the velvet and perfumed depths and looked genuinely bored and annoyed. This was not a pose. And her statuesque withdrawal and aloofness had, if anything, heightened the frenzy of her adorers. When she had unhurriedly alighted at the door of the Astor House, she had not deigned to look back at the great crowd which had roared its final ovation to her, and had not given a single glance to the heaps of flowers awaiting her in her suite. Young Mrs. Rhinelander, and her brother, Dick Thimbleton, had accompanied her to her apartments, and she had hardly been inside the door, and had just begun to remove her long gloves, when she had said to them with that blunt carelessness of hers: "I'm sorry, my loves, but I am tired, and so, if you will excuse me——"

Mrs. Rhinelander had smiled wryly, and had shrugged,

but foolish Dick had said quickly: "Of course, of course! We will go at once, Laurie. Goodnight, my darling."

But Laurie was not Dick's darling. Elissa doubted she would ever be anyone's darling. There was something dreadfully like stone in Laurie. Elissa had never seen her color change, or any thought that was tender or gentle in her face. She was hardly nineteen yet, and her beauty and her incredible voice presaged a magnificent career for her throughout the world. But when these facts were recalled to her, she only stared impassively, and shrugged as she turned away.

She now had in her possession a contract that for munificence had never been known before in America, even in the case of the great Jenny Lind whose voice, it was conceded, had been surpassed by the voice of this young "American" girl. Laurie had sung in *Tannhäuser* in Munich, and had there been given an ovation even more frantic than that accorded her in New York. The great Wagner, himself, had bowed over her hands, and had kissed them in mad gratitude. Laurie had sung in that opera in Dresden also, and the audience, though prepared to be coarsely insulting and derisive, had been silenced by the pure splendor of her Elizabeth. Later, it had become demented. The first presentation in Paris, with another singer, had been a scandalous affair accompanied by cat-calls and howls and whistles. But Laurie's extraordinary beauty, as well as her voice, had conquered the Parisians, also. The Princess Metternich, Wagner's great friend, had invited Laurie to be her guest at her château, yet it was only the pleas of Wagner which had finally induced the girl to accept the invitation. Later, she was also the guest of King Ludwig of Bavaria, and had completely devastated that royal gentleman.

Now Laurie was to interpret *Tannhäuser* to America, and was to sing Elsa in *Lohengrin*. When she signed the incredible contract for her appearances at the Astor, it was with the same ennui with which she had received her ovations. She had risen from the little gilt chair in her suite, and had announced to the assembled and excited gentlemen that "she was excessively tired, and she prayed that they would excuse her." In reality, her friend Elissa Rhinelander knew too well, Laurie never was tired. Her cold vitality was inexhaustible. She experienced no more fatigue than did a mountain or a stony cliff.

Elissa had come to the stupefied conclusion that Laurie cared nothing for her music, her triumphs, her conquests, and that though she sang with the wildest passion and feeling, these were automatic and well-learned rather than from the heart and soul. She was a marvelous actress, but her passions were never involved. Or, were they? thought Elissa, as the train rushed through the darkening landscape.

Laurie was as smooth and impassive as golden metal, and as hard. She shone and glimmered like that metal, and was as impervious. Yet Elissa could not forget the tumultuous passion in her singing voice and on occasion that strange, questing look.

Elissa, straining inquisitively to gaze at her friend's face, saw that look again, fleetingly, as the shoulder of a green mountain flashed by the window. She said: "Are you fatigued, Laurie?"

Laurie turned her head slowly. A sudden shaft of sunlight struck through the window and glittered on her shining head. She smiled. "No. Do I appear so, Elissa?"

"You are so quiet."

The door of the private coach opened, and Dick Thimbleton entered. He had been standing on the platform, smoking what Elissa called "one of his vile cigars." His first glance, as always, was for Laurie, and she regarded him pleasantly. He came to her eagerly, smiling, questioning. But when she only gazed at him with her unchanging graciousness, his thin dark face became thoughtful again. He was a handsome and elegant young man in his thirties, a very eligible and wealthy bachelor, accomplished and distinguished. He had known Laurie for two years, and was completely in love with her. He had pursued her to Europe, proposing, as he said, "regularly every Saturday night." For a young man naturally so well-bred and reticent, he had been singularly persistent, and had at last won from Laurie a very tentative acquiescence. At least she had not any longer forbidden him to propose, though Elissa suspected this was less from any weakening on Laurie's part than from a desire not to expend any more on an active refusal. She was inert, but not yielding.

When Laurie had announced her intention of visiting her family in Grandeville ("where is Grandeville, in the Lord's name?" Dick had asked) Elissa had suggested that she and her brother accompany the girl. Perhaps, Elissa had thought, if Laurie were away from New York and all the excitement and adulation, she would be able to see Dick for all he was: kind, sincere, thoughtful, gentle and superior. In the atmosphere of a raw frontier city, his accomplishments would shine to the full. In the presence of yokels and farm dolts and coarse men, Dick would appear in his complete brilliance and aristocracy. Elissa shrewdly suspected that Laurie, for all her lethargy, was not entirely insensible to money, when it was about her in quantity. She also was coming to believe that Laurie truly liked Dick Thimbleton, and that she was beginning to depend upon his friendship.

It was his private coach, all crimson velvet and plush, with dull-blue velvet curtains and fringe at the windows, and heavy flowered carpets upon the floor, which had been attached to the train that was taking them to Grandeville. He had overcome Laurie's coldly irritable objections. "Why should you travel in discomfort, my love?" he had asked her. "Besides, are you not unreasonable to suggest that my sister and I share such discomfort? Very selfish of you, you must admit."

"I must recall to you, my dear Dick, that your journey to Grandeville was not my suggestion in the first place," Laurie had returned, forbiddingly. And then, quite unexpectedly, she had smiled, and had touched his sleeve gently with her long white hand. She had seemed amused, and he was slightly baffled. Laurie had these moments of inexplicable amusement, and they were not always without cruelty. They gave him twinges of discomfort.

Sometimes he had thought that she looked at him with hidden compassion. And then she had become restless, the apricot color fading from her cheeks, her mouth compressing. She had had hours of silence, and her eyes had been clouded with a curious regret when they had rested upon him.

Elissa and Dick had overcome the thousand and one objections she had raised against their accompanying her on her journey home. "We have no fine hotels in Grandeville," she had informed them, "and my mother's health is not too good." She had written to Janie about her guests, fully expecting to receive an irate letter in reply, tartly advising Laurie that she had no time or room for these strangers. But Laurie, who had half forgotten the resourcefulness of Janie, was surprised to receive an enthusiastic demand from her mother that Elissa and Dick be sheltered in her house. Laurie did not know that Janie had made many frank and entirely indiscreet inquiries about the Thimbleton family, and was all wild excitement at the implications of this visit. Laurie had prepared to show her friends an entirely different letter from her mother, thus discouraging them, and was extremely annoyed.

Laurie's New York and European triumphs were quite familiar to the citizens of Grandeville. Main Street had been decorated with banners, with festoons of colored paper and large posters. Even the war, now one year old, took second place amid this excitement. The Elmwood Theatre, recently built, was being polished and furbished in the firm determination that she should "render" a few selections for the delight of Grandeville. Of all this Laurie was still innocently unaware, and it was just as well.

The vivacious and clever Elissa had not been able to elicit much information from Laurie about her family. She had given only the barest and most indifferent outline. Her mother was a widow, a Scotswoman. She had a brother who was a judge, another brother who had married a wealthy German girl, and was now assistant manager in some shops in which the family was, vaguely, interested. There was still another brother. Here Laurie's face had changed, almost imperceptibly. Bertie. Bertie did nothing but delight his mother. He was a gentleman. Laurie's wide rich mouth had curled just a trifle. She had said nothing more. But Elissa, always shrewd and quick, had perceived that Laurie's attachment to her family was very tenuous, and even disdainful, and that she had no affection for them. Why, then, was she returning to Grandeville for "a rest"? The "fatigue" was only a pose.

Laurie must have been thinking these thoughts also, for Elissa caught her sudden swift glance, curious, hard, diverted. It was not a pleasant glance. It was even a little merciless and malicious. Troubled, and slightly affronted, Elissa tossed her black ringlets, and looked away. She was a young woman in her late twenties, a widow for nearly two years, and very elegant and fashionable in her dark-green satin gown and green satin slippers. A cloak of white ermine was thrown over her shoulders. She was not in the least pretty, for her somewhat sallow long face was very narrow, her mouth mobile and wry, her nose too aquiline, her figure too thin. But all this was relieved by her big black eyes, full of deviltry and naughty laughter and awareness, and by her matchless style. She had that aura of accustomed wealth, culture and fashion which is never acquired, but is inbred.

The large and ornate chairs of the coach, covered with crimson scrolled velvet, were set at angles on the rolling floor. The three were alone. Laurie's and Elissa's maids rode in the public coach just ahead. At one end of the coach was a thick and discreet curtain of thick red plush, beyond which were the beds of the two young women, and their travelling necessities. Near the platform were the sleeping quarters of Dick Thimbleton. Heavy mahogany tables, anchored to the floor, were scattered at the opposite side of the coach, each with its filigreed brass lamp. A crystal chandelier swung from the domed carved roof. There was even a bookcase available, and a polished music-box. Now, as the day darkened, a maid entered and lit the lamps, and the landscape faded from the windows. Elissa could see the faces of her brother and Laurie mirrored dimly in the glass, and the reflection of the lamps was superimposed on the wild scene of mountain and endless meadow and valley.

Elissa, quite suddenly, began to dislike Laurie. She had at intervals these moments of dislike. Then she would have liked to believe that Laurie was stupid, inert, lethargic. But her innate honesty prevented this. What did Laurie want? Apparently she wanted nothing.

Laurie was an enigma. Poor Dick, thought Elissa, with angry and unaccustomed indignation, he ought not to be involved with this strange creature. For in these moments of acuteness, Laurie seemed indeed a stranger, and completely unknowable.

Laurie lay back in her chair, and Elissa, disliking her more and more, and admiring her with equal energy, and loving her, was fascinated by her friend's grace. There was not a single faulty line in the curve of her full young breasts, in the molding of her throat, in the indentation of her waist above the billowing blue taffeta of her skirts. The golden hair, with its hint of ruddiness, was smooth as if carved from metal. There was a large serenity about her, as she slowly turned her head to smile at the ardent if quiet Dick, who leaned forward to talk to her from his own chair. Wagner, the wonderful and terrible Wagner, had looked at Laurie for the first time, and had screamed: "Brünnhilde! Walküre!" It had been excessive, of course, and very extravagant, which was the way with foreigners. Yet, Elissa admitted, she could now see what had provoked Wagner to such ecstasy, and had lighted such a flame in his eyes.

What so absorbed Dick now in Laurie's slow and languid conversation? Laurie had never been noted for swift repartee or originality. Yet Dick leaned towards her, a light on his lean and clever features. Elissa bent forward, also, to hear what so engrossed him.

"You will have a very dull time, I am afraid, in Grandeville," Laurie was saying. "Farmers with round beaver hats, and smelling of the stables, and swarms of strange creatures from outlandish places in Europe, and slaughter-houses and sausage factories and grain elevators and Lake steamers. It's a very stupid town, and a completely gross one. As for my family," and she shrugged her large and exquisite shoulders, "they have never been noted for their sophistication or wide interests. Except, perhaps, Robbie. He is married to a charming girl, the daughter of the Mayor, but even he has that certain harsh outline of the provincial."

Then that queer restlessness came over her again, and she turned away from Dick. "This dreadful war! It was supposed to have been over in six months! What exuberant nonsense! Now when the people realize it is not a lark at all, not all trumpets and banners and fine uniforms, they are restive. Was it really true that many people were killed in the draft riots in New York, Dick?"

The young man's expression became grave. He talked quickly. If the war continued much longer, he would apply for a commission. Laurie's hand absently smoothed a fold of her dress; her head was turned away from him. "The people love fine ideals, and are quite stirred by them," said Dick. "But when they are called upon to sacrifice, to fight, and even to die for those ideals, they begin to lament, to accuse, to deny, to protest. Do they think the love of country should be confined to the maxims in copy-books, and the love of justice and God to the pages of the Bible? Don't they realize that if a thing is not worth fighting for or dying for then it has no reason for existence, even in words?"

Laurie did not answer, and Dick continued with quiet vehemence: "This Republic was not founded by men who considered their safety and their comfort above justice and freedom and manhood. It was founded by those who had a vision, who believed in the rights of man and the fatherhood of God, who hated tyranny and injustice and oppression. Where are their sons now? Where are their voices, in this sullen and resistive Republic?"

He could see only Laurie's profile, and it told him nothing. He put his hand on hers. "Will you miss me, if I go into the Army?" he asked softly.

She moved her hand gently from under his. She smiled. But her voice took away something of the caustic quality of that smile. "Certainly I shall miss you, Dick. But I do hope you will not be too precipitous."

His face darkened. He leaned back in his chair.

He talks to a creature without sensibility, thought Elissa, with angry resentment. What does Laurie care about America? What does she care about anything? She has no heart. Why, then, do I love her? I am a woman, and her beauty does not move me in the least, except, perhaps, to an occasional jealousy. She makes no effort to be charming and agreeable, not even to me. Yet I love her.

Laurie turned to her, and said: "I do hope, Elissa, that you will be comfortable in my mother's house. It is not grand in the least. Somewhat uncomfortable and countrified." She hesitated, then laughed a little, inexplicably. "But I do think you will enjoy Ma!"

As the belching train moved steadily northward, the hills fell away, and low flat land, sometimes empty, sometimes massed with trees, took their place. Moreover, the green became more sparse in the meadows, which had great patches of brown spread through them, and the trees became less lush. They were still hardly in bud, and there was a harsh chill light in the sky, and a look of bleak cold on the earth. Elissa was surprised to see that the streams across which they roared had edges of sharp crystal ice, and that, in the distance, the higher land was patched with old snow. She could feel the cold breath of the North as it filtered through the cracks about the windows, and she ordered the stoves to be replenished. It was a desolate country, she thought fretfully, and she wondered whether her wardrobe would be adequate for it.

CHAPTER 53

IT HAD snowed in the night, not the brief bright April snow of the more southern country, which merely enhanced and refreshed the new lush green of the earth. This was the April snow of the North, accompanied by dark and somber skies, and it had the grim insistence of winter. The trees, which bore only slightly swollen buds, were freckled with hard white fragments, and their scarred trunks were veined with that whiteness. The earth was still brown, though faintly greening in spots. The snow covered these spots, so that only the withered deadness was revealed.

It was only three in the afternoon, but the lamps had had to be lighted. Fires burned with winter amplitude, ruddy and hot on the hearths. About the house the wind groaned and howled, and the skies darkened rapidly. Laurie looked up from her needlework, and glanced indifferently through the glass. She was accustomed to Northern springs, and never heeded them. But poor Elissa was confined to her bed with a bad sniffling cold, and her brother was solicitously with her. Two days in Grandeville had been quite enough for Elissa. The turpentine stupes on her sore chest, her swollen red nose, the desolate scene outside, and the narrow vaulted room in which she lay, had all convinced her that the sooner she left this place the better. Laurie smiled to herself, bent her head a little closer over her needlework.

Janie sat near her, close to the fire. The two women were silent now. They had had a desultory conversation, and it had all concerned Europe and New York and Laurie's triumphs. Janie eyed her daughter. All this grand talk of the Princess Metternich, of King Ludwig, of Queen Victoria, and of the graciousness of President Lincoln! All these casual accounts of ovations at the Astor Place Opera House and Castle Gardens! Janie's lips twisted sourly. She would have liked to believe that the lass was exaggerating, that she was boasting with puerile vanity. But Laurie had spoken of it all with indifference and disinterest, and only on the insistence of her mother. Nevertheless, her smile had been queer, and she had not been as taciturn as Janie had known her to be. She had even volunteered information about herself and her triumphs. Had there been a malevolent and amused satisfaction in those cold blue eyes, and a curious derision in the slow and lovely voice?

Janie's gaze narrowed at Laurie. Laurie sat near the fire, tall, large, too handsome, too chill, too remote, in her dark blue cashmere with the thick cluster of cream-colored ruching at the high neck, her hoops exaggerated in what was doubtless the latest Parisian style. She wore, at the throat, a huge sunburst of diamonds, pearls and rubies, which she had negligently stated, upon Janie's questioning, had been given to her by King Ludwig himself. Upon her wrist was a matching bracelet, almost two inches wide, ablaze with the same gems, and in her ears were the rings which completed the set. Janie wet her lips. King Ludwig, no less! He was very "kind," Laurie had said, nonchalantly, without a smile, and Laurie had been his guest. Janie shook her head as if in sullen denial. It was not possible. Laurie Cauder, daughter of Janie Driscoll and Robin Cauder, obscure farming provincial and wild Highland blood. Laurie had shown her mother other jewels, also, a golden medal personally bestowed upon her by Queen Victoria, a necklace of pearls from Princess Metternich, rings and unbelievable bangles and brooches and tiaras from the "crowned heads of Europe." Janie wet her lips. She must not forget a detail of all this tomorrow, when she would give the astounding news to the Grandeville *Courier*. Had not Janie, herself, seen the contracts presented to Laurie in New York, she would have believed none of it. She had screwed up her eyes at the letters from illustrious personages, though she had not been able to read a word of them, written as they were in French, German or Russian. But she had well understood the coats of arms which had emblazoned them, and the casual signatures. She had been astounded, shaken, thunderstruck, for she had only half-believed the accounts in the New York newspapers, convinced that in "this country" the blatant press was always exaggerating. She had wanted to believe it exaggeration. But the newspaper clippings from London papers had taken her aback.

Laurie had not been in the least reticent, when urged to tell her stories. Why? She had always been enigmatic and secretive, Janie remembered, frowning. What had opened that beautiful grim mouth? Then Janie sat upright. She stared at her daughter. Why, she thought, the lass hates me! She flings these things in my face, not to make me proud, but to cow and confound me!

She said, in a stately voice: "But, after all, you are glad to be home, are you not, lass?"

Laurie looked up calmly from her work. She said: "Yes. Why else am I here?"

"You've not forgotten us, then, with all your wonderful friends, and the grand houses, and the dukes and nobles and kings?"

Laurie looked at her steadfastly. Again she smiled her cold and peculiar smile. "No. I've not forgotten, Ma."

Janie summoned an expression of judicious sternness to her face. "They may bow and scrape before you, Laurie, and clap and give you flowers and these gew-gaws, but I'm still your mother, and to me you're just my little lass that I used to cuff about when you were in pinafores. I don't see you as the marvelous Miss Cauder, but as my own child whom I had to correct out of her witless ways."

Laurie did not speak. But she regarded her mother steadily. And there was something in her regard that startled Janie, made her uneasy. She said: "Don't look at me like that, lass! It's as if you hated me."

Laurie took up her needlework again. She said: "I never hate anyone. I do not find anyone of sufficient importance to hate him."

Janie was shocked again. She felt herself shrink. She said to herself persistently, out of her dwindling conceit: But the lass does hate me. She may put on her la-dee-da ways and airs and graces, but she can't get over it that I'm her Ma and she's only my daughter, and that the hen came before the egg.

She looked up to see that Laurie was gazing at her with strange still derision and contempt. And Janie was frightened. If Laurie hated her, it was with the hatred of a goddess for a worm, and with royal disdain. Laurie in her turn studied her mother. Janie was now more than forty-five, but a shrivelled if lively age. The artfully colored red hair was still in wiry and carroty ringlets about her wrinkling yellow neck and sallow rouged cheeks. She was thinner and slighter than ever, but very stylish, so that even Elissa had been agreeably impressed. Even Janie's coarse and rowdy wit had delighted Elissa, as Laurie had half suspected it might, and Dick had been highly amused by her, and interested.

Janie, trying to force herself to meet Laurie's look unflinchingly, again felt herself dwindling. She had no power over Laurie at all, and it came to her, with furious conviction, that she had never had any power. This tall golden woman was not her daughter, had never been her daughter. She regarded Janie as of no importance at all, and Janie's enraged hatred and humiliation almost strangled her.

All this was very hard for Janie to endure, and she seethed inwardly. She was overcome with self-pity. Was this her reward for her motherly care of this creature, her sacrifices, her "sleepless nights," her "prayers," her "ambitions"? Did this odious young woman think to detach herself from the mother who had given her birth? If Laurie was famous, it was because of the "good blood" that flowed in Janie's veins, and through Janie, into her own. Janie began to think of herself as the true source of Laurie's fame and glorious voice, and to feel much abused and unworthily humiliated.

But Laurie, narrowing her own long blue eyes, only looked at her mother, guessing her thoughts. Her lip curled in a cruel smile. She looked away.

In spite of her discomfiture and hatred and rage, there was a burning question in Janie's mind. Was Laurie to marry this grand Richard Thimbleton, who was so rich and aristocratic, and on easy acquaintance with all the powerful of America and Europe?

Janie smirked to herself, slyly, with bursting pride and excitement. She had meant to precipitate an understanding between what she believed an importunate and obscure Laurie and a hesitant great gentleman. Yet here was Laurie, indifferent, repelling, condescending, and it was the great gentleman who was humbly ardent and entreating.

"You are nearly nineteen, lass," she said, "and time it is you should be married. Have you given thought to it?"

Laurie said, jocosely: "Why should I marry?"

Janie gaped. "And why not, pray?"

"Why does a woman marry?" asked Laurie, with cool and smiling disinterest. "To provide shelter, clothing and food for herself: that is one reason. To escape onerous family surroundings. To have her own home. To keep herself from starving, or to free herself from the odious charity chimney-corner in some brother's house. To acquire a position in society. For wealth. To be with the man she loves." She gazed at her mother with sparkling reflection. "None of these reasons urge me into marriage."

All this to Janie was outrageous heresy and folly. Yet she had no immediate reply. What Laurie had said was true. She need not marry. At last Janie said with asperity: "You consider it proper, miss, to traipse about the world unmarried, an unprotected female, subject to ambiguous proposals, defenseless and unguarded?"

Laurie felt the strong life and vitality in her large and beautiful body, and burst into unrestrained mirth. "Why, Ma, I have the muscles and the strength of a man, and am quite capable of dealing with any gentleman who might harbor improper designs! As for traipsing about the world unmarried, I find it a very agreeable position, and I am subject to no man's whims and pettishnesses and jealousies. I am free." And now her blue eyes darkened and flashed, hardening into bright stones.

Janie stared at her with the deepest hatred and envy. Ah, what a life was this, filled with beauty, conquest, wealth and freedom! Why was it not she instead of this insensitive hulk of a girl who had been chosen for this life!

"Why, then, did this popinjay accompany you into your own home, as your guest, following you about like a mewling calf, and cozening you with his eyes?" she cried, burning with her envy.

"He came because he wished. I gave him no encouragement," said Laurie, tranquilly. She put aside her work. She lay back in her chair, her fine long ankles extended beyond the rim of her hoops, her arms folded behind her radiant head. She began to hum softly to herself, and looked at the fire with abstraction. Lazy, loutish creature! thought Janie. Were it not for the neat French maid, now ensconced with the family servants up on the third and fourth floors, Laurie's hair would be rough and untidy, her clothing mussed and wrinkled, her sandals scuffed, her stockings awry, as they had always been in the days of her childhood in this house. She accepted life, Janie observed bitterly and virulently to herself, like a great indolent cat, casually licking up the cream, indifferent to the desires or the presence of others. Only when she was crossed or annoyed did any passion flare up in her smooth-planed face. When she had been greeted by the vociferous committee at the depot, and had seen the festoons and the decorations in her honor on Main Street, the blackest look had contorted her features as if she had felt disgust and affront. There were those who flatteringly ascribed this to natural modesty, but Janie knew that it was unjust vanity, that Laurie ought to give some decent heed to and express some gratitude for the demonstrations.

And all this, Janie saw with her penetrating intuition, came from Laurie's huge cold hatred for the world and all in it.

Suddenly Janie was afraid of this girl to whom she had given birth.

Their eyes met. An odd flicker leapt up, vanished, in the unreadable blue between Laurie's lashes.

But she said in an ordinary tone: "What has happened to Angus? Has that lump of German lard become intolerable to him? He looks like death itself."

Janie, under usual circumstances, would now have embarked on malicious gossip about her son, but that look in Laurie's eyes, her negligent sprawled position which was like the repose of a big tawny cat, silenced her. Laurie was dangerous. Janie knew this now. So she said, affecting the annoyance of a loving mother: "Such extravagant language, Laurie! Angus is tired, and extremely busy. As for Gretchen, it is now hoped that she is expecting. It has been long enough, Heaven knows."

Laurie was silent. She only gazed at her mother meditatively for a long moment or two. Janie exclaimed irritably: "You and Angus were always such friends! Now you speak of him with contempt!"

"He deserves nothing but contempt," replied Laurie quietly. She turned her head and regarded the fire. The rosy light danced on her features as though they had been carved from golden stone.

"Why?" demanded Janie angrily. "He is furthering himself in the world. He is doing excellently! He is respected everywhere. He is making a fortune."

The subtlest quiver of a smile touched Laurie's lips. "How are his headaches these days?"

Janie frowned. "He wears spectacles when he reads. It was his eyes, doubtless. He was always so studious. He must have strained them." She hesitated. "He had quite a severe collapse three months ago."

She paused, for Laurie had swung her head back quickly to her mother. All through her long and languid body there was the queerest tightening. "A collapse? What was wrong?"

"It was the headaches. He was ill in bed for two months, and then for several weeks could only crawl about. Mr. Schnitzel, who is so excessively kind, and as devoted to Angus as a father, brought a special and famous physician from Chicago to attend him. There was nothing wrong. The doctor was puzzled. It was nerves, and Angus' eyes, he finally decided."

"Nerves," repeated Laurie. And then she laughed, an ugly sound. She sat up, smoothed her hair. She said: "Robbie is doing well, also, I perceive."

"With old Cummings' help, of course," replied Janie ill-naturedly. "And that chit of an Alice is expecting, also, though with that little miserable body of hers she will doubtless have an extremely bad time. It is only old Cummings' influence which makes the city fawn so upon Robbie, I am afraid."

"I disagree, Ma. Robbie has a most brilliant mind. He did not need Mr. Cummings. It might have taken him a little longer, perhaps, but he would have reached his goal eventually. And what was this you told me yesterday, that Robbie might run for Congressman this year?"

"Oh, it is a lot of talk! Nothing will come of it, I assure you. Robbie hasn't the presence for a politician. There is no real chance for him."

You hope, thought Laurie, with malice. She smiled. "I am certain he will succeed. Robbie never fails. He has my best wishes, and any help I can give him."

Janie hated her with fresh energy. She hated her for her remarks about Robbie; she hated the negligent rich sound of her voice, which filled the dark warm room with the very sonorous echoes of music. She hated her for the hatred she felt in Laurie, and the power, and the latent danger, the implacable cruelty.

"There is something that baffles me," said Laurie, amusedly. "What keeps Bertie alive, with all his excesses. He looks like a corpse."

Janie's heart began to pulse with the profoundest pain and grief and bitterness. She looked at her daughter with lethal intensity. How dared this creature speak of death and Bertie in the same breath, and with such malignance and malicious intent? What had Bertie ever done to her? Yet she could stare at her mother with such mercilessly smiling eyes, with such knowing malevolence, as if she guessed at the anguish in Janie's soul, and enjoyed it.

Janie spoke in a trembling voice, and her hands clenched spasmodically. "You never sympathized with poor Bertie. You never understood what he suffers. It will not give you pleasure, I know, to have me tell you that he has not—not—touched a drop for six months, and that he is becoming stronger every day."

"On the contrary," said Laurie smoothly, "I am glad, for your sake, Ma, that he is behaving himself."

She yawned, smoothed her rumpled frock, shifted her hoops. Janie could only stare at her, still trembling all through her slight and withered body, as if she had been struck a vicious and intentional blow.

Laurie was speaking again, in that neutral tone of hers. "And how are the shops getting along?"

It took Janie a few moments to gather her forces to answer. But here was a subject very vital to her. She said in a hard and exulting voice: "Very badly. I receive my money regularly, of course. Stuart would not dare withhold it, even if it came from his purse, or from the purse of that dreadful Jew. He is horribly in debt, Stuart. The war has done him no good at all. His supply of cotton goods has been cut off, naturally. It would not surprise me if he failed very shortly."

In her triumph and elation, she did not see that Laurie had sat up in her chair, that she had paled. She only heard Laurie say: "Why does all this please you? You have money invested in the shops."

Janie grinned, and tossed her red ringlets. "Why does it please me, ma'am? Because when Stuart is forced into bankruptcy, which will not be so long now, Angus will buy him out, and buy out that Jew, also. He will force them out. Though you may have such a high and mighty disdain for your family, Laurie, we are not without friends, who would delight to assist Angus. The day I have long awaited is almost at hand. That blackguard's debts and extravagances, and the war, have finally ruined him. It is only a matter of a few months now."

With one slow and vital movement, Laurie stood up and went to the windows with that long free stride which was so unladylike. She pushed aside the draperies. She looked out at the dark April storm. She heard Janie's exultant voice behind her, going on and on in a mounting frenzy of gloating. She heard the poisonous hatred in that voice, the exultation. Her hand caught a fold of the draperies and twisted it savagely.

So Stuart was ruined. She had not seen Stuart since her return the day before yesterday. All plans had had to be cancelled because of Elissa's illness. Laurie's nostrils widened, and her mouth was pale and evil in its compression. And then she smiled, and the smile, reflected in the polished black of the window, was not a pleasant thing to see.

"I've waited a long time," said Janie, in the high and virulent voice of final exaltation. "I've waited a long time to repay him for his insults and his wantonness and his abandonment of a poor widow and her children. I've waited to avenge myself for his slights to Angus, and to my family." She nodded her head in a kind of malediction.

Laurie broke in: "Where is Marvina? And how is little Mary Rose?"

Janie halted, in the very midst of her pæans. She snorted with contempt. "Marvina, that dolt? She has gone to the mountains, as usual with that dreadful and measly brat. I shouldn't be surprised if it was the end of the child this time. Coughing her lungs out, and Stuart bumbling about her like a frantic bee. And good riddance, too. She's cost him a pretty penny, out of the coffers of the shops, no doubt."

"And Stuart is alone in that house?" asked Laurie, indifferently. The fold of cloth in her hand was crushed and stained with dampness.

Janie burst out laughing, shrill and venomous laughter. "His damned precious house! Well, he'll not have it long. I've a fancy for it, myself, and Mr. Allstairs is not unagreeable. That house, filled with treasures too good for him, and too expensive! I'd like to see his face when it's taken from him, in bankruptcy! It will be a joyful day for me, miss!"

Her eyes narrowed suddenly and cunningly. "He hasn't asked you to repay him for what he laid out for you, has he? Not that it would surprise me in the least."

"No," said Laurie, "he hasn't asked me." Nothing could

have been more bored than her voice. She turned from the window and came back to the fire.

"What do they think of the war, here in Grandeville? They are very excited about it in New York, and there may be trouble. But New York is very excitable anyway."

Janie shrugged. She was still vibrating with her triumph, and was annoyed at this change of subject. She had wanted to continue her song of exultation. "The war? It is making the farmers rich, of course, and Mr. Schnitzel and his friends are doing unbelievably well. Army contracts for their beef and sausage. Mr. Lincoln's call for volunteers went almost abegging in Grandeville. Mr. Schnitzel and the other gentlemen in trade and the manufactories warned their men that if they responded to the call they need not look for employment again after the war. Now the draft has come, and we are determined to resist it. Many of the upper class gentlemen are preparing to buy alternates, which is only sensible."

"What a fine patriotic spirit!" remarked Laurie, with smiling and shrugging disdain. "I doubt the South is in such a happy quandary."

She flung up her arms slowly and deliberately, and yawned. "It is almost time for dinner, is it not? I think I will retire to my room and prepare for it. Elissa may come down, herself, I hope. She is much better."

Janie had another hopeful thought. "Has the war affected your own income in America, Laurie?"

Laurie shook her head. "Not at all. New York is teeming with money and with merrymakers who are profiting from the war. The theatres are packed constantly. You never saw such gaiety, Ma. And such fashion, and such wealth, and such display. Moreover, I expect to leave for Europe again, after this contract. The war means nothing to me at all."

She climbed to her old room. Her little polished rosewood desk blinked in the firelight. She sat down slowly, and then was still. Her hand lay on the desk, large, white, exquisitely formed, glittering with jewels in the light of the lamps. Finally she reached out and took up her pen, dipped it in ink, and wrote on her own engraved stationery:

"I must see you tomorrow. It is imperative that I see you. I shall call at your house at four o'clock, on the hour. Please do not think this request extraordinary. Do not write me it is impossible. I shall be there." She signed it: "Laurie."

She went to the bell-rope and pulled it. A little maid answered it almost immediately. Laurie put the note in an envelope, held a stick of wax to a candle, dropped the melted red fluid upon the paper, sealed it. She turned to the maid, who was gazing at her with profound awe and admiration. Laurie smiled, and the smile was dazzling. She took up her knitted bead purse, and pressed a golden coin into the maid's hand.

"Take this letter immediately to Mr. Stuart Coleman, Bertha, and let no one see you come or go. I'm sure you can manage it."

She waited all that evening, tense under her smiles, her slow easy laughter, her teasing of Dick, her pleasant conversation with Elissa. She watched the clock. But no one came to her with a message. At ten, she retired to her bedroom, and smiled to herself.

CHAPTER 54

WITH that unpredictable and always exciting inconstancy of the Northland, the weather changed during the night. Laurie awoke to see that the snow had dwindled to sparkling light heaps of innocent whiteness, like fleece, scattered over the brilliant green of newly revealed grass. The sky, pure and polished cobalt, shook with blazing cold light. The spruces and other evergreens which crowded about the Cauder house showed tips and fringes of green, and were darkly bright with life. The brown trees stretched their sinewy arms upwards. A freshness blew across an earth full of pungency and exhilaration. The shadows on the street were sharp and purple, and windows sparkled in a riot of brilliant sun and patches of glittering snow.

"I must admit," said Elissa Rhinelander, as she sat, bundled in furs, in the Cauder carriage, "that this climate would never be boring. Yesterday, one would have thought that this was the North Pole; I almost expected to see Eskimos as I looked through my window! And today, everything is teeming and too lovely."

Laurie looked calmly at the vivacious streets through which they rolled. "You ought to be here during the winter," she remarked. "You would never believe it could ever be summer here."

There was color under her fair skin with its golden tinge. She had more animation than Elissa had ever detected in her before. She appeared in a state of suppressed restlessness.

When Dick Thimbleton, who had accompanied the ladies, made some humorous remark, Laurie's laugh rang out, catching itself as if with some secret excitement. She had never before appeared very young to him, in spite of her youth. Now she was a young girl, alive and glowing, and inclined to be kind and attentive. That afternoon, he thought, he would speak to her again, for there was a yielding air about her, and a softness.

But when he looked for her, in the evening, after leaving his sister, he found she had vanished. Mrs. Cauder also was out, in her carriage, and the disconsolate but philosophical Dick came to the conclusion that Laurie must have accompanied her mother.

But Laurie, wrapped now in a hooded black cape, was hurrying rapidly through streets emptied of daytime throngs, her head bent a little, the skirts of her cape and frock billowing behind her in the wake of her long swift stride. The hood almost hid her face; across her forehead was one shining lock of hair.

She waited impatiently on Niagara Street for the passing of the horse-car and its retinue of drays, wagons and busy carriages. Her foot tapped the curb. When an opening in the traffic appeared, she plunged across the street, turned towards the river. Now the freshening wind was sharp and strong against her face and throat, and her hooped skirts swirled about her. She felt the keen breath of the Lakes and the river, and heard the languid hissing of the disturbed waters of the Canal. The river, beyond, had lost its daytime brightness, and was gray and rough. The Canadian shore, a purplish blur, was only a smudge against a heliotrope sky. Yet here was a desolate vast quiet, a wide and limitless horizon of water and sky and earth. Laurie paused for several moments to breathe deeply of the pure and strenuous air. She stood on the bleached stones near the river, a tall and black and blowing figure against all this living wasteland. The hood fell back from her head, showing its vivid and ruffled gold, and her face, turned to the heavens, had that free wildness, that simple and innocent barbarism and untamed savagery which had made the great Wagner exclaim: "Die Walküre!" She was as still as one of the fir trees near by, yet as potent with promise.

She did not hear or see the approach of a short and enormously fat and aging man, also in black, who moved slowly and heavily towards her along the line of the river. But he soon detected her, and stopped short, fascinated by her appearance, by the way her cloak rose and bellied about her like spreading wings, by the brightness of her head and the unearthly look on her lifted profile. It seemed to him, fearfully, that she was a creature not of this world, but something fallen from a more heroic and untamed planet, some creature not all goodness and gentleness, but possessed of a fierce loneliness, a nameless implacability and terrible beauty. His heart, always inclined to superstition, began to beat with a strange fear, and he almost crossed himself. Then he recognized her, though it had been several years since last he had seen her. Not understanding the relief he felt, he hurried towards her, smiling, his hand extended. "It is Laurie!" he cried, his voice almost lost in the roaring voice of wind and water.

She turned her head to him. Her look was gracious, and pleased. "Father Houlihan," she said, and gave him her large white hand, bare and unjewelled today.

She looked down at him, still smiling. Poor man, he had aged, she commented to herself. The strident blue eyes were very sad, and quite dimmed now, and his big ruddy face was lined as if with chronic sorrow. Under the brim of his round black hat his small fringe of hair was white and sparse. His massive shoulders drooped, as if too heavy a burden lay on them. But his smile, full and childlike, still possessed that simplicity and love and kindness which she remembered, and which nothing could destroy.

"Sure, and I did not know you, Laurie, for a minute," he said, looking up at her with almost boyish admiration and diffidence. "It's a fine woman you've grown, and it's proud of you I am. Stuart told me that you had come home, but that he had not seen you yet. I've just come from him."

The world's too much for him, thought Laurie, but he doesn't know it yet, poor man. She had never been particularly fond of the priest, and had not often encountered him. There had always been a steadfast look in his eyes which had disturbed her, even in her childhood. He was gazing at her now with that same honest and open expression, and her golden brows drew together momentarily.

"And how is Stuart?" she asked, in her deliberate voice that never revealed anything. "I am on my way to see him now."

Father Houlihan was startled. He was too simple not to betray his sudden perturbation. He had spent the last hour with Stuart, and Stuart had appeared restless and uneasy, and had said nothing of an expected visit from Laurie. In fact he had appeared anxious for his friend to be gone, and though the priest had been puzzled at this, and a little hurt, he had left as soon as possible. Stuart was weary and harassed, and probably wished to rest, he had thought in his gentle charity. Now he was waiting there alone, in his empty house, even the servants gone, and this young woman, unchaperoned and unaccompanied, was on her way to him.

He looked up at Laurie earnestly. And she was looking down at him with a cold smile that repudiated him. There was a sudden slight darkening of the evening sky, and the roar of wind and water was louder, more threatening, more solitary than ever in its savagery.

He said: "Shall I go back with you, Laurie? It is a little rough along the river, and I've something to say to Stuart which I had forgotten."

"No, thank you, Father," she answered quietly. She did urged him to leave her. But he stood his ground. He not move, but there was a slow impatience about her, which swallowed drily.

"It's wonderful stories I've heard of you, I'm thinking," he said. "Wonderful! I cannot believe this is the little Laurie I knew. And is it true that you are to sing for us in the Music Hall on Saturday? I shall be there, happy and proud." He smiled at her, wistfully, pleading, hoping to soften her, to make her a warm and human woman again.

She inclined her head. Her lips pursed a little, humorously, and with unkindness. "I hope I shall not disappoint you, Father," she said, and his quick and sensitive ear detected irony in her voice. All at once he was afraid, not for her, but for Stuart. Yet, it was ridiculous.

"Good evening, Father," she was saying, coolly. "I hope I shall see you again before I return to New York."

He made an impotent gesture, as if to detain her. She was regarding him impatiently, and he saw, with a sinking of his heart, how inflexible and hard were her long blue eyes, and how unnaturally cynical and remote.

"You are certain you do not wish me to go back with you, at least a little way?" he urged, freely. "Rough men, and such, along the river; one never knows," he added, in a dwindling voice at the sudden amused brilliance in her eyes.

"I'm quite capable of taking care of myself, Father. But thank you, anyway."

She inclined her head, and was going from him with that free swift stride of hers. He stood there, alone and fearful, watching her until a copse of fir trees shut her from his sight along a bend in the river. Now he was all alone, buffeted by the wind, surrounded by the endless desolation of river and faint purple sky and bleak roaring fir trees. Had she really been there at all? She had left no sensitive impress on the air, no aura of her presence. And then the priest crossed himself, involuntarily, and he felt a sharp pang of sorrow in his heart.

Though he did not know it, Laurie had stopped behind the copse of fir trees, and had waited grimly for him to follow her. With all the power of her inexorable will, she willed him gone. She sent out that will like rods of iron, pushing him on his way. After several long moments had elapsed, she emerged from the trees, and strained her eyes after him. He had disappeared. She had the river and the shore and the sky to herself. She continued down the river, smiling a little.

Finally she reached Stuart's house, the "Irishman's Folly." It stood there glimmering in the evening light like a Grecian temple, floating in the clear and trembling air, all its columns gleaming, its windows blue with the reflection from the sky. Was it her imagination that it appeared abandoned, untenanted, and completely deserted, and standing alone in an unearthly circle of despair? She set her hand resolutely on the gate, opened it, closed it behind her, her lips tightened. She ran lightly up the wide shallow steps, lifted the knocker on the door. The echoes eddied about her, desolately.

It was Stuart who opened the door. He reached out his hand and drew her in upon the black-and-white polished floor of the hall. A faint but sharp light poured into that hall from the pellucid sky outside, and she saw him before her, haggard and ravaged, but smiling, and still possessing that large and violent splendor which had always been his. There were very wide patches of thick gray at his temples, and a broad streak of it spreading backwards from his forehead into the still heavy waves of his hair. His face was much too ruddy, too deeply lined with dissipation and weariness, and his full and sensual mouth was more gloomy than she had remembered it in spite of its smile. But, as she looked at him (and she was so tall that her eyes were almost on a level with his) her heart thundered, and a long and thrilling wave, sensuous and disturbing, ran over her body. She felt weak, drifting, and she was filled with a terrible and shaking joy.

They looked at each other silently, their hands held together as if welded by fierce electric impulses, and they only smiled. Then Stuart, after what seemed to be a long time, removed her cloak, and laid it over a gilt chair in the hall.

He took her hand again, and led her into the silent and deserted parlor. She looked about her, almost dazedly. There were the lovely chairs and draperies, the dim pale rugs she had remembered, the profusion of flowers, the rosy trembling fire on its marble hearth. The air was full of the scent of hothouse roses and ferns and the warmer odor of burning coal. The chaste gilt frames of the pictures on the white walls were picked out in streaks of golden light. There was not a sound in the great house, not a murmur through its exquisite corridors and wide delicate rooms. They were entirely alone.

Here again they stopped and looked at each other. Laurie's black bodice and wide hoops set off her fair and golden beauty. Stuart gazed at her in silence, the corners of his lips hard yet tremulous.

She moved away from him, smiling her enigmatic smile. "Shall we sit down?" she asked, and these were the first words she had spoken to him. She seated herself, unhurried, near the fire, and after a moment he joined her in another chair. He bent towards her, his hands, clenched together, between his knees, his head thrust forwards, his black eyes fixed almost fiercely on her face. She played gently with her lace kerchief and regarded him serenely, though her breast was imperceptibly disturbed.

"Laurie," he said, softly.

She fluttered her kerchief languidly before her face, thus giving him only fleeting glimpses of her eyes and smiling mouth. "How are you, Stuart?" she asked tranquilly.

His lips tightened. She saw that there was a spasmodic quivering about his nostrils. He relaxed a little. He shrugged, without answering her question. Now his eyes left hers, flashed restlessly over the room. Her brows drew together slightly.

They were silent again. The dropping of the coals on the hearth, the soft movement of Laurie's kerchief, were the only sounds in the room. She felt again that curious sense of desertion about the house, the emptiness. Even the exquisite funiture appeared to have retreated, so that the room seemed larger than she remembered it, and chillier. Stuart must have felt this odd air also, for Laurie sensed that he had withdrawn from her, and was sinking again into the ominous atmosphere of his house. She moved slightly, and catching this movement, his eyes returned to her, became warm, fixed, waiting.

"You haven't congratulated me on my 'triumphs,' Stuart," she said, ironically, resolutely shutting out from her consciousness the chill bleak light that filtered through the windows. "After all, it is you who are really responsible for them, such as they are."

He said: "I wanted to hear you, at the Opera House, when you made your debut, but Mary Rose was ill." When he spoke his daughter's name, his face darkened with pain. "I had to take her and her mother to the mountains. They will remain there for the summer." He paused, and said, with forced difficulty: "I am indeed proud of you, Laurie. You ought to know that."

But she saw that the magic and enthralled moment had passed, that he was again caught in his wretchedness and preoccupation, and had almost forgotten her. She frowned impatiently; her heart still beat strongly, but with diminishing wildness. "I am sorry about Mary Rose," she said politely, trying to control her impatience. "But surely she is a little better? You wrote me in Europe that she had improved."

He turned to her, trying to smile. "She was better. But she had a bad attack this winter, and the doctors ordered her to the mountains. The last letter I received from her was quite cheerful, the darling! Perhaps I am too worried."

He looked at her listlessly. "You are a very beautiful woman now, Laurie. I am proud of you. But you mustn't forget us here at home."

She was angered. What had gone wrong? She regarded him fixedly, feeling the heat and quivering of her own body, which was aching again. And he looked back at her, his eyes dulled with sadness and impotent pain. It was this house, this house which now was hideous to her. He was caught in it; he could not see her within its walls.

"Is the war bothering you much, Stuart?" she asked, mechanically.

It was entirely wrong, she saw, to have said this, for he stood up, with that helpless violence of movement which betrayed his inner fear and torment. "Terribly," he said abruptly. "If it goes on much longer, I'll be ruined."

She stood up, also. She must get him out of this house, and the memories in it. Her resolution hardened. "It is stuffy here," she said. "Let us go out into the air, if you please, Stuart." She heard dim and booming echoes through the corridors. The room was darkening. She wanted to run from it.

He looked at her, hardly seeing her. Then he said: "Yes, if you wish, Laurie." They went out into the hall together, and in silence he put her cloak again over her shoulders. He brought out his greatcoat and his tall beaver hat, and opened the door. They stepped out into the evening, side by side, without speaking.

Again, there had been a change in the weather. The wind had fallen. The sky was a dim clear ultramarine in which stood the brightening crescent of a new moon, revealing itself through the tall bare branches of a poplar tree, a frail light through iron filigree which was as intricate as lace. The green lawns were too green, almost as artificial as stage grass, about the white and soaring house. Birds twittered and called to one another from tree to tree in a silence completely profound, and as soft as water, and as solemn as the quiet within a cathedral. The earth had a deep and living smell, almost tangible. Below the lawns which ran almost to the shore, the river was dark and restless, its voice muted, and far beyond, nothing could be discerned of Canada but a few twinkling lights. The scene was awesome in its loneliness, and had a religious stillness, sad and melancholy.

As Laurie and Stuart walked slowly toward the river, the crescent moon brightened, seemed to move in that aquamarine heaven, and a purplish shadow ran over the earth. Laurie's head was uncovered; the very slight wind lifted a wave of hair gently, flattened it against her cheek, blew it across her brooding eyes. Her mouth was set. A thousand thoughts ran through her impatient mind, a thousand openings for what she wanted to say. But she discarded them all. She glanced at Stuart sideways. He walked beside her, abstracted and grim, withdrawn from her.

Laurie had a quick and flexible intellect, which few ever suspected. She had come here, across oceans, across endless spaces of land, for this moment. She had come across all her life. And here she stood in silence beside Stuart, who was staring unseeingly at the dark and running water of the river, unaware of her. What had happened?

She was conscious of a humiliating helplessness. She turned swiftly to Stuart. He stood beside her on the broad whitish stones of the shore, and was staring at the opposite shore. Suddenly she could wait no longer. It was her very despair that made her turn to him impetuously, and lay her hand on his arm. To her joy, she felt his muscles involuntarily tighten under her fingers, and she saw the slow turning of his head towards her, the bemusement of his eyes.

"Stuart," she said, and her strong full voice faltered dismayingly, "I've never thanked you for your help——"

Now those tired eyes brightened, warmed, affectionately.

"I never wanted your thanks, Laurie. I was only too glad to help. I can't tell you how proud I am of you. It does seem impossible that my little Laurie has become so——"

Her hand clenched on his arm. Now she felt his quickening, and an inexplicable withdrawing from her. She burst out on a cry: "Stuart! Nothing of all that matters to me! I never wanted it, never cared! I did it only because you wished it, because I knew it would please you, because you desired it! Surely, you must know that!"

He was suddenly as still as stone. Everything disappeared from her sight but his face, heavy and dark with blood, and his fiercely penetrating eyes. She felt the flesh under her hand pulse and throb. She came closer to him. He could see the blue and quivering flame of her eyes, the shaking of her wide red mouth.

All the long control and inertia of her life was swept into brittle fire like straw that had been ignited. She cried: "Don't you understand, Stuart? I've loved you all my life! I've done everything you wished, for I thought it was the way to you! I've loved you since I first saw you, on the docks of New York. All my life, Stuart! Nothing means anything to me but you."

Then, without warning, she began to weep. The tears dashed down her cheeks. She still held his stiff arm. She moved so close to him that their bodies touched.

He moved his head as if strangling. He said: "Laurie. You don't know what you are saying. I am nearly twenty-two years older than you, old enough to be your father. You are only a young girl. You think you love me, but it's only gratitude. Laurie," he added, and now his voice was stifled, "don't talk to me like that. You don't know me, Laurie. You don't know to what you are exposing yourself, out of your ignorance and immature romanticism. Don't tempt me, Laurie," he cried, with sudden violent roughness, pushing her from him with his elbow. His black eyes were leaping. "You don't know what you are doing."

But she followed his one retreating step. He lifted his arm again, as if to protect, rather than repudiate her. She pressed her body to his, and put her arms under his coat, beneath his arms. Her lips were close to his, parted and trembling.

"Stuart," she whispered, with fervid earnestness. "I love you. I've always loved you. Why do you think I've returned here? There was nothing to come to, but you. My studies in New York, my singing in Europe, were only a winding path that led back to you." She looked at his congested and still obdurate face. "Oh, Stuart! Kiss me."

He took her hands away from him. She felt their heat and dampness. All his movements were gentle. But he was trembling strongly. He loomed above her in the darkening light, and it seemed to her that her heart melted, flowed out to him on an irresistible wave of desire. Her ears hummed and roared with discordant sounds. She heard him say: "Don't, Laurie. Don't, for God's sake. Laurie, you must listen to me. I have nothing to give you, or offer you. I'm a ruined man, Laurie. I can't even marry you."

She cried out, loudly: "Do you think I am a child? Who spoke of marriage? I'm a woman, Stuart, and I love you. I came back to you, Stuart. I won't leave you again. I'll be with you always."

His eyes welled, dilated, then narrowed on her. A kind of wonder, unbelieving, lustful and overwhelmingly hot, flashed into them. He was silent, looking at her as if for the first time. This was no longer the young Laurie he had known, and he believed her now. Her uplifted face floated before his, ardent, and desirous, wild and lighted, and her eyes were glowing and soft as the morning sky. She had placed her hands on his shoulders; it seemed to him that their touch burned through the cloth that covered them.

Yet some decency in him still made him pause. What did she know of anything, this nineteen-year-old girl? How could she know what she was doing to him, he a man past forty, dirtied by the years and by noxious experiences and lusts? It was fantastic, frightful. He could take her, easily, and with ecstasy and ferocity and mad pleasure to himself. But, he thought to himself, dazedly, he loved her. Yes, he had always loved her. For the first time in his life he loved a woman, and it was too late.

All his life had been without control. He had done everything he wished, with violence and lustfulness and brutality; he had grasped at everything he had desired, and had taken it. If sometimes this had resulted in disaster, it had always satisfied him. He had never known mercy, been halted by decent hesitancy, when he had desired a thing, whether it had been a woman or money or any luxury.

But this was Laurie, little Laurie, and he loved her. She was not only a woman, but something tender and deeply beloved and defenseless. He saw now that he had always loved her, from the very beginning, from her very childhood. She was infinitely dear to him, and precious and too lovely. He was overcome with his longing and his despair, even though his blood rushed and crashed in his ears, and his heart labored heavily.

She did not know what she was doing, or what it would mean! He must show her, make her recoil with loathing and disgust. He looked into her eyes, almost on a level with his. But he did not look at her mouth. He dared not look at it. With deliberate roughness he suddenly caught her to him, and grasped her left breast in a brutal hand. He pushed back her head with his free hand and pressed his mouth to hers with considered brutishness, forcing her lips apart. He tasted the tears that had wet them; for a moment, before his own terrible passion struck him, he felt a pang of gentleness and sweetness and pity. And then, he was no longer acting in order to disgust and terrify her.

It was a long time before, in his demented delirium, he became aware that Laurie had not recoiled from him, had not cried out, had not struggled or protested or shrunk away. Even in his madness, he felt that her arms were about his neck, that she was returning his kisses with equal frenzy and recklessness, that she was murmuring strange and incoherent things, that she was clinging to him fiercely, laughing deeply in her bare throat.

He thrust her away from him, then, still holding her by the arms. They looked into each other's eyes. His were reddened and suffused, hers were flaming.

Then he lifted her in his arms and turned towards the house. Her head lay on his shoulder. He kicked open the door and entered the hallway. She looked about her, swimmingly. No longer was this a desolate and abandoned place, full of gloom and threat, ominous with the future. It was lovely and warm, enchanted, bright with a hundred dancing colors.

When Stuart mounted the beautiful winding stairway, a stairway of white marble in the dusk, she put her arms about his neck again, and drew down his mouth to hers in ecstatic desire and triumphant joy.

CHAPTER 55

JANIE knocked sharply on Laurie's bedroom door, then entered without further courtesy, not awaiting Laurie's permission.

It had turned quite warm for April during the night, and now a flood of dazzling sunlight fell through the windows upon Laurie's bed. She sat up as her mother bounced in grimly. Janie's mouth opened on a burst of vituperative words, then remained open, in silence. For Laurie, sitting upright against her pillows, was naked, and quite unashamed of her nakedness, even apparently unaware of it. She said: "Yes, what is it?"

Janie, stupefied, stared at her daughter, whose golden shoulders and veined pointed breasts were only partly concealed by her long masses of bright hair. She had not seen Laurie naked since the girl had been six years old, and it was the sudden reality confronting her of a full and voluptuous woman that made her understand at last what a stranger was this in her house. Bawdy and disingenuous though she was, Janie was shocked, and oddly frightened.

She finally caught her breath. She pointed at her daughter. "What is this disgraceful exhibition, ma'am? Why this—this nudeness, in bed?"

Laurie looked down at herself, undisturbed, and slightly surprised. Then she smiled, though she made no effort to draw up the coverlets. "Oh? I always sleep like this, Ma. I can't endure the confinement of a nightshift."

She stretched out her long and beautiful arm and pulled the bell-rope. She leaned back against her pillows, and yawned as openly and as indolently as a cat. She shook out her yellow hair, ran her hands through it, let the heavy masses of it fall as they might. Her lips were blooming. Her eyes were softly blue. She regarded Janie with amusement, but without cynicism.

Janie, quite "gone," sank on a chair. She had become so pale that her brown freckles stood out on her sallow face. Her shock increased. She avoided gazing at Laurie's bare shoulders and breasts, but could not meet her eyes either. She did not know where to look, so fastened her virulent gaze on Laurie's calm forehead.

"I presume," she said, in a hoarse and shaking tone, "that you find nothing indecent, nothing shameful, in this? But, certainly, it is all a proper part of your general behavior."

Laurie laughed. "Shameful? Indecent? Why? I sleep alone." Her eyes twinkled. "And, when I do not sleep alone, I am convinced that my bed companion will not object."

Janie gaped, aghast. "What are you saying, miss?"

But Laurie was impatient. "Ma, what does it matter how I sleep? I find this comfortable. That is all that is pertinent." She paused. "You wished to talk to me this morning?"

In a voice trembling with hatred and fury, Janie answered: "You've rung for your breakfast, I opine? Do you wish the maid to see you in this—this condition? Pray, if it is not too arduous an effort, cover yourself. This has always been a respectable house, and I want no tales carried beyond its walls."

Laurie shrugged. She swung her long and perfect legs out of bed. Fascinated, Janie was unable to look away. She watched Laurie negligently pull a blue silk peignoir over the splendor of her nakedness. Laurie picked up a brush from her bureau and rapidly ran it through the hanging richness of her hair; she did not glance in the mirror. She was as unaware of her beauty, or as indifferent to it, as a flowering tree. She began to hum to herself, and her voice, full and powerful, filled the room and joined in the fresh and boisterous wind that pervaded it. Janie felt a peculiar bursting sensation in her meager chest; all her nerves prickled with unendurable malignance. How hideously unfair was the world, and fate! To give all this to one disinterested and shameless woman, and to give nothing to others!

She shouted, out of the torment of her malevolence and envy: "Will you stop that yowling, you minx, and listen to me?"

Laurie glanced at her over her shoulder with unaffected surprise. She had forgotten her mother. "I'm sorry, Ma. What is it, please?"

Trembling with her efforts at self-control, Janie almost shrieked with brutal sarcasm: "If I may ask your ladyship, is your ladyship aware of the hour?"

Laurie found this question baffling. She stared at Janie, her golden lashes blinking. "No. What time is it?" She glanced at the sky, and laughed. "Why, I should think it is almost noon!"

" 'I should think it is almost noon,' eh?" cried Janie. "And that is all that means to you? Well, let me tell you, you minx, it means much more to me. It means that you did not enter this respectable house until almost dawn. It means that I spent a sleepless night of worry, in the company of your fine friends, one of whom, at least, paced the floor in great anxiety for you, though why, God only knows. Men are such damnable fools! When they finally left me, I waited alone. And then," she paused in furious and dramatic significance, "I heard the wheels of a carriage, far down the street, almost in the wake of the milk wagon. I heard that carriage stop. It came no further. Shortly after that, you appeared, skulking in the lamplight like a trollop, letting yourself in stealthily at the back door."

She sprang to her feet, her sallow face burning with crimson. "Will you condescend, miss, to enlighten me as to these disgraceful events?"

Laurie laid down her brushes. She shook back her hair. She looked at her mother thoughtfully. She said, very quietly: "What I do is my own concern. In the last six months I have sent you two thousand dollars, and numerous presents. If you wish, I shall leave this house at once."

Janie was appalled, stricken speechless at this effrontery. She was not acting any longer. She caught the back of a chair. It slipped from her grasp, overturned. She looked about her, blindly, swaying a little. Then, she sank on the warm perfumed bed which Laurie had vacated. And Laurie watched her all through this, hard and calm and expressionless. She regarded Janie's twitching face without pity or interest. She said: "I am nothing to you, or you to me. You must understand that."

Janie did not know it was desolation that swept over her then, mingled with wild self-pity and helplessness.

"How can you say these things to me, Laurie, me, your Ma?" she asked, and her voice was weak and quivering. "What have I done to deserve such cruelty? Cruelty," she repeated, in bitter surprise that she had never known before that Laurie was cruel. Her fear sharpened, and with it, her desolation.

"I was merely pointing out to you, Ma, that you must not interfere with me," said Laurie. "I do not mean to be insolent or without sensibility. But I am not a child. I am a woman, and have had the experience of a woman. I am not without some fame, nor am I dependent upon you for my shelter and protection, nor upon my brothers."

"Why did you return here, Laurie, then, if your mother,

and your brothers, are nothing to you?" Janie was still overcome.

Laurie raised her eyebrows. "My words were badly chosen. I ought not to have said, perhaps, that you are nothing to me, nor should I have implied that I so regard my brothers, either. I have my attachments. I would not have returned to Grandeville had there been nothing here for me. I am never impelled by sentimentality, nor by those who have set up standards of sentimentality to be followed by other human beings." Her lips curved. The lines of her mouth were less sharp and bold this morning. She even regarded Janie with sudden humor and tolerance.

But Janie stared inflexibly and piercingly at her daughter, and Laurie grudgingly admitted to herself that Janie was no fool, and not to be deceived by smooth words. Janie repeated: "Why did you return here, Laurie?"

This was becoming tiresome. It was also dangerous. Laurie was secretly exasperated and impatient. Her position was too impregnable to be injured by gossip, but there was Stuart to consider. She said: "I thought I told you, Ma. I am even willing to admit, now, that I am not free from a little sentimentality of my own."

"You came to flaunt your triumphs in our faces, then?" exclaimed Janie viciously, forgetting in the extremity of her gall her reason for entering this room this morning.

Laurie laughed slightly. "Perhaps I am only human after all," she said, with lightness.

There came a discreet knock on the door, and the little maid to whom Laurie had given the overwhelming gold-piece entered with a breakfast tray. Laurie graciously directed her to lay the tray on the bedside table. She seated herself indolently on the edge of the bed and examined the steaming porridge and eggs and bacon with healthy interest. Her blue silk dressing gown fell open, revealing her round and perfect thighs. The little maid blushed but could not look away.

But, as Janie looked at the little maid, she was reminded of something else. Here was one upon whom she could pour the vitriol of her rage, humiliation and helpless hurt without rebuff or defeat to herself. She shouted: "Bertha! I have just learned that you absented yourself without leave from the housekeeper on Thursday night, though it was dinner time and the other housemaid was ill, and that you did not return until dinner was almost ready for serving. What is the explanation of this, you wench? Was it your evening off, perchance, or were you under the delusion that it was?"

Bertha, terrified, wrung her hands in her apron, and shot a pleading glance at Laurie. Laurie lifted a silver dish-cover and looked with pleasure at the hot crumpets. She said amiably: "Don't scold Bertha, Ma. It was my fault. I had some legal business to discuss with Robbie, and sent Alice a little note by Bertha asking if I could see the two of them last night for a long business and friendly consultation." She put a buttered crumpet to her lips and tasted it with evident appreciation. "It seems I have disturbed this household unpardonably. First, I take Bertha from her duties, and then I cause my dear Ma to remain up half the night watching for my return. I have learned cosmopolitan ways, I am afraid, not quite fitted for Grandeville and the code of *Godey's Lady's Book*."

Her expression was amiable, but she was secretly irritated. All this nonsense of lying and conniving and plotting which was so necessary in a small city, and among one's kin! It was odious, humiliating. She could not endure it.

Janie stared at her daughter. Now some of the pinched look left her mouth, the virulence, her eyes. Then she glowered at Bertha, but her voice was less harsh when she said: "Go about your work, wench. I see it was no fault of yours, after all. You are to obey Miss Cauder whenever she wishes, naturally, but try no tricks of your own."

Laurie frowned faintly. Just then her own maid entered, lamenting that she had not heard her mistress' bell, and prepared for Laurie's ill temper. But to Laurette's surprise, Laurie greeted her affably.

"Please replenish the teapot for me, Laurette," said Laurie. "I think Mrs. Cauder might like to join me in a cup."

The two maids departed, and Janie and Laurie were alone again. Laurie ate with relish, though her annoyance was still sharp, and Janie watched her, in narrow-eyed silence. Laurette returned with fresh tea, and hovered with servility over Janie as she filled the latter's cup. Her air of solicitude, her excellent service, mollified Janie, who finally dismissed her with a grand gesture. Ah, these New York maids had a touch and a way with them that could never be duplicated in rustic Grandeville. She envied Laurie such a maid. Laurette discreetly retired to Laurie's dressing room, where she prepared her mistress' clothes for the day.

Janie sipped her tea. Laurie demolished all the bacon, the crumpets, and eggs, with gusto. How unrefined it was to have such an appetite, and be so unashamed of it, thought Janie, sipping daintily at her cup. Laurie reminded her, continued Janie's thoughts, of a buxom milkmaid, all coarseness and zest and bouncing vitality. These thoughts placated her.

Laurie leaned back against her pillows and yawned voluptuously. "A wonderful breakfast," she commented. "Even in New York, or London, such fresh eggs are almost unobtainable. As for Paris!" She rolled back her head and revealed her strong young throat. "They give you a hard roll and a cup of abominable coffee for breakfast. Ma, I congratulate you on your cook."

Janie bridled with pride. "Gordon is invaluable. Hearty food, and no nonsense, but the best."

Laurie, still lying on her back across the bed, surveyed the pleasant and boisterous sunshine that poured in through her window. "Imagine such a perfect day, for April in Grandeville," she mused. "Tomorrow, doubtless, we shall have snow again." She swung herself up lithely, and looked at her mother. Laurie's eyes were smiling now, as well as her mouth. Her face became thoughtful.

"I am always ill-natured before breakfast, Ma. I must ask your pardon. I am so accustomed to coming and going as I please that it never occurred to me that I owed you an explanation. I regret that I caused you anxiety."

Her tone was so gentle, so contrite, that Janie's spirits were completely revived. She pursed up her lips with maternal severity. "There are the neighbors to consider, Laurie, not to speak of my natural anxieties. A mother must learn to endure them with as much philosophy as possible. It is the selfishness of children. Nor do I think it proper for a female to roam the streets alone at night. One never knows."

"Ah, but Robbie brought me home in his carriage," said Laurie, her annoyance returning at the thought that she must inform her brother that he had conveyed her home this morning. It was disgusting. "I was not roaming about so casually as you imply. I asked him to stop at the corner in order that the noise of the carriage might not disturb you, as I know you are a light sleeper."

But she was already bored. She had not found it necessary these last three years to cajole or appease anyone. That rôle had been reserved for others. Excessively tedious. Laurette entered just then with a smooth inquiry as to what Miss Cauder intended to wear that night at her recital at the Music Hall. Laurie frowned. She had forgotten. These horrible provincial little cities! She said: "Oh, damn. Anything, Laurette. But not the extreme gowns. I think the green satin and lace would be suitable."

She gave her mother another thoughtful glance, then stripped off her wrapper. Janie was embarrassed. She rose, brushed the crumpet crumbs from her morning dress, and murmuring about the business of the household to which she must attend, she left the room.

Laurie stared at the door which had closed behind her mother. Her peignoir hung from her hand, drifted on the floor. The sunlight, no more golden than Laurie's flesh, fell full upon her body.

The girl smiled, began to sing softly to herself, while Laurette listened, entranced and adoring. Mademoiselle, she reflected, was in high spirits this morning. Her singing voice was the voice of a woman who loved, the voice of a woman with a lover. She, Laurette, had never heard Mademoiselle sing like this before. It was very exciting. Could it possibly be that she had yielded at last to that so adorable Monsieur Thimbleton?

CHAPTER 56

LAURIE was angered and egotistically affronted when a messenger brought her the hasty program for her concert that night. With naïve innocence, the committee in charge of the performance commented copiously on Laurie's race, and beamingly announced that she would sing "a selection of her Scottish songs, always dear to the heart of this American daughter of Celtic birth. Though Miss Cauder is famous for her exquisite renditions of various operas, notably those of Robert (!) Wagner, a German musician of considerable ability, and though she has condescended to interpret these operas to the fashionable and sophisticated society of New York, she will render for her appreciative audience in Grandeville those simple airs and ballads so beloved of the natural heart, and so dear to those who prefer sincerity to arias sung in foreign languages and composed by musicians unacquainted with the rugged honesty and simplicity of the American people. She will be accompanied on the piano by Miss Rachel Ellicott, descendent of the founder of this flourishing city."

In spite of her annoyance, Laurie burst out laughing when she read this note appendixed to the program in the most elegant printing, Scotch songs, indeed! These yokels, these vain dolts, with their "rugged honesty and simplicity"! She despised them. It had not occurred to them that she might wish to rehearse her "ballads" with the proud Miss Ellicott, who probably sniffled and had big feet and worse hands. There was nothing else to do, now, but to go to the Music Hall, catch Miss Ellicott between handkerchiefs and sneezes, and hastily go over the "Scottish songs" with her before the performance.

How dared they mortify her with their adoration! With their assumption that they were doing her honor, she the gracious guest of Victoria of England, of Ludwig of Bavaria, of the Buonapartes! No doubt they would consider that they were condescending to her by their amiable worship, and no doubt they would sit in rustic criticism as she sang. How her New York friends would roar at this when she enlightened them during the coming season. She burned with her mortification even while she laughed.

Then her sense of humor, always strong, returned. She hastily searched through her music. Not a single Scottish air or ballad. However, Miss Ellicott probably possessed them among her mincing repertoire.

It would do no harm to give these raw farmers a little pleasure, she reflected. She came upon two sheets of music, and stood very still, looking at them. They had been written down for her by a friend in Paris, a musician of great skill, an Alexandre Bizet, who was yet to write a certain famous opera. He had arranged the music artfully, yet had not obscured the pure beauty and simplicity of the artless songs. She held them in her hand and stared before her, quite pale, her eyes intent. Her breast was suddenly full of pain.

She thought: Five days, before I return to New York. During that time I must so weld him to me that he will never forget. There is a life for us in the future, together. Nothing has ever defeated me; nothing shall defeat me now. He is mine and I am his, and I must make him see that, forever.

She took the handbill of the Grandeville Music Hall down to Elissa Rhinelander and Dick Thimbleton, and enjoyed their laughter. Elissa's laughter was a little cruel. Dick seemed touched, which annoyed Laurie more than ever. "They love you, Laurie," he said. "After all, they are your old friends, and are proud of you."

"They insult me with their pride," she said haughtily.

Dick looked at her with obscure sadness. There were times, he reflected, when Laurie was quite plebeian, and insensible. Yet these qualities made her what she was: exuberantly healthy, indomitable and robust, full of strength and power. Laurie was returning his look. He did not quite like her narrowing her eyelids this way. The blue between them had now a glint of cold and calculating green. He loved her, yes; but he did not know *this* Laurie, and did not like her.

He looked at his sister, picking her way fastidiously through her breakfast. He said: "Elissa, my love, I am very sorry, but I think we must return to New York before Laurie leaves Grandeville. Please believe me that it is imperative."

Elissa was confounded. She looked from her brother to Laurie. Laurie was smiling indifferently. Elissa did not speak. She made a wry mouth, and shrugged. She did not understand. But she presumed that Dick knew his own affairs.

Laurie left them, then, returning to her own rooms. Dick and Elissa were alone. Elissa raised her eyebrows at her brother. "Well, then," she murmured, "explanations are perhaps in order."

Dick sighed. "I know when I've received my congé. In fact, broadly speaking, I've always understood nothing was of any use, with Laurie. Something has happened to her lately. What it is I do not know, but this I do know: she has suddenly dismissed me as being of no consequence at all. She will be grateful to me when I leave. That is the only thing I can do for her now."

Laurie, in her own room, was writing rapidly. "Tomorrow, I will join you near the river in front of your house at four o'clock. I have much to say to you, for which there was no opportunity yesterday." She looked at what she had written. Even to her, there was a too commanding note, a too uncompromising order, in the words. She carefully tore up the letter, and rewrote: "I must see you again, near the river, in front of your house, at four o'clock. I have something to say to you, my very dear, for which there was no opportunity yesterday. With all my heart, and all my soul, your Laurie."

Why was it always necessary to consider the sensibilities of others? The direct approach, the slashing to the heart of a thing at once, always offended. She compressed her lips, sealed the note, put it in her bodice. She would give it to Stuart that night, when she had the opportunity. She stood up, feeling refreshed and in command of all circumstance, and inexorable. But her heart felt constricted and disturbed, her blood too swift. She looked through the windows. The deceptive spring weather had changed. The north sky was already darkening, and there was a snowy chill in the air. Nevertheless, she opened her window and leaned out, letting the cold wind cool a face suddenly hot and fluid in its expression.

She remembered Stuart's contrition, his gentleness, his fear for her. All at once, she was full of loving scorn. He had hardly believed her when she had cried out her passion for him, her obsession for him, her long path to him. He had thought them the extravagant and innocent ardor of a young girl, of which he was guilty of taking advantage, to her hurt and her misery. For a while, it is true, her wild response to his own lust and desire and savagery had almost convinced him, but they had also taken him aback. He had wished to protect her. Her hands clenched on the wet window-sill. What did he know of her? How could he understand the long desire and dedication which had sent her out on a career which she had believed might inspire him with admiration for her, and pride?

It was hard for him to understand, of course. Laurie, disingenuous, was not entirely dazzled by her passion. Stuart, she knew, was only a provincial merchant, on the brink of ruin. He was extravagant, violent and unprincipled, prodigal and reckless. His appetites would always be larger than his purse, and eventually they would destroy him. He had no brilliance of mind, though his intuition was subtle and discerning. He was disorderly and rampant, and would forever remain unsophisticated, compelled only by his lusts, his tempers, and his gusty cravings.

Why, then, did she love him? What had brought her back to his arms and his despair and his ruin, in this abominable little city which she loathed? She shook her head fiercely to herself. She did not quite know. She knew only that always she had yearned for him with every pulse of her body, every drop of her blood. When she thought of him something in her melted, became pure and tender again, soft and glowing.

What did his ruin matter? What if he lost those ridiculous shops? She had much money. She would have a great deal more. There was no end to what she could do. She saw Stuart and herself in Europe going from one beautiful city to another, the guests of the mighty and the worshipping. They would accept Stuart, at her command. It was expected, by the sophisticated, that a famous singer have her lovers. Stuart would be in the brilliant background of her life, always comforting, always admiring, always proud of her, always loving and passionate. She would return to his arms after each triumph, and lie in them, a girl again, simple and surrendering, soft and beseeching, living only for him.

When the uneasy thought crossed her mind that Stuart might not desire to be the beneficiary of her fortune, she shook her head impatiently. He could not be such a fool. Money was money. He would not be insensible to her fortune, to the riches which would accrue to her. Unknown yet to herself, she grimly wagered everything on the strain of weakness she had already detected in him, years ago. He had made her; it was only just that he accept the rewards of his fashioning.

His life was no impediment to her, or the circumstances of his life. His daughter, that miserable puling little creature? Laurie's mouth became cruel. She laughed, curtly. She hated Mary Rose with virulent intensity, because Stuart loved her. She, Laurie, would make short work of that sentimentality. She felt the strength and resolution in herself, which nothing could ever deny or defeat. She made her plans for Stuart's and her own life, and because of the power in her she saw him accepting everything, surrendering to everything. In return, he would have her in her completeness, melting in his arms, giving up her life and her whole soul to him. How could any man resist such a prospect, such a tremendous future?

Annoyed and irritated almost beyond endurance, Laurie returned to the miserable little "dressing-room" behind the drafty stage of the Grandeville Music Hall. The hour's coaching of the tearful Miss Ellicott had infuriated her. She had browbeaten and bullied that poor creature into some semblance of good execution of the "simple airs and ballads." That, at least, was some consolation. Miss Ellicott doubtless hated her thoroughly now, but she had also terrified the ugly chit. Laurie again felt humiliation that she had been subjected, against her will and previous knowledge, to such a situation. She prayed, with exasperation, that Miss Ellicott had not been so completely demoralized that she would fail in her accompaniment.

When she flung open the door of her dressing-room, she found Robbie and Alice awaiting her. Alice was dressed in ample white lace, and wore a deep Cashmere shawl over her pretty little shoulders. Her condition was very evident, a fact by which she was not in the least embarrassed. She embraced Laurie with gentle enthusiasm. "We received your note just before arriving, my love," she explained, "but could not come sooner."

Laurie accepted calmly her brother's kiss on her cheek. She was still vibrant with her cold rage and mortification. But she smiled equably enough. She sat down with a short and explosive sigh, and looked at Robbie and his young wife.

"Well," she said. She had not seen these two for six months, when they had visited her in New York. She fixed a shrewd eye on Alice. "When?" she asked forthrightly.

Alice blushed. She peeped at Laurie shyly. "In three months," she said. She stretched out her small white hand and took Robbie's hand. He returned its pressure absently. He was regarding his beautiful and overwhelming sister with shrewd curiosity and affection. He respected her very much, and his subtle mind read a great deal in her strong and lovely face.

"From all reports, you are doing excellently, Laurie," he said, after she had wryly congratulated Alice on her prospects.

"I understand that you are not doing so badly, yourself," replied his sister, giving him one of her charming smiles. She sat on the rough stool before the cracked mirror, all splendor and overpowering majesty. The pale green satin of her gown bellied about her; her hoops were enormous, draped in cascades of lace and rosebuds. The lace bodice hardly concealed her lovely breasts. Her shoulders were entirely bare, and perfect. Her golden hair, simply dressed, was softly drawn back from her heroic face to a heavy and shining chignon, and over her right temple had been fastened a cluster of pale pink rosebuds. About her throat was clasped a chain of blazing rubies, which threw scarlet reflections on her smooth skin. Bracelets to match clasped her wrists below her long bare arms. In that miserable and cold little room, all dust and chaff, she was incredible. In one corner stood a mound of roses and ferns, from Stuart's hothouses.

The gentle Alice was virtually cowed in Laurie's presence, in spite of the latter's affectionate graciousness. She shivered a little.

Laurie regarded them steadily in a sudden silence; her blue eyes were quite dark, and welling, with her peremptory thoughts. She said abruptly, directing her words to Robbie:

"It is very tiresome, of course, but I asked you here for a specific purpose. Robbie, yesterday afternoon at four I went to your home to see you and Alice. I wished to discuss some legal matters with you, and to spend some time with your little wife and yourself." She smiled tightly. "You brought me home, almost at dawn. It was a long visit, for I had not seen you for some time, and I had legal matters to discuss with you, concerning some of my properties in New York."

Alice stared at her, confused, bewildered. She said: "But Laurie, this is the first time we've seen you since you came home!"

Laurie flashed her one contemptuous and impatient look, and turned to Robbie. He had begun to smile quietly.

"Indeed?" he said.

Laurie sprang to her feet. Robbie could feel her profound energy, her contempt for all this subterfuge, and her anger. "What an odious little town this is!" she exclaimed. "But all this lying and sneaking seems necessary. Our dear Ma might question you. Also, I may need to visit you frequently during the next five days." She looked swiftly at Alice, who was gazing at her in complete stupefaction.

Robbie was frowning thoughtfully. He had no criticism to make of Laurie. He had no questions. He saw that she was a woman, imperative and strong, and full of power. He did not feel any disquiet for her, or uneasiness. She would always know what she was doing.

"Laurie," ventured Alice, speaking with resolution even under her embarrassment and timidity, "I don't know about all this. It seems—seems unworthy of you—this scheming. Surely you can trust us."

Laurie's teeth clenched. But she said with equanimity: "Doubtless I can trust you, Alice. But I am not one to make a confidant of anyone. I only ask this favor of you, this understanding. My affairs are my own. I consult nobody." She looked at Robbie. "I trust you are not going to reveal yourself in the rôle of authoritative stern brother?"

This is ridiculous, thought Robbie, highly diverted. She is over a head taller than I, and no doubt weighs half again as much. She could push me over with one finger. "Authoritative stern brother," indeed! His strong sense of the ridiculous made him smile involuntarily. What was the minx up to? There was a man involved, or he did not know his humanity. But what man? That aristocratic gentleman in his mother's house? He had read the ecstatic hints in the Grandeville papers. But why did Laurie have to skulk off with him, into the bushes? It could be done easily enough in their own rooms. But, perhaps, he thought satirically, the gentleman did not wish to "violate" the sanctity of Laurie's home.

He was not in the least shocked, as he might have been with a gentler and more obscure sister. His appraising look at her had seen her for what she was.

He leaned back on his inadequate chair, crossed his neat small legs, and contemplated Laurie quizzically. He said, with mildness, as if discussing something which interested him only academically, while Laurie returned his regard with large impatience and uncompromising sternness: "Laurie, it has become evident to me that you have developed quite a propensity for taking bulls by the horns. Somewhere you have learned, with Euclid, that the shortest distance between two points is a straight line. Unfortunately for people like you, an axiomatic theory does not allow for human nature and the capriciousness of others, who might rebel against your striding between two points with the wind at your heels. I wonder," he mused, "whether you follow me?"

Little Alice, who had a mind of her own, nevertheless gazed at her husband in bewilderment. What dear Robbie was saying was not in the least pertinent, she reflected. But Laurie looked at her brother with sudden grimness, and there was an apricot-colored flush high on her cheekbones. The long fingers of her white hand began to tap on the dusty top of her dressing-table, and her foot joined in the tapping.

She said: "Always the man of reason, I perceive. You have mellowed, Robbie. There was a time when you had only derision for those who considered human sensibilities while on their way between two points. Am I to congratulate you on a wisdom born of the years or to commiserate with you on the loss of realism?"

Robbie's pale dark brow, usually so smooth and unfurrowed, puckered. He regarded Laurie steadfastly. He said: "Say, rather, that I have acquired realism."

He stood up. His sister smiled at him sardonically. The restlessly tapping fingers increased their tempo. "This may seem irrelevant to you, Laurie, but I remember a saying of Hesiod's: 'For beasts of the fields and for fowl of the air Zeus has ordained one law, that they prey upon one another; but for men hath he ordained justice, which is by far the best.' "

Robbie took a thoughtful turn up and down the dank and narrow room, his head bent. "Somewhere," he mused, "and under circumstances at which I can only guess with concern, you have learned to 'prey.' You have learned to disregard everyone else. You have set your course by your own desires. That is sad for you, Laurie. You will suffer for it. In a way, too, I am extremely sorry for you."

She listened with smiling scorn and hard lips. "I fail to follow your classical references, Robbie, though I stand with humble admiration before your learning. Yes, I have learned many things. But that is beside the point. It happened that I returned to Grandeville for a specific purpose, the purpose of my life. I shall go away again, very shortly. What that business is, is my own affair. Has it been too odious of me to ask you to assist me?"

He stopped before her, in silence. But she saw his keen black eyes fixed upon her, and they were quite kind, kinder than she ever remembered them. Something stirred painfully in her; the harsh lines of her mouth softened involuntarily. He said: "No, Laurie, it is not odious of you. You are not a child, I see. If we can help you, you have only to ask."

He held out his hand to Alice, whose face suddenly shone at the tender gesture. She rose at once, and childishly clasped her hand in his. From the heights of her love she beamed down upon poor Laurie, whom no one loved despite her beauty and her fame and her great endowment. Laurie watched them; her expression became satiric. She rose, also. "Thank you, Robbie. And now, I believe, I must prepare for my 'appearance before the distinguished audience.' "

The manager of the Music Hall entered after Robbie and his wife had left. He was much flustered, and when he encountered Laurie's hardened eyes, he was even more disturbed. He was very sorry. Perhaps Miss Cauder did not understand the whole program. There were to be four renditions by the choir of the First Presbyterian Church before Miss Cauder's appearance. A very excellent choir, he stammered, seeing Laurie's face darkening with outrage, and if Miss Cauder just opened her door she could enjoy it also. After the choir, the minister of that church would deliver a few sound homilies and worthy sentiments. Miss Cauder would then appear.

"All this will take an hour!" exclaimed Laurie. "Am I to remain in this detestable hole, freezing and shivering, while a choir of yokels bawls to the heavens?"

The manager fled. Dangerously close to the explosive point, Laurie paced up and down the room for several moments. And then she began to laugh, uproariously.

CHAPTER 57

SPECIAL seats near the stage had been reserved for the Cauder family. Janie sat with Bertie at her right hand, Bertie wan and skeletal, but affably smiling as ever, and the despair of near-by young ladies who tried to focus his glances upon them. However, when he was not smiling, the face beneath his thickly curling and ruddy hair was tragic and haggard, and old, and his hands constantly trembled. This was his first appearance in public for several months, and the audience in the vicinity whispered and snickered. He appeared unaware of them, and favored even the most malicious, when his wandering eye touched them, with his absent and brilliant smile. This was effective in silencing them, though that had not been his intention in the least.

At Janie's left sat Angus and the surly Gretchen, his wife, and beside her, her covertly sneering and envious parents. Angus sat as stiff as a corpse propped upright, his pale stern face fixed and expressionless, his gray eyes as cold and dull as lightless stone. Robbie, naturally, sat beside his brother Bertie, and engaged him in amiable and casual conversation, while Alice clasped his hand, unresponsive as it was.

Behind the Cauder group sat Stuart and his two friends, Father Houlihan and Sam Berkowitz. Sam was still and silent, for he had recently lost his mother, and the priest was tense and tired, though there appeared no reason for his state. Stuart actually seemed light-hearted, drunken with good spirits, and there was a glow in his eye, an exuberance, which neither of his friends had seen there for years. Yet they also detected a kind of wild intoxication about him, a feverish restlessness. Even while they talked to him through the dull renditions of the choir, and the prosy and sonorous sermon of the minister, they saw that he barely heard a single word, and that his noddings, the inclinations of his head, were all mechanical.

The audience, the newspapers lyrically announced on Monday, was extremely distinguished, exquisitely attired, and in an exceptionally receptive mood as it gathered to pay honor to its most illustrious daughter and friend. The papers spoke of the bowers of flowers heaped high on each side of the stage, the festoons of flags, the numerous blue uniforms of furloughed officers among the audience, the colorful gowns, pelisses, fans, bonnets and ribands of the ladies, the air of gay expectancy that pervaded the hall.

The hall, however, was chill, drafty and cramped. Municipal money had dwindled to such a point in the building of it that no ceiling had been added, and a confused medley of ropes, rafters, spiders' webs and scaffolding hung high and threatening overhead. The curtain, of cheap red velveteen, was dusty and frayed, and had been imported from an old theatre. From the rafters was suspended a precariously swinging chandelier, spluttering and hissing with gas-jets, which overcame all the ladies' perfumes with its noxious stench. This was such an innovation, however, that it received only admiring and very proud glances. The walls were painted a rough and leprous brown, and were beaded with moisture. The floors were rough, unfinished planks, stained and uneven. The seats, a miscellany gathered hastily from various churches and abandoned meeting halls, were stiff and uncomfortable, and quite out of line.

But under that flickering, flaring and uncertain light, the ladies wielded their feathered fans, arched their bonneted heads, fluttered their kerchiefs, coquetted with their escorts, and preened, quite certain that this was a most distinguished event and a most distinguished audience. They were sure that Laurie would be overwhelmed by the cosmopolitan air of this Hall, and the discernment of its temporary inhabitants. They had firmly decided that they would not be overly impressed by her, that their applause would be restrained, in order to teach her a humility not learned by her in the gilded halls of fashion in New York and Europe. Many of the ladies already exhibited a genteel ennui, languidly sniffed at smelling salts, conversed in a most blasé manner with their neighbors. Laurie had not yet appeared. Some of the ladies murmured that it was quite possible they must leave before Laurie Cauder ventured shyly out upon the stage. Children, you know, and the most odious situation as regards servants, who were flocking to the manufactories making uniforms and bedding for soldiers. One did not know what the world was coming to in these days.

The three-piece "orchestra," composed of one piano, one violin and one insistent drum, suddenly clamored triumphantly, and as if in response, the chandelier spluttered and hissed valiantly. The curtain, which had dropped impressively after the retirement of the minister, parted with violent jerks and creakings to reveal Miss Laurie Cauder on the dusty stage, with a tasteful backdrop of a luridly painted garden scene, all violet and crimson and yellow and blue. The audience burst into dignified and restrained applause, to which Laurie bowed ironically, in acknowledgment. The footlights at her feet flared fitfully. She could smell the gas, the dust, the dankness. She advanced a foot or two towards the footlights, and over her shoulder Miss Ellicott glanced at the famous lady with hatred mixed with fright and nervousness.

Laurie looked at the audience, and the audience, with stateliness, looked at Laurie. She smiled a little to herself, but was mortified again. With the sensitivity of an artiste, she immediately detected their mood. They were "honoring" her, she saw clearly, these provincial sausage-makers, petty manufacturers, grain merchants, shop-keepers, horse-breeders and traders, slaughter-house owners, quarrymen and brick-makers. Their genteel ladies peered at Laurie through opera glasses and tilted their bonnets majestically. Really, they whispered to each other, the girl was too big, and her stride was very unrefined, and her air too assured and bold for a female.

Laurie opened her mouth. And at once, the audience was stunned. They had expected a sweet and trilling voice, very pretty and light and prepossessing, a voice similar to Miss Ducey's, who was much sought after at private parties. Perhaps a little better than Miss Ducey's, they had conceded graciously, before Laurie's appearance, and were now prepared to applaud its better timbre and higher range. Miss Cauder would not find them entirely benighted, or without discernment.

But the voice that poured through Laurie's red and opened lips was like a cataract of pure and blazing gold, molten, effortless, and stunning in its power. It was like a great golden bird, mounting, swinging, rising up against a golden heaven, its mighty wings outspread and brilliant with blinding light. It soared, struck against the rafters, bounded back from the narrow walls, in one astounding volume of unearthly sound, so that the audience quailed under it, and opened their mouths in stupefaction. It was incredible that all that powerful and perfect music could leap from the throat of a single woman, that she herself was not torn apart by the force of it, its strength and wild dynamic might. She drowned out the feeble "orchestra," so that she seemed to sing alone, and it was only in her pauses that one could discern the accompaniment, frantically and faintly a beat or two behind. It was like a quavering camp-follower in the rear of an army with flying banners.

Stuart, who had been smiling, was very quiet, his elbow on the back of Janie's chair. He had turned white, become motionless. He listened to the voice that had enthralled kings and princes and dukes and queens, had thrown into frenzy tens of thousands of distant peoples. It seemed to him that Laurie sang for him alone. He did not hear Father Houlihan's pale-lipped whisper: "My God!" nor Sam's dim exclamation. That voice, which struck triumphantly and with savage beautiful strength against the ceiling and the walls, overpowered him, filled him with terrible ecstasy and pride, and shaking passion. Laurie! Laurie! She was looking at him, smiling even as she sang, and he saw, dazedly, that her breast rose and fell with her singing like the quiet swelling of a wave.

Some of the magic of her voice mysteriously communicated itself to her very flesh, so that she appeared ringed about in light, her face incandescent, her few gestures flashing with radiance. The audience, speechless, petrified into complete silence, stared at her with distended eyes, sucking in their lips, overwhelmed by the "most glorious Elizabeth in the world," as Wagner with rapture had called her.

And then she was silent, and the quaking orchestra was silent, also.

There was no sound at all, except for the hissing of the chandelier. Laurie bowed, smiling ironically again, lifting her brows. The audience looked at her, frozen into complete motionlessness, unable to lift even a hand.

Then Laurie spoke: "And now, dear friends, I have a song which I will sing you, in gratitude for your appreciation. You will not find it in any shop. It was composed and sung by my father, in the hills of Scotland."

A few among the audience, belatedly recovering themselves, feebly applauded. But all the rest were still dumb, still stupefied. Except for one man, whose wife beside him did not feel his sudden convulsive start at Laurie's words, and did not see his stark and shrivelling face.

Laurie unrolled the small scroll of music in her hand, and graciously turned to the bewildered orchestra. "I have no accompanying music for this," she said, gently. "I shall sing it alone."

And then she faced the audience again. She lifted her

head, the uncertain gaslight suddenly flared into her eyes, and the sockets were full of wide blue flame. She did not look at Stuart, now. She sought out her brother's face, the face of Angus, and looked at it fixedly.

She sang her father's song: "O Morning Star!" She poured out the simple but poignant words, the pure and tender and passionate music. Her voice shook; it was a torrent of sparkling crystal, or of tears. It rose with wild supplication, as if to a dark morning sky, in which a star burned with exultant fire. It was like the lifting of marble praying hands, that voice, like a face upturned humbly yet proudly to the brightening heavens. It was the call of a soul, adoring, pleading, communicating with God, full of pride that it possessed the consciousness of knowing Him. It was the wings of angels, turning into light at the touch of dawn. It was the sweetest and most reverent ecstasy, pellucid yet stern.

No one saw Angus leaning forward to listen to her, the gaslight wan on his face, which was wet and slimy with moisture. No one saw him put his hands to his head in one fierce gesture of anguish. No one was aware that he looked only at his sister, and that she looked only at him, crying out to him with all the power and remembering tenderness of her voice, as if, in that moment, she had recalled him and was holding out her hands to him in one last final pleading.

"By heaven!" exclaimed Bertie, when the last note had faded away dramatically. "The girl has a wonderful voice! If Pa could only have heard her!"

Janie was wiping her eyes sentimentally. Robbie was smiling, much moved, at his pale little wife. "Ah, it's a grand thing to know you've given such a voice to the world," sighed Janie. But Angus sat like a dead man in his chair, one hand pressed against a temple that throbbed with the most terrible pain.

Laurie was bowing and smiling and retreating, her blue hoops sweeping the floor. Then she swung about so vigorously, facing the wings, that her lace pantalettes were revealed almost to her knees. In a moment she had gone, leaving upon the stage a peculiar aura brighter than the dusky flickering of the footlights, a kind of faint and quivering halo.

The audience, finally recovering itself, began to murmur softly and incoherently, in a kind of awakening daze. It was

some moments before they became aware that Gretchen
was calling out loudly, and with fear. "Angus! It's my husband! Something's happened to my husband!"

CHAPTER 58

LAURIE and her mother were admitted by a
swollen-faced Gretchen into Angus' darkened room. The
thick red draperies were closed tightly against the flooding
April sunshine, and a hot fire made the room too close, almost stifling. The odors of unaired places were thick in the
motionless air. Janie gasped a little, put her lavender-soaked
kerchief to her nose. But Laurie advanced towards the bed
and stood looking down in cold silence at her brother. In the
background, Gretchen whimpered, wrung her hands, cast
furtive and inimical glances at Laurie.

Angus lay on his white pillows, his face drawn and gray,
his eyes sunken. But his thin hands moved restlessly, as if
groping. Seeing this, Janie whispered shrilly: "O my God!
See what the lad is doing!" and burst into tears. Gretchen,
distracted from her dislike for Laurie, rushed to the bed and
bent over her husband, her whimper now becoming a series
of high-pitched squeals. She sought for the signs of dissolution, but as Angus was doing nothing different from what
he had been doing ever since last night, her terror dissolved
into resentment against Janie, and she glared furiously at
her mother-in-law.

"He isn't 'picking at the coverlets,'" she said hoarsely.
"He's asleep, and is having a nightmare."

"Yes," said Laurie coolly, "he is having a nightmare."

She sat down, bonneted and cloaked, at the bedside. An
oil lamp burned mustily in the gloom. It made threads of
gold of the lock of hair on Laurie's brow. She regarded her
brother without visible emotion, and then looked with
amusement at the flushed Janie and the fat, whitish Gretchen
who were exchanging bayonet glances.

Laurie found Gretchen more distasteful than ever. The
loose violet dressing gown, billowing with lace, did not conceal her "condition" in the least. Rather, it emphasized that
condition. What a dreadful creature! meditated Laurie, revolted. But pathetic, also. It was evident that she adored

Angus, Angus lying there concerned only with his inner horrors and despairs.

There was little room in Laurie for pity. Nevertheless, as she contemplated Gretchen with her usual coldness and detachment, she felt something like compassion. There was a new softness and warmth in her these days, and through it more human emotions could penetrate. She smiled at the young woman, who had completed her baleful study of Janie.

"He does not look so ill," she said soothingly. "What do his doctors say?"

Gretchen, somewhat taken aback by this kindness, and by the clear shining of Laurie's eyes, melted with self-pity and the relaxing of her fear. She began to sniffle. "It's one of his attacks, they say. But worse than ever. It's his head, you know. He has such headaches. He hasn't had an attack for some time now, and we had hopes he wouldn't have another."

Janie gasped again in the heat and closeness of the room. "What the lad needs is a little air and light," she said loudly. "It's suffocating in here." She marched to the windows, hurled back the draperies, flung open a sash. The sunlight swept into the room on the wings of bright wind. The lamp flickered, paled. A bar of light struck across Angus' face, and he stirred and muttered.

"Oh!" cried Gretchen, pounding clumsily to the windows. "You mustn't do that! The doctors ordered quiet and darkness!"

But she stopped, quailing before Janie's vitriolic green eyes. "You'll be killing my lad," she said. "It's air and light he needs, and he'll have them while his mother is here."

"You are unreasonable, Mother," said Gretchen, shrinking. "You will make him worse."

Laurie, seeing that Angus was about to awaken, said: "If you two don't stop bickering, you'll disturb him more than air and light."

Angus was moving his head on the pillows, as if in great torment. And then, very sluggishly, he opened his eyes. There was no recognition in their exhausted gray depths as he looked at his sister, sitting quietly beside him. He looked at her with the empty far weariness of a sick child, still held by feverish dreams. She bent towards him. "Angus," she said gently. "It's Laurie. Are you a little better now?"

But he did not reply. He only stared at her immovably, as if trying to see her face through mists. And then, at last, within his eyes there appeared a faint tired sparkle of recognition, and his lips parted on a sigh. He tried to smile. His hand moved. Laurie hesitated. She touched his hand lightly, and smiled at him with brilliance.

"You are better, I see. We just heard of your sudden illness. But it is not serious, I understand. You must rest."

The hand under hers was cold and damp and feeble. She shrank from it. But her rusty pity broke through its barriers and flooded her. She clasped his hand strongly, willing him some of her strength and health. A bird of pain stirred in her cold heart, lifted its wings, fluttered. She felt a smarting about her eyelids, a weakening sadness all through her senses.

He was trying to speak, moistening his lips, moving them. And then he could only whisper: "That song, Laurie. Dada's song."

The words were simple, and childish, and in her the bird of pain grew to enormous dimensions. She bent closer over him. She murmured: "I sang it for you, Angus."

Suddenly, to her surprise, or perhaps not to her surprise, his face darkened, became tight and accusing, and full of bitterness. He withdrew his hand from hers. "It was a cruel thing to do, Laurie," he said, and his voice was stronger.

She was silent, watching him. At last she exclaimed: "No! it was not cruel, Angus. I thought I might reach you for the last time. I thought I might reach you, for my sake, too."

Janie and Gretchen had approached the bed, and were listening with bewilderment, exchanging perplexed glances, their enmity forgotten. Gretchen said: "You are disturbing him, Laurie."

Laurie stood up. She still looked at Angus. There was a flush on her cheeks, and anger in her eyes, but pleading, also. "It's no use, is it, Angus?" she asked.

He was silent. He turned his head away from her. Laurie sighed, shrugged. "Let him rest," she said to her mother. "That is all anyone can do for him."

She hesitated. She saw his bleak and lonely profile on the pillows. She wanted to leave him immediately. But something made her say, with a tremor in her voice: "Angus, have you forgotten me entirely? This is still Laurie, you know."

He sighed heavily, but did not turn his head to her. "No," he said faintly, "it isn't Laurie."

Her mouth hardened, even while her pain devoured her. "It isn't Angus, either, then," she said.

She waited, but he did not speak again. She looked at her mother, and signalled silently. Janie bent over her son and kissed his pallid cheek with her dry rouged lips. He did not make any sign of acknowledgment. The two women left the room together. Immediately, Gretchen drew the draperies over the windows, shut out the air. She tiptoed to her husband's side again. He seemed to be sleeping.

CHAPTER 59

THE RIVER ran dark and winy, and with a distant sound, under a far gray sky, dimming and eerie. All the colors of the earth had faded and retreated, so that even the near-by grass, the greening trees, the brown flower-beds, had an indistinct and shadowy look as if they belonged to a world of dreams or a strange planet. There was no sound of bird or wind, only a curious hollowness of atmosphere in which all echo was swallowed, or seemed muted and obscure. Even Stuart's white house on its rise of ground retreated to an unreality, and appeared formed of floating mist.

It was an atmosphere, a scene, which depressed and disquieted Laurie. It reminded her of the dream garden of which Stuart had told her long ago. She and Stuart walked along the shore of the river in a heavy silence they could not for some time break, feeling themselves disembodied, moving in a vacuum over a landscape only faintly formed and likely to dissolve at any moment. They stood for a moment, hand in hand, to watch the river, seeing it but not hearing it except for an obscure dulled murmur, marking how each smooth and glimmering wave slipped into another as if made of soundless glass. The Canadian shore had melted into a drifting gray fog, so that the waters had no visible boundary. Though it was near sunset, there was no glow in the western sky, only a shadowlike purple tint darkening perceptibly.

They found a large whitish flat stone, and sat upon it. Stuart uneasily lit a cheroot. Laurie watched the smoke idle away into the air hardly less gray and sluggish. Her eyes were tired, fixed on her inner thoughts. But her hand in Stuart's was the only warm thing in that quiet gloom.

He said gently: "Long ago I decided it was no use about Angus. You are distressing yourself futilely, my love."

She moved restlessly, sighed. Her expression became sadder, darker. "It was foolish of me even to try. He changed years ago, and I could do nothing but watch him change. I don't know what came over me that night. Perhaps," and she laughed drearily, "it is because I never acknowledge defeat, and thought I might break through to him."

She pushed back her hair impatiently, threw up her head, which was bare. Her hair burned, bright yellow, in the dreamlike dusk, but her face was drained of all color. She forgot Stuart, in her gloomy thoughts, and he gazed intently at her heroic profile, all strong clear planes and delicate angles. What a woman was this! He had never known an honest woman before, a woman of strength and purpose and resolution, who could yet be so tender, so sweetly wild and passionate. She made him feel weak and exhausted and irresolute, and he wondered again why she loved him. Was it some delusion that clouded her judgment? He smiled ruefully to himself. No, she was not deluded. She had been quite forthright and blunt at moments, agreeing with him that he had despoiled and muddied his life.

She will go away soon, he thought, and pray God she will forget me. The unselfish thought gave him a strange strength and courage even when it filled him with pain and desolation. He had nothing for her, could give her nothing, not even freshness or hope. And not even the dubious honor of his name. But surely, he reflected, she will forget me! What am I, compared with those she has known, and will know?

But it was a humble wonder to him that she had come so far to be with him, that she had moved through shadows to the reality of him. What tenacity! What delusion! Pity mingled with his sorrow and desolation, and he lifted her hand to his lips.

She smiled at him absently. Her eyes were still dark with restlessness and pain. She was still thinking of Angus.

She said softly: "He, Angus, and I, used to walk by the river. We always had so much to say to each other. How can I forget him, abandon him? He is part of my child life. He was my friend. We loved each other so. And then he changed. I hated my mother, for influencing him to his destruction. But now I am not so sure. Only a weakling can be turned by another human creature to ruination and despair."

With a rare impetuosity, she snatched her fingers from

Stuart's gentle grasp, clenched her hands, and beat them on her knees. She said with a kind of suppressed fierceness: "I don't know why I sang that song! The reason must have been hidden in my mind, for I obeyed the impulse blindly. I hardly knew whether I would sing it or not. And then I looked up and saw his face, I saw the living corpse he had become, and for the first time in years it seemed terrible to me that it was Angus, my brother—that man sitting there beside that stolid stupid woman, with his life all around him like a heap of dead stones!

"I could hear my father singing, and I sang with him, to Angus. My father's hands reached out for Angus, through me. I heard his voice in mine."

She was silent, breathing deeply and irregularly. Then she looked up at Stuart, and her eyes were full of sorrow and tears. "It sounds ridiculous, I know. But I saw my father, reaching out for Angus, trying to save him. I—I believe, perhaps, that there are times when the 'dead' cry out to others, stretch out their hands to them, through the medium of another's voice and flesh. I felt this was so, last night, with my father."

Stuart placed his big warm hand firmly over one of the cold clenched fists on her knee. He said quietly: "It isn't ridiculous." He sighed, and looked over the silently sliding river. "A year or two ago, I dreamt of my mother. She was a poor, good and colorless little creature. I thought she came to me and took me by the hand and drew me out of bed. She said to me: 'Stuart, you have always believed you had enemies. And perhaps one terrible enemy, in particular. You are right. You have a most frightful enemy. Come with me, through your life, and I will show you his face, so that you may know him and never forget him.'"

Laurie tried to smile, to speak, and then was silent. Finally, as Stuart said nothing more, but only stared at the darkening river with the most tragic expression, she said: "Yes, Stuart? Did she show you the face of your enemy?"

He did not look at her, but said only: "Yes. She did. She took me through the most tangled and stinking jungle one can imagine. It was full of snarls and smells and rustlings and pits and creeping vines with horrible red flowers on them. It was night, and there was a crimson moon peering through the choking tops of trees. She finally brought me to a little pool of water in the midst of crawling weeds and stenches, and pointed to it. 'There is your enemy. Be warned against him in time.' I looked in the pool and saw my own face."

He sighed again, tried to laugh. "She was right, you know. And I do believe she came to me that night."

Laurie was very still on the stone on which she sat. She moved restively. All the vitality seemed to have seeped from her, leaving only disquiet behind. She resumed: "So I tried to reach Angus. It was a mistake. I could only give him pain. He hates me now."

But Stuart said quickly: "How can you know what you have done for him? Perhaps the time will come when he will understand." He laughed, wryly. "I, too, worked on Angus, and finally gave up. But perhaps I planted something in his mind which might spring up some day when least expected. At least it is pleasing to my conceit to think so."

She took his hand and held it in her smooth palms. He put his other arm about her, and she dropped her head on his shoulder. She began to speak, very softly: "Stuart, when will you be in New York again?"

The arm about her slackened, but he said with forced lightness: "I don't know, my darling. Why should I go? The shipments I ordered from France and England have been 'indefinitely delayed,' to quote the War Department. As for the cotton shipments from the South, there are none, now. Of course I could accept contraband, but I won't. I can pay huge prices for illegal stuffs, but I won't."

She said: "But the cotton is manufactured in New England, is it not?"

"I used to import my own cotton and then ship it to the mills in New England, where it was manufactured in accordance with my own patterns, at a very reasonable price. That is not possible now, of course. Certainly, however, I could buy regular cottons in the usual patterns from the mills, but the price has gone up so enormously that most of my customers could not afford it. The mills are profiteering by this war; I can buy what I wish at a price beyond reason, and gouge my trade in accordance. In fact, I was so cynically advised. Is not the North in a surge of prosperity brought on by this war, while the South starves? But such prosperity, bought with soldiers' blood and the sweat of underpaid women and children, is not the prosperity I will encourage. I will not deal with such scoundrels." He laughed, bitterly. "Moreover, they demand cash."

Laurie bit her lip. "Are matters bad with you then, Stuart?"

"Very bad," he admitted frankly, and with sudden weariness. "I dare not think how bad. I live from day to day now." He dropped his arm, looked over his shoulder at his house, and a stark expression of hunger and passion stood in his eyes. "If only I keep my house, nothing else will matter."

He added: "I cannot pay my bills on time. In some instances I am six months behind. Only the fact that Sam draws hardly a penny from the shops keeps us in business. If the war ends this year, I shall survive. If not—I go under. But, surely, it will end this year!"

He added: "It must end this year." His voice was grim.

"What do you sell, under these circumstances?"

"I sell what I can. I buy what, and where, I can. Many of my shelves are empty. I have had to discharge almost half my clerks. That was the worst of all. Fortunately many of them enlisted, and others found employment elsewhere. They are not suffering." He forgot her for an instant, and exclaimed almost with ferocity: "I need five hundred dollars a month! I can't exist on less. And so I never look at the books these days. If a day passes without ruin, I draw a deep breath, and wait for tomorrow."

What a witless way of existing! thought Laurie. She frowned, shrewdly. "Angus, however, knows the books," she said. "Doubtless he would inform you if you were approaching the danger point."

"Doubtless," he agreed, with relief.

Doubtless, she repeated to herself, with gloomy and apprehensive irony.

And then her apprehension sharpened, and she saw Angus' face. Surely to God Stuart could trust him! Surely he would remember that it was Stuart who had given him his opportunities, had trusted him, extended to him only the deepest kindness, had expended on him a consideration and affection and regard he had never encountered before. She tried to remember that Angus had at least a high sense of honor and integrity, that he never lied or cheated, that his dour religion would restrain him from blackguardly tactics. She shook her head as if in denial, over and over. Janie might have her schemes, but Angus had his rigid integrity. Whatever else had gone from him, surely he had retained that!

Stuart was speaking again. "Do you remember River Island, Laurie? Sam now tells me he has saved ten thousand dollars. The Island is municipal property, and is up for sale. No one wants it particularly, or has bid for it, except that old spider Allstairs. (My God, do you realize the man is over eighty, and as malignant as ever?) Allstairs thinks it can be developed into farms, though there is the difficulty of transportation. At all events, he has offered seven thousand dollars for it. Sam is offering ten. He hasn't given up his dream, apparently, and now the stubborn old rascal sees an opportunity of realizing it. He has deprived himself, these last few years, of practically every decency of living in order to save that money. You see, there was another pogrom in Poland about four years ago, and he feels there will be another soon, as soon as it is convenient for the land-owners, and the clergy. He wants to bring over at least four thousand terrified Jews and establish them on the Island." Stuart paused; his brows drew together. "I can't forget that if he had not paid some—debts of mine, some obligations, he might have saved those wretched people from death, and torture. I feel—in some way—that I am guilty." He moved away from her a little. "About a month ago he offered me that money, but I can't take more blood money from him. I wish to God I'd never taken the other, which, by the way, I have repaid only to the extent of four thousand dollars."

He was consumed with vivid misery. He twisted his fingers together, his hands hanging between his knees. Laurie was impatient. She said: "But Sam has never asked you to return the money, Stuart?"

"No! Of course not! He never would. He was reluctant to accept what I could repay him. And then came the pogroms, and I realized what my stupidity had cost him. He aged ten years in as few days, when the reports came out in the papers. When I cursed myself, to him, he said: 'If I had not preferred you above anything else, my friend, I would not have given you that money. You must forget it. It is no more than you would have done for me,'" and again Stuart smiled, with bitterness.

Laurie moistened her lips. She looked steadily before her, and said: "Stuart, let us be honest and reasonable. How much have you expended upon me?"

He moved away from her with a gesture of outrage and repugnance. She cried, gathering up her force: "Stuart! Don't look at me like that, as if you were a fool! Did you think I intended to accept your bounty without repaying it—when I could? Am I an object of charity? A disgusting creature without pride or self-respect? It is true you are my kinsman, but the relationship is distant. Do you never wonder whether people don't ask who assisted me, and why? I assure you these questions have been asked. I informed the inquisitive creatures that I was lent this money, which must be repaid."

His nostrils distended, and his expression was violent. She laid her hand on his arm. "I am a rich woman now, Stuart. I demand that you allow me to repay you, or I shall lose my self-respect, my dignity."

She laughed, drily: "If I were a man, there would be no question of this between us. It would be understood."

He stood up, as if to leave her. She rose, also. "Is your own pride hurt, Stuart?" she asked tauntingly. "If so, consider mine."

He tried to speak quietly, but his voice was hoarse: "Laurie, you must not speak of this again. There is more involved than what you know. I will say only this one thing: our words have weakened what self-respect I still possess, what assurance, what mastery of circumstance." He added, as if violently distraught: "Let me be proud of one thing, at least!"

They looked unwaveringly at each other for several long minutes. Laurie saw how shaken he was, how frantic, and how tormented. She sighed, inwardly, then with extreme gentleness she bent forward and kissed his drawn cheek. "Very well, Stuart, I shall not speak of it again, if you wish. I am sorry you will not let me keep my own pride, my darling. It did seem to me, however, that in this emergency you might have allowed me to return to you the money which is rightfully yours."

She tried to cajole him back to his former mood, but she had wounded him in some inexplicable way, and though he was all gentleness and affection as they resumed their walk by the river he was unusually taciturn and abstracted. She said at last: "Whatever I have done, Stuart, has been because you have desired it for me, not because of any desire of mine. I was a lethargic lump of a girl, all indifference and laziness. But when you spoke of my 'future,' I could see that such a future would make you proud of me. It was all for your sake."

His lacerated egotism was artlessly pleased at this, and he pressed the hand on his arm with awakening tenderness. He said: "But what am I, compared with you, my dearest love?" He awaited eagerly for her answer. She leaned her cheek against his for a moment, and said: "But without you, I should be nothing."

He began to speak to her of his anxieties, and she listened with the deepest and most intense sympathy and interest. Two weeks ago Father Houlihan, returning late at night from a sick call, had been set upon in the darkness by certain ruffians who had beaten him badly, had insulted him and called him the foulest names. Two nuns on their way to Mass last Sunday had been vilely accosted by two young men, and subjected to hideous advances in a spirit of obscene mockery. Another window had been broken in the church, and upon the door of the convent had been scrawled lascivious and unspeakable words. For very fear, many worshippers had been kept from their Sunday devotions, and Catholic children, returning home from school, had been accosted and threatened. Sam Berkowitz and the other one hundred Jews in Grandeville had been threatened with physical violence, and tarring and feathering. Nor did the foreign settlement escape. The "anti-alien" feeling was growing dangerously.

"And we are in the very midst of a death-struggle for the preservation of the Republic!" exclaimed Stuart, with furious bitterness and despair. "There is a pattern here which is ominous and significant, if it could be detected."

Laurie tried to soothe him, though she felt no personal concern. "But I understand that Grandeville has given over 14,000 men to the Union Army, Stuart. That does not argue well for what you are hinting, of a nation-wide plot."

"But there is a plot, Laurie! Grandeville is not alone in this. The feeling against 'foreigners' is sweeping the country, South and North alike. So sinister has it become that the President, himself, addressed Congress on the subject. What is behind it? Why did it break out at this time? And, curse it, who is competent to judge what is 'alien' in the country, and deleterious, and what is not? Are we not all of us, foreign-born or native-born, aliens in this country? Are we not all the children of Europeans? They speak of this as a 'new' country. It is not. The land is new, perhaps, but the people who inhabit it are only extensions and descendents of old European strains. Americans did not spring from the soil of America, new-born, newly created, and of a new race. The land is new. But the people are old. They are tied forever to their European forebears by racial cords. But their minds ought not to be tied. We must realize that though Americans are a European people of a hundred races, we have a different destiny together, and we must be one people, whatever our blood."

He was much stirred. He continued impetuously: "We must have no allegiance to any potentate or prince, or to any nation, but America! The moment we call ourselves 'English' or 'Irish' or 'German' or God knows what, that moment we no longer are Americans. We are aliens, even if our ancestors dwelt in America for two hundred years! We have no place in America. We are Americans only, or we are not Americans at all. For nearly a hundred years the people have understood this. Now they are forgetting. Some evil men, somewhere, are whispering of old loyalties, old treacheries, old tyrannies, old oppressions and hatreds, and they have only one purpose: the destruction of the Republic and the death of America."

She had never seen him stirred like this, so stern, so exalted, and so passionate. She marvelled at him, and was mute. She thought to herself: But America has never meant anything to me. No other country has, either. I am just a human being.

He was speaking again, with anger: "Do you know what the Germans in this city have been doing, Laurie? They have actually told their men that if they enlisted in the Army, they would find themselves destitute and unemployed after the war! Oh, they have been very circumspect and discreet in their treachery and disloyalty! They have used brutal hints. So many men who would naturally have enlisted have refrained out of fear for their families. However, the draft has begun. The draft! Is it not a horrible thing this country, conceived in the blood of resolute and martyred men, nourished by their hearts and their ideals, blessed by their prayers and their faith, must resort to a draft to fill the ranks of an Army which ought to have been filled three times over by devoted men? To such a pass has America come, that not even this mortal threat to her very existence can stir the sluggish pulse and the dead souls of her people. If I did not love her so much I would say: 'Let her die, and let these swine die in her death!' "

She was ashamed, and alarmed. She looked at the river, the earth at her feet. This was America. She had never known it before, nor cared to know it. There was a quickening in her blood, a flush on her face.

"I have tried to enlist," said Stuart bitterly. "But they would not take me. I might have had a commission, but they said my health was precarious. My God! I am a healthy man, full-blooded and strong. It is true I have gout, and a rumbling heart, but my resolution would overcome them, I know."

He looked at her. "Your brothers: have they spoken of joining the Army?"

Laurie gave him a twisted smile. "They have all bought alternates, I think."

Stuart groaned in his huge contempt and disgust. "Alternates! Pay a desperate man money to die in your stead, while you fatten on the profits of war! Buy your safety with his life, so that you may continue to lie in a soft bed and breed weaklings, cowards and traitors like yourself!"

Laurie frowned a little. She had very little family loyalty, but the tone of Stuart's voice and words offended her. One did not like to realize that one was related to "weaklings, cowards and traitors." She said: "Perhaps you are not aware of all the circumstances, Stuart."

"Circumstances! There is only one circumstance, and that is the danger to the Republic. There is nothing else."

They walked back towards the house. The mauve twilight, drained and misty, had settled over the river and the earth.

Stuart, with his subtle intuition, felt that Laurie had become cold and distrait. He was filled with compunction, though his unsteady heart was paining him enormous. On the path that led to the house he put his arms about her and embraced her with sad ardor. "Have I offended you, my love?"

She hesitated. Offended her? How could he offend her? The loved one could never offend beyond forgiveness and forgetting. She seized his sleeves and pressed herself to him passionately.

"Offend me? How could you? There is nothing you could do, Stuart, that I could not forgive, or forget, or understand."

CHAPTER 60

MAYOR CUMMINGS sat with Robbie Cauder over their after-dinner glass of port.

They were very fond of each other, and it was this fondness that had made Robbie consent to occupy the second floor of the pretty mansion on Delaware Avenue. The Mayor felt that he had indeed acquired a son in this small, neat, black-eyed and subtle Scotsman, who, though so reticent and reserved, had a kind of wholeness and ironic integrity which pleased his father-in-law. Robbie had become the Mayor's complete confidant, and the older man found it inexpressibly relieving to discuss with him his troubles and tribulations of office.

The Mayor was discussing the powerful upper clique of Grandeville, and it was evident that he did not like them. "They have consistently opposed the coming of various manufactories into the city," he said. "Look at Detroit, Chicago. How fast they are growing, and how progressive they are! But not so with Grandeville, apparently. It is growing reluctantly, but only reluctantly. We have a pack of old fuddy-duddies here, who like dirty cobbled streets, ugly houses and dank lawns, and what they call 'peace.' They live in an orbit of their own. The 'masses,' as they call them, do not exist in their elegant consciousness."

The Mayor smiled wryly. "In a feudal society, which these grand ladies and gentlemen who are the offspring of sausage-makers, slaughter-house owners and tanners would adore, the clique could operate with safety. But we have no knouts here, no fawning police, no subduing clergy, no Praetorian guard or military caste, which would keep the people oppressed and silent. We have a republican society, and fools who isolate themselves from the growth of a republic, or of a city, are in danger of losing not only their properties, but their lives. They stagnate a city; they destroy its potentialities. In a republic, a people must grow or they will die. Dozens of manufactories could come to Grandeville, but the simpering sons of the abattoirs and stinking tanneries say: 'Oh, no! Let us keep dear Grandeville as it was when we were children!' So industry moves westward, to the smug pleasure of Detroit and Chicago."

The little rotund Mayor puffed impatiently at his cheroot. "I might forgive them if they had an authentic aristocratic tradition. Their souls smell of the tanneries and the offal heaps. I could laugh at them, but when I see that Grandeville could become the gateway to the West, a vast industrial center of prosperity and hope, then I do not laugh at all. I despise them, and their pretensions."

He stood up, put his fat little hands under his coat-tails, and walked up and down the pleasant dining-room, from which the ladies had retired. "More than all this, I am worried over the situations they are creating. It is true that anti-Catholic and anti-'foreigner' riots are rampant over the country. But they are especially bad in Grandeville. Why?

Because, perhaps, the people hatingly resent the fact that they are despised and ostracized, that their opportunities are limited, the situation hopeless. It is in the nature of humanity to hate something, always. But instead of hating the injustices and tragedies which have caused this war, and the men who have profited by these things, they must hate something more immediate. A man cannot harbor abstract hatred, though he ought to try to for the good of his soul. He cannot hate cruelties to other men, and intolerances, though again, he ought to try. He cannot be a full human being unless he possesses this salutary hatred. But it is easier for him to hate his neighbor, and oppress him, particularly if that neighbor is weaker and more defenseless than himself."

The Mayor sat down and frowned anxiously at Robbie. "I'm worried, for instance, about old Houlihan, to come back to immediate matters. He was forced to come to me for protection. Last month he delivered a fervid sermon to his congregation on the subject of passionate patriotism. America, he said, has grown upon the bones of devoted and dedicated men, and has been nourished by their blood and their faith. She is deserving of every heart-beat of every man, of every hand, and every soul. If her children desert her, then she must die, and the guilt will be upon us all. He urged every man in his congregation not to wait for the draft, but to enlist at once. He castigated the devourers and the traitors, the evaders and the indifferent. He spoke of the draft riots in New York, and declared that they were a shame and a crime before the face of God. A crime against America, he said, was a crime against all humanity, for in America was the hope of the world. Who betrayed America betrayed all the martyrs throughout the ages.

"Oh, apparently it was a passionate sermon! So passionate, so fervid, that he was met on a dark street one night and again severely beaten. By whom? By those who hate America, of course. Ruffians hired by our Schnitzels and our Schnickelburgers and our Zimmermanns, who hate liberty and tolerance and justice, who hate the common man and his hope for life and dignity. Scoundrels armed by our Kents, our Hamiltons, our Brewsters, and all the 'aristocratic' clique who wish to acquire property and serfs to cultivate and extend that property. To me, the worst of all is that these very ruffians and scoundrels are the oppressed, themselves!"

He resumed: "When a man speaks of preserving America

for Americans, he means preserving America for his private exploitation and greed and hatred."

"Poor old Father Houlihan," said Robbie. "There's a firebrand for you. Frankly, I've never given much thought to America. But when one meets such a rip-roaring and bellicose patriot it makes one stop and think. He has courage, too. Can you extend any protection to him?"

"I've tried. But there are forces here that frighten me. I'm not liked, you know, Robbie, though I've managed to be re-elected frequently," and he smiled.

He went on: "The poor old priest is getting himself thoroughly hated not only by those he attacks, but even by those he defends! It is the history of martyrs, but it never fails to surprise and stun me by its very colossal stupidity and incredible blindness. I understand that some of his wealthier parishioners have even gone to the bishop with a demand that he be removed. The wealthier parishioners prefer that cold white stick of a Billingsley, who has a proper regard for the vested interests. So far as Father Houlihan is concerned, bless his naïve soul, the vested interests consist of God and the people, an error for which he has paid, and will continue to pay."

The Mayor sighed. "If I didn't have some conscience, and some admiration for hot-headed innocents like Father Houlihan, I could be a happy man," he said ruefully.

The July night was hot and sultry. Sheets of heat lightning lit up the western horizon against which trees restlessly swayed their black plumes in uneasy and disordered rhythm.

The Mayor said, as he stood before a long french window and breathed deeply of the freshening wind: "And there's Stuart. I'm worried about Stuart. Things are getting bad in the country. The sudden prosperity is subsiding. The people are beginning to look wan and peaked. It was bad enough for Stuart when the shops were crowded. I'm afraid it is much worse, now that the whole national economy is tightening as the war proceeds."

"Perhaps it will soon be over—the war," said Robbie, watching his father-in-law with affection. The old man, himself, was looking "wan and peaked" these days. What a thing it was to have a conscience. Apparently the little "voice of God" was a disquieting thing to possess, and made for unhappiness and spiritual torment. "The war can't go on much longer, Father. We've captured Vicksburg, and the South must see that the whole thing is hopeless, now. We've got Port Hudson, and as Mr. Lincoln says: "The Confederacy is cut in twain. The Father of Waters now rolls unvexed to the sea."

He added: "Don't worry about Stuart. He is always saved in the nick of time, both from himself and from bankruptcy."

The Mayor hesitated. He peeped at Robbie over his spectacles. He rubbed his chin. He said: "By the way, how is Laurie coming along these days?"

"She is knee-deep in rehearsals. She opens the Astor Place Opera House in November with an opera called *Tannhaüser*, I believe. Written by some impossible old German, Wagner. She sent us some New York newspapers, and New York is purported to be very excited over it. We may go down to New York to hear her, though it is such a distance and not to be undertaken lightly."

He watched the Mayor closely, for the old man was palpably uneasy. He coughed a little.

"Laurie will go far," said Mr. Cummings. "What a sensation she made in Grandeville! They are still discussing it, with venom. Laurie violated all conventions about females when she demonstrated what a voice she has. Her ways, too, are very brusque."

He was still uneasy. Robbie watched him with sudden wariness. But the old man did not speak again, but only eyed his son-in-law with apologetic anxiety.

"Laurie," said Robbie, "will always do the thing good for Laurie. You can depend on that."

The Mayor stopped to gaze at some wax fruit and flowers under a glass dome. They were excellently done, but he had seen them often, too often to be absorbed in them now with such concentration. He rubbed a blunt forefinger over the shining glass. Finally he said: "Where is Stuart these days, Robbie? In New York?"

Robbie's eyes narrowed. He replied casually: "Yes. I believe he is. There is some chance that an English shipment will be coming in for him."

The Mayor was silent. Then Robbie said smoothly: "You mean, do you not, Father, that there is some talk about Stuart and Laurie?"

The old man actually blushed. He wiped his forehead, rubbed his kerchief between his stock and his wrinkled neck. Then he said frankly: "Yes, Robbie. I do mean that. Oh, please don't misunderstand me! I know there is nothing—wrong. But people are talking that they were seen together too frequently, alone, near the river, when she was here, and that one day, the day before she left, they drove together down to Niagara Falls, and spent the night at the Cataract House. That is a canard, a vile canard! I know that, and I've combated the scandal as well as I could. I said that if this were so, her mother accompanied her."

Robbie smiled behind his hand. "Laurie is beyond scandal," he remarked. "Unfortunately Grandeville doesn't concede that, being so provincial. After all, too, Stuart has been like a father to us." The Mayor did not see Robbie's cynical smile. "He is our mother's cousin, and without him Laurie could have accomplished nothing. He gave Angus his position, and worked to have me elected judge. He has devoted much time to Bertie, too. However, people will talk."

The Mayor swallowed. "Yes. Yes, of course. But—but friends of people here have written from New York that Stuart is seen everywhere in that city with Laurie, and that they appear quite—quite loverlike. New York is charmed, they say. But Grandeville isn't charmed, unfortunately. Stuart must live here. He has his wife and child here, and his business. It might be—unpleasant for him."

"Have you talked to Stuart?" asked Robbie, amused.

"I leave that to his family—you," replied the Mayor, with simplicity.

"Me!" exclaimed Robbie. And he laughed. "He would boot me out. You're his friend, Father. Why not try, yourself?"

The Mayor shrugged helplessly. Robbie continued: "Suppose we just leave it in Stuart's hands, and insist all is innocent. As it is, of course. That is the best defense, both for Stuart and Laurie. If we speak of it openly, and with pleasure and affection, as if it were the most natural thing in the world for a middle-aged kinsman to be concerned with the advancement of his protégée, then no one can say much. If I make it a point to announce openly, at our party next week, that Laurie has written that Stuart beaus her about the city, and is very proud of her, and she is devotedly grateful to him, I am certain that much of the scandal will die down, or at least will go under cover." He added: "You are thinking of Alice, aren't you, Father?"

"Yes, of course, my dear boy. She mustn't be agitated just now."

"Alice," said her husband, "is a lot tougher than you know, Father. She has, for a long time, been quite aware that Laurie and Stuart are—fond—of each other."

His voice trembled a little as he spoke of his wife, and his face darkened slightly, as if with pain.

The Mayor said, "I wanted to ask your opinion, Robbie.

There is the matter of River Island. I have approved the sale to Sam Berkowitz. I was not prepared for the storm this has raised. You know what has happened. Handbills have been printed and distributed condemning my action, and calling Sam the foulest of names. I'm afraid there will be some sort of trouble. Old Allstairs was set on the Island, but he offered no more than eight thousand, and Sam, after the approval of the Council, will pay eleven thousand. The Council can't get over that. If they disapprove the sale, there will be many questions why. They have no excuse, you know. Old Allstairs is behind all the popular agitation, of course. In all my life, in my own country, I've never before heard a man cursed for being a Jew. I hear it now. Allstairs has several ministers raving from the pulpits, like demented half-wits. Naturally, Old Allstairs is thinking of his pocket, and to gain his ends he is creating feeling in the city against Sam. What am I to do?"

Robbie's small neat face tightened. "You will stand by your approval, of course, Allstairs or no Allstairs, and his demented friends. I understand that Allstairs wishes to buy the Island for eight thousand dollars, and will then sell it to Sam for twenty thousand. That is his sole purpose in creating this agitation. Once he has bought the Island, and resold it to Sam, you'll be surprised what a good fellow Sam will be once again, in the eye of our psalm-singing old acquaintance."

"The villainy of mankind surpasses my understanding!" exclaimed the Mayor, with passion.

"The villainy of mankind," said Robbie, "comes up to my expectations."

The Mayor was much disturbed. "I shall put pressure on the Council to approve the sale," he said resolutely. "Sam shall have the Island if it is over my dead body. I have always hated Allstairs. He is a bad influence in Grandeville, and though my city has its faults, I still love it."

Alice and her mother were waiting for the gentlemen in the drawing-room. Mrs. Cummings was placidly sewing the christening robe for her expected grandchild. The glistening folds of lace and silk spread over her purple hoops to the floor. But Alice, though her face brightened at the sight of her father and her husband, appeared pale and exhausted. She was fanning herself listlessly. Robbie went to her and took her hand, examining her face anxiously.

"It is the heat, my love," she said, answering his unspoken question.

It was almost her time now, and Mrs. Cummings spent

many quick hours on the robe. Robbie tenderly smoothed the damp brown curls on his wife's head, and ran his hand under them at the nape of her neck. They were quite wet. Alice's gentle mouth was fixed and mauve, her eyes sunken. Her heavy and ungainly body was wrapped in a white lace silk wrapper, and her feet had been lifted to a footstool.

The evening was very hot, and the fresh wind had died. But the lightning brightened balefully in the west, and now there were faint rumblings in the distance. The windows had been closed against the swarm of mosquitoes, and the lamplight revealed myriads of them crawling and fluttering over the polished panes, attempting to enter. The summer had been unusually warm, and very sultry. It was a choice, Robbie observed, of being eaten alive or enjoying the slight breeze. As for himself, he preferred to be devoured in comparative comfort, but one had to consider Alice who had little blood to spare.

Mrs. Cummings sewed. The Mayor read his paper. Robbie sat beside his wife, and talked gently to her. Nothing could have been softer and tenderer than his voice. The girl listened to him, smiling, her little hand in his. Her weary and sunken eyes were fixed on his face with intense love. Sometimes her mouth moved, as if in sad and involuntary yearning. But she said little. However, her heart cried over and over: When will you truly belong to me, my darling? You speak to me with such sweetness and tenderness, but there is something held away from me, which should be mine, too.

She was too tired this hot night to think much of anything except how terribly she loved her husband. His hand, though small, had a strength and firmness in it which she needed. When he touched her, she had to turn her head away to hide her tears. But she clung to his hand.

The storm was coming closer. There was a sudden uneasy threshing in the trees outside, a deeper muttering of thunder. The heat in the parlor increased. The Mayor put down his paper, and his face was crimson. He stood up. Robbie had begun to examine some of his legal papers, but when his father-in-law rose, he also rose, politely.

"Let's have a little turn in the garden, shall we?" asked Mr. Cummings of his family.

Alice shook her head slightly. But she added quickly, as Robbie appeared about to resume his chair beside her: "I'm too tired, I'm afraid. But Robbie, my love, do go with Papa into the garden, for a little fresh air. Mama will stay with me."

The two men left the house and strolled up and down in the dark gardens. The wind had raised late July scents from the earth and the flowers, and they filled the air with smothering intensity. The dark plumes of the trees swayed against the lightning. The earth reverberated with the approaching thunder. Beyond the walls, the street lamps flickered fitfully, and a carriage or two rattled home precipitately over the cobbled streets beyond the gardens. Somewhere a dog barked. In the intervals of thunder and wind the silence was thick and black and hot. "We need the rain," said the Mayor, as he and Robbie walked the gravelled paths, smoking together. "Everything drying up."

They talked of legal matters. Robbie discussed a case or two with his father-in-law. The lightning lit up the western horizons constantly now, so that each could see the other's face plainly. But though the trees and the flowers threshed, no rain fell.

Suddenly Robbie halted. "Did you hear a cry?" he asked.

The Mayor stopped, and listened. Yes, there was a faint cry from the house, and from it came a curious emanation of agitation. The two men hurried back, rushing up the stairs, Robbie ahead, the Mayor panting in his rear. They were met by Mrs. Cummings, very pale and trembling, but smiling.

"I'm afraid it's begun, my dears," she said, through quivering lips. "I'm sending the carriage at once for the doctor. And now, will you please help me with Alice?"

They carried Alice, moaning, but trying to smile, up to her bed. Her head lay on Robbie's shoulder during the journey up the stairs. Her father, in his perturbation, exclaimed over and over: "There, now, there now. Mustn't be excited, my darling. We are all here. We shall take care of you. Don't cry, now. Another step. Easy. Very easy." His face was purple and wet with his exertions. But Alice looked only at her husband, though her eyes were dilated with her surges of pain.

They laid her on her bed, and a maid sent them out of the room while she undressed her mistress. The Mayor and Robbie descended to the hall again. Robbie was pale, but bright-eyed. The Mayor, extremely upset, apparently thought the young man in a condition quite bordering on pre-paternal insanity, for he cried over and over: "Mustn't upset yourself, now! It will soon be over. I've been through this before. Sit down, man, sit down!" He, himself, raced back and forth through the room, while Robbie watched him with secret and affectionate amusement. The Mayor continued: "Nothing in male nature, sir, is equal to such an emergency, and one must leave it to God and to nature!"

"I am quite willing, sir," murmured Robbie. But the Mayor did not hear him.

There was a ringing of the bell, and the Mayor, not waiting for a servant, bolted furiously to the door, crying: "The doctor!" But it was not the doctor, but a maid from Janie's house, who wished to speak to Mr. Cauder. Robbie came into the hall, and the girl exclaimed: "Oh, sir, it's Mr. Bertie, sir! Mrs. Cauder is quite upset, sir, and wishes you to come at once! Mr. Bertie's not been home for two days, and the mistress is quite out of her mind!"

The Mayor cried impatiently: "Please express our regrets to your mistress, girl, but it is impossible for Mr. Cauder to come. There is a matter of—of importance—transpiring——"

But Robbie advanced towards the girl. He was very white and very quiet. He said: "I will come at once."

The Mayor heard this, dumfounded. His mouth fell open. He glared at Robbie, stupefied. His lips moved, over and over, before he could stammer: "But, there is Alice! She needs you. The doctor—the doctor will be here at any moment. You can't possibly mean you are leaving, Robbie?"

Robbie looked at the Mayor. He said in a still, firm voice: "I must go. Alice is well taken care of. Besides, I shall return very shortly."

The Mayor stared at the young man's curiously taut and colorless face, at his strange fixed eyes. He could not recognize him. His heart boiled with indignation and incredulity. He said thickly: "You can't leave your wife, now. Your wife, sir. She needs you. My daughter. Your brother is a drunkard and a blackguard, sir, and is out on one of his disgraceful sprees. You would leave my daughter, your wife, in order to find him and pull him from the gutter, again?"

Robbie clenched his hands. The girl, highly diverted and excited, looked eagerly from one man to the other in the flickering lamplight. The thunder was coming closer.

Robbie said: "You don't understand. My brother has never stayed away like this. It must be something—quite frightful. He may be dead. I've got to find him. I couldn't stay here, wondering what had happened to him. It will be some hours before Alice— I must go. But I shall return immediately, when I have some news of Bertie."

He moved towards the door. But the Mayor, recovering

partly from his stupefaction, bounded after him, grasped him by the arm. His face was crimson, his eyes full of fire. "You cannot go, sir! I forbid it! I forbid this disgraceful and unfeeling desertion of your wife! You must be out of your mind!"

Robbie, with fingers as stiff and cold as ice, removed the restraining hand from his arm. "I must go," he repeated. His voice was like steel, but quicker now. "You may tell Alice, if you wish. She will understand." His eyes regarded the Mayor as if they did not see him. There was a silent and fanatical torment in them. "She will understand," he repeated. "This is a matter of life and death to me."

"Life and death!" stuttered the Mayor, staggering so that he had to catch the newel post to save himself. "It is my daughter who is facing life or death. Your wife. Yet for the sake of your brother you will leave her in her hour of need!" He drew a smothered breath. "If you leave her now, sir, I shall never forgive you, never."

"That I must chance, sir," said Robbie. "But Alice will forgive. She will know."

Appalled, still disbelieving, the Mayor watched him run down the white stone steps of the house, saw his slight compact figure lit by lightning. And then he was gone.

CHAPTER 61

THE WIND, lightning and thunder increased to a pitch of fury as Robbie sat in the carriage his mother had sent for him. He crouched on the edge of the leather seat, as if prepared to spring out the moment the vehicle halted. He was completely unaware of the servant girl opposite him, wrapped in her shawl. He heard nothing of the threshing of torn trees and the mighty cart-wheels of the thunder rolling through the boiling heavens, nor did he see the continuous glare of lightning. Street-lamps flickered and dimmed; clouds of chaff and dust swept through the cobbled streets, which had emptied of strolling summer crowds.

Robbie's delicate jaw was clenched, the bones protruding, his eyes staring ahead. He did not move during the drive. But there was a sickness and faintness in the pit of his stomach, and a pounding ache in his head. He had completely forgotten his young wife, now writhing in labor. He

thought only of Bertie, with frantic intensity. Now, he had
been gone two days and a night, without any word or trace
of him. He is dead, thought Robbie, the sinking sensation
almost overpowering him. His body arched with frenzied
haste; his heart beat so rapidly that he could hardly breathe.
All his muscles were cramped and aching. What had happened to Bertie? Where had he gone? Had he, in the midst
of his delirium, hurled himself into the river? Robbie tried
to calm himself. The negation of life did not always argue
that the harborer of such negation desired death. Those who
had no love for life rarely yearned for extinction. Unless,
unless, he had been swept into death because he would make
no struggle to survive when threatened. He might have
wandered off in his drunkenness, fallen into the river, flung
up his arms with a smile, and gone down as listlessly and as
compliantly as he had lived.

I should never have left him, never, thought Robbie. If
he is dead, then I am guilty of his death. I should have remained with him. He had no real love for me, but he trusted
me. He went where I wished, did as I asked, complied with
everything I suggested. Surely he loved me a little; surely he
had some consideration for me. Surely he would not do this
thing which would cause me such an agony!

All his calm reason was swept away in the wind of his
anguish. He called out in himself: Bertie! Bertie, wait for me!
I'm coming. He felt his urgency leave him like a loud and
imploring voice, reaching across space, holding back his
brother from the ultimate darkness. Now there was a stinging
along his eyelids, an acid burning. His voice could not reach
Bertie; his hands were empty. Always, Bertie had escaped
him with a smile, and when he had grasped him, Bertie had
looked at him with a strange and shining look of warning
which had made Robbie let go.

For the first time Robbie asked himself: Why have I loved
him like this? And there was no answer. There was no answer even in the books of normal affection, nor in the dark
questioning volumes written by men who were beginning to
explore the hidden and shrouded continent of the human
mind. It is an obsession, thought Robbie. But why have I
been so obsessed, or so possessed?

The house on Porter Avenue was lit from top to bottom.
Robbie sprang out of the carriage before it reached the steps,
and he was running fleetly up those steps into the house. He
was met in the hall by Janie, red-eyed, dishevelled, and weeping loudly. She clung to Robbie, moaning incoherently. He

led her into the hot, lamplit parlor, and then cried out: "No news, yet? Have you notified the police? Where was he seen last? When did he disappear? Did he say anything?"

She tried to speak through her tears, and in his wild impatience Robbie shook her savagely. Distracted, even in the midst of her fear and misery, by his look, his vehemence, she could only gape at him for several moments. Then, with a strange stare at him, she pulled herself from his grasp and stepped back a pace or two, wetting her dry and shaking lips. "Robbie," she said, "ye are fair mad, man. Calm yourself."

Still staring at him, she reached behind her for a chair, and sat down. She was shivering, in spite of the intense heat. She could not look away from him. She said again: "Calm yourself. You are demented, Robbie. Don't look at me like that. Be a man. Sit down, and we shall talk of it."

But he stood before her, and she had never seen his eyes like this, so distraught. She tried to keep her hoarse voice low and quiet, for he filled her with fear. Bertie, she said, had told her two days ago he wished to buy some new cravats. That was about eleven in the morning. He had appeared quite normal. He had kissed her that day, as he always did, and with nothing odd in his manner. It had been only two months since his last bout, and one was not again due for at least another month. She had given him some money, and she had asked him to stop in at the shops and request that Angus call on her that evening on a matter of business. He consented. He had also mentioned that he would be back in time for tea, and that he would pick up her copy of *Godey's Lady's Book* on the way home, a copy which she had lent to Mrs. Hathaway. As it was such a fine morning he had not ordered a carriage, and had gone off, whistling, evidently at peace with the world and himself, and showing no signs of the ominous restlessness, silence and abstraction which always preceded his bouts by at least three days. He had had little money, and had not urged her for more.

Robbie listened with passionate attention, his eyes never leaving his mother's face. He said, when she paused: "He did not kiss you as if—as if he intended to go on a long journey, or anything? He took nothing with him? He did not look about him, as if it was for the last time?"

"What are you saying, man?" Janie cried, frantically. "Certainly not. My bonny boy! I would have known it in my heart if there had been something wrong with him, if he had any—peculiar intention. It was all so ordinary. He did not even look back as he went down the street. What are you trying to say, Robbie?"

But Robbie began to walk up and down the room, hurling short fierce questions at her. She replied to them as shortly, through her tears. Yes, the police had been notified. All the taverns which Bertie usually haunted had been visited. He had appeared at none of them. As far as anyone knew, he had not had a single drink. A few people admitted having seen him, walking and whistling down Delaware Avenue, or Main Street. But he had not gone to the shops. Angus had not seen him, nor Stuart.

Bertie had disappeared as if the earth had swallowed him up. The last person who had seen him? A young man, a lieutenant in the Army. Bertie had been spied talking to the young officer at the corner of Niagara and Hudson Streets, at about four that afternoon. Mrs. Fiske had seen him, from her carriage, and had bowed to him, and he had bowed back with his usual graciousness. No, she had never seen the officer before. It was nothing unusual for Bertie to strike up acquaintances with strangers, and converse with them affably and with apparent interest for several minutes, and even to walk with them.

"Has anyone seen the lieutenant, questioned him, found him?" exclaimed Robbie.

Yes, the police had found him at an enlistment center on Niagara Street. He was John Girard, from New York City, stationed now at The Front. He readily remembered Bertie, for he had stopped Bertie in a friendly enough fashion on Niagara Street, and asked him why he was not in the Army. Bertie had affably replied that he was "quite the invalid," and had changed the subject. They had fed pigeons together, and had discussed the war with considerable interest. John had been charmed with his new friend. He had asked him to dine with him at a near-by tavern, but Bertie had politely refused. He had some "business" to attend to, he had explained.

Robbie turned to his mother at this, and something of the gray tension relaxed in his face. His most terrible fear was partly allayed. "Not near the river!" he exclaimed.

Suddenly, over the wind and the rainless storm they heard the opening and shutting of a door. Janie sprang to her feet with a cry, and she and Robbie ran into the hall. But it was only the rigid, white-faced Angus in his broadcloth who stood there quietly and composedly, and something like an involuntary curse upon him rose to Janie's despairing lips.

Angus gave Robbie his usual cold and distant glance of recognition. Then he put his thin black arm about his mother, who strained against his embrace. He said: "So, he hasn't returned yet? This is terrible. Thoughtless, cruel, insensible! But it is to be expected of such a drunkard and blackguard and fool!"

With one fierce and vehement motion, Janie freed herself from him, glared at him with fiery eyes. "Be off with you, you wooden stick of a wretch!" she screamed. "How dare you speak of my darling Bertie like this? Who wants you about here, you heartless praying corpse of a man? Get out of my house!"

She was hysterical, mad, unable to control herself. Angus stepped back from her, blinking, the pallor on his face graying, his eyes sick with suffering. She stamped her foot at him, shrieked at him, cursed him with foam on her lips. The years of her hatred fumed at her mouth, expressed itself in obscene and unspeakable words. Her eyes were insane with her hatred, her despair, her terror and agony. And Angus stood and listened, not moving, his hands hanging slack at his sides, and with such a look on his face that not even the cynical Robbie could endure it. Whatever Angus was, he did not deserve this monstrous tirade of loathing and detestation and repudiation. He had loved his mother, had obeyed and served her, had hung upon her steps and had given her the only devotion of her life.

When Janie paused for sheer lack of breath, Angus said softly: "You really hate me, don't you, Ma?" His voice was strange and wondering, and faint, and his brow was wrinkled.

"Hate you?" screamed Janie, recovering herself. "I've hated you since you were born, you with your prayers, and your kirk, and your psalms, and your mealy-mouthed texts, and your cursed 'duty' and 'honor' and obedience! I've hated the sickly sight of you, the very sound of your voice, your sly steps, your pious looks, your sermons and your parsonish airs! You've never been a man. You've been a stick, a corpse, an idiot, all your life, whining and whimpering like a dog at my heels, wanting me to love you! Love you? Damn you, I say, damn you to hell, you loathsome slimy thing!"

Her face was demented, her teeth and green eyes glistening savagely and with merciless gloating in the light of the flickering lamp. She stamped at him. She mouthed at him.

And Angus only listened, his head bent forward a little, his gaze fixed on her intently, his pale mouth still and quiet.

"I have wished you dead a thousand times!" screamed Janie, with renewed fury. "Why can't you be lying at the bottom of your grave, or the river? You've been like a vile disease in my house, infecting it! It was a joyous day when you left, and I've only prayed that I need never see you again!" Suddenly she burst into terrible tears. "Why can't it be you who has gone, and no trace? Why must it be you standing here, and not my bonny boy?"

Angus stirred. He drew a deep and audible breath, and to Robbie it was an infinitely awful sound, as if a heart was breaking. He appeared to shrink and dwindle in his heavy black clothing. He lifted his hand and pressed it abstractedly to his temple. He sighed again.

A surge of profound and aching sympathy and compassion passed through Robbie. It was absurd to think it of Angus, but there it was: all his life he had sought for someone to love, who would love him in return. But he had been repudiated by everyone. He had been hated and despised by Janie, rejected with cynical scorn by Laurie, ignored by Bertie, laughed at by Robbie, devoured by his wife. Yet he had only wanted to be loved, and to serve. At the last then, he had been rejected not only by the poor and valueless creatures about him, but by God, Himself.

Robbie stepped in now. He laid his hand on Angus' arm, and said, with quietness: "Don't listen to Ma. She's distracted, naturally, at Bertie's disappearance. Let's go into the parlor."

Angus abstractedly shook off his brother's arm. He walked into the parlor. He moved as if bemused, or as if in a dream. His gray eyes were clouded, darkened, with deep and voiceless suffering. Once in the parlor he walked to the cold hearth and stood beside it, looking down at the floor. Robbie led his stormily weeping mother to a chair, and set her in it.

Robbie began to talk again, quietly, explaining to his brother that Bertie had not yet been found, but that there was no reason to fear any violence. Angus said nothing. It was impossible to know whether he was listening. Only the occasional movement of his eyelids testified to any life in him.

"We're continuing the search," said Robbie. He lit a cheroot, and the striking of the lucifer was like a sharp crack in the room. He put the cheroot in his mouth, regarded the ceiling thoughtfully. His own frenzy had disappeared in this

new emergency, and there was an odd relaxing in him, as of
relief and reassurance. "There'll be news shortly, I have no
doubt. Bertie's not been in the taverns, or—or near the river,
and everyone who has seen him has declared that he appeared perfectly normal."

He glanced at Angus. Angus stirred, as if the movement
was a profound effort. He lifted his dead gray eyes and fixed
them on Robbie. But he still said nothing. Janie was weeping
more quietly now, after Robbie's words. She held out a
trembling hand to him, and whimpered: "Ye are the only
consolation and comfort to me now, my little lad."

Robbie looked at her hand, and he thought: It is the hand
of a murderess. This was the one which had struck Angus to
his death, made of Laurie a hard and dominant and remorseless trollop, driven Bertie into his negation of life and perhaps into his grave. It is the hand of a murderess, he thought.
And he looked at her hand, and then into her face, not
moving.

Janie looked back at him, and suddenly her swollen green
eyes narrowed with understanding, and gleamed with hatred
for him. Her teeth bared. But she made no sound.

In that hollow gaunt silence, filled with bitter and frozen
emotions, deadly and unforgiving and heart-broken, no one
heard the quiet entrance of another man, in the uniform of
the Army of the United States. He stood in the doorway,
looking at the three petrified people in the room, smiling a
little, his thin but erect figure clad in Union Blue, his hat
half-hiding the shining blue of his eyes.

It was Robbie, turning his long and piercing gaze from
his mother, who saw the soldier first, and so intense had been
his thoughts that for a moment he could only stare, thinking
confusedly: It is Bertie's friend. And then he saw that it was
not a stranger who stood there, so silent, so smiling, but,
Bertie himself.

Brother looked at brother across the length of the room,
before either Angus or Janie was aware of the newcomer.
And Bertie, still smiling, still motionless, gazed back at
Robbie.

All at once Robbie felt a swelling and pulsing in his heart
which was both pain and joy and fear. He went silently
across the carpet and held out his hand to his brother. Bertie
looked at that hand, and then he took it, not slowly and indifferently, but with strength and firmness, and with warmth.
They did not smile now.

There was a faint sound behind them, a smothered and

gasping moan. Janie was rising slowly and stiffly from her chair, her shawl dropping from her shoulders, her face idiotic with stupefaction, her mouth working soundlessly. And then, with a loud hoarse cry, she was running across the carpet, her arms held out, tears pouring from her eyes. Robbie released his brother's hand; the strong warm tingle of it was still in his flesh. Janie flung her arms about her son, pressed her face to his chest, clutched him frantically, uttering incoherent cries the while, imploring him, blessing him, running her hands over him as if to reassure herself that he was alive and close to her heart again, sobbing her thanks to God in the same voice that had cursed Angus hardly ten minutes before. She was completely beside herself. Bertie was forced to hold her firmly in his arms, or, in her transports of joy she would have collapsed at his feet. She snatched at his hands and kissed them; she strained to reach his cheek. She stroked his face and called him endearing names. Tears dashed from her eyes, quivered over her distended and grimacing mouth.

Robbie turned away. He could not refrain from pitying his mother, even though her ecstasy and joy had in them an element of savagery and violence, and shamelessness. He took a step or two in Angus' direction. Angus was looking at his mother and brother. His face was stark and tragic. But he made no move to go to Janie or to Bertie, or to speak.

Bertie, laughing, trying to calm his mother, half-carried, half-dragged her to a chair. But she would not release him. She kissed his hands, over and over. She ran her hands over his sleeve. It was not for some distraught moments that she realized the stuff of which that sleeve was made, and its color. When she did, her cries and exclamations and sobs halted abruptly, and she stared at the uniform with an expression completely blank and shocked.

Robbie came back to them. His own mind still had an area of stunned numbness in it, and now it slowly returned to life, throbbing dimly. He stood beside Bertie, his hand on his brother's shoulder.

Bertie was talking, easily, with his usual lightness and casual amiability. "I waited in the enlistment office all afternoon and evening, expecting every moment to see the officer in charge. But there were so many before me, and I was afraid to leave to send you a message lest someone else take my place. It was not until ten o'clock that my turn came, and the officer and I became so engrossed in our conversation that I was amazed to learn it was midnight. He invited me to share his lodgings behind the office, where we continued our conversation. I decided not to disturb you last night, but to return this morning, after my enlistment had been completed. It seems there was much to consider——"

He paused. He looked at Robbie now, smilingly, and Robbie, in silence, smiled back, his lips stiff and cold. And then he saw Bertie's eyes. They were no longer untenanted, filled only with their usual blank light. They were quiet and sparkling. But again Robbie saw the warning in them, not repudiating now, but pleading.

Janie held her son's hand to her breast. She did not stir. She only gazed at him steadfastly, every sallow freckle distinct on her sallow cheeks and large nose.

"The enlistment took all day. Many tests were given me. I didn't care about a commission. I only wanted to enlist as a common soldier. Finally, I was persuaded." He paused, then looked down at his mother. His free hand touched her cheek, very gently. He added, with slow softness: "I must leave tonight, for my training camp."

Robbie never knew what instinct made him reach his mother's side and press his hand against her shoulder, firmly, with hard pressure. She had opened her mouth wide, as if to cry out, but at his touch she fell silent, paling even more. She looked at Bertie with a strange and intense penetration, and her features became austere and even dignified with her repressed emotion and the warning Robbie had conveyed to her.

"Bertie," he said, looking full into his brother's eyes, "did you want to do this?" His voice was low and earnest.

Bertie smiled. He inclined his head. "I did, indeed."

Robbie was silent. Had Bertie actually been filled with desire for this? Had he actually been harboring in himself the pangs and passions of patriotism? Had this war truly had some meaning for him? Robbie could not recall that in two years of war Bertie had ever discussed the matter with him or with anyone else. He had read the papers, idly remarked on a battle, turned a page, yawned. What had been transpiring in him all this time? Robbie could not make himself believe that Bertie had hidden a secret excitement, a secret desire and resolution, in himself.

Bertie remained an enigma. He had answered his brother's question politely, and with easy amiability. He had made the conventional reply. Robbie bit his lip. But what lay behind that reply, and its immediate affirmation? What was America to Bertie, who had really never lived at all in this world?

Robbie said, aloud: "This is a wonderful thing, Bertie. A wonderful thing. I haven't congratulated you yet. I will do it now." And again he held out his hand to his brother, thinking: Go your way, Bertie. Try to find yourself, somewhere, somehow.

His thought was in his face, and Bertie saw it. He shook Robbie's hand with hard pressure.

Janie, too, must have had her thoughts. She was weeping again, but very softly now. She rose, stood on tiptoe, and kissed Bertie's cheek. "My braw laddie! My soldier laddie!" she murmured. "My handsome laddie! I'm proud of you, my darling."

Bertie regarded her with pleased surprise. He returned her kiss. He let her embrace him again. But over her head he looked at his brother, and Robbie, though his heart throbbed with sick presentiment, returned that look strongly, and with affection.

They all started a little when they saw that Angus stood near them, and was looking at them, for they had forgotten him. He was glancing slowly and wanly from Janie to Bertie. His gray eyes fastened themselves with inexorable bitterness and cold violence upon his younger brother.

"So this is all you can do, worrying your mother to death, forcing her to believe you had died in some gutter in your drunkenness or taken yourself to the river, and then returning like a conquering hero in a uniform you have no right to wear! A uniform which is meaningless to us, to you. You are a cheap and flamboyant rascal, sir, and I despise you, I repudiate you!"

His voice shaking with passion, with overwhelming and despairing emotion, with jealousy and anguish, rang through the room. He lifted a lean white finger and pointed it implacably at his brother, and there was such murderous hatred in his face that even Bertie lost his constant smile, and became grave and silent.

"All your life you have been a burden and a shame to your mother, a disgrace to your sister, an ignominy to your brothers! All your life you have lain on this family like a black cloud, humiliating us before our inferiors, besmirching our name and our honor. Do you think, sir, to inspire us with admiration for your folly? But I tell you this is your crowning achievement in our mortification, the last act calculated to hold us from our equals, our inferiors and our superiors in complete and disastrous ridicule."

His stern and narrow face, always so white and so expressionless, had become the face of a wild and hating demon. He was like one possessed. He vibrated with his emotions. He looked only at Bertie, who said nothing.

And then, before Janie could awake from her new stupefaction, he had turned and left the room, staggering a little, as if drunk.

Robbie sat beside Alice in the pale dawn light. The girl slept, her young face drawn and haggard, but at rest. Two hours ago she had given birth to a daughter, now lying in her crib in the nursery across the hall where Alice had lain.

For two hours Robbie had sat like this beside his wife, watching her. But he was not thinking of her, or even of his child. He was thinking of his brother. And he said to himself: I know I shall never see him again. He has gone away, forever.

There was in him now a wide and empty desolation in which pain walked like a specter. He looked steadily at the sleeping face of the girl, and saw only Bertie. It was not Alice's hand he held, but his brother's. When she sighed a little in her profound sleep, it was Bertie's sigh he heard.

He felt that he was not sitting in a room where life had entered, but in a room where death waited.

CHAPTER 62

"So," said Stuart, with elaborate mockery and rage, "you'll not be having them, eh? Well, let me tell you, Grundy, that you'll have them whether you want them or not! I'm paying for them, not you."

"I'll appeal to the police!" shouted Father Houlihan furiously. "I'll not be having your bruisers and your skullbreakers following on my steps! I'll have you thrown into gaol, you scoundrel!"

"I think," said Sam Berkowitz slowly, "that you should consider Stuart, Father."

"'Consider Stuart!'" bellowed the priest, all the dimness now gone from his energetic blue eyes, which were blazing. "He'll be having me followed by a corps of cutthroats and bullies, as if I were a criminal, by God! And that reminds me: God is my Protector. I don't need murderers with clubs and guns."

"God," remarked Stuart, "hasn't prevented you from having your skull almost broken three times. Or perhaps you walked into a door, that gave you those two grand black eyes, eh? And it was your worshipping, I presume, that brought that broken arm upon you. Slipped, perhaps, before the altar, when you raised the Host?"

"You dirty blasphemer!" screamed Father Houlihan, half rising from his chair with clenched fists. "I'll not be having a blasphemer and a defiler in my house! Get the hell out of here, before I throw you out in person!"

But Stuart only laughed, for Father Houlihan, in his vigorous movements, had set into loud protest numerous muscles still sore and bruised from his last beating at the hands of masked ruffians. The priest subsided into his chair again, with a groan. But his look was still fiery and suffused.

"I think," said Father Billingsley, in his neutral and precise voice, "that Father Houlihan is quite correct in his objections. No man needs more than the protection of God."

"He doesn't, eh?" asked Stuart contemptuously, and eyeing the younger priest with complete unpleasantness. "The evidence of history refutes you, Father. Or perhaps you are not a student of history?"

Stuart well knew that Father Billingsley was a very learned authority on history, that he had written a scholarly book on Napoleon and another on Gustavus Adolphus, both of which had attracted much attention among pedagogues on both Continents. Father Houlihan, momentarily distracted from his own personal rage, exclaimed: "Well, now, and that's a blackguardly thing to say, I'm thinking! You, who don't know the difference between Mount Etna and St. Helena! Or perhaps, sir, you wish to give Father Billingsley a lesson in history, yourself?"

Stuart was suddenly exasperated. "I could teach him, and you too, confound you, a very fine lesson in human nature, and a grand lesson on the wool-gathering of the Almighty, when He ought to be about protecting fools and children like yourselves! I'm tired of this nonsense. You'll have these—these excellent gentlemen to protect you, whether you want them or not, and they're good Irish Catholics, too, and you won't dare forbid them to follow on your heels right up to the altar. So resign yourself."

"I'll not have it!" shrieked the priest, brandishing his clenched fists.

"You already have it," responded Stuart, grinning.

He glanced at the two huge young Irishmen who were

standing respectfully near the door of the priest's neat little parlor. They returned his grin, touched their foreheads in a casual salute. Father Houlihan glared at them. "And why, may I humbly ask," he said with heavy sarcasm, "why are these fine lads not in the Army, instead of haunting a poor old harmless priest like myself?"

"They've already been in the Army, Grundy, and have been honorably discharged, with wounds. Walsh, here, is blinded in the right eye, and Cullen has a bullet in his hip. But their muscles are still splendid, and they know which end of a gun shoots, and they fire first and ask questions afterwards."

"So it's murderers I have guarding me! I'll be leaving a trail of corpses behind me! I'll not have it." The priest was quite beside himself.

"You already have it," Stuart repeated gently.

The priest exhaled with a snorting sound, and a ferocious look. He tried to quell the smiles of his new bodyguard. They returned his vitriolic glance with bland and innocent and respectful eyes. Sam laughed softly. "Stuart is very right, Father. You need protection. Stuart has no time to waste worrying over you. You must haf some regard for him."

"And Cullen confided in me that he hasn't made a confession for three years," said Stuart, smiling, "and Walsh hasn't attended Mass for nearly four. You can work on them at your leisure."

"Heretics, too," wailed Father Houlihan. He fixed the young men with a stern frown, and began to berate them on their default in duty. They listened humbly, with sad expressions, nodding their heads in agreement as his indignation mounted against them. Suddenly he began to laugh. His arm, only lately released from its sling, ached. He rubbed it absently.

"And who's to feed them, and house them?" he asked of Stuart, trying not to be too forgiving just yet.

"I have engaged rooms for them at Mrs. Murphy's, two doors down. They will take turns guarding you, one by day, the other by night. For instance Cullen, with his gun handy, will curl up on the threshold of your bedroom tonight, like a good dog. Tomorrow Walsh will follow humbly in your steps. You can get him a rosary and a prayerbook, and converse with him on religious matters as you go about your duties. He needs the re-education."

The priest gazed at Stuart, trying to retain his grim and furious expression. But it was hopeless. He sighed, and smiled. His voice shook a little when he said: "Stuart, you are a damned rascal and an obstinate wretch. Stuart, I love you." He extended his hand to his friend, who took it and pressed it warmly. The priest's eyes dwelt on him with obscure sadness.

Stuart said: "It's come to a fine pass when a man of God must be guarded, in America. It's an excellent thing to observe in a free Republic that harmless good women cannot leave their convent without being subjected to filthy insults and threats, and little children leaving their schools must be terrorized. It's a lovely scene to watch one like Sam, here, being spat upon in the public streets and receiving communications menacing his life. It soothes the heart with hopes for humanity and the progress of the human race, to discern these things."

But Father Houlihan said indignantly: "Mankind rises two steps, falls back one. But we've come a long way from the pit, and with the help of God we shall rise still higher. This is a time of stress, and men's passions are maddened. This, too, will pass."

"Oh, you and your love for America! You have me repeating your words all over the place, like a parrot." But Stuart, though his eyes remained somber, smiled a little. "Yes, this will pass. Perhaps. But the spores of hatred and cruelty have a long survival, and what is broadcast on the wind today will find a growing place tomorrow. Do not think that the spores which have settled on the soil of America in these days will die. They may have a long sleeping. But they will awake and grow, twenty, thirty, fifty, one hundred years from now. I feel it in my heart."

"They always grow. The soil is forever infected with them. But faith and love and mercy and justice will always destroy them, wherever they rise," said the priest earnestly. "I have never been afraid. I saw, and knew, the face of one of my attackers, but I brought no charges against him. It was not he who originated the disease. It was a man in one of these grand houses, who is afraid that my words threaten his soft bed, with its numerous occupants, his fine wines and table, his sparkling carriages, his swollen bank-accounts, and his bonds."

Stuart's face darkened uneasily. "And there's another thing. Grundy. When you spoke at Union Hall, and urged the workers in Schnitzel's slaughter-houses to demand higher wages, and to form a trade union against him for their protection, you did a dangerous thing. You've made a very deadly enemy. Oh, it's true that Schnitzel had to disgorge, but you've won a sinister victory. There were those other speeches you made, too, to the workers in Zimmermann's sausage factory, and to the workers on the docks and on the steamers, and in the steel manufactories, and other places. You've made Grandeville unsafe for you——"

"I've made it a more decent place for the workers!" cried the priest. "By God, do you think it is not the work of a priest to protect his people, to make their life more endurable, as well as to guard their souls? I despise those men of God who believe that a priest's work ends at the altar, where he must talk only of transcendental things. A man's belly must be fed before he listens to his soul. Justice must live, if religion, itself, would survive."

Stuart studied him with affection. "All right, Grundy. All right. I agree with you. But not one hundred dastardly workers is worth your little finger. They're the first to turn on you, remember, the first to listen to evil lies against you, even while they devour the more lavish food you've enabled them to eat, and the extra decent money you've put jingling into their pockets. Even while they lie under whole roofs, in reasonably comfortable beds—all procured by your work—they mull over the canards they've heard about you, and hate you."

"I can't believe it," whispered the priest. But the simple suffering on his tired face belied his words, and he turned aside his head. He sighed. "Even if it is so, I must do what I can. Sometime they will know, and understand."

Stuart rose. But Mrs. O'Keefe entered at that moment with the announcement that a light supper was being served for the gentlemen. She glanced at the hulking bodyguards with satisfaction, and graciously remarked that a generous plate of ham and some good beer was waiting for them also, in the kitchen. She gave Stuart a smug wink, which he returned. Father Billingsley rose with austerity, and asked Father Houlihan's permission to retire. The older priest watched his junior leave, and sighed deeply. He said to Stuart: "There is a good lad, a very good lad, and a fine soul. But as removed from the earth as if he——"

"Was spinning on your old proverbial needle point," added Stuart. "By the way, are you and Mother Mary Elizabeth reconciled yet?"

Father Houlihan laughed ruefully. "Ah, there is a very, very clever lady! So erudite. So saintly. She puts me to shame. I am afraid I am a great disappointment to her. My conversation is very vulgar, she believes, and as for the needle point business, I must confess that I still do not understand it."

"You know something much better, Grundy," said Stuart fondly.

They went into the little back sitting-room where Mrs. O'Keefe had laid out a most excellent supper. But Father Houlihan's usually robust appetite was feeble tonight. He furtively scrutinized Stuart. Yes, there was a change in the dear lad. He was thinner, and somewhat febrile, and his eye was very bright and restless. He appeared younger, more excitable and alive, it is true, almost as he had been ten years ago. But he could not rest; he was nervous and intense. Father Houlihan averted his eyes. The wider patches of gray in Stuart's hair had disappeared mysteriously. The priest thought that the saddest and most revealing thing of all. Also, a certain flamboyance and gaudy splendor in Stuart's dress had been subdued, and he was attired with a quiet elegance which had never been to his natural taste. He drank more than ever, but the drink did not make him exuberant as it used to do, but even more nervous and uneasy, and he had a way of becoming absent and darkly thoughtful. Several of his more garish rings had disappeared, and his jewelled watch-chain had been replaced by discreet and genteel links across waistcoats notable for their restraint.

Father Houlihan inquired about Marvina and Mary Rose. Stuart's expression subtly changed. He played with the silver near his plate. His wife and daughter were now at Saratoga, he said. Mary Rose was much improved, the doctors had assured him. But she needed the waters. In two weeks she and her mother would go to the mountains again for a few weeks, to complete the improvement in her health. They would be home in November.

The priest cleared his throat. And how was New York these days? Was the war affecting that city, also, to any great extent? Stuart carefully cut another slice of ham, though two slices still remained on his plate. Sam Berkowitz glanced anxiously and silently from his friend to the priest. Yes, the people were more shabby; they had less money, in New York. The streets were full of troops, and the soldiers improved their furloughs by considerable drunken rioting. But otherwise the city was quite gay. There was not so much to buy, for the blockade and Southern raiders had curtailed American shipping. However, the grand ladies were still lavishly attired, and he, Stuart, had never seen so many jewels.

"You'll be going to hear Laurie in her opera," suggested the priest, with what he considered much casual artfulness.

Stuart took another slice of bread. Of course he would be going to hear her. New York was very excited even now, though it was only September. It would be a fine thing if Grundy and Sam could go, also. It was bound to be spectacular and wonderful. Stuart's hand shook a little. His cheek flushed. His eye had the brightness of a man under the influence of alcohol.

And then he abruptly changed the subject.

It was not hard, the priest reflected, to help a man to the right path if that man could be made to see that the other path was evil, or if the man was evil, himself. But Stuart was not evil. He was a good man. He had only the faults of the excess of his virtues. Prodigal he might be, but his very prodigality in unworthy things sprouted from the prodigality of his generosity, his kindness, his warm passions and his capacity for love. The same rain and hot sun which caused the flowers, the trees, the grass, the fruit and the food of the earth to flourish in profusion also stimulated the growth of the poisonous weed, the tangled jungle, the barbed tree, the venomous berry.

What could he say to Stuart? That he was an adulterer, and in danger of hell-fire? That he had seduced a young woman, to her possible destruction? The priest smiled sadly to himself. Stuart had been an "adulterer" for many, many years, and Father Houlihan doubted very much that he was in danger of hell-fire. Hell-fire, he was convinced, was especially prepared and reserved for those virtuous men who possessed no charity or kindness in their souls, who prayed earnestly with their lips and hated their fellows with their minds, who sedulously haunted the churches and paid into their coffers and had nothing but malignance for humanity in their cold hearts. (Nor was Father Houlihan convinced that these virtuous men were hypocrites, as Stuart would call them. They had intense faith, far more faith than was possessed by the easy, unvirtuous men who would gladly give their lives to help mankind to a better future and a gentler and nobler existence.)

Nor did the priest have the slightest doubt that if any seduction had taken place Stuart was the seduced, not the seducer. He knew for certain only one thing: that Stuart loved a woman for the first time in his life. How could he, the priest, then say to Stuart that he was doing an evil thing? I am doubtless very unorthodox, and completely in error, and my bishop would be flabbergasted, thought Father Houlihan humbly, but I see no foulness in love, if it is truly love, and I see no sin in such a love, whether blessed or unblessed. The power of love, and love itself, comes from God, and nothing evil comes from Him.

When Stuart and Sam had left him, he sat in meditation for a long time, praying for the peace of his friend, and earnestly invoking God's protection for him. It came to him, with naïve surprise, that he prayed more for Stuart than for anyone else in the world! Under the spell of this unique surprise, and quite intrigued by it, he went upstairs to his bedroom. He found that his capable sister had somewhere unearthed a camp cot, and on this cot Mr. Cullen was reposing in a roll of blankets, and very wide-awake. Father Houlihan was taken aback. He frowned at the young man, who rose politely, and gave him an army salute. "You'll not be sleeping across my door?" asked the priest. "I will that, Father," replied the young man genially. "That's my job."

"And a better job you'd be doing sleeping in your own home like a Christian," said the priest severely. "Such nonsense." When he closed his bedroom door after him, he heard Mr. Cullen conscientiously moving his cot across the doorway, and then the creak of the springs.

What dramatics! Stuart had a flair for the histrionic thing. As if anyone would break into this quiet little house with assassination in mind! It was ridiculous.

CHAPTER 63

Stuart and Sam Berkowitz walked slowly home together in the mild and clear September night. A hunter's moon hung, enormously and golden, over the thinning trees, and the black sky was pervaded with a wide and luminous glow. The air, soft and balmy, was warm with spicy scents, flowing over the city. The street-lamps shone on empty streets, the silence of which was broken only occasionally by a voice, a footfall, the rolling of a carriage going home. All the upper stories of the houses were lit, testifying that the families were preparing for bed.

The two men strolled in companionable silence for some

time, Sam smoking his usual pipe, Stuart puffing on his cheroot. They passed a few young officers briskly leaving a home where they had been happily entertained. They laughed and joked with one another. Stuart scanned their faces. Perhaps one of them might be Bertie Cauder. But Bertie was not among them. His family had not heard from him for nearly six weeks. His training would hardly be completed yet. But the vast machinery of war was rolling rapidly now. No one could know.

Stuart glanced sideways at the tired, thin, middle-aged man beside him. It hurt him that Sam appeared so old, his hair so white, his graven face so deeply lined and weary. Yet Sam's expression was quite peaceful, overlaid with thought. He felt Stuart's glance, turned his head, smiled slightly.

"Business was a little better this week," he observed tentatively.

Stuart raised his hand. "Please. No talk of business, Sam. You know I don't like it. I know, and you know, that I'm on the edge of a precipice, but I, in a muddled way, believe that if I ignore the precipice I won't be frightened by it, and might even be able to walk away from it in time, still intact." He smiled wryly.

No, thought Sam, this time neither you nor I will walk away from it. He sighed. Stuart no longer even glanced at the books. He spent his time in the shops, conversing amiably with the customers, closing reluctant sales. He lived in a kind of feverish dream-state, from which he refused to be awakened lest he expire of sheer terror. Sam shook his head. It was almost the end. Only a miracle could save the shops now.

Suddenly he saw Angus Cauder's face, and his mouth tightened grimly. But how could he speak now to Stuart? It was too late.

He, Sam, had come to the end. His work in the shops was done. His money would soon pass from his hands, and River Island would be his. His step quickened; he was less tired. His eyes glowed under the brim of his tall hat. His long dream had at last been called into reality by God, and within a year two thousand harried and tormented and homeless people would find a last haven within the leafy safety of River Island, there to lift their bruised and weary arms to the saving tasks of life.

He said: "Stuart, tomorrow I pay for my Island. My Island. It will be mine tomorrow. It is approved. There will be no more delay."

Stuart replied: "Good! Very, very good! Sam, that is delightful news."

Sam smiled. His voice shook somewhat when he said: "It will be good news for those who expect only suffering and death. I haf written to those who will help. Soon they will be coming, the men, and the women, and the children."

"You are certain the matter is completed?"

"Yes. Of course. It was signed today. Tomorrow I give the money. It will be taken from the bank, by me." He paused. "Today I went to the bank. There was Mr. Allstairs. He called me in. We haf not spoken for years. But he was very amiable. He said to me: 'Sam, it is dangerous just now to do this. Wait a little. I will buy the Island, in my own name, and then you may buy it back from me in a few months, in a year, and pay me only the interest. I will do this for you, a depositor, a client.'"

Stuart stopped short in the street, and shouted, clenching his fists: "Oh, the dog! The dirty dog! The vile, crawling dog!"

Sam laid his hand on his friend's arm. "Hush. You will wake all the street. Let us be quiet. See, they are opening windows now, and peering out. Mr. Allstairs was very friendly. He is an old man, I thought, he must haf forgotten much evil, or repented of it. Perhaps he is sincere. I do not know. Perhaps he thinks of the temper of the people in this city, who prefer tormenting the defenseless to fighting to save their country. I do not know. I no longer think. When a man grows older, he knows there are things he can never know. Only the young ask why. I haf not so many more years, and I shall not waste them in questions. So I only said, with courtesy: 'No, Mr. Allstairs, I must do it now. But it is kind of you.'"

Stuart stared at him incredulously. "You said that, you damn fool?"

Sam smiled again. He shrugged. "It is said that while pleasant words may not avert a blow, or change a man's mind, neither do they invite a blow nor turn a just man against you. As for the unjust man, he has his plans beforehand, and nothing can put them aside. And again, perhaps he has forgotten much of his evil."

Stuart was outraged. "Why, you infernal idiot, you know very well that he is behind the agitation against you, and your plans for the Island! That has been settled by investigation. He paid for the handbills which said 'No Jew Ghetto near Grandeville! Down with the Jews!' And dozens of others.

It was his hired ruffians who attacked old Grundy, and who have threatened to attack you. It was his hand, through another's, which sent paving rocks against your doors and through your windows. And yet you can say: 'perhaps he has forgotten much of his evil'! Don't you know how malignant he is? He is sleepless. He is like a soft leprous spot in Grandeville, growing larger and larger, eating away at the body of this city!"

"He can do nothing now, to me, or to my plans," said Sam with quiet intensity. "Whatever he has tried has been useless. So I do not worry. I do not even think of him."

He added: "Tomorrow, which I forgot to tell you, I am going to New York, where lives a rabbi who is my friend. I shall discuss many matters with him. And I must give you my keys in my house, for my private safe. Do not forget to take them."

Stuart grimly reflected that there was probably very little in the safe just now. Sam continued: "There are papers in that safe, too, for the business which will arise in the next few days. I am asking you to care for it, for me. The business about the Islands, and the discussions I haf outlined which I will talk over with the farmers on the Island. Read them, when you can. Perhaps it is possible you may haf suggestions to offer me, which I haf overlooked."

"They own the farms?"

"No. Only on lease. But we can come to amicable agreement, I am sure. I shall not dispossess them, certainly. I wish only to go into details with them about my plan.

They reached the lonely and silent little house where Sam lived. He looked at it sadly. He missed his dead mother. But she must be glad tonight, thinking of what her son had finally been able to accomplish.

Stuart looked curiously at his friend's face in the light of the flickering street-lamp. It was quiet, and peaceful, but full of gentle resolution and fulfilment. The majestic and tender dream of a lifetime shone in his weary brown eyes. Even as Stuart watched him, Sam lifted his eyes to the dark and silent heavens as if in humble and thankful prayer.

Stuart said good night, and went on his way, humming abstractedly to himself. Sam went to the side of the house, and fumbled for the key in his pocket. There were thick masses of shrubbery here, flowering shrubs all golden and white in the spring, which had been Mrs. Berkowitz' joy. Sam found his key, and prepared to put it into the lock. He heard a slight rustling sound, and by the dim light of the moon saw that he was confronted by two huge men, bulking and bending towards him like gigantic apes.

His flesh prickled, his lips turned cold. But he faced the intruders with quiet resolution. "What is it you wish, please?" he asked politely, his hand on the door.

One of them took a menacing step towards him. "Are you the Jew, Berkowitz?" he asked, in a low rumbling voice. His companion moved swiftly and silently behind him.

Sam hesitated. Then he said: "I am."

For one last blinding moment he saw the upraised club above his head; by the moonlight he saw the snarling and bestial face. And then the universe exploded all about him in a torrent of fire and bursting stars.

CHAPTER 64

STUART had gone only a few short streets when he remembered that he had not taken the keys of which Sam had spoken. He swore under his breath. Sam, no doubt, would be compelled to go to the shops to give Stuart those keys, and so delay his pressing business. Stuart swung about and went back rapidly the way he had come.

He was puzzled to see that Sam's house was still in darkness. Surely in those ten minutes he had not been able to prepare for bed and retire for the night. Also, Stuart knew his friend's habits. Sam sat up far past midnight every night, to read. But there was not a single light in the dark little house with its blank windows, and the shadows of the wavering trees rippling across its white front.

Stuart's exquisite intuition caused his heart to pound with sudden terror and warning. He stood on the walk before the house, trying to control himself, to halt the roaring in his head. But his hand grasped his cane with involuntary firmness. What nonsense! The night was lovely. Perhaps Sam, at the last moment, had decided to take a quiet walk by himself before going to bed, or reading.

"I'll try the door, anyway," Stuart muttered to himself. He went to the side of the house. There was no sound but the thin rustling of the trees, the soft sighing of the wind. The thick heavy shrubbery leaned over the flagged walk, made a pool of darkness along the path. Another window, black and empty, stared at him like a blind eye as he passed it. Insects blundered against his face. His feet crunched on some dry and fallen leaves. He moved cautiously, his hair rising with nameless fear.

Suddenly he stumbled. His groping foot had struck against something soft. He recoiled. He stood, frozen, trembling with strange premonition, and icy sweat broke out over his face. His hand, finally, fumbled in his pockets. It felt like a hand of wood, without joints. It stuck in the lining of his pocket, came away numb, with his packet of lucifers in it. He struck a match. He saw Sam lying at his feet, his head crushed, his quiet face covered with blood, his eyes closed.

The burning match fell from Stuart's hand. He uttered a great loud cry, then fell to his knees beside his friend. He lifted him in his arms, implored him frantically. He threw back his head and called frenziedly for help. All over the neighborhood windows were suddenly flung open, voices called shrilly. "Murder!" Stuart shouted. "Murder! Police!"

Everything darkened about him, swayed, rolled, tilted. His arms were weak and flaccid. He held Sam against his breast, and called incoherently to him, prayed to him, begged him for a word. For the first time since childhood, he wept. He felt the scalding sting of tears on his eyelids; he heard his voice groaning and uttering terrible imprecations. He did not know when he was surrounded by panting men with lanterns in their hands, men half-dressed, demanding, shouting, exclaiming. He did not know that his own hands were wet and running with Sam's blood. He did not feel the grasp of those about him, who were shaking him, commanding that he help them carry Sam into the house.

He knew only that Sam was moaning, stirring feebly in his arms. He held his friend tighter, wiping away the blood that streamed over his face. "Sam! Sam! Tell me. You must tell me. Who did it, Sam? Who struck you down?"

The wan and swaying lantern-light wavered over the dying man in Stuart's desperate arms. It wavered over shocked craning faces and leaning shoulders and rustling shrubbery.

Sam stirred again, opened his eyes, looked blankly through dark mists at his friend. "Stuart," he whispered at last. "Stuart."

"Yes. Yes! Stuart. Sam, who did it?"

Sam's head fell back. His eyes closed again. But his lips moved. He whispered faintly: "Allstairs. They would not let me haf it——"

Stuart's arms slackened. He looked up at those surrounding him, saw them for the first time. And as they looked at him, they involuntarily shrank at the sight of such a frightful expression. One or two, in fear, stepped backwards with their lanterns, as if to hide that face.

But he said only: "Help me. We must carry him in. And someone go for a doctor, at once."

CHAPTER 65

REALITY had taken on the substance, horror, darkness and terror of a nightmare. Sometimes, as he rushed through the quiet midnight streets, Stuart would pause, trembling, staring up at the sky, and repeating aloud: "It is a dream! It is only a dream!" He would look at the heavens, filled with circles of bright silver light, at the rushing plumes of the trees, at the guttering street-lamps and the black houses hidden in their shrubbery, and a hideous long quaking would go over him, a mortal sickness, an insane rage, and he would implore that he might awake and find himself safe in his lonely bed in his own house. The people, in their beds, heard his maledictions, his thin wild exclamations and blasphemies and cried, and would turn over restlessly, muttering, cursing the "drunkard" who had disturbed them so incontinently. And then they would hear his disordered running footsteps, echoing in the warm, wind-filled silence.

Two soldiers passing him on a lonely corner flickering in lamplight, saw his face, and involuntarily they shrank back. They looked after him, uneasily. They saw his tall swift figure moving rapidly into the darkness, and one of them touched his forehead, and the other shrugged. "He's after somebody," said the younger man. "God help him, whoever he is."

But Stuart saw nothing but the face of Joshua Allstairs. He felt himself walking through a long blind tunnel, unaware of the streets about him, seeing only Joshua at the end of it, crouching, waiting, unable to move. He reached Joshua's dark house, the tall dank trees fluttering their leafy shadows over the polished narrow windows, which stared out like empty mirrors. He lifted the knocker and struck it again and again, until all the narrow and deserted street was filled with clattering echoes. And then he banged on the door, over and over, with the head of his cane. He said aloud, quietly: "You must let me in. You cannot hide from me now." Finally he heard dim exclamations behind the door. It opened a crack, and he saw the frightened face of Joshua's butler peering out at him. "What do you want?" quavered the old man. "Go away. Are you crazy? Who are you?"

Stuart without haste set his hand against the door and hurled it inwards. The old man fell back with a thin screech, and retreated. The frail moonlight flooded into the hallway, showing the servant in his frayed dressing-gown. "Police!" he screamed, faintly. "Police! Murder!"

Stuart seized him by the throat with his left hand, and lifted his cane. For one instant the old man saw his face, and he closed his eyes with an incoherent prayer. His legs failed him. Stuart flung him aside like a rag-doll, and went up the stairway. The steps were edged with flame; the whole stairway crawled and undulated before him like a shadowy serpent. He went up steadily, firmly, his lifted cane in his hand.

Above, every room was dark. But from behind the door of one there were querulous exclamations, and then under its edge appeared the wavering light of a lamp. "Who is it? What is it?" exclaimed Joshua. "Judson? Judson? Who is it? At this hour?"

Stuart seized the handle of the door. But the door was locked. He set his shoulder against the stout wood. It resisted him. He did not hurl himself against it. He closed his eyes, and thrust with his shoulder, implacably. His legs bent; his head sank into his shoulders. In that warm darkness he could feel the muscles of his body and of his legs swell, arch, strain. He said softly: "I am coming in, Joshua. I am coming to kill you, Joshua."

There was a sudden ringing silence in the room. Then Joshua screamed. Stuart heard the scrabbling of his ancient feet as they rushed towards the window. He heard the window open. He heard Joshua's shrieks: "Murder! Murder! Police!"

Stuart pressed against the door. It began to creak and groan. It trembled in its frame. "Come now, come now," Stuart urged it, in the gentle suppressed voice of madness. "A little more, just a little more."

In the room beyond, Joshua was screaming, beating his hands together with a frenzied clapping sound, as he leaned from his window. There were sounds from the street, running footsteps. Stuart did not hear them. He heard only

Joshua's cries, and as he strained, and the door quailed under his superhuman strength, he laughed aloud.

There was a sudden thunderous report, a long splintering cracking, a crash. The door burst inwards at the hinges. Stuart was precipitated into the room, like a charging bull. Staggering, he recovered himself. Joshua was crouching against the window, trembling, whimpering. His old face was a death's head of mortal terror, of craven, gibbering fear. His pale eyes were distended, glimmering wildly in the dim lamplight, and his long white night-shirt hung on his withered frame like a shroud. He looked at Stuart, and then he could not even whimper. His stark dry mouth opened soundlessly, webbed with saliva, and the nostrils of his predatory nose sank inwards. He dwindled, his body bent, pressing itself against the window frame.

Stuart looked at his enemy, the man who had killed his friend. He looked across the room at him, and said, very gently: "Pray, Joshua. I am going to kill you."

The shrunken form at the window stirred slightly. The white night-shirt blew in the night wind that came from the windows. Joshua's claw-like hands gathered his garment about him. His large gray head shook as if with palsy. His mouth moved, and he whispered: "They will hang you, Stuart. They'll drag you up a scaffold, and put a rope around your neck."

Stuart smiled. It was like a flash of lightning on his dark and twisted features. "You will not see it, Joshua. You will be in your grave by then."

He lifted his cane, and took one step towards Joshua, who, recovering his voice, screamed madly, over and over. And then Stuart paused. He smiled again. "You killed Sam Berkowitz tonight, Joshua. You hired murderers to strike him down. He had done you no harm. You hated him, for no reason. You are an old man, Joshua, but your greed is not old. You could never have enough, could you, Joshua? And because you could never have enough, you killed my friend. He died in my arms. Look at me, Joshua. Do you see this blood on my hands, on my clothing? It is Sam's blood. I carried him into his house and laid him down. He did not die too soon, however. They thought they had killed him, your hirelings. But before he died, he told me——"

Joshua was groaning. He wrung his hands together. He was slipping along the wall like a gray shadow, his eyes blazing with terror. He moaned: "It's a lie. A dastardly lie. I sent no one to kill him. They lie. Stuart, believe me. I had nothing to do with it. You wouldn't kill me, Stuart? I'm your wife's father, Stuart. I'm your little girl's grandfather. They'll hang you, Stuart. That will be the end of you. They'll hang you by the neck until you die. Stuart!" he screamed, as Stuart advanced silently towards him, crouching a little, head thrust forward. But it was the look on Stuart's face, rather than his advance, that inspired Joshua to emit shriek after shriek of gibbering, inhuman terror.

He clasped his hands together. He continued to sidle along the walls, aimlessly pushing small articles of furniture between himself and Stuart, little tables, a chair, a small commode. His hands fluttered over each article. He shrank behind it. If he could just reach his great poster bed he might slide under it, draw himself together, writhe out of Stuart's murderous grasp. In the meantime, he continued to shriek, his voice cracking, breaking. And the lamplight shone dimly on that scene of horror, the fleeing old man, the younger man gliding silently but without haste after him, their long trembling shadows following them on the high white ceiling and along the floor.

The crazed terror of death was upon Joshua. Between his shrieks, he mouthed lunatic pleas to Stuart, even while he busily thrust small objects between himself and the avenger, and slipped along the walls toward his bed. He sidled into a hanging cabinet of rare old *objets d'art*. The cabinet swayed, then crashed to the floor, with a thin tinkle of shattering glass and china. The gleaming fragments twinkled in the lamplight. And over them, crunching them beneath inexorable feet, came Stuart, closer and closer.

Suddenly he saw what Joshua intended. He stopped, flung back his head and laughed. At that awful sound, Joshua was petrified. He shrank against the white wall. He lifted his shrunken arms and spread them. His failing legs bent. He stood in an attitude of crucifixion, his gaunt head sinking forwards, his fearful eyes fixed on Stuart. He was an old and wicked man, and he had been condemned to death.

He knew, now, there was no hope for him. He sank to his knees. He became a heap of bones covered by a nightshirt. He could not even whimper. He was all silence. But he wound his skeletal arms over his head and waited the blow that would kill him.

Stuart reached him. He stood over the old man. He said, very gently: "Are you praying, Joshua? Or is it that you dare not pray? Are you afraid God might be listening? You foul murderer, you demon, you vicious dog!"

Joshua did not answer. His arms merely tightened over his head. But a long shuddering ran over his body, so that the night-shirt trembled as if struck by wind.

Then he felt Stuart grasp him by the back of the neck. He felt himself swung into air. For the last time he screamed frantically, with rabid terror. He saw Stuart lift the shining cane over his head, the golden knob glittering. He closed his eyes. He hung from Stuart's hand like a gaunt old rabbit, and was still. His mouth fell open. He sagged, his feet aimlessly trailing the floor. He had mercifully become unconscious before a single blow had been struck.

Stuart looked at the ancient night-shirted skeleton in his grasp. The head lolled over his hand as if the neck had been broken. Saliva drooled from the slack lips. The arms and legs hung lifeless.

There was a rapid pounding of feet up the stairway, shouts, the stabbing lights of lanterns. Stuart heard and saw.

He flung Joshua from him violently, and the body of the old man slid over the floor, coming to rest abruptly against the farther wall, a tangled heap of naked bones, obscene and repulsive, and silent.

CHAPTER 66

"HERE he is, Father," said the turnkey. He put a heavy iron key into the faceless door, turned it, opened the lock. "Only ten minutes, now, please."

Father Houlihan hesitated on the threshold of the dank stone cell. There was a high window, barred, in the moist wall. Thin streamers of sunlight fell into the cell; upon the narrow cot sat Stuart, his head in his hands. He did not lift his head; his thick hair, black and dishevelled, was twisted in his blood-stained fingers. His clothing, rumpled and stained, had not been removed during the night. His neckcloth hung, untied, over his waistcoat. Ironically, the jewelled ring on his right hand glittered in the sunlight.

Father Houlihan entered the cell. The door clanged after him. He stood and looked at his friend. Stuart did not move, did not even stir. He was not aware that anyone had entered. On a stool near him stood the meal of bread and water and greasy meat, which he had not touched. Nor had he used the pitcher of water and the ragged towel which had been given him. He sat on his cot like a man of stone, and did not appear to breathe.

The priest sighed deeply, from his heart. He removed the dirty tray from the stool, and he pulled that stool close to his friend. Then he said, in a broken voice: "Stuart. Stuart, my darling lad. Won't you look at me, Stuart?"

Stuart did not move. Father Houlihan's exhausted and red-rimmed eyes filled. The tears fell over his haggard cheeks. He had become an old man. He shivered, over and over. Then he put his hand on Stuart's shoulder, and cried: "Stuart, you must look at me! Have pity on me, Stuart!"

A long shudder ran over Stuart's shoulder; the priest could feel it under his hand. Then Stuart's hands dropped, but he did not lift his head. Father Houlihan saw his stark, bemused face. Stuart's eyes stared at the floor, rimmed in black. One of his cheeks was oozing with blood, and there was a horrible purple bruise on his forehead.

He said, in a far hoarse voice: "Sam is dead. He was murdered. But I did not kill his murderer. He died before I could kill him." Suddenly his voice rose, and he groaned with desperate hopelessness and rage: "Curse God! Curse everything! He died before I could kill him! I was cheated! Sam was cheated! Curse God!"

The priest put his hands on his shoulders, and shook him steadily and firmly. "Stuart. Look at me, my lad. Try to hear me. It's your friend, Grundy." His voice broke. "Do you hear me, Stuart?"

Stuart was suddenly silent. Then his expression changed, became contorted, full of hatred. He flung off his friend's hands.

"Have you come here to mouth your mawkish words over me, you fool? To whimper your ridiculous and insane aphorisms? To exhort me?"

He sprang to his feet. He began to hurry up and down the narrow confines of his cell. He was beside himself. He raved. He cursed. He wept. He struck his clenched wounded fists against the walls like a madman. When his starting and disordered eye encountered the priest, he poured filthy maledictions upon him. Where was his God? he stammered, in the loud thick voice of madness. Where was his God, that He had allowed Sam to be murdered so brutally, Sam who had harmed no one? Where was his precious Jesus in that hour when Sam had died? Who had helped him? Who had defended him? There had been no one to hear his last cry, the cry of an innocent man so evilly done to death for money. What had Sam done to inspire such hatred? Nothing. Before God, nothing! Yet God had not intervened, to save him. He had died in his, Stuart's arms, and this was Sam's blood on his hands. Stuart thrust out his dirty stained hands into the priest's very face. But Father Houlihan did not shrink. He did not look at the hands before him. He looked only at Stuart.

Stuart burst into unhinged laughter. "You don't like the sight of blood, do you, you bloodless priest? You forgive Sam's murderers, don't you? Sam was only a Jew, and the murderers were 'Christians'! Christians! You remember that, don't you? It does not matter what a Christian does, whatever crime he commits, whatever innocent he murders, whatever good man he does to death for money! He can be forgiven. He can be washed in the blood of the Lamb, and taken into a nice cozy Heaven to play hymns forever on a golden harp! He has been baptized, in dirty water! His crime against a Jew will be forgiven, for it was not a crime at all! He can rest at the feet of his simpering God, and be congratulated, as he had been congratulated by the stinking creatures that God has created. World without end, the liars, the thieves, the murderers, the ugly foulnesses, the perverts and the dogs will whisper: 'He only killed a Jew'!"

He paused. The priest was slowly rising, his large old face white as cloth, his eyes blazing. He stood before Stuart, and looked at him steadfastly.

Stuart laughed again. "Why don't you speak? Why don't you say: 'You should not have attacked that vile fiend, for he only killed a Jew'!"

Then the priest raised his hand and struck Stuart full across his convulsed face, not once, but many times, and with calm and steady deliberation. Stuart fell back. He staggered against the wall. And then he stood there, blinking, staring.

The priest said, and his voice was very quiet, and without emotion: "I shall say only this: If you had not gone to Allstairs, I should have gone. I should have gone, as you did. I owe you gratitude."

Stuart stared at him. There was a deep silence in the cell. The two men regarded each other across a space of five feet. The priest stood like a statue, pale, not trembling. He seemed to grow in inexorable stature. His strident blue eyes were full of blinding light.

"What do you think I have in my breast, you stupid man?"

he asked. "A lump of ice? A stone? A piece of suet? Do you not know it is the heart of a human creature, a man like yourself? Do you think these black robes hide a fleshless body? Sam was my friend, more my friend than he was yours. We were men together. We knew each other, as you have never known either of us. We knew each other's soul. When he was killed, part of me was killed, also. I shall never be whole again."

He spoke simply, and without emotion in his voice. He was very calm. Then he sat down again on the stool and looked before him. His lips moved silently, in unspoken and majestic prayer. Then he bent his head and covered his face with his hands.

"God forgive me," he whispered, "for there is murder in my heart."

Stuart stood motionless, pressed to the wall against which he had fallen. He could not remove his eyes from his old friend. Slowly the anguish, the demented fury, faded from his face. He put his hand to his head. Then, with blind steps he groped towards his cot. He fell on it, his head bent on his knees.

Again, there was silence in the cell. The priest continued his whispered prayers, as if he were alone. Stuart heard that whispering. It seemed to him that it pierced every cell in his body with unendurable agony.

There was a grinding in the lock of the door. The turnkey appeared, and with him two men, Robbie Cauder and Mr. Ezekiel Simon, Joshua Allstairs' lawyer. He was a dry tight little man, bald, with twinkling blue eyes, a sardonic expression, and an agile carriage.

"Well, well," he said in a sprightly voice, as the door clanged behind them. "What have we here, eh? A nasty business, a very nasty business. But not one that can't be mended! Judge Cauder, sir, I have discovered we have no place to sit. But no matter. Our business will not take long, I trust."

He winked at the grave Robbie, who was regarding Stuart with concern, and he made a sprightly moue as he indicated the priest, and tilted his head at the door. But Robbie shook his head sternly, indicating that the priest should remain. Father Houlihan turned slowly on his stool, and looked at Robbie with severe questioning, and then at Stuart.

Robbie advanced, and held out his hand, and the priest took it. "Father Houlihan, we have some matters to discuss.

If you have the time, I beg you to remain. I am glad to find you here. I—I am certain that Stuart needs you."

"I shall remain, sir, if it is your desire, and I can help my friend," said the priest with dignity. Stuart had again sunk into his terrible bemused apathy, and showed no indication that he was aware of the presence of the newcomers.

Robbie hesitated, then sat down beside his kinsman. He studied him with sad, stern gravity. Mr. Simon hummed a little to himself, glanced about the cell with pleased disfavor. Robbie spoke: "Stuart. Pull yourself together, man. This is very serious, you know. We must talk to you."

Stuart's stiff hands slowly dropped from his face. Whitish channels had been worn through the grime on his haggard face. He stared at Robbie blindly. Then he muttered: "Ah, so you are here. To prepare my 'defense,' I suppose. To save me from the hangman." And he smiled.

"What hangman?" said Robbie impatiently. He pulled out his clean white kerchief, and thrust it into Stuart's hand. "Wipe your dirty face. Be a man. Listen to me, Stuart. You are a fool. But you aren't a murderer. Allstairs isn't dead. He's very much alive, though he's nursing a broken arm."

Stuart stared at him emptily. "Not dead?" he whispered. "Not dead?" Then his look changed, became distorted and ferocious again. He started to his feet. "Not dead! He's alive! My God!"

The priest rose with a cry. He seized Stuart's arm. "Thank God!" he exclaimed. "Thank God, he is not dead! Not for his loathesome sake, but for Stuart's! I thank Thee, dear Lord, I thank Thee!"

"Stuart," observed Robbie, wryly, and shifting himself with fastidiousness on the dirty blanket, "does not seem to share your exultation, Father Houlihan."

Stuart clenched his fists. He muttered: "I shall have to try it again, then."

Robbie spoke sharply: "Don't be a damned fool, man! You always were, you know. Try to use your reason, if you have any. Try to control yourself. You have a family to think of." He made a disgusted gesture. "I shall see to it that you remain here, safe from yourself, until you come to your senses."

He gestured to the priest, who gently forced the trembling Stuart to sit down again. Mr. Simon had watched this scene with happy pleasure and affectionate interest. "Ah, yes, hot blood. It will be better for him to remain here for a few days. I shall recommend it. A little sentence of ten days,

Judge, for creating a riot, or inflicting assault, or something?"

Robbie nodded with impatience. "That can be settled later. Let us get down to facts, now."

He paused, then spoke firmly and quietly to Stuart: "There were witnesses, half a dozen of them. Neighbors. They are on your side. It is fortunate for you that Allstairs is so universally hated. Now, I have a few questions to ask you, you imbecile, and please try to answer them sensibly. Allstairs fainted in your grasp, before you could strike him?"

It was some moments before Stuart could gather his faculties together, and then he nodded, dumbly. He was dazed. He kept rubbing his forehead, and whispering to himself.

"That corroborates the accounts of the witnesses," said Mr. Simon, pleasantly. "And Mr. Allstairs' own testimony."

"And then you threw him from you, against the wall, so that he broke his arm?" continued the merciless Robbie, who, whatever he privately felt at the sight of Stuart's face and anguished eyes, discreetly concealed it.

"I hoped his neck was broken. I hoped I had killed him," whispered Stuart.

Robbie frowned. He glanced at Mr. Simon. "What he says need not go beyond this cell?" he suggested.

"Oh, quite so, quite so. We are only eager for the matter to be settled discreetly," assented Mr. Simon, happily.

Robbie said, coldly: "The neighbors, and a policeman, arrived in time to see the last act of this disgraceful affair. Several reached the room just before you seized the old—man. They say you reached him, took him by the neck, and he fainted. Then you threw him from you. They fell on you then, just as you were about to kick him, or beat him with your cane. You fought like the mad dog you are, and then the policeman clouted you with his club and they carried you here. Very fortunate for you, all around."

Stuart said nothing. He folded his arms on his knees and stared before him. Mr. Simon cleared his throat.

"Let us be brief. Mr. Allstairs has declared that he will bring no charges against you. You are his son-in-law. He has discretion, and I might suggest, taste. No family scandal, you see. Let the matter subside. Very generous of my client, I may add. Very generous indeed. What do you say, Mr. Coleman?"

Stuart moved. He looked up. "Ah, I see. He is afraid to have me tried. He is afraid of what I might say. He is afraid I shall accuse him of murder!"

"Oh, my dear sir, what nonsense!" exclaimed Mr. Simon,

lovingly. "What excessive charges to bring against my venerable client! How can you prove them? Who are these 'murderers' you speak of? Can you produce them? I am afraid you have a very vivid imagination. The unfortunate Mr. Berkowitz was attacked on his doorstep by anonymous ruffians, who wished to rob him, not kill him. They were a little too—strenuous, shall we say? The fact remains that they did rob him. His purse was not on him, and a certain precious ring he wore was gone."

Stuart's eyes were drained of all expression. His mouth fell open. And then, all at once, he was suddenly seized by a veritable madness of impotent fury and despair.

"So he will not be punished for his murder! He will go free, as he has always gone free before! There will be no hangman's rope for him! He will be free to murder and rob again, to do his foulnesses, and to live out his obscene life! No! No, by God! I demand a trial. I demand my opportunity to accuse him! I know what I know! I know what Sam told me, when we walked home together. I know what he told me before he died." He sprang to his feet again, and confronted the lawyer savagely. He pointed his finger at him.

"And you know what this will mean! You know what it will mean for Allstairs! Allstairs knows, too. That is why he sent you here!"

Mr. Simon's agreeable smile died. His little wizened face was very nasty. He said, coolly: "Where are your witnesses, Mr. Coleman? Who will corroborate your wild accusations? Who will believe you? No, no, my dear sir, you are quite helpless. You can do nothing. Mr. Allstairs knows this, also. Yet, he has magnanimously ordered me to have any charges against you dropped."

But Stuart laughed in his face. "'Magnanimous'! Oh, what benevolence! Look you, if Allstairs were not afraid, he would not have sent you to me, with this loving message! He dares not face my accusations in open court——"

Mr. Simon thrust his little hands into his pockets, leaned against the wall. He regarded Stuart calmly. "Let us be frank, Mr. Coleman. I will not deceive you. Mr. Allstairs is indeed afraid to face your accusations. I grant you that. You see, I am being very honest with you, against my better judgment. In return for your silence, he will also be silent, and the matter will be settled.

"On the other hand, Mr. Coleman, let us consider the other alternative. Mr. Allstairs will not withdraw his charges of assault with intent to kill against you. You are an indiscreet man, and you will not deny that you intended to kill him. Moreover, there are witnesses. You will be brought into Court. You will make your accusations. Matters might be quite unpleasant for my old client for a while, and he might even be held in such a cell as this, while efforts were made to substantiate your charges. But—and you must understand this perfectly—no witnesses to your alleged murder will be found. Do you expect the ruffians to appear, and declare themselves, accuse themselves, and Mr. Allstairs? That is ridiculous, as you know. The police are searching for the nen. I doubt they will be found. Such audacious criminals iave a clever way of disappearing. How will you prove any connection between Mr. Allstairs and the criminals? The words of a dying man? It is true that Mr. Berkowitz has been opposed by Mr. Allstairs, for a reason which Mr. Allstairs genuinely considered important. Mr. Allstairs had planned that River Island be sold in lots to impecunious farmers, on very long and generous terms, and at low interest. Don't you think that the producing of papers to that effect will have considerable weight with the Court, Mr. Coleman?

"On the other hand, Mr. Berkowitz wished to bring a horde of foreigners, strange creatures, to that Island, to set them up in homes and on the land. Foreigners are not wanted here, Mr. Coleman, at least not at present, if ever. The general sentiment of the people is strongly against such a project, my dear sir. The Court will remember that, also.

"You will say, again, that Mr. Berkowitz was opposed by Mr. Allstairs, but Mr. Allstairs will have the sympathy of the community in this position, as he has always had it. So, Mr. Berkowitz tells you of this opposition. Later, you find him dying. You, alone, find him dying. I shall return to that phase of the subject in just a moment, please.

"You allege that Mr. Berkowitz murmured the name of my client before he died. But what proof of that had Mr. Berkowitz? None. None at all. Moreover, no one heard him murmur that name. Again, you alone, heard him.

"You come to a mad, unfounded and melodramatic conclusion. You race off to kill my client, on the alleged dying statement of a brutally beaten man, who had no real justification for his accusation. My client forgives you, for the sake of his daughter, your wife."

He paused. The priest had risen. His eyes were fiery. "Sir," he said in a trembling voice, "you are condoning murder! You would have Mr. Coleman condone it, be an accessory to it."

Robbie eyed the priest with displeasure. "Father Houlihan," he said sharply, "please do not be so quixotic. Surely you are not insensible to the reasonable arguments of Mr. Simon."

Mr. Simon raised his hand benignly. "Mr.—er—Houlihan is obviously emotionally involved with Mr. Coleman. We will let that pass, too."

He took a step towards Stuart, who had been listening with black stupefaction. His voice dropped, lost its pleasantness.

"Mr. Coleman, there is another phase of this which I shall now bring up. I ask you to consider it. In your first incoherent statements to the police, you said that you had forgotten some keys which Mr. Berkowitz had asked you to take from him. Incidentally, those keys were not found on his person. You said that you returned, some ten minutes after leaving Mr. Berkowitz, and found him dying. The neighbors admit they heard nothing until you called for help, and they found Mr. Berkowitz in your arms. You told them he had been murdered. No one heard him speak again, before he died. You, Mr. Coleman," and the lawyer pointed a merciless finger at the aghast man, "found Mr. Berkowitz dying. You were covered with his blood. And, Mr. Coleman, it has been discovered that you owe Mr. Berkowitz fourteen thousand dollars, interest on which you have never paid."

"Blessed Mother!" exclaimed Father Houlihan, turning as white as death. "You are not accusing Mr. Coleman of killing his friend?"

Mr. Simon smiled. He was quite grim. "I am accusing Mr. Coleman of nothing but indiscretion and foolhardiness and obdurate blindness. I am merely pointing out to him that matters can be made very disagreeable for him, and will be made very disagreeable, if he insists upon a trial, and makes his unfounded and ridiculous accusations in Court."

The priest, shaking violently, turned to Robbie. "Robbie, you condone this? You approve of this?"

Robbie regarded him coldly. "Father, I have no alternative. You have heard the facts. Allstairs will eventually be exonerated, even if Stuart persists in his folly. But Stuart will not be exonerated. He will be sentenced to a long term in prison. At the worst, he will be accused of murder. The facts are all against him. I beg you, if you are truly his friend, to persuade him to listen to reason."

He stood up. He glanced at his watch. "We must leave now. In an hour, we shall return. I hope, I sincerely hope, that you will have convinced him."

He hesitated. He looked at Stuart with grim bitterness. Stuart sat as if stunned, his hands hanging slackly between his knees, his features working and twisting. Then Robbie drew a deep breath.

"I must ask Stuart to consider another thing. All dirty linen will be brought into public view. The people will have a Roman holiday. Quite irrelevant matters will be dragged out. Innocent people will suffer, such as Marvina and little Mary Rose, Stuart's wife and daughter. And, very possibly, quite probably, my sister, Laurie."

At this, Stuart started vehemently. His eyes were no longer blind. He lifted them to Robbie, and they were filled with fierce fire. Robbie nodded. "Yes, Stuart. Every effort will be made to blacken you, to fasten your guilt in the minds of the jury. I am a lawyer, and I know. Your character will be made to appear utterly shameless. They will stop at nothing. And, if *you* have not, I do have some regard for my sister. I beg you also to have a little for her. She is young, and her life is before her. It is in your hands to wreck it irretrievably. And for no other fault but that she loves you."

He took Mr. Simon's arm, and repeated, without looking back: "We shall return in an hour."

The turnkey opened the door, and they left the cell.

The priest and Stuart were alone. They stared at each other for a long time. The priest slowly sank upon his stool. Across the little space, they could only regard each other in a terrible and bitter silence.

At last the priest said, in a hoarse tone: "Stuart, we are undone by the powers of evil."

Stuart came to life, maddened. He beat his fists impotently on his knees. But he made no other sound. The priest could hear that drumming, and it seemed to him that those fists beat on his aching heart.

He said: "We have no other refuge, no other court, but God. In that refuge, and in that court, we must rest our case. We, ourselves, can do nothing."

CHAPTER 67

THEY stood by the month-old grave of Sam Berkowitz. The quiet cemetery was full of gentle sunlight, tawny, torn in the scarlet, green and golden foliage of autumn, lying in pale yellow shreds on thick, sweet-smelling grass, sparkling on gravelled paths, flooding the brilliant turquoise of the warm sky. Birds were singing their autumnal farewells in the trees, throwing arrow-like shadows of their winging selves over the basking earth. The wind had a melancholy singing voice as it lifted, and blew, the curled crimson and gold of falling leaves through the shining air. But there was no other sound. The mounded graves lay peacefully under the skies, under the shadows of cypresses and burning maples and dark firs. Here and there sunlight struck a pure white shaft, or glanced away from the simple bare face of a low stone, turning it white as snow.

The priest was murmuring in a trembling voice:

" 'The beauty of Israel is slain upon thy high places: how are the mighty fallen' "

His voice broke; he bowed his head; his eyes were brimmed with tears. Stuart stood beside him with a dark face grooved and bitten with pain, and hopeless misery. He looked down at Sam's grave, brown and clodded in the radiant sunshine, and the blackness in him, the hatred, the despair, was like a lightless tide upon which no moon would ever shine. He moved restlessly, as though he would cry out against the priest and his mournful and tender words, and he clenched his fists as Father Houlihan resumed, as if in meditation:

" 'Saul and Jonathan were lovely and pleasant in their lives,
  And in their death they were not divided:
  . . . O Jonathan, thou wast slain in thine high places.
  I am distressed for thee, my brother Jonathan:
  Very pleasant hast thou been unto me:
  Thy love to me was wonderful,
  Passing the love of women——' "

Father Houlihan had become an old man, dwindled and bent with suffering and grief, his face bearing on it resignation and bewilderment. The younger man saw his tears, his trembling clasped hands. The grave was covered with clods, but over them, almost covering them, Father Houlihan had laid the last of his garden roses, crimson, white and yellow, exhaling a swooning breath on the pungent air.

Pray, mourn over him, thought Stuart, vengefully, but I have not done yet. I will find a way.

The priest was silent for a while, as he wept. And then, slowly, he lifted his eyes to the sky. He murmured again:

" 'I will lift up mine eyes unto the hills,
From whence cometh my help.
My help cometh from the Lord,
Which made heaven and earth.
He will not suffer thy foot to be moved:
He that keepeth thee will not slumber.
Behold, he that keepeth Israel
Shall neither slumber nor sleep.
The Lord is thy keeper;
The Lord is thy shade upon thy right hand.
The sun shall not smite thee by day,
Nor the moon by night.
The Lord shall preserve thee from all evil:
He shall preserve thy soul.
The Lord shall preserve thy going out, and thy coming in,
From this time forth, and even for evermore.' "

The Lord shall preserve thee! thought Stuart, with passionate scorn and desolation. But the Lord did not preserve Sam. He had let him die, brutally, alone, an innocent man. The Lord had punished him because he had had a dream of mercy and love. Vile men had killed him for no other reason than that he had been a good man. Stuart, unable to control himself, walked away to a group of trees and sat down on a white bench under them. The very light about him, the very peace, the very soft and gentle color, enhanced his agony, so that every object was outlined as if with a livid pencil. Sam! Sam! Where are you, Sam? But you are nowhere, except under those clods. There is nothing left of you.

There was only one certainty, and that was death. All the dreams and loves and hopes of men came to this final place, and there was nothing left of them; at the last, there was not even memory. Sam's dream lay with him there, unfulfilled, never to be realized, a jewel encased in clay which would never be found again.

A sick and heavy lassitude crept over Stuart. He thought as he had never thought before in his life, and his thoughts brought him nothing but torture and despair. All desire had left him. Sam is dead, but I am dead, too, he said to himself. All at once he envied his friend, who did not carry this burning stone in his chest.

Father Houlihan wiped his eyes, and looked about him. He saw Stuart under the trees, staring before him fixedly. The priest sighed. Sam was at rest, but this poor man was in hell. He went to his friend and sat down beside him. He began to speak, softly, as if meditating aloud:

"Do not think that he is dead, Stuart. He is more alive than we. I know this, not by faith, but with an inner conviction. Do not think his dream died with his body. The dream of liberation and love and security and peace is a lantern which is handed to the living by the dead, and which goes down the ages forever, glimmering, fainting, blazing out, dimmed, hidden by rocks and the shoulders of mountains, by the shadow of black trees, by fogs and storms—but never extinguished, never broken upon the ground. For the light of God is in the lantern, and who can dash it out? Sam knew this; he knows it even better now. Do not think his work is done. He has only gone to a larger place, where he will labor endlessly, and joyously, with countless others, to fulfil his dream."

He looked at the deepening sky, and smiled tremulously. "Work, Sam. Pray, Sam. We will pray with you, giving you our faint and uncertain prayers, our feeble hopes. We will watch with you, guarding the little light you gave us. We will not forget. Do not forget us, Sam. Be with us when our faith becomes weak, and our eyes are blinded with despair. Do not forget us. Be with us, for we loved you."

Stuart's mouth twisted darkly. He pointed to Sam's grave. "There he lies, and in your heart you know he is there, and nowhere else. In spite of your pious mumbo-jumbo."

"*No*," said the priest, quietly and firmly, his clasped hands tightening on his knees. "He is not there. He is with us, all about us. Can't you feel him, Stuart? When I spoke over his grave, I saw him so clearly, but so much younger and stronger, and with such peace in his eyes. I could even hear his voice. He prayed with me."

Stuart began to speak, and then was silent. A faint shiver ran over him. He said, loudly: "You may feel as you say, but I feel that he is completely dead. I have never doubted it." He added, in a hurried voice: "I hope he is dead. That is the only peace he could have, for if he remembered at all, he could not endure it."

When the priest did not answer, Stuart continued: "I have a much better way than murmuring maudlin prayers over a grave. I, at least, haven't forgotten. Look at this," and he thrust a handbill into Father Houlihan's hand.

The priest read: "*Ten thousand dollars reward for any information leading to the arrest and conviction of the murderers of one Samuel Berkowitz, who was killed in Grandeville, N.Y. on September the 18th, 1863. Signed, Stuart Coleman, River Road, Grandeville.*"

"I have had five thousand of these printed, and there will be more. They will be broadcast all over the State, and into Pennsylvania and Ohio. This same advertisement will be published in twenty newspapers in the larger cities. I, too, have a 'conviction.' I believe I shall get results."

The priest said: "Ten thousand dollars. Who can resist ten thousand dollars? Yes, Stuart, I know you will get results." His dimmed blue eyes suddenly sparkled with fervor. "Yes, yes! You will get results, God grant!"

Stuart smiled bleakly. "At first, when Sam's will was read, and I knew that he had left me this money: 'If I have died before the purchase of River Island, ten thousand dollars is to be paid to my dear friend, Stuart Coleman,' I thought of carrying out Sam's plan for the Island. But, as you know, it was sold immediately to that viper, Allstairs." Stuart's fist clenched murderously. "They lost no time in closing the transaction. So, it was no use. I couldn't take that money. I have laid it aside to be paid when I have information about Sam's murderers."

And badly as you, yourself, needed that money, thought Father Houlihan. He laid his hand on Stuart's arm. "Good, good," he said. "Yes, you will get results."

He continued, gently: "It was good of Sam to leave both of us his shares in the shops, equally divided. God bless you, Sam. Stuart, Sam knew that we needed an extension to the hospital. I shall use the income from my shares to build a new operating room, and to pay the salary of an expert surgeon from New York. I have thought of a young man whom Sam knew well, a Dr. Israel Goodman. I have already written to him."

Stuart smiled grimly. But he held back the words: "Don't count too much on the 'income.' There may not be any, soon."

They were silent again, looking at Sam's grave.

Then at last Father Houlihan said gently: "There are always periods of unreason, cruelty and intolerance in mankind, as if a madness had seized on the race of men. These things are like storms, blowing up from the bottomless pits of hell, and spreading over the world. In each generation, these storms come, devastating, devouring, burning, laying waste. But after they pass, God and men remain, wounded and gasping and bleeding, but still with faith, still with hope. Nothing can destroy the dream of God, a dream of eternal peace and love and work and brotherhood upon the world. We must know this. We must understand this. 'I will say of the Lord, He is my refuge and my fortress: My God; in him will I trust.—His truth shall be thy shield and buckler. Thou shalt not be afraid for the terror by night; nor for the arrow that flieth by day; nor for the pestilence that walketh in darkness; nor for the destruction that wasteth at noonday.' Stuart, Sam was a soldier in the Armies of the Lord. He fell in battle, yes. But he did not fight in vain. His dream, the dream of all good men, goes marching on, triumphant. Some day it will be fulfilled upon the earth, and the whole world will be a shelter and a refuge, filled with understanding and brotherhood."

"I only know that Sam is dead," said Stuart, in a hard and stony voice.

"I only know that Sam is living," said the priest, with gentle surety.

They walked slowly together to the gates of the cemetery. They passed mourners kneeling and weeping at graves, and the priest raised his hand in tender benediction as he walked by them. Some of them looked after him with tear-dimmed eyes.

They turned for a last look at Sam's grave, a mound in the distance, covered with roses, slumbering in the last sunlight.

Again the priest raised his hand, and said, softly:

> " 'The Lord bless thee and keep thee:
> The Lord make his face shine upon thee,
> And be gracious unto thee:
> The Lord lift up his countenance upon thee,
> And give thee peace.' "

But Stuart said aloud, with hatred: "I won't forget, Sam. I will find them. What justice could not do, ten thousand dollars will do!"

CHAPTER 68

As MAN is prone, in his anthropomorphic egotism, to believe that nature, herself, partakes of his racial cataclysms, and surges with his own passions, and that the very "signs" of heaven are concerned with him, so did the inhabitants of the North country dimly suspect that the terrible rigors of the winter of 1863-64 were in some way a manifestation of the forces of nature convulsed by man's own convulsions.

At any rate, it was the opinion of the people that "never had there been such an awful winter." Uneasy, alarmed, bereft, often hungry, always deprived, terrified at the prospects of an unending war which would drain them of sons, money, property and security, the common comforts and decencies of life, they looked out on a winter which in gloom, sunlessness, snow and desolation was an extension of their own misery and darkness of soul.

Coal was "short," food was becoming scarce, the shops were almost empty of materials, oil for lamps was low, money had mysteriously "tightened," and always, always, the young men marched away in their sturdy blue and were not seen again. But the hospital which Stuart had built was now filled with the wounded and the dying, and the nuns worked with pale exhausted faces, tender hands, and uncomplaining voices. The sullen restlessness of hatred and revolt had overcome the apathy of the people. They hated the President, many of them, cursed him for the war which had brought this suffering upon them. But they hated the South more, for being the cause of the war. In the universal hatred, then, the issues of the war were forgotten, and the people settled down to somber endurance of suffering, of privation and hopelessness. The survival of the Union, the Emancipation Proclamation, the suspension of the Writ of Habeas Corpus, the new huge taxes, the draft, were regarded by them with heavy apathy.

"Unless we can fuse together these many alien minds and hearts," said Mayor Cummings to Robbie Cauder on one melancholy evening, "unless we can remove from their consciousness the memories of Europe and the adherence to foreign tongues and ways, the Republic will again, and again, in future years, be in mortal danger. We must make them understand, by a method which is beyond my knowledge now, that America is a new race composed of all races, one people, and that any foreign allegiance whatsoever is not only traitorous, but means dissolution of the very nation, itself, and the end of a long dream."

However, the fact remained that the people were more concerned with their sufferings and the frightful winter than they were with the issues of "a gigantic and bloody struggle." The winter had come early. October saw the first bitter drifts of snow, the first wild gales from the Lakes, the first dark shadow over the land. By December the city was snowbound, a quaking cemetery under white dunes and hillocks, under air as sharp as the crack of a whip, under winds that shook chimneys, snapped off trees, and heaped the streets with impassable drifts. Huge and blazing stars crackled in black skies, but the sun was not seen in the day except for fleeting instants when it exploded through layers of thick gray clouds and flooded the snow with brilliant, strong blue light, its fierce shadows lying in the hollows of dunes and fanged ridges.

Even the houses along Main Street, Delaware Avenue, Franklin Street, Porter Avenue and Richmond, were cold. Only one room was heated, and here the families gathered, shivering, miserable and speechless with fear. As for the poor, they sat about the kitchen stove, and when that cooled, they crept, shivering, to bed.

Joshua Allstairs had sufficient coal. His hearth was a fiery blaze of warmth and comfort. He reflected on the state of his cellar, where over ten tons reposed snugly. Quite enough for the winter. Even for next winter, if necessary. There was a fire in his bedroom, too. As for the servants, they were graciously permitted to fill warming pans from his wide hearth and carry them to their frozen bedrooms. One did not quarrel with servants, these days. There was a dangerous ferment in the air, to which Joshua was not insensible.

His old arm was slow in healing. He still carried it in a black silk sling. A permanent palsy had come to him, also, so that his huge gray-white head nodded in a constant, gentle rhythm. He had never quite recovered from the horror and terror of the night when Stuart had come to hunt him to his death. One side of his face was fixed in a petrified grimace, and, as if to compensate for this, the other side was more malignant and terrible in its expression than ever.

He smiled benevolently on his visitor. But that visitor, who rarely saw others objectively, or even subjectively, was not insensible to the terrifying look of his host. He wondered, faintly, how such an old man, poised on the very brink of death, could retain such an avid hatred, such a sleepless malevolence.

But that was not his concern. He even respected Joshua for his vitality. His own vitality, never very positive, was always cold and tired these days. The pain in his head was almost constant. At intervals he quietly munched lozenges which had been recommended to him "for their soothing comfort and alleviation of the nervous system." They were intended to be soporific. They only dimmed his own grinding pain, however, so that he could allow his mental faculties to emerge briefly. In these interludes, he felt his mind like a quivering bared knife, with light glimmering along its edge. He could actually see that knife. When the vision became too keen, he would munch another lozenge, chewing rapidly, with a kind of terror.

Joshua was speaking, in a soft and affectionate purr: "So, here we have everything before us, my dear Angus. Our dear friend, Stuart, owns fifty-five percent of the stock in the shops now, thanks to the Jew who left him half of his own forty percent. Thanks to the Jew, also, that abominable priest owns twenty percent. As matters now stand, all the stock is worthless. Even, unfortunately, your own, or rather your mother's, twenty-five percent. I commiserate with you on that, with all my heart, my boy.

"We now know that Stuart's personal debts amount to twenty thousand dollars, in personal notes which he gave to New York and Chicago banks—money squandered on—er —reprehensible females, jewelry, *objets d'art*, his house, and his extravagant ways of living beyond his means."

As Joshua struck each of the bony fingers of his left hand with his right index finger, there was a thin cracking sound. Angus shivered. But his face did not change.

"Your affectionate and astute father-in-law, Mr. Schnitzel," resumed Joshua fondly, "has lent you the money to buy up those personal notes in the amount of twenty thousand dollars. He has also bought the mortgage on Stuart's house, and presented it to you. Stuart knows nothing of all this as yet. Am I correct?"

"You are correct, Mr. Allstairs," said Angus politely, in his neutral and echoless voice. He touched his forehead briefly, found it damp, shook out the immaculate folds of a kerchief, and wiped away the dampness. He replaced the kerchief with precise and quiet motions.

"I congratulate you, Angus, on the kindness of Mr. Schnitzel. Mr. Schnitzel has also demonstrated a shrewd faith in you.

"Let us continue. The shops will go into bankruptcy. Not only will Stuart's interest in them be worthless, but yours, also. You know that.

"And now, here is my offer: I will advance you the money to settle with your debtors, or, rather, Stuart's debtors—the merchants, manufacturers and importers—for fifty cents on the dollar. In return, I shall enter into partnership with you. The war cannot last much longer. As your silent partner, I shall take no active part in the operation of the shops. You will be sole manager, at a salary, or a profit, to be amicably settled between us. My only stipulation, of course, will be that you force Stuart Coleman out of the shops, entirely. You own his personal notes; you own the mortgage on his house. You will have no difficulty at all, my dear boy!"

He leaned back in his chair, and smiled angelically. Angus looked at him, and winced inwardly. The young man's face was as cold and fixed as if it had lain under the snow for weeks.

Angus shook his head. He said: "I am sorry, Mr. Allstairs, but I have not planned it that way. Do not think I am insensible to your kindness. I am not. I marvel, indeed, at your generosity. But it cannot be that way. However, I have a counter offer."

Joshua's face wrinkled viciously. He sucked in his lips. He clutched the head of his cane. But he said, mildly enough: "Well, then, I am a reasonable man. Make me your offer."

Angus was silent. His forehead was puckered. He looked at the fire in a long meditation. Then he began to speak quietly, as if thinking aloud:

"I have a deep attachment to the shops, Mr. Allstairs. I might even say, a profound attachment. They are my whole life. I know nothing else. I have dreamed, for years, of owning them entirely. I want no partners, not even a silent partner. The shops must be entirely in my own hands. I have worked to that end for years."

Joshua, who in the beginning had listened with impatience, now listened intently. Respect glimmered in his vulture's eyes. He rested his chin on the head of his cane and fastened his gaze unblinkingly on Angus' face. He nodded tremulously. Why, he reflected, there was even a dim passion in that dead voice! A tremble, a movement, as of life.

"Mr. Schnitzel," continued Angus, "is more than—kind, sir. He is overwhelmingly magnanimous. He has offered to back me in any sum. However, he too has suffered from this war, and the twenty thousand dollars he has lent me to buy up Stuart's notes—in order that Stuart can be forced from the shops—is all he can spare me just now.

"Suppose, Mr. Allstairs, that you decide to proceed on your own, and foreclose on the shops. You will get nothing but debts. There will not even be a manager. The Merchants' Committee, newly formed in New York to conclude the business of the shops, will take everything. How much do the shops owe you, Mr. Allstairs? Eighteen thousand dollars? You will lose that entirely, sir.

"But suppose, on the other hand, that you take my own personal notes, after I have disposed of Stuart, to be amortized during a reasonable period of time from the profits of the shops—say at an interest of eight percent, which is practically illegal." The young man allowed himself a bleak smile. "As you have said, the war cannot last much longer. Then, with cash in hand, I can restock the shops now, from merchants in New York and Chicago. I can have the shops on a flourishing basis, in spite of the war, within six months. I will draw nothing for personal expenses from them, until prosperity returns.

"I think, with your monetary aid, that I can settle with the Merchants' Committee for fifty cents on the dollar. I have sounded them out, discreetly, and they are giving the matter consideration. They must. Otherwise, they will lose everything. They know that if they sell at auction what stock there is on hand, they will get much less in that event of total liquidation, probably not more than five cents on the dollar. I think they will listen very closely, yes, indeed."

Joshua said nothing. But his head was nodding excitedly.

Angus continued unemotionally: "I will reorganize the business entirely. I will call it Cauder & Company. I will be sole owner. Perhaps this is an obsession with me. But I know I must have it that way.

"You have the figures. You know that the shops owe seventy-five thousand dollars to the banks and merchants, the wholesalers, manufacturers and importers. You know what I need. I have outlined my plans to you. It is entirely in your hands, now, to decide what can be done."

There was a long silence in the dark and desolate room.

But the fire was a blaze of scarlet on the hearth. Joshua crouched in his chair, licking his lips, his mesmerizing regard fixed on the younger man.

Then his tremulous hand reached out for the bell-rope. "Shall we have a little tea, eh? A little light refreshment, perhaps?"

Angus nodded. Then he said, firmly: "There is another thing which I must discuss with you. I ask you to listen reasonably, sir. I think, too, in a way, that it will please you, when you consider it." He smiled again, and that smile was like cold moonlight on snow, yet without malignance.

"I need a manager. I shall offer Stuart the position of manager in the shops at a salary, say, of three hundred dollars a month. After all, he is my kinsman. He will receive no other remuneration, however. He cannot refuse. If he does, he will be penniless. I feel it is my duty to offer this, even my religious and Christian duty. Of course, if he does refuse, then I am absolved from any further effort in his behalf."

Joshua's face darkened, lightened, blazed, twisted with evil, as all the potentialities of Angus' words rushed through his mind. He leaned forward, hardly breathing, watching the younger man. He began to chuckle. "Ah," he said, "how have the mighty fallen! What an end! What justice! What retribution! Please me? My dear Angus, this is the final delicate touch, the final revenge, the final righteousness! Please me! Ah, if I could only be present when you make him that offer, which he cannot refuse! It would be a justification of my long suffering at the hands of that blackguard, the very vengeance of God!"

Angus stiffened. He sat even straighter, and thinner, in his chair. Again, he touched his forehead with his lean fingers, and his eyes closed on a spasm of pain. He said quietly: "I cannot agree with any of that, sir. I am an honest man. I believe in justice, and I believe I am being just with Stuart. The shops have been his; he has loved them, been proud of them, lived for them. They are his monument. What I have to offer him—what I must offer him in all Christian compassion and mercy—he cannot refuse. Otherwise, he will see his shops collapse about him, himself reduced to penury, his house lost forever. He will remember the shops—and his house. He will remember, too, how he has neglected the shops, ignored the bills and the duns. I know that he has done this out of fear, out of a craven reluctance to face consequences and grapple with reality. His motto has always been 'sufficient unto the day is the evil thereof.' But he has refused to see that the day of evil always arrives. As for his prodigalities, his sins, his excesses, his follies and his dishonesties, I leave them to the final judgment of God."

CHAPTER 69

FATHER HOULIHAN could not sleep. He could hear the hissing of the snow against his window. He could hear the snoring of Mr. Walsh, stretched across his doorway. He could hear the dolorous howling of the wind, the rattling of the windowpanes. Trees cracked in the iron frost of the winter. Life had retreated from the world.

There was a long sickness of the soul in the priest. He could not even pray. It was as if his very spirit were enclosed in ice, lying at the bottom of a dark crevice in some glacier. His loneliness, his desolation, were unendurable. A dozen times he rose, knelt before his crucifix. But he had no words. The lips of his soul were numb. He could not weep; he could not even think. He felt himself alone in a universe of evil; he felt the winds of black and endless space roaring over him.

He had been suffering like this for several days, and had avoided even Stuart. The disease which afflicted him was nameless. He knew only that he wished for death, as he had never wished it before in his long life. There were no words for his malady.

He was filled with fear and dread and hopelessness. He saw the candle on his table throw wan streamers of pale light on the crucifix. He lay rigid in his narrow bed, cold as death, despite the heaped blankets and quilts. But there was a hot coal in his brain, throbbing, blackening, scarring

He was not given to self-analysis. He could not trace the beginning of the mortal illness in his soul. He tried, vaguely Sam's death, perhaps? Stuart's black preoccupation in these days? The disaffection of his wealthier parishioners? The coldness of his bishop? The war? Each thought made the coal in his head brighten, pain more deeply. Perhaps they were the sum of his misery. But why had God deserted him? Why could no prayer come to his lips? He felt himself surrounded by the hatred of the city. There was no help for him.

Unbidden, terrifying, the words of Job rose up before his eyes in letters of fire: "Though I speak, my grief is not assuaged; and though I forbear, what am I eased?—He teareth me in his wrath, who hateth me: he gnasheth upon me with his teeth; mine enemy sharpeneth his eyes upon me. They have gaped upon me with their mouth; they have smitten me upon the cheek reproachfully; they have gathered themselves together against me. God hath delivered me to the ungodly, and turned me over into the hands of the wicked.—My face is foul with weeping, and on my eyelids is the shadow of death. Not for any injustice in mine hand: also my prayer is pure."

The long sickness in him sharpened, became like the taste of ashes and vitriol in his mouth. He knew now the source of his sickness. He saw the hatred of the people, even those he had helped with passionate hands and voice and indignation, all about him, like a cloud of poisonous insects, stinging him, filling him with disease and suffering. He remembered each of the scores of foul letters, all anonymous, which had come to him. He saw the clouds of venomous and grinning faces he had met on the streets. He heard, again, the curses. He saw the slowly emptying pews of his church. He heard the voices, saw the hands, lifted against him. Why? There was no guilt in him, he hoped. He thought, humbly, I have only tried to do the will of God. Why, then, was he hated?

Suddenly, the priest sat up, his eyes filled with tears. What had Jesus said on the Cross? "My God, my God, why hast Thou forsaken me?" Then, He, too, had felt such a sickness and terror as this, such a hopelessness, such a despair, such an abandonment! At the last, even His own godhead had not been strong enough to prevent His mournful cry to God, His own consciousness of the overpowering wickedness of men! Why then, should he, Michael Houlihan, be so afraid, so ignorant, so terrified? He, who was less than the dust beneath the feet of Christ. If God, Himself, could feel so, in the last supreme moment of anguish, desolation and abandonment, in the last realization of the enormity of mankind, why should he, a miserable priest, feel such guilt in his own anguish?

He pushed himself out of bed. He sank on his knees before the crucifix, his eyes flooded with tears. But he was smiling. He murmured aloud. He prayed. "Forgive me, Father, for I am only a poor and wretched man. I did not accept the hatred, the same hatred which followed Thee.

I thought, in my stupidity, my conceit, that I might be loved for doing, in a little way, what Thou dids't, and for which Thou wast paid with hatred! I, to be loved, and Thou, to be hated! What presumption on my part, what folly, what sinfulness! But, forgive me."

He knelt for a long time in the bitter cold of his room, his head bowed on his clasped hands. But he was at peace. He was filled with pure and trembling joy. The universe was no longer filled with evil, but with love and tenderness, with the presence of God. It seemed to fume and blow with indescribable colors and warmth and music.

He heard shouts, cries, the ringing of bells. He lifted his head, dazedly. He heard Father Billingsley pounding frantically at his door. Then the door burst open, and the younger priest stood on the threshold, trembling, white as a ghost, wrapped in his dressing-gown. He mouthed, unable to speak. Father Houlihan rose slowly to his feet, ice-cold again, shivering. Father Billingsley pointed at the window, and the priest turned in heavy, numb obedience. He saw a brilliant red glow in the sky, the swirling of smoke.

It was the church! The beautiful little white church, which Stuart had built so lovingly, and at such reckless cost. The church was burning. Father Houlihan heard shouts and screams, the frenzied ringing of fire-bells, the galloping of horses, the grinding of wheels.

"My God!" whispered Father Houlihan. "My God!"

He turned, as if in a nightmare, to his junior. But Father Billingsley had gone. His feet were clattering down the bare wooden stairs. Father Houlihan heard the front door open. He heard his junior's frenzied cry: "The eucharist! I must save the eucharist!"

Flames enveloped the white snow of the church. They turned the golden cross to a cross of fire. Every window was a pool of scarlet. The arsonists had done their work well. There was no saving of the church. There was no saving of Father Billingsley, who had eluded the dazed firemen to dash into the gushing church, and to die on the seething floor before the altar, his arms outstretched.

CHAPTER 70

STUART led the appraiser from New York to his cherished buhl cabinet, and waited while that cabinet was scrutinized, tapped, thoroughly examined. His lips were compressed grimly. The appraiser's attention was attracted by some exquisite porcelain French figures in the cabinet, also, and he narrowed his eyes thoughtfully. There was an ivory fan, too, which had belonged to Marie Antoinette, to which the appraiser was not insensible.

A little later Stuart looked at the draft in his hand for seven thousand dollars. He did not look at the corner in which had stood his cabinet, and its treasures. He put the draft in his pocket, threw his coat over his shoulders, pulled his hat down over his eyes, and went out, calling for his carriage. He was driven to Father Houlihan's house. As he had not looked at the empty corner where his cabinet had stood in its lovely glory, so he did not glance at the gutted shell of the little white church near the priest's house, its blackened fragments partially covered by dirty snow. He went into the house, and was greeted by Mrs. O'Keefe, who had become old in these weeks, and whose eyes were constantly puffed by weeping. Stuart frowned at her, while his heart ached. "It's cold here," he said. "Why didn't you tell me? I sent an order for eight tons of coal. Haven't they arrived? Well, then, I could have had some of my own brought over. Such nonsense."

But there was a small fire in the priest's bedroom. Father Houlihan, sunken and aged, lay listlessly on his pillows. It was an effort for him to turn his head when Stuart entered. He tried to smile. His hands were still bandaged, and a healing burn scar marked his cheek lividly. Stuart sat down near him, and smiled briskly. "I've brought you some excellent port, Grundy," he said. "Three big glasses a day, with an egg beaten up in it, remember. Get you on your feet in no time."

"Stuart," said the priest, and then could not speak through his thickened throat. His eyes, so faded now, were almost colorless, drained by his tears and his agony. Yes, reflected Stuart, the world had become too much for this harmless, good old man. He made himself scowl. "You've got to get

525

up, Grundy. You can't lie like this forever. What will your new assistant think, when he arrives tomorrow? You always had plenty of grit, old feller. You've still got it. And Malone says there is no reason in the world while you shouldn't be up and about."

The priest said nothing. He only gazed at Stuart as if the very sight of him was life-giving, and consoling.

Stuart drew out the draft and laid it on the quilt. "There is seven thousand dollars. Enough to begin again, for a church. We'll make it bigger and handsomer, Grundy. Gray stone this time, perhaps, with rich Italian doors. I've already ordered the doors. They'll not keep you down, Grundy, poor old boy."

The priest lifted the draft in his bandaged fingers. He stared at it. He burst into silent tears. "Good God," fumed Stuart, wiping the tears away with his own kerchief. "That's no way to receive largesse. You've taken to weeping like a drunkard to his bottle. Be a man, Grundy, or I'll be sorry I came."

The priest was trying to speak. "Stuart, where did you get this money?" he croaked. "I can't take it lad. You need it. Where did you get it?"

"Never you mind," said Stuart, bluffly. "It—it was an unexpected profit. I've been doing a little something in Wall Street. Very unexpected. You might as well have it. I don't need it, damned if I do."

The priest began to shake his head, his heart too full for speech. "Don't be an ass, Grundy," said Stuart, irately. "Look here. You've always been trying to get me into your confounded church. I'll make a bargain with you. When the church is finished, I'll be the first in a pew. How is that? You can preach to me, and I won't yawn in your face. You can go on with your mumbo-jumbo, and I'll be as respectful as hell. I'll even kneel, confound you."

Father Houlihan's tears flowed more slowly. Suddenly, he began to smile. Finally, while Stuart watched him naïvely, he even laughed. At that strange and unaccustomed sound, Mrs. O'Keefe popped into the room, amazed. Father Houlihan's laughter became somewhat hysterical, and he waved the draft at his sister. She took it, began to cry soundlessly, throwing her apron over her face.

Stuart stood up. "Damned if I'm going to sit here and be drowned," he said. "Don't forget, Sarah. Three glasses of port, with an egg beaten up in them. And, Grundy, you mustn't worry about—anything. I'll take care of your worries.

I only want to see you on your feet again. We've come a long way together, old boy. First you hold me up, then I hold you up. We'll come over all of them yet, Grundy. To-morrow, when I come, I expect to see you downstairs, full of ginger again, receiving your new assistant with proper dignity."

Father Houlihan's face changed, became somber and desperate. "Stuart," he began, "I won't——"

"Now, now, no more talking. You must rest. Didn't I tell you I would take care of your worries? You'll see: there is nothing to be distressed about. Why, Grundy, I'd give my soul to help you, you know that; not that my soul is worth anything. Probably mortgaged to the devil a long time ago."

But the priest's expression had changed again, become solemn and tender. He lifted one bandaged hand, beckoned Stuart to him. Then, very gently, he made the sign of the Cross before his friend's face. "God bless you, and keep you, Stuart," he whispered. "If there is a mortgage on your soul, God holds it, and will redeem it."

The bishop's house was cold also, for all its discreet comfort and austere dignity. He had given away most of his coal to the poor and the deprived. But he sat in his black robes before the smallest of fires, a little thin with a lean ascetic face and bright cold eyes. His ring flashed in the candle-light, as he restlessly tapped with his hand on the carved arm of his chair. He regarded Stuart aloofly.

"Do you not think it impertinent of you, Mr. Coleman, to come into this house requesting, nay demanding, what you call 'consideration' for Father Houlihan? Are you not aware of the impropriety of your—request? I cannot recall such a situation in my experience, which has been long. You are a Protestant. I do not believe that even a Catholic would be so presumptuous in a matter which can concern only my-self and Father Houlihan. I should call this impudence, did I not know that only your ignorance of churchly etiquette prompted your visit."

"Oh—," said Stuart, impatiently, then caught back the oath. He reminded himself that angry words would not benefit his friend. He controlled himself. But his exhausted face became suffused. He choked on his words.

"Moreover," continued the bishop, sternly. "I resent the fact that you have sent to me a delegation consisting of his honor, the Mayor, your kinsman, Judge Cauder, and as-sorted dignitaries and prominent gentlemen of Grandeville.

You imply, in all your acts, that I am incapable of managing the affairs of this diocese. Or worse, that I am personally hostile to Father Houlihan. Really, this is outrageous. I must remind you, Mr. Coleman, that the affairs of this diocese are mine, not yours, and while I am not insensible to your kindness, nor to your love for Father Houlihan, I naturally resent all this impertinence."

"Impertinence, hell!" exclaimed Stuart, unable to restrain himself now. "All these stately phrases. I only know that you've never understood poor old Grundy. You've been too damned severe with him. You've never considered him a gentleman. You've frowned on his activities.

"You've written me letters of thanks, and summoned me here to thank me personally, for what you have considered my 'generosity' to your Church. Hasn't it ever occurred to your Reverence that what little I have done has been done for Grundy——"

"Grundy?" interrupted the bishop, flushing with affront.

Stuart waved his hand irately. "Yes, Grundy. I call him that, for a personal reason. Please let me finish. You've heard me call him Grundy a hundred times, yet you always pretend to be bewildered when I use the name." He drew a deep breath, flashed his angry black eyes at the bishop. "Well, then. I didn't help Grundy because he is a priest, but in spite of it. I love him. He's a wonderful old beggar. He's marvelous. He's a saint. I love the ground he walks on. Everything I've done—the church, the school, the convent, the hospital, has been only for him, not for your Church. Dozens of others, non-Catholics, have helped your Church, at my suggestion and instigation. Because they, too, honor and love poor old Grundy. Because they know he is good and sincere and gentle and honorable. I've told you my plans for a new church. If you insist on removing the old fellow, I withdraw my offer. I'll tear up the damned draft. And I promise you that your Church will get no further help from my friends, either. You'll antagonize every decent man in the city, Protestant and Catholic alike."

"Are you threatening me, Mr. Coleman?" cried the bishop, turning purple. "Dare you threaten me?"

"I'll dare anything for old Grundy," said Stuart, with hard resolution. "And I warn your Reverence that if you stick him away in some monastery or other, in the name of 'discipline,' you'll regret the day. I mean it. I'll fight to the death for the poor old chap, whose only sin is that he loved an accursed humanity, and believed in it, and fought for it."

The bishop was almost beyond speech. He struggled for breath. It was hard for him to control himself, to retain his dignity. Finally, he began to speak, in a strangled voice:

"I owe you no explanation, Mr. Coleman. I need say nothing to you. I could request you to leave this house at once. But I am remembering your kindness and generosity, and am patient with you.

"For years, I have warned Father Houlihan to refrain from his dangerous activities. It is not in the province of a priest to engage in popular, and secular, agitations. His work is the saving of souls, the proper administration of his parish. But Father Houlihan has been guilty of addressing motley audiences of workingmen, urging them to demand what he declares are 'better wages and living conditions.' He has been a firebrand, agitating in causes which cannot, and must not, concern him. He has infuriated influential gentlemen in this city, both Catholic and Protestant. He has gone about proclaiming loudly against what he chooses to call 'intolerance and hatred and oppression.' I have warned him repeatedly——"

Stuart sprang to his feet. He cried out: "'Saving souls'! Why, curse it, what is 'saving souls'? Sprinkling holy water on starving men, uttering pious imbecilities over children who are dying for want of food, urging oppressed laborers to be patient under the yoke of their exploitation? Have you heard of revolutions, your Reverence? In spite of the priests, there have been bloody revolutions because the people could no longer endure their agonies and their starvation, and the cruelties of their masters. And the Church has suffered in those revolutions, because she has refrained from standing with the humble and the desperate, whom Christ loved, against those He hated and denounced. Have you not thought what a power the Church could be, if she set her face against the murderers, the tyrants, the oppressors? The world is full of atheists, non-believers, haters of religion, because the 'men of God' have rarely seen fit to champion the suffering and to denounce those who have inflicted that suffering!"

The bishop, his face convulsed, tried to rise, but before Stuart's wild passion and crying words, he sank back again in his chair, speechless, petrified.

Stuart paused, "You may please a group of bast—, of rascals, if you remove old Grundy from his parish, which he has served so faithfully and so tenderly. Yes, you may please them. But you will really 'infuriate' ten thousand of Grundy's friends, and they, too, are influential, and have power.

Have you considered that? Have you thought of their angry sentiments against you, and against your Church?"

The bishop was silent. He stared steadily at Stuart. His hands had begun to tremble. Finally, he began to rub his chin.

He said, almost gently: "There is much in what you say, Mr. Coleman. I realized, of course, that there was a great friendship between you and Father Houlihan, but I confess that I did not understand how great it really is. There is much to be said for a priest who can inspire such fervid sentiments, especially among those who are not of his Church. I shall take this fact into consideration in my final disposition of Father Houlihan's case. Mother Mary Elizabeth has also pleaded for him, which surprised me, as I was not aware she held him in such high regard." And the bishop smiled.

A huge flooding of relief filled Stuart. He stammered: "Thank you, thank you. And, Monsignor, I ask you to pardon my vehemence, and my disrespectful approach. But I became frantic— If you could have seen him today, as I have seen him so many days since that calamity, you would have been overcome with grief for him. If your Reverence would but send him a word of kindness, through me, perhaps, or by letter, a word of sympathy——"

The bishop spoke austerely. "Mr. Coleman, I beg of you. I need no suggestions."

"I assure your Reverence that I meant no impertinence," said Stuart, hurriedly. "But I know what joy it will bring to Grundy if he receives a word from you, the smallest word of consolation."

The bishop's smile was slightly less bleak. He shook his head with faint amusement. "You must allow me to conduct the affairs of my diocese in my own way, sir."

"Certainly, certainly! I meant no harm." Stuart hesitated. His blotched and haggard face took on the sudden smoothness of youth and simple eagerness. "There is another thing, Monsignor. I understand that you have often spoken to Grundy about my coming into your Church. Damn it, sir, I confess I have no faith in anything, and, to be honest, I never could have faith. But, if it will please you, and incline you to poor old Grundy, I shall be glad to come into the Church——"

The bishop stared. Then, though he tried to restrain himself, he began to laugh, softly at first, then with gathering tempo. Stuart regarded him with affront, frowning. When the bishop paused for breath, Stuart said, with dignity: "I am pleased that I have amused your Reverence, though how, I confess I do not know."

"We strike no bargains for souls, Mr. Coleman," said the bishop, with something quite warm in his august voice. "It is not possible to say: 'If you will do this for me I shall allow you to save my soul.' A man must feel an overpowering urge to come into the Church. He cannot buy a favor with his soul. His soul is not his to use as a bribe."

But he extended his hand to Stuart, and looked up into his face with an affectionate curiosity and a peculiar regard. "You have given me food for thought, Mr. Coleman, though you could not understand in what way. Do not worry yourself needlessly over your friend. With God's help, I shall find a merciful solution."

CHAPTER 71

STUART, as he returned to his house, felt more peace, and more hope, than he had felt for months. He was firmly assured that nothing distressing would happen to his friend. His first impulse had been to return to the priest's house and joyously communicate the news, but some rare and unusual discretion prevented him from this. Old Grundy would probably be more than scandalized, more than appalled. Absurd. These churchmen always delicately hesitated at the direct approach. They preferred to skirt and detour and mince, as if dancing a confounded minuet, and they must be careful to strike the proper attitudes and bow and sidle with the correct gestures. Stuart was exhilarated.

Marvina and Mary Rose were expected home in the next week or so. Stuart, tossing his cane, hat and coat upon a small chair, was tenderly pleased to find a letter from his small daughter, full of childish love and of joy in the prospect of returning home to her father. There were also a number of formidable letters bearing upon them the addresses and names of New York lawyers. Stuart, as usual, flung them aside, covered them with the day's newspaper. Once out of sight, they had little power to annoy him until he accidentally uncovered them again. There was a letter from Laurie, also. He tore it open, eagerly, and by the dim March light creeping through the windows, he stood in the hall and read it.

"My darling Stuart," Laurie had written, and though her words were not impatient there was a harder angle in her writing, a darker stroke than usual in her capitals: "As I have told you before I sympathize with all my heart, and can only wish that in some way I could alleviate your distress. Your last letter contained twelve pages, and nine of them were filled with descriptions of the sufferings and prostration of your friend, the priest, and maledictions against those who inflicted this suffering, and against those who killed poor Mr. Berkowitz. It touches me to read these proofs of your single-hearted generosity and loyalty and faithfulness to your friends, and I am sorry that so far there has been no response to your advertisements. Doubtless, there will be. As you have said: 'Who can resist ten thousand dollars?' However, though I wrote you fully about my notices, and sent you clippings, and described the ovation given me after my last appearances, you mention nothing of them. I understand, most certainly, that more important affairs now occupy your attention, but my vanity is sorely wounded, I am afraid. After all, your praise and sympathy and love are more to me than the applause of thousands, and the adoration of many strangers. But I have told you this before until you must find it tedious.

"You say that when you leave to bring Marvina and Mary Rose home from the mountains you will come to New York first. How delightful a prospect this is! I have not seen you since Christmas. The occasion will be one of exceptional joy to me. In New York the belief is very firm that the war will be concluded early this summer, and then there will be no reason why I should not go to Europe again. Nor have I abandoned by intention of persuading you to go with me, or, rather, to accompany me, for three months. But we shall discuss this when I see you next, which I pray will not be too long delayed. I might say, in closing, that I wear constantly the diamond- and pearl-brooch and the earrings with which you presented me at Christmas, and constantly receive the most extravagant compliments on them. Your taste, as always, is impeccable."

Stuart sighed, as he put the letter in his inner pocket. Even women like Laurie could not disassociate themselves from their immediate and exigent private desires. He had felt a coldness in her letter, a stately chill, a cool offense. He was suddenly bereft, alone, filled with a tired and aching loneliness. Even love, it seemed, was a greedy emotion, and had in it no sympathy or tenderness for the torments of the beloved's soul.

A maid had been trying to attract his attention, and he frowned at her impatiently. "Mr. Cauder is awaiting you, sir, in the parlor," she told him. "Mr. Angus Cauder."

"The devil," said Stuart, scowling. What did that dim-eyed corpse wish of him? Without the slightest presentiment, Stuart marched into the parlor, his scowl deeper than ever. He stood on the threshold, and glared across the space of carpet with considerable contempt and repudiation. "Well, Angus," he said, harshly. "I trust no trouble brings you here?"

Angus was sitting before the fire, his chin on his bent hand. He rose as he heard Stuart's voice, and stood near the fire, dressed in black as always, his face a glimmering white mask in the gloom of the March twilight. He did not smile. He said: "I am afraid, Stuart, that it is very serious trouble."

Stuart forgot his antagonism. He advanced towards his kinsman, and said in a warmer and more concerned tone: "Not Bertie? Nothing has happened to Bertie, eh?"

Angus was silent a moment. Then he said coldly: "No, not Bertie, Stuart, I am glad to say. It is your trouble, Stuart. I thought I would speak of it to you, here, rather than in the offices. It is a matter of the most urgent privacy."

Laurie, then, thought Stuart. He smiled scornfully. His black eyes flickered with disdain over his visitor. He lifted his coat-tails and sat down negligently, drew a cheroot from his pocket, lit it unhurriedly. Only then did he say patronizingly: "Well, sit down, man, sit down. There is no corpse in this room yet, is there? You are not a premature undertaker, I hope."

"In a way," replied Angus quietly. He sat down.

"Eh?" said Stuart, staring blankly. "What did you say?"

But Angus sat stiffly in the opposite chair, and only looked at Stuart. He held a brief-case on his bony knees. His gray eyes had a peculiar glint in them, an impersonal gloating and lofty aversion. It was that look which made Stuart pause in the very motion of putting his cheroot into his mouth. For the first time he felt the faint chill shock of presentiment. "What is it?" he said roughly. "Out with it. It must be very important." He infused a satiric note in his voice, but even to him that note was weak.

"It is very important," said Angus, with no inflection in his words. He opened his brief-case and withdrew from it a sheaf of bills. Stuart recognized them as bills immediately. Hadn't he been throwing the cursed things into his wastebaskets for months? He winced a little. A hot dark flush invaded his face. But he lifted his head arrogantly, and assumed a forbidding posture.

"Those would not be bills, eh?" he asked, with heavy contempt.

"Yes, they would be bills, Stuart," replied Angus, with his deadly quietness. "Bills that can no longer be ignored. Bills in the sum of seventy-five thousand dollars, some of them over a year old, from New York and Chicago wholesalers, manufacturers and importers. Also, urgent communications from various banks." He paused. "Would you like to refresh your memory with them, Stuart?" And he extended the ominous sheaf to the other man.

But Stuart made no effort to take them. Smoke curled from his mouth. His heart had begun to beat with its old rusty pain.

Angus still extended the bills in his lean and inexorable pale hand. He said: "In the preoccupations of the past few months, Stuart, you have not given heed to these bills. I can understand that. But they have become so imperative that I felt I must come to you at once, and discuss the matter with you."

Stuart gazed at his kinsman's face, and was silent. At length, in a stifled voice, he said: "This is a matter for discussion at the offices. I must ask you not to press me today. I do no business on Sundays, as you know."

Angus smiled. Angus did not withdraw the bills. "The matter is so urgent, Stuart, that I must overlook the fact that it is Sunday. Things cannot be delayed any longer."

Stuart aroused himself with difficulty. "You are impertinent, sir!" he exclaimed, with an oath. "You are only my manager. I insist that you no longer discuss this with me in my house, today."

Angus laid the bills on his knees. He gazed down at them thoughtfully. The fire crackled. A storm was rising; the first pallid flakes of snow were hissing at the windows. The voice of the river, breaking through rotting ice, was heard as a dull roar in the wind. Angus said: "I, too, have an aversion for business on Sundays. But, as certain things must be done tomorrow, at the latest, I am compelled to discuss this with you today."

Suddenly Stuart hated him violently. This hatred mingled with a desire to escape, to run out of this house, to flee from the onerous and terrifying burden of his days as he always fled from them. The bills in Angus' hands appeared to him like writs of execution. If he could only throw this corpse, with his bills, out of his house, and close the door upon him, he could forget the terror that haunted his sleeping hours and dogged him all his days; he could forget as he always forgot.

He wanted to kill Angus, this insolent puppy who sat there so immovably and looked at him so strangely.

"We must discuss it," said Angus, and his voice was barely audible. He reached into his brief-case again, and withdrew a smaller sheaf of papers. These he did not extend to Stuart, who felt a nauseous prickling over his flesh, a more terrible premonition. "I have here, Stuart, your personal notes in the amount of twenty thousand dollars. I bought them at a discount. Are you prepared to buy them from me, for twenty thousand dollars?"

Stuart pulled himself up in his chair. Now his breath beat thickly in his throat. Everything in the room moved about him in wide sick circles, dimming. But Angus' calm and rigid face was fixed in the center of the circles, and did not move.

Angus was putting the notes back into his brief-case, with the slow precise movements of an executioner preparing the ax. He was saying: "My question was rhetorical, I can see. You have no way of buying the notes from me."

He allowed himself to lean back in his chair. Now his voice was louder, or so it seemed to the desperately ill Stuart, and it had a curious clangor in it like an iron bell.

"You can see, Stuart, why I had to come to you today. A Merchants' Committee has been formed in New York, to force you into bankruptcy. I shall be very brief with you. You will be forced into total bankruptcy within ten days."

His voice was the only, and the most dreadful, reality in that swimming, darkening, welling room. Stuart heard every fateful word which destroyed him, ruined him, flung him out, brought his house and all his life thundering down upon him in the long upheaval of the final earthquake. Angus' calm and neutral voice went on and on, without hurry or emotion, the voice of a judge who condemned Stuart Coleman to death.

"It is understood, finally, Stuart, that your claims, and the claims of any other shareholder, are absolutely worthless, because in bankruptcy proceedings there will be nothing left, anyway. From tomorrow, henceforth, therefore, you are completely penniless. You must accede to my offers. You have no alternative.

"If you attempt to fight me, out of foolish vanity, or childish determination, I shall press for payment of these notes, and foreclose on your house. If you are reasonable, and I do not doubt you will be after careful thought, you will realize that the offer I shall make you is more than generous, more than you could possibly expect of me.

"You have ignored the business of the shops. Ruin has been steadily coming, and you have run from it. Each time, in the past, that Mr. Berkowitz attempted to discuss these things with you, you put him off, with demented oaths. Finally, he could do nothing. He saw it was useless, as I have seen it. He did not know what to do. I did. I have done all I could. I now make you my offer of three hundred dollars a month, which will help you keep your house, whose mortgage is in my hands. I will adjust matters with you within reason, and with mercy, because you are my kinsman, and have shown me some kindnesses." At this, the palest of convulsions arched Angus' lips, but did not change the even tone of his voice. "As my manager, you will not be forced to attend to details which have always been onerous to you, nor will you have the responsibilities which you have consistently evaded for years. You will have no responsibilities, but you will have only that three hundred dollars a month. With care, you can keep your house. But your scale of living will need to be essentially reduced. That is your affair. You must make your own adjustments. I give you only my advice."

With a shrill rustle he replaced the bills in his brief-case. Stuart did not move. He sat as if dead, struck down, in his chair.

Angus rested his clasped hands on his brief-case and looked at the man he had struck down with his quiet and merciless hand. No flicker of compassion or regret or sorrow passed over his frozen features.

"You can only refuse my offer to make you manager at three hundred dollars a month. That is the only choice left to you. I should regret it. You would make me an excellent manager. You have a way with customers which I confess I do not have. But, should you refuse, you would have no other income, and to protect my mortgage, I should be compelled to foreclose on your house. You would leave me no alternative.

"Stuart, you have often called me a miser, a cold-hearted wretch with no human emotions. But I have always had the highest regard for the shops, and that is why I have persuaded that—interested party of which I have told you to lend me the money to settle with the Merchants' Committee for fifty cents on the dollar. As I have told you, they have agreed. Yes, you have called me a miser, and cold-hearted, but I have had this feeling for the shops. I have had this feeling for you, as my kinsman."

He waited. But Stuart, sinking in his chair, was unable to move.

Angus resumed: "There is another matter. Mr. Berkowitz left twenty percent of his shares in the shops to—Father Houlihan. The priest is in a way of losing any income whatsoever, unless I proceed with my plans. But, to buy the goodwill of the Catholic community here, and of others who might have a sentimental attachment to the priest, I will make him a generous offer: I will give him five thousand dollars for his shares, which are really worthless. I do not have to do it. You know that."

For the first time, Stuart stirred. It was as if he felt the impact of a knife in his very vitals, and writhed under it. He put his hand to his throat, as if strangling. But it was a feeble gesture. Strange to say, that trembling gesture aroused some response in Angus, for he, too, lifted his hands and pressed them suddenly and firmly to his temples. He bent forward a little. His mouth opened, twisted. He gasped, inaudibly. His eyes closed.

Stuart whispered: "You have plotted this for years. You always looked for your opportunity. You have done this to me, deliberately."

Angus' fingers pressed deeper into his thin, veined temples. His long lean body tightened with his private agony. His breathing was louder now, hissing in the silence. He bent his chest closer to his arching knees, with their bony points.

"Always, through the years, you plotted against me, hated me. You waited a long time." Stuart's whisper was louder, more hurried, quicker. "But, you could wait. You had the patience of the serpent. You had the patience of all evil men."

Angus lifted his head. His white face was damp and glistening in the firelight. His voice was ragged, but calm: "You call me 'evil.' It is you who are the evil man, Stuart Coleman. You deserve no mercy, no compassion, no consideration, from me. But because I am not evil, I have given them to you. It is consistent with your nature that you should accuse me of the things which you actually are. There is no good in you. Impious and lascivious man! Consort of wicked and unspeakable people! Your name is a byword in this city, a contemptuous word in the mouths of decent folk who have regard for the laws of man and of God.

"If I were indeed evil, I should seize this moment to ruin you completely, to drive you, with the approval of a respectable community, out of Grandeville. Be careful, Stuart. Do not press me too far."

He rose. But he had to catch the back of his chair, for he staggered slightly. The pain in his head was savage, violent. It blinded him. "I have given consideration to your wife and child, the natural sufferers from your iniquity and prodigality. Being what you are, you would extend no such mercy to others, no such Christian charity. Yet I have mercy upon you. I have given you my offer. Take it or leave it. I am absolved from further pleadings with you."

He gasped, suddenly. He clutched the back of his chair. Stuart looked at him steadily, out of the depths of his own torment.

And then a strange thing happened. Stuart began to smile. It was not a dark, or a cruel, or a hating smile. There was even something gentle in it, and very sad. It was beyond reason, for he had only his intuition and his heart to prompt him.

He said, and his voice was very clear and low: "Go on, Angus. Go your way. And may God have mercy on your soul."

CHAPTER 72

"MORTIFICATION?" said Stuart, smiling at Father Houlihan. "Perhaps I should feel mortification, humiliation, outrage, fury. But, odd to say, I do not. I don't know why. It was his face—you should have seen his face. I could only pity him, then."

But Father Houlihan was looking at Stuart's own face. Stuart saw that loving and sorrowful regard, and he said, suddenly, involuntarily: "I am tired."

He rearranged the hot-house roses which he had brought to his friend, and then stood staring at them sightlessly. "I never knew what it was to be tired this way. Never before. Perhaps I am getting old. I don't know. But nothing seems of profound importance to me any longer, except the finding of Sam's murderers, and their execution." He tightened his fists. "That's all," he said, softly.

He turned to the priest. "Don't look at me as if I were a miserable object, Grundy. I never liked anyone to pity me. Besides, 'let us be reasonable.' The shops have been saved. I get three hundred dollars a month. I have no worries, no responsibilities, no burdens. I have saved my house." He rubbed his forehead, and sighed. "When Sam was there, it was different. But I have lost heart now."

He tried to smile humorously at his friend's mournful expression. "No more diamond necklaces, no more *objets d'art*, no more gold-headed canes, no more bottles of Napoleon, no more fine horses. You think I am devastated? I am not. I am tired." He added: "You think I am without pride?"

But the priest said: "You do not hate Angus?"

"Hate him? My God! I tell you, I saw his face!"

Father Houlihan stretched out his hand to his friend, and Stuart took it, shaking it warmly and affectionately. "Stuart, I've always said you were a good man. It takes a man with God in his heart to pity his enemy who has destroyed him."

Stuart was suddenly somber. "Destroyed me? No. No one destroyed me. I destroyed myself. Well, I do not care. I have had a good life. A very good life." He laughed gently.

Father Houlihan did not entirely believe Stuart. He believed that Stuart was self-deceived. He was exhausted, he was numb, he was too desolate for strong emotion. And, he had one obsession: the finding of the murderers of Sam Berkowitz.

"I shall be away for two weeks, or more, Grundy. Take care of yourself. I will bring back the finest architectural plans for the new church. It will make the old one look like a toy. You'll see."

He went out and untethered his horse. He rode through the dirty rotting snow that filled the streets. He touched his hand briefly to his hat as he passed acquaintances, indifferent to the sly whispers in his wake. He was very tired. He felt the tiredness like dry ash in his body, in his mouth, in his eyes.

He looked at his lovely house, and for the first time his heart beat a little quicker. Ah, he still had his house. He need fear its loss no longer. He would pay Angus one hundred dollars a month on the accursed mortgage. He would have two hundred left. Most of the servants must go. The stables must be emptied. But the nurse for Mary Rose must remain, and one cook. Stuart's eye brightened. He would soon have his daughter with him, and he would have his house. Matters could be much worse.

When he entered the house, after carefully wiping his muddy boots, he found the turnkey from the jail awaiting him, with an excited face. "Mr. Coleman, there is something I must tell you, at once. Very important. And then, perhaps, you will come with me, eh? Is the reward still good?"

Angus sat with Joshua Allstairs in the rich private offices of the bank. All the papers had finally been signed. Joshua leaned back in his chair and chuckled.

"The day I've awaited for fifteen years has come, Angus, my boy. A lovely, lovely day. God's vengeance on an evil man has been given into my hand. Christian probity and piety have been vindicated. I can die in peace."

Angus nodded. He gathered up the papers precisely, scrutinized them with a careful frown. He said: "I see here a certain paper. In the event of your—passing, sir, your interest in this matter is to pass, with the balance of your estate, into a trust for your daughter, Mrs. Coleman, and your granddaughter, Miss Mary Rose. But only in the event that Mrs. Coleman leaves her husband within sixty days after your—passing. In the event she does not, which is only slightly possible, the whole estate is to be held in trust for Miss Mary Rose until she is thirty years old, and is married. A very excellent arrangement."

Joshua chuckled again. "Marvina is a fool. She always was. I had little difficulty in persuading her to visit me secretly. And I love that little girl of hers. Marvina will leave that abominable man, I am assured of that. I have even discussed the matter with her. She agrees to everything. She always agrees to everything."

The tendril of pain fluttered in Angus' brow. He rubbed it, absently. The last few weeks had made him paler, thinner, than ever, so that he was even more corpse-like than before. Joshua eyed him with cruel curiosity and interest.

"Mrs. Coleman is very fortunate in having a father like yourself, sir," said Angus, ponderously. "Forgiving, generous, unforgetting, loving."

Joshua nodded benignly. "But I imagine you will be such a father also, Angus. You have a fine little girl." He made his malignant old face sorrowful. "How sad that her mother did not live to see her reach full estate!"

Angus' face changed. He put the papers into his brief-case, fastened the straps. He thought of his little daughter, Gerda, who was just beginning to walk. His heart did not warm. The child possessed her mother's rough flaxen hair and big shallow blue eyes. She was her grandparents' child, not his. He knew that she did not even like him, or tolerate him. As for Gretchen, six months dead, he felt no emotion at all. She had ostensibly died of "lung fever," when her daughter was three months old, but Angus knew, as did her physician, that she had died of overeating. It had been an odious death.

Joshua watched his young friend's frozen and immobile face intently. He said, with false sympathy: "How are your headaches, my boy?"

Angus smiled bleakly. "They bother me. I ought to wear my spectacles. But I always forget them. However, I can say that they are somewhat improved. Mother uses herb compresses on my head at night, and they assuage the pain considerably. I have hopes that time will cure them."

He looked steadily at Joshua. Joshua was an ancient man. But he was potent. And he had been very kind. Moreover, he was a pious and devout "Christian." Angus felt enormous respect for him. He smiled. "I must thank you again, sir, for everything. Without you, I could not have realized my life-long hopes and desires."

Joshua extended his claw of a hand. "My boy, I was never mistaken in a man in all my life. I knew what you were from the very beginning. We'll go far together, I vow."

They shook hands with restrained regard. Angus picked up his hat and coat. "You will dine with me as usual, on Friday evening?" asked Joshua. "I look forward to those occasions."

"Certainly. It will be a great pleasure." Angus bowed ceremoniously.

He turned to the door. But it burst open suddenly, and revealed the face of a frightened clerk. The clerk was swept away by a vigorous hand, and on the threshold stood Stuart and the Sheriff.

Joshua uttered a faint cry, and grasped the arms of his chair as if to rise. His face became contorted, screwed into a monkey-like expression of ancient hatred and fear. Angus stepped back from the threshold, flushing.

For Stuart's face, for all its wild smile, was terrible. It was black with hatred, with triumph, with maniacal joy and exultation. He advanced into the room and pointed to Joshua. He cried, loudly, to the Sheriff: "There is your murderer, sir, at last! There is your prisoner! Take him at once!"

Joshua fell back in his chair. He shrank, he withered, to a heap of trembling bones. But his eyes were coals of fire. He looked at Stuart, and not at the Sheriff. The Sheriff's face was stern. He held a writ in his hand.

The Sheriff said: "Mr. Joshua Allstairs, I have here a warrant for your arrest for complicity in the murder of one Samuel Berkowitz. You will please to come with me at once."

There was a loud and rasping gasp in the room, but no one heard it. Angus had fallen back against a wall. He stood there, clutching his brief-case to his chest. He looked at Joshua in his chair, saw the horrible evil and terror on the old man's craven face.

"What are you saying?" whispered Joshua. Then he croaked: "What are you saying, sir? Are you mad?"

But the Sheriff stared at him remorselessly. "I am not mad, Mr. Allstairs. This morning we took a prisoner, one Will Dobson. He was pursued in the railroad yards as he was about to board a freight train in order to leave the city. He fell under a wheel. He is terribly mangled. Fearing he was about to die, and wishing to make his peace, he called for me, and confessed that on the night of September 12, 1863, he was hired, with one Fred Engels, to assault Mr. Berkowitz. He was hired, with Engels, by you, Joshua Allstairs. He told us where Engels could be found, and he, also, is in custody, and will throw himself on the mercy of the State. He has confessed his part in this murder, though he states that murder was not entirely the object. He declared that for this heinous crime he and his companion criminal were paid the sum of five thousand dollars, in cash, by yourself."

Joshua started in his chair. His face was frightful. He raised his hand and pointed it violently at Stuart, but looked at the Sheriff. He cried: "It is a lie, a most abominable lie, sir! I had nothing whatsoever to do with this! If there is a murderer in this room, there is your man, not I! Have you forgotten that it was he who found the Jew, his friend, and he, alone, and that he owed this fine friend fourteen thousand dollars? Sir, I demand that his fellow conspirators in this appalling plot be forced to confess who is the real murderer!"

"Why—" began Stuart, advancing to his ancient enemy, with clenched fists. But the Sheriff caught his arm, and said, with odd gentleness: "Easy, Stuart. Quiet, there. Patience, Stuart." He turned to Joshua. "It is no use, sir. The men have confessed. We have their written confessions. They have supplied all details. You will have to come with me at once."

Joshua's dry toothless mouth opened on a ghastly screech. He screamed, over and over. He beat the arms of his chair with his knotted hands. He cursed. He frothed. He went into a convulsion of terror and hatred and madness. The Sheriff waited. Stuart waited, looking at his old enemy. But he was horrified, in spite of himself. He closed his eyes, suddenly. He could not look at that face, the face of a demon.

The Sheriff, composed, though pale, waited until Joshua was still, shuddering, whimpering, weeping, in his chair, wringing his hands. The old man was gray; his staring eyes were bloodshot, starting. He was looking about him now, as a hunted rat stares, looking for a corner, a hole for escape.

Then the Sheriff said: "There is a lesser crime attributed to you also, Mr. Allstairs. The burning of the Church of Our Lady of Hope. The men have confessed this, as well as the more terrible crime. I need not have told you this, except to convince you that there is no possibility of your escaping justice this time."

Joshua was whispering again, and the whisper was like the sliding of a snake through dry grasses: "I demand my lawyer. I must see my lawyer. I will have justice."

"You shall have justice," said the Sheriff, grimly. "Before a jury of your peers. And now, sir, you are wasting my time. Call your carriage at once."

There was a sudden and awful silence in the room, except for Joshua's incoherent whispering, which had an element of dementia in it. He crouched in his chair, wringing his hands. His fiery eyes blazed about him, unseeingly. His lips moved endlessly, over and over. He whispered of strange things, and all were heavy with hatred and insanity and fury.

Finally, the focus of his eyes fastened on Stuart. He started. The two men regarded each other in the dreadful quiet. Then Stuart said, and his voice trembled: "You have lived a long life of evil and abomination. You have stolen, destroyed, ruined. You have killed. But you are an old man. I am sorry for you. I pity you, from my heart."

At this, Joshua uttered a monstrous cry, a shrill, howling and inhuman cry. Stuart fell back. He turned away. "Curse you, curse you to hell!" screamed Joshua. "May all the pangs of hell tear you and devour you! May you rot and die in agony! May all the foul fiends rend you forever!"

Stuart said: "God have pity upon you. You are an old man."

It was then that Joshua uttered appalling oaths and blasphemies. He beat his hands on his knees in a frenzy; he stamped his feet on the floor with a drumming sound. He went out of his mind. He howled, again and again.

"God!" said the Sheriff. "I can't stand this. I shall have to have help, Stuart. Do you go for the police."

And then, as suddenly as he had gone mad, Joshua was silent. He stared before him, at the floor. He began to smile. He chuckled. Convulsions of mirth rippled over his wizened body. He sank far back into his chair. He was completely still. There was the grimace of a devil on his gray, webbed face. The grimace widened. The silence in the room was complete.

Stuart bent forward to scrutinize him. And then he exclaimed: "My God! I—I think he has died! He has escaped!"

CHAPTER 73

STUART was admitted to Angus' bedroom. He entered awkwardly, reluctantly, and with much uneasiness. When Angus had sent for him, he had been incredulous, then apprehensive. Well, well, it did not matter. If the poor petrified fool believed that he had worse calamities to heap upon him, Stuart, then he would be disappointed. There was nothing more anyone could do to him, he believed. He had ceased to fear calamity. He was annoyed that Angus might be plotting fresh assaults upon his kinsman. It was a waste of time, so far as Stuart was concerned. He was immune to further devastations.

Nevertheless, though he smiled drearily to himself on entering Angus' bedroom, he also braced himself. There was a limit, he thought vaguely, to what a man could endure.

Angus was raised high on his pillows. His nurse hovered over him in the stark dim gloom. He was very quiet, his hands lying on the silk coverlet. So dusky was the room that Stuart could not, at first, see the other man's face except for the two dark holes which were his eyes.

"Well, well," said Stuart, with weak bluffness, "we have an invalid here, I see."

Angus' head moved slightly on his pillows. He said in a voice strangely strong and composed: "Good afternoon, Stuart. Miss Crump, you may leave the room if you please. I have some private matters to discuss with Mr. Coleman."

Stuart did not know what to do with his hat and cane, which had not been taken from him downstairs by the sullen maid. He balanced them on his knee. He tried to smile cheerfully at Angus. What the devil! The poor beggar was done in. He felt no animosity towards Angus, only compassion. If the poor fool wished to enjoy his triumphs, to extend them further, and it might give him some satisfaction, let him have them, and be damned to him. It was punishment enough for him to live in this disgusting house with a pair of porkers. If anything could give him joy, he was welcome to it. Old Joshua's death had apparently been a shock to him. Stuart smiled with sudden darkness.

Angus saw that smile. He said quietly: "You hate me, then, do you not, Stuart?"

"Hate you?" Stuart stared. He shook his head. "No, Angus, I don't. Why should I? You acted according to your conscience." He waited. Then he said, with intuitive shrewdness: "You did, didn't you?"

Angus did not speak. Stuart's vision was becoming accustomed to the dusk. He saw that a very sick man lay on those pillows, a man utterly undone, broken, exhausted. Yet there was some inhuman and indomitable spirit in him still.

Stuart spoke frankly: "I don't know why you asked me to come to see you, under all the circumstances. I thought it very peculiar. But I am not one to refuse to visit the sick, and when I heard of your illness, I regretted it. It—it must have been considerable of a shock to have old Allstairs die before you like that." Again his face changed, became dark and hard. "He had an easy escape, Angus, you know. If he was your friend you ought to be glad of that."

Angus' hand lifted, moved, then was motionless again. He said in a low voice: "I understand Marvina has left you. They told me this morning."

Stuart lifted his cane and intently scrutinized the head. He said musingly: "Yes. It was a condition of her father's will. She was very pleasant about it, and very reasonable. I saw her point. After all, I could not expect her—under the circumstances—to forego such a fortune for me. We've not been man and wife for many years. I've gone my way, completely. She has told me she prefers to return to her mother's old home, in Philadelphia, where she has relatives."

He frowned. "But, of course, this is none of your affair, Angus. Unless you have more bad news for me?"

Angus said: "You are not sorry, then? What about Mary Rose?"

Stuart looked at him, steadily. "I have consented not to fight any divorce action Marvina brings against me. In return, Mary Rose is to live with me, when her health permits, for as many months in the year as she desires. It is all very amicable." He paused, then smiled ironically. "If you are distressing yourself over my private affairs, Angus, I am grateful to you. But if you wish to discuss them with me I must decline to do so. I cannot consider them any concern of yours."

Angus moved his hand again. "Will you marry Laurie, Stuart?"

Stuart stood up. He stood beside the bed for a long time, in silence. Angus felt his hardening, his stiffening. But Stuart's voice was gentle and firm: "I am sorry you are ill, Angus. But I will not tire you further. I have only this to say: Whatever Laurie, and I, decide, and that must be some time in the future, it is our concern."

Angus gazed up at him immovably. Was it his illness which gave Angus such a distraught and sunken appearance? Stuart reflected. The planes and angles of his white face seemed less hard and sharp.

"Please sit down, Stuart," said Angus, in a faintly hoarse voice. "I beg of you."

Stuart sat down, frowning, perplexed. What did the miserable wretch desire of him? All at once, Stuart's intuition came vividly alive. There was something else! There was something this frozen stick wished to say, and he had no words with which to say it! Stuart leaned towards him, and said, impulsively: "Why skitter about, Angus? What do you want to say? Can I help you?"

Then Angus said, dimly: "Talk to me. Just talk to me. Tell me anything you wish. Tell me what you think——"

"About what?" said Stuart. And then was silent. His intuition was speaking loudly to him now, but so loudly indeed that he could only hear its loud shouting and not its imperative directions.

Angus closed his eyes. He whispered: "You were very good to me. I remember how miserable and lonely I was, when I was a child. You took me and Laurie in from the garden. Laurie sat on your knee, and you told her a tale. Then, we dined with you. It was a lovely April night. We were all alone."

"Yes," said Stuart, gently. "I remember. I—I was very fond of you, Angus. You were such a wretched little feller. I wish I had had more sensibility, then."

But Angus was still whispering, and his eyes were closed: "You were very kind. I see now how kind you were. You are always kind. It is very hard to speak. I have no words, Stuart."

There was a weak shaking in Stuart's knees. He said: "Tell me, Angus. Tell me anything you wish. I am listening."

But he could see, as if it were clearly and vividly in the room, the huge heavy stone that lay on the flesh of Angus, crushing down his soul, stifling his words. He saw, as if it were actually before him, the struggle Angus was having with that stone, to shift it from him, to free himself of it—a stone that had grown with all his lifetime—and how it was killing him. He saw so many things, vast, tremendous, heartbreaking, and he was stricken dumb, and was awed, by what he saw.

"Talk, Stuart," said Angus. "Only talk. About anything. Your friends. Your life."

"But there is nothing in my life that isn't sordid or useless or futile," said Stuart, devoured by pity. "I am not even successful. I can point to nothing but my poor house, as an accomplishment."

Angus' weary eyelids opened, and his gray eyes, suffused, stared strangely at Stuart. He said: "I never knew how many friends you had. I never knew how much I am now hated, because of you."

Stuart was amazed. He said quickly: "Nonsense. Everyone speaks of how clever you are, how competent, how admirable. If I was in your way, then it was my fault. I deserved it. You saved the shops. I am really grateful. Yes, indeed. I wasn't at first," he added, ruefully. "There was an hour or two I wished to murder you, and could have done it with pleasure. But not now." He thought: Oh, the poor bastard!

But Angus said: "Tell me what you think about, Stuart. Anything."

What the devil! thought Stuart. He began to speak, gently, slowly: "I think about many things, Angus, or, at least, I think I think. But they are feeble things. I think how happy it was to have had Sam Berkowitz for a friend, and your brother, Robbie, who is more human than I thought, and old Grundy. I think how proud I am of Laurie, and how I love my child. I think of the years in the shops, and how I built them up. I think of the soft beds I have slept in, and the— the handsome ladies I have known, the music I have heard, the wines I have drunk, the cards I have played. I think, too, of how much laughter I have had, more than most other men. Damn it," he added, with sudden embarrassment, "my thoughts, I presume, are the same as any other man's. Not pertinent or earth-shaking, or of any significance."

Angus' head moved on his pillows. He sighed. He murmured: "I think, too, of the walks you took with me, when I was a child. I think of the things you said. I remember them all. Do you remember the first night you took me to Father Houlihan's?"

Stuart scowled, trying to remember. He said: "Yes, I think so. You had your Testament with you, and you were very shocked at the card-playing."

He was surprised at the very ghost of a sound from Angus. Surely he had not heard aright! That had not been a laugh! But Angus was smiling, the very ghost of a smile. Stuart could not believe it. He said: "How is your head, Angus?"

But Angus was speaking, and his voice came in weak and hurried gasps: "All my life, my mother impressed upon me that money was everything. That there was nothing but money. It was the power that subdued the world, brought friends and admirers, commanded respect even from kings, surrounded a man with an invulnerable wall, made him honored even before God. If a man was poor, then he was accursed of heaven, and deservedly so."

Stuart thought the words childish, and he was embarrassed again. He said: "Well, well, there is much to be said about money, of course——"

Angus moved restlessly on his pillows. "There are things I cannot say. I cannot even think them, coherently. They are too enormous for me. There is always such a pain in my head. I do not know what is wrong with me. I never know. There is no one to tell me, no one at all. You cannot, Stuart. You have never had my thoughts."

Stuart did not speak. But he leaned forward to look at the other man's deathful face. It was his intuition which made him say: "Angus, I shall send old Grundy to you. Tomorrow. Wait for him, Angus."

He stood up. He felt in feverish haste. "I shall go to him at once! Perhaps he will come today. He always loved you, Angus. He always spoke of—of your capacity for sacrifice. Remember how you wished to be a doctor?"

Angus did not answer him. But suddenly he was gazing full at Stuart, and a glow was on his features, as if they had been struck by a light.

Stuart continued, hurriedly: "Grundy used to say that you had one consuming desire—to sacrifice yourself for others, to live for others. I do not know whether he was wrong, or right. He is so—transcendental. But he is the kindest man. I'll send him to you, Angus. Today. Within the hour."

He reached down, hesitated, then laid his warm hand on the cold rigid fingers on the coverlet. To his utter surprise, Angus laid his other hand on top of Stuart's. The act touched Stuart to the heart. His eyes dimmed. There was a lump in his throat.

He said, hoarsely: "Wait for Grundy. Only he can help you, Angus. And God knows, you need help."

CHAPTER 74

"You UNDERSTAND, sir, that you are admitted to this house under protest, and only by sufferance," said Mrs. Schnitzel, with ponderous majesty, and gazing at Father Houlihan from the heights of her aversion and indignation.

"Ma'am," replied Father Houlihan, gently, "I am not annoyed when it is resented that I enter a place where Jesus has never been admitted."

Mrs. Schnitzel's wits were not excessively subtle, or even normally so, therefore it was necessary that she mull for two hours over this quite obvious remark before the full impact of it assailed her, and took away her breath. By that time Father Houlihan was safely gone.

She observed at this time, however, that his tone was peaceable and full of retiring mildness, so she allowed him to follow in her huge and billowing wake to Angus' room, gathering up her enormous black skirts as if contagion pursued her. She flung open Angus' door and announced loudly: "My dear, the—gentleman you desired to see is here. You must remember that you cannot see visitors for long, and I shall return shortly."

Father Houlihan entered the room, waited until the blackly suspicious Mrs. Schnitzel had retired, and came to Angus' bedside. He smiled down at the young man, concealing his sorrowful shock at the sight of his changed sick face, his brilliant and desperate eyes.

"Well, my lad, it's sad I am to see you like this, in bed," he said, his voice trembling. "But we'll soon have you up and about, eh?"

"Please sit down, Father," said Angus, with a feeble wave

of his hand. His head was swathed in wet compresses. The priest sat down, sighing, but still smiling determinedly.

"It's your head, then?" he said. "It is no better?"

"It is unimportant," replied Angus, in a dull and abstracted tone, touching the compresses.

The priest hesitated. His tired old face was faintly luminous in the dusk. His blue eyes were kind and tender, filled with light. He said: "I have been told I have a way with headaches, Angus. Will you let me try?"

Angus said nothing. He closed his eyes. Father Houlihan gazed sorrowfully at that pale gaunt profile. He had been amazed when Stuart had come to him, urging him to visit Angus at once, but he had also, if incredulous, been overjoyed. Stuart had forcibly pushed him into his carriage, and had sent him on his way, so that he had been conducted to this house in a veritable haze of bewilderment, prayer and conjecture. Stuart's words had been incoherent; he had gathered little from them. Had Angus sent for him, or was this entirely Stuart's idea? He could not know.

He knew only, now, that a desperately sick and suffering man lay before him. And that sickness, that suffering, were the deep malaise of a soul in torment. He put aside his conjectures, his objectivity. He felt, and thought, with his heart. All trepidation, all uncertainty, all awkwardness, left him.

He said: "Will you let me try?"

Angus moved his head weakly, with exhausted impatience. The priest rose, carefully removed the pungent compresses, and laid his veined hands on the young man's forehead. Angus suffered these ministrations, as if he were unconscious. Father Houlihan softly stroked the throbbing and bony brow, but his eyes were closed, and he prayed silently. He felt a peculiar, but familiar, surging in himself, as if he was gathering power from some outer and mysterious source, and directing the focus of that power into his hands and into Angus' head. He felt himself vibrating, pulsing. Moment after moment passed. The vibrating grew less and less, withdrew, the power had gone. A faint weakness came over the priest, and he sat down again. Angus still lay motionless on his pillows. He seemed to sleep.

Then at last he opened his eyes, and they were fixed, as if listening. An expression of surprise moved his mouth. He said, wonderingly: "The pain has gone."

The priest passed the back of his hand over his forehead. He smiled, tremulously. "God is merciful," he said.

Angus started. He turned his head to the priest and gazed

at him steadily. He said: "I had forgotten you were here, Father."

"But you wished to see me, Angus, my son?"

Angus did not answer for a moment. And then he said, in a loud and hurried tone: "Yes. Yes. I always wish to see you! Always!"

He moved on his pillows, raised himself on them. An odd strength appeared to galvanize him. He leaned on his elbow. He began to speak, and his breathless sentences were disjointed. But the priest understood. From the welter of phrases flung wildly at him, he pieced together the whole portrait of a tortured soul, bursting out from its confines, looking about it in madness and misery.

He had heard many strange confessions, but none so strange as this. He had heard confessions from men who had struggled with the evil forces and circumstances about them and had been defeated. He had heard confessions of weakness, of betrayals, of treacheries, of stupidities. But he had never before heard the confession of a man who had deliberately, coldly and with iron calculation, chosen the evil in himself, and had known it was evil, and then had rationalized it and made it a malignant good. Yes, he had taken avarice, cruelty, remorselessness and betrayal, and had sublimated them into virtues, justified of God, beamed upon by Heaven, approved by man, sanctioned by the soul.

He listened to Angus' voice, and he knew that here was a man betrayed, not by his own weaknesses, not by other men, but by himself, and all to the accompaniment of noble phrases, pious texts and rigid virtue. Doubtless, thought the priest, the world is full of such men, yet I have never known it before. He was appalled; he was terrified. He felt his own sense of values thrown together in a disjointed heap. Could a man be so self-conceived, and not be a madman? Yes, he could be so self-deceived, and he need not be mad. The priest was horrified. Was there any saving of such souls? For these souls were armored in the most stringent virtue, armed with sanctity, helmeted with their strong and perverted justice. They did evil things and thought them good, and considered themselves pure in the sight of the angels.

He could not say to Angus: You are a liar and a hypocrite. For this was not true. Angus was full of integrity; he did not know the meaning of hypocrisy. The power of evil had destroyed him with holy words and with the gestures of holiness, and had made him impregnable to mercy and kindness and love, and to holiness, itself.

"I do not understand!" cried Angus. "I still do not understand! And there is none to tell me! What have I done that was wicked? Yet, I know everything I have done has been evil and twisted. I know it, but I do not see where, or how!

"It was in that room, when—Allstairs died, that I first knew it, though I must have felt it all these years." He fell back on his pillows, struggled for breath. He stared at the ceiling as a dead man, who has expired in agony, stares. "I heard him—Stuart—speak. He said: 'May God have mercy on your soul.' His friend had been murdered by Allstairs. He had been ruined by Allstairs. Allstairs had pursued him relentlessly. Yet, he said: 'May God have mercy on your soul.'"

Angus turned his head feverishly, passionately, to the priest. "Why did he say that? When he said that, I saw the most terrible things. I saw myself. Why did Stuart say that?"

Tears stood in the priest's eyes. He said, softly, deeply: "Because Stuart is a good man. You can't understand that, can you, Angus? You can't understand that there is a goodness of the heart which has nothing to do with the acts of a weak body, or the words of a licentious mouth. There is a goodness in some men which the good Lord called 'charity,' the thing which is greater than hope, greater than faith, more beloved of God than all the other virtues. Stuart, for all that he is, is full of love and compassion and charity. In my sight—and I know, in my heart, in the sight of God, also —he is a good and blessed man, and I have no fear for him."

"And I," said Angus, with neutral calm, still staring at the ceiling, "did evil things and called them virtuous."

He lifted his hand and indicated his briefcase on a table beside his bed. "Please give me that, father." The priest brought him the case and laid it near his hand. He sat down again. He could not understand his own trembling, as if portentous things were taking place in that room.

Angus laid his hands on the briefcase and turned his head again to his old friend. "I wanted to be a doctor," he said, listlessly.

"Yes, Angus, I know," said the priest, with eagerness, leaning forward.

"It is too late, now. I—I studied a little. I visited the hospital. But it is too late for all that now. What little knowledge I have must suffice."

"Suffice for what, Angus?"

Angus' eyes were suddenly blazing, filled with vitality and strength. "For what I want to do! For the service I wish to do! Father, only you can help me!"

Amazed, incredulous, the priest listened, wetting his lips grown dry in his confoundment, in the surge of his shaken emotions. He felt the quivering of his heart, as he listened to Angus, who was speaking quickly, but with gathering strength. Again and again, the priest crossed himself. Once he said, in his shaking mind: How strange and lovely are the ways of God. Sometimes he would shake his head, thinking: It is not possible. I am dreaming. Sometimes he whispered inwardly: I thank Thee, Father. All at once he was filled with a blazing joy, and a profound humility.

Angus had ceased to speak now. He lay back in his bed. But he was smiling, his face illuminated, young and gentle again. He held out his hand, and the priest took it. "You will not reject me?" he asked, and his voice was the voice of a child.

"Reject you?" whispered the priest. "Who am I to reject you? God receives you, my son. I—I must think. I must talk to my bishop— Yes, yes, it shall be arranged. What God desires cannot be frustrated."

Angus' hands were fumbling with the straps of his case. He opened it. He held out a paper to the priest. "Read this, father," he said, humbly. "Tell me if it is right."

The priest's trembling hand fumbled for his spectacles. He read the long sheaf of foolscap written in Angus' tiny exact script. He read, and his head swam.

He put down the paper. He looked long and steadily at Angus. They smiled at each other.

Then the priest knelt beside the bed, and prayed. Angus listened. When the priest had finished, and still knelt, with bowed head, Angus slept as he had not slept in a long time.

CHAPTER 75

IT SEEMS to me, thought Stuart, ruefully, as he quietly entered Janie's house on Porter Avenue, that I am always paying visits of consolation these days. What have I become? A damned praying parson? It's not in my nature, and I abhor it.

The dark and shrouded atmosphere of the house enveloped him, shut out the memory of the warm May day outside. The house was also very chill and dank, every window shuttered, every door somberly closed. It was a house of death, though no corpse lay in it. Stuart cursed to himself, hating the gloomy air, the weighted solemnity.

The maid whispered to him. He stumbled up the stairs in her wake to Janie's apartments. He heard no sound. He entered Janie's sitting-room, and smelled the pungent odors of camphor and lavender. He blinked his eyes, for the sun had been brilliant, and it was some moments before he could perceive that Janie, in her bed, was lying motionless, and that her son, Robbie, was beside her with his weeping little wife, Alice.

Robbie stood up as Stuart entered, and extended his hand. The small man was very pale, his eyes sleepless and haunted. But his manner, as usual, was precise and controlled. His hand was cold and lifeless.

Stuart, sweating with awkwardness and pity, bowed to Alice, glanced anxiously at Janie. He asked a question with an inclination of his head. Robbie shrugged, despairingly. "She is taking it rather hard," he whispered. He smiled wearily. "After all, Bertie was her darling."

And you, thought Stuart, are not taking it easily. He looked around uncertainly for a chair, and when Robbie indicated one he sat down, feeling huge and bulky in that room of mourning, and an intruder.

Alice wiped her eyes. Her pretty little face was blotched with tears. Robbie sat beside her, put his arm about her. He did not look at his mother. He looked at his wife, and when he did so, it was with with awakened yearning, with sad passion and devotion, as though he saw her for the first time, and knew her. "Hush, my pet," he whispered. "It isn't good for you, you know." For Alice was recovering from a bout of summer fever, and had not long been out of her own bed.

She leaned her head on his shoulder, and tried to stifle her tears and sobs. She clung to him, and he held her tightly against him, and kissed away her tears.

The single-minded Stuart was interested in this, and pleased. He watched them with the open satisfaction of a child, and forgot Janie.

When he remembered her, it was with remorse. He got up, tiptoed to the bed, and looked down at his old kinswoman, his old friend, his old playmate, and his old enemy. Janie had aged. She was sleeping now, under the influence of a sedative administered by her physician. She was an old and broken hag. She sobbed and murmured feebly in her lethargic slumber. Her red hair was dishevelled on the pillow, her large nose pointed and quivering. Her eyes were swollen and scarlet.

Poor devil, thought Stuart, with overwhelming compassion. This is hard for you. You never loved any other soul. You've come a long way, poor old Janie. We must be better friends now. You have no one left. You never wanted anyone but Bertie, so the whole world has left you, and has only a few reluctant tears for you. Yes, we must be better friends now, damn you, and we'll be friends whether you want it or not.— Janie, do you remember how we roasted potatoes in the autumn leaves, at home? And how we plotted how we'd conquer the whole infernal world? And how we laughed? You had the scrawniest legs, but you were full of ginger, and could swing in the trees like a monkey. Remember how we raced through the meadows? We've got a lot to remember, Janie, and we'll remember it together, and laugh over it.

He accompanied Robbie and Alice out of the room. They closed the door softly behind them. "This is the first time in two nights she's slept," said Robbie, as they stood downstairs in the shrouded parlor.

Stuart went to the windows, flung aside the draperies, opened the shutters. The May sunlight streamed into the room, caught up eddies of golden dust motes. They heard the voices of children in the street. A maid brought in a tray of wine and glasses, and little cakes. She sniffled. Stuart glared at her. He poured the wine, forced a glass on Robbie, and another on Alice. He smiled at them quite cheerfully.

"Well, here's to old Bertie. He did his duty, you know."

Alice said, in a gentle voice hoarse with tears: "Did you see the letter from the President, Stuart? Such a lovely letter! It said that Bertie had died in heroic action, after saving fifty men from certain death. Such a wonderful letter! We're so proud of him."

She stretched out her hand to her husband, and he took it at once, and smiled at her with sad tenderness. She looked at him, and said: "We are proud of him, aren't we, Robbie? It was the way he'd want to die. He was such a fine man, and we loved him so."

Robbie raised her hand to his lips.

Alice regarded Stuart quietly, but there was a glow in her eyes. "There was a medal from the President, too, a Congressional medal. 'For gallantry in action.' When poor mother is better, and able to understand she will be so proud, too."

Stuart doubted it. It would take more than a medal to console poor old Janie. Her heart lay somewhere in Virginia, and it would pulse there forever. Well, she would no longer speak of "going home." She would always remain in America, where Bertie had lived and died in gallant action.

He wondered, briefly, about Bertie. But that young man had always been a puzzle to him, and he shrugged.

Robbie did not wish to talk of his brother. He was very composed. He said only: "I knew we'd never see him again. I knew it from the beginning. So it isn't too great a shock to me."

He stared before him, blindly. But he still held Alice's hand, and from time to time he kissed it, not in absent-mindedness, but with tender passion.

"Perhaps it was best for Bertie," he said, as if thinking aloud. "Best, yes. I can't regret it too much."

Now his eyes focussed on Stuart, and he could not resist a smile. "How are things with you, Stuart? I understand I must congratulate you."

Stuart tried not to look too pleased in this house of mourning. "Damned good, amazingly good, of Angus. I still don't understand it. Leaving me thirty percent of his stock in the shops, leaving me in complete control. Forty percent for your mother, and the other thirty to the Church. Who'd ever think he'd wanted to be a Catholic! It's beyond me. I don't understand people at all."

Robbie smiled wryly. "When Ma has time to think, there'll be an explosion. Her puir wee lad, Angus, going into a monastery, to study to be a confounded missionary to the lepers! She'll have conversation for years."

"It seems such a strange thing for Angus to do," said Alice. "I never really knew Angus. He was so odd. But, if this makes him happy, what does anything else matter? But, it does seem so strange."

"Not so strange," said Stuart, suddenly, with intuition. "He really wanted to do something like that, all his life. He had such a desire for sacrifice. Old Grundy told me that, once. I am just beginning to grasp it. Not very clearly, yet. But I'm getting some inkling."

Robbie eyed him with polite and hidden curiosity. How old was Stuart? About forty-six, apparently. But younger looking than he had been for some time. There was a subdued expression about his eyes, and introspective tiredness and sadness. It was the expression of a man who had suffered much, and could not forget the suffering. However, his face appeared smoother, fresher, younger, and the marks of dissipation were fading. His complexion had a brighter appearance, a youthful and healthy color. There were some men, reflected Robbie, who were like children, or were possessed of unsuspected vitalities. Was it a matter of a good conscience? Robbie was dimly and tiredly amused. Or no conscience at all? He had always believed Stuart was a good man, boisterous and violent, perhaps, capricious, high-tempered and ruthless, and undisciplined. But intrinsically good and kind. He had the capacity to inspire malice and hatred, but only in those who were without true virtue. But, always, fate intervened at the most critical moments in his affairs, as if fate, herself, were a fond and indulgent and loving mother who understood.

Robbie said, absently: "Be more careful, please, Stuart. Do not think me impertinent. But, I beg of you, be careful—about the shops."

Stuart grinned, suppressed the grin. He waved his hand, largely. "How could I be anything else, after Angus so astutely appointed you auditor of the books? I resent that, Robbie, I resent that!" But there was no resentment in his voice. "Yet, I am glad, in a way. It takes much responsibility from my shoulders, especially as you must approve of every purchase I make, and are to inspect the bills."

Robbie hesitated. Stuart was rising. Robbie said: "How is Mary Rose these days?"

"Much better, thank God. Old Grundy's been doing some heavy praying over her. She has some healthy color in her cheeks at last. She is to stay with me until the autumn, when she will return to her mother in Philadelphia. I'm glad of that. She cannot endure our Northern winters." His face became gentle and soft.

He said: "Please tell Janie, your Ma, how sorry I am. Tell her I came. Tell her I shall come to her tomorrow. Sho she mustn't take it too hard. She has a head on her shoulders, and she will soon be proud of old Bertie."

Robbie accompanied him to the door. They saw carriages drawing up, filled with Janie's friends who had come to condole with her.

Robbie hesitated again. He put his hand on Stuart's sleeve. "I am glad to see you looking so well, Stuart. You are not upset about Marvina's divorcing you?"

"No, young feller. You handled that in a masterly way, and I am grateful." Stuart warmly pressed his hand. But Robbie was looking distrait. "Stuart, forgive me, but after all Laurie is my sister."

Stuart glanced away. "I have written to Laurie. Damned

if it's any of your business, but I don't mind telling you. She's been pressing me to leave everything and go to New York to be with her, after our marriage. She's impatient about the shops. She wants me to sell out, or something. The shops! She doesn't realize I have a life of my own! I'm not a lackey, Robbie." He smiled painfully. "So I've written her to tell her that her own career is very vital, that I wish it for her, that she must not consider me. And that, after we are married, I shall remain here, and she will return, after each tour. She will visit me, pleasantly, at intervals, and I shall visit her in New York, when I can."

His face darkened a little, and he sighed. 'That is how it must be. Whether she will agree or not remains to be seen."

Robbie took his hand again, and shook it firmly. "She will, Stuart. And respect you for it. I don't envy you, Stuart. She is a hard customer. But she is also very fond of you. Good luck, Stuart."

Stuart put on his tall hat with a confident air. He smiled. "Thank you, Robbie. Yes, I think she might agree. After all, a man has his pride, too." He moved his shoulders, almost swaggeringly. "A minx, Robbie. But there is something in Laurie which no one has discovered, except myself. She is gentle, underneath all that glitter. She will come around."

Robbie watched Stuart moving down the narrow stone stairway. Poor devil. And in the hands of Laurie, too! Robbie had no illusions about his sister. A hard piece, and an imperious one. There would be hectic storms, recriminations, violences, accusations and rages. But they loved each other, those peculiar two. They would never be bored. Laurie would go her way, when she was singing, and she would not speak of what she had seen or done. That would be very discreet of her. Stuart would ask no questions. He cared only that she loved him. He was old enough to be her father, but she was a woman, and he would always be a child, always young.

The condoling guests were coming up the stairway, but looking after Stuart with mingled curiosity and fondness. Robbie saw them coming. The darkness which in Stuart's presence had lifted, returned to him now.

But in him there was also a strange dim peace.

CHAPTER 76

THE LONELY island lay in its purple mists. A few green fronds of the whistling palm trees emerged from that mist, stirred and clattered against the dawning sky. The small settlement, huddled and white, was still silent in the morning. The heavens were an intense and shadowy blue; in the east, the delicate crescent of the moon was ascending heaven's slope out of the sea, which was pale dim lavender touched with frail silver. Now the voices of birds pierced the warm and empty silence in a very clamor of song.

Above the moon was a star, a single glowing star, vivid and pulsing.

There was a ship offshore, but carefully keeping its distance. A boat was lowered from it. It contained one sailor, and a man in the rough dark habit of a missionary monk. He sat in the prow of the little boat and looked eagerly at the island. A few wisps of smoke were now rising gently from hidden chimneys. The purple mists were brightening, lifting. The island was a jewel of heliotrope, green and gold.

The boat grounded on the coral shore. The monk stepped from the boat. He turned to the sailor, who saluted him. He waved back, smiling. His face was beautiful and pale in the early light, and very sweet. His thin dark hair lifted; his habit blew about him in the first wind.

He watched the boat pull away, return to the ship. Then he turned his face from it, and looked towards the settlement. He stood for long moments, gazing at what would be his home until he died. Joy suddenly blazed in his eyes.

He walked up the slope towards the settlement. He lifted his face to the heavens. He began to sing. The old priest, hurrying to meet his new assistant, paused in astonishment to listen to the lovely sound.

It was Robin Cauder's Hymn to the Morning Star.